ROGUE ETHEREAL

THE COMPLETE SERIES

ANNIE ANDERSON

ROGUE ETHEREAL

THE COMPLETE SERIES

International Bestselling Author

Annie Anderson

Print ISBN: 978-1-960315-04-5

www.annieande.com

BOOKS BY ANNIE ANDERSON

THE ARCANE SOULS WORLD

GRAVE TALKER SERIES

Dead to Me

Dead & Gone

Dead Calm

Dead Shift

Dead Ahead

Dead Wrong

Dead & Buried

SOUL READER SERIES

Night Watch

Death Watch

Grave Watch

THE WRONG WITCH SERIES

Spells & Slip-ups

Magic & Mayhem

Errors & Exorcisms

THE LOST WITCH SERIES

Curses & Chaos

THE ETHEREAL WORLD

PHOENIX RISING SERIES

(Formerly the Ashes to Ashes Series)

Flame Kissed

Death Kissed

Fate Kissed

Shade Kissed

Sight Kissed

Rogue Ethereal Series

Woman of Blood & Bone

Daughter of Souls & Silence

Lady of Madness & Moonlight

Sister of Embers & Echoes

Priestess of Storms & Stone

Queen of Fate & Fire

WOMAN OF BLOOD & BONE

ROGUE ETHEREAL BOOK 1

CHAPTER ONE

MAX

I was burned at the stake when I was fourteen years old. At nineteen, I was dissected by a zealot "physician" who knew less than a pile of cow shit about medicine. I was drowned in a lake when I was twenty-four. At twenty-seven, I was stoned in a public square.

When I was thirty—long after I quit aging—I finally got smart. If I stopped helping people, if I stopped trying to save the humans who were so ungrateful for my assistance, no one would know what I could do. I wouldn't hear the word "witch" from the lips of men who didn't know the first thing about me.

Sure, it meant more people would die, but with as many times as I'd been "killed" for my gift, they deserved it.

I made rules—ways of hiding in plain sight.

One: never, ever, on literal pain of death, live in a small town. There is no hiding there, no way to keep nosy people out of your business. Also, when the town magistrate happens to go "missing," they are going to look at the strange girl who keeps to herself. Yes, I killed him, and no, I'm not sorry.

He deserved it.

Two: no matter how much I may want to, don't cast in public. It doesn't matter if some asshole parent is beating their kid, mistreating their dog, or driving like a blind monkey on uppers. Don't do it. Memory spells are slippery and difficult to execute.

Three: Don't talk about history or politics with people. You run the risk of talking about the French Revolution as if you were actually there (I was), and then some jerkoff history buff—who swears by the books he so ardently clings to—starts getting nosy. It's bad news all around.

I remind myself of my rules—*especially rule two*—as I walk the dark and rather dirty streets of Denver's warehouse district. While I suppose I could get scolded for being a beautiful woman walking alone at night in a big city in a decidedly seedy part of town, I just don't give a fuck. I wasn't leaving my cherry-red Chevelle anywhere but in a highly secure parking garage, even with the three-block walk on five-inch spiked heels. And I'd break rule two in a heartbeat if a man—or woman, I'm equal opportunity—came at me in this part of town. Like the shady-looking fellow giving me the "V" sign as he adjusts his crotch, his tongue waggling through his fingers like some sort of deranged animal.

I contemplate just what I could turn him into. A trash barrel, or maybe a port-a-john, or even a mailbox. Transmogrification spells aren't too hard if you're working with something of equal mass. All it would take is a snap of my fingers and the right words in Latin.

My plans are derailed by my phone ringing in my clutch. Lucky prick.

Someone just saved your life, pal.

I fish the slim, yet annoying device from the creamy pink satin of my bag and answer it.

"You just saved someone's life and ruined my fun. I hope you know I'm going to make the next tattoo I do on you hurt," I grouse, stomping my way down the cracked sidewalk toward my destination.

"No, you won't," Aurelia says, "and sweetheart, if you could make me feel pain, I'd lick your freaking pumps. Why are you planning murder?"

Aurelia Constantine has been one of my best friends for the better part of a century. We bonded over being cast out of our respective families and our mutual love of tattoos—me giving them, and Ari receiving them. Aurelia is a phoenix—like, no shit, flaming-wings-and-everything phoenix. I, on the other hand, am something altogether different.

"Some jackoff is making a rude gesture at me. Speaking of, what would be a worse fate? Life as a port-a-john or trashcan? I can see significant downsides to both," I muse, my fingertips itching to snap.

"Stop plotting the silly human's demise for a minute. Are you coming to my wedding or not, woman? You keep flip-flopping and I can't see what you're going to do." Aurelia is a rare and powerful psychic, and newly crowned leader, along with her twin, Mena of the American Phoenix Legion, and if she can't see what I'm going to decide, it really must be up in the air.

In all honesty, I can't see myself—a Rogue witch—hobnobbing with all of the powerful Ethereal leaders that will deign to be there. It sounds like a sure-fire way to get myself thrown in a dark hole somewhere to never be heard from again.

Yeah, I don't think so.

"I feel horrible, but I don't think I'm going to be able to make it, babe. It seems too risky. All it takes is one coven leader to be there, and then I'll be carted off to some dank hole in the ground praying to die. I really want to be there, but..." I trail off, unwilling to disappoint one of the few people who has made this long, lonely life somewhat bearable.

"I get it, sweetie. Don't beat yourself up. You still planning on coming to the bachelorette party? Evan is cooking up something weird and probably hilarious as hell."

Evangeline Carmichael, Queen Wraith and all-around pixie badass, is an odd duck but a hilarious one. Whatever she's planning for a bachelorette party is sure to be a smashing success.

"This, I can do. You swear you're not upset?" It isn't every day that one of your besties gets married—even though technically this is her second wedding, and she has been bound to her husband Rhys for the better part of two centuries.

"Darling girl, if there was anyone in this world who understood hiding out, it would be me. No worries. I'll see you in a few days."

"You're bringing the twins into the shop, right? I need to squeeze those little balls of baby goodness."

Aurelia's twins, Henry and Olivia, are a solid bright spot in my life. I can't wait to see them grow up. There isn't anything in the world I wouldn't do to keep them safe.

"Yes, if I can get Rhys to tone down the bodyguard detail. Oh, shit! I need to go, babe. Henry is hungry, and if Rhys picks him up, well…" She trails off. Her son Henry inherited some of the Constantine family traits. Namely the Aegis ability—one which shields and electrocutes anything within a ten-foot radius. I foresee his toddler years to be pure hell.

"Okay, babe. Have fun with that," I say as I disconnect, picking up the pace on my black suede peep-toes on the uneven sidewalk. If I wreck these shoes, I will murder Striker on principle.

Striker Voss is my business partner and other best friend. And his ignorant ass convinced me to get dressed up and meet him out here in the ass end of nowhere to get into an exclusive club. How Strike managed to get a plus-one, I'm not sure, and with his abilities, I probably don't want to know.

But here I am in what I think is the perfect club number—a royal-blue velvet, off-the-shoulder wiggle dress from the '50s. The gathered bust and tulip-style pencil skirt make it classy and racy. Plus, the three-quarter sleeves show off a hint of my tattoos—just enough to keep people guessing—and the blue of the dress compliments the freshly dyed indigo of my hair.

The nearly silent purr of the engine pulling up next to me yanks my eyes from my feet and my awareness from the man across the street. The whir of a window lowering is followed closely by Striker's low whistle. He pulls into a parking lot a hundred feet down the road, and exits his Tesla Roadster like he's a model strutting down a runway.

Striker is beautiful in a way that is almost unearthly. Wavy blond, shoulder-length hair, cheekbones sharp enough to cut glass, a jaw dreams were made of, and a pair of lips I know for a fact are just as soft and yet just as firm as one would hope them to be. Eyelashes that would make a model weep brush his cheekbones as he blinks, and I swear, if I didn't already know we weren't compatible in bed, I would hold him hostage and drain him dry.

But I do know how incompatible we are. Margaritas plus an unfortunate anniversary, equaled a solid degeneration to straight tequila and a rather fumbling night together in the 1940s. Striker is a giver—given his species, it's understandable—but in bed, I need a taker. He couldn't be a taker if I held a gun to his head, thus, no more naughty times with Striker. It was awkward for about two seconds until we both laughed about it and moved the fuck on with our lives.

Living as long as we do, little things like sleeping with your best friend tend to get swept under the rug. What doesn't get swept away is the dick move of dragging me out into the middle of stab-central in a club dress.

"Yeah, I know I look good. Could you pretty please tell me why you dragged me out here? I almost turned a thug into a port-a-john for Fate's sake."

Typically, Striker is the one bitching about something, but tonight my back is sore from hunching over one body part or another, inking fresh designs on smooth skin. I love my shop, love my job, but nights like tonight, I'd rather soak in my garden tub and drink a big old glass of wine than go out to this club Strike's been raving about for the last five years.

"All in good time. I swore I would take you to the hottest club in town, but before we go in, there are rules."

Rules, my fabulous ass. What am I, nine?

"I'm nearly four hundred years old, Strike. Not, in fact, the teenager you are treating me as."

Striker gives me the raised eyebrow of impatience and carries on. "As I was saying. Let me open the door for you. Only members can access the building. Don't pay the bartender. Drinks are free and they work for tips only. Do not hand him money, put it in the tip jar. If he touches you, he'll know you're not a member and that is bad news all around. Try and stick to my booth when we get in, and for Fate's sake, do not go on the dance floor. It's like a Roman fucking orgy in there. I plan on sticking to you like glue, but if we get separated, be careful. I swear this place is pure shenanigans. It's like the witches took a look at Fae clubs and decided to go one bigger. Ugh. Like they can compete with Fae clubs."

This rigmarole tells me something hinky is going on. Wait a minute...

"You don't have a plus-one at all, do you? You're sneaking me in? Have you lost your damn mind?"

I may not have ever been to a witch club, but I know enough about them to know only accepted coven members are allowed admittance for one, and two, they have a rule about no Rogues. Striker assured me he could get me into the local club since he had an in.

"You know me, it's better to ask for forgiveness, blah, blah, blah. Just come on. Have I ever steered you wrong?" he asks as he pulls me by the elbow.

"Yes. Several times in the last century, fucker."

"Okay, but"—He pauses, opening the creaky warehouse door which seems to have appeared out of nowhere—"look at this place."

Striker is about to get me in a world of trouble, I just know it.

CHAPTER TWO

MAX

Striker pulls me one step into the warehouse, and the outside streets of Denver fall away, the door sealing shut behind us as if it were never there.

Well, that isn't creepy at all. If I were by myself, that little move would have me running for the door which is no longer there.

There isn't a doorman or entryway, just a vast, dark room, teeming with people dancing and drinking and laughing. Multicolored spotlights make intricate patterns on the black ceiling, seeming to shimmer and move of their own accord unlike any strobe light I've ever seen.

Elegant naked men and women are suspended from swaths of fabric, hanging from the ceiling and performing some sort of erotic acrobatic act above the dance floor. Beyond them is a large bar with shirtless bartenders of both sexes mixing drinks. Striker wasn't lying. This place is like one huge orgy.

"So noted," I murmur, and Striker laughs as he leads me through a throng of revelers to a red leather semi-circular booth, tucked in a corner away from the loudest of the music. It's dark, lit only by the light of a small candle sitting on a slight stainless-steel table, but it has a great view of the dance floor and the pure unadulterated hedonism happening out there.

At first, I just sit and stare. I'm not a prude by any stretch of the imagination, but I was born in the freaking 1600s so it is a bit of an adjustment. I'm a tattoo artist, not a fucking nun, but damn—this is definitely outside of my wheelhouse.

As soon as we sit, a waitress in a gold gossamer dress, thin enough she might as well have been naked, sets two martinis down on the table for us. Mine matches my dress, and Striker's matches the exact shade of his crimson tie. I give our waitress a sweet smile, staring at her face and not her assets in an effort to be polite, and pass her a twenty for the swift service. I keep Striker's words in mind and make sure I don't touch her skin. I'm not sure if the bartender rule trickles down to the waitresses or not, and it's not the time to ask. Striker frowns at me for tipping, but as a rule he knows if I don't pay for my drinks, I always tip.

The waitress is thin and pixie-like, her flaxen hair a fine sheet down her back as she gives me a grateful grin on crimson lips and flounces away. Striker and I tilt our heads to see if she's wearing any underwear beneath her thin toga-like dress. She isn't.

I feel very overdressed in a club like this—like I should be naked, or at least wearing a teddy or something. It's ridiculous. Other than Striker, who is killing it in a well-tailored navy suit, I'm wearing the most non-see-through fabric in this joint. I raise an eyebrow at Strike, giving him my best "what the fuck" face.

"When you said orgy, you weren't lying."

"You act like I exaggerate on a regular basis."

"You do, and you know it."

"Okay, but I didn't this time, so it should lower my average."

"So lowered."

Striker nods, grinning as he sips his martini, and the pair of us settle in to gawk at the sheer debauchery going on within our field of vision. The dance floor is like a conga line—if that particular conga line just so happened to involve penises. I tilt my head this way and that. There are big ones, curved ones, regular-sized ones.

So many. And I'm pretty sure there are a couple of acrobats getting it on in the ribbons. Seriously, this is better than porn.

"Is this a sex club? Did you honestly bring me to a witch sex dungeon, Strike?"

"Of course not! This is a regular club. The sex clubs are way worse."

How in the high holy fuck could a club be any more depraved than what I'm seeing blows my mind.

We're in the booth for maybe ten minutes when Strike gets a visit from a statuesque blonde woman begging to dance with him. By begging, I mean instead of talking directly to him, she drapes herself across his lap and plants a hot kiss on his lips. I'll give her credit where it's due because she's rocking the shit out of a pair of black leather pants and a baby pink see-through lace bustier. Plus, her assets are substantial. I don't even have to strain to see her nipples, so I know Striker is practically salivating after her. I don't even swing that way, and I am.

What is in these drinks?

Striker raises his brows at me, and I'd be a shitty friend if I didn't let the man blow off some steam. I shoo him, letting him off babysitting duty for a little while.

Pink Bustier Girl doesn't lead Striker to the dance floor. She diverts at the last second and directs him to a tall man in a dark suit with a faint mobster vibe, but in a hot way. With dark hair pushed back off his forehead, paired with piercing blue eyes, I get the feeling he's someone you'd like to look at, but isn't a man you'd want to cross in a dark alley.

Striker seems to know him, though, and his posture doesn't suggest he's in any trouble, so I let him have his privacy and go back to people-watching. Everyone is having a good time. Usually in a club there is at least someone pissy or a chick crying or someone arguing in a corner, but here there's nothing like that. Is it the drinks, the atmosphere, or the lack of humanity in the room?

I take another sip of my drink and watch some more.

I'm sitting by myself sipping on my third electric blue martini when a man plops himself down in our booth. It's so dark and tucked away here, I can't quite make out his face, but I can see the fullness of his lips and the blinding white of the smile against smooth, dark copper skin. His voice is deep and rough when he asks for a sip of my drink.

"I don't think so." I laugh incredulously. I mean, who in the hell does this guy think he is, sitting in my booth and begging a drink off of me? It doesn't matter how cute he seems. Or how well his pecs and biceps seem to fill out his shirt. Okay, maybe it matters a little, but dammit. This is my drink.

"And why not, pretty lady?" His voice is a purr of a jungle cat, and he is just as lithe as he scoots closer. He smells divine. Like man and a subtle hint of really good cologne. His dark-brown eyes seem black in the low light, but regardless of their shade, I'm pinned to this slick booth like a butterfly on display.

"You can get your own drink." I'm pretty sure I don't mean for my voice to sound so husky, and I definitely don't mean to be as flirty as I am.

"Not without tipping off the bartender I don't belong here," he denies, sliding closer into my bubble of space. I lean into him a little, and I don't know if it's because we're surrounded by a hundred people having sex, or the seriously potent liquor I've consumed, or maybe it's just him, but I am seriously drawn to this mystery man who seems to have fallen into my lap.

Get it together, girl.

"That makes two of us. The waitress brought me mine, just wait for her to come back and we can order you one," I offer trying to get a handle on the situation, taking a sip to fortify myself.

"That will take forever. What do I have to do to convince you to share?" he asks, his lips brushing mine as he speaks, his tongue tasting the bite of alcohol still on them.

And then we're kissing. I'm no shit kissing a complete stranger I probably could not even identify in a police line-up, but at this point, I'm either drunk from whatever juju they put in the martinis, or just on him since I find myself pulling up the skirt of my dress pretty fast so I can straddle him.

The heat of his body against mine, of his lips against mine, scratch an itch I didn't know I had. His fingers dip into the gathered bust of my dress, and he nearly makes it to one of my nipples when a huge bang and screams ring out. The pair of us freeze, the heat of his hands at my hips before I'm yanked off the man's lap. Striker's warm touch circles my bicep as the fog lifts from my mind, and I yank my skirt down.

The man I was straddling let loose a wicked-sounding growl, but Striker is already pulling me away from him and toward a side door.

"We've got to go. Fast. It's a raid. We do not want to be within five miles of this place," he shouts, and hauls me away from the throng of people streaming away from the dance floor. People are screaming, and men are shouting. I trip, nearly falling on my face, but Striker hauls me up before I can biff it.

I don't know what's going on, but I know enough to know it's bad. Is this club not allowed? And who in the hell is raiding a place like this? It isn't like we have witch police out to stomp out fun. Or maybe we do, and I just don't know about them due to the fact I got kicked out of my coven ages ago.

The red of magic light flashes past us, exploding against the wall—sealing a side door shut and cutting off our immediate escape route. Striker lets loose a growl that vibrates down his arm, and I know we're in the shit now. We break left, skirting around naked revelers as they flee to the exits. I nearly fall again, and this time, Striker's ready for it, seeing as he hauls me over his shoulder in a fireman hold, knocking the breath right out of me. He moves much faster without me slowing him down.

Before I know it, I'm plopped onto the passenger seat of Striker's Tesla and he zips off into the night, leaving that weird little club and a ton of questions in the dust.

But I won't forget what I saw there or the kiss that woke me up.

CHAPTER THREE

MAX - ONE YEAR LATER

Unlocking my shop and setting up is one of the best parts of my day. It took a long time to get back to a place where I didn't freak out when I woke up, didn't panic every time I tried to fall asleep.

Six months ago, I died helping my friends. It wasn't the first time it's happened, but it was the first time in a long time that I wasn't sure if I'd come back. Another witch drained my energy trying to break one of my wards—a ward which was keeping my friends safe. Stupidly, I'd tied it to my life force, so when my heart stopped beating, the ward broke.

Dying that time was the worst one of them all. It was worse than the first time by miles.

I check my calendar, making sure I have designs drawn up for my girl, Alice, who plans on getting a skull made entirely of flowers incorporated into her sleeve. I pull the design and get my area set up.

When she comes in for her appointment, Alice tells me all about her boyfriend who she thinks is cheating on her. I wish I could help, but the last time I cast a truth-telling spell it backfired big time, so I'm hesitant to stick my neck out on this one. Instead, I act the way any normal person would and nod in the appropriate places. When her art is finished, I spray a paper towel with green soap and wipe away the excess ink, revealing the vibrant colors of the flowers.

This. This is why I do what I do. A tattoo artist is almost like a priest or a therapist—without the stuffy school or shitty rules. I can tell Alice already feels better after getting new art. I put that smile on her face. After settling up, I welcome a new customer, and on and on it goes as the shop fills with my other artists.

When the evening shift starts, I check my book again. Striker has a late appointment, and my last appointment of the day isn't one I remember making.

Odd.

I sit on my stool, the buzz of the tattoo machine in my hand. The guy in my chair is the worst kind of asshole, and I'm tempted to fuck up his ink on principle.

I won't, but I want to.

The design—made by yours truly—is a nautical theme reminiscent of old Sailor Jerry tattoos but with a solid twist toward realism. I'm also tempted to use my special ink for the waves I'm still working on—the ink I use when I'm weaving a spell into someone's skin. The kind of spell that keeps dicks in pants, fists away from women, and makes rude remarks taste like dirt in their mouths.

I have never been very good at following rules—even my own. Hell, especially my own.

"So, pet, what do you say?" The guy leers at me, his eyes laser-locked on my ample cleavage. His name slips my mind. Mark? Mike? Matthew? I swear I saw it on his paperwork earlier, but was too skeeved out by the air he had around him to properly check. Despite the attractive mask and British accent, I am not sold.

He totally misses it when I roll my eyes and wash more gray into the body of his tattoo. At first glance, he seems good-looking. Dark, expertly coiffed hair, ice-blue eyes, chiseled features, decent set of muscles, dressed in cool-guy chic of a well-worn band T-shirt and a pair of jeans. If you didn't hear him speak in that misogynistically condescending tone, or maybe if his facial expressions didn't completely give him away as the twat waffle he really was.

But I know his kind—know exactly what they're capable of. I'd been killed by his kind more times than I could count.

Normally, I would shrug him off. Assholes are everywhere, and I get my fair share of them by being a female tattoo artist with a D-cup and a penchant for low-cut tops and tight pants. I can't kill all of them, right?

But this particular one has a very pregnant girlfriend waiting for him on my shop's comfy couch. I can see said couch through the opening in the Japanese screens that separate my workspace from the next one and give privacy to my clients.

It sits directly adjacent to the mirror-fronted counter, and sitting at the counter waiting for his next customer's appointment is Striker. He's solicitously keeping her company, offering her water, and chatting with the seemingly sweet—if a little clueless—young woman. All the while his tawny eyes look her over.

He meets my gaze and gives me "the look."

I hate "the look." That freaking look has gotten me into more trouble over the last century than my normal shenanigans combined over the previous two. Fuck that damn look. But if he's giving it to me, I know for a fact, I can't deny him.

This best friend shit is for the birds.

I'm still pissed about the witch club he took me to—and incidentally the last time he gave me "the look." It reminds me of another man's lips and tongue and teeth—reminds me of the scant passing minutes we spent clinging, writhing together at a little-known underground witch club and how I wished I remembered his face better. It had been months—almost a year—since I saw him last. I hated that the club we were in was damn near pitch black. I hated that the strobe lights and fog effect obscured his face. I hated that I was too drunk or too stupid to never get his name. I hated how I only remembered the way the scant light caressed his dark skin and the way his lips stretched into the best smile.

I hated that I couldn't remember more.

Disgruntled, I flick my attention back to my best friend—a best friend that is presently looking more and more concerned with each second that passes as he scans the girlfriend.

Striker is an empath—a breed of witch that nearly died out in the fifteenth century. Striker's family was murdered by a rival coven of witches who didn't want the empaths spying on them. It didn't matter to them that empaths typically try to shut out emotions so they don't go crazy, and they for damn sure don't try to manipulate them unless absolutely necessary. Given that emotion magic is the only kind they can do, empaths are usually considered to be the equivalent of long-living humans. I know different, but I'm one of the few.

Striker wouldn't be this friendly or attentive if the woman didn't need it—pregnant or not. He only gives what people need and must sense the same thing I do. She's in a bad situation with this guy or with the baby or with her family. The possibilities are endless for what could be wrong, but I know for certain the man in my chair is the root problem.

The same man who is currently trying to get a better look down my shirt, and if he moves one more millimeter, I might forget my tenuous relationship with the coven leaders of this stupid country and snap his insipid little neck.

"Take a nap," I tell the asshole in my chair as I snap my fingers, and his eyes instantly flutter closed, his head flopping to the plastic-covered head rest with a decidedly satisfying thump.

Ahh. Much better.

I leave him to his snooze and rise from my stool on my favorite pair of electric-blue patent leather peep-toes. The heel on them is bigger than the average man's dick and pairs nicely with my cuffed black pedal pushers, magenta tank top, and my signature blue hair.

"Okay, we don't have a lot of time before he wakes up, so what's going on? He beating you? Doesn't want the baby? I know for certain he's a dirty, lying cheater since he just proposed a long night of me giving him 'what he needs' which he described in explicit detail. So, what else is it?"

"Wh-what? What's going on?" she stutters, unable to wrap her head around my questions.

Maybe it's the fact I surpassed her by three hundred years several decades ago or maybe I'm just jaded, but she seems so young to me. If I were to guess her age, I'd peg her at twenty at a push, but more than likely she's closer to eighteen. Her hair is a shiny sable color, her skin has the rosy glow of an overheated pregnant woman, and her eyes are a pale blue, offsetting her summer tan perfectly. If her eyes weren't wide with panic, and the general deportment lying in wait behind her long-gone smile wasn't leaning toward bald despondency, no one would know she wasn't happy as a clam.

Striker breaks in with his usual calm demeanor and soothing voice, stepping around the mirrored counter to sit next to her. This catches me by surprise. He isn't known for getting too close to a person in pain—it just makes his worse.

"We know you are in trouble. We know you are severely depressed and in pain. We are willing to help get you to safety. Let us know how we can help you," he says in the 'voice.' This one is the one he uses when he wants people to calm the fuck down. This one is laced with power and only works on humans. I swear to Christ if he weren't one of the best tattoo artists in the country, I would tell him to be a hostage negotiator. Better people have spilled their secrets to Striker without even knowing it.

"Ye-yesterday he found the money I'd been hiding to run away with the baby. Before I got pregnant, he beat me all the time, but now that he knows he's having a son, he wants me to give birth and then take him from me. I heard him talking on the phone to someone. He's going to kill me as soon as I give birth. He wants to sell my baby. I don't—I don't know what to do. I've tried going to the cops, but..." She trails off for a moment. "I know he'll find me. I know he will." Her voice is a trembling whisper as her shoulders heave, and she begins to cry.

Striker must not have given her enough juice, because typically when someone gets hypnotized, their voice is all monotone and flat. And there are for damn certain no tears.

"What's your name, Sugar?" I bend down into a closed-knee squat by her quaking knees.

"Me-Melody. Melody Danvers," she stutters as she takes the pristinely white handkerchief Striker offers from his back pocket. Mopping up her face, her eyes float back down to rest on her knees. I know that look well enough. It's the look of the beaten, of the shamed. I wore that look plenty when I wasn't much younger than her, and I wore it for much longer than I cared to.

I'm getting this girl out of this if it's the last damn thing I do.

"All right, Melody. Striker and I are going to take care of you. Don't you worry. Do you have family? Friends you can go to?" I'm hoping for a little bit to go on. I sure as shit didn't have a family I could fall back on. If she does, then she should count herself lucky.

"Yeah. My family is back east in a smallish town in Indiana. Even Micah doesn't know where. He still thinks I'm from Kansas, the idiot." Melody swipes at her nose with Striker's hanky and smears her mascara. "Shows how dumb I am, right? My good-for-nothing boyfriend doesn't even know where I'm from." Her eyes begin to fill with tears as she stares off in the distance. She shakes her head and sets her jaw. The girl has grit, I'll give her that.

"That's good. It means he won't know where to look. Striker and I are going to have a little logistical discussion and then we're on top of it. You want something to eat? Drink?"

"No, no, I'm good," Melody responds gratefully, her voice meek.

"All right, Sugar. We'll be back in two shakes." I grab Striker by his elbow, leading him to the office we share.

"Tell me you have a plan, Strike," I whisper furiously as I cross my arms underneath my rather generous chest.

His eyes flick down for a split second before a slow grin spreads across his lips. "I didn't, but I do now."

This does not bode well for me at all.

CHAPTER FOUR

MAX

"No. Never gonna happen," I half-shout and then shush myself before I lose my damn mind. "There is no fucking way I am seducing that shitbag. I put him to sleep. Let's just throw his ass in a dumpster in a random alley and give her a really good head start. It doesn't have to be too complicated."

Crossing my arms, I give Striker the death glare—the one that he's seen maybe three times in the last hundred years. The one that says there is no freaking way I am getting any closer to this dude, especially now that I know what he's capable of. Who in the hell hurts a pregnant woman? Honestly? What the hell is wrong with people these days?

"Fine." He throws his hands up in surrender. "We'll go with your plan. I'll go in the safe and grab her some traveling money, but you're going to owe me. My plan would have played on his feelings and made sure he didn't follow for a while, but you're the boss."

Ick. Just ick.

"You're damn right I'm the boss." I stomp to the door while he spins the dial on the safe. I'd snap my fingers to open it, but it's a special anti-magic safe, spelled with enough enchantments to zap the fingers off a deity if they tried to open it without the combo.

I may be self-taught, but I'm a prodigy. *Thank you very much.*

Crossing the room, I peek at Micah, making sure he's still asleep and gently pull Melody to her feet.

"All right, darling girl, we're going to get you out of here. Okay?" I confirm before tucking her under my arm and snagging my purse. We head to the back entrance, ready to slip into my car in the back parking lot, when everything seems to happen at once.

A red-hot hand seals over my wrist and yanks me back, just as Striker busts from the office at my blood-curdling scream.

But I can't look at Striker. I can't process anything except Micah's distorted face and glowing red eyes.

I don't know what he is, but Micah is definitely not human.

Houston, we have a problem.

I've been around for quite a while—not nearly as long as some—and I am well aware of my ignorance at the majority of Ethereal dealings. Almost everything I know is self-taught, so I could fill a freaking library with the shit I don't know. But the current and most important thing I don't know is why in the holy fuck this man's touch burns, and how in the hell did I not realize he wasn't human?

Micah's grip tightens on my wrist, pushing the agony deeper in my tissues—into the bones of my wrist and up my arm—into the very heart of me. I feel the burning everywhere, so much I can barely speak, I can barely think. All I think is *pain, pain, pain,* and then my mind is pulled, sucking into the deep void of my memories. I'm trapped in the one I try the hardest to block out —the memory of the last time I died.

My head aches and my body burns. I've finally done it this time. I don't know if I'll wake up when this is all over. I don't know if this is my last thing. I wish I was smarter. I wish I knew a better way to keep everyone safe.

I wish I learned more before I died the first time.

Something is draining me, and if I had a guess, it's someone stronger than I am, breaking the ward I so stupidly tied to my life force. Like an idiot, I thought no one could break it.

"Umm, guys?" My voice is thready as I sway on my feet. This is happening faster than I thought it could. Before I can go down, Ian is there to hold me up.

"Som-someone is trying to break the ward. Someone is trying to get in the house." I warn my friends. Aurelia has to get out, she has to protect her children.

Everyone braces, but my vision has narrowed down to just my best friend and her daughter in her arms.

They need magic, but I can't help them anymore. I don't have anything left of me and I tell them so.

"You didn't. Please tell me you didn't," Ian begs as he shakes. His face is ravaged, a mask of disbelief and pain so acute he can barely breathe, and I don't know why. I don't know why he cares. This is the same man who hated me on site, who bickers with me at every opportunity. Who insists on tossing insults my way any chance he gets.

But he's so sad right now.

"I can't... do that. Had to make it stronger. Couldn't... leave you unprotected. Had to do my part," I gasp as I fade, the tunnel of vision growing smaller and smaller.

"What did you do?" Aurelia begs.

"I reinforced the ward. Tied it to my power. When she breaks it... Well, you're going to be a man down." I'm trying to make it a little funny, but my friends don't know. They don't know how many times I've died. They don't know what I would give up just to make sure they were safe.

Even if this might be the last time. I've never died like this. I don't know if I'll come back. This is worse than the first time. I didn't have anything to live for back then.

"I had to keep your babies safe, didn't I? It's better me than them. I've lived longer. Sybil's right, you know. Magic. Use it. Get creative, and get those babies out of here. She's coming. Take them, and be safe," I warn, and it's the last thing I say.

I suck in one last breath, and then I can't pull in another. My body wilts, the last of my power leeching from me as my vision dims.

Everything is blackness.

Nothing but an empty void I cannot escape.

The scream coming out of my mouth seems to snap me out of the memory of my worst fear. Dying doesn't scare me. Staying dead does. And this man—this thing—is pulling it from me against my will. I know he is, because it's carved into every line of his face—the joy he's taking by making me scream. It's enough to wake me up, enough to make me block the pain for a moment and gasp a spell which could slow him down.

"*Mille vulnere,*" I mutter as I snap the finger of my left hand. *One thousand cuts.* I'm not optimistic it will do much more than give him a paper cut, but I have to try.

At the snap, Micah hisses, his grip loosening a fraction as cuts open up on his face. The open wounds pour blood as black as night—another notch in the "What the fuck" column—so I repeat myself once more, until his grip is loose enough for me to snatch my arm back.

But even though I've injured him, I'm not the only one in his grasp. Striker has Melody behind him protecting her with his body, but he's frozen, held up by his neck with an invisible hand, his toes barely touching the floor. My cuts on Micah are doing exactly jack and squat.

Getting us out of here is my top priority, but I don't have enough juice to do much about it. I could transport us all at full strength, but right now, I feel about as powerful as a wet noodle. My brain feels scrambled, everything is distorted and jumbled.

I open my lips to mumble the spell again, my brain frozen, but before I can utter another word, I'm thrown back—flying across the room until my back slams against the wall, the tips of my toes dangling above the floor—held by an invisible hand at my throat.

Micah is smiling now, the red of his eyes glowing bright with a magic I've never seen before. I don't have the first clue what he could be, and, honestly, I'm not sure I want to know. He gave me the creeps before, and now all I feel is fear.

The incorporeal hand at my throat squeezes, but I manage to choke out the only spell I can think of to save my ass from dying. "*Exilium.*" *Banishment.*

Micah is shoved back, the hand at my throat falling away as I suck in a staggered breath. "*Exilium,*" I croak, and Striker collapses at my back, coughing.

Micah's shoved back again, and the taint he leaves on the air lightens. I feel the magic rising in me, bubbling up like a volcano about to erupt as I scream, "*Exilium!*" one last time. The green casting light of the spell explodes from my hands. Mirrors and glass shatter, the plaster of the walls crack, light fixtures hum before exploding spraying shards of glass and sparks all over us. And I take a small amount of satisfaction at Micah's face as he's thrown through the plate-glass window of my shop and into the street.

I feel the burning tickle of blood seeping from my nose as the world tilts. *Too much. That was too much magic*, I think as I wilt to the floor. My only solace is the blaring horn and sickening crunch of what I hope is Micah being run over by a truck sounding in my ears before the world tilts one last time and my body gives out.

Everything is blackness, and I'm starting to hate the dark.

I wake up to a blistering headache, draped on a very familiar couch. It's mine, a comfy slate-gray leather that's buttery soft. I'm uncomfortable, my burned wrist trapped underneath me, but my shoes are off, at least, which is a considerate bonus.

I hear the rumble of Striker's voice somewhere deep in the recesses of my West Highlands ranch, and the faint yet hysterical tones of Melody asking him what the hell is going on. I get it. Everything she has ever known has just been turned on its ear. But I'll leave Striker to explain it to her. Hell, he might even be able to calm her down, but even his abilities have limits.

I abandon the couch and my shoes, searching for my best

friend and our new charge. What I find is Striker holding Melody in a gentle embrace, his lips brushing her forehead. It's sweet and heart-wrenching, and I hate that this happened to her, but I'm glad she made it into our shop today.

I abandon my guests and walk right out the front door. I don't know what Micah was, and I don't want to know. What I do know is this house has to be re-warded and pronto. I pick my way through the cool grass, stopping at the stone retaining wall surrounding my property and start the chants.

I don't ward the same way other witches do. Which makes sense since I'm not a regular witch. We are supposed to be taught spells and castings before we can even read—the natural magic flowing through us like water. But Mama never taught me the right way to do anything. I wasn't instructed on how to do even basic things that every witch knows how to do. Mama was more concerned with hiding my innate abilities and keeping her seat at the table.

She said I was too powerful—my body held too much. She couldn't trust me, she'd said. Told me if I didn't stop flaring my power, she'd bind me—stealing my abilities away and leaving me as defenseless as a human.

I'm actually surprised she never bound me, never took my power away to keep her precious status. I suppose coming back from the dead only to be cast out of my coven was punishment enough. To this day, I still don't know if I was too powerful for her or if my abilities just embarrassed her.

I suppose I'll never know.

I curl my toes into the wet grass, muttering the protection spells which should keep us safe. Whatever Micah was, this should keep him out. My only hope is, he was either dead or too out of it to follow us. But knowing what I do about the Ethereal, I don't trust Micah is anything close to dead.

I walk the perimeter of my property three times, marking the dirt every ten feet or so with a sigil for protection. I'm on my fourth pass out of ten when Striker finds me.

"Overkill much?"

"You and I both know this isn't overkill. This is barely the tip of the damn iceberg." Something in my gut tells me we are in for a world of hurt.

CHAPTER FIVE

MAX

Taking another look at the quiet residential street my house sits on, I wonder if any of them know what I am. Wonder if any of them are even a little like me. Alone. Outcast. Plodding along day by day, still stinging from a hurt that refuses to go away. I sometimes wonder what my neighbors must think of me—the blue-haired tattooed woman pacing a circle around her yard, burned and bloody.

It's a miracle no one calls the cops.

But then I remember the illusion charm I put on the four points of the retaining wall when I moved in four years ago. They don't see me broken and bloody. They only see me walking around my yard. They also get the impression I don't want visitors, so they don't talk to me.

Hiding is a lonely life indeed.

"I hate to break it to you, but you're going to have to come inside at some point," Striker insists at my back as I complete my tenth pass of warding my house and property. Yeah, I'm acting like a nut job, but Striker didn't see what Micah put in my head.

He didn't relive the worst moment of his life at the whim of a sick fucking asshole. His mind wasn't invaded and defiled. I shudder and wipe my nose. It comes away red, but I don't have the luxury of stopping right now. I need to make an obfuscation charm for each of us and get Melody the hell out of here.

"You and I both know you're better with people than I am. You explain it to her. Better yet, explain it to me. I haven't a single freaking clue about what that was." I'm half-hysterical as I throw up my hands and head to my greenhouse. The arid Colorado weather isn't conducive to growing some of the more sensitive plants I need for spells, so I had it built when I had the kitchen redone. For about a month, my wards and my sanity were total shit.

The matte-black steel frame bisects thick-paned glass walls all butting up against an eight-foot stone wall that was already on the property when I bought it. I had the foundation and frame specialty made by an expert welder who had a general contracting business. He made the entire thing by hand in under three weeks, constructing everything else with a team. The back wall was a pain in the ass to work around, but yards in this part of town aren't exactly huge, so I had to make do with what I had.

Concrete counters hold my heaviest beds, and the cedar shelves carry the smaller pots of herbs. I managed to get running water and a sink in here, but only because Striker charmed a guy with his voice voodoo.

Striker leans against the sink—the product of his handiwork and crosses his arms. I recognize this as his serious stance, but I'm not prepared for what comes out of his mouth.

"If I had to venture a guess, I'd go with an incubus. The red eyes are a dead giveaway. He's got some juice, too, if he could hide enough that neither of us realized he was an Ethereal when he walked in."

My brain buzzes for a second before the betrayal sets in. Striker knew what Micah was all along. I've known Striker Voss for more than a century, and never—not once—did I ever hear him talk about an incubus to me. Honestly, we don't talk much at all about Ethereal business.

"Incubus? A—there's such a thing as an incubus? And, B—

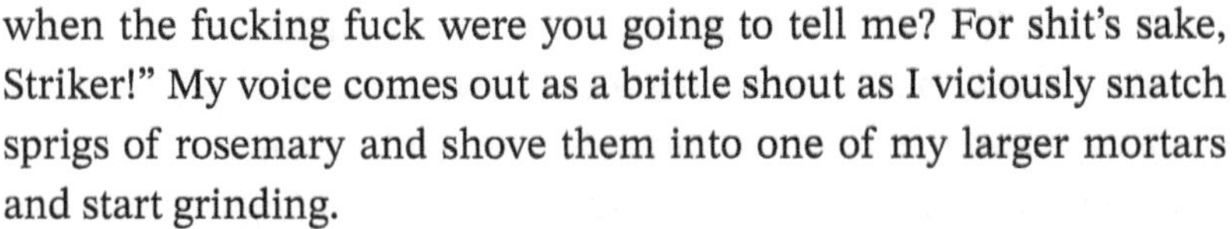

when the fucking fuck were you going to tell me? For shit's sake, Striker!" My voice comes out as a brittle shout as I viciously snatch sprigs of rosemary and shove them into one of my larger mortars and start grinding.

I can't even look at him right now.

"Well, excuse the shit out of me. It is not my fault your mother taught you exactly dick about being a witch or being a member of the Ethereal altogether. And it isn't like I purposefully hid it from you. Incubi are rare. It isn't like they're on every street corner and I failed to point one out. I haven't seen one in longer than I can remember. Jesus. Calm down."

Oh, no, he did *not* just tell me to calm down.

"Calm down. Calm down? Were you just shown your worst memory? Did you have to relive it? Did you have to relive dying? No? Then shut the fuck up with your calm down," I snarl, the pot of the rosemary plant cracking under the weight of my power filling the air. If I don't stop, I'll bust the windows of the whole greenhouse.

The horror on Striker's face is what does it. He's the only one who has been here for me since it happened. I shut every single person out of my life but him. He's felt it, the fear that claws at me. Fear I hadn't felt since the first time I died.

"Jesus, babe. I-I'm sorry. I didn't know that's what you saw. I just thought he was burning you."

This takes the wind out of my sails. Of course, he couldn't know what I saw.

"Well, he was doing that, too. Speaking of, I need to make a poultice to fix this shit, or it will get infected."

"Which you have in the house. Along with your candles. You can do just as many spells in your kitchen as you can out here. Quit stalling. I know why you won't come inside, but you're just going to have to get over it."

Striker is reading me—which I hate—but he isn't wrong. I don't want to go inside because I know I'm going to have to face Melody. She's going to be looking at us to tell her what to do, and I have no freaking clue.

"I don't know what to tell her. We said we'd take care of her, but this is way bigger than just an abusive human. That I can fix with a spell and an amulet. This shit I cannot fix, man."

Striker throws an arm over my shoulders and steers me out of my greenhouse, across the courtyard, and toward my kitchen door. Despite the difficulty with the climate, I still have several pots of flowers on the cobblestone patio which serve precisely zero magical purpose. I just love pretty flowers, and witches by nature are typically kickass at gardening.

"Just because you can't fix it, does not mean you get to bitch out when you said you'd help. I know I got you into this mess, babe, but you're just going to have to suck it up for a minute and get your shit together, got it?" Striker lands the truth bomb I did not want to hear.

I grumble something unintelligible and stomp through the doorway, bypassing Melody sitting at my breakfast table and heading straight for the liquor cabinet. I'm going to need a big glass of bourbon to get through this shit. I pull the bottle down and slosh three fingers into a whiskey glass, downing it in two swallows. I refill the glass and take a seat at the table across from Melody and reluctantly meet her eyes.

"He isn't dead, is he?" she asks, starting off with the hard shit. She looks so young, yet the fear and pain in her eyes tell me she's lived through enough hell to last a lifetime. Striker must feel the waves of fear coming off of her, too, because he's right behind her, rubbing her back.

"Doubtful, darling. Very doubtful."

"That was..." She pauses to try to wrap her head around it, I assume. "He isn't human. I thought I was going crazy, but I'm not, am I? He has red eyes. I didn't imagine that." She sounds almost relieved, and I wonder how much of the stress Striker felt coming off of her was her worry that she was mentally ill.

"No, sweetheart, he isn't human. In case you were wondering, we aren't, either." I don't know if she realizes this, and honestly, I don't want to have this conversation later.

She rolls her eyes in a "no shit" way, which only people under the age of twenty can truly master but seems to soften it with a little half-smile.

"I caught that part. But you're nice, right? I mean, you aren't going to hurt me. You aren't like Micah."

She seems so young to endure what she has—what she's still—facing. Too young to have the weight of a child coming into the world, too young to have a man beat her. Not that there is any age where that would be a good time, but for it to happen to her so young…

"No." I repress a shudder. "We aren't like him. I've locked down the wards, so we should be good for the night. How about I get you some food and set up in my guestroom for tonight, and in the morning, we can figure out how to get you out of here? How does that sound?"

Melody's smile is grateful as she nods, and I hope by the time she actually needs me, I can come through for her.

I toss and turn throughout the night, finally giving up on sleep at about two in the morning. I should be exhausted. I should be passed the fuck out in my massive bed, but the curling pit of dread in my belly isn't having it. Typically, I sleep in the nude, but the fact I have guests in my house nips it in the bud. The stretchy silk camisole and matching sleep shorts should be comfortable, but unfortunately, they're binding. Maybe that's it. My tits are pissed they can't roam free and are punishing me with no sleep. I'd like this better than the alternative.

Because the alternative is the nagging worry my wards aren't strong enough. That the amulet I put on Melody isn't strong enough. That I need a lot more help than I'm willing to ask for. I love my friends. I love the whole Constantine Clan. But the fact of the matter is, I died and came back in front of them, and I just can't face them if they think what my mother thought. I couldn't stand it if they didn't give a shit about me anymore because they think I'm something I'm not.

My mother thought I was cursed or a necromancer when I

woke from being burned at the stake. She didn't even ask me. She just cast me out without a second glance. As if I was dead to her—as if I meant nothing.

I couldn't bear it if the only real family I have did that, too.

I throw the covers back, grumbling at the misfortune of runaway sleep and abandon my room in search of ice cream. And maybe some more bourbon. The house is quiet, not even the usual settling of the house due to the dry Colorado heat. It's eerie in a way I don't like, and I can't tell if it's my body's way of recognizing danger, or if I just locked my wards down so tight even the summer heat decided to fuck off.

Opening the freezer drawer, I pull the triple fudge gelato out and contemplate just eating directly from the carton. I live alone, and other than Striker, rarely have guests, so it isn't exactly out of my wheelhouse to eat the whole thing by myself. I reluctantly decide on a bowl and spoon since if I were a pregnant lady in a house full of strangers, I wouldn't want someone's germs while I ate fudgy goodness.

The hair on the back of my neck stands on end as the prickle of one of the wards breaking flashes across my skin. *Son of a cock sucking motherfu...*

"Striker! Melody!" I have to get them up. They need to be awake, and we need to get the hell out of here. How am I going to get them out of here? Striker doesn't have the ability to transport himself like I can—the freaking slacker—and this is when I have enough juice.

But I can't do a transport of three people. I sure as shit can't do it after what happened in the shop. I knew I was powerful, but I've never destroyed a room like that. I've never had to exert that kind of power—drain it, sure—but not like that.

Snap. Another ward breaks.

Striker bounds into my living room, wearing a pair of striped pajama bottoms he seems to have conjured from thin air and nothing else, with Melody trailing behind him in what I'm assuming is his T-shirt stretched over her pregnant belly.

I'd be half-tempted to give him shit if it weren't for the third ward break whipping against my skin. Wards are no better than a deadbolt. Anyone can pick anything if given enough time.

The fourth ward breaks. This time, I actually feel the snap of it cutting into my skin as a rivulet of blood drips from an open cut on my cheek.

This isn't picking the ward like a lock—this is bombarding it with enough brute-force magic so it falls like a domino. And even though I tied it to the earth and not myself, I may be in some deep shit.

I wipe away the blood and show Striker.

"Shit," he rumbles, his eyes flashing.

Shit is right.

CHAPTER SIX

MAX

Striker's tawny eyes focus on the red staining my fingertips, and a preternatural growl slips past his lips. Strike isn't mixed with any form of shifter—I don't think—so that growl is pretty impressive. And my focus on it is my coward-ass way of not dealing with the shitty situation right in front of me. I'd rather contemplate the supernatural quality of Striker's pissed-off growl than deal with this.

Because I can't really process all my wards breaking. I can't process the blood on my face. I cannot fucking handle this. It isn't what happened the last time I died, but it is too close for comfort.

I promised Melody I would take care of her—promised I would help her see this through—and here I am losing it at the first freaking turn. I'm ashamed of myself. How in the hell did he find us, anyway? My place was warded out the ass.

Did someone follow us? And how does he have the juice to break through a ward like this? The only time my ward has been broken was by a host of evil souls—hundreds, maybe thousands of souls bound for Hell by a witch determined not to die.

That, I totally get. This? Not so much.

The fifth ward breaks, and this time it nicks the skin of my neck—a thin stream of blood runs right across my windpipe. It isn't deep, but it's enough to hurt.

At my pained gasp, Striker goes into damage-control mode—something which is usually my job—and looks out the windows, assessing the situation while I try to get my shit together.

"There are five pairs of red eyes out there. Your baby daddy have buddies, Melody?" Striker's voice comes out calm, but I know he is pissed beyond all belief.

"Y-yes. He has friends. I didn't know they were like him." She shudders, rubbing the large swell of her belly. None of this can be good for her. Neither will murder right after giving birth, so I need to fucking focus.

"We need to get the hell out of here, Max. Please tell me you have a plan."

Is he high? A plan? I'm lucky I'm not pissing in my pants right now, and he wants me to come up with a plan?

But it's true that out of the two of us I'm usually the one to get us out of a mess. Sort of. Sometimes. Okay, it's usually fifty-fifty.

My expression must convey my thoughts on the matter because he grabs me by the shoulders and gives me a little shake. Not enough to hurt, just enough to snap me out of it. Hell, at this point a solid slap to the face would be welcome. I'd really love to wake up and have this be some shitty little nightmare.

But I know it isn't.

"What about a doorway? You can make one of those, right?" Striker offers the idea like he's trying to calm a feral cat.

I haven't made a doorway in ages. I quit making them after I figured out how to transport myself. But I still know how to make one. I might have the ingredients to do it, but I can't even start the spell until all the wards are down.

"I'd need yarrow and angelica flower from the greenhouse. Salt and chalk, and a bowl of chicken blood. And I couldn't start it until the final ward is broken." My voice is weak and I freaking hate it. Why hadn't I learned how to defend myself? Why wasn't my magic working on this guy? It works on every other type of Ethereal.

"Do you even have the chicken blood?"

Oh, no, he did not just ask a practicing witch if she has chicken blood. That's like asking a chef if he has fresh garlic.

"Of course I have the fucking chicken blood. It's in the fridge next to the other chicken parts. What do you think this is, amateur hour?" I snap, which is likely the intended response.

"Well, excuse me, Miss Maxima, I had no idea we were working with an actual witch who had her shit together. Welcome back." His tone is snide, and he's only ruffling my feathers by calling me Maxima. I hate that damn name. What in the high holy hell was my mother thinking?

The sixth ward breaks, splitting the skin of my back and causing me to cry out from the pain. This one is deep, and it kicks my ass into gear.

"Striker, grab the yarrow and angelica flower. Melody, grab a stone bowl from the kitchen."

"On it," he says, and I follow Melody in the kitchen and grab the mason jar labeled "CB" since I do *not* need to explain that shit to a visitor, even though I don't really have visitors except for Striker.

In the next moment, Striker stomps back into my kitchen with a terra cotta planter in each hand, and the three of us head down the stairs to the finished basement. Finding the innermost room, my casting room, I snap my fingers and fire blazes from the six tall pillar candles I set strategically around the room. There isn't a light switch here or a real altar. Just a long wooden table with a thick grimoire, vials of salt, chalk, and a hammered metal bowl.

I can't cast this spell with a metal bowl. It jacks with the polarity like a compass going bananas, and then the direction gets really messed up. I pluck the bowl from Melody's hand, and get the set-up started, rather than wait to see what other horrors another ward breaking will do.

I don't have to wait. The seventh and eighth wards break in quick succession in the form of a pair of slashes forming an "X" on my belly, cutting into my camisole pajama top and splitting my skin enough to have me doubled over.

Shit.

If this keeps going, am I even going to be able to do the damn spell?

I suck in a huge breath, grunting through the pain as I struggle to stand. I draw the doorway on the wall with the chicken blood, whimpering as I stretch to make it big enough. Striker's right behind me, drawing a circle of salt around us before handing me the chalk. I shave some chalk dust into the bowl, followed by the rest of the chicken blood, three sprigs of yarrow, and a full bunch of angelica. I have to burn it all together and say the words, but I have two wards left before I can start.

The ninth ward breaking splits the skin of my thigh, the tenth the length of my left forearm through the already-burnt flesh. It's enough to make my vision dance.

I can't bitch out now, though, so I shake myself and begin.

Mumbling the Latin phrase, I barely get the words out to open the door—the pearlescent light folding this reality to create the portal. Striker goes through first to make sure it's safe. He gives us the high sign, letting us know it's clear, but I know I don't have enough time. The pounding of booted feet are on my stairs. They know where we are, and with no barriers, they can come as fast as they wish.

I look to Melody. She hears it, too—the thunder of them coming. The fear on her face guts me.

I promised I would help her. I swore. And I don't go back on a promise. Ever. I didn't when I was a teenager and it cost me my first life, and I sure as shit won't do it now when it could cost someone else's.

I do the only thing I can think of. Grabbing Melody by the upper arm, I yank her toward the door, which I hope leads to the upstairs apartment of my tattoo shop, and shove her through. She stumbles a bit, but Striker catches her before she can fall. Just like I knew he would.

They'll be good for one another. The way he takes care of her... He'll be a good dad. He'll take care of her, and she'll take care of him. They'll be safe and happy.

I can do this. *I can.*

Then I set out to close the door—keeping them both safe from the men whose only instinct is to kill, to take. Men who will hurt them, kill them, steal Melody's baby as soon as it breathes its first bit of air. Steal her happiness and his. They will take it all away if I let them.

Striker's face right before I close the door behind them tells me all I need to know. This time, when they kill me, I might not come back. He knows this just as much as I do. His expression cuts at me worse than the wards breaking. I'm hurting him, yes, but I'm saving him, too. He might not see it that way, but I can live—or die—with that.

Before the door seals shut, Striker's growl of betrayal reaches my ears. If I don't make it out of here, he'll never forgive me.

If I save them, though, it will be worth it.

CHAPTER SEVEN

MAX

Staggering out of my casting room, I leave a blood trail on the wall holding me vertical.

I am so fucked.

The best I can do is try and get the hell out of here to give Striker and Melody a head start. I don't have enough time to make a doorway, but I might have enough strength to get upstairs.

But I don't make it that far. Micah's red eyes meet me when I turn to the back corner of my basement, and his smile as he wraps his burning hands around my forearms is as evil as it gets. And those awful hands take me back to a day I never wanted to go to again. The day I lost everything.

VIRGINIA 1642

It felt as if ants were crawling across my skin. That urge—that need to get up, to get out, to go away was back. I hated that feeling, but the older I got, the more often it came.

I was born in Spain, but my mother took the voyage to the New World when I was a baby. The Americas were all I knew, and I wondered if this place was any good for people like us. It didn't seem to be. Witches—or more often than not, humans accused of witchcraft—were being killed left and right, and I feared for our safety. If it weren't for the wards which were pressing in on my skin, we would be known to the humans who colonized so close to us.

Despite the climate outside our wards, I could not stay in this bed or this house or this commune one more second, and although my stupidity would be monumental, I still tiptoed on stocking feet across the freshly polished floor to the thick wooden door which led outside.

I'd polished that floor, and every other piece of furniture and bit of silver in our house. I polished shoes, too. I milked the cows, I tended the chickens, I fed the pigs.

What I did not do, was learn anything other than how to tend a house. Valuable information—but not valuable enough.

Mama did not let me practice with the other girls my age. I did not learn the spells I needed to—the spells I should have been taught since I learned to speak.

Which was not to say I did not know some things, but what I knew scared me. I was stronger than the girls my age. I was stronger than all of them put together. I could do things even my own mother could not do. I could do things this entire coven could not—like walk right through a ward as if it wasn't there.

Unlatching the door, I snatched up the boots from their tidy row and stepped out into the night, careful to stick to the shadows wrought by the flickering flames of torches on the walking path. The coven was working something big—every girl my age was attending a ceremony.

Every girl except for me.

It hurt to know I was never going to be included, never going to be the woman my mother wanted me to be, but a large part of myself screamed to get out from under these wards, out from under my mother's thumb.

I was suffocating here under a weight which did not seem to be mine to bear. It didn't seem right that I was the one always on the outskirts of my own family.

Making it to the edge of our land was easy, the only hiccup was walking through the ward hexes without breaking them. As much as

I needed to be free, leaving my family unprotected was three steps past stupid and reckless on a scale even I wasn't capable of.

Fifteen wards—one from each of our elders—guarded our land. Not only did humans not cross into our property, any Ethereal would be shocked into unconsciousness and likely trapped in a magical snare very few could escape. Plus, anyone who came within a stone's throw would feel a gut-wrenching urge to leave.

But not me.

Picking my way through the wards, I took my first breath of fresh air. Mist was falling, and I tilted my face to the sky. I wanted to stay there breathing in the cool autumn scent of the forest for a moment before I headed back inside the boundary.

Before I could bring myself to head back in, a man's pained groans caught my ears. I should have gone back inside the wards. I should have, but I didn't. Instead, I followed the sounds of agony to find a man clawing away from the warding snare. It didn't matter that he flashed back and forth between what I assumed was his true form of semi-solid black smoke and his glamour of a human man—the snare still caught him.

His human form was of a well-dressed older man. Wavy light-brown hair fell across his face obscuring his features except for the bright luminescent golden glow of his eyes. The buttons on his waistcoat were polished brass, and his boots were supple leather. He was likely wealthy or at least appeared so, but I knew appearances could be deceiving.

I appeared to be a defenseless fourteen-year-old girl, and I most certainly was not.

Something about the man called to me. I'd never seen an Ethereal like him. Not even in passing. Our coven was secluded—hidden away from everyone and everything else who moved in the shadows of our world. He felt familiar in a way that I could not deny.

I had to help him. Had to.

But the only way to help him was to drop the wards—to put my family in danger. It was wrong. It was the worst idea I could think of.

"S-s-s-save m-m-m-me..." The thought hissed through my head, but I knew I hadn't heard a sound. It wasn't my voice, it was his.

"I will," I promised, but I didn't tell my mouth to do so. It was as if my mind had been taken over by someone else. The closer I got to him, the more I needed to do whatever I could to make sure he lived.

Without my mind telling my feet to do so, I pivoted toward the hex marks of our coven's ward, snapping the protection spells one by one, until the snare around the man's foot fell away.

"S-s-s-s-save m-m-m-me..."

Then I found myself whispering words of healing—spells too advanced for my young body to handle. A smarter part of me screamed to stop, but I couldn't halt the Latin falling from my lips or the charged green light flickering from my hands.

I was not in control, and I had a sinking feeling that this man, whoever he was, had taken over my body and my powers to free himself. Blood dripped from my nose, and I crumpled to the wet bracken of the forest floor—my legs too weak to hold me up before I regained control of myself.

The man lay there—his form still, glamoured as a human. He appeared to be sleeping, his eyes closed, and his brow unfurrowed, but a large part of me knew better.

I had to get away from him—whoever he was—before he took control over me again. But I didn't get the chance. The sound of hoof beats hit my ears, and their simple squelching echo was enough to put a pit of fear in my belly.

Horses meant men. Men meant humans. Humans who could have seen me do magic. Humans who all too frequently burned women alive for even the assumption of practicing magic.

I didn't have enough time to put the wards back up. I didn't even have enough time or energy to run.

A pair of footmen grabbed me by my elbows, wrenching me from the forest floor and away from the man who was anything but.

They shouted at me, calling me witch and demon. They spat in my face and tore at my clothes, searching for a devil's mark. It wouldn't have mattered if I didn't have one. The footmen were in the employ of a magistrate who rode in the coach, which happened to be passing by.

They thought I killed the man who was lying so still in the mud and leaves that he appeared dead. They saw the green light coming from my hands—they saw my magic.

Without a chance to speak for myself, they tied me to a tree, took a lantern from the coach, and threw it at my feet—the glass and fuel exploding as it hit the base of the oak.

Flames caught the cotton of my dress first, and sooner than I thought possible, I was left to scream out my dying breaths alone as men watched me burn.

Blackness consumed me for what seemed like eternity. I was alone in the dark and I worried over every wrong I'd done and every mistake I'd made in my short life. I was stuck and freezing, and so, so scared.

Eventually a pinprick of light came in the darkness, and I followed it until I could open my eyes and take a new breath.

The forest looked different. A circle around my naked and freezing form was black as night. As black as the void where I had come from. A folded stack of clothes and a pair of boots sat just outside the ring of charred earth, and I fell on them, wrenching the dress and stockings on as fast as I could.

Once I was dressed, I noticed my mother standing not far off, but she didn't seem happy at all to see I was alive.

In fact, when I took a step toward her, she took a step back.

"Mama..." I trailed off, not knowing what I could say for myself. I didn't know how I could even survive the hell of burning and come back unscathed. I didn't know anything anymore.

"You are not my daughter. You are not a member of this coven. You are banished. You are Rogue. No coven will take you. No coven will accept the abomination you have become."

Every word from her mouth was a blow. I knew I should not have dropped the wards, but I wasn't in control. And abomination? How?

"I don't know what happened. What happened to me?"

"You are not a witch. You are something else, and I will not let you taint us any longer."

"But, Mama. I don't understand. How am I alive? I burned. I died," I whispered through sharp sobs which seemed to cut at my chest. "What happened to me?"

"What happened is, you put us all in danger. You took our home from us. You nearly killed us. You tore away every protection we had and now we have to settle somewhere else."

"But I wasn't in control. There was a man made of smoke. He was trapped in the ward snare. He made me free him. I didn't want to. He took over my mind, Mama."

The color leeched from my mother's face, but she didn't answer me. She didn't do anything but snap her fingers, and in a flash of red light, she left me in that forest alone.

Micah's smile is the first thing I see when the vision of my past fades. Red eyes and the smallest glimpse of white fangs peek from the sneering uptick of his mouth. Good to know I'm amusing at least.

"So, I'm not the first demon you've met. Interesting. I'd wondered…"

The man from my past—the one who got me killed, the one who ruined my life—was a demon? There are demons?

It didn't really matter. The vision was long, and his power to see my worst memories had an added benefit he didn't anticipate—they made me angry. An angry witch—at least this angry witch—isn't someone to be trifled with.

Micah still had my forearms in his grip, but every red-blooded girl knows the best way to break a man's hold on her. Kneeing Micah in the balls is as satisfying as one could expect. Good to know that part of his anatomy is equivalent. By the time he can catch his breath, I've transported myself out of my basement.

I land on my hands and knees in a glittering pile of shattered glass. Not my best landing, but I still give Striker a tremulous smile when he makes it to me, sliding through broken glass on now-booted feet.

He doesn't catch me, though. The floor does when I lose my fight against the dark.

CHAPTER EIGHT

MAX

The crick in my neck is what hauls me from the blackness. That and the gentle rocking of a moving car. I pop up from what appears to be the back seat of an SUV and panic for a second, until my eyes land on Striker's blond curls and square jaw.

Calming down, I gauge my surroundings. First off, my wounds are bandaged—white gauze and medical tape cover the majority of my forearms. Aches and pains make themselves known throughout my body, and I'm in a new outfit—a decidedly less bloody one of loose black linen drawstring shorts and a gray T-shirt, with a little pocket over the right breast. Said breasts are encased in a black camisole, and based on the level of squish, it has an attached shelf bra. The clothing is familiar since it's mine, and likely procured from my spare closet in the apartment above the shop.

I could be embarrassed about the fact that I did not dress myself, but if Striker did it, then he's already seen everything. Hell, he's done most of the artwork on places which are only accessible by way of complete nudity. He did the dragon that spans from my left shoulder blade over my ribs and down my abdomen to wrap around my left leg. I was pretty much naked for about a month.

I spy Melody in the passenger seat munching on beef jerky and I figure with the heaviness to her belly, it would be unlikely that she would have helped the unconscious woman into new clothes.

"Oh, good. You're alive. I worried I was going to have to bury your rotting carcass in one of these Fate's forsaken corn fields," Striker quips as he passes back a bottle of water, his eyes never leaving the road. He's right. We are beset on both sides by never-ending cornfields on a straight highway which seems to go on forever.

I take the bottle and chug half of it in a few gulps.

"So happy I didn't inconvenience you too much. Where are we? How did I get here? And holy shit on a stick, darling, your ex is the fucking worst," I address Melody. She gives me a sidelong no-shit stare as she shoves another piece of jerky in her mouth.

"We're somewhere in Iowa on the way to Indiana. I figured the further we were from Micah the better, considering every time you tangle with that dickhead, you pass out. Speaking of, everything but the burns have healed. I don't know what the hell is up with that nonsense."

"How long have I been out?" The not-healing bit isn't great. I don't know what's going on there.

"About twenty-eight hours." Granted, I don't heal exceptionally fast in comparison to other Ethereals, but at the twenty-eight-hour mark I should be pretty close to good. And if I died, well, I typically don't come back with injuries.

"Was I unconscious or the other thing?" I pitch my voice lower since I don't know how much weird Melody can handle.

"You mean dead?" Melody accuses. "Yeah, we had that scare already, but no. You were just unconscious. Thanks for that, by the way. I so enjoy feeling like shit because people stepped in to help me and got hurt. What the hell?"

Melody may be an infant compared to me, but impending motherhood has turned her into one round-bellied mama bear complete with a glare only a real mom could accomplish.

"Well, excuse me for saving both of your lives and getting out in one semi-charred piece. Reliving being burned alive was super fun," I shoot back, my snark at peak level.

"No one asked you to do that. You could have come with us. You could have closed the door and been on the other side. You could have been safe. Instead, you decided to play cowboy and got yourself hurt. Again. Not. Cool." Striker's low voice hits me like a slap.

My leaving really hurt him. I didn't assume he'd like the fact I put him in charge of Melody, but I honestly didn't think I had enough time to get through and close it behind me. I honestly didn't think I could keep them safe.

I didn't think, and that more than anything is the problem. He has been stewing on this for a while now, and even with Melody here, he can't control the venom in his voice.

"What would you have had me do? I put the both of you first. I made sure you were safe. I could barely stand, so I knew I couldn't walk through anything, let alone the doorway. I did what I thought was best, and I'm not sorry, so we'll just have to agree to disagree. Now, is there a rest stop in our future because I haven't peed in over a day and I'm about due."

After another thirty minutes of tense silence, we finally find a rest stop. I race Melody to the bathroom, and I manage to get there first, pee, and wash my hands before she can waddle her butt to the door with Striker keeping pace so she's not alone. Dammit, they are so cute together, I can't stand it.

We make a stop at the nearby convenience store for snacks and coffee before piling back into the SUV and hitting the road.

It takes us another eight hours, ten rest stops, and three driver changes before we arrive in Melody's hometown on the outskirts of Fort Wayne, Indiana. The sun is setting on the green rolling hills of her family's farm, and I'm hit with a pang of loneliness I didn't know I could have. This farm makes me homesick for a home I've never even had.

The scene is idyllic with a sprawling ranch house, a painted red barn in the background, and clear pond close to the road that reflects the summer sky. It looks like a home—something I wouldn't really know about, nor have I experienced in my long life. The dirt road that leads to a farmhouse is enclosed by a horse gate, which Striker jumps out to open so we can pull through.

An older couple—maybe early fifties—meets us at the mouth of the driveway that curves just to the left of the porch stairs. They fall on Melody like a pair of love-starved wolves, as they hug her and kiss her hair. Her mother puts gentle hands to the large swell of her belly, and a sick part of me can't handle it. It can't possibly handle a show of this much love and support.

It isn't to say that I'm not happy she's safe, I am. I am thrilled beyond fucking measure. Unfortunately, I am also a jealous cow because I cannot stop the bitter pang in my chest that wonders why I've never had this.

My mother hated me from the gate, and my father was nowhere to be found. I've never heard my mother speak of him, and if I had a guess, he was the reason we left Spain in the first place. The only place I've had love at all is in Striker's friendship and the Constantine's family. How sad it must be for me to be jealous of a child's love. I manage to get myself under control before I step out of the SUV, but not before I get a look from Striker that tells me he read every single emotion that has ran through my body.

I don't like being read. I don't like that he knows how weak I've been in the last forty-eight hours. I don't like that I've been weak at all. Maybe it's due to the fact I've been forced to relive the deaths that have marked me so, but I feel as if I've been cursed for a very long time.

Scott and Nadine invite Striker and I into their home without a second thought. Genuine hospitality seeps from their every pore and action. Nadine fusses over my injuries, which we were very vague about when recounting the story to Melody's parents.

The pair of them swear up and down that Striker and I saved their baby girl from an evil man (*very true*) and refused to hear another word about it. Well, Nadine didn't want to hear another word. Scott took Striker and I aside and wanted to know what Micah looked like, and whether or not he should tell his county sheriff about him.

This was a quandary, because if Micah were human, I'd say hell yes. But since he isn't, Striker and I were going to have to be real smooth with how we protected this family. Finally, it was decided that I would walk the grounds and ward as I went.

"Melody, how about you show me around?" I offer as a cover as I usher her outside, and we make a small circle at the main perimeter of the lawn.

"I need to do this circuit ten times. Can we do that and not wig out your parents?" I ask, muttering in Latin as I stop every ten feet.

"Probably. Honestly, I think we should just tell them. Mama is part Cherokee. My grandma taught us the old ways. She'd take it to heart, and we'd be safer if we knew where to step and where to stay safe."

Melody's offer has merit. I've never been a big fan of keeping people in the dark—especially about their own safety.

"Are you sure?" I hedge, unwilling to make a decision without Striker's assessment. He's better at reading people than I am, obviously.

"I'm pretty sure. Plus, who knows what abilities this kid will have. I'm going to bring a child into this world, and I have no idea what he'll become. I'll have to contend with more than may be rational, and they will, too. At least if I tell them now, I'll have you two as backup in case they want to cart me off to the mental institution," she says with a self-deprecating smirk. She's joking, in a "ha-ha, this could really happen so don't leave me," kind of way.

Just then, Striker sidles up to us and wraps an arm around Melody's shoulders. She sort of melts into his side for a moment, and I can't help but smile. Striker is at least four hundred years her senior, but in that tiny bit of time, his eyes don't take on the weight of the centuries he's spent on this planet. For the first time, he appears almost content.

For the first time in a long time, I wonder if I could live without him. I think if he were this happy, I could.

I so could.

After a nice home-cooked meal, Striker and I sit Nadine and Scott down and explain what really happened to their daughter.

"This is nonsense!" Scott shouts as he shoots up from his seat. He paces his living room, his face red with indignation. Personally, I don't blame him. Who wants to know that the world as they knew it is a lie?

"I assure you, I am not a liar," I murmur, but the volume of my voice doesn't matter. What matters is the green casting light weaving around my fingertips like a sentient yet weightless liquid. Scott's eyes lock on my hands until I snap my fingers and the lights go out. I snap again and they come back on. I flex and relax them, and he watches as the lights in their living room dim and brighten enough to hurt our eyes.

"Th-this is a trick. This has to be a trick," Nadine whispers, her voice tremulous as she watches a lamp she's had for probably twenty years, like it will jump at her at any moment.

"No trick. And I'm not here to hurt you. Or your family. Melody came into our shop afraid and alone. We took her away from the man who hurt her and brought her home. The only reason we are telling you anything is because we want to keep her safe just like you do." This seems to placate him a little, and in the end, Scott and his wife believe us—that their safety is all we want.

But when the time came, I didn't keep anyone safe at all.

CHAPTER NINE

MAX

Munching on a likely cancer-causing bit of snack food, I fiddle with Striker's phone, trying to find some good music. His taste in music is questionable at best, but finding a quality radio station during a road trip is a pain in the ass. Every fifty miles or so, the station craps out and I have to switch it again.

Plus, I have a solid aversion to top-forty music. The stations just outside of Chicago weren't bad, but the farther we get from the sprawling city, the less the good stations tune in.

I'm giving Striker shit for his questionable taste in music, trying to perk him up after we left Melody, but I'm not having much luck. He merely stares at the stretch of highway in front of us and periodically grunts at me.

I offered to make my own way back to Denver before we left so he could stay, but Striker's been with me so long, I don't know if he could handle letting me go out on my own. The last few times I did, he was not pleased with the shape I came back in.

I get it, but I wish he would have stayed with Melody. She made him lighter—made him happy. Even though he barely spent more than two days with her, he'd been less bogged down with the emotions of everyone else, and instead, found his own happiness.

It pisses me off that he chooses me instead of himself, but Strike wouldn't be him if he *didn't* sacrifice himself. A part of me recognizes that same irritating quality in myself.

What a pair we are.

When the phone rings in my hand, I fumble and nearly drop it on the floorboard. Melody's name flashes across the screen and for some reason—even though I haven't answered the phone—I know it's bad. I answer the call, my heart sinking to my feet at her panicked whisper.

"Max! You have to come back. He's here. I do-don't know what to do."

I look at Striker. He can't hear what she's saying, but he can feel my emotions well enough. I mouth "turn around" as I try to affect my most calming voice. Inside, I'm screaming.

"Okay, darling. Here's what I want you to do. Find some salt. Your mother keeps a ton of it in the kitchen, right?"

I pull my mouth from the receiver. "Find a building, whatever. We need cover," I tell Strike, noticing the knuckles of his fingers turning white as he grips the steering wheel hard enough to bend it. I need to make a doorway, and I can only do that against a wall or building. I sure as shit can't do it on the side of a busy highway for everyone to see.

"Y-yes. But he has Mama and Daddy. He-he says he'll hurt them if I don't come out. Max, I'm scared." The pain in her voice is like a lash against my skin.

Micah will most likely kill them either way, and that fact hurts so much. She has to know that. She can't do what he wants—not ever.

"I know, baby girl, but he'll hurt them even if you do what he wants. Find the salt, Melody." I try to stay calm. I don't want her to hear the guilt. I don't want her to know that I'm just as scared as she is.

I hear some rustling around and a cabinet slamming before she comes back.

"Okay, I've got some."

"Good. Make a ring around yourself. Thick as you can. It will offer some protection. Striker and I will be there in two shakes, you got it?"

"Ye-yes. You're coming for me, right? Striker's coming, isn't he?" Her voice breaks on the end, and it whips at me like another lash.

For some reason, I'm so glad Striker can't hear the desperation in her voice. The fear. I'm glad these words won't be what wakes him up at night if we don't make it.

"Striker and I are coming. We will always come for you, okay, darling girl? Always. You hang tight."

I disconnect and grab the oh-shit handle as the SUV fishtails when we take the next exit a bit faster than recommended. Still, Striker manages to not roll us and pulls into a storage facility. One of those places for people who have too many things.

"Please tell me you packed my shit," I pray to myself more than asking Strike if he has. I doubt he would have stopped if I didn't have what I needed.

He's at the liftgate before I am, pulling out a black backpack. I don't need much for this spell, but I do need chalk. It isn't like before when I didn't have enough of my own juice to make a doorway and had to resort to using chicken blood. I have more than enough now.

Digging in the pack, I produce the white chalk and draw a rectangle on the brick of one of the storage units. Murmuring the spell, I feel Striker's urgency radiating off of him.

I just hope we aren't too late.

The portal opens into the Danvers' living room. Coming through the doorway, the first thing I smell is blood. Lots of it. A man in horse-working clothes appears to have been disemboweled where he sat on the couch. He isn't Scott, but might have once been a farmhand of theirs. He's young, maybe Melody's age, sweet-looking even in his final rest.

This is who Melody should have been with. She should have stayed in this idyllic country home. Married the sweet farmhand

and had his babies. This blood-soaked scene shouldn't be her life.

Over the stench of the recently dead, I try to focus and send my senses out, but the house is still.

"Search the upstairs. Yell if you need me."

Striker is already halfway up the staircase before I get a grunt of assent. He doesn't give one single shit about anything other than finding Melody, and I can't say I blame him.

Moving to the open Dutch door separating the kitchen and living room, my sandals crunch and scrape the broken crockery and salt littering the floor. I skitter to a stop when I see the salt circle in the middle of the room.

It's empty.

The scattered grains are peppered with drops of fresh blood. Melody should still be in that circle. Nothing could have broken that protection that quick. Two minutes. It took us two minutes to get here. It should have been enough time. We should have made it.

Why didn't we make it?

Looking past the circle, little droplets lead to the kitchen door, and I can't stop myself from following them. I feel it against my skin—there isn't another live person here.

I can't figure it out. Why didn't the wards protect them? Why couldn't my magic save them? What makes this guy so much different that my magic does nothing?

The droplets grow more significant as they lead to the porch and turn to puddles that soak the dirt driveway and parts of the grass. In the middle of one of the pools is what I can only guess is Melody's dad. I don't know for sure since Scott's missing his head. And his vital organs. But the fabric of his T-shirt is the same as this morning when he gave me a tremulous hug before we left.

I could tell I made him slightly uncomfortable, which given the light show last night, was warranted. But he still hugged me. Still thanked me for helping his little girl. And the scent of his shirt caught my nose. It snagged my notice because I found it strange that he could have been working before the sun came up, but his shirt still smelled like pipe tobacco and earth. It's funny what one remembers. I still have that smell in my nose, but I can't get my brain to figure out why the man I knew for such a small measure of time is dead.

I've seen death many times over in my long life. I've seen torture and malice and every concoction of misery a person could think of. But never to this degree.

Never so much violence at once.

Nadine is close by, her puddle slightly smaller, but her evisceration much, much worse. Nadine died last, and Melody had to watch. If not watch, then she heard her screams. I stifle a sob, pressing my palm to my mouth, so I don't start screaming myself.

A trail of blood and gore leads in the direction of the barn. I don't want to follow the path left for me. I don't want to know what lies in wait for me. I just want this all to be a bad dream I can wake up from. I want Melody to be safe.

I don't think I'm going to get what I want.

I pick my way past the gore and follow the trail to the horse barn, danger pricking at my skin with every step. I don't think I'm going to like what I find in here.

At the wide-open entrance, I feel someone coming at me, but I'm ready. I turn to look, and the red eyes are enough to have me snapping my fingers. I watch as the man's head twists on his neck, effectively breaking it as if it were a dry twig.

A faint memory bubbles up. I remember telling Ian once that I could snap his neck with a flick of my fingers. I was half-joking at the time, irritated at him for using my full name. I wouldn't have hurt Ian, but the amount of satisfaction I feel at the crunch of bones makes me a little sick.

I shouldn't want to smile. I shouldn't feel good for killing someone—even if it is likely temporary.

But I do.

I'm lamenting over my own morality when a knife slashes across my upper back. I was too busy focusing on my own shit, I didn't pay any fucking attention to the fact that Micah had five friends. Yeah, I "killed" one, but there are potentially four others ready and waiting to kill me.

The agony of the blow takes me to my knees. The pulsing lash of white-hot pain flashes across my brain. The kick to the ribs and the subsequent gut twist of a bone breaking catches me off guard. I have yet to see my attacker, but he's kicking my ass something fierce.

Bile fills my mouth as I try to scramble away, but all too soon, burning hands snatch one of my feet right out from under me. My face smashes against the concrete before I'm airborne—tossed like a rag doll into the door of a horse stall. The boards give way under the force and I land half-in and half-out.

One of my arms isn't working, and my burned leg is probably broken.

I'm fucked. I am so fucked.

Adrenaline courses through me—fight or flight my ass. I need to get my shit together or this bastard is going to kill me. I don't want to know what happens if he succeeds.

I can't die right now. I can't. I can't let this thing kill me.

I spy a black double-barrel shotgun propped against the wall in a little cubby next to the open barn door. I need that gun. Using what little power I have left, I snap my fingers, the gun flying into my hand almost faster than I'm ready for.

I press the latch and open the barrel, thankful the damn thing is loaded. I aim, vaguely aware that this might be my only chance.

Pulling the trigger is harder than it should be. Hell, breathing is harder than it should be. But I never hear the gun go off.

I don't hear anything at all.

CHAPTER TEN

STRIKER

When Melody came into the shop, I never expected to be here in her childhood bedroom trying to glean something—anything—about where she is.

It's as if she's just gone.

Not dead.

Gone.

Max thinks I'm merely an empath—a dying breed of witch that no one really gives a shit about unless they are trying to hide something. And in a sense, she's right. It's true, I can feel every single person's emotions as if they are my own. If I didn't ward my mind like Fort Knox, I'd be batshit insane by now.

But I can do things that I don't have an explanation for. I can do things that scare the shit out of me. One of them is the ability to tell where a person is—on this side or the other.

If I have a strong mental connection with that person, it is as if I can follow their emotions no matter where they are.

But not Melody. It didn't matter that my gut was filled with worry. It didn't matter that my heart physically ached in my chest every single second since I left her here.

It doesn't matter, because no matter how hard I have tried, I can't find her.

And it pisses me the fuck off.

I'm still trying to glean something from the objects in her room when the blast of a gun rings out, echoing its death knell across the rolling hills of the farm.

I can't say how I made it down the stairs. Or across the lawn past the dead bodies that barely seemed to register. But standing in the doorway of the barn, the scene before me is crystal clear.

Max is unconscious, hanging half-in and half-out of the debris remnants of a horse stall door with a shotgun loosely held in her arms that don't seem to be working. Across the walkway lies an incubus, still as death, and another incubus screaming and clawing at what appears to be the melting refuse of what used to be his face.

And the smell... Sulfur mixed with ass mixed with horse manure.

If I didn't care about whether Max was still breathing, I would give into the bitter urge I have to put my boot in the melting leftovers of his neck and snap it, but Max means more to me than my revenge.

I have to get her out of here. I need to get her to help, and there is only one person I can ask.

Transportation was a problem at first, but I figured Max wouldn't mind if I hijacked her powers for a little while to get us the hell out of here. Another one of my dazzling and altogether unexplainable abilities. I can't exactly use much magic myself, but if the need is great and I put my mind to it, I can play puppet master for a few seconds to get what I need.

I don't like doing it. It makes me feel sick to use someone, but desperate times and all that.

Arriving on his doorstep with a broken Max in my arms doesn't exactly seem to be a good plan, but I don't have time to rethink it before the door opens to reveal the man I caught Max making out with almost a year ago on that long-forgotten night before the world turned to shit.

"Hey, Ian. I know you're going to have questions, but a little help?" I kind of jiggle Max at him to maybe unfreeze him somewhat.

I don't know if he can't quite figure out how we bypassed the doorman, if he is pissed we're here at all, or if he just can't process, but he's solid as a statue while Max just keeps bleeding on me.

"Ian!"

My shout seems to snap him out of it, because before I can track it, Max is out of my arms and into his. He turns, hauling ass into his apartment, and I follow, slamming the door shut behind me. A hipster-looking man I've never met jumps to his feet from a black leather couch that looks like it belongs in a frat house, roughly tossing his beer to the coffee table. By a wing and a prayer, the bottle stays right-side up. And he's in a beanie. Who the fuck wears a beanie in July, for shit's sake?

I have no idea at all why I'm focused on that stupid amber glass or his choice of fashion accessories and not my friend.

The shock, I guess.

I think I'd rather think of just about anything but my friend being hurt, or my woman being captured. Maybe I'm stuck on trivial details because if I don't, I'll plan precisely what I'll do to the men who took Melody when I catch them. I'll end up going off half-cocked and screw myself over for sure. Me, I'm not so worried about, but Melody...

"What happened?" Ian sets her on an empty pool table, yanking a black medical bag from underneath it. This preparedness isn't exactly surprising. Ian Moran is known in certain circles as a top-notch doctor, and he doesn't really care which side of the law someone is on as long as they pay.

I doubt I'll have to cough up the dough for Max, but I will if he needs me to.

"I'm not exactly sure. We got separated. Short answer? I have no fucking idea. Long answer? Incubi."

An aghast whistle sounds from the man I've never met, and I

nod. A single incubus is a pain in the ass. More than one is a major fucking catastrophe of epic proportions. I was vague as shit when Max asked about them, and not explaining it to her may make me a dick, but I never expected there to be more than one.

Let alone five.

Ian assesses Max, checking her airway before taking a pair of shears to her shirt and bra. What he sees doesn't make him happy at all.

"Aidan, get my surgical equipment. One of her lungs is punctured," Ian barks before hauling ass to the kitchen sink to wash his hands.

He doesn't care that Max has bled all over his once-crisp white shirt. He does not give that first fuck. His manner is a cold-blooded unemotional bag of focus I can appreciate in a medical professional. Aidan grabs a plastic box with a pull-away vellum lid. Inside is a pair of surgical gloves, plastic tubing, gauze, and a scalpel.

Ian dons the gloves before pressing two fingers against Max's left side feeling for her ribs. Then he takes the scalpel and pushes it into her skin.

"Make yourself useful, huh? Grab a bucket," he commands, and I have no doubt he's talking to me. I do what he says, searching his obviously bachelor kitchen for something close to bucket-ish. I find it in one of those plastic margarita buckets one gets in Panama City Beach during spring break.

"Get the lead out!" he calls.

At that moment, I choose not to judge Ian for his obviously sophomoric youth and get the lead out. I offer Aidan the bucket. Ian is already inserting the clamped tube into Max's chest as Aidan holds the bucket at the edge of the table and puts the other end of the tube into it. When Ian unclamps it, a rush of blood runs through the plastic, burgundy lifeblood staining it red.

"Get over here," Ian commands and I hop to. He passes me a face mask with a bag attached. Luckily, I've seen enough re-runs of every single medical drama known to mankind, so I know exactly what I'm supposed to do. Two squeezes of the bag are all it takes for Max to abandon those shallow, panting breaths for slower, deeper ones.

Ian watches her for a few minutes before taking a suture kit to the tube in her chest, and I've never been happier that I don't actually have to look at something that gross.

"Okay, now that Max is breathing again, I'm gonna need you to tell me what the fuck happened to her. Because if you're at fault, I'll find a way to kill your ass, I don't care if I have to make one up." Ian seethes as he ties a knot in the sutures and moves down Max's body to check for more wounds.

A part of me wants to punch him in the face, but I'm finding it difficult to fault the guy. I can sense the love he has for Max—she's it for him. It's likely a wraith bonding trait that he just can't shake. Or maybe it's more. I hope it's more. At least for Max's sake.

"A couple came into our tattoo shop a few days ago. The woman pregnant, the guy a total fuckwad. I could tell the woman—Melody—was in trouble. Max put the guy to sleep, and Melody told us she'd overheard him telling his friends he was going to kill her after she had the baby. Max and I thought we'd just get her out of town, right? But then the guy—Micah—woke up, and he grabbed Max. We got out of there, but he tracked us back to Max's house. We made it out and carted Melody home to Indiana. But, uh… He found her, anyway. Killed her family."

I have to stop there for a moment to clear my throat. I shouldn't be here explaining everything to Ian. I should be trying to locate Melody. I should be using every contact I know to get her back. What if he hurts her? What if she has the baby…

"I was looking for something of hers so Max could locate her. Max was in the barn. Two waylaid her. She took one out, but the other did some serious damage until she got him in the face with a shotgun blast of rock salt."

Aidan whistles again. "Which brings you here."

"Which brings us here."

"What I want to know is why you didn't protect Max. Demons can't touch you—not physically at least. Why didn't you keep an eye on her?" Ian seethes, his eyes flicking back and forth between black and dark brown.

Honestly, I'm stumped. I have no idea what's going on, and I tell Ian as much.

"What the fuck are you talking about?"

"The Armistice, stupid. Demons cannot touch angels and vice versa. Doing so would bring a war no one wants to be in the middle of. You could have protected her if you just stuck with her. They would have left her alone. Sure, she's half-demon, but with an angel in the mix, they wouldn't have even touched her."

"One, I have no bloody idea what you're talking about. Two, it didn't matter if I was right next to her, they attacked us all at first. Burned her arm. Made her see her worst memories. Something about the last time she died. Three, you're like a freaking toddler—how the hell do you know this shit?"

Ian's brow furrows in confusion for a hot second before understanding dawns. "You two have no idea what you really are, do you?"

I guess not.

CHAPTER ELEVEN

MAX

Sure, she's half-demon, but with an angel in the mix, they wouldn't have even touched her...

I know that voice, but it takes a minute for it to come to me. Ian. Why do I hear Ian? Where in the holy frick and frack am I? My eyelids take their sweet ass time opening, and it takes a while for me to realize I'm looking at the high ceiling of an apartment.

Then the pain makes itself known in a big fucking way, and I have to focus on the world around me, so the white-hot agony of healing bones and closing cuts doesn't take my breath away. The raised male voices grate on my nerves, but I'll take it.

Well, until Ian's words actually filter through my brain.

Sure, she's half-demon... Then, another little gem. *You two have no idea what you really are, do you?*

This has me popping up from whatever the hell it is I'm lying on like a jack in the box.

My voice is made of broken glass, but I manage to croak, "Who's half-demon?"

I can't really pay attention to the answer to my question due to the fact the white-hot agony I felt earlier has now morphed into some sort of soul-searing, mind-bending form of torture, and I nearly pass out. I also vaguely realize that I'm naked as a jaybird from the waist up, a fact I'm not even remotely fond of, but I can't quite process that right now. What I can process—and it's freaking me the fuck out—is the thick tubing coming from my ribs. It's sutured in such a way that my skin puckers around it.

I don't think I'm supposed to be awake for this part of healing. I think humans have it right and comas are probably best for all involved. Yes. A coma would be really nice right now.

"Jesus Christ, Max!" Ian moves in my direction and reaches for me, reclining me back down to what I now realize is a pool table before rummaging into his bag. I hope he has some really good drugs in there because I don't think Ibuprofen is going to cut it.

At this point, I'd take a hammer to the head and suffer through the brain damage. Plus, there is a wounded animal somewhere in this room. The sound coming from it chills me to the bone.

"I'm gonna take care of you." His dark eyes meet mine for a moment before he moves back to rummaging through his bag. It's then that I notice that sort of keening whimper is coming from my throat. I'm making that horrible sound.

"You're going to be fine, baby. I promise."

I feel a needle stick in my arm, and it takes less than a count of two before I'm off in floaty land.

It's then that I realize that no one answered my question, but I don't think I really need them to. I'm pretty sure the answer is something that has plagued me for nearly four centuries.

A truth I never wanted to admit to myself.

If I had a guess, I'd go with the half-demon is me.

But that could be the drugs talking...

I wake up again in the plush softness of a well-made bed. The room is dark, likely the middle of the night. Gingerly sitting up is my sole focus, and I manage to accomplish it without the blistering agony from before. Also, I'm clothed in a black T-shirt and blue boxer briefs. The tube is gone, and it is one of the few things I can mark in the win column.

This is the second time in forty-eight hours I've been dressed by someone *not* me, and I'm finding it rather irritating.

Disembarking the monster of a bed is next, and while I'm not a small woman, the distance from the surface to the floor seems a bit steep. I manage it, though, taking my best guess as to where the bathroom is and handling my business. At this point, I'd kill for a toothbrush, but I make do with the mangled toothpaste tube on the messy counter and my finger.

Then I peruse the bandages on my arms that seem to have gotten bigger, not smaller. That doesn't look good.

I take a gander at myself in the mirror and decide I've definitely looked better. My tan skin has a solid sallow look to it, and the bags under my eyes are big enough to go backpacking around Europe. Plus, my hair is a complete disaster of snarls, dried blood, and Fates know what else.

I need a shower. I need a day off. I need a vacation.

Melody. *Oh, god.*

Tearing out of the bathroom, I open the bedroom door and smack into a tall man in a beanie. I know this tall man, though.

"Who wears a beanie in July?" I stare at Aidan, and it all comes flooding back. I was hurt. Striker must have brought me to Ian.

"Don't judge me for my fashion choices, and I won't judge you for yours, Smurfette."

"Real original. Where's Striker? And Ian? Ian was here, right?" My recollection of events is a little vague.

"In the living room trying not to kill each other, most likely."

I move past him before his words actually register. "Wait, why would they be trying to kill each other?"

Aidan just shakes his head and mutters something along the lines of, "not my circus, not my monkeys."

I make my way down the sparsely decorated hall to an open-concept large room that seems to serve as a living, dining, and kitchen area. It's decked out in a Spartan-meets-frat-boy style. A pool table instead of a dining one, a leather couch that looks like it could seat fifteen, a TV bigger than some billboards, and an entertainment center with every single gaming console known to mankind spilling from it.

If I didn't know them better, I would assume Ian and Aidan were twenty, not over a hundred.

"You'll go in there over my dead, rotting corpse." Ian's low, rumbling growl sounds through the open room.

Ian's standing in Striker's way, a clawed talon pressing into the center of Striker's chest. Striker is holding one of my overnight bags with what I hope is all of my makeup, hair supplies, and a fresh set of clothes, and shoes. For some reason, he isn't letting Striker pass.

"Is there a magic word my best friend needs to say to get past you, or what? Because we can leave. In fact, leaving sounds like a fine option. I got shit to do."

Both men turn to me, Ian's phase fading away before I catch his eyes, but I don't miss the sliver of hurt in them before he masks it.

"I wanted to get you up and dressed so we can go, and Dr. Moran here didn't feel up to releasing his patient while he spewed a bunch of bullshit. But you're awake now, so the argument is moot."

A growl erupts from Ian, but I talk over it.

"Spewed what bullshit?"

"I don't—"

I cut him off before he can give me some excuse. "What bullshit, Striker?" His tawny eyes glow for a second before they narrow, his jaw clenching in that way of his that means he won't tell me unless I beat it out of him.

Striker won't say, but Ian will. "Cough it up." I pierce Ian with my stare. He's all too willing to oblige.

"You're half-demon. Your friend here is half-angel. I don't know what you stumbled in, but those burns on your arms are part of it."

This doesn't throw me for the loop I thought it would—to have it all but confirmed.

"And you're sure about this?" I cross my arms despite the nagging ache in them.

"Pretty sure. I got it from a rather reliable source." Ian mirrors my stance as he gives Striker his back.

"What I want to know," Aidan interjects from behind me, "is what you meant by 'the last time she died.' Are you a necromancer or something?"

His questions sting. It isn't the first time it's been asked, and likely won't be the last.

"No, I'm not a fucking necromancer. I'm not in service to a damn demon. And you two should know what he meant by that. You were both there." I fling out a hand in anger, causing the lights to flicker some. *Whoops.*

"At Mena's. When the ward broke. I didn't save you, did I? I didn't keep you alive. You died." Ian's pained murmur causes my chest to ache.

"If it makes you feel any better, I didn't think I'd come back that time." My voice nearly peters out. "I'd never died that way before, so your efforts were appreciated."

Ian looks at me like I've lost my damn mind, and Striker's eyes start glowing again. Way wrong thing to say.

"No, it doesn't make me feel any better!" Ian scolds. "Why didn't you tell anyone?"

How could I condense a lifetime of pain, suffering, and general despondency into a single sentence?

"I was kicked out of my coven at fourteen for coming back after being burned at the stake. I have emotional damage. Excuse the shit out of me."

Ian just rolls his eyes. "I'm a half-black Irishman who also happens to have been born over a hundred years ago. Not to mention, I'm also half-wraith and half whatever the bloody hell my mother was to create the amalgamation of abilities that seem to screw me over at every turn. No, I couldn't possibly know what discrimination looks like." His voice is straight deadpan as he blinks at me like I'm an idiot, the Irish in his accent flaring.

Okay, he has a fair point on a multitude of levels.

"So, I should have told you. Agreed. I apologize for withholding pertinent information about myself."

Both Ian and Aidan seem to ponder on my apology for a minute while Striker seethes. I get it. Melody is in the hands of the very men we vowed to protect her from. Getting a move on would be awesome at this point.

"You said everything had to do with Max's burns. You going to elaborate?"

"I can't. I don't know enough about it to say either way. But there's someone we can talk to, and he could help to get your girl back. But if I were you, I'd get dressed up."

"Why?" The question falls from my lips.

"Because we're going to Aether."

I can't figure out why that name sounds familiar until it dawns on me. It's the witch club we went to ages ago.

I hope Striker packed something good in that overnight bag. *I think I'm gonna need it.*

CHAPTER TWELVE

MAX

It took over an hour for me to get my shit tight enough to attempt to walk back into that club. I likely wasn't actually welcome in Aether, but Ian promised us he knew the owner, and could get us in. Luckily, Striker either already planned on going there to ask questions, or he grabbed the first outfit he thought would make me feel pretty after almost getting dead.

I choose to believe option two when it's probably more like option one.

I fidget, pulling the sleeve of my black leather jacket further down to cover the white of the bandages on my forearms as I inspect myself in the lone floor-length mirror in Ian's apartment. Getting ready for a club night isn't my normal, but since my day-to-day look is full makeup and hair, I'm a pro at making myself up in a hurry. Striker helped by drying my rolled hair while I did my eyeliner, so my typical hour and a half get-ready time was cut significantly.

I paired the jacket with a black deep V-cut, loose-fit silk tank and cropped black leather pants. The kicker was the Christian Louboutin five-inch, silver studded, spike-heeled pumps. They are shiny and a little dangerous. I love them, even though the price tag was fourteen steps past ridiculous.

My thick, blue glam waves make me feel a little more normal, even if my whole life is more than a little upside down. Plus, I feel weird. Not sick, not hurt, just weird. Drained, maybe?

"Are you going to look at yourself in the mirror a bit more or are you going to get a move on?" Striker asks from my left as he adjusts the cufflinks of his starched white shirt. He's dressed in a suit again, even though he likely could get away with the outfit he was wearing an hour ago. Like me, he doesn't want to risk getting thrown out before we know something substantial.

"Get a move on, I guess. I feel weird, though."

"You just had a tube in you, draining blood from vital organs. I'd feel weird too. Now, let's go."

Nodding, I follow him to meet Ian and Aidan in the living room. Aidan gives me a wolf whistle, and Ian elbows the taller man in his ribs. No idea what that's about.

Since he's supposed to take us where we need to go, everyone puts a hand on Aidan. Aidan is a full-blooded wraith, and unless his position has changed, he's a guardian for the crowned king and queen of his species. His abilities are a bit of a mystery to me, but the one I'm familiar with is the one where he can smoke in and out of anywhere at any time. One second he's a man, and the next he's a swath of black smoke and gone. It's creepy as hell. Without so much as a count to three, the wraith uses his gifts to transport the lot of us to the Denver warehouse district.

Aidan's wraith gifts are made of suckass, I think as I wobble on my spike heels and try not to vomit on the cracked pavement when we land. Transport the wraith way kind of feels like every molecule in your body is being ripped apart and put together wrong. I am not a fan.

I manage not to lose the contents of my stomach on the sidewalk and follow the men to the warehouse door that seems to have sprung up out of nowhere. Ian slides it open to reveal much the same as the last time I was here. This time, however, the acrobats are on rings suspended from the ceiling that seems to match the starry night sky, and instead of being naked, their bits and pieces are barely covered in peacock feathers. They swing and twirl above the dance floor, and I'm amazed for a second, before my hand is tugged and I stumble forward.

Ian has my hand in his, and instead of flowing around the crowd, we're skirting it completely to find a less crowded section and a solid black door that reads, "Management." Ian knocks, and a woman I recognize opens it. She's tall and blonde, and I distinctly remember her plastering herself on Striker's lap the last time we were here.

"Doctor Moran. I don't recall inviting you. Do you have an appointment?" Her Australian accent curls around her words in a seductive way I don't really appreciate.

This isn't a woman who is unaware of her assets. No, she uses them like a weapon. Her wide blue eyes have a fake innocence to them that I know all too well, and paired with her outfit, I'm pretty sure I have her pegged.

She's wearing a woman's loose-cut tuxedo jacket, but she's missing the blouse underneath. Coupled with a cropped pair of tux pants, and a collared necklace that looks like it's made of golden feathers, this woman knows exactly how she sounds and how she looks. Not that I hate that about her, in fact, I'm dying to know where she got that necklace.

"You and I both know I don't need an appointment, Ruby. Please tell him I would appreciate an audience."

"Very well." She sighs before closing the door. A minute later it opens wide to reveal a long hallway filled with bookcases stuffed to the brim. Every row has its fair share of books. The hallway opens up to what appears to be a library office. The ceiling and walls do not seem to fit in a warehouse but more appropriate inside an opulent mansion somewhere in Europe.

Given the nature of the club, that is totally in the realm of possibilities. The hallway doesn't have even half as many books as the wall-to-wall bookcases that are only sparsely interrupted by a fireplace here and a wet bar there.

A man sits behind a rather sumptuous mahogany desk. I

remember this man, too. He's the dangerous, yet attractive guy I saw Striker talking to. His brown hair is swept back from his face as if the strands themselves are too obedient to move out of place. His eyes are a piercing vibrant blue, at odds with his dark hair. At this point I'm glad I put on makeup, since these two are ridiculously gorgeous in a way that has me feeling like a troll.

"Ian, Aidan, Striker. Pleasure to see you. And who is this?" Caim inclines his head to me.

"Caim," Ian nods, "I would like you to meet Maxima Alcado."

I try not to cringe at the use of my full name, but my eye twitches, anyway. This seems to amuse Caim, and a half-smile emerges on his full lips.

"And why have you brought a Rogue into my establishment?" Caim pins me with his steely eyes. They seem to have an X-ray quality I'm not at all comfortable with.

"We have a demon problem." Ian tightens his grip on my hand just a shade.

"Obviously." Ruby stares at me as if I'm a cockroach she is considering stomping on with her pointy-toed shoe.

"While I can see you haven't heeded my advice, what would make you think that I'd help you?"

"Because an incubus attacked an angel, and I was under the impression that was against the Armistice. I kind of thought you'd want to know."

Ian's bold statement seems to catch him by surprise, his eyes widening a mere fraction before he schools himself. Caim manages not to appear ruffled as he steeples his fingers.

"Interesting. That is a very serious accusation."

"It is if what Ian claims is true. That I am somehow half-angel without my knowledge. I believe he got that information from you, and since I've known you for several years, I wonder why I didn't know this."

"One, you didn't ask. Two, I'm not quite sure what your lineage is, I just know that you are most definitely not an empath, and if I had a guess, I'd say you were a seraphim of some sort. Maybe? You're definitely angel mixed with something. But... Your parents are not registered on my list, so I can't say for certain." He shrugs at this, as if informing someone that their entire life has been a lie is no skin off of his nose.

"What list?" Striker sputters. "What registry?"

"I keep the lists of all Ethereals—the ones registered with the Council, anyway. Like you, Maxima Alcado—daughter of witch, Teresa Alcado, and the demon, Andras. But you already knew you were a little different, didn't you? What, with the dying and coming back to life and all? What is it, one hundred and thirty-eight now?"

"One hundred and thirty-nine, and if you would be so kind, please call me Max."

"A demon with manners. How intriguing." Ruby sneers from her perch on the side of Caim's desk.

"Oh, don't listen to Ruby, she's just prejudiced. Plenty of demons have manners. Plenty of angels are outright scoundrels. What we are does not dictate what can be. Ethereals, just like humans, are inherently neutral. Just like me."

"Good to know I won't turn into a murdering psychopath. I was worried there for a minute," I joke, my wry smile mirroring Caim's. "Just so you know, those one hundred and thirty-nine times I've died? Those were because I was helping people. I've never, not in four hundred years, taken a single innocent life. Not one. I would appreciate it if you didn't look at me like I was scum on the bottom of your shoe. The only reason I'm Rogue is because I came back to life after I was burned at the stake at fourteen."

Ruby appears contrite for a second before muttering, "Shitty," under her breath. She gives me a commiserating nod. I'm not the only one with a shitty past, I guess.

"Give me the particulars of your situation, and I will be happy to see to your claim."

Striker tells him every detail, starting from the tattoo shop, to my home, to the Danvers' farm in Indiana. He doesn't seem surprised except for once, when he learns that they infiltrated my home. Caim nods, makes notes on a legal pad as he listens.

A waitress comes in the middle of Striker's story, supplying Caim with a fresh cup of tea. I meet her gaze for a second. I vaguely recognize her as the waitress who served us, but she was much happier then. Now, her face is pale as a sheet. Ruby dismisses her, and she scurries off, but not before she gives me one last haunted look.

"I'll get this squared away very soon. In the meantime, I suggest you try to locate your Melody using any bit of skin you have touched her with. Try and flex those angel powers of yours, Striker. You'll be surprised what you can do. And Max? You have temporary access to my club, and I'll look into your Rogue status. Your mother is a prickly one, isn't she?"

He doesn't even know the half of it.

I give him my best wry smile, not disparaging her in mixed company, but not denying it, either. My mother is the freaking worst, but I don't know Caim well enough to know if I could speak freely about her to him.

I'm untrained, not stupid.

I simply shrug, and Ruby leads us out of the office and back to the raucous club filled with revelers. I don't make it two steps past the threshold before someone grabs my forearm. I hiss in pain as I yank my arm away from the waitress from before. Her corn-silk-blonde hair is slightly disheveled, her skin sallow with fear.

"I know where your friend is. The pregnant one. She was here. In the basement of the club. I saw her."

She must see disbelief on my face due to the fact she grabs my arm again, making me hiss in pain.

"She was here. I swear!"

But I believe her, and the sheer rage I feel makes it easy to blow Caim's office door to pieces and stomp inside.

He'll look into it, my fabulous ass.

CHAPTER THIRTEEN

MAX

It hits me about ten seconds after I blow the door that my actions may be classified as rash. But given the sheer amount of shit I've gone through to protect Melody only to have her held captive in the very club where we chose to select help, I prefer to overlook it. It probably doesn't help that I'm also dragging a waitress by her arm down the hall to give Caim a piece of my mind.

There are not-so-quiet murmurings at my back, but I'm pissed enough that I don't focus on them.

At the mouth of the corridor in between Caim and me stands Ruby. I'm smart enough to know that I cannot possibly best her in combat, but I'm also dumb enough to test out my abilities on her.

"Everyone needs to calm down and take a fucking seat," I command, my voice thunderous. When I snap my fingers, Caim parks his ass in his sumptuous leather wingback, and Ruby seems to fly back through the air, landing in a rather comfortable-looking club chair. I hear feet shuffling behind me, and I have to assume it's my friends caught in the same spell.

Well, that is unfortunate, yet, probably for the best.

At this point, Caim appears mildly ruffled, but Ruby is

probably contemplating on how best to remove my head from my shoulders. Which is fair.

"Now. We are going to discuss this calmly and rationally, because contrary to popular belief, I don't actually enjoy making enemies. Your lovely waitress overheard our conversation and claims that a woman fitting Melody's description was in the basement of this club. Today. Which means at some point in the last twelve hours you have had a kidnapped pregnant woman in your establishment. Now, I'm all for an errant coincidence, but this smells fucking foul. Care to explain?"

Caim's eyes narrow as his face reddens, and it occurs to me that the only reason everyone is silent is due to the spell I cast. I may have put a little too much juice into that one.

Whoops.

I snap my fingers again. "Sorry," I mutter. It may sound like an afterthought, but I really mean it. If Caim and Ruby have nothing to do with this, then I most definitely don't want to be on their bad side.

If they are, however, I may have just bitten off way more than I can chew.

"In my club?" Caim fumes—his words sound like the faint hiss of a snake right before it strikes. "I want to know exactly what happened, and I want to know exactly where you saw her. Tell me, Silver. No harm will come to you for telling the truth."

The waitress, Silver, shakes in my grip, but I'm hesitant to loosen my hold. If she bolts, I've lost my witness.

"T-there was a man in the back room talking to the new bartender—Vincent? Victor? I don't know his name. Umm... They were arguing about something I didn't hear. But when I went to the stock room to make sure there was enough cocktail napkins before my shift, I heard a wo-woman, and she was crying and screaming. So... I f-followed the sound, and the basement didn't look like our basement, you know? There were people down there, and they were packing up stuff and shoving people in cages. There was a pregnant woman, she was screaming that she wouldn't go, and they hit her in the mouth and she f-fell." Her voice breaks as she covers her mouth.

"Th-they just shut the door on her. I made a noise, and someone was coming to look for me, so I just went back to work, you know? I wanted to tell someone, but it didn't make any sense, and then I thought I'd imagined it, or if I didn't, then I needed to get out of here and never come back. I just-just didn't know if I was gonna get killed because I saw too much." Silver shrugs as she wipes her nose with the back of her forearm. She's still shaking, but somewhere in the middle of her story, I wrapped an arm around her shoulders.

"Can you show us?" I can tell Caim's trying not to snap his desk in half as he asks the question. He didn't do this. No way. If he did, then he deserves an Oscar.

Silver nods and burrows herself under my arm. Poor girl. She's shivering her ass off in her next-to-nothing outfit of some sort of mesh and peacock feathers, so I shrug out of my jacket and drape it over her shoulders.

"Maxima, this will go a lot faster if you would give me back the use of my fucking body," he reminds me.

Shit. I snap my fingers again, allowing everyone to move, mumbling another contrite "Sorry."

Caim sweeps past us, stealing Silver from me and tucking her under his arm as he leads us out of his office. I'm the last one out except for Ruby. As we cross the threshold, I snap my fingers again, turning the obliterated door back into the solid black surface it once was.

Ruby says nothing, but her raised eyebrow tells me volumes—up to and including that she'd really like to wring my neck right about now. I can't do much about that, but I still give her a repentant smile and follow the men to the back of the club. I missed most of this the last time I was here, but I get the feeling the nightclub changes quite frequently.

I catch Striker's blond waves in the crowd and Ruby, and I haul ass to catch up, following them down turns and hallways until finally catching up to them in a secluded back corridor that seems to go on forever. We can't even hear the music from the club or feel the bass of the speakers.

"Ruby, if you would be so kind, secure Vaughn from behind the bar. I have a feeling we'll need to find out exactly what he knows." Caim eyes the door to what I assume is the basement. Ruby nods, and she's gone before my eyes can track it.

Impatient, Striker tries to move past us to get to the door, but Aidan and I manage to grab him by the scruff and yank him back.

"What the shit are we waiting on?" he growls.

"This door does not belong here. The door to my basement is at the end of the hall. This door"—He punctuates his words with a finger point—"goes somewhere else, much like my office does. Since I didn't make the Fate's forsaken thing, I'm checking to see if there are any traps. If you want to get dead because you're too impatient, be my guest. If not, then shut the fuck up and let me work."

I wonder if I should speak up and let him know there isn't warding around the door, but my mouth makes the decision for me.

"There aren't any hex lines. It looks just like your door. The magic is a little cruder but similar. No traps," I mutter as I inspect the door.

Caim stares at me like I've grown another head.

"What? Am I not supposed to be able to see hex lines?"

Caim just blinks at me. I guess not.

He gestures for me to open the door, and despite Ian's growled warning, I actually do it. When nothing happens, I start down a rickety set of stairs and turn the corner to a nearly empty basement. Striker's thunderous footsteps follow me, but his growl in frustration is the real kicker.

We missed them. Detritus of the space being recently used is everywhere. Dirty bare mattresses mixed with the smell of piss and shit, food wrappers, and trash. It smells to high heaven, but no one is left.

Caim seems to churn in his own blind fury as I try to get a glimpse of warding or clues of some kind. I try and fail. The place has been wiped of anything of value. Soon, we all flee the scent of despair and human waste and head back upstairs.

By the time we get there, Ruby is on her way back, and she's frog-marching a young man in front of her. He's shirtless and pretty in that dumb, single-dimensional way that only seems to come from too much magic, too much recreational drug use, or too few brain cells. Based on the somewhat vacant expression on his face, maybe all three.

"Vaughn?" Caim prompts, but he doesn't get a response. Vaughn is vacantly staring down the hall, a floaty unbothered expression on his face.

This smells fishy. No, literally. Magic like this smells like dead fish to me. But not everyone can smell and see magic like I can, I'm guessing.

"Someone jacked with his brain." I gag at the smell. "Forgetting spells smell like rotting fish."

Now *everyone* is looking at me like I grew another head. What?

"You can smell magic, too?" Caim's brow furrows, the question not really a question. His eyes pierce me in that way I'm not comfortable with again.

"Some. Not all. But memory-fudging ones are especially repugnant." I try not to inhale the stench and fail. "Oh, my god, could you put him downwind or something?"

"Can you fix it?" Ruby asks, and I'm tempted to give her the real answer.

On the one hand, this dude is more than likely a member of a black-market smuggling ring of some kind, so fuck him. On the other, I don't know that for sure, so I can't just hand him over to almost certain torture. Plus, just because I get something from him doesn't necessarily mean he'll be all there when I'm done. It's more like deciding if we want his brain fried or scrambled.

Either way, the yolk ain't going back in the egg.

"It depends on what you mean by fixed. With something this bad, this crude? I could pull his last few memories before he was wiped, but there is no real fixing it. His brain is either going to be a vacant mess or a drooling mess. So, unless you want to kill him or get him the best possible care, I don't want to mess around in his noodle too much more than it's already been messed with."

"He's a part of this, get what you can out of him," Caim orders, and I reluctantly do as I'm told.

Muttering in a bastardized version of French Creole, I whisper the spell I learned from a pair of ancient grimoires last year as I touch two fingers to Vaughn's forehead. In the next second, images and emotions flood my mind, flashing and melding together.

Blackness, fear, mixing drinks, anxiety, getting ice from a bar back, anger, arguing with Micah, walking down a hall and down a staircase, being horrified at what is in the basement... nothing... nothing...

"Shit!" My eyes squeeze shut to try and glean a little bit more information. "He was part of this, but he didn't know... He was horrified when he saw what was going on in the basement. Micah was using his house as a base of some sort but didn't tell him what for. Paid him money, but Vaughn didn't ask questions. That basement is really in a home in Provo, Utah."

When I open my eyes, Ruby is holding Vaughn up, his limp body in her arms as blood trickles from his nose and eyes. Oh, no. Vaughn wasn't innocent, but he wasn't evil, either. I didn't mean to hurt him. Yeah, I knew it was a possibility, but...

Tears well in my eyes as Ian throws an arm around my shoulders. I don't know how I feel about Ian being the one to comfort me for killing a man, but at this point, I'll take it.

"Like you said, babe. He was part of this, and there was no way to save him," Ian whispers in my ear as he runs a warm hand up and down my arm.

"Yeah, well, then why do I still feel like shit?"

"You're a good person. Duh." Ruby grunts as she hefts Vaughn into a fireman's carry before discarding his body in a doorway I didn't realize was there. "I'll come back for him. Unless one of you wraiths are hungry?"

"He's not appetizing, but thank you," Aidan diplomatically supplies, and I know what that means. He wasn't evil. Wraiths only eat the souls of the evil.

Shit, now I feel worse.

“There are matters to discuss, ladies and gentlemen. I suggest we retire to my office to hash them out. And Max?” Caim turns to me.

“Yes?”

“Next time, knock.”

I doubt I’ll be living that one down anytime soon.

CHAPTER FOURTEEN

MAX

For some reason, Caim's office seems much smaller when we file back into it. I don't know if it is Caim's anger that fills it, or if it is Striker's wrath. Either way, the air is decidedly unfriendly.

Ruby took the liberty of ordering us some food, and while I know it's been ages since I've eaten, I can't seem to make myself take a single bite of the juicy hamburger and fries I requested. Typically, I can eat my weight in burgers. Fries are never turned away, and top it all in guacamole and hot sauce, and you have yourself one ravenous witch. But right now, I just can't make myself eat.

Odd.

I look over at Striker, and even though he hasn't eaten too much in the last twelve hours either, his plate is full, too. The penny-pinching, miser part of myself wants to slap the shit out of both of us for wasting food. Too many times have I been without to be wasteful, but I just can't do it.

Abandoning my plate, I sidle up to Striker. He hasn't so much as said a single peep since we got back to Caim's office. Not that I can blame the man. His world has officially been tossed on its ass.

"Hey, Strike." I rest a comforting hand on his arm. Striker and I have always been kind of touchy—probably from a lack of real families growing up. We needed that comfort from someone, and when we became friends, that comfort came from each other.

But right now, my touch is not welcome. I realize this about a millisecond after my hand makes contact. Striker's shoulders seem to lock, his jaw solidifying to solid granite, and I don't think he realizes it's me before he grabs at the arm attached to the hand touching him—grabs and squeezes with all of the incredible strength and supernatural juice he can possibly manage.

Were I able to get my body to move faster than my brain, I probably wouldn't be in the agony I'm in right now. But alas...

My scream is silent. Striker's is not.

He squeezes out a "don't fucking touch me" through gritted teeth before his body turns and his eyes widen, and he finally lets me go. When his fingers fall away from my still-gauze-wrapped forearm, I feel the blood rushing back into the limb. Then red begins to stain the cotton, and that's when everyone moves.

Somehow, Ian and Aidan are between me and Striker. Ian is in his face—fang and talons at the ready to rip Striker a new one. Aidan is at his back prepared to haul him out of there if need be. Ruby and Caim are behind Striker, and their eyes are all glowy and luminescent—doing the same thing that Striker's do when he's pissed—which he is right now due to Ian being right in his face, threatening some sort of disembowelment with a red-hot poker.

Huh. I guess Striker, Caim, and Ruby are a little more alike than I initially realized.

Silver seems to have hidden somewhere, and here I am bleeding on Caim's Persian rug.

Ian coming to my defense, I don't precisely get—well, I can gather a fucking guess, but I still don't understand why he's doing it. Ian and I have never really gotten along. In fact, the first time I met him, I'd just gotten into a car accident after being rammed head-on by a pair of bloodthirsty werewolves after springing my girl Nicola from a hospital.

I got knocked out for most of the action, but when I came to,

Ian was there. I didn't know he was a friendly, so I blasted him with a dose of magic.

He's hated me ever since.

Or so I thought.

"I do realize tensions are high, but I'm ruining what is likely a forty-thousand-dollar rug, so if someone could help me, that'd be great," I half-shout to be heard over the posturing and male fucking ego.

My words have the desired effect, and Ian stands down, turning back to check my arm. He pulls me over to a pair of leather club chairs and gets to work on me.

"Rancid piece of shit." Ian peels back the tape to look at the wound. I've never really looked at the burns Micah left on my skin, preferring to keep the contents of my stomach right where they were. But since I haven't eaten in a while, the likelihood that I'll chuff is low, so I reluctantly take a gander at the damage.

It doesn't look anything like I thought it would. Sure, it's a burn, but it isn't raised flesh and bubbling skin. It's bloody and isn't healing, but it doesn't look like any burn I've ever seen. Instead, it is a design—a marking burned into my skin, obscuring the tattoo underneath. It looks like two linked crescent moons with an arrow flowing through it. There are cubes and triangles inside triangles, dots and dashes. It's simple yet intricate, like some of the dot and line tattoos that I've done on a few college kids who've pulled a random design from some website.

"That's new," Ian remarks, and the way he does it makes my skin crawl. He knows more than he's saying, and in no way, shape, or form is that good for me.

"Here, I got your bag." Aidan stands beside us, dropping a black duffle at Ian's feet. It takes a second for me to realize he went back to Ian's apartment to grab his med supplies in the time it took me to internally analyze and freak the fuck out over this burn.

A part of me already knows what it is. I don't know what it means, but I know it's really bad.

I want Ian to reassure me. I want him to read the freak-out in my mind and tell me that everything will be okay—that I'm fine.

But Ian can't read my mind at all. He can't possibly know that despite my stony expression, I am a jittering fucking mess inside.

Striker is the one who is supposed to know this, but when I glance up from the markings on my skin to the room around us, he's already gone.

Him being able to sense everyone's emotions in a room this small, plus Melody being gone... I get it. I do. I totally understand why he did what he did, why he doesn't want to be touched and why he lashed out. Granted, I wish it hadn't been at me, but I can see his side.

But then again, I don't see it at all. He fell for Melody in the blink of a freaking eye, and while I'm not one to judge, I'm still shocked that the former man-whore of the Ethereal fell so hard so fast for a woman he barely knows.

What I also can't get is him leaving. Never, not once, have I ever abandoned Striker in the middle of some shit, and there have been many a shit storm in our past. I've been bleeding or damn near dying, or hell, actually dying, and I've never left him.

Dick.

Ian takes his time, cleaning the wound and rewrapping it to give it a chance to heal. The fact that it isn't healing is another concern altogether. I have died and come back in less time than it's taking this stupid burn to heal. When he finishes with the bleeding forearm, he switches to the other, checking the skin for infection, he says. I know it's bullshit.

He wants to know if the other burn is a design, too. It is.

I think I had a little hope before Ian pulled that gauze back. Like maybe it was a fluke, or I was high on adrenaline and shitty situations and my mind made it up.

No such luck.

I turn my mind back to Striker and his problems, seriously not wanting to deal with my own right about now.

"What do you think Striker's mixed with?" I blurt, Ian's head coming up in surprise at the question.

"Why do you ask?" Ian's voice is wary for a second, but I don't know why.

"Well, because it isn't like him to fall this hard, this fast. I was kinda wondering if there might be a biological reason for it, or… I don't know." I shrug. "Like how wraith's mate. What is it? It's the voice, right? You have to hear your mate's voice to trigger it, and then you guys turn into territorial crazy people. Like that. Are there other Ethereals like that?"

Ian just blinks at me for a second, his face like stone. The silence is drawn out enough for me to feel a little uncomfortable before he gives a swift shake of his head and answers me.

"There are a few. Dragons, wraiths, of course, a few species of demon, pretty much any kind of shifter. But each trigger is different, and since we have no idea what he is, other than half-angel, it's anyone's guess."

He doesn't say anything more, his demeanor almost walled-off from me as he collects the detritus of medical supplies in his hands.

Did I say something wrong? Is it rude of me to want to know more about other Ethereals?

Ian gets up to go take care of the blood-soaked gauze and alcohol pads, and Ruby plops down in his vacated chair.

Her face is pensive, her brows drawn in such a way that I think she's about to tell me I'm about to die. She even opens her mouth only to snap it shut a second later, as she seemingly debates with herself.

"Spit it out, darling, am I dying or something?" I command, exasperated.

Ruby's eyes are pitying, but she shakes her head no. Ian begins to head back to us, and Aidan is somewhere behind me. Striker's gone, and I just can't deal with this shit all at once. Irritated, I pop up from my seat and haul her up with me, stepping away from everyone so I can get whatever she has to say to me out without an audience. We're in the hallway of books before I stop.

"Okay. I'm listening."

"You're not dying, but… you might wish you were. I know we got off to a rocky start, and you might not like me, and I might not like you, but as a sister, you have to know what's on your arm."

"I'm all ears, doll."

"It's a demon brand. A mark of ownership." She's telling me this like she's delivering a terminal diagnosis. And shit, she might be right.

"The demon who branded you, essentially owns you. He can do just about anything to you, against you, and under the Armistice, under the rules of the Council, he has the right. I know you don't have a reason to trust me, but he can do anything to you, and you have no recourse against him."

Right this second, I kind of wish I hadn't abandoned that plush club chair since the ground seems like quicksand ready to suck me up.

"It's how he found me, isn't it? And how he broke my wards?" I ask the question, but I don't really need to. This is so much worse than I thought it would be—to know what that design meant. I thought I was so smart, trying to protect Melody. And who led him there?

Me.

I'm such a freaking idiot.

"Well, thanks for letting me know. Any pointers on how to get it off?"

"There isn't a way to get a brand off, per se. Once it's there, it's there. There is a way to break the brand, and the hold the demon has on you, but it isn't easy."

"Well, sister, I'm all ears. I would fucking love to know how this murdering, woman-beating, human disemboweling, black-market trafficking psychopath can be removed from my life. Please, tell me."

Sure, my voice is snotty, but the answer isn't just yes. The answer is, hell yes. Please, dear god of all that is holy, yes. She raises an eyebrow at me, but, I don't care if I have to hitchhike naked in Antarctica until my tits fall off, I need to break this damn brand.

"You'd have to kill him," Ruby admits, "and killing a demon isn't easy. It's damn near impossible, trust me. But I have a contact you can go to. She's... eccentric, but she knows her stuff. Crones typically have the knowledge the Council refuses to keep or refuses to share."

"The Council?"

"Just a group of old Ethereals who's mission in life is to make rules that no one adheres to. I wouldn't worry too much about them."

Ruby pulls a slip of paper from her back pocket and passes it over.

"Use the information she gives you wisely. Crones don't see good and evil the way you and I do."

What the hell am I about to get myself into?

CHAPTER FIFTEEN

MAX

In the unlikely event I make it out of this mess, I'm going to kill Ruby. Based on her directions—which I really should have read all the way through before embarking on this Fate's forsaken trip—I'm supposed to leave the trailhead located two-point-four miles past the parking lot at Hanging Lake, and make my way down into the valley gorge. At four in the freaking morning.

This must be a joke.

I don't camp. I don't hike. The most outdoorsy thing I do is grow herbs and flowers in a greenhouse and drink wine on my freaking patio.

I also sure as shit do not want to jump into a pitch-black valley from this outlook spot since that is the only freaking way to get there. Oh, and it's the only way to get there because the cliff face is a ninety-degree slope.

Ruby's note specifically says no magic. Well, Ruby and her note can go eat a dick.

There is no other way to get down there besides rappelling off the freaking cliff, and I can't exactly do that in Chucks. It's bad enough I have to walk this path in the pitch-black dark armed only with a backpack full of spell ingredients and a flashlight by myself, since Striker is nowhere to be found.

Yeah, I'm four hundred years old. Yeah, I can take care of myself. But... there are bears and cougars out here. And snakes and creepy crawly...

Fuck it.

I'm not spending one more second out here in the damn dark. Snapping my fingers, I transport myself to the tree-laden gorge. Granted, landing in a stream was not my intended destination, but I'll take the soaked Chucks over almost certain death. I slosh my way out of the stream, snapping my fingers once again to dry my feet.

I should have listened to Ian. *Don't trust Caim and Ruby,* he'd said. Did I listen? Nope. Did I even give him the time of day when he tried to talk me out of this shit? Double nope. I'm the dumbass who said I needed to go to "the bathroom" and freaking left him there. Honestly, I'm no better than Striker.

Survey says? I'm an asshole.

Maybe I'm still reeling from what Ruby said. Maybe I can't deal with being that close to Ian. Maybe Striker really hurt my feelings. Maybe a little bit of all of the above is making me a little out of sorts.

But hurt feelings aren't going to get this brand off, that is for damn sure. Hopefully, this random-assed trek in the mountains will do that.

Now that I'm down here, I can faintly see the pale-white hex marks surrounding the perimeter of a warded rickety-looking cabin. Smoke wafts from a crooked chimney, filtering through the ward and disappearing off into the night.

I can walk through the ward, but most witches don't like the violation, so I do the only polite thing and knock, touching a tiny bit of magic to the warding lines. I have to be careful, or I'll bust the ward, and then everything will be shot to shit.

It wouldn't be the first time.

The door opens, and, immediately, I'm confused. When Ruby said crone, I half-expected an ancient woman hunched from the years, maybe blind or crotchety or both. Okay, I more than half-expected. But what I get is an elegant lady with silver hair, warm brown eyes, killer eyeliner, and a pretty cocktail ring with a giant aquamarine in the center of the setting.

I only notice the ring when she sweeps her chin-length bangs off her forehead in an old Hollywood-style classic move. It looks equally elegant and likely practiced with the level of effortlessness it takes to look that classy.

"Maxima, darling, do come in," she offers via a posh-sounding English accent. "I've put on a fresh pot of tea, and I have biscuits cooling on the counter." She waves me into her cabin with a flourish of her hand.

After all I've been through, it's tough to not be wary when someone I don't know, knows me, but I suck it up and give her a smile. Outside, the cabin appears to be a one-room shack. Inside, however, it's more like a luxurious cabin mansion. Thick beams span the vaulted ceiling that I know couldn't possibly fit under the piddly offerings of the tiny planked roof.

Magic is a trip. Four hundred years later, and it still catches me by surprise.

The crone ushers me toward a silk damask armchair, a pair of steaming cups of tea sitting on the coffee table in front of it. Its twin sits opposite, and she relaxes into the plush offerings. I feel stiff and formal until the crone picks up her tea, slides off one of her ballet flats and tucks a leg under her, settling in.

"Thank you for your hospitality. I apologize for calling on you so late."

"Oh, it's no bother. I so rarely get visitors. You'd think I'd have cannibal tendencies with the way I've been avoided. I don't, by the way. People just forget, I suppose."

O-kay.

"You know my name, but I don't know yours. I suspect calling you 'The Crone' is a little…"

"Coarse?"

"Yes, that works."

"My name—not that anyone has asked me in some time—is

Bernadette. I say this with the caveat that I've had several names over the years. I've lived a very long time. For the sake of our conversation, however, Bernadette will do."

"A pleasure to meet you." I nod. "Did Ruby tell you why I was coming here or..."

"Ruby? That little wench? No. Decidedly not. She and I try to stay as far from each other as possible. I find her and her ilk very irritating." Bernadette waves her hand in dismissal before taking a delicate sip of her tea.

"They can be, but so can anyone. She directed me to you for help. She said you had 'the knowledge the Council refuses to keep or refuses to share.' Now, I don't know anything about a Council, but if you have information that could help me, that would be appreciated."

"While I'm glad she sent you to me, it really depends. What information do you seek?"

I can't help but sigh before I pull back the tape and gauze covering my forearm and show her the brand.

She peers at my arm. "Oh, dear."

"Pretty much. Ruby said you knew how to break a brand."

"Well, of course I can break a brand. You can, too, *if* you do it right, but it isn't the breaking that's the problem, is it? You don't have the right tools. The action is easy, but if you don't have the tools for the job, well, then you're fucked, I suppose."

"Well, by the look of things I'm fucked one way or another. I'd really love to not be fucked by this particular asshole."

Bernadette whips her hand out and latches onto my forearm, inspecting the lines and symbols behind a pair of jeweled reading glasses she pulled from I have no idea where. Her hands have the thin, papery quality of an aging grandmother, but are also imbued with enough strength that I know there is probably no way to get out of her hold.

"An incubus I take it? Parasitic little buggers, aren't they? Oh, dear, he made you see your deaths? Well, that is just rude. No one wants to relive dying." She inspects the lines from one end to the other, practically having a conversation with the information she gleans from them.

"There are two brands, if that information helps."

"It does, let me see."

Pulling back the bandage on the more healed of the two, Bernadette sucks in a breath as she latches onto the other arm.

"This is not good, my dear Maxima. I need to slow the healing process for these burns. If they heal all the way, there will be no breaking the brand. This is going to hurt, child, but it's the only way to give you a little time. Brace yourself."

I don't think I processed how bad this is going to hurt before she rakes her thumbs over the injured flesh. Breaking the skin, blood wells from both designs running down my arm. Before the drops can reach the plush rug, however, Bernadette snaps her fingers and a silver bowl appears underneath my arms, catching the rich red droplets. A few seconds later, my arms are rewrapped in fresh gauze, but the stinging refuses to go away.

Honestly, I think I might hurl. I can't even hiss in pain, it hurts so bad.

"Okay, okay. I know it hurts. I know, darling girl. Just breathe through it." Her calm voice floats through the fog of agony currently surrounding me. Managing to take some mildly hiccupping breaths, the pain abates a bit. Oh, my god, this is so much worse than when Striker squeezed it.

"All right, doll, we have less time than I thought we did, so you're going to listen to what I have to say and not give me any lip. Deal?"

"I'll make an effort as long as you don't do that again."

"I can work with that. What you want to do—breaking a brand—has consequences. Killing a demon isn't easy, but living after you've done so paints a target on your back. In more ways than one. Trust me on this. You need to decide if this is something you can live with. I know your lineage, dear. Your family's history is rife with turmoil. You, yourself, have been on the receiving end of Fate's cruel hand. This might not be something you can come back from."

"I understand."

"No, dear, I don't think you do, but I've said my piece. Now, you need to stay hidden. I can help with that. You see this ring?" She offers her right hand to me, showing me the large aquamarine cocktail ring. The large oval stone spans nearly the entire length of the base of her finger to the first knuckle. The pale-blue stone glistens from the bulky geometric setting. Line and dot designs along with sigils decorate the thick metal setting and the wide band.

I've seen something similar, yet very, very different in my past. Something a bit larger—a cuff—hid a very troubled woman and stole her mind along with it. But Bernadette is not the woman I knew.

"This ring has kept me hidden—from demon and angel alike—for more than five hundred years. I want you to take it." She slips the wide cocktail ring off her finger and puts it in my palm.

"I couldn't. Don't you need it?" I try to offer it back. Yeah, the ring is killer and would be really freaking nice to have right now, but... I don't want to take something away from a woman who has been nothing but kind to me.

"I think my solitude is about over, don't you?" She plucks the ring from my palm, grabs my right hand, and slides the still-warm metal on my third finger. "You need the blood of a member of his line, the bone knife I gave your mother in 1627—which she never returned by the way—and the spell I gave her. I am not allowed to recreate the spell for another, but it can be passed down if your mother will be willing to part with it."

"You want me to go talk to my mother? *My* mother? You want me to go ask the woman who banished me from my coven and made me a bloody Rogue after being burned at the stake, for a favor?"

Bernadette winces at me before nodding.

Fabulous.

CHAPTER SIXTEEN

MAX

Finding my mother has never been a problem. I've always known where she was. Typically, I use her position in this country—or even on this planet—as a pinpoint of the exact place I do not want to be. We've crossed paths maybe ten times in the last four hundred years, each time somehow, some way to my own detriment. Still, I somehow find that little beacon inside myself a comfort. Despite the way she's treated me, I like knowing my mother is alive somewhere. Even if I want to knock her into next year.

Likely, this attitude will come to bite me in the ass at some point.

My cream and black T-strap heels make tiny puffs of dust as I stroll up my mother's front drive. For some reason after talking to Bernadette, I felt the need to wear my armor to speak with my mother. Decked out in a tight-as-sin, black-and-white polka dot wiggle dress, I feel almost myself. I'm mostly covered from neck to knees except for the dainty cap sleeves and square neckline, but I'm pretty sure my mother will have a problem with it. Likely the tattoos, blue hair, and the general "I don't give a fuck" attitude will cause a stir, too.

I am way too sober for this.

Hell, if I could, I'd have brought a flask and pre-gamed it until I was half-trashed before I set a single toe in Idaho. Unfortunately, Teresa Alcado has the nose of a bloodhound and the capacity for more judgment than a Baptist preacher's wife. I could be wearing nipple pasties and a G-string or a nun's habit, and my mother would probably look at me the same way.

Walking up the drive of my mother's Coeur d'Alene home at six in the morning will grant me exactly zero favors from her, but I can't seem to resist watching her security people lose their freaking minds as I stride right through her wards.

My mother excels at a lot of things—warding around bloodlines is not one of them. She seems to forget that Rogue status or no, we still share blood.

I don't make it to the porch before she whips open the front door of her house, clad in a bathrobe and pajamas. Her bronze skin is just as flawless as I remember it, her dark coffee-colored eyes under expressive black brows all under solid black waves that are pulled up into a messy morning bun. One of those expressive brows arches and I feel about ten years old.

Now, here is the real test of how this could go. She could either shun me from her property —which will not go very well for her security people—or she'll let me in. I'd almost take the shunning at this point so I can avoid the scrutiny of her stare.

I can see her turning it over in her head as she looks me over before her eyes narrow on the bandages on my forearms. I knew I should have worn a jacket.

The silence stretches on and on before she lets out a long-suffering sigh and raises a brow. "Have you had breakfast?" It's like she expects me to lie or something.

"No, ma'am."

"Well, come on in." She steps away from the doorway, and immediately, her security seems to relax.

I give her a sidelong glance as I cross the threshold. "Don't let them relax. I have trouble after me or else I wouldn't be here in your hair."

I walk past her, heading for what I think might be the kitchen to wait for her. Plopping down on a barstool at a rather beautiful marble island, I resist the urge to go in search for a cup of coffee or a bottle of bourbon.

My mother follows me into the kitchen a few minutes later. “Thank you for the heads up.”

“No problem.”

“Would you like a cup of coffee?” I nod, because, caffeine, and hell, yes. “How do you take it?”

“Black’s fine, thank you.” She pours the glorious black liquid into a vibrant turquoise mug and passes it over. I’m able to take a single fortifying sip before she starts the questioning.

“Why are you here, Maxima?” That right there is the reason why I loathe my full first name—the way my mother says it like an accusation. Like my mere existence is an inconvenience.

Hell, it probably is for her.

I have to debate with myself whether or not I want to tell her everything. If I don’t, she’ll try and sniff it out of me. If I do, she can use any little bit of it against me.

For lack of better options, I pick door number two.

“A few days ago, a pregnant woman came into my tattoo shop with her boyfriend. My business partner, Striker, sensed she was in trouble, and we decided to help her. In the middle of trying to get her to safety, we discovered the boyfriend was an incubus. Since I didn’t know that demons even existed until three days ago, I was ill-equipped to handle such a situation. In my attempts to get her and Striker to safety, I was unfortunately branded. Since I have absolutely no intention of being an incubi’s plaything, I would like your assistance in the form of the bone knife and spell Bernadette gave you for killing a demon.”

By the time I finish with my request, my mother’s face has gone from her usual bronze to a sickly white. That can’t be good.

“Also, I would love to know why Caim informed me I was half-demon and not you. Granted, I’ll take the spell and knife, the information is more of a bonus request.”

“Wha… Why didn’t Bernadette just give you the spell?” She

blows right past my request for information. Granted, I did tell her she could, but I kind of hoped she wouldn't.

"She said she couldn't recreate the spell, but you could pass it down to a relative. Since my Rogue status does not revoke a familial tie, here I am. Plus, you have the knife I need."

"And you want me to give you the only spell in history that can kill a demon?"

"Well, it's either beg you for help or become a demon's plaything. I've seen how this demon plays with its toys, Mother. He does it by disemboweling them. Since I can't exactly die, that means torture over and over again. Forever. And that's if I'm lucky. I think bringing myself here when I knew how I would be received is testament enough. How's this? If I happen to die for real this time, I'll put a rider in my will that you get them both back. Happy?"

"Not even remotely." She crosses her arms. "Where does Caim fit in all of this?"

Oh, I'm in for it now.

"My friend Ian is familiar with him through business and suggested we go to him for help. It turns out the incubus has been running an underground smuggling ring out of Caim's club, and Caim is pissed. I figure I'm not the only person looking for this guy, but I'm the only one with the actual means to kill him. Caim likely won't because of the Armistice, and if I don't get Micah before the wounds heal, I'm screwed."

"That or Caim is getting you to do his dirty work. I wonder what he's getting out of all of this."

"I have no illusions, Mama. I know that Caim is likely getting revenge and using me to do it. The bonus is I won't be a slave to a psychopath. It sounds like a solid win for me."

"Interesting."

"Plus, Caim said he would look into revoking my Rogue status. I think it will be a very beneficial partnership despite the risks."

At that statement, she narrows her eyes. Jesus, here we go. My mother is a lot of things. Power-hungry is at the tippy top of the list. Ruthless is a close second. She has fought tooth and nail to get where she is in this world, and despite our bad blood, I don't want to jeopardize that.

"I don't want your coven, Mother. I know I'm powerful but being in a coven was never going to work for me. I'm too different. You and I both know that. I scare people, and I can't live with people who fear me. I just want a chance to not be alone. To have access to everything I was denied since I was labeled something when I was a child."

"You put us in danger!"

I'm so pissed, the panes in mama's glass-fronted cabinets start to shake. If I don't get a handle on myself, the glass will shatter in three... two... one...

I manage to pull myself back before everything explodes, but not before every single pane of glass is decorated in a spider web of cracks. I can't say I'm sorry about it one bit.

"You made a ward that drove away anything that wasn't a witch and then wondered why I chafed under the strain of it, even though you knew I was half-demon. A demon used me to drop the ward and free himself from the snare. Men saw me, stripped me naked and burned me alive, and what did you do? You cast me out from the only family I ever knew and turned your back on me. Even before then..." I trail off before finding my voice again.

"You refused to teach me anything about being a witch, so I couldn't protect myself. Even the simplest of spells. Everything I know today, I taught myself, and I still make mistakes because I don't know the basic fundamentals that every single other witch knows. You neglected me and your responsibility as my mother. You did not protect me—or if you did—not in the ways you should have."

I don't want to dredge all of this up, but just the thought that I would be out for her position pisses me off, and I cannot stand her blaming me for my first death.

"Really? I didn't protect you? Okay. So, I didn't keep you away from your father? I didn't hide you under ward after ward so he couldn't find you? I didn't keep you away from the craft so your power wouldn't grow, and he'd be drawn to you like a beacon? I didn't stay your sentence with the coven so they wouldn't try to kill you? No. I didn't protect you at all, did I?"

Now she tells me. This info would have been great four hundred years ago.

"Had you told me any of this, our lives would have been different. How was I to know what was beyond the ward? You wouldn't even look at me. You told me to shut up and sit down and not ask questions. How could I have known the danger? You kept me ignorant and secluded and unloved. Why did you even have me? Why keep me? Even now, you struggle to look at me."

She does. Her chocolate-brown eyes are staring at my forehead, not my face.

"You look like him, okay? You look like Andras." Her voice breaks as she shakes her head. "He never loved me. He used me to make that blade for him. Seduced me. When I fell pregnant with you, I thought we would be a family, but he left on his quest to find the demon he needed to kill. I had you before he came back, and I was so excited to introduce you to him. But when he came back, he wasn't the Andras I knew. He was cold and cruel and used his compulsion on me so I would hide the blade for him. So, I did, I took the blade, and I took you, and we all went to the New World to hide."

"He broke your heart." She nods. "He broke your heart, and you took it out on me."

"Yes." She swipes at the tears under her eyes. "I'll give you the blade and the spell on the condition that you never attempt to overrule my position on this or any other coven."

"Fine."

"Then we have a deal. But I suggest you watch yourself and the people you surround yourself with. Caim has trouble delivering on his promises. Trust me on that."

This makes me more than wonder what in the hell Caim promised my mother.

CHAPTER SEVENTEEN

MAX

Tracking Striker down in a city the size of Denver is not my idea of a good time. Considering the only sleep I've gotten in the last three days has been while I was rendered unconscious due to blood loss, I'm not exactly my usual chipper self. Better known as, if I don't find Striker in this bar, I'm going to go fucking nuclear.

I silently debate the ramifications of said temper tantrum as I inspect the dank façade of the shitty little hole-in-the-wall bar that I'm about to enter. Don't get me wrong, I love shitty little hole-in-the-wall bars, but this would be the thirtieth such bar I've searched in the last sixteen hours, and I'm getting cranky.

I knew I never should have given him that shielding amulet in the '60s. I knew one day it was going to bite me in the ass.

A part of me wants to go it alone on this. I have just about everything I need to kill Micah —except for his blood of course— but roping Striker in on this might help him get his shit together.

I hope.

I don't particularly enjoy being irritated at my best friend, but right now, I kind of want to kill him a little bit. I've done everything I can to try and find the little shit, but after my third attempt at scrying, my tenth attempt at a locator spell, and kicking in his front door, I quickly realized Striker didn't want to be found. My only option was going door to door to locate his wayward ass.

He's just lucky these pretty shoes are comfortable, or I'd kick him in the nads the next time I see him. Hell, I still might.

I yank open the door, giving it a little elbow grease since the hinges might have been forged the same year I was born, and slip inside. Inside, the smell is stale beer, old cigarette smoke, even though no one has been allowed to smoke in a bar in over a decade, and orange soap. The place is practically empty except for a tired-looking bartender, a drunk couple of men playing a rather pitiful round of pool, and an old man in a corner booth staring at a glass of amber liquor, and Striker.

He's sitting at the bar, his blond head in his hand as he draws lines in the condensation on the bar top with his finger. A sweating tumbler of Scotch sits next to his hand, and the bottle not far from it. If I had a guess, Strike is completely shitfaced.

Goody.

I begin my long-suffering trek to pick up my cargo when the pair at the pool table finally notice my entrance. I understand that I'm beautiful—this fact has never been lost on me. But I'm also a firm believer in look, don't touch—an adage these gentlemen have either not learned or choose to ignore, considering the pair of them are now standing in my way.

They are possibly in their thirties, but hard living and too much alcohol have aged them considerably, stealing their likely once-good looks. One is blond, the other dark. Wedding rings on their fingers glint in the low light.

Their poor wives.

I have a lot of respect for humans. They are typically more aware of their surroundings than other species, and more often than not, they get a trill down their spine when they cross an Ethereal's path. They know to stay away from us.

These two dipshits, not so much.

"Today is not the day, gentlemen," I warn, not in the mood to get into it with them.

The blond one just smirks at me, his sneering half-smile pissing me off so bad I've snapped my fingers before I can even really think about it. The next second he seems to slip on nothing, falling just so, his face smacking the pool table on his way down.

I don't look at him. Instead, I lock eyes with the human barring my way, raising my eyebrow in challenge. His expression has the wide-eyed quality of a frightened child, so I give him a sweet smile.

"Like I said, today is not the day. Move. Or I'll move you."

He moves out of my way, not even bending to help his friend who is still holding his nose, blood seeping in between the gaps in his fingers. The dark-haired one has some brains, I'll give him that. I step over the groaning man, making my way to my drunk best friend.

It takes Strike a solid minute to realize I'm even standing there, and another thirty seconds or so to blink his bleary eyes at me.

"Well, aren't you a sad sack of shit."

"I can't find her, Max." Striker's words come out in a slur. "Looked everywhere, used my powers n'evrthing. Call'd in markers..." He shrugs and takes a swig of his tumbler. "She's just gone. Miss her, Max. She was the first girl I thought I could have something with, you know? I saw her and her pregnant belly, and I wanted that. I wanted a family of my own."

"So, you're giving up then? Okay. I'll just get rid of this spell that makes a demon-killing blade, and we'll drown our sorrows. You, your lost love, and me because as soon as this brand heals, I'll be a demon's plaything. I mean, I have almost everything to defeat the prick, but sure, let's bitch out now."

Striker blinks at me, and my words seem to register because he blinks again, his gaze going from bleary to sharp.

"What did you just say?" His voice is no longer slurred.

"I don't know, it must have slipped my mind after searching for your dumb ass for sixteen hours after you left me at Caim's. I had to go talk to my mother. By. My. Self, you asshole." At each point, I drive one of my well-manicured fingertips into his chest.

"Max, don't fuck with me on this. What did you say?" he demands as he struggles to stand, knocking his stool over in the attempt. As far as intimidations go, I find it somewhat lacking. Especially since he still needs to hold onto the bar to stand.

"I'm not talking about this shit here, so you need to decide if you're done drinking or not." I cross my arms and give him my death stare. I can't believe I had to track him down. I can't believe I had to do all the legwork. I can't believe he abandoned me at Caim's.

What am I, his fucking mommy?

"I'm done."

"You damn well better be. Let's go."

"You're telling me you walked through Teresa's wards, hashed out some emotional family drama, and she just handed over the knife and spell? We are talking about your mother, right? The same one who made you a Rogue in the first damn place?" Striker gives me his most skeptical eyebrow raise as he takes a seat in his terrycloth bath towel.

After the bar, we headed back to the apartment over the shop to hash everything out. Mostly because Striker is not a small man, alcohol and standing for him is not advised, and my upper-body strength is somewhat lacking. I have enough ingredients here for just about anything, so it was just as well. I didn't feel safe going back to my house, anyway. Freshly showered, he seems half-sober, but I trust his sober status about as much as he trusts my mother—meaning, not at all.

"She made me promise not to go after her seat." I shrug with a bit of indifference. I can't quite look at him, though, and that is a red flag if there ever was one.

"Yeah, right. She didn't make you do a vow-binding spell or anything? You honestly think she'll just take your word for it? I don't think so."

"You really think she'd screw me over?" When I ask the question, I mean it for real this time. Am I really an idiot for trusting my mother?

"Yes. Yes, I do. I trust Teresa Alcado about as much as I trust

Caim or Ruby. Did you know I've known Caim for more than a century, and this is the first I've heard about being an angel? Ian knew before I did, which means it can't be that much of a secret."

"At least it explains why none of my hangover cures ever worked on you. I was calibrating for the wrong species. Now quit stalling and chug-a-lug. I need you sober before we hash this out."

"I don't wanna. It smells like moldy feet." He pouts and stares at his glass of sickly purple potion with serious trepidation. I agree with him on the smell, but it's his own fault he's still hammered.

"Plug your nose, then. Make it snappy."

Striker's brow furrows as he dutifully plugs his nose and downs it in one long gulp. His face turns a sickly shade of green for a moment, and then he hauls ass back to the bathroom. The retching I hear sounds violent. Oh, well.

A few minutes later, Striker hobbles out of the bathroom sweaty and gray. "Did you poison me? Sweet Jesus." He collapses into the chair with a groan, covering his face with a hand.

"No, but you needed to get the alcohol out of your system. The potion will take care of what's not in your stomach. Should take about thirty minutes or so. I think. I'm not quite sure with angels. Shouldn't you have self-healing abilities or some cool shit at least?"

Striker peers at me through the gap in his fingers before sliding them down his face. "I may have some things up my sleeve that I haven't told you about. I feel bad about it, but..." He trails off with a shrug. "I knew it was weird and I'm not comfortable with them, you know?"

I force myself to blink and give him a reassuring smile, but that admission hurts a little. There is nothing about me that Striker doesn't know.

"I get it."

"You don't get it. I hurt your feelings."

"I can understand where you're coming from and still be hurt that you didn't trust me, babe. It's called seeing both sides. Now go put on some clothes, brush your teeth, and we can get started."

"Bossy bitch," he mutters but gives me a half-smile so I know he still loves me. He'd better. I don't search the bowels of Denver for just anybody.

"Stubborn asshole."

He smiles for real then, climbing to his feet and heading to the spare bedroom where I keep some clothes for him. I conjure a toothbrush with a snap of my fingers and hear a "thank you" called through the thin walls.

I hate that I didn't know more about Striker. I hate that I probably can't trust my mother. I seriously dislike that Caim and Ruby aren't exactly on the up and up. But more, I want this to work. I want to be able to get the drop on Micah. I want Melody and her baby safe.

I can want all damn day. It's the getting that hasn't exactly been my style. Here's hoping that part of my life is over.

CHAPTER EIGHTEEN

MAX

"I want to go over it one more time." Striker snatches the vial of salt from my fingertips.

"Are you kidding me? We've gone over it ten times already." I snatch the vial back, but I stuff the stopper back in the top.

That's a lie. We've probably gone over the plan twenty times, but the first ten, Striker was still a little hammered, so they don't really count.

He runs his hand through his hair as he winces before pleading, "Just one more time?"

"Fine. What stage of the plan are you unclear on?" Oh, yes, I am in full-on pissy bitch mode complete with my hands on my hips and everything.

Striker purses his lips, giving me the squinty glare I so hate seeing on his face. "The part where we just leave and don't immediately kill him. I'm real fucking unclear on that particular point."

For the love of all that is holy. If I didn't need him on this, I'd just leave him here. "The plan requires us to get his blood, do the spell, and then we can kill him. Do you want him to kill me before I can get the spell done?"

"No," he grumbles.

"You seem torn on that. Are you sure? Because it isn't like I can do the spell with him just standing there. Which means we need to grab the blood and Melody and get the hell out of there. Spell's done, then we can kill him, okay?"

"Fine."

"Striker!"

"I said *fine*."

Right. Like that petulant "fine" meant dick. I swear to the Fates, my eye is actually twitching. He has pissed me off enough that parts of my body are moving of their own accord with zero prompting from my brain.

"Please keep in mind that you killing Micah will start a war. I haven't read this Armistice, but enough people are bitching about it for me to know it's bad news. It doesn't matter what goes down. You aren't killing him. We're going in, getting Melody and his blood, and getting out. Don't screw us over for revenge, Striker."

"I won't!" His tone is adamant, but for the first time, I wonder if I can actually trust my oldest friend.

I give him a long look, trying to figure out if he's even capable of this. All things considered, I could ask Ian instead. I probably should. Then again, he'd more than likely slam the door in my face for leaving him at the club. Which would be fair, I guess.

"Learn a little patience in the next thirty seconds, or I won't take you, do you understand?"

"Fine. Whatever. I'm a pillar of fucking virtue. You and I both know that Melody doesn't have a lot of time, so if you could get over the fact that I'd really like to kill him despite how much it dicks with the plan, that'd be great. I want to, but I won't because that would likely hurt you both. Are you happy now?"

"Immensely." I scale back the snide just a little. He's worried this won't work, and hell, if I'm being honest, so am I.

I draw the circle with salt, muttering a locator spell in Latin, modified a touch so I can use it for my own ends. The magic of the brands currently burned into my forearms have their own power, all I need to do is trace the thread back to Micah. It's an easy enough trail to follow, and I grab Striker's hand, pulling him with me as I transport us there in a flash of green light.

As soon as our feet touch the dew-damp ground, I know something's wrong. I can't tell you what state we are in or what country, but I know without a doubt my plans have already gone up in a puff of smoke.

Caim said that demons aren't inherently evil, but I'm having a hard time wrapping my mind around it.

Striker and I are on the edge of a two-lane highway. There is a dense forest behind us, but that isn't the worry. The trouble comes from what lies ahead, across the road. Set back off of the highway is a sprawling two-story house, with a wrap-around porch. On that porch is a woman sitting in a rocking chair.

Her shoulder-length blonde hair is cut into a stylish long bob, pair that with her equally stylish slouchy T-shirt and skinny jeans, it's likely she's the owner of this establishment, which appears to be a bed and breakfast. She seems nice. Probably ran the local bake sale to raise money for the church or elementary school. Maybe even ran a carpool or led a Girl Scout troop or something.

It's clear those days are over, because even from this distance, it's shockingly easy to see her throat is cut. Well, cut is the wrong word. Cut would imply that some form of blade was used when more than likely it was claws or talons that ripped her flesh apart.

"Jesus. Fucking. Christ."

I can't help but nod at Striker's words.

"Okay, new plan. Get Melody out and then go. Screw the blood, the spell, *and* the blade." I don't know why exactly I'm whispering, but I am.

It isn't like this is my first dead body—or even my twentieth—but shit, this whole situation is way less hospitable than I hoped it would have been. I thought, hey, I can totally seduce the dude who originally wanted to get into my pants, right? Then, surprise! Bing, bam, boom, steal a little blood, Striker grabs Melody, and ta-da! We're done.

Murdered B&B owners were not part of the plan.

"Agreed."

The trek across the street and through the yard is one of complete silence, and it's one of the longest walks I've ever taken. I've never been happier in my life to be wearing flat shoes than I am right now. A part of me knows that Micah is in this house, knows that he killed this woman, but the only bright spot in all of this is the near certainty that Micah is alone. But the same section of my brain that has all this information also knows for a freaking fact I'm going to have to run at some point.

Striker pulls ahead of me, going up the porch stairs first to the front door. The poor woman—be she the owner or a patron—has been dead for a few hours at least, based on the amount of congealing blood beneath the motionless rocking chair. In the middle of the largest puddle is a set of keys that I pray we won't have to use.

Striker draws a dagger from the inside of his jacket before he turns the knob. In a stroke of luck, we find the door unlocked, filing inside as quietly as we can. But this house—while beautiful—is probably at least eighty years old. My feet hit a loose board, creating a grating creak that seems too loud for the stillness of this space.

Then, the squeaks of my Vans on the hardwood or the clunky latch on the door don't matter. Because there is a baby crying in this house, a newborn by the sounds of it. I can't stop Striker from following the cries up the staircase or down the hall.

I don't want to follow him, but I do it, anyway. The pit in my stomach grows with every step I take closer to that sound. I've seen too much death at Micah's hands to believe this will all be okay. I'm only an arm's length behind Striker, but when he freezes in the doorway of the far room, I wish I would have protected him better.

I wish I would have gone alone.

Because he makes this grief-filled howl that has tears falling from my eyes before I even know what is going on. I pull him away, shoving him from the doorway, so I'm between him and whatever it is that's making him make that sound.

But what I see, no one should ever have to see.

Micah is there, holding his child swaddled in a bloody bath towel, but that isn't what has me gasping for air. That is saved for the massacre he has made of Melody. She didn't have this baby naturally, or if she tried, it didn't end that way. The gaping maw of her belly tells the tale well enough. Micah cut that child out of her womb, and by all accounts was just going to leave her there to bleed to death.

I make a decision—which is probably the wrong one, but I don't have the luxury of a real choice—and rush to Melody. Well, I start to, but I don't make it. My feet freeze about three steps into the room, glued to the floor by whatever magical hold Micah has over me.

He comes closer, and for the life of me, I want to snatch that baby from his arms. He doesn't get that child. He doesn't deserve that innocence, that joy he's stolen from Melody. He doesn't.

Micah's eyes flash red, his mouth pulling up into a boyish half-grin.

"I'll come back for you later, Maxima," he taunts. "Maybe when I'm done with you, you'll fare a little better than she did." Then he slides a single finger along my temple and down my jaw, cutting the tender flesh under my chin with his newly formed talon. He shifts even closer, sniffing at the skin of my neck.

"Yes. I'll enjoy making you my pet," he whispers in my ear, and it is everything I feared. That brand is real, the bond that makes it almost impossible to move is real. Ruby didn't make it up, and Bernadette wasn't lying.

He means every single thing he says.

I can't speak, frozen in the horror of every single atrocity committed here today as Micah just smokes out of the room, leaving the smell of blood and sulfur behind him. As soon as he's gone, my body relaxes for half a moment before I'm ripping off my zipped hoodie and pressing it to Melody's middle.

"M-my b-baby. He t-took my baby," Melody stutters as her body is wracked with shivers from blood loss. Her lifeblood soaks her ripped maternity top and leggings and the bedding around her.

"We're gonna find him, baby. We are." Striker helps calm her, appearing at my side. I can't fix this. I don't know if this can be fixed.

"P-promise me you'll f-find him. Promise you'll get him somewhere s-safe."

"I promise, Mel. I swear." His eyes are wide with fear when he turns to me. "Get us out of here, Max, now!"

His words snap me out of my fog of adrenaline and fear. I grab both of their hands, and with everything I have in me, I take us to the only place I know that will help us. In the next second, we land in Ian's living room, shocking the shit out of Ian and Aidan as they stare open-mouthed, with game controllers in their hands.

In a blink, Ian's up and working on Melody, sending Aidan to get blood from a local hospital, doing everything he can for her.

But looking back, I shouldn't have taken Melody there.

I should have let Striker and Melody have their last moments.

I should have let him say goodbye to her. Because in the end, Ian can't save her.

No one can.

CHAPTER NINETEEN

STRIKER

There was a time in my life when I didn't think I could survive in the human world. Their emotions were too raw, too acute for someone who felt every single one of them but didn't have the same urgency of time. Time is what made those emotions so tangible, but time itself has always been a joke for me. I know I'll live an unending number of years, likely losing myself in the passing of them.

Melody was a bright spot of light in the dull, dreary days where I faked happiness because it was easier than answering questions. She was someone I could reach for—someone I could take care of. Max didn't need me. Not in the business, not in her life. I pulled my weight, sure, but she took care of me more than I took care of her, save for a few scrapes here and there.

Melody needed me. Me. Not Max, not someone else. I knew it the second she stepped into the shop. I saw the curve of her cheek and the light in her eyes and the swell of her belly, and I knew she was mine to keep safe. Instantly I hated the man she was with. Hated him more than I could possibly hate a complete stranger who'd never done me wrong.

In the scant minutes I had talking to her while Max was inking a fresh tattoo, I recognized the light in her. It warmed me when I'd been cold for so long, and I knew I would die to keep her safe.

So, when I climb the stairs searching for her and the baby, my brain can't process what I see. I flip straight to denial.

That can't be my woman. That can't be her blood soaking her T-shirt and the pale bedding underneath her. That can't be.

My brain can't process, but my body knows the truth when a howl of the fiercest pain rips up my throat and out of my mouth. I'm frozen in the doorway, but not for long. Max grabs a hold of me, yanking me out of her way, and at first, it's a good thing because I can't get my body to move, even though I want to kill Micah.

This isn't happening. Not to her. I refuse to believe it. She's not dead. My sweet Melody isn't dead. No.

I pull myself together, willing my legs to move, to bring me closer to her.

"M-my b-baby. He t-took my baby." She shudders, her sweet voice slurred and distorted by blood loss and shock. Her once-tan skin is gray and clammy as she shivers, reaching for my hand. I give it to her, feeling her fragile fingers in mine.

"P-promise me you'll f-find him. Promise you'll get him somewhere s-safe," she begs on a panting breath, her pale-blue eyes boring their way into my soul. Of course I'll find her son. If it's the last thing I do on this planet, I'll find him.

"I promise, Mel. I swear." I reassure her the best I can. Her body seems to wilt further into the mattress as her eyes turn glassy.

I scream for Max to get us out of there, and she takes us to Ian. Ian, to his credit, jumps in to help, sending Aidan to get blood, Max passing him instruments and supplies as he works on Melody. Somehow, I'm shoved out of the way—either as a result of my own inaction or on purpose, so I don't have to see just what they are doing to the woman I love.

But I want to see what they are doing to her. I want to know if her eyes ever open, or if she's in pain, or if she's breathing. I want to know if the ultimate dread I feel will ever go away.

But a minute later when Aidan comes back, Ian is giving her

compressions, and Max is pumping oxygen into her mouth with a bag, and I'm still just standing there, motionless, because I cannot fathom a world where this beautiful, wonderful woman isn't alive.

Soon, everyone stops. They stop compressions, and Max stops squeezing that stupid bag, and Aidan stops hooking up her IV with his filched O-negative. They just stop because Melody isn't breathing, and she won't start anytime soon.

I push them out of my way so I can see her. Her skin is so lifeless, so gray. Her lips no longer the blushing rose I loved so much. A tiny smudge of blood dots her cheek, so faint it could probably be a freckle. And it's that tiny little nothing smudge that drives me over the edge.

Crawling up on that pool table that served as Ian's surgery slab, I wrap Melody up in my arms, her lifeless limbs dragging against the felt as I pull her to me. Pressing my lips to her forehead, she seems so cold already, and the grief finally hits me. I can't handle the wrenching in my chest that tells me she's really gone.

But this can't be how this ends. There has to be a way, there has to be some way to bring her back. Melody was carrying a half-demon, maybe she can come back like Max does. Maybe…

"Take me to Caim's." My voice is a guttural form of agony ripping up my throat, but that doesn't matter right now. What matters is getting Melody to someone who can help her.

Max just stares at me, her eyes filling and spilling over as she shakes her head no, matted blue whips of hair shaking with it. There's blood smeared on her cheek, and it kills me that it's there.

"I'm not taking you there, babe." Her voice is trembling as she denies me.

"Yes, you are."

"No. I'm not. I know what you're thinking, and I don't want to know what Caim's price will be to bring her back. I'm not letting you do this to yourself, and I'm not letting you do this to her. She died, Strike. Humans die."

Anger pulses through me at her words. "And what would *you* know of death?"

"Not enough to say I've lost someone I've loved. I've never felt anything like what you feel for her, but that means I can see clearer than you can. I don't feel the same grief you feel, so my mind isn't clouded by it."

It would hurt less if she'd just stabbed me through the heart. I reluctantly lay Melody back down on the felt, careful not to disturb her body before I jump off of the pool table, getting right in Max's face.

"My mind is not clouded. Everything is perfectly fucking clear. Melody is gone because we couldn't protect her. She's gone because I was too slow to find her. Because we didn't find her in time. So, I'm going to fix this shit. And you are going to help me."

"You're right. It's our fault, but Striker, she's dead, and I'm not letting you lose yourself to Caim—whatever the hell he is—to bring her back," Max argues, and I swear everything in me seems to burst into flame with the rage coursing through my body.

I feel a strange ripping sensation at my back as the inferno under my skin reaches critical mass, then a heavy weight where there wasn't one before. Then a sharp bite on my palm, but right now, I don't give a shit about any of it. I only care about getting to Caim so he can fix this mess and bring Melody back.

Max's warm-brown eyes go wide, and she backs up a step, and then Ian's there in front of her, all fangs and talons and black eyes like I'm going to attack her. It burns that this is the third time in so many days where it's Ian in between me and my best friend. And what does that say about me, where a stranger looks at me like I'm going to hurt her?

"Striker, look at your hands." Fear laces through Max's voice as she peers around Ian.

Black talons have sprouted from my fingertips, and my hands seem to be coated in thick red scales like the hide of a lizard.

What the actual fuck?

"Umm, babe, I don't want to alarm you, but you have wings, too."

That explains the weight, but honestly, I don't give a shit if I stay like this, or if this is just some fever-dream hallucination brought on by grief.

"You're taking me to Caim." The guttural growl of my voice rips through the room. It's deeper, louder than what I'm used to hearing. But it doesn't really matter. The influence I've used almost every day of my life seems to be doing exactly dick to convince Max she should take me where I want to go.

"No, she isn't, but I will," Aidan offers, sidling up to us, getting in between his brother and me and farther from Max.

I back up, giving Aidan a nod and he grabs my upper arm, smoke surrounding us like a blanket as I feel like my body is being ripped apart. I land on my hands and knees on a plush Persian rug I've seen before. I have a hard time not puking all over it.

"What the hell, Aidan? Is this really necessary?" Caim complains. "What's th—" His voice stops like a record scratch when I climb to my feet and look him in the eyes. Caim's face turns gray for a second before he drops his gaze and gulps.

I must look pretty hideous if he won't even meet my eyes.

"I need a favor," I begin. "The woman you said you'd help us find? She's dead. I want you to bring her back."

"No." His response comes immediately, and it hits me like a blow. This was my shot, my one chance to bring her back and he won't even hear me.

"No negotiation? No questions? Just, no?" I ask in disbelief, denial rising in me by the second.

"I'm not in the business of resurrecting dead humans. So, again, no." His words are like a slap in the face. Caim has been trying to recruit me into his rather secretive business for ages.

"Please, I'm begging you. I'll give you anything. I'll do anything. Please." I'm begging, but I couldn't give a single fuck. Screw pride. Fuck everything but whatever will give me Melody back.

"You don't have anything I want, Striker. And if you need the explanation, resurrecting your Melody would take someone else's life, someone whose time has not yet come. It would screw with the Fates, and I make it a point to never mess with those women. It would be like telling my bosses to go fuck themselves. I choose to keep my head right where it is, thank you. I can't help you, son. No one can."

"I'm not your bloody son. I'm no one's son, remember?"

A blanket of rage settles over me, but instead of the frenetic fire racing over my skin, it makes my mind crystal clear. I know exactly what I'm going to do. If I can't bring Melody back, I'll for damn sure have the next best thing.

Micah's head on a fucking spike. Armistice or no, I'll have my revenge if it's the last thing I do.

CHAPTER TWENTY

MAX

I have no idea why I thought actually having a plan would work out for us. In my experience, having a plan meant utter and complete disappointment. I've had my plans dick me over, but never in all my years have they done so in quite such a fashion.

Melody is dead.

Striker is gone.

And I have no way to get Micah's blood to make the demon blade without killing myself in the process. I'm not just fucked.

I am *fucked.*

Not just that, but I failed this sweet girl. I failed her son. I failed her family. I failed Striker. And I'm about to become a demon's plaything to do with whatever he wishes. With the burning ache in my chest and pit in my stomach, I'm half-tempted to use the blade on myself.

Getting rip-roaring drunk seems like the best course of action.

"Please tell me you have alcohol in this frat house you call an apartment."

Ian turns, looking at me with an expression I can't read. His brow is furrowed, his eyes still the phased inky black, talons and fangs galore. I don't know why he doesn't phase back to normal, but I've got my own problems right now, and Ian isn't one of them.

"Why do you care so much for a man in love with another woman?" His question catches me off guard. He asks this like he has the right to know, which since he's put himself between Striker and me a couple of times now, I guess he might.

"He's my best friend. And we're not like that. Sure, he's hot, but Striker and I don't work together that way. I care about him because he's one of the few people on this planet who doesn't treat me like I'm a freak. Being Rogue is hard. No coven will accept me. I can't go to a lot of Ethereal places—can't be among my own kind. I can't shop at certain stores. And if someone hurts me, there is no one I can go to, and no one to help me. I'm fair game. Striker doesn't care about any of that. We've been watching each other's back for a while now."

Striker also never seemed to care what being friends with me did to his social standing. He was covenless too and just didn't give a shit.

"So, you're like family?" he asks, his phase bleeding right out of him.

If by family, he means we screwed once and hated it, so we decided platonic was the way to go? Then yeah. But I don't say this to him. There is no scenario where telling Ian I screwed Striker once in a fit of drunken misery is a good plan. Just no. Plus, there is this whole thing about it being none of his bloody business. But a tiny part of me wonders if that's true.

"Yeah, and right now he's with your brother probably asking Caim for something impossible, and Fates know what he'll offer as payment. I can't help him, and I can't get revenge, and I can't get these fucking brands off. I am well and truly screwed. Plus, I have a mountain of guilt piling on my soul and don't have the blood I need to avenge her. So, alcohol? That would be awesome right about now," I remind him, but he doesn't move to get me the sweet oblivion I need, the dick.

"What blood do you need? Show me the spell, maybe I can

help." While his offer is nice, and it's cute that he thinks he can help, I'd rather be drowning in bourbon right about now.

Snottily, I pull out the folded parchment, pointing out the ingredient in question. "It says 'blood of the demon's line.' Which means I could get it from Micah himself or his child. I don't have either, not that I'd take blood from a baby, so I'm pretty much shit out of luck."

Ian frowns at the ancient piece of parchment I pulled from my back pocket. Yeah, I probably should take better care of it, but it's not like a grimoire exactly goes with this outfit.

"Why don't you take the blood from Melody? The baby came from her—wouldn't that make her of Micah's line?"

Something inside me revolts at the idea of using Melody at all. Like I would be violating her in some way. It must show on my face because Ian's expression turns pitying.

"She's dead, Max. There's nothing you can do for her now except take down the bastard who did this."

He's right, I know he is, but my face still crumples, and my eyes still pour rivers of tears at the thought of using Melody in any way. Dammit, she's suffered enough. Taking from her now that she's gone seems… wrong somehow.

"It could work." My voice is clogged with shame, but I still wipe the wetness from my face. I don't have time to be a guilt-ridden whiner right now.

"You don't have to do it, Max. I'll draw some blood from her body with a syringe. We won't hurt her, okay? Why don't you fix yourself a drink? I think there is some bourbon in the cabinet next to the fridge."

He's giving me an out, which I really freaking appreciate, and I take it, spinning away from the dead body on the pool table and the kindness I can't seem to absorb right now. Ian's kitchen overlooks the living and dining spaces, but I try to keep my eyes on their task of searching for booze. I find a bottle of bourbon in the designated cabinet, along with a tall tumbler and get to pouring.

But the burn of the alcohol only seems to make the hollow feeling in my chest worse. I should have looked for Melody before searching for the weapon. I shouldn't have wasted so much time looking for Striker and went off on my own to get her.

It makes me wonder if Melody and her family would still be alive right now if I just kept my nose out of it. But then I remember her words.

He's going to kill me as soon as I give birth.

No. I remember her fear, I remember her pain. If I'd have left Melody alone, there would be no one to find that child. Her parents didn't even know she was pregnant until we brought her home to them. There would be no one to avenge her. No one to stop him. And dammit, I'm going to do what I have to do to make sure he never does this to another woman again.

I take another swig of bourbon and set the glass down. I need my wits about me if I'm going to outsmart that bastard.

"Okay, it's done," Ian calls, but I can't make myself turn around. Can't I take a nap? Or maybe go on vacation? Why is it me doing this and not someone else?

I mentally slap myself. Melody arrived on my doorstep. I said I'd help her, and that's what I'm going to do, dammit.

Put on your big girl panties and suck it up. No one is going to save you. No one is going to protect that child. Get it together.

My self-induced pep talk complete, I turn to Ian. My eyes catch on a white sheet covering Melody's body, and I can't help but be grateful he took that small bit of time he had to respect her body.

"What else do you need? I have supplies here..." He trails off, his eyes assessing in a way that makes me uncomfortable. I think that has always been my problem with Ian. He is forever looking at me like he's waiting for me to understand something, waiting for me to clue in on the joke.

But I can never seem to grasp this unspoken whatever it is between us, and I'm forever feeling like an idiot.

"You're going to do something stupid, aren't you?"

I shrug. "I think we've established that this whole plan is stupid, so, probably."

"No. I mean you are going to do something to get yourself killed."

I choose not to process his words, and instead, listen to his voice—reveling in the faintness of Ian's Irish accent. He still has a bit of a lilt to his words—or at least he does when he's pissed. Kinda like he is right now.

"Haven't you heard? I can't die." I state the obvious truth he knows all too well, still not meeting his gaze.

Then he's there in my face, so I have no other option but to look at him. His dark eyes assess me, and if I didn't know better, I'd say he knows what I'm going to do, even though the plan in my head has barely formed.

"You know what I mean, Max."

Something nags at my brain with him being this close. It's like I remember him from somewhere else but don't, all at the same time. It pisses me off, and so do his questions.

"I'll do what I have to, just like I've always done. And if that means dying, then it'd be par for the course. But I don't plan on getting myself killed if that's what you mean."

My answer is brash and filled with more bravado than I currently have in stock, but so what? What's that saying? Fake it till you make it? Well, I'm going to have to fake it all the way to the end on this one because I have serious doubts about the "making it" part.

Ian gives me his most dubious stare until I almost cave.

"Why don't we see if I can even make the damn blade before you go into protection mode? Okay?"

"Fine. We get the blade taken care of and then we can kill this asshole."

"What's this *we* shit? *We* aren't doing anything. *I'm* making the blade, and I'll take care of Micah. *You* are staying here and alive. Because only one of us can come back from the dead, and sweetie, that's not you."

"We'll see about that."

Is he high right now? No, honestly, is he? How many deaths does he expect me to have on my conscience? I take a few steps back, needing the clarity only space will provide.

"Ian, I can do many things with my abilities. Honestly, the

possibilities are almost limitless. What I can't do, however, is worry about one more person that I care about getting hurt because of me. So, I can put you to sleep. I can paralyze you. I can make you think I never came here for help. Hell, I could make you forget you ever met me. Don't test me on this because the options are endless, and I don't think you'll like what I'll pick."

"I'm just supposed to stand here and let you run off to get yourself killed? As far as I know, you have zero hand-to-hand experience. What happens when you can't use your magic, Max?"

"That's what the blade is for."

"Are you kidding me?"

"Why do you even care?" I throw my hands up, exasperated with this whole conversation.

"I give a shit about you, Maxima." Ian growls in my space once again with fire in his eyes. He's so close I can feel the heat of him through my clothes. Something about the way he says those words makes me think he really means it. He cares about me. Funny, when he says my name like that, it doesn't make me cringe. It doesn't bring the hurt I've become so accustomed to feeling.

He gives a shit about me.

But why?

The question almost falls from my mouth when he moves closer, his body flush with mine. His hands find their way to my hips, pulling me, pressing me against him. I can't look up. If I look up into his eyes, if I stare into those fathomless brown pools, I'll kiss him. If I kiss him, something tells me I won't want to stop. Hell, I know I won't want to stop.

And I can't do this right now.

My body revolts, my heart thundering in my chest, my breath short little pants of want, but still, I manage to pull away.

"Okay," I concede, my voice like broken glass, "I'll make the blade, and then we'll make a plan."

"That, I'll agree to." Disappointment mixed with a bit of hurt laces his words. I don't want to hurt him, but I can't focus on it right now.

I can't abandon my promise.

"Then pass the blood so I can get cracking. This blade isn't going to make itself."

Step one: procure a way to kill Micah.

Step two: try not to die.

Step three: figure out what the fuck is going on with Ian.

Should be a piece of cake.

CHAPTER TWENTY-ONE

MAX

The spell to make the blade demon-ready is easy—a little too easy, if you ask me. Every step of this saga-of-shit has been awful, so I kind of thought the spell itself would be a significant pain in the ass.

It isn't. In fact, the Aramaic text even has the phonetic spelling written underneath it in Teresa's terse scrawl. I guess Mommy Dearest didn't want me to screw this up. In all honesty, this is probably the most helpful she's ever been in her entire life, so I'll take it.

I couldn't stay at Ian's—not with Melody there—so instead of wasting more time waiting on Striker and Aidan to do whatever it was that they felt they had to do, Ian took me to my shop. It's Monday so the shop is closed—not that I've even taken the time to think about my business or my employees since Micah steamrolled all over my life.

But someone has. The front window has been replaced in the few days I've been gone, and the walls and light fixtures have been repaired. There isn't a smell of fresh paint, so magic has to be the culprit. The room has a scent to it, the slight ozone of spent magic and the unique spice of the person who cast it.

"You fixed my shop, didn't you?" I turn to Ian, who is still frozen in the middle of my little waiting area, staring at the hand-painted mural I'd done ages ago on my walls. It's a blooming cherry blossom tree, the pinkish-white blossoms caught in a windstorm, floating off into the beyond. The walls are uncracked, the plaster smooth as a baby's butt, and the light fixtures that used to be reduced to shards of broken rubble are gleaming and intact once again.

"Striker said he'd called everyone and told them there'd been a break-in. Let them know to cancel their appointments for the next week so everything could be repaired. But no one was here to help you fix what was broken, so I thought I could."

He doesn't even know the half of it. But a part of me believes Ian could probably fix anything if he has a mind for it.

"Thank you." I manage to croak out, unable to meet his eyes. Sure, my vision is a little wobbly from fresh tears, but I power through.

It's one of the nicest things anyone has ever done for me, and I decide that when this is all over, I'm attacking Ian Moran and kissing the shit out of him. Probably more than that, but I can't think about it right now.

That will have to wait until I do the damn spell. Oh, and kill the demon who branded me and murdered an innocent woman.

You know, no big.

"You're welcome," Ian says at my back, and the rough timbre of his voice does some things to me. Some floaty, girly, lusty things that I'm totally unprepared for. The sound of his voice pitched this way nags at my brain once again, but I can't place why.

Finally, I manage to unstick myself and coast to my office, spinning the dial on the handy-dandy magic-proof safe, and grab the carved bone blade my mother so reluctantly bestowed upon me. She was also reluctant to tell me exactly where the weapon came from, but I managed to pry a few details about it from her. She wouldn't say when it was created, but based on the thin leather wrap on the hilt, I'd go with a few decades past ancient. More than likely, it should be stained brown from age and use, but it remains pristine as if it were just carved from the humerus bone my mother said it came from. She wouldn't disclose who or what species provided it or if it was taken by force, and at this point, I'm lucky I don't know so I won't feel any guiltier than I already do.

I skirt past Ian and through the shop, up the back set of stairs to the apartment above, heading straight for my supplies and altar. Unfolding the parchment from its home in my back pocket, I go over it one more time.

I'll need a salt circle, the blood Melody's sacrifice provided, and the blade.

I have everything I need, but I can't seem to start. I hate to even think it, but I'm scared. So much more than I am pissed. But then I remember Melody's voice on the other end of the line whispering how scared she was.

She was brave when she had every reason not to be.

She was brave even though I failed her.

I can be brave, too.

Sucking it up, I set the blade in a large hammered bronze bowl, drawing a circle of salt on the wide-planked hardwood floor around it. I hold my hand out to Ian, and he places the thick syringe in my hand, filled to the brim with Melody's blood. Depressing the plunger, I douse the pristinely white tang in the lifeblood of my fallen friend.

We'll get him, baby girl. I promise. I'll get him for you.

Next come the chants in a language I don't understand. Aramaic hasn't been on my list of languages to learn, but I may need to start. I use the carefully crafted phonetic guide my mother provided, haltingly at first, but my words get clearer the more I say them. I immerse my fingers in the thick, red liquid, cupping my hands to pour the blood over and over the blade, careful not to nick my fingers on the surprisingly sharp edge.

A strange vibration starts pinging its way through me, almost making my words falter, but I power through, chanting the phrase over and over. Then, the bowl starts spinning, and I yank my hands back before the blade can cut me. The blood pooled in the bowl's depths seems to funnel into the blade, the bone sponging up the lifeblood as if it were dying of thirst. Candles that were not lit before, burst to life, their flames peaking high into the air before snuffing out altogether.

Snapping my fingers, they come to life again as I peer into the bowl. The blade sits there, pristine as ever, not a drop of blood left in the basin that holds it.

Well, that isn't creepy at all.

"I think it worked," I hesitantly say aloud, praying that somehow my words don't jinx me.

"Good. Now you have to find him. How did you do it the last time?"

I glance down at my bandaged forearms. I haven't looked at them uncovered since Bernadette abraded the flesh, too scared to know if my time was up.

"I followed the link to him from the brands he made on my arms."

Admitting that hurts somehow and I don't know why. Well, I do because without uncovering them, I already know that the burns are healed. I grasp the fact that my time is all but gone.

"So that's what they are." His voice is like glass over gravel. He might have suspected, but he didn't know. And now it is too late for me.

Too late because I know where he is. I know he's looking for me and I can feel it. A tiny siren's call tapping at my brain, begging for me to come to him.

"Yeah. But I don't need to follow the magic. I already know where he is."

This catches Ian by surprise, and his gaze on me turns sharp as a razor's edge.

"How do you know?" It isn't a question, more like a demand.

"The brands are healed, Ian. I'm too late." My voice cracks as I confess my death sentence—the awful thing I have tried so hard to prevent. I've failed at everything. Four hundred years on this planet, and what do I have to show for it?

"What do you mean, too late?" a voice calls from the stairwell, a voice I know all too well.

Striker moves into the wide-open room, his wings and talons gone, but his wrath is still there in full force. Aidan is behind him, hanging back, and already the place is wired, the frisson of his rage pinging against my skin.

I don't like that I can feel Striker's emotions. It means that he is too out of control to harness them. Even if the phase he couldn't hold back is concealed under his skin, it roils underneath his flesh, just waiting to come out again—waiting for the rage in his blood to ignite once again.

I don't know what Striker really is. I don't think he does, either. But the violence finds its target when his eyes fall on the blade still sitting in the bowl on the floor.

I know if Striker gets the blade before I do, he'll start a war—a war I don't think either of us will survive.

I don't know who gets to the knife first, or why I feel the excruciating pull yanking us from that room, draining me. All I know is when Striker and I land on the still-warm pavement of a suburban sidewalk, we're no longer in my shop.

It takes a second before I recognize the turquoise door attached to the pretty white house, but once I do, I know exactly where we are and why we came.

This is my house, and without a doubt, Micah is behind that door.

And worse?

I don't have the blade. Striker does.

CHAPTER TWENTY-TWO

MAX

Looking at my house from the sidewalk, no one would ever know there was a demon lurking inside. I suppose that was the goal of the illusion charm, but the magic hiding my house doesn't work on me, and still, my pretty house with its wide wrap-around porch and navy shutters call to me. Even though my skin, my brain, my bones know that Micah is inside, I still want to follow Striker in through my front door.

I still want to trail behind my best friend and go inside.

Well, I do, and I don't.

As much as I want to kill him for what he's done, want to run that blade deep in his gut, being this close to Micah is beginning to seem like a mistake. My wrath is muted, my thoughts wrapped in the fluffy cotton swaddling of the brand's magic.

It has to be the brand, right?

I want to go inside even though I no longer have a weapon, even though my magic seems to have been dulled, but there is a part of my brain that's screaming. It's a woman's voice that sounds so much like mine, but it gets farther and farther away, drowned out by a sudden lethargic pall that makes me want to go inside and lay my head down on my pillow.

Yes. That's it. I'm tired, and I want to go to bed.

The heat of the sidewalk scores at my fingers as I struggle to stand, but then my hand brushes cool metal, and I manage to focus for a slant second. A pale-blue stone winks at me from the pavement, glittering from the streetlight.

It's pretty, so pretty.

As soon as my fingers close around the ring, the fog from the brand burns away. The ring Bernadette gave me must have slipped off during the struggle over the blade, and Micah is using his control to try and trick me.

The dick. Both of them.

Shit! Striker has the blade, and if I had a guess, he's already in the house. I can't see him from my inelegant crouch on the sidewalk, but I'm not as dumb as I look. I have mixed feelings on this. On the one hand, Micah is in there, I don't have the blade anymore, and I'm pretty sure he just tried to mind-fuck me. On the other, if I don't stop Striker from killing him, he'll violate some ancient treaty and start a war. I think.

Somehow, I think out of everyone, I'm going to be the person who gets screwed over in this scenario.

The more my mind comes back, the more I know I didn't bring us here. I just wanted the blade, and to keep Striker from doing something stupid. And if I didn't take us here, that means Striker used me. He used my power as if it were his own. I feel as if he must have siphoned off some of my energy, and that knowledge feels like a hard slap when I'm already knocked down. That must be one of his tricks that he's kept from me.

It hurts that I've been used so callously by someone I trusted. Someone who has been vital to me for so long.

I have to go into the house. I know I do, but there is no way I'm walking in the front freaking door like Striker did. Instead, I make the likely idiotic decision to snap my fingers, arriving in my living room. It looks exactly the same as it did a few days ago.

Was it days? It feels like a lifetime since everything got turned upside down. I decorated this house and every single room in it. I painted those walls the brilliant peacock blue. I picked the slate-gray couch and every single goldenrod, plum, and teal throw pillow. I chose the plush area rug and the funky but cute art on the walls. I made this house my home, and while nothing seems out of place, it feels like a stranger's. It doesn't feel like mine anymore, and I hate that the home I spent so long creating for myself seems lost to me.

It almost feels as if I've been robbed.

But haven't I?

Deciding to find Striker before he screws us both over, I try and sense where Micah is. If his earlier mind-control taunts are any indication, my bedroom is a solid guess. I have to suppress a shudder as I try to gauge where Striker could be. After this long together, I should be able to feel him, right? I should be able to sense where he is using whatever demon juju is locked inside me, shouldn't I?

The faint whimper of a baby crying has me turning my ear to it. I can't tell if it's coming from the door that leads to the basement den and casting room or the dreaded flight upstairs where I know Micah is.

I close my eyes, trying to isolate the sound, knowing I'll go for Melody's son long before I try to save Striker. Striker is older than me, and he's armed. The baby isn't. Plus, the baby is innocent in all of this. If I see Striker, I'm punching him right in the balls first and then getting his dumb ass out of here.

Even in the back of my brain, I get that he's running on rage and not using his head, but shit, can't he just stop and think for one Fate's forsaken second?

I don't get an answer to my question because a rough hand closes over my mouth as a strong arm clamps around my stomach from behind. I can tell by the tattoos and combination of height and muscles behind me that this isn't Striker. Oh, and the general putrid 'I'm screwed and not in a good way' feeling I've got going on.

Without warning, Micah snaps us from the living room, popping into my bedroom without a second to spare. My stomach pitches, and I deduce demon traveling is no better than wraith traveling.

"I said I'd come back for you and look at that, you've come for me instead." Micah's thick British accent presses into my ears, inciting a body-wracking shudder.

It doesn't help that his lips—which I want nowhere near me—brush the shell of my ear as he says it. I don't want to be in his arms. I don't want to be this close to a bed. I don't want this man to keep breathing.

"Oh, come now, pet. I'm not that bad." His voice is honey on gravel, but he doesn't fool me.

"Tell that to Melody." I seethe, gritting my teeth as he tightens his hold.

"Melody was human. Simply a host for my seed." He rubs his lips along the column of my neck. I used to find that attractive in a man. A man could kiss me there, and I'd become pliable. When Micah does it, my stomach roils. "You, on the other hand, are much different. Practically royalty, you are. But no one protected you, did they? Let you be named Rogue so any demon could snatch you up and make you theirs. As long as you've been around, I figure it's a damn miracle you haven't been claimed by now."

"I don't know what you're talking about."

"Don't you know who your family is, love? Your father, the demon Andras, only son of our High Queen Lilith. You know her as Bernadette."

"You're saying that Bernadette is my grandmother?"

"Yep. I'd recognize this ring anywhere." He snatches up my right hand to get a better look at the ring that saved my mind. "If you looked at the sigils, you'd know what family you belong to. Spells it out good and proper. Why do you think I want you? What better trophy to have than the granddaughter of the High Queen and daughter of the Crown Prince?"

"So that's what this is? I'm a trophy. I guess it doesn't matter to you that I'd rather burn at the stake again than be your pet?" I growl, testing the hold he has on me as I try to yank away.

Unfortunately, I don't get anywhere but held tighter. Shit.

"It's 'cause I can't get into your head, if I could you'd be begging me to take you."

"Aww, did I hurt your fragile little ego? You can't mind-control me, so you decide kidnapping and enslavement is a good option?"

Micah's talons grip my chin, slicing into the fragile skin just under my jaw as he cinches his arm tighter around my waist. His actions tell me I may have struck a nerve. Whoops.

"You think a challenge will best me? No, pet, I'll take this ring off you, and you'll do exactly what I want you to do. I'll complete your branding, and no one will be able to take you away from me. Not even your high queen granny."

I hope he's not lying—that the brand isn't complete. That I'm not his—at least not yet.

But then I can't hope for much of anything at all because even though I struggle, even though I yank and stomp and kick, Micah rips that ring off my finger, damn near breaking it in the trying.

I feel his influence almost immediately, the cotton-candy fog of it clouding my mind. My limbs relax, my fear fizzles out, but with it, goes my sense.

"Come now, pet, let me see your brands."

The smart part of my brain is screaming for me to run, to snatch that ring back, to shout for Striker. Fucking anything but sit here in Micah's arms and let him mind-control me into slavery. But I don't, and the longer I stall, the more I forget why I'm worried about Micah in the first place.

I reach for the white surgical tape that holds the gauze to the healed brands, when a baby's cry sounds through the room. The woman in my head, her screams are getting louder.

Melody's son is in this room. You promised to help him, to keep him away from Micah.

You promised, you promised, you promised.

Micah's grip is lax, so this time when I yank, I manage to get free.

But only for a second.

In the next, my hair is wrenched, bringing my head back and clotheslining me faster than I can blink.

"You think I'm going to let you go that easy, pet?" His voice is a coy sort of whisper that makes the pit in my stomach grow wider, blooming into pure dread.

Then Striker's in the doorway of my bedroom, his phase a shining beacon of hope that fizzles out when he doesn't move to help. His fiery eyes glaze over as Striker stands stock-still, immobile, except for the breathing.

Micah's sudden laugh brings gooseflesh to my arms and a chill down my spine. It's a joyous kind of sound, and coming from him, it's a harbinger of pure fucking evil.

"Oh, how adorable. He thought he could save you both."

That's when I know. Striker can't help me.

He can't even save himself.

CHAPTER TWENTY-THREE

STRIKER

I screwed up. I know I have, but getting out of the mess I made is going to hurt more than just me.

I shouldn't have gone to find Max in her shop. I shouldn't have fought her for the demon blade. I shouldn't have siphoned her energy, making her take us to wherever Micah was.

I shouldn't have, but I did.

Blinded by the rage that courses through my body, I dicked over the one person who has never left me behind. My need for revenge had me leaving my best friend in all the world, dazed and drained on a sidewalk where I knew Micah could get to her.

The cry of Melody's son echoes through the house, a siren's call slapping me in the face with all the wrong I've done. All the vengeance in the world won't bring her back, it won't let breath and life flow through her. She won't grow old, watching her son grow up. She won't be with me.

Killing Micah won't do anything but snuff out another life. While that is appealing on so many levels, somehow, I still seem to lose.

Melody's son cries again, the baleful whimper of a hungry child, and instead of looking for Micah, I change direction, searching for the child instead. The staircase to Max's room never seemed so steep as it does right now, each stair taking me closer to the child I'm afraid to fail.

My hand trembles as I push open Max's bedroom door, my phase rippling over my flesh before the wood even leaves the doorjamb. But what I see isn't what I thought I would.

Melody is sitting up in the middle of Max's bed, her back against the tufted headboard, her son in her arms as she pats his diapered bottom trying to soothe him. At first, my heart can't take the sheer joy I feel. I must have dreamed her dying, or maybe she came back like Max does. Maybe it was the worst nightmare I could have, the vision of her bloody and gray, the life running out of her body one faltering heartbeat at a time.

My legs can barely hold me as I stagger to the side of the bed.

"M-Mel? Baby?" I can barely speak as my hands find her face, cupping her cheeks as I press my grateful lips to hers. I can't believe it. The thought she could come back was always a pipe dream in my head. A part of me never really believed she could come back at all, but having her sitting on this bed when I thought she was gone forever is the only wish my soul could ever ask for.

"Isn't he beautiful?" She smiles, and then her eyes fall back to her son as she runs a fingertip over the line of his cheeks. I follow her gaze, memorizing the way her fingers graze the line of her son's flesh, the way she holds him, the way she protects him. I could watch her forever.

"You holding him is the most beautiful thing I've ever seen." My voice breaks, still unable to get myself under control. The love on her face. Fates, I never thought I'd see her again. Never thought the crevasse left in my heart would ever heal. I've never been more grateful for anything in my entire life.

We sit in silence for a few minutes before a niggle of doubt hits me. I want to know what happened to her. I want to know if she's really okay.

How did she get here? How did she find her son? Why didn't she come to me?

"Baby, what happened to you?"

“I died, Striker,” she says simply, but her voice, her tone is wrong.

“But you’re here now. How did you get here?” As soon as I ask the question, dread filters back into my chest. She sounds like an echo, a copy.

“I don’t know, you tell me.” She continues to stare at her son, content in her own ignorance.

Or maybe it’s something else. This is wrong. This feels wrong.

I look up at the sun streaming through the window, filtering through Max’s curtains and highlighting the soft beauty in Melody’s cheeks. But her face is a little too full. Her nose a little too rounded. Her lips a little too wide.

I don’t want to pick this blessing apart, but…

It was night when I got to Max’s house, but it’s day now.

Did I miss the sun coming up?

No. I don’t think I did.

“Melody, baby, can you look at me?” My voice is pleading, and when her eyes meet mine, I know, the clawing ache of loss hitting me all at once.

My Melody died yesterday. She bled out on Ian’s pool table after a barbaric cesarean. She was left to die after she served her purpose. She was used and discarded as if someone that beautiful, that precious was disposable. My Melody was sweet and sassy and wonderful. She didn’t accuse, and she didn’t blame.

But most importantly, unlike this Melody, my Melody had blue eyes. They were the very first thing I noticed about her when she walked into the shop—the pale icy blue of them a stark contrast to her dark hair and tan skin. I looked into her wide eyes, and I was lost.

This isn’t real. None of it.

And it’s like I’ve lost her all over again.

Keeping the piercing agony off my face is almost impossible. My greatest wish, everything I would have bargained or stolen for, is crumbling to dust and I have to sit here and smile.

Because I’m going to get out of this trap, and I’m going to take Micah down.

If it's the last bloody thing I do.

MAX

"Let's complete that brand, shall we?" Micah murmurs, more to himself than to me. His influence on my mind is heavy, a thick leash of evil making my body do exactly what he wants it to do.

Unfortunately for him, the baby makes a plaintive cry again, and it clears my head some. Trying to catch him by surprise, I elbow Micah in the gut, yanking away from his hold.

But I don't run. Not this time. I already know running won't work. He has my ring, and without it, he can find me anywhere on this tiny little planet.

What I need is a distraction, a way to incapacitate him long enough for me to either get my ring back or search Striker for the damn blade and cut his stupid murdering head off. I would pick door number two, but it's a question of time at this point.

I try my first spell, muttering the Latin phrase I've used several times in my past as a method of interrogation. *"Mille vulnere." One thousand cuts.* Micah just smiles at me. My spell does nothing. Not even a paper cut this time.

I try another. *"Flumine sanguinis." River of blood.* This one isn't one I've used much. One, because it is freaking disgusting, and two because it's a shitty way to die and I'm not fond of killing people—at least people who don't deserve it.

Nothing.

Again.

"River of blood? Pulling out the big guns on that one, aren't you? Sorry, pet. Those spells won't work on me. Not anymore." He smiles venomously, his hand latching onto my forearm faster than my eye can track.

"None of your spells will work on me. Don't you get it? I own you." Micah's lips curl around the words like a lecherous caress. His power presses in on me, nearly taking away my will again as he shoves me against the wall, caging me in.

The more I fight him, the more pissed off he gets. Then, both of his burning hands latch onto my forearms. While there are plenty of shitty memories he could make me see, I know his game and I fight back, forcing him out of my mind, his own head rocking back as if I'd slapped him.

"You don't own shit."

The shock on Micah's face is so precious, if I had a camera, I would've stopped to take a picture.

"You bitch! You think you can keep me out? You think you can say no to me? No one says no to me, pet," Micah growls, his eyes glowing red, fangs peeking from beneath his lips.

Then, it's me who is shocked. Micah's face twists in fury as his power washes over me, flooding my body with his influence, with his fire. But something is different this time. Either Micah has flexed a little too much muscle, or I'm finally getting some mileage out of the half-breed demon status.

I'm drowning in his power, my mind clear for the first time since this mess started. I feel the energy pulsing out of him and into me. I'm draining him. Not on purpose or with any conscious thought on my part. No. It's him. He's trying to bend my mind to his so much he's flooding me with everything he has.

So much, he's losing his hold on everything else. Over Micah's shoulder, I watch as Striker comes back to himself, his body slowly becoming less frozen, his eyes focusing on the room instead of what was inside his head. I don't know what he saw, but whatever it was is enough to have my heart burning in agony just in response to the expression on his face. He's more than wounded. Whatever has cut into his soul was made of the worst sort of poison.

Striker is silent as he draws the demon blade from his belt, stepping toward us like a ghost. I never realized before just how quiet Striker can be, just how lethal. The furrow of his brow, the set to his lips, the wrath on his face, I wonder not for the first time if I really know my best friend at all.

I can't help the tendril of fear that steals through me as he comes closer, sidling behind Micah without so much as a whisper.

When the blade finds a home in the meat of Micah's shoulder, I don't expect the blinding agony that rips through my body. I really don't expect the warm wetness of blood pouring from my own shoulder. Micah staggers away from me, his talons scrabbling at the wound in his shoulder. If I could move, I'm sure I'd be doing the same, but all I can do is slide down the wall that can't seem to hold me up, landing with a jarring thump on my hardwood bedroom floor.

The room tilts on its axis as I try to pull in a breath. I didn't know it would hurt this bad. I didn't think killing Micah would be the end of me.

But I think it might be.

Striker drops the blade, skirting around Micah and pressing his hand on my shoulder to staunch the flow of blood weeping from the wound. His touch only makes me cry out, unable to hold the agony of it inside me for one more second.

I know what I have to do. It can't be Striker who kills Micah. I can't let my best friend in the world start a war when I won't be here to help him fight. And I won't be here. I've already figured that much out for myself. If a cut on Micah does this to me, what will killing him do?

I'm not stupid. I know if Micah lives, he'll kill me or Striker, or worse, sell off that baby to the highest bidder to do Fates know what. He won't stop until he gets his trophy. I don't know what my family did to Micah to make him hate us so much. If my demon side is anything like my witch side, I can see where making enemies isn't exactly a new thing.

But it's a debt I'll pay if it means my best friend gets to live. I'll pay it if it means no war. I'll pay it if it means I finally get to keep my promise to a young pregnant girl who never even asked me for help.

I'm saving her son. I'm saving her love.

And I'll get vengeance on the man who stole her life out from under her.

I tilt, pulling away from Striker and sliding closer to Micah. The blade is close, but the white-hot agony ripping through my shoulder make three feet seem like a mile. Striker tries to stop me, but I think he's more worried about hurting me more, so his touch is gentle.

By the time I get to the blade, Striker's already figured out what I'm going to do.

"No, Max. No. We'll find another way."

"Th-there isn't another way, Strike. He'll just keep co-coming. He'll just t-try again," I stutter, my fingers closing around the wrapped leather hilt.

"No. Please don't."

Micah jerks pitifully, trying to scrabble away, but at this point I'm half-lying on top of him to reach the bone knife, the sharp double-edged blade coated in his blood. Then I feel the barest inkling of his power trying to filter back into him.

He's trying to escape. Not if I can help it. Tightening my grip, I heft the knife that seemed so small an hour ago into my hand.

"Love you, Strike," I whisper, trying to convey all of my remorse for what I'm about to do. I'm leaving him. I promised I wouldn't do that to him. I promised so long ago that I wouldn't abandon him the way everyone else had.

At the time, I didn't think dying was an option, so it was an easy promise to make. Now, breaking that promise is just as easy.

As the blade pierces Micah's chest, Striker's scream is the last thing I hear.

CHAPTER TWENTY-FOUR

MAX

A man's voice filters in my ears, calling me from the blackness that has swaddled me in silence for far too long. He's singing softly in a tune I can't place, but the song doesn't matter, the light that seems to seep through my eyelids does. Forcing them open, it takes a minute for the room to come into focus.

Softly lit by a bedside lamp, Ian's bedroom feels familiar and comforting after clawing my way back from the dark. My eyes drift to the side, falling on worn jeans and a pair of rather attractive bare feet crossed at the ankles.

"Maxima? Baby?" Ian's voice is a pleasant mix of surprised and relieved, but the words themselves trip a hair trigger in me I didn't know I had.

"Why do you call me that?" I snap, not really meaning to, but my full name plus the endearment grates the shit out of my nerves.

"Maxima or baby?" Ian's tone is neutral. He doesn't sound hurt, but his face tells another tale.

"Both."

"Well, I call you Maxima because you're a chick and Max is a dude's name, and I call you baby because I'm totally and completely enamored by you, and it's my subtle way of showing it." Ian's wry answer makes me chuckle.

"So noted, but no endearments, please. No baby or honey or darling. Just don't, okay?"

After Micah, I'm not sure I can handle another man calling me anything other than Max.

"You wake up after two damn days, and it's 'don't call me honey'? Are you kidding me?" Striker gripes, and I whip my head to my right to see him sitting in a leather club chair with a burp cloth on his shoulder patting a diapered baby booty.

"Two days? That's... excessive." I don't think I've ever been out for more than a day.

"Excessive? That's all you're gonna say? Not 'sorry you had to watch me kill myself' or maybe 'sorry I played martyr for the seven thousandth time and got myself killed'? Jesus fuck, Max."

Striker's eyes flash gold. He's pissed, but he doesn't have any right to be. I didn't take us to Micah. I didn't put us there at all.

I put a hand on the bed to shove myself up to sitting. Striker's aching for a fight, and I'm just pissed enough to give him one.

"Look, I'm not the one who put us in that situation in the first damn place. I'm not going to argue with you about what went down because I did what I had to do, just like I always do what I have to do. You don't like it? Don't go off half-cocked with a weapon that can start a war. Sound good?" I spit through gritted teeth, and it takes a second for me to realize that the shaking bout of rage I feel isn't just me, it's the whole damn room, probably the whole freaking building.

So my abilities have kicked it up a notch. Interesting.

Honestly, it's a giant slice of shit cake on top of a shitty couple of days. Why not add to the power I already can't seem to control? That won't backfire on me. No, surely not.

Worry pings in my brain for the first time since I woke up, and I scrabble to search my skin for the brands Micah left. Both arms are the smooth tattooed skin, the brand that had burned my skin just days ago missing. I run my fingertips over the skin, just to reassure myself that they are indeed gone.

Melody's son fusses a bit, drawing my eyes to the tense way Striker clings to him.

Oh, no. No.

"You can't keep him. You know that, right?" My words are harsh, but unfortunately, they are also true.

"Why the fuck not?" Striker snarls, both arms circling around the baby as he clutches him closer.

I don't want to be the bad guy here.

But the both of us made Melody a promise. We promised we would save her son. We promised we would get him away from Micah. We promised we would keep him safe.

Safe isn't with us.

"He isn't yours to keep. You aren't a demon. You don't know what his powers will be or what instruction he'll need. You have no idea how to raise him, nor are you equipped to do so. Look at me. Look at how I was raised. Do you think I would have been killed so many times if I knew what I could do or what I was capable of? Even you. You have no idea what you are. How can you raise a child when even you have no idea what you can do?"

Striker's eyes, which were filled with anger just a second ago, turn wounded. Jesus, I do not want to be the bad guy.

"But I'll love him, isn't that enough?"

"For some, love can conquer everything. But you can't choose the course of a child's life based on just love. You need to be smart. You need to choose him instead of playing into your own grief. You can't keep him just because he's that last bit of Melody you have left." My tone is soft, but my words are barbed. There just isn't another way to say it, and it has to be said.

"Fuck you, Max. Fuck. You." Striker seethes because I'm about to take away the one thing that could dam his grief. I get it, but I shouldn't have to be on the receiving end of this horse shit.

"Fuck me? What happens when Micah's friends realize he's dead, hmm? Won't they come looking for us? How are you supposed to keep him safe then? Answer me. How?"

But Striker doesn't have an answer for me because the answer is, he can't.

. . .

Walking into Caim's office with a newborn in my arms goes over about as well as one would expect. After three days of wearing Striker down, I finally got him to see my side of things. Sure, the brands were gone, and Micah was dead, but I didn't trust that we were safe.

I couldn't let Melody's son pay the price if I was right.

"What the hell are you doing here?" Ruby demands, "And what the hell is that?"

I ignore her. For someone who tried to help me stay alive and out of slavery, she sure is surprised I'm here. I don't think Ruby and I will be braiding each other's hair anytime soon.

Instead of giving Ruby the time of day, I lock eyes with Caim. "I would like to speak to you without an audience." I keep my voice as bored as I can make it. Letting either of them know just how much I need them seems like a bad plan. Caim and Ruby feel like predators to me now, and I don't understand why. If I show either of them the least bit of weakness, I have an inkling they could smell it. I wouldn't be here at all if I could avoid it, but Caim owes me a favor.

Caim's lips quirk just so, a subtle upturn of the mouth so quick Ruby misses it. "It's fine, Ruby. Leave us."

I hate to admit, but I get a sick sort of satisfaction out of her stomping off in a huff. Yeah, no. We're never going to be besties.

"Your problem has been taken care of, which means you owe me a favor and I'm here to collect."

"I owe you, huh? And how is that?"

"Without me, you would never know about Micah running a black-market site right under your nose, and now that he has been handled, you won't start a war. Sounds to me like you owe me big." My words are blunt and to the point.

Caim assesses me for a minute, steepling his fingers as he looks the baby and me over. Melody's son fusses for a second, so I drop the diaper bag on my shoulder and start rocking him. All things considered, he is probably easy for a newborn, but I haven't gotten the hang of him yet. Readjusting his pacifier and cooing at him for a bit seems to do the trick, and he settles back down. I think he looks like Melody with his pale-blue eyes and light-brown hair that will no doubt darken with age, and somehow it gives me comfort to know a piece of her lives on.

"What is this favor?"

"I want you to find him a good home. A place where they are kind, and safe, and won't eat him or make him feel like shit for being half-human. I want him to be brought up knowing what he is and how to use his powers. I want him loved. You have in your possession every single registered Ethereal, right? Find someone on that list who wants a baby who can train him and love him. You do that, and I'll call us square." It's a big ask, I know, but I killed a damn demon and almost died to prevent an all-out war. A big ask is par for the freaking course around here.

Caim's forehead furrows in confusion and he sits just staring at me for a moment, while I adjust my little bundle so he's sleeping on my chest. I wish I could give him a name, but it just doesn't feel right. He's not mine, and he's not Striker's. We don't get to bless him with something so precious.

"You could ask me for anything, literally anything, and with what you've done for me I'd have to help you, and you pick helping this boy over any amount of riches or power you could possess?" Disbelief is clear in Caim's tone.

"I made a promise to Melody that I'd keep her son safe. I keep my word, Caim. Always." And I don't make promises I don't keep, I want to say, but I don't. Who knows what he promised my mother —or didn't promise her for all I know? Out of the two of them, so far, Caim hasn't dicked me over, so I'll take his word over hers at the moment.

"You are nothing like your father." The statement catches me by surprise. I don't know Andras, but I do know Teresa. If I'm nothing like my mother and nothing like my father, who the hell am I like?

A question for the ages, I bet.

"You know him? Is he a bad man?" I ask the child-like question slipping out of my mouth before I can stop it.

"The worst. But he's a good man, too, just in his own way."

Well, that clears everything right up.

"You're better off not knowing, Maxima. Trust that at least."

"I'm pretty sure he's known where I was for the last four hundred years. I don't think he has any plans to get to know me, so I'll take your word for it."

"Good. Now give me the child. I know exactly who to give him to." He rises to his feet, pushing away from the desk and holding out his hands for Melody's son.

I give his forehead a gentle kiss, muttering a blessing for him that I hope will take before handing him over.

"Does he have a name?" Caim adjusts the little bundle in his arms with practiced ease. This isn't the first child Caim's held, not by a long shot.

"It didn't feel right to name him. Striker wanted to call him Ronan, but..." I trail off, shrugging. "It didn't feel like my place."

"I like Ronan." Caim coos to the baby, running a single finger down his chubby baby cheek. I've done that a time or two over the last couple of days, fighting with myself to not get attached to something so precious.

"You'll make sure he's safe, right?"

"Of course, Maxima. Children are to be protected." Caim's eyes meet mine for the first time since I handed the baby over.

His words give me a little comfort as I leave them to it, the aching loss I feel lessening just a bit.

Goodbye, Melody. I hope you are at peace.

CHAPTER TWENTY-FIVE

MAX

"Again!" Aidan shouts, and I can't help but groan from my flat-on-my-ass position on the awful blue mat.

Fuck training, fuck bokkens, just fuck them all.

"You were the one who came to me to learn how to fight, Max. No one forced you, now get your ass up and do it again."

Who thought Aidan as my trainer would be a good idea? Oh, right, this girl.

Peeling myself off the mat, I question my sanity for the hundredth time.

"You do realize I could crush you with a snap of my fingers, right?"

Aidan just raises an eyebrow at me, not breaking a sweat, even though he's wearing a beanie.

Still. In August.

I sometimes wonder what's underneath. Does he have a bald spot? A random growth? I may make it my mission to check one of these days. After my body quits hurting from the beat downs I've been getting.

"You realize that having a guardian train you is about as good as it gets, right? Magic doesn't always work. You can't rely on it. Isn't that what you told me when you asked me to train you?"

"Yeah." I sigh, snatching up the stupid wooden katana that has been the bane of my existence for the last three weeks.

"You're a natural, Max, probably one of the quickest studies I've ever seen. But you're lazy as hell. Now get into a fighting stance and let's go."

One of these days I'm going to kick his ass.

Probably won't be today, though.

After our session—and a shower—I haul my tired ass back to the shop. Ever since the ordeal with Micah, I can't seem to make myself go back to my house in the burbs, so the apartment over my tattoo shop is getting a fair amount of use.

It feels weird now, coming into work without Striker here. He tried to come back after everything. He did, but I could tell it was killing him. He'd look at the counter separating the waiting area and the rest of the shop, and the sadness would just wash over him. Everything in this place reminded him of Melody. Hell, I probably did, too. So, one day I let him off the hook.

"You don't have to be here, you know." A brilliant opener, but it was what I had to work with. Striker didn't have to be here. He was immortal (probably) with enough money to last until the end of time. He didn't have to be stuck with me in Denver. He didn't have to be in this shop with me, and he didn't have to be reminded every day of the love he lost.

"My name's on the deed right next to yours, Max. Of course I have to be here." His lifeless tone was killing me.

"You're going to let a piece of paper tell you how to live your life? You're miserable, and your sadness is killing me. How the hell are you supposed to heal if you're reminded of her every single second of the day?" I asked, mostly because I wanted to know.

I had the resolution of giving Ronan up to Caim. I had the closure of fulfilling Melody's dying wish. Striker never really had that. He wouldn't even let Melody have a funeral. I ended up calling Aurelia to help me inter her. No one knows more about funeral rites more than a phoenix, and given that my other best friend was a pile of depressed shit, I needed the help.

"I don't think I'll heal from this, Max. Melody wasn't a girl you just get over." His voice was hoarse with the pain he had shoved deep down inside.

He was probably right.

"But you're right about one thing, I don't have to be here." He nodded to himself before walking across the shop to brush a kiss on my forehead, sparing me the hug, even though I would've probably accepted one from him.

He left without another word, and in the last few weeks, I haven't heard from him. As much as I know it's for the best, I really hate it. Striker and I haven't gone more than a week without talking to each other in a century, so the distance sucks hairy monkey balls.

Letting myself into the back entrance, I climb the staircase, my sore legs crying with every step. I hate being sore. I loathe sweating. But the confidence of knowing I can take care of myself is something I can't quite pass up. I need to know what I can do without powers, without magic. I need to be able to defend myself if...

For some reason, a tear falls down my cheek. It's been happening a lot lately, stupid random bouts of crying. I hate it. I feel so weak when I just start leaking out of the blue. But I get why it's happening.

One of my besties is off on his own. My house is probably going to have to be sold because I can't even look at the front fucking door without having a panic attack. Melody's dead and her son is gone—off to live with a couple who hopefully loves him.

But I can't stand to be touched since I've woken up, and I can't really sleep at night. I'm trying so hard to get my life back together, but it's like overfilling a paper bag.

The bottom always falls out eventually.

I park my butt in the middle of the staircase, delaying the inevitable lesson with Ian just a little so I can get myself under control. Along with Aidan training me in hand-to-hand combat, Ian is going over the basics of being a witch. Sure, a lot of the lessons don't apply to me, but I like knowing all the things I should have been taught by my mother. Even if the lessons are mostly a ruse so I can get to know Ian a bit more.

I thought I would be able to just jump into a relationship—or at least sex—with Ian after everything was over, but the no-touching rule is screwing me over, and not in a good way. I just don't want to shudder if he touches me, and I can't seem to make that happen right now. At least with the lessons, I get to have him in my life. Even if they are about as chaste as a ninety-year-old nun. Ian doesn't seem to be going anywhere for the time being, so at least I have that.

I haul myself up, contemplating what I can cajole Ian into picking up for takeout as I slog up the rest of the stairs. Before I even get the key into the lock, I know there is someone here. The ward hexes are gone. I understand it isn't Ian because he knows better than to waltz into my home without asking.

Not after Micah. Not ever again.

"You broke into the wrong fucking home," I call into the dark. "Show yourself." This isn't a burglar, that's for damn sure.

I snap my fingers, igniting every candle and turning on every light. I won't attack if I don't have to, but I want to see what I'm working with. What I really want to know is how they broke my wards.

Ruby is lounging on one of my tufted armchairs, her legs crossed as she inspects her nails in a show of boredom.

Oh, good. I need this tonight.

"You about gave me a heart attack, Ruby. What the shit?" Dropping my purse on the console table behind my velvet peacock-blue couch, I wait for an answer.

Ruby rolls her eyes before finally looking at me. I'll give her credit, the woman is beautiful, but Jesus, I wish she wasn't so... mean. She reminds me of my mother, and Teresa Alcado is no one to emulate.

"How many times have you dropped into Caim's without so

much as a hello?" she accuses, and she's right. I've been a little lax in the manners department, but give a girl a little warning, why don't you?

"Popping into someone's home is rude. Lesson learned. Any other tidbits of wisdom you wish to impart before you tell me why the hell you broke into my house?"

"I'm here to bring you in."

That doesn't sound good.

"Bring me in where?"

"To the Council, Maxima. You broke the law. You have to be punished." Ruby doesn't look too broken up about this. Hell, if I had a guess she's probably smiling on the inside. She has got to be dicking with me.

"And what law was that?" I scoff, not impressed.

"You murdered your Master," she says simply as if I'm supposed to know what the hell she's talking about.

"As far as I know, I have no Master. Good talk, though. You know where the door is on your way out," I bite out sarcastically, skirting around the couch to the kitchen. This day calls for bourbon and some ice cream. I'll worry about dinner later.

"Micah Goode. Ring any bells? You killed him, and now you have to stand trial."

I'm glad I'm not looking at her when she says his name, and I think I manage not to show any outward sign of fear. I really do need bourbon. A whole bloody bottle of it.

I reach into the liquor cabinet for the bottle of amber liquid. "Really? Are you fucking with me?"

"Afraid not." Her tone doesn't say as much. She sounds like she's suppressing a snicker, the bitch.

"Well, Ruby, I don't know much about Micah Goode except for he isn't my Master," I declare, just barely avoiding lying through my fucking teeth. I've lived for four hundred years, so my poker face is spot on. "No brands, see?" I show her my forearms.

I don't know why the brands are gone or how they left my skin. Bernadette said they couldn't be removed, so the reasoning behind it doesn't make much sense to me. Maybe when Micah flooded me with his power, he messed with the branding somehow. I don't know.

"Be that as it may, you're coming with me, Maxima," Ruby orders, and I know I'm going with her whether I like it or not.

Because Ruby is an angel, and if everything they say about me is true, then I'm a demon. If I harm a hair on her little head, it will start a war—a war I damn near died to prevent once already.

I've already been burned at the stake.

How bad could it be?

DAUGHTER OF SOULS & SILENCE

ROGUE ETHEREAL BOOK 2

CHAPTER ONE

MAX

There are some things I'd have hoped to never experience. Being eaten alive by carnivorous ants, missing a shoe sale, being forced to watch *Gomer Pyle* reruns—you know, the really evil stuff. There are other things I didn't even think to put on the list. Being dragged by the arm by a bitchy angel into a room full of Ethereal elders probably should have been at the tippy-top. Had I known it was a thing, I probably would have written it down or something, but alas...

"You know, that 'never harming the other side shit' goes both ways, Ruby," I warn my captor as she drags me through the hidden halls of a club the pair of us are very familiar with. Her definitely more than me.

One could say Aether was where everything started, and they'd be right, in a way. This underground witch club was my first real introduction to my kind in a very long time.

But they weren't all my kind, now were they? Witch DNA only accounted for half my makeup. The other half was a bag of cats even I didn't want to get in the middle of. And truth be told, if Ruby Sinclair wasn't dragging me through the place, I probably wouldn't even be allowed to grace these halls with my presence.

From what I'd gathered in the weeks following my parental reveal, demons weren't welcome most places. In my case, being half-demon made it so I wasn't welcome in my own family.

Go figure.

"Oh, please. It's no worse than you throwing me across the room, Max, and you know it," she snarls, which is a feat considering she's about as menacing as a tabby cat. Blonde hair, big boobs, porcelain skin. I had a feeling she wasn't *just* an angel. I also figured she was probably a bit more threatening to people who weren't me.

But Ruby had a point. I did toss her across the room like a rag doll, and keeping the smile off my face as I recall the memory is harder than I thought it would be.

"Yes, but you landed in a very comfy chair with exactly zero bruises, and that stunt helped suss out a black-market dealing asshole. This right here"—I return while tugging my upper arm out of her grip—"is just you being a dick."

More like it was her way to push the limit of the law as far as it would go. I couldn't harm her without starting an all-out angel-demon Armageddon. But then again, she couldn't harm me, either. I wonder how much leeway she could get, since she was essentially taking me to jail or to a judge, or whatever. All she'd said after she broke into my home was that she was taking me to the Council.

Not that I really knew what that meant.

"*Fine.*" Ruby turns down a hallway I'd yet to traverse. "Follow me and stay close. I don't have time to hunt you down if you decide to rabbit on me. I have shit to do."

What shit exactly *she* had to do, I had no idea. As far as I understood it, Ruby was Caim's bodyguard, bounty hunter, lap dog, and all-around gofer.

Rather than roll my eyes, I follow her down a shadowy hallway away from the revelers and music—away from the safety a crowd of that size provides—and step closer and closer to a place I have no desire to be.

They say I broke the law by killing Micah, the incubus who

branded me. Maybe I did, but deciding between killing a man, or becoming a slave to him for the rest of my long life, well… it was really no decision.

Too bad I didn't read the fine print on the bone blade my mother gave me.

Ruby stops at a door that seems to have popped up out of nowhere. The wood is an ornately carved mahogany. In the dim, it takes me a minute to recognize the words etched into the frame. *Numera omnes qui ingrediuntur ad iudicium.*

Judgment comes to all who enter.

Well, that isn't ominous or anything.

Ruby's corn silk hair falls in a sheet down her back, highlighting when she fidgets, hesitating before opening the heavy door. Ruby doesn't fidget, and she doesn't hesitate. Not ever. Her pause causes the hair on the back of my neck to stand up, and I don't like it one bit.

She shoves it open, revealing a bright room, nearly blinding after immersing myself in the dark pockets of the nightclub. She steps aside, waiting for me to enter. Just like Caim's magical portal of an office—*which skeeves me the fuck out*—this room seems to be here, and then again *not* here. We've all done it—made a temporary portal when we don't want to bother with something so pedestrian as actual travel—but permanent portals like this one are on my long list of things that are probably not so good for the balance of magic.

I look back down the long hallway, catching glimpses here and there of club-goers living it up, and I wonder if I'll ever be like them.

Carefree.

Accepted.

Doubtful.

"Any day now," Ruby gripes, and I have the distinct urge to put my fist in her face. I don't, but I really want to.

I heave a longsuffering sigh and step into the room. The snick of the latch closing just behind me does absolutely nothing to help my rising trepidation at what is a huge, honking unknown. Immediately, I feel underdressed. The space is wall-to-wall marble, the bright white of it threaded through with waves of gray. To my right is a room that seems to go on forever, the shadowless whiteness reaching on and on in a vastness that my eyes just can't seem to comprehend. To my left, is a raised dais with what seems to be a judge's bench.

Only there isn't just one judge.

There are eight seats, but only six are filled. Large expertly carved wooden thrones, each with a totem above the headrest. In the first seat is Caim, his blue eyes blazing as he grinds his teeth. He is a bit less poised than I'm used to, which doesn't spell good things. The totem on his seat is a pair of spread wings.

Next to him is a tiny, fine-boned blonde. On the street, I wouldn't put her past thirty. On this dais, with her eyes assessing me in the way that they are, I'd say she was ancient. Her rosy lips quirk into a half-smile that isn't comforting at all. Her totem is a dragon, its mouth open in a snarl.

Beside her is a giant, thin in the extreme, his expressionless face seeming to see me and see through me all at the same time. His totem is an hourglass. Next to him is an open seat, the wood of the totem molded into the fluid form of a phoenix.

Down the line is a quite attractive but scowling man, his sable-brown hair brushed from his face in an artfully messy way that is made to look effortless, but in no way actually is. His totem is a pentagram. Next to him is my grandmother, Bernadette—or Lilith if we want to get technical. She's wearing a white suit jacket with pearls. I can't tell what is behind the bench, but I'd lay money on her being in a skirt. Her totem, frighteningly enough, is what appears to be a gargoyle's head, its mouth open in a screaming hiss, fangs bared, tongue lolling. But Bernadette's face is carefully blank.

Not good.

Beside her is a gruff-looking man with silver eyes and weathered skin, dressed in flannel and looking like he'd rather be drinking a beer at a pub than be within a hundred miles of here. His hair is long and shaggy, falling into his eyes. The hair on his chin is three days past scruff and entering scraggy-beard territory. His totem is a wolf baying at some unseen moon.

Next to him is the other empty chair, the totem on it a haunting version of *The Scream* only with less abstractness and too much abject realism.

Angel, dragon, warlock, phoenix, witch, demon, shifter, wraith. The heads of all the Ethereal factions sitting in one place. Well, almost all of them. I knew the two that were missing personally, but my "in" with the leaders of the phoenix and wraith faction would probably do little to help me now.

Especially since the remaining six—well, except for my gramma—were all staring at me like I was a puppy who shit on an heirloom rug.

Fuck a duck, I am screwed.

They don't start with pleasantries, no one introducing themselves to me or even attempting to be civil. The brown-haired witch snaps his fingers and a hard-backed wooden chair springs up out of nowhere. I assume he wants me to sit, but I ignore the chair out of spite and cross my arms, my bravado hopefully hiding that I feel mighty underdressed and at a loss. Had I known I was going to meet what was inherently Ethereal royalty, I would have at least done my hair.

As it stood, I was in black, skinny jeans with the cuffs rolled up, electric-blue Converse, and a hot-pink semi-see-through tank that said "Adios Bitchachoes" with a lacy black bra underneath and a messy bun on top of my head. Yep. I probably should have asked Ruby for a timeout so I could at least put on something presentable.

Why didn't Bernadette tell me, warn me? Why didn't Caim? Did I mean so little to the both of them that they wouldn't give two shits about me sitting—well, standing—right where I am?

"Do you know why you're here?" the blonde dragon asks. Her accent is thick, maybe Russian or Ukrainian perhaps.

"I have an idea," I drawl, my left eyebrow hitching up without permission.

Oh, I have more than an idea. I know exactly why I'm here. It probably has something to do with the demon I killed.

"Good, then we'll dispense with the pleasantries. Maxima Alcado, born Maxima Christina Arcadios, Rogue witch, denounced member of the former Arcadios Coven, shunned daughter of the demon Andras and Pacific Northwest Coven leader, Teresa Alcado, sole heir to the royal seat, you are hereby accused of murdering your Master, Micah Goode, with a forbidden instrument."

A high-pitched buzzing takes over my hearing as a biting cold seems to seep into my limbs. I hate that name. Hate the way my body betrays me every single time I hear it. Both his name and the one I was given when I came into this world. *Arcadios.* I thought I'd buried that part of me just like my mother had. I guess not. And Micah's. I hate the way just the specter of him makes it so I can't go home, can't even look at my house without my breath coming in these same short pants of an impending panic attack.

It isn't fair. I didn't ask to be branded. I didn't ask to be born in the family I was. And that's why Micah wanted me. Because of who my family is. Because of the blood running in my veins.

I guess the self-defense excuse was probably moot here.

I open my mouth to say just that when I hear my gramma's voice in my head, her crisp English accent echoing through the edges of my brain.

Don't say a word, Maxima dear. I'll fix this. I swear to you. I'll fix this.

I meet her warm brown eyes, knowing she means it, but also knowing that if it came to it, I might be beyond saving.

"Have you nothing to say?" The witch's tone is snide as he sneers at me.

I shift my gaze from Bernadette to him, keeping my face impassive, looking him over. Yes, he's attractive, but his sneer sours his looks. My assessment must unnerve him because he shifts in his seat.

Probably used to a bit more groveling, I bet.

"So be it." He pauses—probably for effect—taking over the speaking for the dragon, a little upward crook of his mouth. "The sentence for your crimes is death. Do you have anything to say now?"

It turns out I didn't.

CHAPTER TWO

MAX

I feel a hysterical giggle bubbling up my chest as I utilize the wooden chair to take a load off. I'd stopped my bestest friend on this planet from killing one fucking demon—which prevented the Fate's forsaken Apocalypse, I might add—and this is the thanks I get?

A death sentence? Were they fucking high?

Bernadette's crisp voice echoes through my brain again, and I wonder if she'll teach me that trick in the few minutes I have left on this earth.

My guess is probably not.

I want you to remind them of a little thing called consent. It isn't just for prom dates, pumpkin. Even demons require it.

Consent. Is that going to be my saving grace?

"Really? A death sentence. And may I ask, can you prove that Micah was my master?" I question the silent panel of judges. "I don't think you can. Because I don't see any brands on my arms, and I know for a fact that his death would not erase them. If he were my master, then his death would have meant my own. And

I'm still breathing," I snarl, my arms open wide to show them the smooth, tattooed skin.

"All I see are tattoos. Maybe you covered the brands." The witch's snide slips a bit when I call him on his bullshit. What am I, a rustler trying to cover up a horse brand?

"You know good and well I can't cover up those marks. You can't prove he was my master, can you? And if you can't prove it, then you can shove your death sentence up that tiny little pinprick you call an asshole." I'm addressing them all, but my eyes are focused on the witch who gained so much pleasure from announcing my death sentence and my Rogue status as if I was slime on his shoe. I get a little thrill when his face turns indignant as he sputters.

I don't think anyone has ever talked that way to him probably ever. I love being the first to do things.

That was not what I meant, Maxima, and you know it.

I shrug at her, giving an unrepentant smile.

It takes precisely two-point-five seconds to come to the realization that if they wanted to kill me, they would have done it already. There would be guards or something. My magic would have been suppressed.

I snap my fingers to test my theory, watching as the green of my power slides like a molten fire over my fingers. I snap them again and an ottoman springs up under my feet. I cross my ankles and my arms at the same time as I level them all with a hard expression.

I'm tired, I'm pissed. It's been a long day, and this bullshit isn't making it any better.

"There is also the issue of consent. Micah for damn sure didn't have it, and I was under the impression it was required for one to be enslaved for all of eternity. And you're telling me, he branded the next in line to the royal demon seat or whatever against her will, and I'm the one sentenced to die? As far as I'm concerned, the only one here who broke the law is Micah, and I cut out the middleman and took care of him for you. You're welcome. Can we just cut the shit already? You all want something from me. So instead of bullshitting me with this asinine death sentence that I know for a Fate's forsaken fact you will not carry out, why don't you just tell me what you want?"

What I'd really like to know is where exactly these people were when Micah was off murdering humans and butchering his baby mama. I want to know where they were when he was trying to make me submit, when he was taking over my mind, when he was making me afraid of my own skin.

Sitting here up on high, I suspect.

Bernadette raises an eyebrow but can't hide the way her lips decide to curve up at the corners. A few months ago, I might have smiled with her, but today I've had about enough of this bullshit.

I'm missing my lesson with Ian for this malarkey. Ian. I hope he doesn't worry about me. That's a lie. I kind of hope he does a little, but not enough to cause real harm. I'm in that weird, selfish place where I want him to give a shit but don't want him to be inconvenienced.

Feelings are weird.

"We... You..." the witch sputters. *Oh, dear, I think I broke him.*

"What Barrett is trying to do even though he insofar has bungled it up royally, is to ask you for help. There was a vote earlier on how this would go because your grandmother suggested using fear as a motivating tactic would be unwise. The five remaining voted, and you can see how that's going," the shifter explains. "My name is Marcus, by the way, and if you'd be so inclined to hear us, I'd like to ask you for a favor."

"This is *not* what we discussed!" Barrett hisses around my grandmother.

"And what was your threatening her going to do?" Marcus retorts. "Piss her off so she'll never help us? Were you going to attempt to kill her and then get your ass kicked by someone a quarter your age? Fear doesn't work on everyone, you know." I get stuck on the age thing. I'm nearly four hundred. That would mean

Barrett is edging on twelve hundred. I've never met a witch over eight hundred.

Old as fuck or not, Barrett is still a dick. "She *broke* the law." If anything, he is persistent, and at this point, I wish I had popcorn because this is better than reality TV.

"No, she didn't. Micah did not have consent. Not only that, there is no way on any plane of existence Micah Goode should have ever tried to enslave a princess. And what are you defending him for?"

"I defend the law. No matter who breaks it, it is our job to uphold it. If there is no law, then there will only be chaos." Barrett bangs his fist on the bench like a gavel. "She killed the demon who branded her—with a forbidden weapon, no less—and you want to ask her for a favor? Are you getting senile in your old age, Marcus?"

Marcus rolls his eyes in a way that would make a teenager proud, turning his body back to me. "As you can see, we still have somewhat of a debate on the validity of your supposed breaking of the law."

"If we're getting technical, I've been a Rogue since I was fourteen. I don't know any of your laws, and as far as I can tell, you should be thanking me. Because if I didn't kill Micah, Striker Voss would have. Which if I recall correctly, would have started the fucking Apocalypse. *Again*, you're welcome."

This earns me a sharp stare from the dragon lady, and I have a hard time keeping my chuckle to myself. They have to tell me their names, so I'm not just thinking of them by their totems.

"Can you guys maybe introduce yourselves? I know Caim and Bernadette and now Barrett and Marcus, but the rest of you..." I trail off, shrugging in the hopes that they understand why I wouldn't know them. Being cast out of my family at such a young age means I know less than I probably should about this world. The warlock takes pity on me first.

"I am known as Gorgon, child," the warlock murmurs. Warlocks have always been very interesting to me, typically bald even as children no matter the sex, taller than even the tallest human, and thin in the extreme, warlocks aren't as mainstream as your average witch or shifter. In my four hundred years, I don't think I've seen even a handful, and their abilities are something out of a *Dr. Who* episode. Warlocks bend time to their will, shaping it and molding it to their needs. Or at least that's what I've heard. I'd never actually met one until today.

I give him my most polite smile. "Pleased to meet you, Mr. Gorgon." My impromptu manners must catch him by surprise because I get a shocked sort of laugh out of him.

"And I am Cinder," the dragon says, and something about the way she moves seems familiar somehow. I give her a nod in deference.

"Again, pleased to meet you all."

"I'm sorry about the circumstances, Max, but like Marcus said, we need a favor," Caim starts, and I swear I almost forgot the angel was here. "It isn't one we ask lightly, and it isn't one we want to ask at all. But there are only two people on this earth that can carry it out, and there is no way we could ask Bernadette to do it." His face is ravaged as if he in no way wants to ask what he's about to, and it's slowly killing him. Shit.

"There's a reason you are next in line for the royal seat even though you're a Rogue. Your father, Andras—"

"He might be my father by blood, but I don't know the man." I cut Caim off, rage tinting my vision red. I hate being associated with that man. I hate being associated with my parents at all. I don't know them, not really. The both of them abandoned me in their own way since birth. My father in all the ways that mattered, and my mother…

She might have birthed me, and she might have housed me for the first fourteen years of my life, but she never, not once, loved me.

"Be that as it may, he is your father, and the reason I'm in this seat right now is that he killed his brother, your uncle, Samael. He… murdered my youngest son," Bernadette admits, her voice breaking at that last bit as if the truth of it has just hit her.

Pain streaks across her face as she grits her teeth, and the toll all of this has taken on her starts to show. Her expression that was once so warm is now hollow with the ravages of grief.

"In light of the fact that you are probably the only being on this plane who could kill Andras, we are willing to pardon your murder charge and trust that you will use your weapon within the parameters set forth by this Council—if you dispatch him for us. Then, and only then, will you take your rightful seat," Barrett informs me, his bearing as if he's doing me a big favor.

"Let me see if I have this right. You want me to avenge the murder of a man I've never met by killing another man I've never met? And then join a Council I've never even heard of until a few months ago? Oh, and on top of that you will 'forgive' my self-defense against a woman-beating, black-market dealing sociopath who branded me against my will. Am I just supposed to roll over like a dog and say thank you, sir, I'll be sure to get right on that?"

"Andras killed your uncle," Barrett tosses back as if that means something.

"So? He's a man I have never met and didn't even know about until a minute ago. Maybe the politics of this world are a bit more important to you than they are to me. Did you seem to forget that I'm a Rogue? I have no family or a home or laws that protect me. As demonstrated by your bullshit murder charge."

"It won't just be your uncle he goes after, Maxima," Caim warns.

"You know, I think it's hilarious you have the gall to ask me for a favor when the last time I did you one it almost got me killed."

Caim rears back as if I'd slapped him, which is good because he deserves it.

I'm not a tool. I'm not a pawn. If they want something done, they'll just have to do it themselves. Despite the grief I know Bernadette must feel, this is asking way too much.

"The answer is no."

CHAPTER THREE

MAX

My eyes barely adjust to the dim as I storm from what was likely my own personal band of executioners. No one is in the hallway when I emerge from the all-white high courtroom, which is a freaking boon in my book. Maybe that isn't what it is, but the bright, colorless room makes me think of the pearly gates they talk about in stories. I was seriously expecting Barrett to transform into Saint Peter somehow and punt my ass to Hell. I'm just happy Ruby isn't here. I would slap the taste out of her mouth, Apocalypse be damned. It isn't long before I'm outside Aether, breathing in great gulps of air as the panic that I managed to stave off hits me like a sledgehammer.

Ruby was in my home. She just walked right in without so much as a blip. She found me—anyone could find me.

You weren't hiding, remember? You took the ring off. And P.S., you didn't do anything wrong. The sensible part of my brain pipes up, and I stop to wonder if that's true. Did I take off my grandmother's ring—the one that had the power to hide me from any magical being with the added double whammy of shielding my mind—because I wasn't hiding? Or was it more because I couldn't stand the reminder of why I'd needed it in the first place?

And am I really not hiding? I don't go back to my house. I practically sent Striker away. I can't bear to touch Ian...

Ian. Shit. I stood him up. With shaking fingers, I pull my cell phone from my back pocket, the simple act of it sending a hysterical giggle up my throat. His voicemail picks up, and despite my aversion to public speaking in general, I leave a message.

"I'm so sorry I stood you up. I didn't mean to." I pause, not quite knowing how to explain. "I promise to make it up to you. Call me back." I hang up, while I check my surroundings. Just to be sure I won't catch a human off guard, I turn off the cracked sidewalk and duck in between the warehouse that conceals Aether and a burned-out remnant of a building that I faintly recognize isn't really a building at all, but the thought is there and gone in a moment. Snapping my fingers, I let my magic transport me back to the alley entrance of my shop.

I learned not so long ago that transporting oneself from one place to another isn't just for wraiths, other Ethereals can do it, too. But typically, witches can only accomplish it if they have a full coven—all working on the spell together.

I can do it easily by myself. It made me wonder what else I can do that other witches can't and vice versa.

I inspect the warding lines—or lack thereof—of my building, knowing I'd strengthened the wards as I left. Was it Ian who broke them all? It doesn't seem to be a thing he'd do—torching all of my wards—but I don't really know what Ian would do...

Not really. I'd always been too selfish to really see him the way I should. I probably still am.

I sniff the air, catching the scent of the ozone of spent magic that could be from the wards coming down. Or it could be from something else altogether. I don't like it one bit, but if someone tripped my wards, I need to know who it is and what they want.

Oh, and I need to make sure the super-duper magical ring is still in my jewelry box, and the bone blade is still in my safe. Yeah, that wouldn't hurt either.

My nerves are shot, but I sack up—or I would if I had a sack—and reach to turn the knob of the reinforced steel door I'd installed after the whole Micah mess. I'd needed the security, or at least the illusion of it. I probably still did—the little security blanket wouldn't hold off the ghosts, but would let me pretend they wouldn't touch me, anyway.

The hallway opens up to the back staircase, stairs I'd already trudged once tonight, but I bypass them to head to my office. Flicking on the desk lamp, I peruse the room. There isn't a paper out of place on my desk, no drawers knocked akimbo, nothing. But I have every certainty there was someone here. Maybe not now, right at this second, but my wards came down on purpose, and someone was in my office.

My safe hasn't been tampered with, nothing has been touched, but someone has been here all the same. I spin the dial combination, the same one that could blow the arms off a deity if they so much as looked at it wrong. Using every bit of magic I had, I'd made that safe so it was coded to only two people on this planet. Only two people could touch it.

Striker and me.

Anyone else would be blown to kingdom come and rightly so.

The locking pins disengage, and I swing the door wide, the bone knife—the same one I'd used to kill Micah—sits on the velvet-lined shelf, not even a millimeter out of place. The low light catches the slight sheen of the ancient leather-wrapped hilt, the blade itself the length of my forearm, and the pristine color of freshly carved bone.

I know for a fact the blade is as ancient as it feels, carved from the humerus bone of an Ethereal a millennium or two ago. My mother never said what kind, but if I had a bet, I'd go with either angel or demon. Either way, I probably don't want to know. All I know is that blade makes me very uneasy, and the way it meets out death is sadistic and cruel. It makes me hate it and everything it stands for—everything it is.

It makes me ache in places just thinking about it, all the hidden places in my soul that I so rarely shine a light on. Great bleeding places that hold all the hurt and hate and pain. I hate how it was me who got free from Micah and Melody didn't. How I failed her so spectacularly. Hate how her son will never know her, never know what his mother went through so he could live. I hate how the brightest light in Striker's life is dead and gone, lost in a way she can never be found.

My skin begins to itch, and I shudder, the pain and heartbreak washing over me, threatening to drown me if I let it. I'd never failed someone like I'd failed Melody. Never messed up so bad that someone died who didn't deserve it.

I've never had collateral damage before. Not in four hundred years. I find I'm not too keen on it.

I shut the safe, leaving the blade right where it had stayed for the last few months. I'd been unwilling to touch it. Hell, I still didn't want to. Spinning the lock, I study the safe, looking at the hex lines of magic that still seem as strong today as they were yesterday. I inspect them, making sure there are no breaks, no open spots, and just for kicks, I send another jolt of my power into the ward, strengthening it just a bit more.

I have power to spare lately, power I don't want or need, but what I accidentally drained from Micah. It's wrong, accidental black magic, but like so many things about myself, I can't change it.

I can only hope that one day I'll be able to get rid of it.

The trek upstairs seems longer the second time as I whisper the warding words of protection on my temporary-ish home. After ensuring the giant aquamarine ring my grandmother gave me for protection is right where I left it, I slip it on my finger before bedding down for the night.

Can't be too careful.

A tap on my shoulder the next evening causes me to nearly maim one of my best clients. My customer, Jet, is a man of few words and seriously opposed to small talk. We also differ greatly on what we call music, so as is custom, the pair of us have in our own earbuds —him with his preference of death metal, and me with a mix of just about anything else. I've been alive for quite a while, so my taste runs along the eclectic, but that is a genre of music I just can't seem to get into.

My new receptionist, Della, takes a few steps back, either frightened at the expression on my face or just jumping because I found my feet in a not-so-nice way, brandishing a dirty tattoo machine.

Not cool.

I set down the machine so the needles won't stab anyone, flick off my gloves, and pop the earbud out, looking Della over for a split second. Medium-brown hair pulled into a wispy yet complicated chignon, small build, fair skin so very different from my darker golden bronze. She's cute in a mesh of class and the everyday-girl way that I will never be. I will always be different, other. The blue hair and tattoos just make me feel more at home in my skin.

Virgin-skinned and proper with a Frenchie-Catalan accent that drives my male customers absolutely wild, I hired Della on the spot after searching for a receptionist for weeks. She'd whipped my appointments into shape and had me booked out into the next year using some sort of administrative sorcery I'd never be able to cobble together. And she makes the best damn coffee I've ever had. She is a quiet little mouse of gloriousness, and I don't want to upset that balance.

But I feel like a first-rate idiot, especially since Della's green eyes are wide in fear.

Whoops.

"Sorry. You startled me," I murmur apologetically, taking a deep breath to calm down. It's completely possible that the PTSD-suffering person—me—should not be wearing earbuds in public. Noted.

"So sorry! *No va ser la meva intencio espantar-te*. You have a phone call." She's flustered, pointing behind her to the phone. My first language was Catalan, but Della speaks the more modernized version of the one my mother spoke to me four hundred years ago, and it isn't one I regularly use. Just like English, every language changes over time. I think she said, "It was not my intention to scare you," which is nice enough and makes me feel like a dick.

"Sure. I'll be right there."

She nods and backs away, and I tap Jet on his meaty shoulder to let him know I'll be right back. He gives me a shrug, which could mean anything from "sure" to "whatever" to "I hate you."

Jet doesn't say much.

I get to the fancy new phone Della requested so she could do her job properly and pick it up, waiting for her to press the button for whichever line my call is on. I didn't hold the super expensive phone request against her. Before we only had a vintage rotary phone that would probably be at home in an old-timey whorehouse. Given the number of calls we get for appointments on a daily basis, her request for an upgrade wasn't too outrageous.

She presses the third blinking light—how she remembers which one is which is a freaking miracle to me—and the voice of my best friend comes through the line. I'm not even sure he's really my best friend at all—not sure if he has ever really trusted me the way I did him once upon a time. Not sure if it hasn't just been a convenience for him to hang out with me all these years. I hope not, but hope is pretty much all I have at this point.

His voice is husky as if he's just getting up, and I'm so happy to hear from him that it takes a few words for me to wonder if the huskiness isn't from disuse, but from screaming.

"Max! Max, Jesus, I'm so glad you're all right. You have to ge—"

His words are cut off as the power goes out. No more than a second passes from the lights spluttering out to my front picture window blowing in, glass flying everywhere right before the flames engulf the walls, the floor.

I soon realize what Striker's words should have been.

They should have been "get out."

CHAPTER FOUR

MAX

I *never should have come back here.* That is my very first thought as I stare at the flames licking their way closer to me. The bite of glass against my palm only serves to prove that thought true.

The words "collateral damage" flash like a neon sign in my brain, proving to me once again that maybe I'm not as good a person as I thought I was. Would a good person bring trouble to those around them? Would a good person stick around when they knew death was on their heels? Would a good person taunt their betters into firebombing their shop?

Probably not.

I sit here frozen, figuring I probably deserve the heat of the flames, deserve to burn. But it's the whimper of fear behind me that snaps me out of my self-deprecating thoughts. Reminding me it isn't just me in this room or this building.

In this fire.

I whip my head to the side and take in Della. She's crouching behind the mirror-fronted receptionist desk, the glass cracked in some places, shattered in others. But Della isn't the only person in this shop. I have two other artists here today, plus their customers and mine, Jet. Bellows of fear meet my ears for the first time since the fire started, but they seem far off, distant somehow.

A buzzing whine overtakes the yelling, the tinny, warbling sound making me wince, my fingers reaching for my ears before I can stop them. My hands come away red, blood thick at my fingertips. It's then I feel the slight tickle of a drip coming from my nose.

Was there a blast and I missed it? Or is this a spell? The world goes dark for a second, but I manage to shake my head enough to clear it a little.

The way out the front is completely blocked, the fire spreading up and out like fingers searching for light in the dark. I whisper a blessing of protection for Della and me and snatch up her hand, hauling her up with me as I search for a way out amongst the now-smoke-filled shop. I used to think I'd know my way around this place blindfolded, but the acrid smoke filling my lungs tells a different tale.

Crouching low, I manage to slam my shoulder into a doorjamb of the hallway before seeing the outline of the back door. "Do you see the door?" My voice is a guttural rasp, but she doesn't answer me.

I shake her hand, probably squeezing her fingers too hard. "Y-yes." Her voice seems a whisper when it probably really isn't. Everything is a whisper. Everything is a muted form of gray when I know it is really vibrant oranges and reds.

This is a spell. I look down, sluggishly searching my hand for the ring that was supposed to bring protection. Naturally, it's missing.

I glance back into the now-black void of my shop. "Go. Call for help." I need to go back. I need that ring and the bone knife, and I need to save those people—the innocents who were so foolish to find themselves close to me.

"No. You need to come with me." Her hands now becoming the firm ones, pulling, dragging me to the door. The air hits my face, fresh and clean and the pair of us huddle, gulping in the glorious oxygen.

"Here. You dropped this. Keep it close." Her words are coming in between gasps, my grandmother's ring in her palm as she offers it to me. "The working in the smoke is meant to confuse, I think."

I nod my head for a second, plucking the warm metal from her hand until her words register, and I focus on her face. Della's human—or she's supposed to be. How in the hell does she know about workings?

Who the hell is she?

I don't have the time or energy to figure out exactly what species Della is, or what the fuck she's doing in my shop. She's helping me, and at the moment, that is really all I can ask for. Sliding the ring on my middle finger, my mind becomes clear again, like a fog lifting. Before Della can move, I have her throat in my hand.

"Who are you?" My hand is gentle but insistent. I want an answer before I give her my back to get my people out.

"Not your enemy. Your grandmother sent me to look after you. I'm an ally." Her voice is calm and soft but firm in a way I know her mouse routine was just that—a routine, a mask. Or maybe not. Eyes wide with fear, she unsuccessfully tries to hide her trembling. The faint scent of fear is in the air, and it's coming from Della.

"Good," I mutter, dropping my hand. "I'm going back in there. You helping?"

She shifts her feet, eyes sliding to the door and back to me. With a twist to her lips, she nods.

The door is warm to the touch as I throw it open. The heat and flames not yet reaching the hallway, but the sickly smoke wafting from the fire feels like fetid oil on my skin. Rancid, spoiled, sour. The air is ripe with it, the smoke like rotten fingers poking, prodding. Trying to get in my mouth, my nose, my lungs. The working is strong, meant to confuse, intended to reach into one's mind and make them sit there while they burn to death. It feels like old, forgotten magics. Not Celtic, not Santeria, not anything I've ever seen, but familiar all the same.

I hold the breath in my lungs, praying Della's doing the same. Without knowing the origins of the spell, I can't stop it, but I might be able to hold it back enough to get my people out.

Blowing the last of my breath on my fingers, I mutter every Latin word I can think of for "Stop" as I spin the working breath on the tips of them, the spell strengthening with every widdershins —or counterclockwise—revolution. Undoing, unraveling. *Subsisto, tardo, confuto, concesso, subflamino, insisto, conquiesco, finis...* Over and over, driving the fetid smoke back inch by inch, the green of my magic shines like a beacon in the dark.

All too slowly, the smoke recedes. Problem is, the fire itself isn't magical, so smoke or not, my shop is still a big ball of flame. I can't push the smoke back and douse the flames at the same time. The faint wail of sirens sound in the distance, but they feel too far away. We could all burn before I could even get anyone out of here.

Della moves around me, stepping close in the scant space between us and the spelled smoke weaving her way to the booths. Everything seems to move in slow motion. The smoke, Della, my nulling spell.

The smoke is too powerful. I feel it pushing back against me, searching for a break in my power, like a sentient thing. Intelligent in a way that means only one thing—the person who cast it didn't just throw the spell and leave.

They're still here. Pushing against me. Searching for a weakness, a break. Any fissure in my powers that they can weasel their way into.

I don't have the luxury of time. Whoever is casting this is stronger than me.

"Get them out." I choke. "I can't hold this much longer." The sweat at my brow isn't just from the heat of the flames. This working is kicking my ass in a way that I've felt before. This isn't witch work. This is a freaking demon.

I'd bet on it.

Della comes from behind a hand-painted silk screen, a man thrown over her shoulder in a fireman's carry. From the tattooed back of his head, I know it's Jet, and Jet isn't small. Confused customers and both my artists trail like a line of ducks behind her, heading toward the back.

I don't know if I should be confused or relieved. I'm sticking with relieved. Whatever super-strength mojo Della has, it's helping me out in a huge way. My only hope is Jet and the rest of my people are okay.

The sirens get louder, but the spell doesn't abate. The caster doesn't care that humans are in here, doesn't care that they could have killed someone. They want something, and they really don't care who they hurt to get it.

I can think of only one thing in my possession someone would kill to have. Something people have probably killed several times over to have, throughout time, and space, and worlds.

A shiver works its way through me.

All of a sudden, I feel cold. The spell I'd been pushing against falters, and I almost sag at the reprieve. But it doesn't last.

The sirens, once so close they were screaming, fizzle out as if someone turned the sound off on the world. The roar of the fire, the way it ate through my shop, the crackle and fizzle and pop of flames all silent.

My body trembles and I scramble back, half-searching and half-escaping to the office.

Whoever they are, I know what they want, and I'll be damned if they get it. Not from me.

I spin the dial on the safe, my shaking hands missing the last number and I have to start all over again.

Shitshitshit.

The locking pins make a shuddering snap when they release, but before I open the safe door, I yank the silver chain from my neck. Wrapping it twice around my right wrist, I pull the blade from the protection of the safe and loop the last bit of chain around my hand and the knife, pricking my finger on the tip and smearing the blood along the hilt.

Whispering ancient words of a magic I barely understand, the silver liquefies, the links transforming into a rope of metal, binding the knife to my hand. The hot metal burning my skin in a way that I know I'll scar, maybe in every healed body that comes back.

I try to think of the vanity of it instead of the pain. Instead of the smell of burning flesh. Instead of how this binding might be permanent. Instead of the blood and death magics I just used to protect the very thing I hate.

I whirl, watching as the flames freeze in place—unmoving, unwavering. The smoke itself like gray fog clouds hanging in the air. My shuddering whispers are the only sound, my lips the only movement.

Until I see the shape of a man, his form made up solely of black smoke, flickering and wavering as if he has no corporeal form. Only his eyes are solid, unflinching, glowing yellow and piercing through the dim. They follow the length of my arm, tracing down my body until they latch onto the blade practically soldered to my hand.

The blackness rushes me, and I scramble back, scrabbling in a truncated crab walk until my back hits the plaster of a wall. And still he comes, a screeching scream of rage and wordless command vibrating through the ruins of my shop.

I slash with the blade the way Aidan taught me to, aiming for where the soft spots would be on a human. I know full well it won't kill whoever it is who seeks it, but a knife is a knife, and any weapon is better than nothing.

Aidan taught me that, too.

The screech of command morphs into one of pain or rage, the form backing away, retreating at my paltry slash.

And somehow someone turned the sound back on in the world. The sirens scream, men yell on the street. The roar of flames return.

I snap my fingers on my left hand, the action smarting a bit with a cut finger, but that's the least of my problems.

Traveling from my burned-out wreck of a shop, I arrive at a door in the middle of a dim hallway. *Numera omnes qui ingrediuntur ad iudicium.*

Judgment comes to all who enter.

Before I destroy the carved mahogany of the high courtroom door, all I can think is, *you're fucking right it does.*

CHAPTER FIVE

MAX

The wood splinters, exploding into the too-perfect high courtroom, making my lips tip up just slightly. The ghost of a smile flits across my face and it's gone in an instant. Rage wars with the betrayal in my gut. How could they do this to me?

I know I told them I wouldn't kill Andras, but burning out my shop? Putting all my people in danger just to steal a freaking weapon? If they wanted the bone knife, they should have just fucking asked for it.

Barrett's surprise as he recovers from his cowering crouch in front of the dais warms my cold dead heart. Shards of wood pepper the floor, and his expensive loafers slip on them, making him unsteady on his feet. If I were to guess who on the Council ordered the firebombing of my shop, Barrett would be at the top of the list. Hell, Barrett would be the entirety of the list.

"I want to know why," I croak, the soot and smoke still clogging my throat even though this air is fresh as a damn daisy. It pisses me off. I want to rub my soot-covered self all over the pristine whiteness. I want to smear it with my blood. I want to spill it, too. Maybe Barrett's, but maybe not.

The dark side of myself, the one that I try to keep buried, wants to know if Barrett has friends or family. It wants to put them in danger instead so he knows how it feels. It wants the equal and opposite reaction, wants true vengeance. True reparations.

Fury like I've never felt courses through me. It should feel warm, right? It should be a fire under my skin, but it isn't. It's cold, icy. A frozen tundra of rage ready to exact my will.

"Why what? Fates, child, what in the name of perdition happened to you?" He appears almost... concerned? The fake worry on his face makes me want to slap him right across his snooty freaking mug. Maybe with my right hand—the one with a knife attached to it.

"For a man so keen on the rules, you sure know how to break them. I want to know *why* you firebombed my shop. *Humans* were in my shop. *Humans*, Barrett." I watch the ambient white of the room take on a green cast, my magics rising in and out of me so much I tint the room in their glow. The heat of them feel like soothing flames, masking the agony of the blade in my hand, the smoke left over in my lungs.

"I didn't—" He scrambles back a step, slipping on the wood again.

"Then you made someone or bribed someone. You want this blade so bad, you come and get it."

As I speak, the path from me to him cracks and shakes, the floor vibrating with my powers as it continues to rise in me. I've always hated a bully.

The marble floor shifts, peaking at the crack, the movement tossing Barrett off his feet. He scuttles back, trying to get away from me, muttering something under his breath. Not Latin, not French, something I've heard before but can't place.

Other than a zing of heat flashing over me, his spell does nothing. No blood, no broken bones, no flames, just a big load of fuck all.

My power rages again, shaking the foundations of whatever this place is. It feels neither here nor there, not on Earth, but not in Hell. Not Heaven. It feels like nowhere and everywhere, and me and my rage, my power is breaking it apart. The sick part of me smiles, happy at the destruction. It's hard to hold back on this newfound bloodlust, this call for vengeance and death. The siren call of retribution.

"Stop, Maxima. I didn't hurt your people. I didn't."

Then the distance between us is gone, the fingers of my left hand around his throat, pinning him to the cracked dais. "You wanted me dead from the moment I walked in here. Told me as much. Why should I believe you now?"

"Because I believe in the law, and hurting humans is above all the worst thing I can do."

The truth of his words take a minute to filter through the bloodlust, through the call in my brain that tells me to rip into his flesh with the bone blade and watch as his innards paint this stupid white floor red.

Truth. His words smell of truth.

My magics flare again, and I wish I could say they were healing me, but they aren't quite doing the job anymore. My stomach pitches suddenly, nausea and pain bleeding back into me bit by bit as my adrenaline wanes.

Barrett looks afraid, and I don't know if that fear is guilt or something else. All I know is I feel tired.

Tired of it all. Tired of fighting and getting nowhere. Tired of people dying. Tired of never being accepted, never really having a family. My rage peters out, and all I'm left with is...

"You sneaky little shit." I level Barrett with what is probably my best glare. "A tired spell mixed with what? A depression or self-loathing one? Fates, you're diabolical. I didn't even see your lips move."

A wry grin peeks out of the cloud of his face, and he straightens fully away from my hand that has fallen from his throat, and that's when I notice Marcus sitting in his seat at the dais, his feet crossed at the ankles on top of the table, a bag of chips in his hands. He munches on one as he surveys us, the crunch of it practically echoing through the room.

"She could have killed us both, and you're eating bloody

crisps?" Barrett dusts off his suit jacket and straightens his tie. His cultured British fading away to a less-polished version that he seems to hide.

"I told you she was going to kick your ass one day. Didn't think it was going to come so soon. I didn't want to miss it," Marcus says around the food in his mouth.

"No help at all. Sitting there eating bloody crisps. She could have *killed* me."

"And if you sent someone to hurt her humans, you would have deserved it. I was doing my Council duty to act as witness to either your sanctioned death or her crime. You're a twelve-hundred-year-old witch against an untrained Rogue a third your age. I assumed you could handle it."

"You're a right tosser is what you are. Against a witch and demon hybrid that shouldn't even exist! It's like a house cat going after a Bengal tiger. One of them is an apex predator and the other *is not*."

His words are like a blow, a sucker punch when I was already going down. *Shouldn't even exist.* I feel my face go slack, the laugh at their exchange falling off my lips. Marcus catches my expression before I can wipe it clean.

"That isn't what he meant, Maxima. Barrett wouldn't be Barrett if he didn't accidentally insult someone every five minutes. You'd think he would be a better conversationalist by now, but he kinda sucks at it." Marcus' tone is consoling, and if Barrett's words didn't echo what I already thought about myself, it probably wouldn't sting so bad.

I give Marcus a tremulous smile, the spell Barrett cast still pinging every horrible thought I've ever had about myself through my brain, making his words fail to ring true.

"If you don't mind, please call me Max. The only person who calls me Maxima is my mother, and she doesn't like me much."

Barrett whips his head back to me, the anger sliding off his face as he winces. "Oh, *damn and blast*. That wasn't what I meant at all. And after that spell... bollocks. Maxim— er... Max, I didn't mean *shouldn't*." He sighs, covering his face with a hand in exasperation. "But existences like yours are rare. As in you're the only one I've ever heard of. Demons and witches can't reproduce. The babies die. Every time. You just being alive is an anomaly."

"Just what every girl wants to be called, Barrett. An anomaly," Marcus grouses, uncrossing his feet and setting them back down on the floor.

"Fates, save me. That is not what I meant."

"You going to hoard all the chips? I think I'm going to need some if we're going to watch Barrett try and pry the foot from his mouth." I hold my hand out to Marcus for a chip but smile at Barrett so he knows I hold no ill will.

Plus, if Barrett didn't send that... thing to set my shop on fire, he isn't my enemy. I don't need to make him one. I have a feeling I have enough of those just being me without adding to it.

My eyes fall to my feet, and I finally grasp the full scope of my destruction. Broken marble, shards of wood, and rubble litter the floor. Like an angry child, I broke this room, shattered everything in my path.

I know it might just be from Barrett's spell, but the urge to cry hits me. One of the only things I learned from my mother all those years ago was that once you cast a spell, you have to be prepared for the fallout. There is no reversing anything—not really. All spells have to run their course. I can fix something once it's broken. I can give someone a memory back. I can even heal a papercut if I really concentrate.

But spells like the one Barrett hit me with will always run their course. Knowing that makes the sting in my eyes fade just a little.

Breathing a spell on my fingers, I snap them, watching as the green fire of my magics flare. Then the rubble moves, going back where it came from like an explosion in reverse. Every mote of dust, pebble of marble, and shard of wood go back to their original homes. The peak in the floor where the marble fractured flattens, the crack in the stone sealing before my eyes. The mahogany shards and splinters piece together before sealing back into the door as it once was. As if I was never here. I turn back to them, and Marcus stares at the door slack-jawed while Barrett looks at the floor as if it's about to jump up and bite him.

"What?"

"You do realize a whole coven of witches your age couldn't do that? Not to this place and not to that door." Barrett doesn't take his eyes off the floor as he talks, and I'm almost glad. But that last bit of magic seems to have spent all that I had left. My rubbery legs carry me up to the bottom step of the dais, and I plop down hard on my ass.

"We've already established that I'm a freak, Barrett. No need to rub it in. And while we're at it, can someone get this thing off?" I whimper the question while waving my charred ruin of a hand that still clutches the bone blade. I've tried not to look at it, but now that I have, I don't feel so good.

The blood starting to drip from my nose doesn't help matters, either. The bright white of the room begins to dim and then cants a little to the side.

Then it's lights out.

CHAPTER SIX

IAN

24 HOURS EARLIER...

My hands shake a little as I smooth the close-cropped hair on my head before doing the same to the goatee on my chin. It is a nervous tick my brother points out every opportunity he gets —usually when we're playing poker, and I'm losing.

I lose a lot. Kinda like I'm losing now, but only at a much different game.

I'd lied those many months ago—by omission, sure—but lying all the same. I never told her I knew her, knew the way her lips tasted, knew how her body fit to mine. Knew her scent when she was aroused.

I know lots of things about Max that she never told me.

At the time, she'd been nothing but an insanely beautiful girl sitting alone at a booth where she definitely didn't belong. In the midst of the chaos around us, she wasn't trying to sex-up a random stranger or make a deal when no one was looking, which was usually what places like that were for. All she did was people-watch and sip her drink. But the closer I got to her, the more I realized she wasn't a girl. Despite her young, unlined skin, this woman was old—older than me and probably wiser than me, too. Her eyes were the dichotomy of young and ancient, having seen too much and yet not enough.

I found myself sitting at her table without a real thought in my head, only that I wanted this beautiful woman with the intricately tattooed skin and blazingly blue hair to smile. I can't rightly remember what I said to her, only that I flirted and charmed and crowded her in the way wraiths do when they see a mate. Testing, teasing for a reaction.

And I got it.

But I never got her name, and a few weeks later when we came to Kyle and Nicola's rescue, Max was there. Broken and bleeding, she didn't remember me. And it hurt to think I didn't leave the same impression on her that she did me.

In the light of day, we hated each other. Well, that wasn't true. I hated that she didn't remember me, and she hated that I was an antagonistic asshole.

Until about eight months ago when she died in my arms.

The fear and agony of that day echo through me as I stare at the back door of Max's shop. She lives here now, instead of the craftsman over on Lincoln, and a part of me hates that for her but loves how close she is to me all at the same time.

But all that could change tonight. Her closeness might be an agony instead of a balm. Because I have to tell her about that night in Aether. I have to tell her, and I really, really don't want to.

It takes another five minutes before I sack up enough to get out of the car, the threat of losing her creating a vicious noxious hole in my chest where my heart used to be. The trek to the back entry is long, each step weighing me down, but eventually, I get the door open and traverse the stairs even though my feet feel like lead.

At about the third step from the top, a hint that something is wrong trickles into my brain. There is no music. No movement. Nothing. I can't rightly say how she lived her life before, but every time I have ever come to visit her, Max always has a TV on or music playing. Always. As if the silence physically grated on her, she methodically made sure there was something going on in the background.

And there is nothing.

The second? I can't feel her magic anywhere. Max has an aura, a presence that physically presses in and lets you know she's there. It's comforting when she's happy and almost grating when she's angry. It's the light caress of her magic even when she isn't using any. It just is.

I've only felt it gone once, and any time she isn't where she said she would be, I lose it a little. I should have noticed before now that I couldn't feel her. I should have noticed before I ever walked through the door, but I was so worried about how she'd react to our history, I wasn't paying attention. Now my senses are on high alert.

Pulling in the scents from the hallway, I get a faint hint of someone who shouldn't be here. Ruby's signature fragrance filters through my brain, but it's nearly gone now as if she left in a hurry. Max's, however, lingers, her scent clinging to almost every part of this building. But there is something else, too. Something made of smoke and death and… something I can't place.

I take a few more steps up the stairs, my feet light this time, instead of my idiotic plodding when I wasn't paying attention. I strain to hear something in the building—breathing, walking, anything.

Something's wrong. Someone's here, I'd bet my life on it, and it's not Max. Calling on the power I assume I got from my mother, I cloak myself in the darkness around me. Sometimes I think this is the dumbest ability I could have gotten. I'm half-wraith, and I can't travel. I'm half-witch—*I think*—and I can't do half of what witches my age can. The only thing I can do that they can't is make myself essentially invisible. When compared to traveling, healing, and soul-eating, it's a neat party trick but has few practical uses.

This just so happens to be one of them.

But pain lances through my head before I can take another step, ripping a groan from my lips. I manage to duck the heat of the next blow, but my cloak of darkness falls from me as soon as I can no longer concentrate on it. Blood trickles down the back of my neck as I haul myself up the last few steps. Like an idiot, I don't have a weapon on me. How long has it been since I've gone anywhere unarmed? And yet—when it comes to Max—I never seem to think straight.

Despite my best efforts—and the lucky instance of my wraith eyesight—I can't actually see my attacker. The scent of magic rising fills my nostrils, cloying smoke-filled power like a perfumed house on fire. My whole body freezes, caught in a web of control, agony lighting up my senses so much it steals my breath. Whispers—low, commanding murmurs bombard my brain, but I can't quite make out what they're saying.

Odds are, I don't want to know anyway.

My eyes frantically comb the stairwell, searching for a hint—something, anything to tell me who or what's here.

My power flickers, sputtering once, twice before I'm able to cloak myself again, wriggling from the invisible binds of magic to Max's door. Turning the knob, I fail to feel the zing of magic that usually accompanies just knocking on it.

It's unwarded. Unprotected.

Max hasn't had an unwarded anything since Micah Goode attacked her. Not that her wards did much to keep him back in the first place, but that doesn't stop her from checking and rechecking them. Making sure they're as strong as she can make them.

But before I have a chance to let the worry fully consume me, the agony hits me again, and all I see is blackness.

MAX

Barrett's face is the last thing I want to see when I open my eyes, but that doesn't stop the man from being three inches from my face when I finally regain consciousness. Granted, Barrett is pretty if you don't mind the giant stick up his ass. Shockingly clear-blue eyes set in a pleasingly attractive face, square jaw, not too overly bushy eyebrows, decent medium-brown hair. Problem is, his face is perpetually dialed to disapproval.

Even now. I just woke up from a major magical cat nap—

okay… I passed out from using too much magic and probably shock—but still. No relief. No "thank the Fates you're not dead."

Nope.

Barrett and my mother probably get along like freaking gangbusters based on their general level of disapproval alone.

"Don't look so disappointed, Barry. I'm sure I'll die at some point, and you'll get the joy of watching me come back to life. It'll be a hoot." I groan, planting a hand in the soft plushness of a pale linen couch to sit up.

It's then I notice I'm no longer in the white high courtroom, but what appears to be a stately office, and not Caim's, either, even though the courtroom and his office are both somehow located in Aether.

And yet not.

Then I start giggling, and Barrett's eyebrows begin their ascent up his forehead.

"I just got it." I'm still chuckling. "Aether. Everywhere and nowhere. The road to all places. No wonder there are so many pockets here. Speaking of, where the hell am I? I mean really. Is this Aether or somewhere else?"

"Somewhere else," Barrett murmurs, sitting down on the edge of the carved mahogany coffee table. "And you're right. Aether is like a hub. It connects places, makes the world smaller, and all that. Not everyone can travel like you, so we needed a thin place where we could move easily."

I find it more than a little disconcerting that he knows I can travel, but I decide to stay on task.

"A thin place?"

He rolls his eyes up, scanning the ceiling as if it holds all the answers. My guess is it doesn't because he heaves out a sigh before answering me in a cautious tone as if he doesn't want to say too much. "Places where the barrier between this world and the next is thin, where it's easy to traverse along the ley lines to get where we need to go."

"You mean the Veil? Because the Veil is a person—three people, actually."

His eyes fall back to me, the blue in them blazing.

"Yes and no. The Veil keeps the dead on the plane they're supposed to be on. They are the barrier that keeps our worlds separate. But demons don't need to use the Veil to go to Hell, just like angels don't need it to go to Heaven. We aren't bound by it because we're alive, hence thin places."

His expression turns speculative and assessing, and I don't like it one bit. I obviously know more than he expected me to, and rather than wallow in just how uncomfortable that makes me, I decide to go for moxie.

"You're telling me I could open one of the doors in Aether and walk right into Hell? Please remind me never to come back here, mmm-kay?"

"I'll make a note of it."

The door behind Barrett opens, and Marcus strides through, a black old-timey doctor's satchel in his hand. "How's our patient?"

"Alive. And inquisitive. You got the things I asked for?"

"Yes, I got your frankenbag," Marcus grouses, passing over the satchel. "You sure I didn't need to bring chicken blood and a sacrificed goat, too?"

"Nah, not this time," he mutters in all seriousness—either in sarcasm or just not realizing Marcus' joke, and I can't decide which one is more frightening.

"All right, Max, I need to get that blade off your hand, which means I need to perform a *break*. Have you done one of those before?" Barrett asks as he starts pulling items from the bag. A small silver bowl no bigger than my hands cupped together, a squat black candle with runes etched into the wax, a large vial of salt, and a few bunches of dried herbs tied together with twine.

"Kinda," I hedge. I mean, I have performed a *break*, but it didn't exactly go well—for me. The last time I did one, I had a demon compelling me to do his bidding, and I ended up burned at the stake, so you know…

Not exactly a point in the win column.

"It's a simple spell, but the blowback can be anywhere from infinitesimal to life-threatening. It is better if the person who cast the spell in the first place performs the *break*. It minimizes the blowback."

That doesn't sound good at all. More like it seems like an excellent way to fuck this up royally.

Here goes nothing.

CHAPTER SEVEN

MAX

I should have gone back inside the wards, but I didn't. Instead, I followed the sounds of agony to find a man clawing away from the warding snare. It didn't matter that he flashed back and forth between what I assumed was his true form of semi-solid black smoke and his glamour of a human man—the snare still caught him.

Something about the man called to me. I'd never seen an Ethereal like him. Our coven was secluded—hidden away from everyone and everything else who moved in the shadows of our world. He felt familiar in a way that I could not deny.

I had to help him. Had to.

But the only way to help him was to drop the wards—to put my family in danger. It was wrong. It was the worst idea I could think of.

"S-s-s-save m-m-m-me..." The thought hissed through my head, but I knew I hadn't heard a sound. It wasn't my voice, it was his.

"I will," I promised, but I didn't tell my mouth to do so. It was as if my mind had been taken over by someone else. The closer I got to him, the more I needed to do whatever I could to make sure he lived.

Without my mind telling my feet to do so, I pivoted toward the hex marks of our covens' ward, snapping the protection spells one by one until the snare around the man's foot fell away.

"S-s-s-s-save m-m-m-me..."

Then I found myself whispering words I didn't know—spells too advanced for my young body to handle. In my head, I screamed to stop, but I couldn't halt the Latin falling from my lips or the charged green light flickering from my hands.

I was not in control, and I had a sinking feeling that this man, whoever he was, had taken over my body and my powers to free himself. Blood dripped from my nose, and I crumpled to the wet bracken of the forest floor.

I had to get away from him—whoever he was—before he took control over me again. But I didn't get the chance. The sound of hoofbeats hit my ears, and their simple squelching echo was enough to put a pit of fear in my belly.

Horses meant men. Men meant humans. Humans who could have seen me do magic. Humans who all too frequently burned women alive for even the assumption of practicing magic.

I didn't have enough time to put the wards back up. I didn't even have enough time or energy to run.

A pair of footmen grabbed me by my elbows, wrenching me from the forest floor and away from the man who was anything but.

They shouted at me, calling me witch and demon. They spat in my face and tore at my clothes, searching for a devil's mark. It wouldn't have mattered if I didn't have one. They thought I killed the man who was lying so still in the mud and leaves he appeared dead. They saw the green light coming from my hands—they saw my magic.

They tied me to a tree, took a lantern from the coach and threw it at my feet—the glass and fuel exploding as it hit.

Flames caught the cotton of my dress first, and sooner than I thought possible, I was left to scream out my dying breaths alone as men watched me burn.

"Max. *Maxima.* Max!" Barrett's voice filters through the haze of the last time I performed a *break*. But I'd never done one on my own—never of my own free will. Never without that man or demon, or whatever the hell he was speaking for me.

Ruining me. Destroying everything I was and everything I would be. My sight finally focuses on Barrett, and I debate on whether or not I should tell him the truth.

"I—I haven't performed a *break* in a long time. The last time..." I trail off, almost unable to say it, the tremor of my past fear and agony rippling through me. "I was burned at the stake, and even then, it wasn't me who did the spell. More like it was done through me. So I'm more than a little rusty."

Barrett takes a moment to digest what I just told him.

"This was why you were named Rogue, isn't it?" Barrett whispers. "A demon compelled you to perform a *break*, and you got caught by humans. You burned for a crime you had no intention of committing." His voice is like ice, his blue eyes burning like the coldest of flames.

"I woke up in a charred circle. My mother threw me some clothes, told me I was Rogue, and I've been on my own ever since. Later, I figured someone thought I was a necromancer or something. Because I came back. But my mother never taught me any kind of spells, so me summoning a demon didn't seem to be on the table. Until a month ago I didn't even know I was half-demon."

The room seems to go cold—which honestly, I don't mind because my hand feels like it's on fire, but then it's Barrett who's looking at me, so, defensive positions may be necessary. Marcus also doesn't seem to be faring any better in the anger department.

"Ummm... guys?"

Marcus' voice is garbled, like his teeth don't quite fit into his mouth when he growls: "Your mother is on my shit list, Princess. I really hope I don't meet her in a dark alley anytime soon. I might have to get my mate to teach her some manners." His palm gently lands on Barrett's shoulder and squeezes, his touch appearing comforting rather than painful.

It takes me a solid minute to realize he means Barrett when he says "mate," and even longer before I realize he means that they both are pissed on my behalf. I'd always known Teresa had done the wrong thing—banishing me, blaming me for something I didn't mean to do—but I didn't realize how validated I'd feel. My nose starts stinging, and I have to blink away the hot tears that are just begging to fall.

"You know, your bickering makes so much more sense now," I crack, trying to bring levity to the room. Barrett's lips tip up, but it doesn't mask the outright sorrow on his face. It isn't pity, more like an empathy I didn't believe him capable of.

His voice is gentle, a murmur. "I'll walk you through the *break*. Step by step. It's simple. I've seen you do much more complex magic, so I know you'll be fine. Quite honestly, it wouldn't be safe for me to do it for you, or I would."

"Now, don't go getting soft on me."

"Wouldn't dream of it."

Barrett walked me through the steps of the *break*, going over the proper pronunciation of the Latin. He didn't have to tell me that performing a *break*, especially this close to an object that was probably darker than the pits of Hell, was a little sketchasaurus rex —even for me.

I examine the Celtic runes carved into the black candle. There are three: one for protection, one for breaking obstacles, and one for water. Why there is a water rune on a candle, I'm not sure, but if we're washing away a spell, it sort of makes sense. I've always found runes odd in a way. Forgetting their names, but always remembering their definitions.

"Quit stalling." Barrett raises a chiding, knowing eyebrow. It reminds me of one of my mother's patented disapproving stares. I manage to slip off my grandmother's ring from the tattered ruin of my right hand and switch it to my left before I start, afraid the *break* will kill all the spells on that hand. Hell, I'm afraid of what the *break* will do to the blade itself.

I begin by drawing the circle with salt, whispering a blessing of protection before placing the bowl in the center. Dried angelica, rosemary, and sage go in the bowl before I snap my fingers to light it on fire, using the flame of the cleansing herbs to light the *break* candle. I blow the herbs out, letting them smoke enough so I can wash myself in the breath of the protection they offer. Only then do I start the chant of Latin, only part of my brain wondering why it is always a dead language used for spells and not English or French or Spanish.

Conteram hoc opus. Hoc carmen subsisto. Break this working. Cease this spell.

The more I say the words, the hotter the chain circling my wrist and forearm become, the metal burning my flesh until I smell it cooking. I try to shove the pain down but there is so much of it, it grows, builds, overflows my senses. I grip the bone blade tighter, needing to hold onto something, anything. But still, I continue my words, halting but true.

Conteram hoc opus. Hoc carmen subsisto.

The metal begins to melt, dripping onto the coffee table in a plink, plonk, splash. It's everything I can do to not start screaming.

Conteram hoc opus. Hoc carmen subsisto.

The metal is gone, freeing me from the blade, but I can't seem to stop chanting or let go of the dagger. The spell is in me now, working through me, taking control. Blood runs from my nose in a steady drip, drip, drip, and I still can't stop chanting the *break*.

Conteram hoc opus. Hoc carmen subsisto.

Oily black smoke begins to pour from the blade, hundreds of screams echoing off the walls as the room fills with it, dimming every light until the only source is from the flickering candle. Women's screams, children's, men's—all of them writhing together in a sea of pain.

Then everything stops. The pain, the screams, my chanting. Barrett seems to freeze in his half-sit, half-crouch on the ottoman to my right. Marcus, too, is frozen, only his is mid-shift. Gray fur sprouts from his arms and face, the bones of both misshapen with his change. The bone blade falls from my hand in slow motion, tipping end over end until it lands hilt-down before falling flat in the center of the salt ring, knocking the bowl of still-smoking herbs to the side.

My break didn't just free my hand. It freed something or maybe hundreds of somethings from the blade. The smoke begins to move, churning through the room until it finds an outlet—the fireplace. There, it funnels from the room until there isn't even a hint of the oily blackness. Only when it is completely gone does the candle finally flicker out, the room seeming to come back to life.

The light from the modern lamp at the side table flickers back on. Barrett finishes his jump to his feet. Marcus' phase completes, twisting his bones until a giant gray wolf is now standing where he originally stood. I look down at what was once a burned ruin of a hand. The flesh is knitted back together, only a red raised scar where the metal of the necklace once was.

"What in the fresh hell was that?" a terse voice calls from the door. The voice belonging to my very pissed off grandmother.

"I get a call from Della losing her mind about your shop being damn near burned to the ground, search for your impudent little arse for ages, only getting a blip on you before it disappears, and I get here—in Barrett and Marcus's house, no less—and you're doing arcane magic? Explain. Now."

I'm at a loss as to which part of her rant I should address first when Barrett, of all people, comes to my defense.

"Someone came after the blade, and she protected it, Bernadette. But she hurt herself. I instructed her to perform a *break*, and in doing so... Honestly, I don't know if we did a very good thing or a bad one. The *break* freed souls from that blade. Tortured ones."

Bernadette's face goes white at his words, and she half-sits, half-falls into the closest chair.

"Then it was a good thing," she whispers, her voice clogged with either fear or sorrow. It makes me wonder how many lives have been taken with that blade.

Makes me wonder if it stole their souls along with their lives.

Makes me wonder who made the blade in the first place.

Bernadette raises a shaking hand to her forehead, her voice husky as she speaks. "I came to warn you, my girl. You need to check on the people you love the most. Because if you think bombing your shop is the worst he can do, you haven't been paying attention."

My body goes cold, which is a fucking feat in and of itself since I still feel like I've been thrust in an oven set to broil.

"The worst *who* could do?"

"Who else, child? Your father."

CHAPTER EIGHT

MAX

My first thought is Ian. The one I couldn't get on the phone. The one I was supposed to have plans with last night. I give my body a full pat down searching for the annoyingly slim device that means I can contact anyone at any time. I sometimes forget to be amazed on a daily basis with just how far we've come since the 1600s.

Yanking it from my back pocket, I'm freaking astounded to find the phone is not only charged, but it still fucking works. All the magic that's been thrown around just in the last five minutes alone, you'd think the EMP the workings give off would fry the fucker.

Thankfully not.

I try him again only to be shuttled directly to voicemail. His phone is off, or destroyed, or…

I can't even begin to try to contemplate that one. Instead, I do the next best thing and call his brother who picks up after only two rings.

"Joe's pizza shack. You got the cheddar, we got the dough."

There are times when I want to punch Aidan Keenan right in the face. This is one of them.

"Have you talked to your brother today?"

"No. Why?" Aiden's worry is practically palpable down the line.

"My shop was firebombed. I haven't talked to him in twenty-four hours, and we were supposed to meet last night. I got roped into some bullshit with the Council, so I didn't show." I glance toward Barrett and give him my best "you know it's true" eyebrow. "I tried calling him and his phone is shuttling me right to voicemail. Either he's so pissed he's blocked me, or something happened."

"First, the Council? What the fuck did you do? And second, have you even attempted a locator spell?" By my pregnant pause, he gathers the answer. "And you call yourself a witch. Isn't that Woo-Woo 101? Finding people?"

"I don't have anything of his."

Aidan scoffs, sounding like he's rolling his eyes better than any man over three hundred has a right to. "*You're* his, dumbass. If you haven't figured that out yet, you're dumber than I thought you were, and after our last session, that's saying something."

Yep, punching him right in the face the next time I see him.

"Considering I haven't even kissed your brother, I'd say the possession bit is a little premature, but I'll try." I say it trying to act blasé about the fact that Ian is fucking missing, but my tone must venture too far into bored for Aidan's liking.

"You'll do better than try, Maxima. You find my brother, or else." *Or else* from a wraith guardian means a sight bit more than from just about anyone else. It means he would book me on a one-way ticket straight to Hell if I didn't find Ian. He'd suck out my soul and eat it.

Literally.

"I'll find him," I whisper and then hang up, carefully placing my phone on the coffee table before I smash it.

Ian. I should have looked for him last night. I should have called Aidan sooner. Why didn't I call Aidan yesterday?

"You happen to have a pendulum in that frankenbag of yours? I need to find someone."

But when the pendulum finally falls, I find I don't want to be within a mile of where I know Ian is.

Looking at it from the street, the house seems no different from others on the block. The white, two-story craftsman shouldn't seem foreboding, but it does. I haven't been within fifty feet of my house—a place I used to think of as my sanctuary—in over a month. A cold chill races up my back as I stare at the cerulean front door I'd painstakingly repainted last June, which is a feat in and of itself since it's blisteringly hot for an August night. Denver cools down considerably in the evening, but not enough to cause the gooseflesh racing up and down my arms.

No.

That is caused by the blind panic that has me poised to run from what used to be my home instead of going inside to rescue Ian from whatever brought him here. There is no way he'd come here on his own. He knows how I feel about the place—as if the ghost of Micah Goode might be waiting in one of the darkened corners to come and snatch me up. But the grass is cut, the flowerbeds weeded, as if someone has been keeping the place up for me. As if I'm on vacation or something instead of afraid of a silly pile of bricks.

I don't want to be here. Not on this street, not on this sidewalk, not anywhere close to here. But Ian is inside, and if I follow my gut —which I'm prone to do, even though it has brought me nothing but trouble—Ian is in danger or hurt, or a prisoner, and I don't have the luxury of the time a panic attack will take.

A bird's hair-raising shriek has me looking over my shoulder to scan the dark street. The call is close, and my eyes drift up to the lamppost where a falcon sits. In Colorado, it isn't uncommon for falcons to roam, but I've never seen one in the city, and sure as hell not on my street.

Another shiver races up my spine, focusing my mind on the task at hand. I assess my property lines, knowing the warding that keeps people away is long gone. I wonder what someone looking out their window at this hour thinks of my getup. Before my shop was firebombed, I was in my usual work attire of a tight tank, sailor-style pedal pushers, and heels. Now, my hair has fallen from the painstakingly styled victory rolls, my clothes are covered in soot, and somewhere along the way my shoes came off, so I had to conjure myself some flats. Plus, the black leather belt with the dagger sheath containing the bone blade doesn't exactly go with this outfit.

I've never been so thankful for nightfall.

Keeping my eyes peeled, I make my way to the front door, hesitating only a moment or twelve before I manage to turn the unlocked knob. Convenient, and creepy as fuck, because while I don't have my keys, it isn't like I coded the front door with my fingerprints. Someone wants me to be able to enter, and that just feels icky on a bevy of levels.

Then the door swings open and sitting in the middle of my living room is Ian, bound to one of my dining room chairs. He's unconscious, battered and bloody, his once-white-T-shirt spattered with the rusty brown of dried blood. It feels as if my heart has shriveled up and died in my chest, and I find myself rushing to him, sliding on my knees on the hardwood just so I don't knock him over.

"Ian. Ian, can you hear me?" I pat his face until I realize that I quit patting three pats or so ago and now I'm outright slapping him to get him to wake up.

"Ian!" I shake him in between untying the ropes that bind him to the chair. But he doesn't respond, and the only hope I have is the fact that he's breathing, albeit shallowly.

My brain goes into damage-control mode where it offers anywhere from easy to ridiculous ways to solve a problem, and the best I can come up with is to call Aidan.

"Where is he, Max?" Aidan barks down the line as I try to hold Ian's unconscious body upright in the chair.

"He-he's at my house." I shiver, the pain and shock and sheer weight of the day crashing down on me. "I-I can't get him to you.

He's been knocked out, beaten. His breathing is shallow, and I don't... I don't know what to do. Help m—" I don't get the word out before the call disconnects and Aidan appears in my living room.

Aidan looks livid—a wickedly sharp sword in his hand glints in the meager light as he scans the room. Without so much as a hello, he grips Ian's shoulder and seems to think about it for a moment before snatching up my wrist. Aidan does that wraith-style voodoo smoke-out thing and transports us to the brothers' living room. Vomit rises in my throat when we land, me on my hands and knees, and I try not to chuff on Ian's carpet.

"I swear to the Fates, Maxima, if you don't get your shit together, so help me..." Aidan trails off through ground teeth as he lifts his brother onto the pool table.

I know that pool table intimately.

I damn near died on it.

Melody *did* die on it.

Staggering to my feet, I shuffle over to the table as Aidan cuts open Ian's bloodstained shirt with trauma shears and starts checking him over.

"What happened to you?"

Resting a hip against the solidness of the table, I ignore his question. "Is he going to be okay? Do I need to do anything?"

"You just stand there and tell me what the fuck happened to you. Had I known you'd look like you'd been drug through a tree backward, I would have had a bit more sympathy." He pulls a stethoscope from Ian's black doctor duffle, pressing it to different spots on Ian's ribs.

"My problems are less important than your brother's life, so just focus on him and don't worry about me."

Aidan pops the earpiece out of his ear, leveling me with a hard stare. "I have to worry about you, because for some reason, your shit keeps landing my brother in hot water. I have no doubt Ian was handed over to you like a present, giftwrapped and everything. So you'll tell me exactly what's going on."

Forgiving his delivery, the man has a point. Ian has been

through one thing after another, and while it hasn't always been my fault, I certainly don't help matters. "The Council picked me up last night for the murder of Micah Goode. Sentenced me to death and everything until I reminded them I was an unwilling participant in Micah's schemes. Then they asked me to kill my father. I said no, and then today my shop was firebombed by a black smoke demon thing who tried to kill me."

I don't even want to tell him about the blade and the souls I accidentally released. Or the fact that I blew up the Council's front freaking door. Yeah… Aidan is pissed enough.

"I swear to the Fates, I rue the fucking day he met you in that stupid farce of a club. 'Go to a witch club,' he said. 'We'll meet hot chicks,' he said," Aiden grumbles as he check's Ian's pupils. "Well, he makes out with a woman who doesn't even remember him, and I damn near get my ass blasted off in that raid. Seriously. Ian should have listened to Caim and left you alone, but *nooooooooo*."

Ian made out with a woman in a witch club and then there was a raid. A woman who didn't remember him. The puzzle pieces all click together.

"You're telling me it was Ian this whole time? And no one thought to tell me? I ought to punch you right in your stupid face, Aidan Keenan."

The look of surprise on Aidan's face would be pure gold if I didn't want to murder him so bad.

"Is he going to be okay?" I nod toward Ian, sparing him the briefest of glances so my heart doesn't decide to wrench right out of my chest.

All this time.

I've been so hung up on that guy. The one that woke me up, made me feel. And he was right in front of me the whole time. I feel like an idiot.

"A concussion, maybe a bruised lung. He should be okay."

"Good," I murmur, my voice as soft as I can make it before I throw my fist right in Aidan's stupid face.

CHAPTER NINE

MAX

The line rings less than once before one of my best friends on this planet picks up.

"I really hate it when you wear that stupid ring, Max," she says by way of greeting.

Never one to mince words, that one. Aurelia hates it when she can't see me, and by see, I mean *see*. As a phoenix seer, Aurelia is a weird sort of psychic. If she's close to you, she can tell where you are, what you're doing, and, sometimes, what you're about to do.

If she's not close to you—and I mean emotionally—then she can only tell when and how you're going to die. More the how than the when. But all that death makes my BFF a might bit odd. If PTSD and emotional family drama had a baby, that baby would be Aurelia Constantine.

"Well, not wearing it seems kind of stupid right about now." I examine the ring that I've moved back to my right hand, the skin still red and raised where the metal burned through my flesh. It will, without a doubt, scar, and I wonder if I die and come back if those scars will stay with my body.

"That doesn't sound good. Why don't you tell me what happened?" She says it in the form of a semi-demand. Yep, that's my mother hen of a best friend. It doesn't matter that I'm twice her age, Aurelia would boss me around even if I were a hundred times her age.

"My shop got firebombed, Ian got attacked, and the Council is up my ass. Did you even know we had a Council? I can only assume whoever did it—and fun fact, the person who did it is more than likely my absentee father—wants to make an example out of the people I love, so... This is my friendly check-in to make sure you and yours are alive and well."

Silence permeates the line long enough to make me wonder if the call dropped, and I begin to pace the length of Ian's room, the only quiet place in this joint. Well, the living room is pretty quiet, too, but that comes with Aidan's bitchy stares, and I can't deal with that right now. I'm too amped up from everything; I can't deal with his pissy silence.

"Nope, we're all good. At least so far. I'll put Tweedle Dee and Tweedle Dumbass on alert, but whoever wants to tangle with a houseful of Aegis is going to be in a world of hurt. Is Ian okay?"

I can only assume Tweedle Dee is her husband, and Tweedle Dumbass is the Wraith King—AKA Aidan's boss. That should be a fun conversation. I sometimes forget Aurelia can electrocute just about anything, and her twin sister Mena is probably the most powerful phoenix to rise from the American Legion in two thousand years. And that doesn't even take into account the fact that my tiny friend could take the head right off a man's shoulders with one precise strike.

"He will be." I rake a hand through my wet tresses, the cleanliness of my shower leaching away as reality sets in. My friends are in danger because of me and my fucked-up family.

"Then I want to unpack some of that shit. Your *dad*? I could have sworn Teresa hatched you like the bitchy reptile she is."

I was afraid she was going to ask that.

"Not something I want to get into too much depth about. He's like a former crown prince of demondom or something. I need to do some research, but the consensus is that the Council wants me to kill him and then take the demon seat. And by the way, I saw the seats, babe. Phoenixes and wraiths have them and they're empty, so maybe you should check into that when this whole thing blows over." I huff out a breath, amending, "*If* it blows over."

"Why do I get the feeling you're trying to distract me from the fact that you've got some big shit going down and you're not asking me for help. Just because I can't see you doesn't mean I've lost all sense, Max." Her exasperated "Mom" tone is barbed enough to grate on me.

"Well, do you or do you not have two little ones in your care? Do you or do you not have a husband that will no shit fillet me alive if I get one tiny scratch on his beautiful wife? You're benched from hero duty until your babies can fend for themselves. Hunker down and spread the word. I have a few more calls to make." I want to explain this gently, but I'm too hurt from Ian and Aidan's betrayal to be nice. I'm too sore from the cut of my father wanting to kill me. I'm an open festering wound and I just can't be nice about her safety right now.

"I'll do that, but you be safe, too. I love you, Maxima, and watching you die was the worst thing I've ever experienced. Don't make me do it again, got it?"

"Got it. Love you back," I murmur before disconnecting and plopping my ass on the edge of Ian's bed.

My eyes drift to the man under the covers. A part of me wants to crawl under them and snuggle next to him, and the other part wants to patiently wait for him to wake up so I can give him another concussion.

I feel like a joke, but I can't seem to make myself leave this apartment until I know he's okay. I need to see his eyes open, and then I can leave. Maybe Denver isn't the city for me anymore. My shop has already been busted up twice, and people I thought were friends aren't who I thought they were.

And Striker. His betrayal still stings, and I still don't know how deep it really goes. He knew the shop was going to be attacked. Was he with my father? Did he hear something? I have too many questions when it comes to Striker and not enough answers—

especially for a man I'd lived and breathed and worked beside for a century.

And then Ian keeps the club shit under wraps. It's just one betrayal too many. The very last straw to break me. I thought I'd found a home here, but if the last four centuries have taught me anything, it's that no home is permanent.

Not for someone like me. Not for a Rogue. Not for someone who has never had a home or a real family. One would think I'd be hardened to it by now, but every time, it still hurts when I have to leave. I've probably stayed here too long, anyway. I just need to make sure Ian is okay first.

A soft finger tickles the shell of my ear, and I can't keep the smile off my face if I tried. I'm warm, snuggled in the softness of a down comforter, unwilling to open my eyes to assess exactly where I am. Who I am. I could be this girl for a few more minutes. I could be safe and warm and so, so loved. But then the hurt and betrayal and all the poison of the last few days seems to filter through the happy haze my brain so desperately wants to hold onto.

I pull away, out of the ball I seem to have curled up in at the foot of Ian's bed, my feet on the floor and ready to run before rough, callused fingers close around my wrist, pulling me back. I fight the urge to fall onto the bed, but his touch alone is banking the fire that has blazed for years. The fires of hurt that never seem to really die.

"Where are you going?" Ian's voice is husky as if these are the first words he's spoken all day, and maybe they might be. But it's a question I don't want to answer. I pull my wrist from his grip, no real feat since he isn't giving me much resistance.

"Away." The word is curt, but no less true. "You're awake and healing up. I don't need to stay any longer."

But true to form, Ian is up and out of bed and in front of me, barring my escape.

"Wait, wait, wait. You're just leaving? No, 'I'm glad you're alive.

Sorry you got your ass kidnapped and beat to shit for me.' Just going. I'm real glad you actually give a shit, Maxima, or my feelings might be hurt right about now."

Rage ignites in my belly, and I have to clench my fingers so I don't claw his freaking eyes out. "Oh, we're gonna talk about who hurt who?" I abruptly stand, ready to face off with him if I need to.

Ian moves closer, in my space, in that tiny little bubble where he shouldn't be. "Yeah. I want to talk about who hurt who," he murmurs, somber. Watchful.

"I know about the club, Ian. *I know.*" Pain leaks into every word. "Why didn't you tell me who you were?"

"I—"

"No, I don't really want to hear what bullshit reason you have for why you didn't tell me. It doesn't matter. Because if you actually gave a shit, you would have before now."

"But—"

Again, I cut him off. "Save it. You made me feel like an idiot. How many people knew, and I didn't? Huh? How many?"

How many people saw me as the moron who made out with a guy in a club and didn't remember him? How many people were in on the joke?

"I was going to, but... When you saw me again, you didn't know me. I figured you didn't care as much as I did, so I didn't say anything. Then the Fates kept throwing us together, and the longer I went without telling you, the more it would hurt when I did, and..." He trails off as he turns away to plop into the striped bedside chair. "I didn't want to lose you. Even if I didn't really have you."

His answer thaws the wall of ice around my heart just a little, and all the rage and anger and fight bleeds out of me.

"I thought about that night so much, I figured I must have dreamed you. But your face was hidden in the dark, and you never gave me your name. I didn't know who you were. You should have told me."

I skirt around the chair, needing to get the hell out of here. Ian doesn't need me, and if he actually gave a shit, he might have told me sooner.

"You're still going to leave?" he murmurs before his fingers clasp around my wrist again, pulling me around and back to him, my chest pressed against his. I focus on his throat until I see it bob in a swallow. Somehow that one tiny nervous action pulls my eyes up to his. Then his lips are on mine, the softness of them contrasting so beautifully with the coarse hair on his face. His palms cup my cheeks, holding me still as the pair of us sink into the kiss, and it's just like I remember.

Fast. Frenzied.

Our hands drifting anywhere and everywhere we can touch. Pulling on clothes, trying to reach skin. He really is the man from the club those many months ago. He really is the one I couldn't believe I'd lost myself with—lost and found myself. Found the woman who had just opened her eyes to how wonderful this world could be.

And then in true Ian fashion, he ruins it.

"You about done with that running bullshit?" Superiority leaks into every word. It's all I can do not to punch him just like I did his brother. The floaty feeling of happiness evaporates in an instant.

"Running keeps the people I love safe. Running keeps me safe. Running keeps my dumpster fire of a father away from everyone I freaking care about, so how about we don't kick running out of bed just yet, mm-kay?" I pull from his arms, his warmth, ready to bolt.

"It won't help. And as much as I want you safe, running now just means more running." Ian squeezes my hips, trying to get me to see his side. But he doesn't know.

He can't know.

My laugh is bitter as it spills from my lips. "Running is all I know how to do."

CHAPTER TEN

MAX

Leaving the bedroom is the only course of action I can possibly fathom. But in the finding of my phone and the bone blade and trekking through the apartment in Ian's T-shirt and boxers, I realize that I have nowhere to go. My shop could be burned to the ground for all I know, my house is tainted with the specter of Micah Goode, and I have no one else. No one that I would thrust the burden of my presence upon, no one I would endanger by asking for help.

My footsteps falter in the living room just feet from the front door, Ian on my heels.

"Max! Don't leave," Ian pleads as Aidan sits back on the couch, undoubtedly to watch the show.

"I just figured out I have nowhere else to go," I tell the door, letting my once-proud shoulders droop. "I can't go back to my house, my apartment burned to the ground along with my shop, and if I burden someone else, my father could hurt them, too."

The silence of the fire rockets its way through my brain. I would have just sat there. I would have just burned. How can I put the people I care about in danger like that?

That would make me the monster my mother always thought I was.

"What do you mean your father? What do you mean your apartment burned to the ground?"

Aidan's dark chuckle echoes through the silence. "You've been out of the loop, brother. A lot has happened since yesterday."

"Yeah, a lot has happened. You guys are just going to get hurt if you help. I *can't* ask you to help." Heaving a resigned sigh, I reach for the door.

"You said it yourself. You have nowhere else to go. So why not let us help? You too proud for help?"

I think of how Aidan blamed me for Ian's kidnapping. There is no way in hell he's going to let his little brother stay anywhere near me, and honestly? I don't blame him. The knob turns easily in my hand, as if locking it never even entered their minds. Or maybe it's my sign to keep going and never come back.

"Yes," I whisper, but I don't give Ian a chance to try and stop me this time. As soon as I clear the door and the warding lines I placed last month, I snap my fingers—heading to the last place I want to go.

I'm trying to stay here the least amount of time possible, so the frenzied stuffing of all my shit in a duffle bag is looking a bit more like a tornado than I'd care for. This room in particular gives me the creeps, and if it weren't for the fact that the last vestiges of my wardrobe are here, I wouldn't step foot in the place. Plus, trying to pick which shoes to leave behind is becoming more of a nightmare than originally anticipated.

I don't want to leave Denver. I don't want to upend this life I've built for myself. But then again, I didn't want to be burned at the stake, or cast out of my coven, or have a murdering demon as a dad.

I don't always get what I want.

I sigh as I glance between the pair of electric-blue peep toes in my left hand to the sensible black wedge booties in my right. Neither of them will fit in the bag, and only one pair is even remotely comfortable. I put them both back on the wooden rack in my closet, and whimper at the fashion sacrifices I'll have to make in the coming days.

I suppose when this all dies down, I could have Aurelia send me my things, but I have a tough time wagering free tattoos and warding spells for that big of an ask. I move to the final thing to pack—besides weapons—that I always bring with me to a new place. The last scrap of fabric from the dress my mother gave me after I was cast out. It seems stupid that I've carried it with me for so long, but I can't seem to let it go.

It's a reminder.

A beacon.

A way to remember to never get too comfortable. Never drop my guard. Never trust that everything will be all right. This scrap is the perfect reminder that even family will leave you in the dust.

I pull the plastic bag from the keepsake box I usually keep on the top shelf of my closet, careful to keep the nearly four-hundred-year-old fabric from creasing. This is all that's left of the dress, the cloth decaying over time. The first time a piece crumbled to dust I cried for a week. Now, there is so little left, I fear I won't have it for much longer. I gently stuff it in an internal pocket of my duffle and return to the closet to pick from my small cache of weapons.

Aurelia loves Christmas, and her favorite kind of gift to give is bladed weapons. I can't blame her, each weapon gifted is as beautiful as it is functional. She even taught me how to use some of them. My personal favorite is the rope dart. Silver and gold braided through thick twine all attached to the ringed handle of a carved iron push-dagger. Better than just pretty, I spelled the blade ages ago with a working to keep a wound made by the blade from closing.

I also pick up a trio of throwing knives spelled with a *rue de sanguine* working that is lethal to most Ethereals. That is if I don't miss. I put them in the bag along with the bone blade, unwilling to carry it on my person.

Not after I freed those souls. I may never use it again.

The only other thing I need is in my casting room, a spiral-handled athame that has been with me since my first day of my new life. I nicked it from the refuse of where our encampment had once been before I was kicked out. Someone had left it behind. For a long time, it was the only tool I owned, and that blade, and my power and the scant amount of knowledge of witchcraft I had was all that kept me alive back then.

I turn the blade over in my hand, knowing the secrets it carries.

How many lives it's taken. How many lives it's saved.

Slipping the athame into a small sheath at the base of my spine, I gather up my duffle, not surprised in the least at how heavy it is. I glance around the casting room one more time before walking through the basement, up the stairs, through the kitchen, and out the back door. Passing my now-unkempt greenhouse, I snap my fingers, carrying myself to my shop.

I arrive on a rooftop across the street from the burned-out wreck of what used to be my tattoo shop. I haven't called my artists or the insurance company. I haven't dealt with the police or informed our customers that we were no longer in business and wouldn't be for some time. I didn't do any of those things in the scant time since the fire, even though it feels as if it happened ages ago.

The brick still stands, but every single window has been blown out, glass still littering the sidewalk below. The wide-arched antique panes of glass are now nothing but rubble. The brick stands tall, blackened with soot that still seems to smolder. I remember buying this old wreck of a building years ago. It took forever to restore it—make it new again.

And now it is nothing. The roof yawns wide with big gaping holes, the support beams sticking out like toothpicks into the night sky, blackened and charred. It feels as if a piece of me burned to ash right along with my building.

Too focused on what remains of my livelihood, I don't notice the man behind me until he's a little too close for my liking. Closing in fast, I'm not sure how I can feel him, but just knowing that I can, sends a chill down my spine. But chill or no, it's not like he gives me a head's up before he strikes, all fangs and claws.

Sloppy.

Aidan taught me how to duck strikes the hard way, so this bumbling man is a bit easier to evade than, say, a wraith guardian. I duck him and quickly reassess that he might not be as unskilled as I originally thought. His flailing attack puts me right in the scope of another man I didn't sense. A man whose touch is pure ice—so cold it seems to burn through the thin fabric of my shirt.

I want to scream, but I can't. All I feel is coldness, all I sense, all I see, is the frigid ice of my own torture. Then a wicked specter of a chuckle floats to me on the high winds of the rooftop. It's a bitter, mocking sort of laugh I know well—even if the only place I hear it now is in my dreams.

The last time I heard it, I was in my house trying not to die.

Then the cold is gone, and my body wilts to the pebbled surface of the roof. It can't be. My nightmares can't be real. There is no way this can possibly be happening.

But it can, can't it? I performed a *break*, now, didn't I? All those souls, hundreds, maybe thousands of souls trapped over the ages. Stuck in the putrid home of a bone dagger.

And I set them free.

I set *him* free.

Micah. Goode.

Had I known when I wielded it that the blade trapped souls, I'd like to think I wouldn't have used it. I'd like to think I couldn't be that cruel.

But I know what I've done in my past to men like him. I know what lives I've taken when there was no other way to survive. When it would save a life. When it would stop an evil.

I know—for Micah—I would always, will always pick up whatever weapon I could use to stop him. And maybe this is my comeuppance. My punishment for knowing such a horrible thing about myself and refusing to stand down.

But Micah isn't alive, I know that much. His body—such as it is

—is only slightly opaque. The colors just on this side of gray, his flesh just on that side of sallow.

But he can touch me, hurt me, burn me.

And we both know it.

"Did you miss me, Maxima? I sure missed you."

The hope I held that I wouldn't hear his voice again crumbles to dust. I thought the laugh would be the worst of it, but *noooooo.*

This motherfucker has to be able to speak too. Micah Goode is proof positive that no good deed goes unpunished.

"Nope, I didn't. I figured the knife in the chest would have been a big enough sign for you, Micah, but even from the fucking grave you want to torture me. What is it? My birthday? Are you the Hell gift that keeps on giving?" I try to keep him talking long enough to grab the small vial of salt stashed in my duffle.

But just like in life, he intercepts me, latching onto my hand as his clumsy friend wraps his cold arms around me and squeezes.

"I think I might like this better, Maxima. I'm not hungry, I'm not thirsty, but I have a need, and that is to make you pay."

In all the time I've walked this earth, I've never seen a spirit like this one. When souls aren't claimed, when they aren't sent on by a phoenix to be reborn or a wraith to writhe in the pits of Hell, it isn't like they just stay with their bodies chilling in their graves until someone gets to them.

Ghosts move, but they aren't aware. They don't interact with us —not really. Some might follow their family, their loved ones. Some wander, searching for that one thing, that last piece of unfinished business.

But Micah… he's aware. He knows who I am and how he died.

He is vengeful.

Spiteful.

And drawn to me.

The cold steals my breath, and in my desperation, I haltingly mutter the only spell I can think of. *Exillium. Banishment.*

Micah's spirit doesn't leave exactly, but the spell—as halting as it is—does push him back a few feet, his shoes solid enough to make twin trails in the graveled rooftop. The weaker specter, the one holding my arms, lets me go, and I fall.

And I don't waste the scant opportunity I've found. I rip the zipper open on my duffle, finding the vial of salt and the rope dagger. I manage to pour a handful of salt in my palm and run the braided metal and twine rope through the grains. Salt in the rope, iron in the blade. I may not be able to banish or even kill Micah Goode.

But I can hurt him.

From my knees, I toss the dart. And miss. The blade sails past Micah, hitting nothing but air. But my wide shot isn't without its virtues, because even though the dart misses, the rope finds Micah just fine.

His howl is uniquely satisfying, but my good fortune doesn't last. I pay too much attention to Micah and forget his bumbling friend. He spins me so I'm facing him now, and for the first time, I see why he might be so awkward.

Half his face is gone, his body burned and crippled in his mask of permanent death. He doesn't speak, only moans his happiness as he burns me again and again with his icy clutches.

"*Ex—exillium,*" I whisper through the bitter pain, praying the spell works even for a second.

But I don't get that second—not with two players in the game. The grotesque spirit lets me go, but Micah latches on, and even in death he got to keep his talons. And his fangs.

He strikes with both, cutting into my arms, his fangs piercing my neck, spilling my blood onto the rooftop, unable to drink it. He swallows again and again, but the blood falls through him, drip, drip, dripping.

Water, water everywhere and not a drop to drink.

I don't realize I've said the words aloud, until his hand scores icy fire across my cheek.

"Shut up! Shut your fucking mouth, you stupid bitch!" He drops me back down to the rooftop as he rakes his hands through his hair. Even as a ghost, Micah sure is vain. In his frantic pacing, I manage to slip my hand behind my back, latching onto the handle, drawing the athame.

"Aww, wassa matter, Mikey?" I slur, the pain and blood loss seeping into my bones. "Can't finish the job?"

He growls, ready to hit me again until I throw the athame. This time I actually hit my mark—even if it isn't his heart where I aimed. True aim or not, the athame remains lodged in Micah's belly, the silvery blood staining the blade when he draws it out.

"How many people have you killed that way? And now you can't get the job done. Must sting a bit, huh, Mikey?"

Micah drops the athame, moving to rush me, but he stops so fast the pebbles beneath his specter feet skid. His eyes go wide before his mouth twists into a rueful sneer, and just like that, Micah Goode runs for his life… or his undeath, if you want to get technical.

I want to look behind me, but as dumb as it sounds, I'm just too scared. I don't have much else in my grasp except for the rope dart, and honestly, I don't think it will do much for whatever it is Micah would rather run from than take his shot to kill me.

Heavy footsteps fall, slow at first and then faster, and still I can't make myself look. Squeezing my eyes tight, I brace for the killing blow.

A killing blow that never comes.

Warm hands fall on me where cold ones once were, and I know exactly who scared Micah Goode into running.

Opening my eyes, I prove myself right.

Ian came for me.

CHAPTER ELEVEN

MAX

I want to ask Ian why Micah ran. Was it just because I had backup? Or was it something else? Something wholly Ian that made Micah run for the hills.

I know he'll be back. I know Micah isn't done with me. He has an eternity worth of time and nothing better to do. It might be time to ask Gramma how to banish a ghost.

Ian murmurs, "*Salutaris.*" *Health, to heal*. It's a spell I've never been able to get to work on myself, but when Ian murmurs the faint Latin, I feel the blood start to clot on my neck. The working doesn't close the wounds entirely, but at least the bleeding stops.

"Fancy seeing you here, handsome," I slur slightly, the healing spell doing nothing for my other wounds or the blood loss.

"You didn't think I was going to let you leave town and not say goodbye, did you?" He clucks his tongue. "You and I have unfinished business, kinda like those specters I seem to have run off. You picking up strays?"

He seems awfully calm for a man who's just seen a ghost. This isn't his first time seeing ones like that, and I don't know if I'm relieved he came to my rescue, or miffed I don't know this about him. I settle on relieved because, hey, I'm breathing, right?

"Not picking them up. They found me."

Ian's lips form a tight line but he doesn't say another word, his silence edging me out of grateful and into miffed.

"Care to share with the class why two ghosts ran for the hills just seeing you coming?"

His lips turn down in the universal sign of "nope" right before he grumbles, "Not particularly."

"Tough shit."

"I don't know why, okay?" His voice is like a whip as he throws up his hands. "I have a theory, but it's unproven and a shit one at that considering it's based on nothing but a guess. You're not the only one who doesn't know their parents, Max."

He has a point. I don't know the entire scope of what I can do because the only demons I've seen have tried to kill me. It's not like I had the time to ask them exactly how my abilities work. And from what I gathered? Ian knows even less about his parentage than I do. His only benefit is he has a sibling he actually talks to.

"Let's get you up and back to the apartment. I can treat you there." He helps me stand on my unsteady legs, then his eyes fall on the athame still silvered with Micah's blood.

He inspects the blade, turning the corkscrew handle this way and that. "You managed to cut him?"

A flash of alarm has me standing on my own two feet and reaching for his hand.

"Don't get your face too close. If you turn that blade just the wrong way—"

The added feature of that particular blade springs free, a specially carved rune in the underside tang of the first turn of the corkscrew—a preloaded spell that lengthens the blade from dagger size to short-sword size. All of which that just manages to miss Ian's face. But he doesn't seem to be surprised so much as peeved.

"How about you don't mess with my weapons? I have a couple of secrets that don't need to come out in the form of your death, mm-kay?" I gently remove the athame from Ian's grip, pressing the rune again to shrink the blade.

He lets me go and reaches for my duffle, giving me a pointed look as he removes both the athame and rope dart from my hands. "I take it this was your doing? Altering the weapons?"

"Some, but the athame came like that."

"Interesting. Where did you get it?"

Why he's asking this while I'm beat to shit on top of a building after being attacked by fucking ghosts isn't just irritating, his tone is more accusatory than I'd like.

"Virginia. 1642. I picked it up from the refuse of a burned-out home. Left behind by my coven after they left me to rot. Any more veiled accusations you want to make?"

He only shakes his head, still eyeing the blade as if I stole it. As if it shouldn't be in my hands. I suppose I did technically take something that wasn't mine, but possession is nine-tenths of the law and all that. Whomever the athame belonged to, they didn't care enough about it to keep it, left it behind in the ashes of one of our coven homes, so it became mine. Bigger things have been claimed with less.

My cell phone buzzes in my back pocket. I swear the thing is indestructible at this point. The number is one I sort of recognize, a Coeur d'Alene area code, meaning it could be one of two people. My little sister or my mother.

I cross my fingers, answering, "Hello?"

"Ma—Max," Maria whispers, her voice aching and strained, making the tiny hairs along my arms stand on end.

"Ria? Baby girl, where are you? Are you hurt?"

Maria was ten when I was cast out. Neither of us really know our fathers. In my case, that's a good thing, but in Maria's not so much. At least hers was a good man, even if he left this world much too soon. One of my biggest regrets is leaving her to the iron rule of my mother, even as involuntary as my going might have been.

"Man... came... took Mom. Need help. Hurts..."

"*Ria*!" I want to smash something when the call disconnects. I'd rip a hole in the world for that girl, even if she isn't a little girl anymore. Even if Mom would rather pretend I never existed, and Maria just followed her lead.

Even if she never really loved me at all.

I wrench the duffle out of Ian's hand with probably more force than necessary, raking through the bag for a pendulum and an old road atlas from 1997. I use one of the throwing knives to pierce the flesh of the outside of my forearm, coating the edges of the blade in the fresh, untainted blood. This blood doesn't have spectral traces, wasn't drawn by ghostly fangs or claws. It's as clean as I can make it.

Smearing the blood on the pendulum, I pray this works. While we're only half-sisters, the bloodline is surely pure enough and close enough that the casting shouldn't be a problem. I spread out the paper map of Idaho on the pebbled rooftop, wishing that Google Maps worked with spells. Hell, the thing is magical enough on its own, how hard could it be to upgrade it a scosche for locating purposes? I mean, I can find the best Thai food in town, but locator spells are out of the question? Shenanigans.

"Max, what are you doing?"

"Shh! I'm busy."

Swinging the pendulum, I gather myself and my power, focusing on Maria's face, on my love for her. "*Ea invenio, invenire soror mea.*" *Find her, find my sister.* The trouble with casting a locator is every single one is different. The spell is tailored for each person, each relationship, each circumstance. It depends on who you're looking for and on what plane of existence they're on.

So, when the pendulum stops swinging, the magic in the spell halting the rose-quartz crystal without dropping, without the pull to any one location, I fear the worst.

Tears track down my face, but I don't have the time or inclination to wipe them away. Maria asked for my help, she went to me when there are about a dozen other people she could have gone to.

She asked me, and I'll be damned if I let her down.

I try two or three more times before calm, warm hands find their way around me, softly pinning my arms down to my sides. At this moment, it doesn't matter if the hands are soft. They're stopping me, and Maria doesn't have the luxury of time.

"Max. Max! How about we try a bigger map? Maybe she isn't in Idaho." Ian whispers the last part in my ear, and it takes a second to register before I stop trying to claw my way out of his arms.

I nod, and his arms fall away, flipping the pages to a larger-scale map. If this one doesn't work...

I set the pendulum in motion again, murmuring the spell over and over. "*Ea invenio, invenire soror mea.*"

The pendulum falls inside the confines of the state of Colorado, so I flip to the Colorado map and do it again. This time the crystal drops, the cut tip pointing to Denver.

I swear to the Fates, if this stupid thing points right back to me, I'll lose my damn mind.

Moving to the Denver city map, I swing it again, this time the pendulum is yanked out of my hands, the brass chain slipping from my fingers as the sharp crystal's point embeds in the map, landing in the warehouse district.

It's near Aether, and if I drive, I can be there in twenty minutes. Just snapping my fingers and traveling there isn't going to happen. Not after Micah. Not after however many times I did that stupid locator spell. My car should still be parked behind the burned-out wreck of what used to be my shop. Since my keys are more than likely still in what used to be my apartment, I might be able to use magic to start it.

Maybe.

I rip the crystal from the map, stuffing it back inside my bag. I'll need to get a new road atlas, but that's the least of my problems right about now. I need to figure out how to get off this roof. Preferably without dying.

No one has time for that.

Standing, I try to pull the duffel up with me before my weakness makes itself known. I sway, nearly going splat on the rooftop. *I guess it's better than going splat on the sidewalk.*

"Whoa, whoa, whoa. Where do you think *you're* going?" Ian tries to take the duffle handle from my grip.

I may be weaker than a day-old kitten, but he can fuck right off. "I'm finding my sister."

"No, you aren't. You can barely stand up. Let alone help anyone else."

"I'm fine." Even *I* know it's a lie. My whole body feels like it has been simultaneously frozen and set on fire. My bones ache, my skin feels raw, and that's not even taking into account the scabbed wound on my neck.

I feel like smeared dog shit.

But my little sister needs me, and that supersedes everything else.

"Do I look blind to you?" he snarks, and I kinda want to swing this duffle hard enough to smack him in the face. I want to, but I won't. Because I'm a weak ass right now and I fucking can't.

"It's my sister, Ian. Would you leave your brother behind? Would you let him die alone and scared because you were a little hurt? No. You wouldn't. So, don't tell me I'm not going. I'm going. Either with you, or through you, but I'm going to find my sister." I seethe through gritted teeth.

"I'm not saying don't help her. Let me and Aidan go. We can find your sister."

He's talking reason, but I'm not having it. I don't know what mess my sister is in, and I'm not leaving her Fate at the hands of Ian and Aidan. At this point, Aidan would rather let me and my sister die just to protect his brother. I can understand the sentiment, but it doesn't instill much confidence in me being left behind.

"Aidan would rather throw me off this roof than let you go back out there and stick your neck out for me."

Can I blame him? No, no, I can't. Ian's face is still healing, the purple, almost black around the inside of his eyes, the swelling still there is faint. There are probably even more wounds I can't see under his black T-shirt and green hoodie. More than I can even dare to think about.

A concussion and probably a bruised lung. That's what Aidan said. Ian might be up and around, but he actually isn't much better off than I am.

"Let's call him, then," he taunts, tugging the bag fully out of my hands while he dials the phone. This time I don't try to get the bag back. It's too big of a feat to stay standing, the dizziness seeming to seep into every part of my brain.

Blood loss can just fuck right off.

Not a second later, Aidan arrives on the rooftop in a swath of black smoke.

"Weren't you leaving town?" He offers in greeting as he traipses to us, the confident swagger of a man with zero fucks to give.

Even if he's wearing a beanie on his head.

In August.

"My sister needs my help, but your brother won't let me go alone. Since standing is a bit of a problem, I can't exactly say no to the offer. You coming?"

Aidan's expression goes from taunting, to speculative, to concerned. Ahh, so he still does have a heart underneath it all. Good to know.

"Lead the way."

CHAPTER TWELVE

MAX

Touching down on the pavement, I barely avoid giving into my burning need to vomit. I hate traveling with Aidan, and the sadistic bastard only seems amused by my inherent motion sickness where this particular wraith ability is concerned.

Resting my hands on my knees, I take deep breaths to avoid all my internal organs hitting the sidewalk, and pray a little to any God, deity, or power that be that will keep me from chuffing on the pavement. Luckily, someone listens—either that, or my equilibrium finally settles from having all my molecules ripped apart and put back together wrong.

When I can breathe again, I take stock of the deserted street. There are two very different parts to Denver's warehouse district. The trendy, gentrified parts, and the deserted war-zone-looking parts. Every city has them, the places no one up to any sort of good wants to go. It makes so little sense why my family would be here, but since we're less than a full city block from Aether, the stretch isn't exactly thin.

I examine each building, looking for the tell-tale signs of

warding sigils or hex lines. Something, anything that says a witch has been there. I'd take a neon sign spelling out the word "Trap" at this point. Walking west is my only option on this dead-end road, and I begin scanning each building for the luminescent pale-silver hex lines that only I seem to be able to see.

I'll never forget when Caim found out I could see and smell magics. I'd never felt so odd before, and that's saying something. Honestly, tattooing "freak" on my forehead would be a time saver for everyone.

Each building has the façade of a crumbling wreck, and no doubt some actually are, but others aren't what they seem—I know that much. I might not be able to completely see past their glamours, but I can see enough of the magic to know they are there. Granted, there is enough "go away" magic to fill the ocean, but those spells don't always work on me.

I blame the half-breed demon mojo for that.

But I'm looking for something specific: the silvery warding lines from a witch, which would surpass any glamour for security. But it's tough to see past the two men who seem to be trying to keep me from my end goal. Aidan and Ian both shadow my unsteady steps, one behind and one in front, in a dumb-as-shit protection sandwich that I want no part of.

I catch a bright spot out of the corner of my eye: flickering hex lines of a ward that is slowly dying.

"There." I point and take off running, drawing the energy from pure adrenaline alone. Or maybe from the scant amount of hope that still lingers in me.

I make it ten feet from the deserted husk of a building before Ian drags me back, his thick arm catching me by the middle. As someone who has never required permission from anyone, this new turn of events pisses me right off.

"That's a warding line. I see the hex marks." I try to explain before losing all patience and whisper-hiss, "Let me go, you idiot!"

Ian's arm goes slack, but he doesn't quite let me go.

"Do you have any idea how many Ethereals are in this part of town? Hundreds, maybe thousands. Just because you see warehouses and crumbling buildings, doesn't mean they are actually there," Aidan chimes in, and I'm so happy to have a wraith explain witch things to me.

For real. *It's my favorite.*

This takes mansplaining to a whole new level.

I resist rolling my eyes and punching him in the jaw again by sheer force of will alone. "I know. I can see past the glamours. I can also see the hex lines of a ward, and the sigils look familiar, so..." I trail off, staring pointedly at the arm still circling my middle.

Aidan gives Ian the man nod, a pretentious little chin tip, and I have to force myself not to light them both on fire. I maneuver closer to the building, careful not to step on a hidden ward or sigil, which is tough to do when there is trash and grime everywhere. Carefully, I approach the peeling wood of a door that looks like it's holding onto its hinges by a wing and a prayer, as I study the familiar hex lines keyed only to a specific bloodline, a hopeful smile curving my lips.

Teresa Alcado never could figure out how to keep me out.

Debating for half a second, I try to decide whether I should pluck the lines and let everyone in, or just walk right through the ward and leave the brothers behind. Tickled at the thought, I pick door number two, their curses following me in the building as I turn an ancient knob to the equally old door.

Inside, the furnishings are quite a bit nicer, that is to say, the ceilings are complete, and I can't see the sky. But while the walls and floor are new, freshly painted or papered, the room is a total wreck.

An antique red velvet settee is turned on its back, one leg hanging precariously by a thin splinter. One lone overhead light casts deep shadows on the broken remnants of the room, the smell of ozone from spent magic is high in the air. Walls are cracked, the plaster bowed or in rigid peaks as if it were exposed to a flash fire or an extreme heat. An upholstered chair lays on its side far from the circle of seating, its fabric slashed to ribbons. Smashed glass from broken lamps litter the thick pile on the Persian rug, their remnants lying broken, their cords wrapped around table legs like coiled whips.

But Maria isn't here.

Not in this room anyway, and I'm hesitant to carry on further if this is what the living room looks like. I can't sense another presence, and that is the part that scares me most of all.

Retracing my steps, I head back out of the ward and begin plucking the hex lines apart. I can feel the brothers' stare, but I don't explain—can't explain what's inside.

They have to see it for themselves.

"Are you out of your fucking mind?" Ian's hot whisper hits my ear along with the warmth of his breath. But it isn't just his breath I feel—no. His rage presses into me like a smothering blanket.

"Nope. Just tired of you two keeping me from doing my job. I thought I could go in there and get her but..." I trail off, shrugging as I pluck another hex line and watch as it fades away.

"But what?" Aidan asks from behind me.

"She isn't in the living room, and the place is blown to shit," I murmur, plucking four or five lines at a time, trying to get the ward down faster. "If she's in there, I can't feel her. If I can't feel her, then something else could be in there, too. Hence me unraveling these stupidly complex warding lines so we can all go in to be murdered."

Last one, I think and pluck the lone remaining hex line.

"Okay, it's down. Give me my weapons," I order Ian, who's holding my bag.

He unceremoniously drops it at my feet, and I crouch to dig through it, grabbing the throwing knives, bone knife, rope dart, and the athame. I don't know what's in there, and honestly, I hope I don't find out. But just in case I do, I want to be armed. I tuck the athame back in its spine sheath, stuff the throwing knives in my bootie, snap the clasp on the bone knife holster around my waist, and wrap the rope dart around my wrist, tucking my index and middle fingers in the loop of the push-dagger.

Aidan seems to be already through the door, and I move to follow him when Ian stops me.

"You be careful. Stay behind us, and no cowboy-martyr bullshit. I will knock you out to keep you safe, don't fucking try me."

More wraith bullshit.

Like my life matters when Maria is hurt or dying. Like my breath is more important than hers. I feel my magic rise in me, the crackling sort of power that flows from my chest, down my arms manifesting in green-hued molten fire skating over my fingertips.

"You get in between me and finding my little sister, so help me, I will put you down. I can't die. She can. Don't fuck with my family, Ian." My threat is palpable in the scant space between us.

Ian takes a step back, hurt tracing over his face before he masks it. I want to be sorry, but I'm not. I'm not sorry for needing to protect my sister. I'm not sorry for being willing to give my life —such as it is—for hers. Ian might not realize it now, but he'd do the same for Aidan. He'd steamroll anyone in his path to keep his brother alive.

Even me.

He heads into the building behind Aidan. The room is just as decimated as before, only slightly more illuminated by the green tinge of my magics that I can't seem to suppress.

And I feel nothing.

Not my sister, not another presence.

Just... nothing.

That is until a tiny flare of something to my left pricks at my consciousness. Like a flickering flame, it sputters, ready to die out. I don't think, I run—past Ian and Aidan, and wrench open a battered door. Only with the added light of my magics do I now notice the faint smear of blood leading to the door as if someone was either dragged there, or maybe... if someone crawled there herself.

I don't see her at first, the closet too dark that even the feeble light from the room and my magic does nothing to penetrate it. Icy chills rake up my spine. This blackness is too big, too thick.

Something is here, cloaking her, hiding her. My only hope is I have enough juice in me to knock the darkness back.

"*Detrahet me in lucem.*" I mutter a faint, breathy whisper of hope. *Bring me light.*

And then she's there, curled up in a bloody ball covered in heavy coats and furs. If it weren't for the blood, she'd look so much like the sleeping child I left behind all those years ago.

"She's here," I whisper-yell, alerting the boys so we can get the hell out of here.

I reach for her, ready to pull her from that abyss of a coat closet when a hard body knocks me away, slamming me into the floor. I try to breathe, but all the air is sucked away by a putrid, rotting-flesh-smelling... *thing*. I can't see what attacked me, but if I were to take a guess, a zombie wouldn't be far off.

Not that I think zombies are real, but if they were, this is exactly what they'd smell like. I reach for the rope dart, re-coiling it around my wrist, ready to let the dagger fly as I scan the room for what hit me. All I see is Ian and Aidan back to back, blades drawn and braced. Aidan is bleeding from a gash on his upper arm, and Ian is unsteady on his feet.

There are too many shadows in this room. Too many places for things to hide.

"*Detrahet me in lucem,*" I command, my magic rising in me and exploding from my fingers like the sun.

The spell bathes the room in light, the sources coming from all directions, all angles so that there are barely any shadows, and oh, how I wish I could unsee what resides in them. Crouched in a corner is a monster if I ever saw one. Naked, pasty flesh of a human body, the head of a crow missing its feathers, talons instead of fingers, hooves instead of feet. Ripped from the very depths of Hell, this is something that should have stayed in the dark. Its talons grip the sheetrock as if it is gearing up, preparing itself to launch.

And then it does, pushing off its great hooves, bypassing the brothers, talons reaching not for them.

But for me.

It's fast, darting toward me like a missile. The rope dart leaves my fingers before I ever tell it to fly, sailing around the monster's neck, the short blade of the push-dagger imbedding into the flesh there. Black blood as thick as tar pours from the wound, but all I've seemed to do is give it a leash for me, a tether to yank me from my feet.

And it does, it so does.

It reels me in until I have enough sense to let the rope go, but my hesitation means I'm down again, and all too quickly it's on me, taloned hands gripping my upper arms as it looks me over. Intelligent, ruthless eyes assess me and quickly find me lacking, the crow's head emitting a coughing sort of bird chuckle. It's mocking, derisive, and if the human shaped part of him had anatomy, I'd kick him right in the nuts.

Too bad he doesn't have any.

You think you can best me, child? I've been rending flesh from bone before humans even existed. There is no torture that I cannot create and no punishment out of my reach. You will not kill me, child. Not with your puny witch weapons.

"What do you want, then? A cookie?"

"Who the fuck are you talking to?" Ian whispers, and it takes a second to realize that they can't see what I can. They can't see this monster holding me hostage.

They cannot see me, silly girl. That's part of my charm. People fear more what they cannot see, cannot perceive, so much more than what they can.

I highly doubt if someone saw this monster they wouldn't fear him. Not unless they were stupid.

Tell them to leave. You can even have them save your baby sister. But you're staying here with me. We need to have a chat.

I nod, and the bird-human-horse man lets me go.

"Aidan, get your brother and grab my sister and get the fuck out of this house. Now." My voice is low and as calm as I can make it. Ian won't do what I need him to, but Aidan? I know he will—he won't even hesitate.

"What the hell are you talking about?" Ian hisses as his brother herds him to the closet.

Aidan reaches, pulling my sister's limp body from its depths, and I breathe a sigh of relief. Not because I'll be okay. I highly doubt I'll come out of this unscathed.

But because the people I care about will.

CHAPTER THIRTEEN

MAX

I don't bother looking behind me. I know what I'll see if I do. Ian's hurt, maybe enraged expression as his brother pulls him from the room. Maria's blood-covered face, her body barely clinging to life.

I don't need to look. I'm too busy standing in between the monster and my family. Too concerned with keeping his beak on this side of the room.

"I'm coming back, Max, and you better be alive when I do," Aidan calls from the door, his voice like an ice bath of vengeance and promise.

The last traces of my power crackles in my hands as I look over my shoulder, Aidan's coal-black wraith eyes taking over the green, bleeding into the white sclera, piercing me where I stand. I only say one word, but it's enough to shock even Aidan who probably cares the least about anyone except his brother.

"Don't."

I turn back to the crow demon, staring him down. Preparing myself in case he decides to go back on his offer of letting them go. If it came down to it, he would win. Probably. Aidan might have taught me a few new tricks in the last month or so, but training with him is a far sight different than fighting a demon in real life. Thankfully, this demon in particular doesn't seem to want to feast on my flesh.

At least not right now.

I feel it crackle in the air when they leave, my body bereft of them, even though I wanted them to go.

"Okay, they're gone. What do you want?" I cross my arms over my chest. It's a dumb stance, Aidan has told me so on a number of occasions, telling me to always be loose, ready. But I can't right now.

Relax, child, I am not your enemy. I take that back. I could be your enemy if you don't give me what I want.

No shit. That's the beak of a carrion bird if I ever saw one. Mr. Crow Man would eat me without a second thought and we both know it. "And that is?"

The blade, girl. Why else would I drag myself up to this frigid place? My master wants, I retrieve. It's not that complicated.

He's right. It isn't complicated at all. I don't even consider it. Not after what I saw come out of the bone blade, not after what I felt. It is a soul stealer, and I won't let it fall into the wrong hands.

Not again.

"No."

Miraculously, the naked crow face morphs into what I assume is shock. I didn't think birds could have expressions, but hey, you learn something new every day.

What do you mean, no? This isn't a negotiation, girl. Give me the blade or I'll make you.

His talons reach for me, but I dance out of his way, the pair of us circling each other, searching for the right opening.

"What? You can't grab it yourself? It's right here." I point to the bone blade in the specialized holster Barrett gave me. Big Bird doesn't know it, but no one but me can remove the blade from its sheath, so I don't feel as worried about flashing it to my enemy. "Ahh, that's right. Demons need permission, even the lowly slave ones, isn't that so? Well, I'll make it as uncomplicated as I can. I'll never give up this blade. Never. Go back to your master and tell him I said so."

I don't think so, child. My master wants, I retrieve. I'll take you down to Hell with me if I have to, but he'll get that blade.

I don't doubt him, but even in death, I won't give him what he wants.

"Then we don't have anything else to talk about." I drop my crossed arms to my sides, adjusting my stance. My throwing knives are too far away in my boot, the bone knife is too precious to pull from its sheath.

But the athame, that can help.

I just manage to pull it when the demon is on me again, his talons digging into the flesh of my shoulders, his beak open and hissing right in my face. I didn't know crows could hiss, or maybe this amalgamation of species gives it abilities above and beyond that of the animals it portrays.

The speaking inside one's head thing is a major upgrade.

His beak lunges for my face, trying to pluck the eyes from my skull, or just eat me whole. His putrid breath speaks of the worst pits of Hell, of torture and rot. I swipe the blade, grazing him, but the pain is enough for him to let me go. My reprieve doesn't last long before he's on me again, ripping me off my feet and throwing me into the tatters of what used to be an opulent sitting room. *At least the Persian is soft,* I think as I suck in a breath, trying to find my feet. In the struggle, I dropped the athame, and I scramble to find it. My fingers close around the hilt and I slash blindly, forgetting everything Aidan taught me, managing only by luck to catch him again with my blade.

It isn't enough. I'm not enough. My body is too spent, too tired from the toll of today to use any magic, and my strength—such as it is—is too weak to take on something like this.

His huge, hulking body knocks me off my feet, and I didn't even see him move that time. His talons pin my shoulders to the floor, before drawing me up off the rug. The sharp edges dig into my shoulders, cutting the flesh, but my hands are free, and I spin the handle in my fingers, pressing the rune as I bring the athame up between us.

The blade expands just like when Ian accidentally pressed it, driving up and through the soft spot on the crow's head, just before the hard beak erupts from his face. It drives deeper, through his head and out the top of his skull, pouring the black-tar blood all over us both.

His talons fall away, his body going slack as I wrench the blade from him, the tine sticking a bit in the bone until I yank it free. I guess *one* witch weapon was good enough to kill him. Pressing the rune again, the blade collapses and I wipe the black blood off on one of the ruined upholstered chairs and slip it back into the sheath.

Then I take a gander at the rest of me. Sticky black blood covers my shirt, soaking it somehow, even though the blood doesn't even seem thin enough to do so. I yank off my outer layer, peeling the thin Henley from my skin. At least the tank underneath is black. I won't be winning a beauty contest, and I might be a touch cold, but it'll do.

I take stock of the room again, wondering what happened here, wondering what happened to Maria and Mom. Could this demon do this much damage? Probably. But it feels like more. It feels like I'm missing something big and I don't know what.

Keeping a watchful eye, I head back out the ancient door into the cool night, taking my first deep breath once the rancid smell of the demon is behind me. My bag is gone, but that isn't a huge surprise in this part of town. My only hope is one of the boys snagged it before they left, but I don't have much hope on that front. They had bigger problems than my stuff.

I pull my phone from my back pocket and start laughing. For as much as I thought the thing was indestructible, I guess it couldn't stand up to a fight with a demon. The screen is cracked, spiderwebs of broken glass and missing pieces. I'm amazed I didn't rip my hand open just pulling it from my pocket.

I guess this means I can't call an Uber.

That thought has me giggling. In the middle of the night in a human-deserted part of town that likely has plenty of not-so-nice Ethereals teeming to fuck with the Rogue. There is a good fucking reason I never come to this part of town. I need to shut up, but still the giggles come, competing with the clicking of my booties on the pavement for loudness.

A man appears on the sidewalk not fifty feet in front of me, stealing my laughter. The dark swath of smoke curls around him and then dissipates, melding into the darkness around him. Hands in his pockets, he heads in my direction. I'd be scared in any other circumstance, but the beanie on his head gives him away.

"I told you not to come back for me," I nag, unable to say I'm glad he ignored me. Glad at least I have one person in my corner. Ian might not forgive me for what I had to do here tonight, and a part of me doesn't blame him. But I'm not sorry, either.

"Yeah, but I never listen to you, anyway, so why start now? Ready?" He doesn't let me nod before he takes us both off that street, the faint cry of a bird the last thing I hear before the darkness swallows me.

I hate traveling.

This time when I land, I don't have the strength to hold back, finding the closest receptacle to vomit in. Unfortunately for me, that receptacle is one of my lavender planters. Aidan, the kind soul he is, leaves me to my misery.

When my stomach finally gives up the ghost, I stagger through the back door of my house, not even a little afraid of the place. I guess that's fighting a crow demon from Hell for you, it will cure you of just about anything. My bag is sitting on the kitchen table, but otherwise the kitchen is empty. I follow the rustling sound of feet to my guest room where Ian is tying off the final stitch to a long gash in my sister's arm. There are stitches along her hairline as well, and if the mounds of bloody gauze and detritus of medical equipment are any indication, I owe Ian one.

Using the doorjamb to prop myself up, I ask, "How is she?"

"She'll be fine. Some deep lacerations, maybe a concussion. She'll be okay in a day or two."

"Thank you. For helping her," I whisper, grateful he was there, that he could help her when I couldn't.

He nods, not looking at me even though he's finished sewing her up, collecting the trash and bloody towels to avoid it.

"There was a demon in that room, Ian. You couldn't see him, but he wanted you gone. Be pissed at me if you want to, but I did the best I could under the circumstances. Everyone's alive, so when you're stewing on it, please remember that."

He stuffs the rubbish forcefully into a trash bag pilfered from my kitchen, shoving the gauze unnecessarily hard into the plastic. Still not looking at me like a damn child. And in the grand scheme —at least compared to me—he is young. Maybe too young to understand why I would keep him out of harm's way.

Fed up, I sigh, skirting around him to reach Maria. Her skin is sallow with blood loss, but her breaths are even, and she appears peaceful in her sleep. I bend down, kissing her forehead, away from the stitches and leave her to rest.

When I look up again, Ian is staring at me, a mask of fury on his face. He sees my cuts, probably some bruises, too. The burns from Micah's too-cold touch, the blood both from me and the crow demon. He takes it all in, barring my way out like he'd love nothing other than putting me in a padded cell and throwing away the key. I feel a trickle of warmth at his concern.

But then it all comes crashing down.

"I can't do this anymore," he murmurs, not meeting my eyes. Instead he studies my injuries, cataloguing them, tallying them up in his brain. I can practically see it behind his eyes.

That trickle of warmth is long gone, replaced with a burning cold even Micah's touch couldn't surpass.

"Can't do what anymore?"

I want him to look me in the eye when he says it, when he tells me I'm not good enough. When he says that I'm too reckless, too crass, too different, too something. That I'm chaos and calamity, a disaster just over the horizon.

His brother has said as much, so why wouldn't he?

"I can't watch you throw yourself into one scrape after another with zero thought to who might miss you when you're gone. Aidan and I will help you with your father, but after that..."

He doesn't have to say it. I understand him just fine. *He won't help me anymore.*

"Don't worry, Ian. I know when I've worn out my welcome." I choke out, managing to hold back the worst of the pain.

Skirting around him, I'm barely holding onto the last bit of strength I have when I catch Aidan watching me from the hall. His face is an impenetrable mask, and I can't tell if he's happy his little brother gave me the boot or not.

It doesn't matter anyway.

I have a scrap of fabric in my duffle that tells me everything I need to know about people. A three-inch by three-inch square of wisdom stuffed in a Ziploc bag. Everyone leaves. One way or another.

I shoulder past Aidan, the shame and hurt and everything else hitting me all at once. And four centuries old or not, I still feel like a kid when I catch the trickle of tears starting their descent down my face. My mask breaking even though I thought I'd hardened myself enough over the years. I guess not.

I make it to my room, locking the door and heading to the shower. I crawl in fully clothed, only stopping to remove my weapons and boots. The water is ice when it hits me, but I don't really feel it.

All I know is no one can hear me break over the rush of the water.

And that's all I wanted anyway.

CHAPTER FOURTEEN

MAX

I sit crusty-eyed and cranky, curled up in the bedside chair next to my sister. If I weren't leaving town, I would set this chair on fire on my front freaking lawn. Hell, since I *am* leaving town I still might. I don't have any groceries here, so the coffee situation is dire. The whiskey situation, however, was just fine last night, hence the cranky, crusty-eyed hangover I'm rocking now. I more than likely need another shower, but at this point I'd kill for some takeout and a cup of Joe.

Ian left last night before I got out of the shower, and Aidan made himself scarce in my other guestroom.

I have three guestrooms in this house, and it makes me wonder why I even bought a home this big. Unless there is a crisis, there will never be a need to fill them. It's not like I'll get married or have kids. I don't know if children are even possible. What if I'm a sterile offspring of two species that were never meant to come together? Like a horse and a donkey making a mule. A genetic freak never meant to reproduce.

And why am I thinking about having kids? My only romantic prospect in a freaking century just walked out on me. Babies are farther away than the moon at this point.

Tired, disgruntled, and grudgingly heartbroken, I peel myself from the chair to raid the takeout drawer. Making my way to the kitchen, I pull the overfull-drawer open, rifling through the disorganized menus. There has to be a place I can call... with no phone because mine is broken into a bazillion pieces. Shit.

The back door opens, Aidan pausing at the threshold with bags in his hands. His eyes are wide, and it really isn't any guess what he's gawking at. Stained pajama pants, rat's nest hair, last night's makeup smeared under my eyes. Yeah, I know I look like a train wreck, but honestly, it's my house and I can be a mess here if I want to. Granted, he's seen me look worse, like the time I was topless with a surgical drain coming from my chest.

Yeah, I've definitely looked worse.

"Please tell me there is coffee somewhere in one of those bags." My voice is like gravel, ready to pout my lower lip if it means I can guilt him into getting me some. I'll even use tears. I'm not above it, and hey, they'll be easy to create.

He coughs to mask his chuckle, but he answers in the affirmative, so I'll allow it. "There is. Creamer too. I got a few groceries and replaced your phone. You can call to get it activated."

And now I want to cry all over again. Aidan just saved me from braving the phone store and the grocery store and the coffee shop. Swallowing hard, I manage to nod before I reach for the bags, unloading them in a hurry.

"Thanks," I murmur, but my voice is broken, as if the kindness is just a little too much, even for that single syllable. It's possible it might be.

Pulling the coffee from the bag, I set about to make us a pot, thankful for something to do.

"When you're up to it, you need to look at the warding around the property," Aidan suggests, pulling egg cartons and packages of bacon and sausage from a plastic bag. "I know you threw a band-aid one up last night, but if we're going to be here for any length of time, it's going to need to be stronger."

Nodding, I pour water into the reservoir, filling it up to the tippy-top. "I'll get on that after I start this."

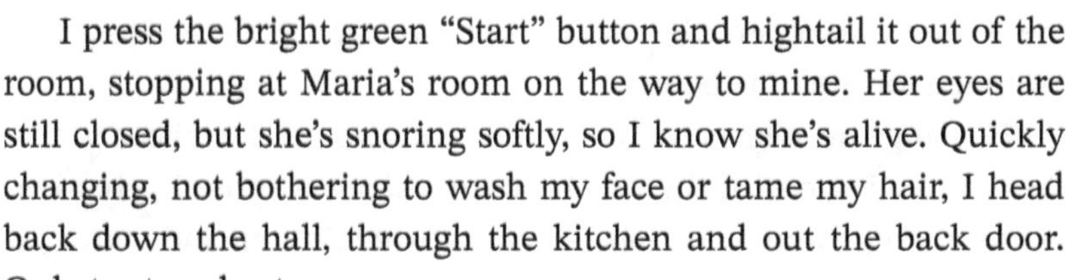

I press the bright green "Start" button and hightail it out of the room, stopping at Maria's room on the way to mine. Her eyes are still closed, but she's snoring softly, so I know she's alive. Quickly changing, not bothering to wash my face or tame my hair, I head back down the hall, through the kitchen and out the back door. Only to stop short.

Ian's sitting on one of my teak patio loungers, his ankles crossed as he stares out over the fence line to the sky beyond. He glances up at my stutter step, gives me a nod, and then looks away.

At this point I don't even want to be nice to the man, but I take the high road by not setting him on fire and resume my trek, heading for the greenhouse. I snag some pruning shears, and clip a bundle's worth of sage, careful not to cut the stalks too low. My greenhouse needs a lot of attention. Some pots are overgrown, some thirsty from the automatic drip system failing in a few places. I should have taken better care of my garden, shouldn't have let a man worth so little of my time keep me from my home.

And even though I killed him, I've somehow set him free once again.

Too many problems, not enough solutions.

Bundling the white sage with blessed twine, I hang it next to the dried bundles, the old habit of replacing what I use so ingrained, that I didn't stop to think.

I was leaving town, wasn't I?

It's not like I have a reason to stay. My shop is gone. My friends are gone, or don't want me. But even with all of that, just being in that greenhouse makes me feel better. Feeling the small spark of nature in this tiny patch of home feels like a gift—like I was given back something I lost. Nodding to myself, I step into the dry air, light the bundle of sage with a spark from my fingers, and get to work fixing the boundary to my home.

My feet rasp against the pavers as I take trudging steps up the stairs to the back door. Knowing Ian is probably only here to check on Maria doesn't take the sting out of his presence or make things any less awkward for me. But the kitchen is empty when I gather the bravery to open the back door, so my reprieve has been extended for the time being.

Hearing the television on in the living room, I make my way there, knowing out of the two brothers, Aidan is more likely to be in the living room than Ian. Aidan is watching an old movie, a black-and-white mystery I'm fond of. I say watching, but he's more like napping, his face soft, almost peaceful as he rests on the couch. I don't think he got any more sleep than I did last night, and for that I feel horrible. I softly fling the throw blanket over him, hoping the action doesn't wake him up. Nothing else to do, I head back to Maria's room to check on her.

I can't avoid Ian forever.

Ian sits at Maria's bedside, a stethoscope in his ears as he checks her heart rate or blood pressure or whatever the hell he's checking.

"How's she doing?" I break the awkward silence of Ian refusing to look at me, even though I know he knows I'm here.

"Her vitals are good. She should wake any time. Witches heal a bit faster than humans, so she may not even scar."

I'm not sure Maria would care if she did scar or not, not that the cuts to her face are grotesque —just that I don't know if my sister is vain. I don't remember her being that way, but it's been a long time.

With nothing else to say, I reply with, "Good."

Since he's taking the only seat, I rest on the edge of the bed, careful not to disturb another sleeping person in my house and take her hand. The hand itself is fine, but deep lacerations crisscross her forearms—so deep it's a wonder she kept her arm.

I hadn't noticed her right hand last night, only focusing on her left side. The wounds are closing quickly, and I don't think she'll have permanent damage, but the pain... It must have been unbearable.

Her fingers twitch in mine, and I grip them harder.

"Maria?" I call softly, not wanting to startle her. "Baby sister, you're safe. Please wake up."

Her dark-brown eyes flash open, and she frantically looks

around the room. Skittering back into the headboard, she sits up, fear embedded in every line of her face until her eyes land on me.

"Maxima," she breathes. "You came for me."

"Of course I came for you. You called, didn't you?" My tone is too light for our past. Maria has never once called for my help, not since I was cast out. She never tried to go around our mother.

A part of me doesn't blame her. I wouldn't go against Teresa if I didn't have to—if it weren't ingrained in my very DNA.

Then her arms are around me, and she's crying—huge gasping sobs of a woman at the very edge of her sanity, the very end of her rope.

"Shh, Ria. You're safe. I made you safe. You're okay." I rub her back gently like I used to do when we were kids. It helps some, but she still sobs, shaking like a leaf in my arms.

"You don't know. You can't know." She says the words over and over, a faint whisper and then louder as if she's warning me away. But I do know—probably more than she does—about the dangers that once lurked in that building.

"Try me, Ria. I found you, remember? I know exactly what was in that building."

Maria pulls out of my hug, wiping her eyes and nose with a handkerchief Ian unearths from his back pocket. Since when did this man have a fucking handkerchief? Did I drink myself into a stupor and he became an adult overnight? I try not to frown at the scrap of white fabric, and watch my sister's face instead, ignoring the man beside me.

"A man came for Mama. Walked right through our wards as if it were nothing. He wanted to talk to Mom, but she was so mad at him. Not that I blame her. They talked but she shooed me out of the room like I was a child. I'm less than a decade shy of four hundred and she shoos me out of the room. I got pissed off and left them alone. Then, when I was on the stairs, I heard a boom, and the whole place shook. I thought the building was going to come down on us. The stairs collapsed, and I went through wood." She pauses, gesturing to her right arm where the damage is the worst. "Landed on the bottom floor. Then something cut me again. I couldn't see what it was... But it was big, Maxima. So big, so strong, it threw me across the room."

"A Corax demon," I supply, to her bewilderment.

I may have looked through all of my grimoires last night to find the devil bird, but I found him. It was in the one grimoire I should have looked in first, since it was a Demonology text from Gramma. But I was drunk and not thinking straight when I started.

"A what?"

"That's what attacked you. Be happy you couldn't see it in the flesh, little sister." I try and fail to suppress a shudder. "Head of a crow, body of a man, legs of a stag. Invisible to all Ethereals and humans except for ones of demon lineage. And it smelled like rotting meat. That for sure wasn't in the textbooks."

Maria looks horrified.

"Is that thing still out there?" Hysteria begins to rise in her voice.

"No. I took care of it. It is very, very dead. Do you remember anything else?"

She nods and continues with her story. "I managed to get up, but th-the Corax thingy kept throwing me. I managed to make it back to the living room—back to Mom, but then the man grabbed her and took her."

"Who was the man? Did he have a name? Can you describe him?"

"I don't need to describe him. I know who he was. Andras. Your dad took her."

I figured as much.

CHAPTER FIFTEEN

MAX

"Don't do anything stupid, Max."

I can't believe he has the gall to say that to me. In my own house, in this room, in front of my sister. Like yesterday didn't happen. Like he didn't just throw me out like garbage. Like him refusing to even look at me, but still thinking he can tell me what to do.

Fuck. That.

Without a thought, I snap my fingers, the skin of his lips melting away and turning into one piece of flesh with no opening. I snap them again, and his butt parks in the chair, his back slamming into the upholstered wingback.

I sniff and don't spare him a glance but catch him trying to struggle from my hold out of the corner of my eye.

Maria's eyes go wide before she curls her lips into her mouth. Either from trying not to laugh or to discourage me from doing the same to her.

I turn my cold stare to him. "Don't. Tell me. What to do," I threaten through gritted teeth, seething in the wrath I've held back for far too long.

Surprise lashes through his face, and I realize he doesn't know this side of me. He doesn't know how much care I took not to hurt him, not to hurt the people around me. To fit in and be welcomed. He doesn't know how vengeful I can be or how far I've gone in my long life.

He doesn't understand what being a Rogue really means. Doesn't get that I have been used and abused, left behind in the ashes, scraping by with nothing but my grit and will to survive.

But I've always had my freedom. Always.

And I won't be told what to do.

I give him five more seconds and snap my fingers again. His lips returning to their original shape, he parts them to speak, but I cut him off.

"I have no intention of doing anything stupid. I have no intention of doing anything at all. Andras wants Teresa? They can work it out by themselves. I have no interest in what my parents need to hash out. I'm only pissed they left Maria behind. Now that she's here safe, it's not my business. Clear?"

"Crystal," he murmurs, and once again he won't look me in the eye. I'm really starting to hate that.

I snap my fingers again, letting him up from the chair, and he doesn't hesitate to get the hell out of the room. At least he's smart.

"Do I want to know why you disfigured that guy to prove a point?" Maria asks, the mirth in her voice shoving bricks of pain off my heart.

I think about it, debating whether or not I want to get into the whole Ian situation with her. "Nope. You mad?"

"Why again would I be mad at you?" She seems genuinely confused, and I hate to be the one to break it to her that when she came to me for help, I only ever intended to help *her*. Not Mom.

"I wasn't lying to Ian. I won't go look for Mom." A thread of shame skirts through me as I say the words.

"I would never expect you to." She grabs my hand. "That would *never* be your job."

She sounds compassionate, but there is a thread of something else. Something that just doesn't sound like Maria being Maria. I blink at her, surprised that she sounds... like she knows what happened.

No. She knows *exactly* what happened to me.

"You know why I was kicked out, don't you?" I don't intend it to sound like an accusation, but it does all the same. She knows more about what I went through—maybe from my mother's own mouth.

She knows. And I don't.

Maria's face would be a mask of pity if she had any for me, but that was never how my little sister rolled. Her heart hurts for me, and I almost don't want to know what it is she's about to say.

But the other part of me prays it's a good reason. Craves that it's something I can forgive my mother for. Hopes beyond hope, that for once, I'll feel even an ounce of love from my mother—even tangentially.

"And it wasn't for breaking a ward, either. Mom did it to keep you safe. To keep you out of the Royal Court and away from your family. If you were Rogue, they couldn't accept you, couldn't pull you into the fold, so the first time you messed up..." She trails off, sympathy in her every expression.

I want to cry, but my mouth forms a smile instead, even though tears fill my eyes. This is so much worse than I thought.

"She tanked my life to save it?" I chuckle, but it's a laugh of disbelief.

"I'm not saying she did the right thing. Hell, when I found out I almost went to the Witch Conclave to have your status reinstated. But she told me who your family is, told me exactly who they are. Trust me when I say, you may prefer your Rogue status after all."

"I guess I won't know, now will I?" I shrug, wiping the stubborn tears that refused to stay confined, trying to pass it off as if it doesn't burn through my gut in the worst way.

"So why did you call me? Don't you guys have a houseful of minions at your disposal?" I ask in a roundabout way what the hell they are doing in my city in the first place.

"Not anymore. Not after what happened last year," she murmurs, reminding me of the massacre in their coven home. Last year a pair of witch siblings and their ilk ripped through the witch world, slaughtering coven leaders in an attempted coup.

While some of my blood family survived, many didn't.

"You guys didn't beef up security?"

"We did, but it isn't like they travel with us. We employ other Ethereals, too. Shifters and wraiths. But we came here on witch business. It wasn't prudent to take security with us. We thought we could handle it on our own. We thought wrong." Her hand trembles as she wipes her mouth.

"Are you hungry? I'm not much of a cook, but I make a mean breakfast."

Her shaking stops, and a smile emerges from the fear lining her face. "That would be great, thank you."

"You're full of shit," Maria says as she shovels another forkful of French toast in her mouth.

I take another sip of my coffee. "What?"

"Not much of a cook, huh? I thought I was getting toast and butter not cinnamon French toast with blueberry compote and sausage links."

She also got German potatoes and biscuits, but I can't take credit for those. I didn't make them from scratch. "What? Aidan bought me groceries. I didn't want to waste them."

"I'm not complaining," Aidan says around a mouthful of food. "But explain the takeout menus to me. I thought this food was going to rot in your fridge. Instead, I get the best breakfast I've had in a while. But don't tell Aurelia I told you that or she'll kill me."

Shrugging, I set down my coffee mug, collecting the forks and butter knives, stacking them on top of my plate. "I work too much, and I work late hours. I don't want to cook food at midnight when I finally get off. Those are all the places that deliver until two."

I collect the plates, setting them into the sink and starting the water. It's almost comforting to have people in my house, sitting at my table. Feeding them. It's been so long since I've had that. It relieves the burn in my gut that I've had since Striker left, even though I was the one who told him to go. It does nothing to cure Ian's absence, but that's a whole other wound to heal.

"Where did you—" Maria begins, but her words are stolen from her by a blast in my living room. I feel it in my bones, in my teeth, through every tissue in my body.

That blast is every single one of my wards breaking at once, snapping against my flesh like a whip. At least this time they don't break my skin. Not like last time when Micah was the one breaking through them.

Once I catch my breath, I run to the living room, wanting to see who is ballsy enough to blast their way into my home. But it isn't a person at all. It's a silvery orb of light. From the light steps a specter of a man—not a ghost, but a reproduction like a recorded message.

I've seen a few of these, but not for some time. Manifestation Lights. It was something used in olden times when one wanted to send a message but didn't want to travel. Obviously, it predated the telephone, and I haven't seen one done in at least a century. Maybe two.

How someone could bust through my wards for a message boggles my mind. The man turns in a circle, the spell seeking the recipient before the message will start. He's tall, with long dark-brown hair past his shoulders, his face scruffy as if he's deciding whether or not to grow out a beard. A scar bisects his left eyebrow, cutting high on his forehead and ending mid-cheek. His eyes, though, they are what sets him apart. They aren't hazel or brown, but a piercing glowing gold that can never pass off as human. Even in this grayed-out form, they search, their power flowing through the room, even though this is nothing more than a trumped-up recording.

Something about them niggles at my brain, but those glowing orbs finally find me, and he begins to speak.

"Daughter. I have taken your mother from you. Give me the bone blade and I will return her unharmed. Fail, and I will not be as generous. Don't make me ask twice."

So, this is Andras.

His voice is calm and succinct British, and just like any other absentee dad, he knows nothing about me. If he knew anything at all about me, he would have taken Maria instead of my mother. He would have known there is exactly zero things I would do for Teresa Alcado.

Maria, however, is a whole other story.

The message fades, the silvery orb winking out of my living room much the same as it came in. I fight the urge to shrug and continue on with my life, because while I loathe our mother, Maria seems to still love her despite all her many, many faults.

That and a muttered "meh" would be considered rude.

Everyone else in the room stands frozen, like they're waiting for me to freak or issue orders or something. I skirt them both, heading back to the kitchen and start the dishes, ignoring them and their stares completely.

"That's it? Your dad breaks through your wards, informs you he'll hurt your mom to get what he wants, and you're just going to do the dishes?" Aidan asks, incredulous.

I squeeze the dish soap on the scrubby sponge and start attacking the now-cool griddle. "Yep."

"Wow. You really hate your mother, don't you?"

I think about it for a second. Do I hate Teresa? Maybe, but more, I'm indifferent. She's all but admitted hating the fact that my father left her. Hates that I look like him—even though I can't really see a resemblance. Maria said that she threw me out of the coven to save me, but I just can't see her lifting a finger to do me a favor. Every favor from Teresa has consequences. Every single one. Take the bone blade for example. I had to ask for it, beg for it, even. And what has that blade brought me? Nothing but pain and a personal poltergeist that I have to figure out how to kill.

Again.

I can't say I hate her. But love her? Want her safe and unharmed? Want to stick my neck out to help her, even though it would surely earn me not a stitch of gratitude in return?

Yeah, no. Hard pass.

"I don't hate her," I finally respond, not turning to look at him. "I just don't care about her. He should have picked a better bargaining chip."

Water sluices the suds off the griddle, and I arrange it in the drainer so it won't fall out.

Suddenly, all the windows in my kitchen crack at once, the glass making an audible creak before it shatters, blowing into the room like shrapnel.

Now what?

CHAPTER SIXTEEN

MAX

My fingers make a bloody smear on the white of my kitchen cabinets as I pull myself from my defensive crouch. Ears ringing, I glance around the room, the edges of it fading in and out. Aidan's down, Maria at his side, her jean-covered knees in the glass as she tries to rouse him.

In the fading daylight, it's harder to see, but the source of the trouble is a face I know well. In the dark, he was gray—somewhat solid. But in the light, his specter is barely there. I have a barely tangible hope that he's somehow fading away, but even I know my luck isn't that good.

I reach behind me where I feel nothing but an empty sheath, and I take my eyes off Micah to search the floor for my athame. This is a mistake. Micah doesn't care about a wounded wraith or my sister. He doesn't pay them any mind at all.

All he wants is me and my pain.

When I look up again, he's right there, pinning me against the counter, his icy hands once again burning my flesh through my long-sleeved shirt.

"I should thank your daddy for breaking your wards. Maybe after I'm done with you, I'll hunt him down and give him a big kiss," he whispers, the words hissing on each "s" like a snake. Fangs rake my neck, their frigid points not breaking the skin, but digging in all the same.

He won't bite me again, knowing he can't drink, can't consume me like he would his other victims, but he wants to. I can feel it. I was unaware ghosts could get stiffies, but here we are.

I'm afraid to even murmur a spell, knowing the pressure of my throat merely swallowing could cause the fangs to pierce the skin. I'm stuck. Pinned. Weaponless. Helpless.

"*I exilium sive spectra*," Maria calls, the red glow of her magics high in the air. It doesn't do much against Micah, but pulls him back just enough so I can move.

The light catches the silver of the athame, and I dive for it, cutting myself on broken glass to get it.

I don't throw it this time, instead I keep my hand on the hilt, slashing at Micah, driving him back, out of my kitchen. The blade slices his flesh, but it doesn't seem to really hurt him, just spilling silvery blood on my glass-covered floor. I try punching, but my fist only finds air, so unlike when he touches me.

Well, that's just unfair.

I move to slash again, but Micah spins, shimmering out of the way and appearing three feet from where he was standing? Floated? Do ghosts really stand?

I whisper the words my sister called, "*I exilium sive spectra*." *To banish a ghost.* A little on the nose, but I'd never begrudge Maria a spell that's working in a pinch. My power is greater than Maria's ever could be. Not hating on my sister, but her blood is pure witch, and she's a moon witch at that. There is no way Maria could have my power at dusk except for the three days of the full moon, and even then, it would take a full coven of witches to do what I can.

Sometimes demon blood has its privileges.

This time Micah skids back, his body losing its spectral balance and he rakes his hands across the floor, looking for purchase as if he's forgotten he's dead, all the while he curses me. Yelling at me every single thing he'll do to me.

I want to murmur the words again, but something in his cursing perks my ears up.

"You think I'm your only enemy? You think I'm the only one who wants you to burn? That blonde bitch who sent me after you? She's watching you. Always watching you. You'll never find peace. I'll make sure of that."

It's the blonde bitch comment that snags my attention. I only know one blonde bitch.

"*Immobilis exspiravit.*" I snap my fingers. "What blonde. Who sent you to me?"

Micah's face is frozen in his expression of rage, but his eyes dance as if he knows he can't speak while under this spell and removing it will set him free.

I am so going to regret this.

"*Exspiravit mobilis,*" I mutter, and he *moves*, launching himself at me like a sprinter hearing the starting pistol, ready to tackle me if he has to.

Splaying my fingers just so, I press the rune on the underside of the hilt, the athame springing into its true length, and I swing just like Aidan taught me, catching Micah under his left arm. If he were alive, that swing would have taken his arm off, but since he's a ghost it only makes him howl at me.

And then I'm not standing in front of Micah. I've been yanked away, spinning from the momentum as Ian takes my place. I didn't see him get here, I didn't hear him, but here he is fighting a battle I didn't ask him to fight. I wish I could be mad at him, but I can't.

Unlike me, Ian can touch Micah, and he does. Gripping Micah's neck, Ian shakes a rattling totem at him. The top of the totem is made from an animal's skull—a bird of some kind, possibly a raven or crow, but I've had enough of those animals to last a lifetime, so I hope not. The rest is feathers and a carved wooden handle, engraved with sigils I've only seen in my French Creole grimoires that freak me way the hell out.

Ian's speaking an old bastardized French Creole, a dialect I haven't heard before, so I have no fucking idea what he's saying.

But Micah does. He's screaming obscenities at him, cursing him and his children, promising vengeance in all its forms.

But one word catches my attention.

Messorem. Harvester. Reaper.

"Don't kill him." The ache of Micah's touch is seeping into my bones. "Someone sent him after me when he was alive. I want to know who."

Ian's chanting stops, the shaking of the totem along with it, but his hand at Micah's throat is like a vice.

"The question isn't who sent me to you. The question is who pulled the angel's strings to send a demon to your door," he rasps. "Think about that."

A blonde bitch who is also an angel? *Yeah, I only know one of those.* Rage courses through me, but by a force of will, I manage to choke it back.

"Ruby sent you to me. Did she happen to inform you why?"

Micah smiles, loving the banked rage shining in my eyes. "I didn't ask."

"Then you're of no use to me."

Micah's eyes go wide, fear in their grayed-out pools. He struggles, shoving at Ian, managing to catch him under the chin and Ian's hand loses its grip. Micah doesn't waste what is likely his only opportunity to escape. The house rumbles as he fades out, the glass levitating from the floor before exploding outward once again.

I don't come out unscathed. Ten or twenty shards of glass are embedded into the arm I used to cover my face and neck. Even more are entrenched like darts in my cabinets and walls. Maria and Ian have a few, but I seem to have taken the brunt of Micah's rage.

Lucky me.

Aidan picks that moment to startle awake, just as his brother is checking him over.

If Micah's little attack has taught me anything, it's that I need to get my wards back up—and pronto.

"Maria, can you cast?" I want to get in the yard before the sun goes down. The last thing I need is to try warding this place in the dark.

She looks up from Ian's hands as he checks his brother's vitals, her eyes a shocky kind of wide I know all too well.

"Y-yeah. I can cast."

Giving her something to do will help us both, and maybe, just maybe, I'll be able to figure out why the hell Ruby sent Micah to me. "Good, follow me. We need to re-ward this place now."

"I have plywood in the garage. See what you can make work if you can't repair the back door. This place needs to be secure and now," I tell Ian, earning me a terse nod in response.

He might have thought I created this kind of havoc on my own, but Micah's confession is proof positive that someone started this mess, and it wasn't me.

Maria follows me out the back door, into the greenhouse where I pick up my smudge stick.

"Is this all you're warding with? A smudge stick?"

I look from the burnt end of the smudge stick and back to her. Her eyes are incredulous, mouth a grim line. "What else am I supposed to use?"

A strangled sort of croak falls from her lips. "No wonder people have been breaking your wards left and right, big sister. You suck at warding. Let me show you how it's done." She brushes by me and my puny sage, snagging my pruning shears on the way.

I guess I'm about to get schooled by my little sister.

Warding her way is complicated. And takes about a bazillion ingredients—luckily, I have them all, but Fates, she has a laundry list of crap. Stones, fetishes, and so much salt. Seriously, she might make quarries go out of business.

"And then we're supposed to set it all on fire?" It may or may not be my fifth time asking.

I've done wards so complex even Aurelia can't get visions through them. So airtight wraiths can't feel their mates through them. So badass cell signals won't work. I have never, not once used a single stone, rose petal, or bird feather in any of them.

But I don't tell her that.

"Yeah. One at each corner of your home."

"Well, that will go over well with the neighbors," I mutter, but do as she says, arranging a bowl at the northern point, light it on fire, and move to the next one, trailing a line of salt from one to the next.

"I know you think your way is better, but if you have ghosts after your ass, you might want to try it my way—just for a little while. Your way keeps out living things. Not dead things."

Okay, so she has a point.

I move to the next and the next, setting a small bowl of blessed oils, dried herbs, feathers, and rocks on the raised retaining wall surrounding my property. Fucking rocks. Do rocks even burn?

"Point taken."

She takes a deep breath as if she's gearing up for something. Then she lets it rip.

"I want you to at least consider trying to find Mom," she says in a rush, as if she wants to get all the words out before I say no. She used to do the same thing when we were kids.

Pursing my lips, I pretend to think about it. "I'm not giving up the blade."

"And I don't expect you to. But if we don't find her, Andras might kill her. I know you don't like her, but Mom is really important to our coven and to the American covens. Losing her would be a blow."

"I know someone who might be able to help us, but she's not going to like us coming to her with this any more than I like having to ask her." I try to warn Maria before she gets her hopes up.

In all likelihood, Bernadette isn't going to help us. Not once she finds out who took Mom and what he wants in exchange. But she's crafty enough that she just might put aside her duty and help me. Even if it's to deceive her son.

"I'll take it."

CHAPTER SEVENTEEN

MAX

"You have got to be shitting me."

Maria has said this at least four times since we started on the trek to Bernadette's cabin in the valley, walking the two-point-three miles in the dark. I don't tell her we probably could have traveled here, and trying not to laugh at her is likely going to give me a hernia. I say "probably" on the travel bit because I have no idea what kind of booby traps Gramma has set up in this place, and I'm really not willing to find out.

I've got juice, but Bernadette, AKA Lilith, AKA all hail the Queen, AKA the baddest bitch in Hell, has *juice*. I don't know if she has traps or if she even thinks it's pertinent to set any, but I'm not going to piss her off if I don't have to.

Just like the last time, it's pitch dark when we make it to the trailhead, which looks out onto a ninety-degree cliff and the valley below. And just like last time, there is no way on this earth or any other I'm belaying down that bitch.

I look over the cliff, the moonlight catching the tips of the razor-sharp rocks just right, and start busting up laughing, unable to hold back any longer.

“Yeah, there is no way we’re climbing down there. We travel from here. It’s the reason I brought Aidan.”

Well, that and Ian refused to come. He hasn’t said much to me since he decided to end things, unless it’s to try and tell me what to do.

“I can’t take you, but Aidan can. But the ride is going to suck, so don’t bitch out and puke, deal?” The last thing she’ll want to do before meeting who we’re meeting is to puke right before the introductions.

“Fine. How bad could it be?”

Famous last words, little sister. I think those words and manage not to say them, which is good, because the veil between what I think and what I say is usually pretty thin. I only manage a shrug, and then snap my fingers, landing in the stream again, soaking my Chuck’s and startling a falcon on a nearby tree branch. Its feathers ruffle as it shrieks at me.

Sorry, bird.

Grumbling, I snatch my flashlight from my pack, signaling to them that it’s safe and to give Aidan a visual marker of where to land. Not a second later, Aidan and Maria are in the stream, and Maria is trying not to gag. I pass over my water bottle so she doesn’t heave.

“Fates, that is awful.” She sucks down more water to wash away the likely heaviness on her tongue.

Been there.

“Okay, like I said. Be nice. Don’t be an asshole, and wipe your feet. I’m going to knock on the ward. Don’t go ahead of me and cross. I have absolutely no idea what that thing will do.” I leave out the part where it won’t hurt me because I’m a blood relative.

Them, however…

I gently tap-tap-tap on the pale luminescent hex lines of the ward and wait. Not ten seconds later, the door pops open, and Bernadette flies out of the cabin.

“Maxima, dearie, I’ve missed you. I was afraid you’d hate me after that whole blade nonsense.” She rushes, stopping only when she notices I'm not alone. "Oh! You've brought guests. Come in, come in. I have brownies just out of the oven."

Bernadette gestures to Aidan and Maria to head in, but Maria stops and whispers in my ear before she passes me, "She isn't going to fatten us up and eat us, is she? Because Grimm fairy tales are there for a reason."

I bite my lip to keep from giggling and pray Bernadette didn't hear her. I shake my head "no" and give my sister big eyes. The ones that say she's going to get us in trouble. Maria got "big eyes" a lot when we were kids. Half the times I was reprimanded for being insolent, Maria was the one who made me laugh.

"Bernadette, this is my friend, Aidan, and my sister, Maria."

Bernadette takes each of their hands in turn, clasping their right hands in both of hers. She's smiling while she does it, but her eyes take a far-off quality that makes me wonder what she really sees. Does she see the future like Aurelia? Does she see the past like she did with me?

Or does she see possibilities?

I suppose I'll never know unless I ask her, but now isn't the time for that conversation.

"It seems you never visit me with good news, Maxima, and never at a more reasonable hour. Are you nocturnal? Some of us are like that," she offers, not unkindly.

"No… well, I might be. When my tattoo shop was still standing, I worked until midnight most nights, and didn't typically get home until two a.m." I say it offhandedly, but Gramma's eyes narrow at my use of the word "was" in reference to my shop.

She presses her lips together as she gestures to a light-colored sofa and a pair of chintz chairs offering us a place to sit. "Yes, well, we know who is responsible for that, don't we? I had no idea he would go after you so quickly, dear. I had no idea he even had the thought in his head."

She's referring to Andras, but everything about how things have played out in the last few days makes no sense. Why tear down my wards only to leave the safe behind? Why attack my shop? Was it to get the blade from the safe? And if it was, why use my mother as bait? Why not strike me once it was out?

And Ruby.

I'd guessed it was her, but I didn't know for sure. Micah never said her name specifically.

"I know you didn't, but there is something we need to talk about."

"Of course, dear." She sweeps her hand in the air in a circular motion, then snaps her fingers. A full tea service appears on the coffee table. "Drink your tea. It's a nice oolong."

I take a teacup and a cucumber sandwich, nibbling on the end more from nerves than actual hunger.

I've never actually seen Bernadette pissed off before, and well, if there was anything to take a normally genial person straight to the edge, it's family bullshit.

"Andras sent me a message." I pause, waiting for her to digest what I just said. I can't imagine what she must be feeling. One of her sons killed the other. To be in this position in and of itself must be torture. "He has my mother and wants the bone blade in exchange for her."

"No." The clink of her teacup hitting the saucer is slight but still makes me jump.

I spare a glance at Maria, and her eyes fill at the abrupt denial. "I understand your position, but could you tell me why he wants it? If he killed Samael, then he already has something that will kill a demon. He doesn't need the blade. So why is he going through so much trouble to get it?"

Bernadette sighs and relaxes her rigid posture, leaning back on the cushions. "Because he can? Because he's killed with it before? I made that blade ages ago in a very dark time in my life. Hell had just been made, and our tasks there made me frightened of what I would become. Hell is a place for punishment, and demons are the punishers. We were chosen by the Fates to dole out our power only to the most wicked, and at first it seemed righteous. But as the years went on... I couldn't separate myself from the punishment I gave. I made the blade and the spell, but I never married them.

And when my husband started hurting people not remanded to Hell, hurting my children, myself, started talking of war with the angels, I gave my son the blade and Teresa the spell. Your father killed my husband. Not necessarily at my request, but he had my help. The blade I planned on using to kill myself took my husband's life. That blade might not be the only one with the power to kill a demon, but it is the only one that can remand a soul, taking the soul's power for itself."

It takes a full minute to digest what she's saying. The blade that currently sits at my hip killed my grandfather and however many it took to get to him.

And that wasn't even its real purpose.

"Why did you make it so it would take the soul?"

"Because I feared with all I'd done, with all the punishment I gave, I wouldn't be worthy of the Otherside. I would go back to Hell, and I would rather be trapped in a vast nothingness than go back to that place. Spirits that have been housed inside it seek it for its silence."

A weight heavier than I would have expected settles on my heart.

I freed them.

All of them.

All of those souls.

"The break. It let them all out. Some have already come for me. Micah in particular. He said someone sent him to me—when he was alive. A blonde angel. I worry that the person who sent him to me is Ruby." Admitting this out loud is something that could get me killed. The demon-angel no-touch rule is serious. I have no doubt that if it's proven Ruby did send Micah to me it could violate the Armistice.

"If it was Ruby, then the Council will let it go. She got a demon to do her dirty work for her, that's how we've dealt with our enemies for eons—by getting someone on their side to pull a little friendly fire. Plus, dear, I hate to remind you, but you're a Rogue. No Council member could rule on the side of a Rogue, and you know it as well as I do. I don't like it, but I can't change it. I can't start the war that will end this world for just one person —even if that person is you, dearie. I'm sorry for that, but it's the truth."

I know it isn't intended to feel like a slap, but it does. Although I know why she feels this way, it still stings a little, even though in no way do I want the world to end just because Ruby is a dick.

It's the indifference that really hurts.

"I can accept that. She'll at least lose her job, right? I'm all for the world not ending, but she shouldn't have as much power or be as close to someone with power as she is if she's sending out demon kill squads. And moreover, why, though? Why me? I didn't even know her name when Micah came to me. Why send him my way when I'd never even met the woman?"

"I suppose I'll make sure Caim asks her." Her reply is curt, and I fear she's leaving something out. Like she's keeping something from me. Everything about her answers just haven't seemed right at all.

Nothing about this night is right.

It takes a full minute of silence before Aidan stands—having said almost nothing since he got here, he only nods in deference to Bernadette, and walks right out the door. The line of his shoulders vibrates in anger, and while I'd like to think it's on my behalf, I know it probably isn't.

I'm a Rogue. Why should I expect anyone to really give a shit about me? Even family.

Maria manages a polite, "Excuse me," before she follows suit.

"I know you'll do what you think is right, Maxima, but giving him that blade will surely mean all of our deaths. You must see that."

I stand, skirting the low coffee table and pressing a kiss to her forehead. I do see how giving up the blade could mean my death, but it makes me wonder how much of a stain I'll have on my soul if I don't.

I attempt to rise when Bernadette reaches for the sheath that holds the bone blade, her fingers latching onto the hilt before the spell that keeps it safe slams her back. Her face is awash in shock with threads of anger and a little bit of shame, but I can feel nothing but disappointment.

Disappointment and disillusionment.

Like I'd been robbed when I thought I had nothing to steal.

"I would have given it to you if you'd only asked."

Rising, I turn my back on my grandmother and walk out.

Once I follow Aidan and Maria outside the wards, the pain ripping a hole in my chest only growing worse as I leave Bernadette behind.

Toeing off my Chuck's, I walk in the pitch-black stream, the water cool on my feet as I stare up at the clear sky. Stars—so many and so vast—sprinkle the night sky with just enough beauty to keep me going.

Just enough goodness to wash a little of the hurt away.

I don't look at my sister, and I don't look at Aidan. I can feel their eyes on me as I make this decision—the one I don't want to make but have to.

"Okay, I'm in. Let's go get her."

CHAPTER EIGHTEEN

MAX

What does one wear when they go off on a quest to kill their father? I ponder this as I try to decide between a 1960s mod-style wiggle dress and a pair of gray skinny jeans, thick leather boots, and a tank top that says "Sunshine and Fucking Rainbows" in a circle surrounding a skull and crossbones.

I know which one will be more comfortable should the evening not go according to plan, and I know which one will irritate my mother the most. Spoiler alert: they're the same outfit, and that thought makes me smile.

It really is the little things.

Getting dressed, I make sure the sheath at my spine is secure and adjust the weapons so they can lay right under my jacket. Walking down the hall, I hear the brothers arguing in the living room, their voices carrying through the house.

"You're going to get her killed. You're going to get yourself killed. You didn't even want me to be a part of this, and now you're what, just along for the ride? What the fuck, Aidan?" There is a thud of flesh hitting flesh, but only once and no more.

I hear Aidan whisper, but I can't quite make out what he's

saying. I'd hate for someone—*cough, Maria, cough*—to catch me in this hallway eavesdropping, so I quit my hiding and walk into the kitchen.

Maria is sitting at the table, a bottle of bourbon in one hand and a glass in the other, listening to the guys bitch at each other from the safety of the breakfast nook.

"...I'm not the one who threw her away, brother. That's all on you." Aidan's deep growl is clear as a fucking bell even from in here, and I turn my eyes from the hallway leading to the living room to my sister. Her expression likely mirrors my own, eyes wide, mouth gaping open like a fish.

Maria starts snickering first, and then I follow, busting up laughing for I have no idea why. I'm not even sure I want to know why—at least not right now.

All I know is it keeps me from thinking Ian would rather I go alone than have help, and I keep laughing to make sure that particular hurt doesn't stick its barb right in my heart.

Once my laughter dies down, I focus on Maria. She has emptied that glass twice since I came in the room, and I wonder if I should be worried.

"You mad?"

She focuses on me—a little drunkenly, but I'll take it. "Why would I be mad at you? I know why you don't want me to go"—She raises her glass—"I'm a liability."

She can't quite mask the hurt in her voice, though, and that really sucks.

"Baby girl, you aren't a liability. I have every faith you can hold your own. You are strong and capable, and a fucking badass. But you're my weakness. If Andras had taken you, there would have been nothing I wouldn't have done to get you back. If he takes you now, I won't be able to kill him. I won't be able to do anything but get you back."

Her eyes mist over, and she takes another sip of bourbon. "Even though you got left behind?"

"Even then." I tilt down to kiss her forehead. "Always."

"But you'll have my brother out there with you." Ian's voice lashes the air behind me.

"Yes, and you'll be here protecting my sister. Even-Steven."

Ian levels me with a glare that could cut glass. "You'll bring him back."

"Or die trying."

"That's what I'm afraid of."

We manage to track Andras—or rather my mother—to Savannah. Savannah is a witch "hub," of sorts. The Southeast Coven leader even has a home here. I'd met her once after she'd been attacked in said home, nearly all of her security taken out on the same day my mother and sister were attacked.

That wasn't a great time to be a witch leader.

The locator spell tagged my mother in the middle of the historic district, and I'd taken great pains to map out the area since I was in no way familiar with the city.

I tend to stay out of witch hubs.

"You sure you want to be here?" Aidan asks under his breath as we traverse a sidewalk of the canopied street. Savannah is known in some circles as "spook central" with its ghost tours and such. A lot of battles were won and lost here, a lot of dead, and not just old dead. I assume just like in Denver, the veil is thin here, and there has been enough death, enough blood soaked into the ground to power the ley lines until the end of time.

"No, I don't want to be here. At least if we run into a spook, you can eat him. What the hell am I going to do? Stab at him? Make him run away? I swear to the Fates this place is creepy." I try and fail to suppress a full-body shudder.

"I meant with your parents." Aidan gives me a sideways glance like I must be some special form of stupid.

"Oh."

"Yeah, *oh*."

"Honestly, I'm almost four hundred. I should be over my parental issues by now, right?"

Aidan stops walking. "Why should your age have anything to do with it? They're your parents, and they failed you."

Unable to give him a good answer, I simply shrug and keep walking, leaving him to trail behind me. My mother is in one of the dozens of houses that border Forsyth Park, and I won't know which one until we get a bit closer.

Maria spelled one of my rose-quartz crystals to get hotter the closer I was to her, which is fine in theory, but only works if you're really close.

"Anything yet?"

"A general warmness. Let's get closer to the spot I pegged on the map and see if this thing actually works. It's not like I can just keep an eye out for warding lines. This place has magic out the ass, almost every house is lighting up like a damn Christmas tree."

Witch hubs. It's no wonder I picked Denver as my home. Shifters and angels roam those parts. Sure, there are a few witches thrown in, but they tend to stay in cities with a bigger base of power like New Orleans, Savannah, and Boston.

Forsyth Park is all but deserted, there are a few people out giving Fido his last stroll, a few revelers still cackling about a ghost tour they just took, but everyone else is smartly hanging up their hat for the night. I snap my fingers, arriving a few hundred feet away from the pin in the map, Aidan arriving beside me.

"How come you don't puke when you do that, but whenever I take you anywhere it's chunks city?"

Just thinking about it makes me want to dry heave. "Because I'm not using another species' magic?"

"But demons and wraiths aren't far off from each other. It shouldn't be that bad."

He's probably right, but then again, I'm not all demon, now am I? Shrugging, I keep a lookout for visitors. "Don't ask me. I just work here."

Moving closer, I can peg the house. To call it a mansion would be too broad a statement, and yet there is nothing else I could call it. Built probably in the 1800s, everything about the home is a work of art. From the moldings to the columns to the garden. Everything is arranged to be pleasing to the eye, and yet... That house holds two of the worst people ever created.

It's a wonder how many Ethereal families are just like mine. Where the cast-offs are always on the outside looking in.

I feel the coldness first, a freezing caress on the back of my neck. It stops me in my tracks, afraid that I've just imagined it, and even more afraid that I didn't.

"Aidan." His name is barely a breath on my lips.

"I feel it."

Trembling, I pull the athame, pressing the rune to expand the blade. The streetlights flicker, barely keeping lit under the strain of power heading for us, the city practically vibrating under my feet. What sounds like the wind howling perks up my ears. I know it isn't really the wind, even though I have a distinct hope that if someone were to peek out their window, they don't see what I am.

"What the hell is that?" Aidan shouts over the din, and I hate to have to tell him the truth.

"Souls. Hundreds, thousands. Micah brought friends."

It's a trap. Andras never wanted to exchange the knife for my mother. All he wanted was for me to get close, to leave the safety of my city and pounce like the dickhead he is. He wants the blade, but leaving me alive is just too much of a liability.

The ground vibrates hard enough to nearly shake me off my feet. I can't stop this. I can't even fight against it. I was stupid to come here in a place soaked in so much death, in a place where the dead are celebrated.

I close the distance between Aidan and me, not using him like a shield, but the fact that he's bigger than me and is a better fighter, well...

"How many souls can you eat at a time? Is it like a one by one thing, or can you unhinge your jaw like a snake?" I'm only half-kidding. I'd take a wraith with indigestion over dying in the midst of this shit any day.

Aidan peers down at me, his face awash in what I can only peg as regret. He's fighting his phase—his eyes flickering back and forth from full black to pale green. Against his will his fangs lengthen, his jaw popping and reforming. Black mist cradles him in its embrace, swirling around his legs, his arms. "I can't take them all. Sssome of them don't desssserve to go."

His words hiss as he says them, the snake-like quality of all wraiths coming to the surface. He means to Hell. Some of them are good souls tricked into doing the bidding of someone else. After what Bernadette described of Hell, I wouldn't be able to send someone there unless they really deserved it. Meaning we could die if we stay.

Meaning we *will* die if we stay.

"Max, we need to go," he shouts, and I glance back to the house my mother is likely in. Where she's waiting for me to come get her. I promised I would do this—save her—but I also promised I would keep Aidan alive.

And I can't do both.

Aidan grabs my hand, pulling me, running farther from the house that holds my mother. I feel the lift, the pull of his wraith ability tugging on me, ripping me apart bit by bit.

Then Aidan's hand is ripped from mine, and all I feel is cold—the frigid aching burn of the clutches of a spirit. The warmth of the August night is all but gone, all that is left is cold, hard hands tearing at my hair, my skin. Micah's face appears right in front of me, and all I can do is hope Aidan got out, and he's smart enough not to come back.

"You're some kind of stupid, aren't you? Instead of staying behind those wards where I can't get to you, you come here of all places. Don't you know, Maxima? The dead have power here," he murmurs in my ear, chuckling.

I scream when he presses the tip of his freezing finger against my cheek. This time my skin doesn't just burn with a bout of frostbite. This time I can actually feel the skin cells die.

"Why? You said someone told you to go after me. Why are you still doing their bidding? You're dead!" I scream in his face, wishing he was actually corporeal so I could spit in his face too.

"You should know, Poppet, even death doesn't break a contract." He seems so pleased with himself, as if death makes no difference to him. As if he might be getting something out of the deal.

Micah's fingers latch around my throat, the burning, squeezing strength in them cutting off my breath, freezing my skin and deeper. Reaching into my body and snuffing the flame that is me. My body goes slack, and some of the cold on my arms fade away. I can't tell if it's from spirits letting me go or from shock. The tips of my boots frantically scrape the pavement, the athame falling from my loose fingertips.

In the distance, I hear Aidan's roar of frustration, of pain. Wherever he is, he's losing—the honor he clings to so fiercely is failing him this time.

I only have one weapon I can reach, and I swore I wouldn't unsheathe it unless I had to. This seems like a "have to" kind of situation. My fingers scramble for the hilt of the bone blade, pulling it free. Micah doesn't notice me moving, his once-ice-blue eyes focused more on my throat where his hands are squeezing the life right out of me.

I slash at his arm, doing anything to break the hold he has on me, and I'm rewarded with sweet air when his grip loosens and falls. Falling to my hands and knees, I take a second to catch my breath before I slash and stab at anything I can reach, the black specter of the souls swirling around the pair of us.

"He said the blade couldn't touch me anymore." Micah cradles his wrist, disbelief written all over him as he stares at the wound the blade created. Blood—black as night and twice as thick—pours from the gash in his arm.

"I guess he lied." I stagger to standing, ready to face him head-on, prepared to kill the demon who has haunted me since the day he came into my life.

Since the day he was hired to ruin me.

Micah bares his fangs to me. Forgetting his arm, he braces himself, ready to take me on. Out of the two of us, I'm definitely the worse for wear, and I don't know if I'll be able to win this time around. Micah strikes, his talons slicing through my jacket and the thin fabric of my shirt into my belly, the warm gush of my blood cooling while tainted with his spirit.

"This is how I killed Melody. Just like this," he hisses in my face, the agony of that statement worse than the killing blow he's made to my middle.

And then he's gone. I'm out of Micah's clutches and in warm arms while another man—a man made of darkness and glowing golden eyes attacks him with a sword made of pale bone. The ally flickers back and forth from human-shaped to smoke, and I recognize him.

Andras.

I don't know why he's helping us, but I can't worry too much about that right now.

Turning from the melee, I look up to see Aidan hovering over me, keeping me warm as my blood leaks from my body. He's crying, his tears carving tracks down his filth-covered face, and I don't know why. My death doesn't mean much to anyone but Aurelia and Maria, and even then, Maria's lived almost her whole life without me. Ian might care for a minute, but my death is to be expected. He won't mourn for very long.

But of all people, I would have thought Aidan would take my death in stride. The fact that he isn't is a balm on my battered soul. I want to reassure him, but I'm a little too focused on breathing to think up anything particularly profound.

"Don't wo-worry. I'll be right b-back," I mutter, the heat and strength and life pouring from me as I struggle to drag the blade into its sheath.

"You damn well better be," he orders, guiding my fingers so I can seat the blade.

I want to tell him to be careful.

But I never get the chance.

CHAPTER NINETEEN

AIDAN

Max's mouth parts as if she's about to tell me something when her eyes roll back in her head, and her body goes slack. Blood stains her full bottom lip like one of her lipsticks, and I feel the loss of her light like a gut punch. Shaking her, I plead for her to wake up.

But just like in our lessons, she doesn't listen to me.

I don't have much time. If I want her safe, if I want her to come back, I need to get her out of here.

"Answer me!" the man—Andras—shouts, his fingers around Micah's throat. I've never seen anyone but my brother able to touch a ghost, but Andras is. "Tell me where my brother is."

Micah's lips tip up, black blood staining his teeth in a grotesque smile. Andras growls at him before taking Micah's head with the edge of a bone sword. How he can do that to a man that's already dead I don't know, and I don't care. I'm just sorry I didn't get to do it myself.

Andras wipes off the blade and slips it over his shoulder into a sheath draped across his back. When he sees Max, he does a stutter step, his nostrils flaring, scenting the blood. He rushes us, and my instincts kick in. I gather Max in my arms, protecting her and baring my fangs to the bastard also known as her father.

"Give me my daughter, wraith."

"Over my cold, dead body."

I know I can't beat him. I know it would be the dumbest thing I've ever done to try. But I also know there is no way I'm leaving this woman unprotected. There is no way I'm letting this man take her from me.

Not now, not ever.

"Look, I know you don't trust me, but I can save her. I can heal her. Just..." He trails off, "Just let me try, okay?"

My nostrils flare of their own accord as I take in his scent. And I feel nothing. No hunger, no thirst for the soul of an evil man.

Just nothing. It doesn't make sense. An evil man kidnaps. An evil man sends spirits to do his dirty work. An evil man orders the death of his daughter.

"You... you aren't evil." It comes out as an accusation, and it is. His scent doesn't make sense with all the wrong he's done. For all that he's taken.

"I know I'm not, but that doesn't stop people from believing it. Look, these spirits aren't going to just go away. They're drawn to the blade." He nods to the bone blade sheathed at Max's hip. The one I had to help her put away because she was too weak to do it. "We need to go inside the ward."

The screams of the swarming souls circle around us, spirits teeming, roiling to come closer but they don't.

"Why aren't they coming closer? Why don't they just attack?"

He taps the hilt of the blade across his back. "Because they know if they do, I'll cut them down. It's kind of what I'm known for."

"Fine. Lead the way." I gather Max in my arms once again and follow Andras.

I don't trust him. I probably won't ever trust a man who could leave Max behind—a man who could treat her like nothing. But I don't have to. All I need is for her to be healed, and she can drive this train when she wakes up.

If she wakes up.

I feel the burn of it when we cross the ward, and stutter to a stop when I see a woman on the porch who wasn't there before. She looks eerily familiar.

"For Fates sake, Andras. You bring her back to me like this?" The woman reaches for Max, but I pull her away.

"I'm her mother, wraith. Give her to me."

I know all about Teresa Alcado, and I'd trust the demon with Max over this woman.

"Never." I growl with as much menace as I can muster, flashing my fangs. "Not you. Never you. She'd rather die and come back than have you touch her."

I only know this because she told me as much. Max had said those words in the middle of a session. I'd tried to piss her off, not realizing her mother was the ultimate trigger. She almost took my head off that day, and I never brought her up again.

Her mother will never touch Max on my watch. Not as long as I'm breathing. Teresa looks like I've slapped her, but I don't give a flying monkey fuck.

Andras steps in between me and Teresa, tucking her hands behind his body. "She needs my blood. We can do this inside where she'll wake up comfortable or out here, but either way she doesn't have time. She's fading."

Following him inside, I settle on a deep-seated couch with her on my lap, the blood staining the light fabric. I'm not letting her go, and no one says a word to me telling me I can't.

Not that I'd listen.

Andras holds his hand out for a blade, and Teresa passes one over. Immediately, he slices his wrist lengthwise, pouring blood on Max's stomach. Andras even presses his fingers into the wound at his wrist and wipes some of his blood over the blackened burn on her cheek.

I watch as the wound on her face lightens, turning the pink of scar tissue before evening out to the deep tan of Max's skin. Her stomach is a whole other story. There is organ damage, tissue damage. Andras has to slice the skin of his wrist several times, draining himself to save his daughter's life.

Maybe he doesn't know how many times Max has died and come back. Maybe he doesn't think she'll come back this time. Maybe he's just trying to gain her favor.

Either way, I still don't trust the man. I'm just glad he wasn't lying about healing her.

The rest we'll deal with when she wakes up.

MAX

Rolling over in the arms of a man you have no idea you fell asleep on is hella awkward. Eyelids flashing open, I take stock. I'm looking at a throat. A very handsome throat, but a throat, nonetheless. Said throat is attached to a bearded chin. Then I lose sight of the chin because arms tighten, legs pin, and I'm stuck, plastered to a considerable man chest. I resist the urge to fondle said man chest, but the urge is strong.

Wriggling, I free a hand, pushing it between us so I can use it as a fulcrum to lever off Aidan's pecs. Sweet Fates, please don't let me start perving on Ian's brother. I seriously don't have time to deal with the drama that would come from me having a crush on my pseudo-ex's family members. No one has time for that.

Aidan's eyes flash open, and I'm crushed against said chest. Again.

"Freedom!" I yell, muffled by Aidan's shirt. Then I'm snapping my fingers and he's on the floor.

"The fuck?" he grumbles from the hardwood floor... that I've never seen before. This whole place is unfamiliar.

Peeling myself from the couch cushions, I clap eyes on my parents sitting side by side on the opposite love seat, their hands entwined.

Together.

I'm dreaming. I have to be. I've never seen my parents in the same room. Ever. I've never even met my dad, and except for a Manifestation Light, I wouldn't even know what the man looks like. My mother said she hated him, but she doesn't seem to mind him now.

Confused, I meet my mother's eyes. "Explain."

Before my mother can open her mouth, Andras starts laughing. "Fates, Essa, she's just like you."

While I'm sure he's having a good old time with his "bonding moment," comparing me to my mother is a sure-fire way to get on my bad side.

"Take that back right now." Somehow one of my green sparking fingers finds its way pointed at Andras as he keeps laughing—harder now that my ire has surfaced.

"I'm sure this whole family reunion shit is long overdue, but we have bigger problems than who resembles who. Mass of souls. Right outside the door." I lean over the side of the couch and give Aidan a grateful look, throwing a hand out to help him up since I was the one to toss him off in the first place.

"What the fuck happened, and why are we in the same room with the man who tried to have me killed?" I mutter under my breath as Aidan takes his seat next to me.

"He didn't. He saved your life. Let him talk and then we're out of here. Deal?"

Meeting his eyes, I see the honesty in them, and I can't help but give him a nod.

"A horde of spirits attacked. You were injured, Andras saved your life." Teresa's words are succinct, but they paint a good picture of what happened.

"Thank you? But why? I'm immortal. I die, I come back, rinse, repeat. Unless someone decides to kill me with one of those bone blades, I'm unkillable. Why save me? Unless you want something."

"While I confess I do want a favor, saving you seemed like the honorable thing to do. Your mate had no qualms about it."

"He isn't my mate," I contest, and then Andras' eyes take on a weird sort of glow, bumping them up from just yellow to a luminescent golden, and I remember where I'd seen those eyes before.

The man at the ward in 1642.

"You." My voice is a low growl of indignation. "You got me burned at the stake. You were the man trapped at the ward. You made me save you."

At least he has the good sense to look ashamed. "I never meant for that to happen. Fates, this is such a mess. Can we start over? Hi, I'm Andras, your dad. I'm known in most circles as a gigantic ass, but I'm a delightful person once you get to know me."

I play along. "Nice to meet you. I'm Max, your daughter. I'm a Rogue because you forced me to take down a ward that protected my entire coven, which got me burned at the stake. Great. We've done the introductions. What's it going to take to get my mother out of your clutches?"

"I was looking for you," he lies.

"You were looking for the bone blade you had my mother hide. Try again."

Andras explodes, standing from the couch as if he has the right to be angry with me. "She wasn't hiding you well enough! My family was coming to look for you. So..."

Realization dawns and I find my feet. "So, you worked together to tank my life. You two set me up. How did you even know I would survive? Huh? Did that even cross your minds? Did you even care?"

"We knew you would survive," Teresa whispers, tears gathering in her eyes. "You died once, on the crossing from Spain. I held you in my arms for two days, hoping you would come back to me. On the second day you drew breath again as if you were never sick, and I knew you were more like your father than me. It was the last time you were ever ill."

That only takes away a minor facet of the pain. All this trouble to get me out of the family line, but who in the family is left?

"Your father is dead. Your brother is dead. Your mother has been relatively decent to me. Who are you keeping me from that you haven't already killed?"

"You speak of what you can't possibly know. I didn't kill Samael."

"Then who did?"

"No one. He isn't dead."

CHAPTER TWENTY

MAX

N*o one. He isn't dead.*

Then what the hell am I doing here? Why would the Council order Andras' death if he hadn't just killed his brother? Why would they send me to kill him if he'd done nothing wrong?

"Then why does the Council want you dead?" Aidan asks the question that has been brewing inside my head for the last few minutes.

Andras seems as if he is being overly taxed by having to explain the current mess we're all in. "He faked his death with the help of one of the Council's minions. They believe he is dead. He's trying to pin the murder on me to keep me out of the Council seat."

"And how is that going to work? He pins the murder on you, you get killed, and then he what? Just shows back up with a 'Just kidding!' act and no one's the wiser? I smell bullshit."

Andras chuckles as if I've said something cute. "He doesn't plan for there to be a Council at all. He wants me out of the way so he can murder them one by one and start the bloody war. You know, the one that will happen when a demon kills an angel?"

"Then why pin it on you at all?"

"Payback for killing our father, most likely. It's a way to drive me out of hiding so he can keep me out of the way. He plans to kill our mother *and* every other Council member *and* their second. I'm the diversion."

And I thought my drama with Teresa was bad. I can thoroughly attest that as bad as it got with us, at least I never plotted her murder.

"So, was it you who burned down my tattoo shop or your brother?"

"Samael. He knew you had the blade"—He nods at the bone knife in its sheath—"He needed it out in the open."

"I kinda wish he would have tried to open that safe. It would have saved us all a lot of time. Let me guess, you need it to kill him. Why this blade? Isn't there another weapon to kill a demon? Didn't I see you slaughtering souls with one?"

"I was the chief torturer in Hell once upon a time. My blades only harm the dead. There are a few weapons to kill a demon, but the one at your hip is the only one on this plane, making it the only one I can get to."

"But why—"

Andras stands again, his power and rage growing, filling the room. This isn't the genial man I met just a few minutes ago, the one ready to tell his side. This is the man I expected him to be. "I've answered enough of your questions. Samael has already attacked me more than once. I need that blade. Give me what I asked for."

But he never asked, not really. He swindled, tricked, and threatened. He never asked me for help, only demanded. That's all he's ever done.

"No. And fun fact, that's the same answer I gave the Council when they asked me to kill you. Having this blade out in the open is just going to get people killed. You said it's the only one on this plane that can kill a demon, meaning he plans to steal it from you once you have it. I should lock this thing back up in the safe and drop it in the fucking ocean."

It's meant as a threat, and he takes it as such. His eyes glow bright, showing that underneath the man before me, he isn't much more than the devil I always assumed he was. Then I'm talking to no one, Andras disappears, reappearing behind Aidan, one hand on Aidan's chin, the other on the top of his head, ready to snap Aidan's neck. Aidan's a big man, but my father is bigger.

"No! Andras, what are you doing?" Teresa screams, disbelief in her every move. She didn't think he was capable of this.

Honestly? I didn't either. I also never expected the ripping of my heart when I see Aidan in danger, never thought I'd feel this weight of helplessness and dread. I've never had to protect him before, and I find the need of it more than I can bear.

"I will snap his neck like a twig, Maxima. You don't know me, but I know you. Being Rogue, you have so few friends, and this man is one of the only ones left standing. It won't hurt me to kill him. But it will hurt you. Give me the blade, and I'll let him go."

Aidan tries to wriggle in Andras' hold, but Andras only tightens his grip, hard enough for his talons to break skin on Aidan's neck, making him wince.

"Don't do it, Max. Don't you give him shit!" Aidan commands, and I want to do what he says.

I really want to, but I can't. My eyes trail over the blood dripping down his neck, back up to Aidan's pale-green eyes. He's always been the brave one. The stoic one. The one to show no fear.

But there's fear there now.

Andras tightens his grip again, and a pained gasp escapes Aidan's mouth. I don't expect the wet to hit my eyes, the fear dragging the tears from me against my will.

I pull the blade from the sheath Barrett spelled so only I could remove it, balancing the knife in my palm and hand it over. I don't spare Andras a glance. I'm still staring at Aidan as Andras lets his hold go lax to grab the blade. When the heat of Andras' gaze leaves my face, I do the only thing I can, I wink at Aidan. As luck would have it, he catches my hint, smoking out from Andras' grip, traveling out of danger and giving me just the diversion I need.

Reaching behind my back, I rip the athame from its sheath, slicing his arm just as his fingers close around the bone blade.

What I'm not prepared for is the backhand that comes afterward. Andras has enough power in that single strike to knock me across the room and into a wall.

And then it's lights out.

My mother's concerned face is the absolute last one I thought I'd see.

"Maxima, honey, I need you to get up!" She shakes my shoulders, her hands hard on what is likely a monster of a bruise.

"I'm up, I'm up." I groan, pushing myself up from my crumpled heap behind the love seat.

The room sways a bit and I blink once, hard, trying to reorder what I see now to the room it used to be. Honestly, it looks like a bomb hit it. The couch is a smoking ruin, the walls half-charred and still smoking. Aidan's nursing a bloody nose and a gash on his upper arm. Teresa's cheek is slightly burned, and she's holding her body just so, meaning her ribs are either bruised or broken.

"What the hell happened?" I ask, more to myself than anyone else because I can tell what happened. Andras kicked our ass, that's what happened.

"After Andras hit you, well... I got a little upset." There's the mother I know. Teresa Alcado has never been one to answer a direct question. "I might have set him on fire a little bit."

"I'll say. He got away, or am I going to find him vaporized under the couch?"

"He got away," Aidan answers from across the room. Oh, he's pissed, and I really hope it's not at me.

"Shit. What are the odds of him winning against Samael? Ball park?" I ask my mother, who probably knows what we're going up against better than either of us do.

Her wince is all the answer I need. Aces.

At just that second, someone pounds at the front door, and I've never prayed so hard that someone called the cops in my life, and I start to wonder where the hell my life went wrong that I'd hope it was a cop instead of another Ethereal. I stagger, pulling myself the rest of the way up, ready to fight if I need to. But when no one answers the door, a voice calls that I never expected to hear.

"Max, open the damn door!"

Striker. Then, I'm jumping over the tattered remnants of furniture and yanking open the door so fast it bangs against the wall and bounces back to knock me in the shoulder. Which hurts like a bitch.

Striker looks scruffy and worn, tired in a way only grief can accomplish. His blond mop of curls never looked so good, though, and soon I'm wrapped in the biggest bear hug ever. I didn't realize how much I missed the big lug.

"You sure know how to cause a ruckus, Maxie. I heard from a little bird you needed help."

"Gramma?" I wonder if his little bird is my grandmother.

"No, Maria. But I was already on the case. I've been tracking the situation for some time—since a little after I left actually. Your family tree is a little fucked up, Princess."

Ugh. I hate that word. I'm a Rogue. I'm not princess of shit.

"Well, you're not wrong. Striker, you know Aidan, and this is my mother, Teresa."

Striker eyes her up and down like a snake about to strike, and my mother does the same, only one better.

"Which one of these men are you with, Maxima? Or are you creating a harem of men at your disposal?"

If only she knew my sex life has been as dry as the Sahara for what seems like years.

"Not to be a bitch or anything, but fuck you very much, Mother. Just because covens are usually all female doesn't mean I have to surround myself with a bunch of women. Just because that's how it's always been done doesn't mean that is the only way it can be done. I have friends who I don't sleep with who also come equipped with penises."

I turn to Striker. "Is it penises or penni?"

Striker chuckles. "Penises, sweet cheeks."

My mother looks like I just hit her in the face with a baseball bat. That'll teach her.

"You said you've been tracking the situation. Do you have any idea what's going on?" I ask Striker, because honestly, I have absolutely no idea who to trust. Do I trust Andras who has shown he would rather hurt me and mine to get what he needs?

"I've been tracking Samael. He is alive. Caim and a few of the others never believed he was really killed but needed to keep their reservations quiet. I've been following him for weeks. We're going to need that bone blade of yours if we want to stop him."

I huff out a sigh, perching on what's left of the couch. "That'll be a problem. Andras has the blade. Maybe we can go to Bernadette, see if maybe she can track it since she made the damn thing."

Striker shifts his feet, adjusting the collar of his shirt like he doesn't want to say what he's about to, but in true Striker fashion has to say the thing even if the thing is going to start some shit. "I wouldn't do that."

"Why not," my mother pipes in, finally over her shock of penis talk. "She would be one of the few who could track it."

Striker steps back, really looking at my mother. I see the debate warring behind his eyes. No one would know this but me, no one who hadn't known Striker as long as I had. He was questioning whether or not he could trust her. Whether or not she was worth his time or trust. "Because I just left Samael, and he was headed right for Bernadette. We can't trust her."

Aidan and I exchange a glance. In it is a single solitary thought. *Fuck.* Knowing what we know about Samael's plan, Striker has it wrong.

Bernadette isn't with Samael—I saw her face when she told me her son was dead. No one can fake that kind of grief. And if I know my father, he knows exactly where his brother is. With that Fates forsaken blade in his possession.

No. Bernadette isn't in league with Samael at all.

What she is, however, is a sitting duck.

CHAPTER TWENTY-ONE

MAX

"Where are Andras' weapons?" I ask my mother while searching the floor for mine. Aidan helps me move what's left of the couch where the athame seems to have escaped.

I remember dropping it when Micah nearly killed me, and I can only assume Aidan was the one to snag it for me. The sheath at my hip feels empty, and I realize I am the biggest idiot on the planet for handing the blade over to my father.

"I—I don't know."

"You mean to tell me you've been here for twenty-four hours, and you haven't searched the place yet?"

And then my eyes go wide as I catch her blush. Teresa has been too busy diddling Dad to look too hard at her surroundings.

"You were hate-fucking your way through four hundred years of drama while my baby sister was bleeding to death in a damn closet, hiding from a Corax demon? What the fuck, Mother? Do you not give a shit about either one of your kids?" I didn't start that tirade yelling, but I damn well finish it that way.

My mother wrings her hands, staring at her feet instead of

meeting my eyes. Shame. This is what shame looks like on my mother. I thought I'd never see the day.

"The demon attacked and Andras picked me up and got me out of there. I couldn't get to her in time and then when we were safe, I tracked her. I knew she was with you. I knew she was safe, and it wasn't like Andras was going to let me go anywhere."

"You didn't try to leave, did you? Your baby daddy broke through all my wards, leaving me defenseless while he delivered the message that he was holding you hostage. You weren't a hostage. You were a willing participant to his fuckery."

I swear to the Fates if she tells me she wasn't I will punch her right in the mouth.

"I don't have time for this. You are staying behind. Inform the Council of what we've learned. Make sure they know Samael is alive and is coming for them." I bang out the front door like my ass is on fire, Striker and Aidan at my heels. Dawn is fast approaching, and for some reason, the light on the horizon doesn't make me feel any better.

"Oh, and Mother? Say hi to Barrett for me," I toss over my shoulder. Let her make of that what she will.

I don't quite make it down the little sidewalk to the gate where the ward ends, before I slam into an invisible wall of magic that halts me before I can go anywhere. I know exactly what this is. This is Teresa Alcado not getting her way and throwing a temper tantrum.

I don't even turn around before the door opens, and my mother's voice whips the air behind me even though it is just over a whisper.

"I love you, Maxima, even if you think I don't." She huffs a breath before she begins speaking again, this time the words taking my breath away. "I bless you with all that I am, and all that I will be. May you have safety on your travels. May your aim always be true. May you see what others cannot. May your victories far outweigh your losses. May your losses teach you, and may your love guide you."

In her blessing, Teresa walks barefoot, circling us seven times.

At the end, she slices her thumb with an athame, pressing the bloody digit into the skin of my chest just below my collar bone. I don't look but I sense she does the same to Striker and Aidan, blessing them just as she has me.

She stops right in front of me again, and it's then I notice my mother is far shorter than I am. She always seemed larger than life, but now I see her, really see her. She makes mistakes, she's stubborn, she does what she thinks is right even if it seems wrong. Ugh. We are more alike than I'd care to admit.

She presses her lips together so hard they turn white around the edges before she lets them go. "Be safe. Be smart. Survive. Understand?"

I blink through tears and nod. She presses the athame in my hand—the same one she used to cut her thumb—snaps her fingers, and then she's gone in a flash of red light. I glance down, noticing the athame looks a lot like the one in the sheath at my spine. Pulling mine free with trembling fingers, I compare them side by side.

They're identical.

The athame I've carried for years—through everything—has been my mother's all along.

"Am I hallucinating, or did your mother just do a nice thing?" Aidan asks behind me, lightly dropping a hand to my shoulder in comfort.

"I'd like to think it was a dream, but I'm not that lucky. Does this mean I have to start liking her now?" I'm joking, but only a little.

"Nah," Striker says, letting me off the hook.

I notice his Tesla parked at the curb. "You got anything decent in the trunk?" I point to the ostentatious vehicle. "I don't think a pair of athames are going to cut it."

"Oh, *sweetheart*." His grin turns positively evil. "Do I ever."

This time I don't make Aidan walk the two-point-three miles into the ass end of nowhere before the three of us travel into the valley, me on my own and Striker with Aidan, picking a spot further in the trees instead of out in the open near the stream. Unlike my usual reaction to wraith travel, Striker is no worse for wear. The fucker doesn't look even a little green, and I don't know if I should be irritated or proud.

Dawn is still a few hours off in central Colorado, and my eyesight isn't as acute as Aidan's, but I still catch the crouched, malformed demons lurking in a perfect circle around Bernadette's cabin just outside her ward.

My breath catches as I grip Aidan's wrist. "Can you see them?" I murmur, trying not to move, not to breathe. Corax demons are invisible to most Ethereals, and I don't know if my mother's blessing helped the boys see what they normally wouldn't.

"Yes. This was the thing you sent us away to fight on your own? I ought to tan your ass for letting us leave you like that."

I peel my eyes from the dozen Corax demons just chilling, waiting for us to arrive to ring the dinner bell, to check if Aidan's serious.

He is. He so is. His green eyes flash with indignation and something else. Something I can't place. Not fear, not anger. I don't know *what* it is.

"You should have left with us," he growls, his eyes flashing wraith black.

Honestly, he's probably right, but I can't change the past.

"At least I'm not heading into this fray by myself?" I whisper, wincing, trying not to shrug it off. Aidan looks like he might wrap me in bubble wrap and mail me home if I do that.

Striker sidles up beside me. "What do you think? Knock-out spell? Slowing spell? Any fucking spell that makes us not those monsters' dinner, I'm all for it."

"It's not like I can just pull a spell out of my ass," I whisper-hiss, trying not to alert the gigantic scary monsters that torture people in Hell for a living that we're there. "I need their blood, tissue, something."

Hang on. I stabbed one through the skull with my athame. I don't know if I killed it true dead, but that isn't the point. I might still have some blood on the blade. I yank the athame free, pressing the rune to expand the blade.

There.

In a groove that runs the length of the top of the blade is a long black streak. Corax blood.

I examine the blade. "Never mind. I have some." Reaching into the pack of witchy supplies Striker had in his car—bless him—I pull a vial of salt. Maria can have all the ingredients in her spells if she wants to, but nothing beats raw power, fire, and salt.

"I don't have enough blood to knock them all out, but I can slow them down."

I murmur words I'd used on another demon not too long ago, slowing his magic to a crawl, and this time, I'm not wounded. Drawing a circle of salt, I snap my fingers, letting the flame of my magic rise in my hand. Muttering the words, I let the flame of my magic heat the blade.

Subsisto, tardo, confuto, concesso, subflamino, insisto, conquiesco, finis.

I pour salt over the tang of the blade, letting the granules stick to the thick, tar-like blood.

Subsisto, tardo, confuto, concesso, subflamino, insisto, conquiesco, finis.

Passing the flame of the blade again, the blood bubbles, boiling until there is nothing left.

Smiling, I peer around Aidan's bulk, spying on the big malformed barriers between us and the cabin. One of them staggers.

Yep, it's working.

"I don't know how long we have, so be quick. Beheadings are hard to come back from, trust me, so go with that. Also, Striker, you may want to phase," I suggest, remembering the thick hide of scales that covered his arms the last time he sprouted wings. "Those talons are sharp."

At my statement, Aidan lets out a slow, building growl as he yanks a thick sword from the scabbard at his back. *Okay...* Someone is cranky.

Edging closer to the end of the tree line, I keep a close eye on the Corax, making sure the spell actually took. The demons stumble on nothing, each one finding their knees in the dirt.

Then everything goes straight to Hell.

As soon as we reach the stream, a falcon screams, taking flight from a low branch, circling the demons, the piercing shriek waking them from their induced stupor. One by one, their plucked raven heads turn right to us.

I've never wanted to murder an animal out of spite before, but today is that day. But then I recognize that fucking bird. It was on my street when Ian was kidnapped. I saw it the last time I came to Bernadette's. Hell, I even heard a bird's shriek when I was bloody and broken after the last time I tangled with a Corax.

That isn't a bird. It's a spy.

"Go! Take the demons out. I've got the bird."

Breaking off into a run, I reach for the bag of spelled rocks Maria gave me. I'd scoffed at the time, but beaning one of these motherfuckers against that damn bird's skull is going to be fucking glorious.

My feet are sure on the uneven ground despite my choice of shoes, and my mind falls to my mother's blessing. *I really hope Mom laid a good whammy on me,* I think as I pull a red agate from my pouch and gear up for a toss. The falcon is perched in an Aspen, the fluttery green leaves, half-concealing it, but still I let the rock fly.

The red ones are powered with a disabling spell. Meant for small things like guard dogs. Don't try it on powerful Ethereals. It'll just piss them off.

That's when I stopped listening to Maria, but dammit if she didn't come through in a clutch because the rock hits the bird right in the chest, knocking it from the tree. It falls, landing in the dirt in a great puff of dust, unmoving.

Thanks, little sister.

"*Ipsum revelare.*" I snap my fingers at the unconscious animal, praying I'm wrong. *Reveal yourself.*

If it's a shifter of some kind, I want to know. I want to know if a sentient being that knows right and wrong just sold us—sold me—out. I want to know if it's who I think it is.

The transformation is slow, but that's expected. I'm forcing a shifter to change at dawn, my magic going against their very nature, but feathers soon fall away, and flesh grows in their stead—the phase back to human-shaped, crumbling my sister's spell to dust.

But the bird is exactly who I thought it would be.

When the blonde stands before me it is all I can do not to drive my athame right into her skull.

"Hiya, Ruby. Having a rough day?"

CHAPTER TWENTY-TWO

MAX

I don't know at what point I wanted to be wrong about Ruby, but the betrayal coursing through my veins takes me by surprise. I still remember the woman who pulled me aside and told me where to go for help when she saw my brands. I remember the woman who found out how I was named Rogue and commiserated with me.

Then I realize, I'm looking at a completely different woman than the one who faked her way through our meeting at Caim's. The woman before me now is a rage-filled shell of the woman I met those few weeks ago. Micah's words fill my brain.

You think I'm the only one who wants you to burn? That blonde bitch who sent me after you? She's watching you. Always watching you.

I'd thought he was lying, but he wasn't at all.

Micah was a murdering psychopath, but he wasn't lying. Not about this.

Ruby's blonde hair falls down into two disheveled plaits, dressed in now-dirt-covered jeans and boots, she seems almost normal outside of Caim's club. Wholesome. And the disparity between what she looks like and what she is almost kills me. Ruby has always used her looks like a weapon, and as bitchy as she is, I never expected this from her.

She doesn't even appear sorry, the delicate jut of her chin turning mulish in her silence.

"I could make you tell me why, but I'd rather you offer it freely. How could you do this?" My voice breaks on my whisper.

But Ruby doesn't heed my warning, she begins her phase, bones cracking, her spine bowing with the strain. I don't wait for her to strike.

"*Constringitur in locum.*" I freeze her where she stands, the spell halting her mid-transformation, the angel wings I expected to see budding from her back like flowers about to open.

"I can't hurt you because of what you are, even though you hurt me. But I'll make sure Caim knows about this. I'll make sure Barrett and Marcus and Gorgon and Cinder know about it, too," I threaten, and then turn my back on her, not sparing her another glance. I've got bigger problems at the moment than a bitchy half-breed angel.

Corax demons swarm the entry point to my grandmother's cabin, clashing with Aidan and Striker. Striker is phased into his other form, a mix of angel and whatever the hell he's mixed with. Given the scales—and the knowledge that they actually fucking exist—I'd go with dragon. He has come into his other form, wielding the half-feathered, half-scaled wings like extensions of himself, using them to strike the Corax before he takes their head.

Aidan's fighting style is less flashy, and more about stealth. Using his abilities, he slides in and out of sight, popping behind demons only to take their heads and popping back out again.

About a half dozen lay in the dirt missing their heads, but the rest are staying just outside the warding lines as if they can see them, fending off Aidan and Striker less like they want to kill them, and more like they are just fodder for keeping them out of Bernadette's home. I can't imagine what would happen to the Corax if they touched the pale luminescent hex lines of Bernadette's ward, and at that thought, an idea forms at the same time a smile stretches my lips wide.

Instead of wasting my time by running, I snap my fingers, traveling from the rocky shore of the stream to the demon unfortunate enough to be closest to the hex lines. Catching him by surprise, his talons flail, bird eyes going wide as I drive my athame-turned-sword into its chest. The demon falls, lighting up like a Christmas tree against the ward before he explodes in a spray of demon guts and sludge I only manage to avoid by an inch.

The smell—*Fates, I forgot about the smell*—is enough to make me gag. The stench of rot nearly bowls me over, which is why the demon's buddy catches me by surprise. So much for Aidan's lessons on situational awareness. Talons catch me at the shoulder, ripping an agony-inducing swath down my back.

Blood pours from the wounds I'm probably glad I can't see, driving me to my knees. Then a bird head falls to the ground independent from the humanish body it was previously attached to. A hand appears in front of my face, and I lever myself up off the ground with it, the bulk of the heavy lifting done by the man attached to it.

"Remind me to re-teach you how to *not* be snuck up on in our next lesson," Aidan quips, not quite able to mask the concern leaking into his tone.

"I'll get right on that." I try not to hurl at the agony filling me.

Then I move, or should I say, Aidan moves me. Curling me around his back, he parries with another demon's talons, fighting off strike after strike. But this demon isn't alone. No, this motherfucker brought friends. Two more Corax head for us, the pair of them galloping on their hooves faster than any horse.

Pulling deep, I flex my magics. Breathing on my fingers, I let the spell weave through me, letting the power build. I can almost see the striations of gold in their black beady eyes before I let my fingers loose, the magic snapping like a rubber band through me and outward. The spell circles them in a shower of green magic, whipping the pair of demons up and away, into the hex lines of the ward.

The pair of them look like mosquitos on a bug zapper before

they go boom, sending black, tar-like blood and sludge raining over us.

"For Fates sake, Maxima, was that really necessary?" Striker yells while taking the last demon's head. I can't blame him. He and Aidan caught the brunt of the spray, being so tall. Striker most of all since his wingspan is a greater surface area.

"Three were attacking at once. I was helping!" I yell back, only slightly sorry for dousing us all in demon guts.

Aidan stares down at me where I wilted once the spell left my fingers, black sludge covering his beanie and half his face. "Don't help anymore, okay?"

"Fine. Next time you can take on three Corax demons at once by yourself." I huff, trying to ignore the pulsing torment also known as my back.

I try to stand, the ground shifting beneath my feet, and at first, I think it's just me. Just the blood loss making my legs shaky, but Aidan throws a hand out for balance, too. A rumble from inside the ward grows, spilling out through the hex lines so much, the light of them bends with the strain.

Then the world goes white, the blast of the ward breaking sending us flying, careening into the stream. The water hitting my face is a shock, and I try to claw my way to the surface, but there is a weight on my back holding me down. Pushing as hard as I can, I scrabble my way to the surface, breathing fresh air in what feels like too long. I discover the weight on me isn't something I can just throw off. It's Aidan's limp body that must have taken the brunt of the blast. I feel him breathing, feel his heartbeat through the fabric of my shirt.

Thank the Fates.

Letting him rest on my back, I pull my knees under me, dragging him along with me as I yank us both out of the water. Once the sand sifts through my fingers, I shrug him off, letting him hit the ground as I catch my breath for a second before checking him over. Other than the goose egg that he will definitely feel later, he seems fine.

I search for Striker, finding him on the bank of the stream, his head still in the water. I manage to pull his heavy ass to the bank and make sure he's actually breathing. Luckily, only his hair was in the water. One thing I can say for our impromptu bath, at least it washed some of the demon guts off me.

Turning, I look back at my grandmother's cabin, the ward now a gaping hole of dissipating magic, and grasp just why the ward blew in the first place. Souls swarm the cabin, gray and black trails of smoke and darkness. Their screams are piercing even from this far away.

Aidan said they were drawn to the blade. That means Andras is here.

Samael's here.

Grandma's here.

Might as well make it a family reunion.

Walking through the spirits, I marvel at how they don't even look at me. Since I don't have the blade, they aren't even remotely interested in me—just the way I like it. Ghost problems are bullshit.

My entry into Bernadette's cabin goes mostly unnoticed. Spirits swirl inside the walls, the bulk of them inside rather than out. Bernadette is on the floor, the bone blade protruding from the meat of her shoulder. My father and uncle clash in the kitchen, the pair of them with bone swords that had to come from a giant or a dragon or something. I've never seen either up close, but nothing human sized could produce a bone that big. My uncle appears similar to my father. The same dark hair, same nose, same glowing gold eyes.

But that's where the similarities end. Samael is dressed in a dark suit, fighting with precision and class like a champion fencer. Andras is in jeans and a flannel, fighting like a bare-knuckles backroom brawler. Either way, neither one is winning.

The specters hover over Bernadette, slashing at her with hands I know are so cold they burn. Her skin is black in some places where the cold is so bad it's decayed the flesh, and for the first time, I see her other form. She fades in and out of the cultured but aging lady to a beautiful raven-haired young woman, her face so beautiful it almost hurts to look at her.

Sliding next to her, I reach for the blade, ready to pull it from her shoulder, but she stops me.

"No, Maxima." Her breaths are fast and labored as if it's taking everything she has in her to stay conscious, to stay sane. "Do-don't take it. The spirits, the-they'll kill you. They're dr-drawn to the blade."

Meeting her eyes, her pain brims from her every pore. "I know. Samael put that there?" I ask, drawing the blade from her flesh.

She nods, her eyes filling. "Andras saved me. I never should have doubted him."

I can only nod. She might be able to trust my father, but I sure as fuck can't. "I'll take care of it."

As soon as the blade is free, the spirits swarm me, their hands cutting into my flesh, the cold stealing my breath. But I've thought of the only way to stop them.

They have to go back where they came from.

"*Veni in domum suam, vacui hoc imple. Reperio tenebrae tuae in hoc loco.*" The spell is simple, the words flowing from my tongue as if someone planted them there. *Come home, fill this void. Find your place in this darkness.*

The souls howl, blowing apart before swirling faster, harder, tighter against me, ripping into my flesh with cold fingers. They draw blood, they burn me.

Veni in domum suam, vacui hoc imple. Reperio tenebrae tuae in hoc loco.

A soul solidifies in front of me—a young woman cut down too soon. She screams in my face, wrapping a freezing hand around my throat, squeezing, stealing all my air. They don't want to go, but there is nowhere else. Stuck between planes, stuck between worlds, left to rot in a cage they were never meant for but can't escape.

Bernadette grabs my hand, repeating my words, lending me her voice when mine is gone, lending me eons worth of power to draw from.

Veni in domum suam, vacui hoc imple. Reperio tenebrae tuae in hoc loco.

Then the hand at my throat is gone, the soul tugged back by an invisible thread, they swirl closer to the blade, the power in the blade growing as souls start to fill it.

"Now, Maxima. Give me the blade!" Andras screams, his arms wrapped around Samael's chest and neck, holding my struggling uncle in place.

I don't need to even consider it to know Andras can't be trusted, so I don't give the blade to him. Instead, I let the dagger fly, throwing it with all my strength and pray that my mother's blessing holds steadfast.

May your aim always be true.

Watching as the tang turns over and over in the air, I feel the souls drawing away from me. Feel them follow the blade, feel them fill it with the power of hundreds, thousands of deaths. The point of the dagger pierces Samael's heart, the weight of the power driving the blade home.

He stops struggling, his body wilting in Andras' hold. Andras lets his brother slide to the floor, and I stagger to my kill, yanking the dagger free once the last of Samael's breath leaves him.

I stare at the bone. That's all it is. Just a bone from some creature filed down into the most basic of weapons. What once held something full of life, now takes it without compunction.

This doesn't need to be here.

"No one needs this blade. No one needs this kind of power," I croak, my voice a bitter husk of breath.

The power I shied away from fills my hand as I stare at my grandmother, her form once again the aging beauty. "I know you wanted it for a rainy day, but you'll just have to keep on living a while longer."

A ghost of a smile flits across her lips, and she gives me a subtle nod. I don't bother looking at my father as he stands staring at me as if he's never seen me before. I suppose he hasn't.

The old Max wouldn't have to step between two family members.

The old Max didn't have a family.

But I suppose he never knew the old Max, either.

I draw some of the magic into me—just enough to do what I need to. Then using that little bit, I grip the bone, tossing the magics back into it, overloading it, cracking it, crushing the blade until it's nothing more than bone shards and dust in my hand.

Then, and only then, do I look at my father. I hold my hand out to him, but he doesn't take the bait.

I sprinkle the floor with the bone dust. "Here's your blade, Father."

I hope you choke on it, I think, walking out of the cabin into the sunshine.

CHAPTER TWENTY-THREE

MAX

Barrett stares me down as I sit right back where I started in a velvet green armchair in the middle of the high court room. At least this time when I was escorted to the witch club, Aether, by an Ethereal Guard, Ruby wasn't the one to have her mitts on me. No, that was reserved for the twenty or so witches, angels, shifters, and even a few *no shit* dragons waiting for me when I strolled —okay, hobbled—out of Bernadette's cabin. The cavalry had arrived, even if they were about an hour too late and lost Ruby in the shuffle.

At least Mother actually listened to me.

"You're telling me you killed Samael, didn't kill Andras like you were supposed to, put a freezing spell on an angel, and destroyed the bone blade." He checks the facts of my story, making sure he has them all.

"Yep." I cross my feet on the matching ottoman I conjured for my own personal comfort. Hell, I was bleeding, covered in Corax guts—*still*—and I was pretty sure I was half-delirious. Barrett could ask me if I killed the Queen of England, and I'd probably answer the same, but at least he's keeping to relevant topics.

Aidan and Striker were whisked in and out of here with a pat on the head and a "good job," but not me.

Noooooooo...

I was stuck getting the evil eye from a man who might like me, might respect me, but also might kill me if the need arose. I was too tired to give him any more details. Personally, I was hoping Bernadette would swoop in and save me from the interrogation brewing behind his eyes.

I need a medic.

And a bottle of bourbon.

Preferably not in that order.

"Do you care that Samael wasn't actually murdered by Andras, Ruby was a spy for Samael, and the bone blade was going to cause the Apocalypse? Because I feel those are all important facts to remember here."

"And we should believe you, why exactly?" Barrett asks, the snideness slipping heavily in his tone.

"Knock it off. Can't you see she's bleeding all over the place?" Marcus comes to my rescue, and I kinda want to hug the shifter. I also kinda want to sleep for a week, so hugging is probably out.

Barrett smiles at his mate. "Fine. Ruin my payback for the door incident why don't you."

"What door incident?" Caim leans around Cinder and Gorgon, the gaping hole of the demon seat only highlighting my grandmother's absence. If Caim was surprised Ruby was working for the other side, he didn't show it. But then again, he was one of the few who sent Striker off on his mission, so he might have already known how treacherous she could be.

"Max blew up that door," Barrett says almost proudly, pointing to the entrance to the high court room, "like it was nothing, and then *poof*, put the damn thing back together again like she never blew it to smithereens in the first bloody place. We need to talk to your Fae builder. If that thing can be blown apart by a bloody child, we're all in trouble."

"Oh, give it a rest. I'm fucking bleeding over here. I know I'm not in trouble. You know I'm not in trouble. Just give me my damn cookie for saving the world as we know it *again* and let me get stitched up," I gripe, ready to blow up that stupid door again.

And this time I won't put it back together, either.

"As you wish," Barrett murmurs, breathing on his fingers before rubbing them together.

Heat washes over me, stealing the bitter cold still lingering on my skin from the spirits who attacked so mercilessly. It steals away the ache in my back, the burning agony of the open wounds. I feel it knit my flesh back together, feel the power of Barrett's magic heal me, finally breathing easy for the first time in what feels like a week.

"Thank you," I breathe, wilting into the chair.

"I was wondering when you'd snap. You lasted far longer than I thought you would," Barrett says, a laugh not quite breaking free. "Maxima Alcado, born Maxima Christina Arcadios, former member of the now-defunct Arcadios Coven, daughter of the demon Andras and Pacific Northwest coven leader, Teresa Alcado, sole heir to the royal seat, your Rogue status is hereby rescinded. Any action against you is now considered a direct threat to the Council and will be dealt with as such."

Barrett pauses, likely letting me digest this new information. *Your Rogue status is hereby rescinded.* How long have I wanted to hear those words? Forever, maybe? And yet, they don't feel real. Like this is some sort of trick, some sort of treachery just winding up for the pitch. Shaking, I can barely blink, barely breathe.

"We offer you the vacant demon seat, child. We offer you what should have always been yours." My eyes stray from Barrett to Gorgon, the warlock's kind pronouncement hitting me square in the chest.

If this is a trick, Gorgon isn't part of it, but I know what too good to be true looks like. I've seen it more than once.

Too good to be true is me getting sent to kill one man, when another is responsible. It's me being turned Rogue in the first place. It's the maneuvering and politicking. It's the vagueness, the half-told truths and the bold-faced lies.

"Will anyone be offended if I say I'll think about it? While I appreciate my status as Rogue being rescinded, the Council seat is a very important job—one I'm not sure I'm ready for," I say as diplomatically as I possibly can. Actually, I'm quite proud of myself.

"Don't tarry too long," Barrett advises. "And keep a watchful eye on your assistant. Vampires are nearly extinct, you know."

Barrett drops that bomb, and then just like that, I'm dismissed to digest the mythical fucking creature on my payroll.

Thanks, Gramma.

Walking out the high court room into Aether proper, I spot Striker in a seat on the outskirts of the club. Even in the middle of the day, the place is packed, and I can't quite figure out if these people have jobs or lives. It all feels artificial and weird like most clubs do once the shine wears off.

"Let me guess, you're here for the food."

Striker startles and then turns his head, looking away from the naked acrobats and topless bartenders, away from the nakedness and fun. "Just enjoying the entertainment, boss."

Everything from the slope of his shoulders, to his voice, to the way his eyes seem a little lost tell me his grief over Melody's death isn't gone—not by a long shot. But I don't know what to do for my friend. Being in the human world didn't help, and even here—in this fake, superficial place —filled with glamours and flesh and magic and sex, he seems better than he was. Even if it's only a little bit.

Maybe he needs the superficial right now.

"Yeah, well, I'm going home. Don't stay too long. Too much of this place will rot your brain," I warn. As if it will do any good, as if he'll even listen to me.

I leave him behind, finding the door and getting the hell out of this place. Leaning against the glamoured warehouse wall, Aidan lounges, his feet crossed at the ankle, his face turned up to the sun. I'm half-tempted to leave him there, he looks so peaceful.

"You waiting on me?"

One of Aidan's eyes slowly opens, giving me the perfect side-eye for a man who probably has a concussion. "No, I'm waiting on some other chick. Tell me when you see her, she's hard to miss. She's about yay high, blue hair, covered in demon guts." He gives me a crooked little smile. "They throw the book at you?"

"Nah. Just got my Rogue status revoked is all." I smile as I turn and start walking toward the right side of town—where people and coffee reside—leaving Aidan to trail after me.

I showered until all the hot water ran out. Then I called Della for the first time since my shop burned down. Turns out that while Bernadette was a little lax on who she sent to watch out for me, Della's benefits far outweighed any downsides.

Della was a little vague on the details, but the human side of my building being burned down was taken care of. I don't know how, but every single customer thinks they weren't there that day, or in Della-speak: "I handled it, boss."

And the building? Well, the repairs were already under way. I wasn't sure I wanted to ask questions, so I didn't.

Some things I just don't need to know. So I have a vampire on staff who can walk in the sun? I'm a demon-witch hybrid who seems to be the only one of my kind.

Who am I to judge?

In fact, the only person I am fit to judge is Ruby, and I'm going to find her feathery ass if it's the last thing I do.

Apocalypse be damned.

LADY OF MADNESS & MOONLIGHT

ROGUE ETHEREAL BOOK 3

CHAPTER ONE

For the hundredth time today, a fist was aimed at my head, rocketing toward me with enough power behind it to knock me into next week. That was, if it hit me, which considering the luck I had today, was entirely likely. Managing to duck the fist coming for my face at the last second, I scrambled to the side before swinging up and returning the favor, landing it in his not-so-soft middle. Honestly, it was like I was bare-knuckle punching a brick wall.

I only got to enjoy the pained "oof" for a second, though, because another fist or a leg or an elbow was coming, and if any of the above hit me, I'd be a mushy stain on the floor. My opponent was much better than me on every level—except for the magic one—but I cared too much about the opinion of his pack to fight dirty. Plus, he had a set of sharp fangs he could use to level the playing field at any moment.

A leg came out of nowhere and swept mine out from under me. I landed on a hip—the pain of the bone meeting mat knocking the breath out of me. But I learned early on that staying still was just about the worst thing I could do. Scrambling so I wasn't on the receiving end of the haymaker aimed my way, I managed to dodge another fist.

"I swear to the Fates, Marcus, if you let her get a black eye today of all days, I will hurt you in ways you can only dream about." Barrett's voice echoed through the gym.

A strangled wheeze made it past my lips which only pissed Barrett off more.

"And not in a good way," he added, the threat hanging in the air.

Barrett really was the nicest. I should send him a fruit basket or something.

Marcus, Barrett's mate, periodically took time out of his busy schedule to beat me into something more than the weak, combat-challenged hot mess I'd been for the last four hundred years. And when he thought I actually learned something, he set members of his pack loose on me while he critiqued my technique.

Kinda like right now.

Finnegan Lorenson was a beast of a man, and as his name suggested, practically a Viking. With his white-blond hair, bulging muscles, and can-do attitude, he was one of the larger men I'd fought today. Oh, and by "can-do," I meant more like a "I'm gonna fuck shit up and eat your entrails for breakfast" attitude. The majority of Marcus' pack were of the happy, family oriented, inclusive sort. Not all of them were wolves, not all of them were able to shift, but all of them were included, taught, and protected. It was what I would imagine the Weasley's would be like if they were a pack.

But not Finn.

He didn't like fighting me. Hell, it would be more accurate to say he was offended to be fighting someone like me. I couldn't figure out if it was because I was a woman, a witch, or because I was half-demon. Maybe it was all of the above. Either way, it didn't feel like Finn was sparring—or after that last hit, not anymore.

I ached everywhere, from the tips of my toes all the way up to my scalp, and I was about done with my "no magic" self-inflicted edict. There wasn't a way on this earth I could beat Finn without a little magical backup.

What happens if you can't use magic, Maxima? What are you gonna do then? Aidan's voice ran on an auto-loop in my head every single time I sparred. This used to be his job—teaching me how not to be a weakling—but I'd distanced myself from him over the last six months. I wanted to think it wasn't me being petty, but since his brother, Ian, kicked me to the curb, it was more than likely.

The rejection still stung, the pain of it fading slowly like the pink of a brand-new scar. It wasn't going away anytime soon, and the reminder would always be there. I wasn't the kind of woman he wanted. Those latent wraith traits of his made him need to protect the "little lady" when I was anything but. I didn't need for him to tell me what to do or how to do it. I didn't need him to protect me.

All I'd needed was a partner. And that was something he didn't know how to be.

Honestly, I wasn't sure I was the right woman for anyone, but damn if it wasn't lonely.

The musings over my joke of a love life stole my concentration, and I landed on the mat once again, the breath that I so desperately needed whooshing out of me in a single pained gust. But then Finn aimed a kick while I was still down, and I realized I'd had about enough.

Served me right for mentally whining over Ian.

Before his foot could connect, I wheezed out a command in Latin. *Subsisto.* Snapping my fingers, Finn froze, his foot reared back to strike, malice on his face. No, Finn wasn't playing at all.

Gingerly, I rolled away from his stationary foot before heaving my body to standing. The world spun for a second, but I managed not to upchuck or pass out. And then I noticed Finn's foot inching toward completion, my stopping spell barely holding him. No, that just wouldn't do.

Gathering myself, I decided to give the spell a little more *oomph.* Instead of snapping my fingers, I whispered my commands on the palms of my hands before stretching my arms wide and then brought my hands together. The clap that echoed through the room not only made Finn stop, it knocked him on his ass, his body sliding across the canvas from the momentum of it.

The pack of wolves on the risers watching Finn and I "spar" snickered like children as their packmate slid across the room like a big, blond hockey puck. I looked up just in time to see Barrett's face turn an alarming shade of crimson.

"It's not my fault she was holding back," Marcus grumbled, not expecting Barrett to hear him.

Barrett and Marcus held seats on the Ethereal Council. Barrett maintained the seat for all the witches in North America, and Marcus for all the shifters. When I first met them, I had no idea they'd already been mated for several centuries. Now that I knew, their bickering made so much more sense. It was even kind of cute.

They wanted me to take the demon seat, but I'd been on the fence about it. Until six months ago, I'd been a Rogue. Putting me in a seat of authority seemed to be a bigger leap than I was ready for.

"It's your fault if I say it's your fault," Barrett scolded his husband. "Spar means light touch to no touch, not tear each other to shreds."

Wolves could heal a hell of a lot faster than I could, so their definition of "sparring" was more along the lines of fighting for my life. And while I would heal, a black eye would put a cherry on the shit pie I was about to eat.

"Come on, Max. Wipe yourself up off that mat. You've got a big day ahead of you."

Barrett didn't have to remind me. I knew exactly what was in store for me later tonight. The presentation to the Fates. Only the "p" in presentation was a capital and came with a laundry list of rules and regulations that chafed against me like sandpaper.

I really hated rules. Especially when I had no choice but to obey them.

Groaning, I blew a wayward strand of blue hair from my face.

Half my hair was falling out of the messy bun—messy meaning it took me thirty minutes to make that shit look cute—the sweaty tendrils plastered themselves against my neck and the side of my face like I'd glued them there. Which totally explained why Barrett gave me a bitchy tongue-cluck of derision.

"You had to pick a fight today of all days?"

Of course I did. If I was going to walk into a room full of Ethereal upper crust and let them look me over like a slab of beef, then I was getting all my rage out now. Really, it was safer for everyone that way.

"What? You don't think you can make me presentable in the twelve hours we have to get ready? Some fairy godmother you are."

Barrett's lips parted to answer me just as I felt a frisson of magic rake across my skin. I wasn't supposed to be able to feel magic being spent. I wasn't supposed to be able to see the motes and hex lines or catch the way each spell's scent differed from the other. I perceived all parts of magic —how it looked, how it smelled, how it felt. Everything.

The sensation of a wolf jumping to his other form had a very specific composition. It was part moonlight and part the breeze flowing through a thatch of trees. It was wildness and blood and freedom.

And death. Lots and lots of death.

It wasn't like in the movies where the human side of a wolf would bend and shape into another form, cracking bones and growing hair. No, that was movie magic and a load of crap. Real wolves were two parts of the same soul, fighting for dominance and dominion on which side of the Ethereal coin would fall. Or at least that was how Marcus explained it. Not that it made any sense or explained where the hell the human side went when the wolf appeared in a puff of magic smoke.

But that didn't matter much right now. All that really mattered was that there was a wolf in the room.

Not that it was technically a problem right this second, and not that it was my job to deal with it if it actually became a problem. Or at least that was what I told myself so I didn't start some shit in the Alpha's house. I wasn't in charge here, and as far as wolf politics went, I knew exactly dick. Yeah, I'd been fighting wolves all day, but that was at the Alpha's behest.

I knew without looking at Marcus that this phase was not sanctioned, and judging by his growl, it wasn't welcomed, either. I slid my gaze to Marcus, giving him a little head shake to signal I would handle it on my own. He grinned, likely remembering the time I nearly exploded the high court room with a snap of my fingers.

Turning slowly as to not agitate the apex predator, I surveyed the animal before me. Pure white fur from the tips of his ears to his toes made him seem cuddly at first, the texture soft and plush like a puppy. But letting my guard down even a little would be a huge mistake on my part.

Especially since this particular wolf was closer to three hundred pounds rather than two, and the top of his head probably reached my chin. Not that I'd let him get close enough to measure. Only one of Marcus' men had hair that color, or eyes that shade of ice. And only one I'd just knocked on his ass.

Finn.

I'd only managed to subdue him with a stasis spell that barely succeeded in holding his human form. Something told me that same spell wouldn't work so well on his wolf—if it worked at all. My only real hope here was if I didn't have to fight him in the first place. An evil smile stretched across my lips as it finally came to me.

"And who's a pretty puppy?" I used the exact same voice I'd use when I came across any old dog.

Denver was super dog friendly. They weren't allowed in my tattoo shop because of cross-contamination rules—but coffee shops, restaurants, and libraries? Puppers were everywhere. And while I shouldn't let my guard down for even a millisecond, teasing Finn seemed like the best course of action.

"Look at you all floofy and beautiful. You are a big old ball of gorgeous, aren't you?"

Hoots and hollers erupted from the risers along with a few

belly laughs, signaling my cue to keep going despite Finn's vibrating growl.

"Now, Finn, are you going to bite my arms off if I pet you? Because that would be rude."

Finn's growl got louder as he showed me his teeth—razor-sharp canines dripping saliva.

"Finny-boy, if you don't play nice, you won't get a treat," I said in a singsong voice, breaking away from Marcus and Barrett and slowly circling back into the room in a wide arc.

I wasn't giving my back to this wolf, and I sure as hell wasn't letting Barrett take the brunt if Finn decided to charge me. Marcus would kill him for letting his wolf go free, and for some reason that seemed like a waste.

Finn's claws dug into the mat, ripping the plasticized fabric, yellowish mat innards spilling out around the sharp talons.

I opened my mouth to make another verbal jab, but old Finn wasn't having it. He charged, coming at me straight-on like a man instead of how a wolf would. Wolves were pack hunters: sneaky, skillful. Finn was all brute strength and zero finesse. He fought like a man in wolf's clothing rather than ceding to his animal.

He barreled toward me, refusing to heed Marcus' bellowed shout, ignoring his pack's yells to stop. But I knew better than to flinch.

Finn was playing chicken. I'd bet on it. Granted, I didn't want to be munched on by a three-hundred-pound wolf, but since my other option was to be presented like a show pony to the bougie Ethereal upper crust, it was really shit or diarrhea at this point. And while I couldn't help my galloping heart, or the flash fire of adrenaline racing across my skin, a part of my brain—the one with a little bit of a death wish—only whispered a single word.

Fun.

CHAPTER TWO

Planting my bare feet, I waited for Finn to leap—waited for him to strike—keeping my face a bored mask. I saw the exact second he realized I wasn't going to move. Alarm crossed his wolfy face as he skidded to a stop, the tips of his front paws barely millimeters from my bare toes.

"Trying to scare me, Finn? *Tsk, tsk, tsk.*" I clucked, assessing the magic of his wolf.

Motes of pale-blue magic danced around his head like an aura. It made me wonder if I could manipulate them.

"*Ipsum revelare,*" I murmured sweetly, snapping my fingers. *Reveal yourself.*

It was a spell I'd used only a few times, and one that made my gut ache every time I used it. It reminded me of betrayal and a hurt that soured the triumph of staring a werewolf down and not flinching.

It reminded me that not everyone was my friend. Not everyone cared if I lived or died. Hell, some of them even thirsted for it. It reminded me that even the good guys could turn on you.

The ice-blue motes above the wolf's head roiled, darkening to midnight with threads of silver before he seemed to fade and melt into the shape of a man. I could feel the crowd around us react to me bringing a wolf back to his human form with a snap of my fingers.

I could feel their unease. Their panic. Witches weren't supposed to be able to do that—weren't supposed to be able to control a shifter's phase. But I wasn't all witch, and they needed to remember that.

"Do you know why I perform non-lethal spells, Finn?" Even to my ears, my voice sounded damn near dead.

I should be safe here in Marcus' home. I shouldn't have to defend myself or worry if some idiot will get a wild hair up his ass and attack me. All of the mirth of teasing, all the happiness crumbled to ash on my tongue.

I should have known better than to let my guard down. That was how I got hurt.

"No." Finn's voice was little more than a breath of wind across my cheek as I stared *up, up, up* into his ice-blue eyes.

"It's because I consider you my friend, and I do my very best not to hurt my friends. Are you my friend, Finn?"

His eyes flitted to the side for a second as his nostrils flared, scenting me. Finn was the kind of handsome you'd only see in movies, a shock of white hair atop his tanned face. His icy eyes seemed to glow like stars. His full lips pulled into a smirking sort of smile, and I knew he wasn't as scared as he should have been.

None of them were.

And I already knew his answer—whatever it was going to be—was going to be a lie. Just like his sparring, Finn was dirty, shady. He was a cheat, and he liked inflicting pain. He would kick a man when he was down. And the more I looked into his eyes, the more I knew, he didn't just hate me for being a witch. He hated me because I was a woman, and I'd beaten him.

He was a small-minded misogynist and hated other Ethereals.

"No," I answered for him. "You're not, are you?"

What was likely a prank or a chance to poke fun at me incited an urge in my belly that I couldn't name. Maybe it was bloodlust, or maybe it was just a dire kind of need to make him pay. This was my demon side at work—the side that thirsted for something I couldn't pinpoint. Not blood. Not revenge.

Justice.

"Do you know what a demon does, Finn?"

He shook his head, the smirk falling off his face.

"They make people pay for their crimes. Unfortunately, it's after death, so there is no chance to learn from the mistakes you made. There is no chance to choose another path."

Finn's eyes widened just slightly, realizing too late that I wasn't just some woman he could push around. I wasn't the weak witch that sparred with his Alpha.

Turning my head, I met Barrett's eyes. "I'll take the job."

Barrett's mouth stretched into a sly grin, his blue eyes sparkling like I'd just given him the best birthday present ever. I'd been hounded for the last six months about taking the demon seat of the Ethereal Council. Who knew all it would take was this lone wolf to shove me off the fence? Granted, six months ago, I didn't know that it was one of seven Councils on this plane.

If I didn't know Barrett better, I'd say he arranged all this, but I did know better.

Marcus, however, looked like a proud papa. He put Finn in my path, knowing full well what I'd do when I figured out what a sack of shit he was. He knew I couldn't sit idly by and watch as he did it to someone else.

This was a test—one I'd passed without even knowing how I'd done it.

Turning back to the wolf in question, I nearly reveled in the confused horror on his face. Nearly, because enjoying this would make me no better than him, and I knew without a shadow of a doubt that reveling in his soon-to-be misery would sour my soul. But Finn couldn't go on like he had been. He couldn't keep preying on those he considered weak. He couldn't abuse his abilities like that without consequences. Not anymore.

"Finn, are you familiar with physics? Specifically, Newton's Third Law?"

His confusion only grew at my seemingly left turn to nowhere. Or maybe it was the physics talk.

"That's okay. I'll just tell you because I have a feeling you'll remember it for the rest of your life. Newton's Third Law is one of the cornerstones of modern physics. It states that every action has an equal and opposite reaction. Now, you've had too many actions with no appropriate reaction. Too many times where you have abused the power bestowed on you by the Fates. And today," I tsked, clucking my tongue at him, "you finally fucked with the wrong woman."

Finn's body coiled as if he were preparing to launch himself at me, but I was prepared for that. Before he could strike, I jabbed my three center fingers into his shirt at the line of his sternum just under a bronze pendant with a familiar symbol I couldn't place. I ripped that pendant off his neck, breaking the clasp at the same time, and threw it aside. Pressing the tips of my blunted fingernails in his chest, I forced myself not to rip the fabric or his skin, managing it by only the faintest of margins. My thumb and pinky fingers were spread wide, while the three center fingers pressed close together. Hand placement was key if I wanted to do this right.

At the touch of my fingers, Finn froze. He didn't blink. He didn't breathe. I didn't know if it was the power that flowed through my hands or his fear that solidified him to the spot.

"You attacked a Council member in full view of your pack and in witness of two other Council members. You attacked demon royalty and an unarmed woman without cause. You abused your power, against the orders of your Alpha and your pack. Punishment for these crimes is death, but I'm going to do you a favor. I'm not going to kill you. I'm going to give you the chance to change."

At those words, I pivoted my hand to the right like I was turning a key in a lock, feeling my power rise in me—not witch power, but something else. Something that I couldn't name, or maybe, I didn't want to name. This was the demon side I tried so hard not to tap into, the side that fed my witch half, made it so I didn't need an affinity to the moon or water or earth or fire or air. I didn't draw on anything but myself.

The ground beneath my feet began to quiver, and I hoped it wouldn't be like the courtroom incident. I didn't want to break the whole room apart just to teach this one man a lesson, but the walls stayed true, and the floor refused to crack. And even though I could feel the fear of every single wolf sing through me, I carried on.

I watched as the ice-blue aura above Finn's head sputtered and died. When the last flicker of light blinked out, Finn fell at my feet in a heap, sucking in a breath for the first time with his new lungs.

"Finnegan Lorenson, you are bound to this form, unable to reach your wolf. You will have a human lifespan, healing, senses, and strength. When you learn your lesson, when you understand that this life is a gift to be cherished, when you no longer wish to hurt those who you deem as weaker, come find me. Until then, make sure you work to learn from your mistakes. If you don't, you'll meet some of my family members in Hell, and I guarantee you they won't be as lenient."

Finn gurgled, a mix of rage and fear stealing his speech, and because he tried to kick me while I was down, I refused to do the same to him. Instead of stepping over him—which I really wanted to do because the bastard really had tried to kick me when I was splayed on the mat like a two-day-old fish—I skirted around his heap of man meat. That didn't stop me from skipping like a kid back to Barrett and Marcus, despite the voices buzzing like bees behind me.

I just did something impossible. Again. In front of a boatload of people who might like me a little but didn't have a single reason to be loyal to me at all. Making enemies wherever I went—that sure was a specialty of mine.

Marcus' warm hand circled my bicep, stopping me from bolting from the room which was my only plan past neutralizing the Viking asshole. His hold was gentle but insistent, and I couldn't bring myself to look at him. Instead, I met Barrett's gaze, the pride there soured a little by the fear.

"Settle down." Marcus' words were clear, his voice only barely raised, but the Alpha in him, the command in his voice, silenced the room in an instant. "If you think Maxima did this without my consent, you are sorely mistaken. Finn has been begging for punishment since he came to this pack, and his actions today against her should have earned her the right to take his head. She gave us all a gift by punishing him without the loss of life."

That's when I realized Finn had been more than reckless. If he hadn't charged me, if he'd waited to attack and I hadn't judged him then, I wondered if Marcus would have had to kill him later. Suppressing a shudder, I homed in on the almost grateful tone to his voice weaving through the Alpha command.

"I want you to remember how few wolves there are in this world. I want you to remember our numbers. We are many here, but so many packs are few. This is a gift, a way not to lose another brother. Remember that."

I did a good thing. *I did*. But why did I feel like even though my actions were just, I was still going to pay for them anyway?

CHAPTER THREE

The same shifters who smiled at me yesterday looked anywhere but in my direction as I stalked down the hallway. Hell, they practically parted like the Red Sea. Just what I needed. A whole pack of shifters either scared of me, or worse—pissed off. It didn't matter if Barrett wanted me to start getting ready, I was leaving this house before Marcus' entire pack decided I was a better option for lunch.

Sweat-stained and bedraggled, I decided I couldn't look much worse than I already did. Why not add a hike through a valley in the middle of Colorado during the ass end of June on top of it? I raised my hand, ready to snap my fingers for all they were worth. How many times had I transported myself this way? A hundred? A thousand? More? It was as easy as blinking and just about as fast, letting the magic that coursed through my veins do the dirty work.

"Not so fast," Barrett called before I followed through. "Where do you think you're going?"

Did I want to explain? *No, I did not.*

"I wanted to see Bernadette," I offered lamely.

What I really wanted to say was that I missed my grandmother and wanted her to tell me everything was going to be okay. I hadn't spoken to her in ages, not since me and a couple of friends slaughtered a horde of Corax demons and stopped one of her sons from murdering her. My father was MIA—standard, really, after a lifetime or ten of him bailing unless he needed something —and she was the only person I really had to teach me what I needed to know.

About being on the Council. About being a demon. About what it was to be this freak of nature anomaly that shouldn't even exist.

You know, *the basics.*

"She isn't there."

My heart fell, but what did I expect? She hadn't been there the last ten times I tried to visit—why would she be there now? The cabin always appeared tiny on the outside, but under heavy cloaking and some probable time-slash-space continuum wizardry, it was anything but small on the inside. Nestled in the middle of a gorgeous valley barren of roads, very few people knew it was there. Or at least they didn't before an angel that shall not be named opened her big, fat trap.

Letting out a sigh that could rival a teenager's, I relaxed my fingers. I wasn't snapping my way out of this one.

"She isn't coming tonight, is she?" I already knew the answer.

She loved Samael. And I'd killed him. I'd gone into that battle knowing there would be repercussions. I just never expected her refusing to talk to me to be one of them.

"I don't think so," Barrett whispered, crossing the length of the corridor to me.

I'd like to think he was offering comfort, and maybe a part of him was, but I had an inkling that he was trying to keep me from bolting and blowing my entire Ethereal future to smithereens.

"She blames me for Samael. For destroying her escape. Doesn't she?"

Of course she did. Not only did I kill my uncle, but I also crushed the bone blade to dust. I'd taken away her only chance to die in peace. Hell, I'd hate me, too.

"She'll get over it."

I rolled my eyes. "I killed her son, Barrett. That isn't a thing you just get over."

Barrett's expression went from consoling to grave. "If you hadn't done it, if you hadn't killed him, one of us would have. He earned that death." Barrett's hands landed on top of my shoulders, holding me in place so I actually met his eyes. "You saved the lives of hundreds of thousands, maybe millions of people. You stopped a war that has been brewing since the dawn of time. She'll get over it."

I shrugged, and Barrett got me moving, steering me to the room I'd be tortured in for the next twelve hours.

"No more stalling. It's time to get this show on the road."

"I'm sorry, Max."

Marcus' gravelly voice broke through the swirling deliberation bouncing around my skull, and I stopped staring into the mirror for a second to really look at him. This was the third time he'd apologized, and unless I got my shit together, he was just going to keep doing it.

It wasn't his fault. None of it, but he would shoulder the blame all the same because that was what an Alpha did. Also, his husband was a fucking menace.

I was sitting on a spindly-looking stool in what had to be a great aunt's wet dream of a dressing room. Staring into the Hollywood-style mirror, I assessed the damage. I was all for getting dolled up, and I could do a painted lip and winged eye with the best of them, but this was something else. This was a level of primping I had yet to achieve, and still, I looked about the same.

Or at least, I saw myself under the layers of gold eyeshadow, false lashes, and gold-inlaid body oils that made my already-bronze skin practically glow. I'd been buffed and shined like a new penny, my hair had been curled and tamed, and through all of it, I hadn't gotten one lick of a say.

But this was going too damn far.

"You want me to do what now?" My voice cracked a bit, but I didn't blame myself in the least.

"It's tradition. Everything I've done so far has been tradition," Barrett insisted, exasperated, even though he wasn't the one being pulled and stretched like a damn Thanksgiving turkey.

I called bullshit. "No. In no way is this dress, these shoes, this makeup, tradition. This ceremony is for babies, Barrett. Unless you're putting false eyelashes on an infant, none of this has been tradition. There is no fucking way I am—"

"They insisted."

They. The Fates had screwed with me yet again, only this time, it was in a super-gross way. Everything would be hunky dory if I weren't about to get painted with blood.

"Of course they insisted. It's gross, I don't want to do it, and it's going to piss me off. It's their *modus operandi*. Do they have it out for me, or is this just for kicks?"

Barrett sighed for approximately the three thousandth time. "This is tradition. Every babe that goes through those doors has to be claimed by blood."

He was talking about the doors to the grand ballroom, the same ones I would walk through by myself because Bernadette wouldn't be there with me. Neither would my parents or my sister or my friends. Sure, Maria, Striker, and Della would be there at the end, but I was walking in alone.

Focusing on the bowl of familial blood in Barrett's hands, a thought struck me. "Whose blood is that?"

An expression crossed Barrett's face like he would rather be boiled alive in a vat of oil than answer me. "Andras donated to the cause."

Andras. My father. The bastard who'd gotten me burned at the stake. The giant flaming asshole who tanked my life on purpose. I parted my lips to protest.

"Don't. Just don't. Do you think you're not going to walk in there with every single person judging you? Do you honestly think I'm going to let you walk into that ballroom without every single facet of your appearance on point? You are a former Rogue,

Maxima. Add on top of that your lineage, and every single molecule of your being will be weighed and measured and assessed. By every person who is there tonight. Including the Fates. Hell, especially the Fates."

"And if I don't let you primp me within an inch of my life, I'm going to offend some ancient Ethereal being who will probably want to skin me alive on principle. Right?"

Barrett sighed for the three thousandth and one time. "Essentially."

Just pretend it's chicken blood. *Gag.* No, pretend it's paint. *Yeah, that's better.*

"Fine." I conceded, but I could tell I looked green.

"Oh, give it a rest. It's only a few drops mixed with face and body paint. No need to get all squeamish."

He probably could have told me that at the beginning instead of dragging out all this drama, but whatever.

Something else occurred to me, but I had to wait until Barrett dragged the broad, ornamental brush down the center of my face before I could ask, the coppery tang filling my nostrils. *A few drops, my ass.* He whispered as he painted a thick, straight line down the center of my face, words so faint I couldn't make them out, but hoped it was a blessing.

"Because I'm dual-natured, will both sides of myself be represented or only the one? I know I'm a freak of nature anomaly and everything, but walking in there denying my witch heritage seems..." I trailed off, unable to articulate precisely why not representing my witch side would be a bad thing.

"Wrong?" Marcus supplied the simplest of answers to the question still rooting around in my skull.

I nodded. "Wrong."

Barrett pressed his lips together, indecision on his face as he set the bowl and brush down. "You know that means asking Teresa, don't you?"

My mother and I would never be best buddies or have the sort of loving relationship rom-coms were made of, but sometime after she blessed my friends and I, we managed to find some kind of a truce. This was something she should have done four hundred years ago when I was born. Now she could finally make good.

That was, if she'd do it.

"Which one of us has to do the asking?" I threw the question out there, letting it settle. And if I also happened to shamelessly put my brown puppy-dog eyes to work, I had no regrets.

Barrett assessed my pleading expression, harrumphed, turned, and then gave blue puppy eyes to his husband.

"Oh, come on!" Marcus groused, before catching the full force of both Barrett's and my pitiful stares. I even threw in a whimper for good measure.

"Fine! I'll ask her, but if she says no, you two are just going to have to deal."

"Thanks, Marcus!" I called to his back as he slipped from the room to call my mother.

Not five minutes later, Marcus stalked back into the room with my mother striding right behind him, the short train of her burgundy dress trailing behind her.

I couldn't recall my mother ever wearing a dress like this one. It had a high, jeweled neckline and long sleeves, but the major thing that kept it from being frumpy was the way the fabric hugged her curves all the way to the top of her hips before falling in a straight column.

Then she walked past me to an altar set up inside one of those roll-top desks, and I got a load of the rest of it. Backless. Completely backless. Mom looked hot.

Once I got over her dress, I paid attention to what she was doing.

Pulling a knife from who knew where, she cut her palm just like they did in the movies, letting the blood flow into a small stone bowl. First off, why? And second? That spot was just about the worst place to cut, ever. It took forever to heal, and the scars jacked with all the palmistry lines.

I wanted to ask, but as soon as she got the nod from Barrett that she provided enough, she snapped her fingers, and the blood slowed before stopping altogether, the cut healing in a matter of seconds.

She really needed to teach me that one.

Once her cut was a thing of the past, she spirited the knife away into a sheath at her thigh, and turned to walk back out of the room without ever saying a word to me or acknowledging me at all.

"Mom," I called before she could leave, and at that single word, she halted in a stutter-step as if my lone word was a command.

Teresa turned back to me, her eyes shiny with unshed tears. "I'll see you out there, okay?"

I wanted to ask her if I was doing the right thing. I wanted to know if she was proud of me. I wanted to know if she cared at all.

But I didn't ask.

And she didn't say.

CHAPTER FOUR

My heels clicked on the pale-blue marble floors of the grand ballroom, a room I'd never seen in Aether—which didn't mean much. Too many of the rooms in the underground witch club didn't actually belong to the building itself but were doorways to somewhere else. The vast ballroom seemed to go on forever, the ceilings domed and painted and at least three-stories high. Wide marble columns sat at thirty-foot intervals along the sides of the room, and in between each stood groups of well-dressed partygoers.

Was that the right term? Partygoer? This was a ball of sorts, but more than that, it was my presentation to the Fates. Should I call them spectators, revelers, witnesses? In all likelihood, they were here for the free food, free drinks, and the spectacle of a four-hundred-year-old demon-hybrid finally showing up to what was sort of like an Ethereal christening.

This was for babies. Not grown women. It showed in the fact that I hadn't had a say in what I wore, or what makeup I had on, or the painted line of demon blood that bisected one side of my face from the other. That and the trail of witch blood that ran from one temple, over the top of my cheekbones, across my nose, curving up to the other temple. I didn't choose the crown on my head, or the shoes on my feet, or the jewelry at my ears. None of it.

That wasn't to say that the dress, jewelry, shoes, and the crown weren't beautiful and of the highest quality. They were. Barrett had excellent taste.

But they weren't mine. This place wasn't mine—these people weren't mine.

The only thing that *was* mine was the ink tattooed into my skin. That, they couldn't take away, but somehow it made me even more of a spectacle than I already was. This dress—Grecian in style —had a wide V-neck and back, reaching almost to my navel, my skin exposed to the room. My tattooed sleeves, the mandala under my breasts, the flowers and vines on my back, hell, even the giant dragon that started at my ribs and wound down and around my hip to the top of my left thigh, peeked out of the indigo fabric. The slits of the floor-length skirt parted with every step, showing more skin than I liked. And while the dress itself was beautiful, a part of me wondered about the golden scales at my shoulders that held the fabric together—wondered if they were real dragon scales or if they were replicas. I prayed they weren't real, but I didn't have much hope. Given the blood painted on my face, I wouldn't put it past them at this point.

I felt naked and exposed and on display—when given the fact that this was a presentation, made sense, but I didn't like it.

My heels—sky-high, golden, strappy, flimsy little things—still clicked, echoing through the silent room. I'd never been in a room filled with so many people that was this quiet. It was eerie and proof positive that there couldn't be a single human in the bunch. They all aped human well enough, and even though I kept my face forward, I saw the glamours and magics out of the corner of my eye.

Power buffeted me on both sides, the shiver of it all buzzing against my skin, but never more than the energy I was walking toward.

At the center of the room, a compass was laid into the marble, the giant spines pointing north to the three women I was here to meet. The trio was perched on a raised dais with three golden thrones, each at an equal height which felt significant for some reason, as if they ruled in concert and not separately. But I knew this already, didn't I? Barrett made sure I read up on all the lore regarding those three. Not because I would get tested, but so I wouldn't stick my foot in my mouth and shit all over his meticulous planning.

As I got closer, I realized the three women looked nothing like what I thought they would. For starters, they didn't appear to be women at all. At best I would classify them as adolescents, but even I knew that looks could be deceiving. I supposed looking like a teenager would be preferable to looking like an old crone. Many a person would underestimate a teen, not so much a seasoned lady with the roadmap of time written across her face.

Sneaky.

The one on the left was white-blonde, the middle one dark-haired, and the right one a redhead. None of them appeared older than eighteen, and even that was a push. They sat with a teenager's irreverence, lounging on their golden thrones without a care for the fancy clothes they wore or the importance of the situation. The Fates. The Moirai. Clotho, Lachesis, and Atropos didn't give a blue fuck about any of this. Well, neither did I, but I had to make a show of it, didn't I?

As I neared the end of my trek, my family and friends came into view. Dressed to the nines, my motley crew of supporters was a sight for sore eyes. Unlike the others in the room that stuck to their own kind, my group was a mix of nearly all species of Ethereal. My sister, Maria, a full-blooded witch, stood front and center, buffeted on both sides by Striker, an angel and something mixed that was probably dragon, if I had a guess, and Aidan, a full-blooded wraith. Next to them was Aurelia Constantine, my phoenix BFF, Della, my vampire assistant-slash-bodyguard, and my mother, Teresa. I was amazed Aurelia was standing that close to my mom, but since neither of them were bloody, I wasn't going to question it.

I had so many who were here to support me, I tried to stomp

down the hurt that Bernadette was nowhere to be seen. My father was here, why couldn't she be?

Ten feet from the dais, I stopped to let my parents step forward, the choreographed steps Barrett had hammered into my brain for the last six months, my mother to the left, my father to the right, and we walked in step the last little bit, waiting for the three women to acknowledge us. Then we waited a bit more.

I racked my brain to try and remember the steps Barrett had gone over and over and *over* to make sure I didn't mess up, but no. I wasn't supposed to do anything else. These women—Deities? Gods? Assholes?—were the ones who were supposed to get this show on the road. I had a nearly irresistible urge to tap my foot, but I figured that wouldn't be too good for my health such as it was. The whole reason I was here was so I *didn't* piss these women off, and it was a reason I had to repeat in my head so I wouldn't let my mouth get me into trouble.

"All this fuss and she disrespects us so," the redhead hissed, her voice not carrying much past where my parents and I stood. Shifting in her seat to lean over to the dark-haired one's ear, she whispered there for a second before the dark-haired one finally glanced up from her inspection of her nails.

"Is this the thanks we get for putting up with this drivel? Tainted blood on display for the world to see?" the dark one asked as if I knew what the hell they were talking about.

"Can't you two see she has no idea what you're talking about?" the white-haired one joined in, removing her legs from her armrest and sitting up to examine me. "The poor little child has no clue what it means to be what she is. The least we can do is ask her why she decided displaying the cursed Arcadios blood was a way to honor us."

Great. Arcadios blood. My mother's blood. Why in the holy hell would they be offended at the sight of my mother's blood?

"Fine, Clotho, but the offense has been noted," the redhead replied.

"So be it, Atropos, note away."

So, the white-haired one was Clotho, the spinner, the favorite.

The dark-haired one was Lachesis, the measurer, the forgotten, and the redhead was Atropos, the cutter, the inflexible.

And somehow—without even speaking, mind you—I'd already pissed them off. Aces.

"We reside here today to accept the presentation of a child. Who amongst you is here to give over your child to the will of the Moirai? Who here is prepared to give your child over to the Fates of man and Ethereal alike?" the three Fates asked in unison.

My parents linked their arms with mine and took the last step forward.

"We present you this child, Moirai, born many years ago, so you may see to her thread, so you may weave it as you will." Andras said the words Barrett said he would.

"We present you this child, sisters of Fate, so you may guide her on her journey, and measure out the longest of threads," Teresa said her part.

The three had no problem when my father spoke, but when Teresa said her part, two of the three sneered the way only a teenager could, full of ripe condescension and distaste.

Now it was my turn, and I didn't know if their contempt of my mother would transfer to me. I had a feeling it would. "Clotho, Lachesis, Atropos, I present myself to you, in witness of these fine families, so you may determine my worth and measure accordingly. I present the blood of my father, Crown Prince Andras, and the blood of my mother, High Priestess of the Pacific Northwest Covens, Teresa Alcado. I present the blood that makes my family, both lines of it, so you may judge *both* sides of me. The demon side and the witch side."

That last bit wasn't in the script, but with their distaste, I had to make a stand for the blood painted on my skin—had to let them know that even with their objections, that blood was still mine.

Lachesis seemed appeased at my explanation, but Atropos narrowed her eyes, irritation blooming across her fair skin like a rose—and this rose had some mighty big thorns. It seemed like a bad sign that the "cutter of the thread" was pissed off at me.

Before Atropos could decide my thread needed an immediate

shearing, Clotho spoke. "You honor us, child. By displaying both of your lines, you show us where your heart lies.

Lachesis picked up where her sister left off. "You honor us as you stand united as a family."

Atropos paused before she opened her mouth, a calculating little smile on her face. She seemed eager to draw out this game as long as possible. Maybe to see if I'd break and tell her to fuck off, maybe to see if I could actually act like an adult. Who knew the mind of an ancient woman stuck choosing when everyone would die?

Irritated that I picked today of all days to act like a full-fledged adult complete with self-control, she said in the most monotonous voice ever. "You honor us with your presentation."

Then her face twisted into an evil grin. "As a favor to the Moirai, we request that you dance with any male that asks you on this fine night. You may not turn a single one away."

Request. This wasn't a request. This was an order thinly veiled as a favor. Denying her, pissing her off even more, didn't seem like an option I was willing to entertain. I was going to have to just suck it up. I'd been doing it all damn day—why not just keep the charade going?

But by the reception in this room, I had a feeling Atropos just set me up for one crapshoot of a night.

Yippee.

CHAPTER FIVE

My father was the first man to ask me to dance, which given the severe faces in the room, was almost a blessing. Andras and I weren't on too good of terms. You know, after I killed his brother and made sure the bone blade everyone and their momma was fighting over was destroyed. To my credit, his brother was an evil douche canoe who wanted to start the Apocalypse, so I didn't feel too bad. Honestly, I'd killed for far less.

But Andras didn't seem bothered about the last time we spoke. He had an almost dewy-eyed glow to his face that made me pause for a slight moment once the music started. He clasped my hand in his, wrapped a sure arm around my back, and led me out into a waltz so perfect, it was proof he'd been around long before the dance was invented.

He led me through the paces of the slow ballad remake of an '80s song. "You look confused."

"Not confused, I just don't know what that expression is," I answered honestly.

Andras smiled, his eyes glowing yellow for a moment. "It's pride, sweetheart. I'm sorry this is the first time you're seeing it.

I'm proud of you, of what you did. I was pissed at the time, but you did what I couldn't. And this is all I wanted for you. To take your place here, to be recognized once the danger had passed. It took far longer than I wanted it to, but I'm glad I'm here to see it."

Parental pride was a new thing for me, and I wasn't sure what I was supposed to say back. Unable to find the right words, I nodded as he led me through the first turn, then settled on snark. "No offense, but who are you, and what have you done with my dickhead of a dad?"

Andras chuckled, a rueful smile tempering my insult. "I suppose I deserve that. To be honest, being a good guy isn't my normal setting. But this is the first time I'm not in the middle of preventing a war, so maybe this is who I'm supposed to be. Who knows?"

He paused, leading me through another turn. "I just wanted to make sure you knew all the good stuff, because some of the men you dance with tonight are going to be complete dicks to you. They're going to look down on you because of your bloodline, because you're a woman, because of who you are. They are going to say shit to you because you killed Samael, and Atropos knows it. She hates your mother and her bloodline, and if she can fuck with you, she will."

"Goodie. I so wanted to be on the bad side of the woman who controls my death," I said dryly.

Andras stifled a laugh but couldn't prevent his lips from turning up at my sarcasm. "I wanted the first thing you heard out here to be good, because you're about to get a whole truckload of unpleasant. Do your best not to lose it. That's the end goal, you know. To make sure you display that you're unfit for the Council seat."

My father held me closer, an almost hug in the middle of the formal dance and whispered in my ear, "Don't let her win."

Andras was warning me, and if Atropos' sneer was anything to go by, he was right to. All too soon, the song ended, and a youngish brown-haired man bowed to my father before holding his hand out to me. I took it without hesitation, refusing to let my reluctance show. I wouldn't give Atropos the satisfaction.

"Maxima Arcadios. At last, we finally meet."

His voice was smooth as silk and just as rich, knocking up his attractiveness at least five degrees. His shoulder-length hair bogged him down, but his eyes were kind enough.

"It's just Max. And I don't use the Arcadios name."

He seemed bemused at my correction. "All the same, it's Arcadios blood in your veins and on your face. You're an Arcadios witch whether you call yourself one or not. Bold move, by the way."

"What?"

"Nodding to your witch half. The Arcadios line isn't as accepted as some, but the honor is there. We witches won't forget it."

"So you're a witch, then?" I asked only because I had to. My dance partner was cloaking himself in the most epic way possible, and I couldn't even see the magic he was using to do it, a fact that was less and less comforting the more I thought about it. But he only nodded and didn't offer any more information.

"Are you in a coven? I always wondered how those really worked. Is it like a family?"

Bemused, my dance partner smiled again. "In all the best and worst ways. You have backup, but no privacy and everything is run by committee. But no, I'm not in a coven."

"Oh, sorry. Was my question rude? I'm afraid I'm a bit ignorant on Ethereal social norms."

"Don't worry about it. I'm sure you'll learn soon enough."

My mind went fuzzy for a second, and the next thing I knew, I was dancing with a new partner. My steps stuttered, and I accidentally stepped on his toe.

"Sorry," I whispered, trying not to catch the attention of the other dancers swarming around us.

When had the dance floor filled up? And who decided sea salt cologne was a good idea? A ton of humans thought it was a pleasant smell, but the scent always made my hackles rise. The stronger it hung in the air, the more likely someone was fucking with someone else's mind. I shuddered again, and I tread on my partner's other foot.

"Fates, woman. Can't you do a simple box step?" my partner growled through his teeth.

My new dance partner was tall and broad. Fiery dark-red hair was brushed back off his face, highlighting the spray of freckles peppering his skin, and his eyes were an unearthly shade of orange that I'd only seen on one other kind of Ethereal.

Demons.

Still puzzled on how I'd gone from dancing with my father to this gem, I concentrated on my steps and tried to ignore him. Sure, he was attractive, most Ethereals were, but adding in his attitude with the general contempt on his face, I figured we probably wouldn't be friends.

"You try dancing on these toothpicks called shoes. *Excuse* me."

He sneered, his orange eyes glowing amber, either with his power or from the eerie lighting in the ballroom.

"Complete waste of my time. There is no way someone like *you* is taking the Council seat. This whole thing is a complete farce."

Someone like me? You mean the woman who already took the damn job? I wanted to inform him of that fact but decided against it. If Barrett hadn't told anyone that I had the job, I didn't want to spoil it.

"Golly gee. Tell me how you really feel." I rolled my eyes. "What was your name again?"

"Donovan." He seethed, his jaw clenched tight enough I saw the flex in the muscle.

"Let's see, you don't like me for the Council seat because I have a vagina, right? Or it's because I've been a Rogue for the last four hundred years? Oh, I know, it's because I'm a half-breed, and my tainted-bloodness is stealing the seat out from under you?"

His eyes widened at "vagina" but went positively glacial when I mentioned stealing the seat. *Ding-ding-ding. We have a winner.*

"That's it. But see, they like someone like me for the seat because I'm not a flaming asshole with a superiority complex.

Maybe you should work on your people skills, and you'll get it next time." I smiled, just waiting for my dance partner—*err—Donovan* to lose his mind in front of all these people.

Before Donny could lose it, a handsome Asian man swiftly cut in, stealing me away and leaving Donovan standing on the dance floor in the middle of the twirling masses.

"Aww, no fair. I wanted to see him explode," I whined, and my new dance partner chuckled.

"That is the exact reason I stole you away. It's for your own safety, Princess," the man said, but it seemed more like a joke to him than anything else, so I let the princess name-calling slide.

"You don't sound American. Where are you from, mystery savior?"

A smile bloomed once again on his strikingly handsome face, his eyes crinkling and everything. "England by way of Malaysia. And as much as I like the title 'mystery savior,' I prefer the name Felix if you don't mind."

"Felix, like the cat?" I tried to get a rise out of him. I'd never seen someone so carefree.

"Felix like the cat," he returned without even a hint of derision. "I work with Donovan and have for some time. He isn't suited for the Council, and he knows it, but he's one of three others —myself included—who are in line for the seat. Now, I don't see myself as a Councilman, so you won't be hearing a cross word from me."

Interesting. I didn't know there was anyone else in line for the seat other than myself, but leave it to Barrett to neglect to tell me these things. But Felix didn't need to know I'd already taken the seat, and he also didn't need to know I had no idea if I even should have. He seemed to know way more than I did about Ethereal goings-on.

"So you work with Donovan. What do you do?" I asked instead.

Felix grinned, full of pride, the smile colored with just a hint of evil. "We're Knights of Hell. All three of the potentials are. Donovan, myself, and Alistair. We guard the gates keeping damned souls in where they belong."

I fought not to raise my eyebrows in complete disbelief. I found it hard to believe this smiling, happy man was a guardian of the gates of Hell. He didn't look mean enough to guard the doors of a Chuck E. Cheese.

"And I suppose that impresses all the ladies."

Felix shrugged noncommittally as he led me through another turn. "It doesn't hurt."

"So Donovan is the surly one, you're the pleasant one—what does that make Alistair? Is he going to bite my head off and feed me to a Corax?"

Felix winced, his pained expression making me wonder if it was the Corax talk or Alistair himself that was causing his discomfort.

"Alistair is the perpetually irritated one. Donovan is just a hothead who didn't want to come to this thing in the first place. Alistair actually wants the job. He's pretty pissed off you came onto the scene since your claim is higher than his."

Felix was a veritable fount of gossip. I needed to keep this little gem in my hip pocket. Barrett might not know all this demon-y hierarchy nonsense.

"I did stop the Apocalypse. Doesn't that earn me some brownie points?"

"Depends on who you talk to. Demons love a good war." Felix sighed wistfully as if war was something to pine after.

Soon, the song ended, and another man asked me to dance. I endured three minutes of judgment from a man who was probably older than dirt. My feet ached, the shoes ill-suited for constant wear and little to no sitting time. Luckily, after that song ended, I stole away before anyone else could ask me to take another spin. Plucking a champagne flute from a passing waiter's tray, I slowly sipped it even though I really wanted to chug. Positively parched, I glanced around for a non-alcoholic option once my glass was empty. The last thing I needed was more champagne on an empty stomach.

"Looking for the hors d'oeuvres?" a man asked from behind me, and I couldn't help the sigh of defeat that passed my lips at the sound of his cultured British accent.

I was going to get asked to dance. Again. And probably mocked. Super.

"Yes," I said almost pitifully, turning to get a better look at the man I would probably be dancing with in a few minutes.

After I got some food, of course.

Since I was in heels, he wasn't too much taller than me, maybe six feet or so with a pair of baby blues that could make a girl weep. Artfully tousled reddish-brown hair accentuated his high cheekbones, and then adding in his damn near pouty lips, well, let's just say he wasn't hard to look at. Plus, the man filled out a suit.

He was hot, but it seemed all Ethereals were hot. Looking back at all my encounters over the centuries, every single Ethereal had been attractive, and since most of us didn't age, we would all just go on being hot forever. The orgies in Aether were starting to make more sense.

It took me a second to realize the man had just been staring at me, and me at him. In silence. Awkward.

Shaking myself, I started talking, and just couldn't stop. "I haven't had a thing to eat since sparring with a bunch of werewolves this morning. This is my first ball or dance or gala or whatever, and no one tells you how long it takes to get ready or how long these things last. I mean, really, I could eat a steak as big as my face right now."

My potential dance partner seemed like he was holding in a smile.

"Sorry. That is probably the single glass of champagne working its way through my system. If you would like to dance, I promise to try not to talk your ear off."

He let his smile go, and I swear to the Fates, I almost swooned. Dimples. The man had dimples. He held out his elbow for me to take and led me back to the dance floor where one of my favorite songs by Bonhom was playing. Mystery dance partner led me into a waltz, which was standard fare for the night, the long steps a perfect placement for the haunting song.

"I'm Max, by the way," I offered when he didn't say anything for what seemed like a full minute.

"I know." A smile stretched his mouth again, as if he knew a secret I didn't. Of course he did. He actually knew his name.

"You see, I told you my name in the hopes you would tell me yours. Unlike everyone else in this room, I haven't been around the upper crust for the last bazillion years, so I don't know anyone. Including you."

"You could just ask, you know," he said offhandedly as he led me into a turn and then back into his space again.

"Fine." I sighed, trying for stern. "What's your name?"

He chuckled. "I don't know if I want to tell you. You probably know it already and all the gossip that follows it."

"I promise I don't. If we haven't met before, I probably know nothing about you. Honest."

"All right. If you insist on knowing your dance partner, I'm Alistair Quinn."

I was wrong. I did know that name.

This was the man who wanted my job.

CHAPTER SIX

"So, you do know me." Alistair assessed my expression, a smug half-smile pulling at his lips. "Good. Then you know why I'm here."

Why he was here was the unknown part. Did he just want to square up to the person who had the job he wanted? But he didn't know I'd already taken the job, did he? He thought he was still in the running.

Did I want to tell him?

I took in his dimpled half-smile and arrogant expression. *No, I didn't want to tell him.* I wanted him to put his foot in it and then brandish the mother of all trump cards, watching his face as it crumpled in defeat. Yes, that would be much more satisfying.

"I know your name and profession. And I learned both of those tonight from your friend, Felix. I understand you're irritated I was asked to take the position?"

Alistair's expression hardened like I expected it to. "You mean, am I irritated that some upstart with exactly zero knowledge of our ways and customs was asked to take the most venerated seats available for our kind? No." He mocked sarcastically. "Why would I give a ripe shite about demon politics?"

"I might not know all the ways and customs, but can't you even for a second consider that maybe that's a good thing? I don't know the history, so I will always choose what is right and wrong. Not based on history but based on now. I won't have eons of prejudice clouding every decision."

"How could you possibly know what is right and wrong if you have no understanding of the reasons behind the actions you'll be judging?"

I scoffed. "Because I won't be the only person doing the judging? It's a Council, it's not like I'll be alone destroying lives willy-nilly." A man like him wouldn't even consider that someone like me could have anything to offer. "You probably think I'm being served this job on a damn platter. I've been on this planet for four centuries amongst humans, watching every war, every atrocity. If you think I'm some vapid little child, you're sorely mistaken."

"Yes, amongst humans. You don't know the first thing about demons." He sneered, ignoring my argument altogether while he expertly led me through and around the other dancers. His form was perfect, which irritated me almost as much as his snobby attitude.

But he had to know just how evil humans could be. He was a Knight of Hell. His job was to keep the vilest of souls right where they belonged.

"Maybe so, but weren't demons created to punish the wicked? Isn't that our purpose? Humans can't be all sunshine and roses if the powers that be deigned to create a whole realm just to weed out the bad seeds. You even have the job of keeping the craftiest from escaping. Even if I think you're probably horrible at your job, you have to agree humans are nothing to sneeze at."

Alistair's pale face reddened in affront. *Yeah, I said it.* If he were any good at his job, I wouldn't have died in front of all my friends two years ago. I wouldn't have lost so much. I wouldn't still dream about the life leaking out of me that night.

"What in Fate's name makes you think I'm not the best at my job?" He seethed through clenched teeth.

"Do the names Baron, Bella, and Tessa Bishop mean anything to you?" I saw his sneer and raised him one. *Knight of Hell. Pfft.*

Alistair's steps stuttered before his surprise morphed into something akin to rage. Leading me off the dance floor, he grabbed my upper arm in a blisteringly hot hand, the ironclad grip brooking no argument. I was following him. Or else. Damn demons and their penchant for burning. Alistair steered me toward a darkened corner of the ballroom, assumingly where he could chastise me without prying ears.

Well, fuck that.

Ignoring the pain, I picked right up where I left off on the dance floor. "Those names should sound real familiar. Baron and Bella tried to spring their mother from Hell by attacking the three pieces of the Veil. You know, the three beings that keep Heaven, Hell, and the Otherside from crashing into this plane. You remember those, right? I died trying to stop them. In fact, I still remember exactly how it felt, still dream about it. If you were any good at your job, you would be protecting both sides of the gates, and not leaving us to do your work for you. *That's* how I know you're shit at your job."

I snatched my arm out of his hold. "And watch your temperature, *Knight.* Burn me again, and it won't be Andras you'll need to fear." I stepped into his space, making sure my threat was clear as crystal. "It'll be me."

Stepping back, I tried not to let the fear fill me as I scanned my arms for brands. Micah managed to brand me with a single burning hand. I'd hate to have to kill Alistair, but I would before I let anyone own me.

"I didn't"—He paused before clearing his throat and lowering his voice—"I didn't mean to burn you. Please let me see."

His touch was gentle as he inspected my bicep. Red, raised skin in the shape of his large hand encircled my arm, and he let out a hiss under his breath. "I'll fix it. I swear. I didn't mean to hurt you. I didn't know"—He paused again and let out a sigh—"I forgot you are not inured to the heat."

"You thought I wouldn't burn." I chuckled, even though the

scorched skin hurt like a sonofabitch. "You don't know much about me, do you?"

Confusion clouded his expression. "Why would burning be comical?" he asked as he inspected the skin.

"Because I was burned at the stake? It's how I became a Rogue in the first place. All this piss and vinegar about me taking your rightful spot, and you don't know the first thing about me, do you?"

His jaw clenched as my point hit home. "I know enough. I also know how to fix this, but you'll have to stay still."

He raised a thumb to his mouth, and I caught the barest glimpse of fangs before they sliced into the flesh. He brought the bloody digit to the burn, and before I could protest, he'd drawn a full circle of blood through the middle of the wound. Instantly, the pain abated, and I watched with wide eyes as the red, raised skin melted away to my normal bronze coloring.

"This didn't bind me to you or magically marry us, or some other bullshit, right? Because I've had about enough of that to last a lifetime."

Alistair's eyebrows raised again as if I'd surprised him. He really *didn't* know anything about me.

"A demon bound you?" At my nod, pure malice washed across his face. "Who?"

"Don't worry, Knight, it didn't take." I brushed off his concern. The last thing I needed was another man worrying about me, even if it was this prick.

"So, you killed him, then?" Alistair accused, and instantly, I bristled.

I didn't deserve that tone, but I couldn't erupt on the man in front of all these people even if we were off the beaten path. I didn't feel an ounce of guilt for killing Micah, and I never would. I'd have killed him twice if I could have. Too bad Andras beat me to the punch.

"Wouldn't be the first man I taught not to take things that didn't belong to him. Study up, Knight, there's a whole host of stuff you don't know about me."

With that, I eyed the closest exit and made my way there. I didn't care where the doors actually took me, I just needed to get the hell out of here. Maybe to a place with food and a seat. But I didn't make it that far. Instead, a warm grip snagged my hand and pulled me back around.

Alistair. Again.

Only this time his grip was gentle, and his expression wasn't accusing. It was open—*and I daresay*—even honest. And still, he pulled me closer to him.

"I want to know who bound you." His voice was a gravelly husk of the posh British accent he'd had just minutes ago. His irises glowed amber, and the tips of his fangs flashed just behind his lips. "Tell me who did that to you."

"Why do you need to know? It's none of your concern, *Knight*." I used his title like a slur, but Alistair wasn't taking the bait.

"I give a shit, that's why. No one deserves to be bound without their consent. But especially, not someone like you."

"You mean a Princess? Like those of a lower station don't matter?"

Alistair sighed. "You could aggravate a saint, couldn't you?"

He had no idea. "It's a gift. Now let go of my hand and let me go get some food."

His grip tightened just slightly before his hand fell away. But that didn't mean he let me go. Oh, no. He just stepped closer, getting in my space in a way I couldn't ignore him, holding me there without even touching me.

"I'm not letting you go anywhere until I know the demon who did that to you is dead. And if he's not, I plan to make him that way post haste."

I didn't know why he cared. As far as I knew, Alistair Quinn wanted the job I already had, and other than that, he didn't have one thing to do with me.

"Don't worry, I took care of it."

He rolled his eyes. "Just give me the name, Max."

He wanted his name? Sure, I'd give it to him. I supposed he didn't need to know it was never Micah's idea to come after me. It was Ruby's. And it probably wasn't her idea, either. The list kept growing into a web of people I couldn't trust, couldn't find, or couldn't forget. Micah and Samael were dead, but Ruby… I'd been looking for her for six months, and it was as if she'd dropped off the face of the map.

But she didn't bind me, even if she'd sent him after me. Micah did that all on his own.

"Fine. Micah Goode."

Alistair hissed in recognition. Good to know the man of my worst nightmares was famous. At least Ruby sent the cream of the crop after me.

"Don't worry about killing him, I took care of that already, and when he came back as a spirit, Andras finished him off. But I'll tell you what, if he manages to come back another time, I'll let you have a crack at him."

"You've been taking care of yourself for a long time, haven't you?" His voice was little more than a whisper, but I heard him anyway.

He had no idea. I'd been taking care of myself long before I was ever a Rogue.

"You bet."

Something washed over his expression, and it took everything in me not to take that tiny step forward, not to get just that little bit farther into his space. But I couldn't go there with this man. Not now.

Maybe not ever.

"You're safe, right?"

Probably? Maybe? No, I most likely wasn't, but this man didn't need to know that, and it sure as hell wasn't his responsibility.

"Of course I am. Who'd want to kill me?" I smiled, but the fact of the matter was this whole thing was a joke. I didn't belong here in the middle of the ball or gala, or whatever the hell it was. I wasn't aristocracy, not really. I was a tattooed outcast who liked to make sure people paid for picking on the little guy.

And that's all I'd ever be. An avenging angel—or demon, as the case may be.

I managed to break away from Alistair, each step from him bringing clarity and a coldness I hadn't felt earlier. I needed more of it. I needed that chill in my blood and the sense that came with it. I needed a clear head and a free heart.

But most of all, I needed a quiet room. Chair optional.

The door led back to Aether proper, the pounding music rattling through my ribcage, and I struggled through throngs of bodies toward my destination. Strobe lights flashed, the heat filtering into my closely guarded chill. I headed toward the one door no one in their right mind would go to.

The Latin inscription above the door to the high courtroom called to me. *Numera omnes qui ingrediuntur ad iudicium. Judgment comes to all who enter.* I wanted to be here, a place I felt I belonged—a place where I could do a little bit of good, keeping an eye out for those little guys I cared so much about.

But the normally all-white, blindingly bright courtroom was dark.

"*Detrahet me in lucem.*" I snapped my fingers in the gloom. Light bloomed in my palm, and what I saw had me backing up to make sense of it.

A large swath of the formerly white courtroom was splashed in red, the copper tang hitting me full in the face now that my brain supplied the word.

Blood.

A red-haired woman was splayed in the middle of the largest puddle, and it took me far too long to realize her hair wasn't red at all. It was blonde, stained scarlet from her blood.

I knew the woman, too. It was as if my mind conjured her from my most hideous of thoughts and plopped her exactly where I didn't want her. I'd longed for revenge on this woman, but in all my plans, I never wanted this.

But it seemed Ruby had one last "fuck you" for me, especially with the message, "A gift for the princess," spelled out in blood, painted on the steps of the dais of the high court.

I was going to get blamed for this. I just knew it.

CHAPTER SEVEN

I wasn't looking at the dead woman on the floor. Nope. My eyes were trained on the crudely drawn message staining the white marble dais.

A gift for the princess.

That cold chill I'd desired a minute ago had turned into an arctic freeze. A shudder wracked my body as the realization of what I was seeing finally hit me.

Someone did this *for* me. Someone sought Ruby out, drew her here where she was wanted for treason, and then murdered her without anyone noticing. Under all our noses. It was well known to those that mattered that Ruby and I weren't friends, but I'd caught a glimpse of the iron spikes nailing her body to the floor.

No one—not even Ruby—deserved to die like that.

I needed to call someone, tell someone. Yes. That was what I needed to do. I was about to turn to do just that when hard hands clamped around my shoulders and yanked, pulling me from the room and back into the hallway. Those same hands spun me before I even had the chance to kill the ball of light in my palm, so I caught his face before the light died.

Alistair.

"I didn't do it," I blurted, shock stealing all my sense. Could I sound any guiltier?

Alistair stared at me like I'd just gone off the deep end. "Of course you didn't. You weren't out of my sight for more than thirty seconds. I've heard stories of how lethal you are, but even you can't butcher a woman in that scant of time."

I couldn't put my finger on the "why," but relief stole through me at his staunch assuredness that I couldn't do that. Flashes of what I just saw blinked like strobe lights in my brain. The blood, the broken and tattered wings—or what was left of them—her naked body run through with spikes. I shuddered again, and this time, Alistair ran soothing hands down my arms. I was edging on hysteria in front of this poor man, and there was nothing I could do to stop it.

"We have to tell someone." I managed to choke out before my eyes welled, and I covered my mouth before a sob could fall from my lips.

I'd seen horrible things in my life. I'd seen women butchered before. I saw Melody nearly cut in half. But I had someone to blame, had someone to punish. Now, my mind was still stuck on the shock of it, the sheer brutality of what was done to a woman I might not have liked, but sure as I was breathing, never wanted something like that for her.

"Barrett. I'll get Barrett. Or Marcus. Or my father. Fates, who am I supposed to go to, Alistair? Are there Ethereal police?"

Alistair continued to look at me like I'd lost my mind. Maybe I had. "The Keys are our... Think of them as investigators, like Scotland Yard, but regular citizens can't call them. They're in the employ of the Council. No. We need a friend here. The sooner, the better. This doesn't look good for us."

I didn't understand him at all. "Why? We didn't do anything. I just found her like that. I could never..."

"We're demons, Max. She was evidently an angel if those mauled wings are anything to go by. Unless we get someone to believe us and soon, we are about to be in the middle of a war."

No sooner were those words out of his mouth, was the corridor flooded with people. And I quickly found out the hard way that Aether—or some offshoot of it—had a jail.

The cement slab under my ass might as well have been a glacier. Given my flimsy dress, I had nothing to protect me from the freezing stone, and no way to heat myself. The stone, the bars, the ceiling, everything was warded against magic. Runes of nulling were carved into nearly every inch of my cell, the magic of them grating against my skin worse than any sandpaper. Everything about myself, everything that made me who I was, seemed stripped, tattered, pulled from my very bones as I sat shivering in the silence. Even my innate demon magic seemed muted, muffled, ripped away. Alistair sat in an adjacent cell, his tuxedo jacket rumpled from the not-so-polite way we were hauled down here.

The only good thing I could say for the place was they didn't skimp on the security. A guard was posted outside both Alistair's and my cell, and we'd been forcefully requested not to speak. AKA, they slammed Alistair against the bars of his cell to shut him up when he'd only asked a question. I didn't want to know what someone had to do to get permanently remanded to one of these cells.

Footsteps echoed through my cell block, but I didn't look. This was the fifth time I'd heard steps coming my way, and every time I glanced up, the disappointment of no one coming for me tore me more.

"You sure know how to ruin a good party," a cultured British voice called to me, and I finally raised my eyes.

Barrett. Thank the Fates.

"Barrett! Please tell me you're here for us. I didn't—couldn't—do something like that. Not even to her."

He sighed, nearly touching the bars, but remembered what they could do and thought better of it. Instead, his hand fell on the knot of his tie, loosening the fabric from his neck. "How many times have you died preventing innocent deaths? It's up to a hundred and fifty by now, right? Sure. I totally believe you could kill someone like that."

I was a little too freaked out to fully catch the sarcasm. "Sarcasm is only funny if I'm not being drained of all my magic, Barrett. I'm going to need you to be as literal as possible right now."

"And that brings me to why I'm here. Macallan, unlock these cells. The Fates would like to speak to both of them."

"Sir?" Macallan didn't seem like he wanted to unlock either cell, in fact, his expression said he'd like to conveniently lose the key.

Barrett narrowed his eyes. "Is there a problem?"

"They're demons, sir. An angel was killed, surely the Fates wouldn't want them released." Macallan was whispering, but I heard him all the same.

"I can promise you that neither Maxima Alcado nor Alistair Quinn has ever harmed a single angel in their lives. Just because you're prejudiced against demons, doesn't make them murderers. Things like facts and reason take part in convicting someone, Macallan, not blind propaganda and bullshit. Now, do you want me to tell the Fates why they had to wait, or are you going to open the fucking door?"

Reluctantly, Macallan opened my cell, but I waited for him to get out of the way before I walked through the opening. Once I was out, the relief of my magic coming back had me almost giddy, and I really looked at Macallan. Abnormally tall, probably close to seven feet or so, bulky in the extreme, barrel-chested with a trunk of a neck, his general demeanor screamed malice. But his face told another story altogether, it said fear, insecurity, not hatred.

He feared demons. Given some of us were right bastards, I couldn't blame him.

"Macallan, is it?" At his stiff nod, I continued, "The stories about demons aren't true for all of us. We are protectors, punishers of the wicked. Some of our kind go a little crazy, but that's true for all Ethereals." I sniffed, catching his scent, the light of his magic telling me what kind of Ethereal he was. I knew what he was before the door opened, the runes unable to take that away from me at least. "You're a shifter. Plenty of your kind have turned, haven't they? But no one blames the whole for the actions of a few. We only ask for the same courtesy."

Macallan gave me another stiff nod. "Your Majesty, I know you are better than some. I heard about what you did to Finn Lorenson. You were within your rights to kill him, and you didn't, so I know there is good in you. But you might want to watch out who you spend time with." His eyes flashed to Alistair and back to me. "Not everyone has a reputation like yours."

I almost giggled. Did he mean Alistair had a shitty rep and mine was the good one? No fucking way.

"I'll keep that in mind."

Macallan nodded to the other guard whose name I didn't catch, and Alistair was freed. He didn't have the same hesitation I did about getting out of his cell. As soon as the door was cracked, Alistair bolted from the rune-carved room. He also spat at the guard's boots as he left, the red-tinted saliva hitting the floor just shy of the guard. Alistair couldn't heal in the cell, so his mouth was still bleeding from the brutal shove against the bars.

Alistair squared up against the guard, looking like he'd rather throw a couple of punches rather than get the hell out of here.

"Hey, Knight?"

Alistair's body didn't move, but his glowing amber gaze slid from the guard to me.

"Want to get the fuck out of here before they figure out a way to make us stay? Get your shit together, and let's go."

His eyes narrowed in contempt, the animalistic growl rumbling from his throat made the hair on my arms stand on end. With a flash of fang, he took his leave of the guard and followed us down the almost never-ending corridor, up the stone steps to a set of heavily guarded double doors. We had less trouble with these guards. They opened the doors as if they were glad to see the backs of us, and then we were back in the sea of pulse-pounding music and writhing bodies.

I'd never been so happy to see the overcrowded club in my life.

Barrett had to keep me steady when I nearly lost my feet in relief, but we never stopped moving. The Fates wanted to talk to us, and, dammit, I wanted to talk to them, too. They had to know who did this, didn't they?

Atropos cut the threads of life, right? That meant she had to know when someone died. Was it too far a stretch to think she'd also know how?

Barrett led us to an office I knew well. The brass "Management" plaque was familiar enough to ease my nerves a bit, until I remembered the last time I was here outside Caim's office—Ruby was, too. That thought brought flashes of the high courtroom painted with her blood through my brain with enough force to cause me to stumble again.

Before he opened the door, Barrett turned me to face him, his hands coming down on my shoulders. Whispered words I couldn't make out poured from his lips, and the lingering queasiness from the null wards fell away.

"Do not, under any circumstances, let them see you flinch, Maxima." Barrett's words were a fierce whisper of warning. "You are strong, you are capable, and they need to see you as such. You did nothing wrong, so don't let them see you think otherwise. Do you understand?"

At my nod, he released my shoulders, and I stood straight, pulling on a cloak of confidence I certainly didn't feel.

"And you," Barrett addressed Alistair, "keep your nose clean for five freaking minutes while Max talks her way out of this mess. Do you think you can do that, or am I going to have to send you back to the holding cell?"

Alistair seemed to want to argue, and that's just what he did.

"I want to be in there with her. I'm her alibi. I know she didn't do anything."

Barrett rolled his eyes. "No, Junior, I'm her alibi. Ruby was murdered hours ago when Max was with me. Speaking of, where were you between the hours of 4 p.m. and 8 p.m.?"

Alistair took a step back in affront. "In Hell. At my post." A growl escaped him—the same animalistic rumble that made all the hairs on my body stand on end.

"You'd better have been."

Barrett looped his arm with mine, pulled open the door, and dragged me through with him. I gave Alistair an apologetic glance before the door closed, but the expression I got back was nothing if not resolute. This wasn't the first time someone had slighted Alistair, and from the look on his face, it wouldn't be the last.

"What the *hell* was that about?" I leaned into Barrett and hissed.

"I'll tell you later. You have bigger fish to fry." Barrett kept his voice a whisper as he led me through the archway of books and into Caim's office.

The same three women I'd spent all day getting ready to meet, the same ones I'd been presented to like a slab of beef, the same ones who thought my mother's blood was an affront, sat with their asses perched on the edge of Caim's desk, calm as you please.

Atropos, my brand-new nemesis spoke first, her words just about as damning as they could be. "You, my little princess, are in some deep shit."

I had a feeling she was right.

CHAPTER EIGHT

I'd wanted to be cool and collected. I'd wanted to handle this situation with the grace of my station. Wanted to show these three women—deities, gods, whatever—that I was fit to lead my people, to judge them. Instead, I was my regular sassy self and pissed people off.

Go figure.

"I'm in deep shit? Yeah, apparently, I've got a benefactor who thinks murder is an appropriate gift. I'd say the shit is about waist-high." My particular brand of cheek was not appreciated by this group. Barrett, to his credit, elbowed me in the side, but I ignored him. I was too busy staring at Atropos' face to see if she'd give anything away.

She didn't, so I continued, "You're supposed to be the cutter of the thread, right? So why don't you tell us who did it? Because it sure as shit wasn't me, and it wasn't Alistair, either." I finished off my rant with a defiant crossing of my arms coupled with a hip jut. Yeah, it was a defensive posture, but screw it. If these women were trying to imply I had something to do with Ruby's murder, they were dead wrong.

But something passed over Atropos' face. It was a little bit of fear mixed with uncertainty and general malcontent. *Oh, this is worse than I thought.* As the silence lingered, my feeling of dread only grew.

Clotho huffed and pushed off the desk to pace the length of Caim's office. "We don't know who killed the angel." She broke the silence with *that* admission. Both Lachesis and Atropos seemed shocked she would say as much.

"But knowing that information is typical, correct?" I needed to clarify that point before it got lost in whatever they were about to hit me with.

Atropos snorted, rolling her eyes like the teenager she definitely was not. "Yes. Usually—as in every other death since the beginning of time—I've been able to see the causation and circumstances of death. Not only was this angel's thread cut, but it wasn't cut by me. Someone killed this woman right under my nose."

Which seemed like a kind of big thing for her to admit, and also seemed like something I probably shouldn't know. Not if I wanted to keep breathing.

"So not only do I have a murdery benefactor, I have one that seems to know how to circumvent a Fate." I murmured this revelation to myself, but that didn't stop Atropos from narrowing her eyes at me.

"We know Max didn't do this." Barrett chimed in at my defense. "She was with me all day. In fact, Atropos herself made it so Max wouldn't be alone the entire evening with her 'don't turn a man down' shtick."

Glad I wasn't the only one who thought that edict was bullshit.

"If it weren't for the stasis spell cast on the body, maybe the timeline could be proven, but it can't," Lachesis countered. "We have no idea when Ruby Sinclair was murdered. It could have been six months ago for all we know."

I wanted to tell them how long I'd been searching for Ruby, how long I looked without even so much as a blip. If she'd been under a stasis spell, it was likely she'd been dead the whole time and brought out when it would be most convenient for her killer. I wanted to tell them, but I didn't. I had no illusions that the admission would make me seem more guilty and not less.

But they wanted to talk to me for a reason, and I was done catering to this merry-go-round of bullshit. "You ladies sprang me from jail, that must mean you want something. What is it?"

Atropos almost smiled at my blunt question. Almost, but not quite.

"We want you to find the murderer. Since it seems the act was presented as a gift to you, you are the person best to investigate it. We want you to resolve all of this. Immediately. You have forty-eight hours to bring the killer to us," she ordered in an airy way that told of eons of getting exactly what she wanted.

Was I supposed to fall on bended knee and do her bidding? It didn't matter if I was or wasn't supposed to, I wasn't gonna.

"Say what now? You want me to solve a murder you have no information on in less time than it takes to make good tamales. Or what?"

Atropos and Clotho seemed a little taken aback at my question, but Lachesis covered her face with her hand to hide her smile.

"What do you mean, or what?" Atropos asked.

"Exactly what I said. I have forty-eight hours, *or what*? Why shouldn't I just give you the middle finger and move on with my life? You know I didn't kill Ruby, because I've already prevented the war this would start twice already. You know I didn't kill her because if I had, not only would I not have bungled it in such a fashion, I sure as hell wouldn't have arranged the evidence to point right back at myself. Forty-eight hours. Or. What?" I demanded through gritted teeth.

Atropos' face turned an unhealthy shade of red, but honestly, I didn't give a ripe shit.

"How about if you don't find the murderer, we'll blame it on you. A demon killing an angel wouldn't go over too well, Armistice and all. Or maybe we'll blame your friend Alistair. Clotho has had it out for him for ages, I'm sure she wouldn't mind thrusting an entire war on his shoulders. Maybe we'll divvy it up between the two of you, really throw you under the bus."

I wanted to tell them they couldn't do that, but I knew better. They could and would. Out of spite, out of boredom.

"So the three of you have no honor whatsoever. Good to know. Anything you can add so I can find this bastard, or am I completely on my own?"

Atropos gave me a beatific smile. "You're on your own, Maxima. Don't fuck it up."

I was momentarily tempted to snap my fingers and light her and her sisters on fire, but Barrett snatched my elbow before I could act on my impulses.

"What in the fresh hell was that?" He dragged me from Caim's office back to the too-loud club, the thumping base and strobe lights only serving to fuel my anger.

"That was our bosses being assholes, Barrett. What part of that was unclear?"

Barrett's grip grew tighter, enough for me to know he meant business but not enough to really hurt. "You openly challenged the Fates, Maxima. Are you high, or do you have a death wish?"

He knew better than that. He knew exactly why I challenged them, and if he had less to lose, he would have, too.

"They were acting like scared bullies. Do I bow down to bullies, Barrett?" I didn't even give him a chance to answer. "No, I don't. I didn't bow down to Finn Lorenson this morning, and I'm sure as shit not going to bow down to three women who can't see the forest for the fucking trees. Not today, and not any other damn day."

Barrett pinched the bridge of his nose, dragging me away from the thumping music and down a semi-quiet hallway. I really didn't have time to deal with his judgment. Before I could tell Barrett just that, Alistair picked that moment of tense silence to appear out of thin freaking air and insert himself into the conversation.

"What happened? What did they say?"

How, exactly, did I explain that the Fates were trying to blame it all on us? How did I explain that the forty-eight-hour deadline to find the real killer was a joke? That it was a way to get me to chase my tail long enough to screw me and mine over?

"I have forty-eight hours to find the killer."

He frowned, probably just like I did not five minutes ago when the Fates told me and asked the same damn question I did. "Or what?"

My laugh was bitter and a little hysterical, making Alistair's eyebrows crawl up his forehead. "Or they blame me, or you, or the both of us. Turns out they have no idea who did it, and now, it's my job to find out. Plus, we have to hope it wasn't another demon, or it's going to start the end of the world. Wish me luck, Knight, because I believe the both of us are just about fucked."

"Wha—" he began, but I cut him off. What part of the time limit thing did he not understand? Did he not comprehend just how short forty-eight hours was?

"Alistair, I don't have time to explain. The clock is ticking, and unless you say you killed an angel and my investigation is moot, I have a job to do."

With that, I gave him my back and addressed Barrett. "Where's Caim?"

Caim was the owner of Aether, an angel, held the angel seat of the Council, and was the keeper of the records. On top of that, he used to be Ruby's boss. If anyone knew anything about the circumstances of Ruby's death, it would be Caim.

Before Barrett could answer me, Alistair spun me to face him. Since I wasn't obligated to be nice anymore, I wasn't. A snap of my fingers had Alistair's arms involuntarily bound to his sides, his legs sticking together so he couldn't take a single step. Shock warped his face, which was supremely satisfying.

"What in the bloody hell did you do to me?" He seethed, flashing his fangs and amber eyes.

Interestingly enough, Alistair had upper and lower fangs, the second incisor and canine of both sets pointed, meaning eight razor-sharp teeth to fight with on top of who knew what else. They didn't look like wraith fangs or even the ones on Micah, the murdering incubus.

"I don't like being manhandled. Keep your hands to yourself, Knight, or I will remove the use of them altogether. Now what do you want?"

Alistair narrowed his eyes as if my spell was somehow an affront when he was the one who kept grabbing people. *Idiot.*

"You shouldn't be doing this alone. Or at all, for that matter. You know nothing of our world, Maxima. You're just a witch in a demon's body. You're going to get yourself killed."

"I wouldn't—" Barrett began, but I didn't let him warn Alistair.

No, this was a lesson the man needed to learn. And fast. Snapping my fingers again, I watched his lips mash together. I didn't remove them completely like I did with Ian that one time, but only because I wasn't nearly as mad.

Alistair didn't know me. He had no idea what I was capable of.

"This witch knew enough about our world to put down Samael, a demon that had been sowing doubt and contention for years. This witch destroyed one of the only ways on this plane to kill a demon. This witch has been on her own for a long fucking time. How about you don't tell me what I can and can't do?"

Alistair's irritated scream was muffled by his closed lips. Too late, buddy.

I turned back to Barrett. "Caim?"

"He's at our house."

I nodded and began walking down the hall toward the portal to Barrett's home.

"Are you going to let him out of that spell, or are you going to wait for one of the other witches to take pity on him?"

I debated the ramifications of Alistair being left helpless in a club full of witches on the verge of an orgy. Yeah, even I wasn't that cruel.

"Oh, fine. If you insist." I snapped my fingers once more, enjoying the thud of Alistair's body hitting the floor and the resulting string of curses flowing from his lips like tap water.

"There, I fixed it." I threaded my arm through Barrett's. "Now take me to Caim."

"Your thirst for revenge really scares the shit out of me. I hope you know that."

Me too, Barry. Me too.

CHAPTER NINE

To my ultimate irritation, I couldn't corner Caim the second I arrived with Barrett. Once we reached the sitting room, I quickly realized there was more than just Caim and Marcus waiting for us. The entire Council was there, perched on the available seating, sipping whichever brand of alcohol Barrett and Marcus kept in stock. I sincerely hoped they had a glass of Scotch with my name on it.

Marcus was the first to speak as he enveloped me in a hug. "Thank the Fates. I worried when Barrett told me you were taken to holding."

Holding? Is that what they called it? If that wasn't the entrance to Hell, I didn't know what it was.

"I'm fine. But I'd love to know what the hell is going on. An update and a big glass of whiskey would be fabulous."

"I've got you covered." Barrett held three fingers in a cut crystal tumbler at my elbow.

"You are a prince among men. Did anyone ever tell you that?" I murmured before I tossed the burning liquid back in one swallow. It scalded my esophagus, but the warmth it brought made me feel whole for the first time since I was shoved into that cell.

"What did the Fates say to you, child?" Gorgon asked, his giant warlock's form folded into one of Barrett's leather club chairs. Gorgon was one of the few beings I would let get away with calling me a child. He meant no harm by it, and since he had probably lived a thousand lives, I had no problem with the moniker.

I swallowed air, wishing I had more whiskey. "I have forty-eight hours to solve this." I avoided the word murder solely for Caim's benefit. I didn't know how he felt about Ruby or her passing, but even I was scarred by what I'd seen. "If I don't bring Ruby's killer to the Fates in that time, they will blame her murder on me, Alistair Quinn, or the both of us. They don't seem too concerned that this will shatter the Armistice and start a war." In fact, it kind of seemed like Atropos would love to see me fail.

"Why can't they tell you who did it?" Caim's voice was like broken glass and gravel. "Why are you looking into this and not them? Why..." Caim stood, and single-arm threw the closest bit of furniture into the wall. The chunky wood end table didn't stand a chance, shattering upon impact, the wood paneling of the wall cracking with the strain of the blow.

"They don't know who did it. Somehow, Ruby's thread was cut without Atropos knowing," Barrett answered for me since I was still staring at what used to be a solid piece of furniture.

I had questions for Caim, but I didn't know if I could ask them without him throwing something else.

"How could she not know who cut the thread?" Cinder, our resident dragon, asked in her thick Slavic accent. "No one in the history of forever has died without her knowing it. No one. Just like no one is born without Clotho knowing."

I walked to the wet bar and refilled my glass. No one lived without Clotho knowing, and no one died without Atropos knowing. Did that mean Lachesis knew all the rest? I wanted to ask, but I had a feeling Lachesis wouldn't answer me.

"And they want the youngest of us, the only demon, to investigate an angel's murder?" Caim scoffed. "If they don't know who cut her thread, how in the shit are you supposed to find out?"

He wasn't wrong, but I didn't have the time to let him rant.

"You going to let me ask the things I need to ask? Or are you going to lose your shit again?"

Caim seemed to ponder my questions for a second before he feigned calm and took his seat. "Fire away."

I hesitated for a moment, waiting to see if he was actually holding his shit together, or if he'd lose it. He managed to fake his calm, so I began my interrogation.

"The Fates said Ruby was killed, but I thought angels and demons were the same in that they could be temporarily dead, but not permanently. Not without a special weapon. So, I guess what my question is—is how did Ruby die?"

Caim sucked in a breath, his eyes flashing golden, the same way Striker's did now that he'd come into his abilities. Caim was a hair's breadth away from losing what little composure he had, but still, he answered me.

"Typically, we are just as resilient as demons. But even we have ways to die. Whoever killed her did use a special weapon. The three spikes that nailed her to the floor are one of the few artifacts capable of rendering an angel powerless. Thank Perseus for that one."

"Perseus? You mean the demigod who killed Medusa, Perseus?"

"That's the one." Caim nodded before sipping from a fresh refill of whiskey. "You see, Medusa was innocent. She was just going about her life, worshiping her chosen god, and then Poseidon comes along and rapes her in Athena's temple, right? Athena blames Medusa for defiling her temple, and curses her with snakes in her hair and a gaze that can turn a man to stone. Well, old Perseus needed Medusa's head for a weapon, so he snuck in her lair and cut her head off while she was sleeping, used the head to kill the monster, and everything was hunky-dory, right? No one ever says what happened after that. No one remembers that Medusa had two immortal sisters."

I had to admit the story of Perseus and Medusa always pissed me off. "The sisters killed him, didn't they?"

"Yup. Tortured him for a while, too. With iron spikes. Thirteen of them."

The mental image of a man impaled thirteen times made the whiskey in my belly want to come back up.

"Please tell me I don't have to go find ten more of those things."

"No. Just three more. Seven of them have been recovered over the years, held in a null room similar to our holding cells. The three used to murder Ruby will be heading there after they have been rendered inert."

I wondered if the person who killed Ruby had the other three spikes. I wondered if those weapons were even something I could find.

"Okay, so I can try to find those spikes. Maybe the person who has the remaining three is either the person who killed Ruby or knows who did."

"That would be a dark path to take, child." Gorgon interrupted my musings. "Weapons like that have been outlawed since their creation. Anyone who has them in their possession isn't someone you want to cross. Spikes like those can kill more than just angels."

"Plus," Cinder added, "the Keys have been searching for forbidden weapons for ages. If they haven't found them, you are not likely to, either."

This was the second time I'd heard about the Keys tonight, and I still didn't fully understand who they were.

"The Keys are the Council's investigators, right?"

Cinder bowed her blonde head in a nod. "Correct. When they aren't investigating crimes, they search for forbidden weapons. We have been trying to prevent the violation of the Armistice for a very long time."

It made sense. No one wanted the angels and demons to go to war, especially not me, even if I didn't know what something like that might mean.

"So, I'm back to square one," I muttered.

Then I remembered the feather, the same one I'd been using for the past six months to try and find Ruby. The same feather she'd dropped when I'd knocked her out of the tree in her Peregrine form. I now knew the spells I was using weren't completed because of the stasis-working Ruby was under. But now that it was lifted, it was possible I could use the feather as a beacon to find out where she'd been.

Maybe.

Okay, it was a long shot, but it seemed to be the only one I had.

Sighing, I raised my glass to the other Council members. "Less than twenty-four hours. To the shortest Council sitting in history." I tossed back the remaining whiskey. "I'm going home to pore over a grimoire or twelve. Call me if you guys have any info you want to share."

"We'll come by in a few hours to help." Barrett stood from his seat. "We need to wind the party down. Do you want me to tell your sister you went home?"

I wanted to tell him no, but I knew if I texted her, she wouldn't get it until she left. Electronics went wonky around the wards in this place.

"Sure. She's probably living it up, so don't cock-block her if you can help it. But if you see Della or Striker, send them my way, will you?"

With that, I took my leave of the Council and headed back to Aether, so I could make my way home. With the wards around Barrett's home, I couldn't just snap my way out of there, and even if I could, I wouldn't. I let Barrett and Marcus have their privacy.

But when I stepped back into the corridor, I had a visitor waiting for me.

Andras stood leaning against the wall, his tuxedo bowtie undone, his hair in complete disarray.

"Please tell me you told those bitches where to go. Please tell me you turned them down."

He could only be referring to the three women I had no choice but to obey.

"It wasn't exactly like I had a choice. They said they would blame the whole thing on me and Alistair if I didn't. What the hell was I supposed to do? Say no?" I half-yelled, tossing my hands up.

"I have forty-eight, no, I have less than that. I have less than two days to find out who killed Ruby. I wasn't afforded the luxury of a 'no.'"

Andras pushed off the wall and advanced on me. "They can't do this to you. To me, maybe, but not to you."

"They can, and they did. Now, I need to get home, search a spell book or two, and get cracking, because from what I hear, the Armistice is at stake. Yay on being half-demon. Glad that could come through for me in a clutch." I gave Andras a sarcastic double thumbs-up and skirted around him to the exit.

"You aren't doing this by yourself, Maxima. Not ever again. Not if I can help it."

I wanted to see his side, to think of him finally stepping up and being a dad. In fact, his words were kind in his own weird way. But they were too close to Alistair's, too close to another "you can't" instead of a "how can I help?" They were too close to Ian's rejection, to Aidan's protectiveness, to Cinder's warning.

Those words grated in the absolute worst way, and I turned back to face off against my dad.

Wouldn't be the first time.

"If you're just going to come in and take over, you can just stop right there. I don't need you to tell me what I can and can't do. I don't need you to tell me I'm ill-equipped to take this on. I know, trust me," I admitted with a mirthless chuckle. "But what I am not, is alone. I have a family I made all on my own, Andras, and at no point did that include you. You want to help? Fine. But get the fuck out of my way while you do it."

I gave him my back again, stomping down the corridor, and out of the obnoxiously loud club with too many people that all needed some damn clothes. The summer Denver air smacked me in the face, too hot, too dry, too something.

But I couldn't blame Denver, just like I couldn't blame the sun threatening to come up on the horizon.

I needed to get home, get changed, and get food. Then I was attacking this problem head-on.

Because it wasn't a question anymore of would or wouldn't I. It wasn't even a question of if I'd have help, or if I could bring the killer to the Fates.

It was more a question of what would happen when I did.

CHAPTER TEN

Walking down the sidewalk of a sleepy residential street at dawn would probably be normal enough if I weren't dressed in full presentation regalia—including the crown. My strappy shoes quietly clicked with each step as I walked the half-block from my brand-new snapping spot toward my house. This past winter, the ancient oaks that had shaded my front lawn—and hid my arrivals —fell during a freak ice storm.

I no longer felt comfortable just popping up on the exposed sidewalk in front of my house, so I picked a new spot down the street where the light didn't reach, and no one cared to look. A place where the oak trees converged in a canopy of leaves in between two stately properties, the houses almost angling away from one another. Neither family was in town that often, and the house across the street contained a crotchety blind man that was nice to his daughter, but an old bugger to everyone else. I paid attention to my neighbors, even if I made sure they didn't pay much attention to me.

My only hope was no one looked out their window to see me stalk home. My look-away spells only worked on my property, so if any of them saw me out here, I'd likely be the talk of our block's gossip hound, Mrs. Robicheaux. So far, I'd been off her radar, but my luck could only take me so far.

About three seconds into my trek, I realized I was being followed. Not because I heard footsteps, or because I could see anyone. Nope, that was for rookies.

I could feel eyes on me, sure as I was breathing, and I had to decide if I was going to glance over my shoulder or not. If I peered over my shoulder, I could no doubt see a glamour of some kind, but then I would give myself away. Then again, if I didn't look, then I couldn't tell how close they were, or if I could even defend myself, or if I should run. There were too many cons in the "not look" column. Not letting my steps falter, I inspected every darkened corner, allowing my eyes to lose focus on a few so I could maybe catch the shimmer of a cloaking spell out of the corner of my eye.

The faint webbing of light snagged my attention. Carefully hidden under the streetlamp across the street from my house, the hazy strands of the spell cloaked the figure of a man. Casually dressed in a T-shirt and jeans, he leaned against the lamppost with one shoulder, his ankles crossed, calm as you please. It was his lax stature that pissed me off.

"I know you're out there," I yelled loud enough for him to hear me, but I didn't tip my hand and look directly at him. "I can feel you staring at me. You have until I count to three to get off my street before I make you."

The man didn't even flinch as he nonchalantly plucked a stray piece of lint off his shirt before giving a jaw-cracking yawn.

"One." I began taking a step past him. "Two..." I never said three. Instead, I snapped my fingers, transporting myself directly behind him.

"I gave you until the count of three," I said in his ear, causing him to practically jump out of his skin.

The man whirled, surprise coloring his face as he looked me up and down. Too preoccupied with the fact that I could see him, he didn't notice my heel coming for his knee until it was too late. The sharp crack of his knee dislocating was louder than I thought it would be, but I refused to feel sorry for it. I also refused to feel an ounce of remorse for the left hook I aimed at his temple.

Well, until he blocked my fist.

But I'd been sparring with wolves all damn day followed by one of the most tedious, rage-inducing days of my life. I almost smiled at his gentle block before I seized his wrist, and then he was up and over my hip, and flat on his back on the ground in a move I'd been aching to use for ages. You could say what you wanted about this flimsy dress, but the abundance of slits sure made it easy to move. Before he could raise a hand to stop me, I had a knee in his neck, and my finger bore the green cast of my magic rising.

"You are not welcome, and no offense, buddy, but I gave you ample warning. So, you're going to tell me why you're here, or I'm going to make you cry for your mommy. Am I making myself clear?"

"Crystal," he wheezed, his air mostly cut off from my knee. His dark, coffee-colored eyes rolled back in his head.

I lifted some of my weight off of him, letting the man suck in a breath. "Why are you lurking outside my house?"

"I was sent to look out for you. It's dangerous times, Majesty."

So, he was a demon, but I knew that much already. He appeared fortyish, the faint creasing of laugh lines around his mouth and eyes telling his age, but his dark-brown hair was absent of any gray.

"By who?"

He seemed to think it over for a second until my knee made itself at home against his windpipe.

"Mister Quinn, Majesty," he croaked, his tan skin mottling to red.

I narrowed my eyes at him, and he elaborated, "Alistair Quinn."

At my growl, the man almost chuckled, or he would have if I hadn't been cutting off ninety percent of his air. I removed my knee from his neck, but since I didn't trust him at all, I whispered a word of binding and snapped my fingers. Incidentally, it was the same word of binding I'd used on his boss. His arms and legs snapped together as if bound in invisible ropes.

He seemed affronted at my lack of trust, but so far, Alistair Quinn had brought me nothing but irritation and a jail stint.

"You got a name?" I asked, mostly so I could stop calling him "the man" in my head.

"Ren, Majesty," he answered, causing my eye to twitch.

"Ren? Quit calling me 'Majesty.' It's irritating. Now, if I give you back the use of your legs, are you going to walk into my house without a fuss, or am I going to have to do something drastic?"

"No fuss from me, ma'am." Ren's smile was almost indulgent.

"Good." I snapped my fingers, letting him have the reins for half of his body.

Ren awkwardly stood, and we walked side by side toward my front door, the ward that surrounded the property only letting him pass once I put a hand on his shoulder and guided him through the webbed magic. Once inside, I escorted Ren to my kitchen.

"Have a seat." I waited until he relaxed as much as he was able, before snapping my fingers again and binding him to the chair. "No offense to you, but I need to change, and I can't have you snooping in my house. Add that to the fact that your boss is currently on my shit list, and well, you understand."

Ren gave me an exasperated sigh but didn't complain. I left him bound to the chair and raced upstairs, kicking off those stupid strappy shoes as I went. I was kinder to the dress, as delicate as it was, stripping it off and hanging it up, but the spiky crystal crown got a careless toss on top of my dresser. After I was clothed in jeans and a tank, and the makeup and blood were finally washed off my face, I padded back downstairs to raid the fridge.

There was a bunch of leftover pancakes in there from breakfast the morning before. Maria constantly scolded me for making so many, but I didn't see the need for not using up the entire box. Leftover pancakes were the best. I peeled the parchment paper off of four, popped them in the toaster, got out the butter, honey, and whipped cream, and set the table.

When they popped up, I dished two onto a plate for Ren, and then belatedly remembered to take him out of his binding.

"Breakfast?" I asked, passing over a napkin.

Ren narrowed his eyes at me.

"It's not poisoned," I said around a mouthful of hot pancakey goodness.

Ren carefully picked up his utensils and cut into the fluffy yumminess. His eyebrows did the talking for him as he tasted them. "This is good, Majesty."

"We talked about this. Majesty is not me. I was a Rogue for four hundred years, and I'm probably never going to like being in a position of authority. I'm just Max."

"You'll have to forgive me. I have been with the Quinn family for many centuries, and they aren't as lax with their titles."

"You've been with the Quinn family? You mean, you work for them?"

Ren gave me an indulgent smile, the kind you give to kids when they're being adorable. I hated it.

"I'm a paladin. Think of us like butlers, only a touch more lethal. My family has been with the Quinn's since the beginning."

It kinda sounded like ownership, which made me bristle. "Like they own you?"

"No. Paladins live to serve. It is our purpose. We protect our charges, keep them on the straight and narrow. But no one owns us."

I calmed slightly. "And Alistair had you look out for me. Why?"

"He said a murder was committed at your presentation, and it was portrayed as a gift to you. He wanted me to make sure you arrived home safely."

So, Ren had the same information I did. But that wasn't exactly true. Ren knew a lot more about Alistair than I did.

"Tell me more about Alistair."

Ren swallowed before wiping his mouth with a napkin. "What do you wish to know?"

"Why Clotho hates him, for starters."

"Ah, yes. Clotho." Ren sighed. "Clotho hates the Quinn family as a whole, so I suppose she dislikes Alistair on principle. Several thousands of years ago, there was an arranged marriage that didn't go according to plan. It was supposed to bring the gaining family many children which Clotho foresaw, but the suitor from the Quinn family refused to go through with it. The union was never cemented, and the babies never born. Clotho has never forgiven the Quinns."

"So, someone didn't want to marry a person chosen for them. Makes perfect sense to me. I'd have probably done the same thing and likely flipped them off while I did it."

Ren chuckled. "The Quinn family is keen on irreverence. However, the offending party was cast out of the family, cut off, but still, Clotho refuses to forgive."

That explained why Clotho was pissed, but it didn't illuminate why the holding cell guard hated him. It honestly didn't explain much at all.

"I spoke to a man earlier today who said Alistair had a reputation. The way he spoke, it sounded unsavory—especially since apparently my rep is better than his. Care to elaborate?"

Ren huffed out an incredulous chuckle. "Unsavory? Unlikely. Mister Quinn is a Knight of Hell. His reputation is flawless. His brothers, his parents, his cousins? Not so much. The Quinn family is known in some circles as..." He paused to search for the right word. "Infamous. In all matters. Alistair cleaves to the spirit of the law because that is what is expected of him and his station. His family, to the letter of it. Alistair is honorable but will make exceptions. The majority of the Quinns are not, but since they have followed the law to the letter, they can't be prosecuted. Add into that their high station, and well, few would go after them at all."

It surprised me that Ren was just offering up the information on a silver platter, and I asked him as much. "You are awfully forthcoming for a man I dropped on the sidewalk. Why cough up so much info?"

"You are our princess, Max. It would be like one of the humans snubbing the Queen of England. It just isn't done."

If that was the case, then I could ask really prying questions. The ones he probably didn't want to answer.

"If that's true, then tell me—did Alistair really send you to protect me, or did he want you as a spy?"

Ren winced, the answer clear on his face. Alistair sent his minion to spy on my house, and report back my comings and goings.

Red washed over my vision, my rage clouding every thought. Ren shoved himself back from the table, getting as far from me as he could in my small breakfast nook.

"I'm going to need to have a word with your boss," I ground out through gritted teeth.

Oh, I'd do more than have a *word* with Alistair. He wasn't going to know what hit him.

CHAPTER ELEVEN

"Maj—" Ren cut himself off. "*Miss*, I don't think Mister Quinn meant any harm in it. He only wanted to know if you left and who came to your home. I was supposed to guard you if you left the premises."

I felt the floor shake under my feet. "You mean he wanted to know when I got here, when I left, and who visited me. And that doesn't sound at all stalkery to you?"

"I was supposed to be under cloaking, hidden. Just to keep you safe."

What that really meant was Alistair didn't know I could see magics, didn't know I could see through glamours, and he wanted to keep his man under wraps. He wanted to spy on me and have me none the wiser.

High-handed, patriarchal, *motherfucker*.

"Ren, not only does that not make it any better, I'm having a very difficult time not ripping you limb from bloody limb where you stand. I suggest you leave. Do not come back to my house without an invitation from me, do you understand? There is no cloaking spell I can't detect, no glamour I can't see under. If you are here, I *will* know."

Ren nodded before falling to a knee. "I meant no offense, Majesty. I know you don't like to be called that, but you are what you are. I was under the impression you only wished not to see your guards, not that you didn't know I was there. It was only after you knocked me on my ass, did I realize you weren't in the loop. Please, just let me watch out for you. I won't report back to Mister Quinn."

Absolutely fucking not.

"You have been with the Quinns for how long? And I'm supposed to believe you'll do what I ask after meeting me for a half hour? I know my pancakes are fabulous, but even I'm not naïve enough to believe they can sow dissention that fast. No, you need to leave. Now."

Ren's face fell, his dark eyes turning sad, shame coloring his expression.

"As you wish, Majesty," Ren murmured, and I watched him rise, stalk through my kitchen and out my front door.

I followed him, tracking his every step as he made his way down the pavement and to the sidewalk. Then I saw him disappear as the first rays of dawn reached the street.

One problem down.

Still seething, I went back inside my house, locking the door behind me, and stalked down to the basement. My casting room had gotten a workout in the past six months searching for Ruby. The spacious internal room had no windows and no electricity. The only modern thing it did have was an HVAC vent to combat the Colorado extremes of summer and winter. I was all for purity until it made me sweat. Snapping my fingers, all the candles in the room flared to life, their flames peaking high before dimming to a respectable flicker.

The drywall was covered in weathered wooden planks from the starboard side of a Spanish ship, *the* Spanish ship my mother and I boarded as we crossed the Atlantic in the 1600s. The *Corazon de Oro* only made two voyages—one to the Americas, and one back to Spain before it vanished from the ship logs. I had a feeling my mother had something to do with that, but I tracked pieces of the galleon down a few months ago. All that was left of her was on these walls, and something about the aged wood made me feel like I could do anything, could be anything.

On the east wall of the casting room was my altar, dried herbs, moon-charged crystals, several pillar candles of every color, an empty stone bowl, and my book. I hesitated to call it a grimoire. It was mostly a journal with a few spells thrown in.

No novice witch could follow it. Maria had tried some of my spells with little luck, and Maria was no apprentice. She'd said my spells didn't draw on the elements the way they should, and that was when we realized I wasn't like any witch that had ever been. I didn't draw on the earth or on fire. I didn't need a moon, or wind, or water. I only needed myself, and the demon power that coursed through my veins.

Somehow, I didn't think that was a good thing. It sounded like I was a necromancer, but the demon tethered was me. Maybe Aidan had been right those many months ago. Maybe his insult was the truth. Maybe I really was like all those damned witches who either served to do a demon's bidding, or tethered demons against their will and drew on their power until they were nothing more than husks.

Shoving those disparaging thoughts out of my mind, I considered what to do about Alistair. Should I just move on with my life, put solving Ruby's murder as my priority, and figure out how to get him back later? Or should I give in to the cloying need I felt to slap the shit out of the high-handed demon post haste?

Snatching a vial of salt from the apothecary cabinet on the south wall, I drew a large circle on the floor, my mind still whirling with the rage I felt. The sheer gall the man had to use one of his staff to spy on me. My whole body roiled with the need to bring Alistair to me, the need to draw him here, the need to trap him in a circle so I could teach him a lesson.

Once one end of the circle met the other, I capped the vial, sloppily returning it to the apothecary cabinet as I imagined slamming my fist into Alistair's aristocratic face.

It was no more than a thought, no words were spoken, no

snapping fingers to signal my will, no incantations thought. Not a single Latin word passed my lips. Not that it had to be Latin to cast, it could be any language when used with intent.

But the earth still shook under my feet as if I'd cast a working, as if I was the one doing this. Wind whipped in a maelstrom in the closed room, the candles extinguishing with the gusts. Herbs and crystals fell to the floor, a few of the more fragile ones bursting into a thousand little pieces as they hit the ground. Burned-out candles toppled from their stands, the pages of my book fluttering wildly.

A ring of green fire sprung up from the circle of salt, the flames waist-high as they danced to the tune of the wind. But they didn't spread throughout the room like a normal flame would. It was as if the magic of the closed circle kept them contained. And still, the earth roiled and pitched, nearly knocking me off my feet.

I had a sinking feeling this was me. All of this, the earth, the flames, the wind, was all me.

Before I could figure out how to make it all stop, a ball of black smoke formed in the center of the circle. It grew from the size of a baseball to the size of a cantaloupe in a matter of seconds. Then it bloomed, growing larger and larger until it coalesced into the shape of a man.

The smoke dissipated, leaving the crouched form of a man in the center of the flames. His tuxedo jacket smoldered, as if he'd run through an inferno. On the shoulder of his right side, the fabric was torn. Three crooked horns or spines seemed to have punched through the jacket, glowing fiery runes carved into the bone. Other glowing runes were etched into the blackened skin of his neck, his face, his hands. His entire right side was as if he was made of fire and soot. His hair, windswept and curling in the heat of him, seemed to be immersed in water. It floated in a nimbus cloud about his head defying gravity as if it were a personal affront.

But the left side of his face looked very familiar.

He stood from his crouch, first coming to his knees in a staggering move that made me realize that whatever I'd done, I'd hurt him. Glowing amber eyes burned with the same fire that lit the runes on his face, the lines seemingly etched in flames. But I knew that clenched jaw. I knew those lips. I knew that scowl.

Alistair.

"What have you done?" He seethed through gritted teeth, his hands clenched into fists at his sides.

I honestly didn't know, and I had exactly zero clue what I could tell him to explain the situation. What helped matters none at all was the fact that I was standing there completely dumbfounded, staring at the half-phased demon in the middle of my casting room.

"Play dumb all you want to, but you, Maxima, have royally fucked up. An Arcadios witch summoning a demon? You should have brushed up on your history, love. What you just did is a capital crime. As in, punishable by death."

Summoned a demon? Well, it was what I'd done even if I hadn't meant to. I didn't even know someone *could* summon a demon, let alone it was a punishable offense.

"But..." I trailed off, still completely shocked at the man standing in my casting circle. "I didn't summon you. I didn't—"

I couldn't even finish the sentence. What was I going to tell him? That I'd thought of punching him in the face and then he suddenly appeared? I'd manifested *things* before, but never *people.*

"You did. You pulled me across space and time. You pulled me not from this world, but from Hell, Maxima. You think that won't go unnoticed? You think after the stunt you pulled in Aether, I won't go directly to the Fates with this?"

I didn't even mean to do it, and the little shit was going to tattle on me?

"Maybe you will and maybe you won't. All I know is, I didn't mean to summon you. But you know what I didn't do? I didn't send a servant to spy on you. I didn't send a cloaked paladin to stand outside your home and report your comings and goings. Who did that?" I tapped my finger on my lips.

Shock creeped over Alistair's expression, followed by doubt. He didn't know if I was bluffing or not.

"I talked to your friend, Ren. Nice enough guy if he weren't perched outside my house. He didn't like it too much when I dislocated his knee, but since he's a demon serving the Quinns, well, I figure he'll heal."

Resolve colored his features. "And I'm supposed to believe you summoned me by accident? *Tsk, tsk, tsk*, Maxima. You are in deep trouble, Princess."

If he was right, if Arcadios witches were forbidden from summoning demons, then wasn't I in some deep shit? Would anyone believe that I'd done this by accident?

I had a feeling only one person might, but that meant making a call I did not want to make.

I needed Barrett.

CHAPTER TWELVE

I eyed my phone like a coiled snake. Calling Barrett was admitting defeat, guilt, and a whole host of other things I did not have the time or inclination to deal with. But with the summoned and bound demon in my basement, this was a problem I just couldn't ignore.

I hadn't taken a purse to Aether when I left to go spar with the wolves, so fortunately, I had my phone here. Unfortunately, I had about a zillion missed calls and texts, mostly from my father. Whoever gave him my phone number and taught that man how to text, deserved to be shot. I reluctantly went to Barrett's contact and hit the deceptively malicious "Call" button.

He answered on the second ring. "Hey, we're already on our way, and I come bearing gifts of coffee and grimoires. And pastries. I think we cleaned out the entire case at that shop on Washburn. I almost feel sorry for their morning rush."

"Umm," I replied dumbly, unable to tell him the reason for my call. *Sack up, Maxima.* "I, umm, have a huge problem."

I got a beat of silence on the other end of the line, then the sound of an engine speeding up.

"What now?" Barrett's voice was knowingly accusatory. I didn't blame him. I kind of screwed up a lot.

Waffling for a moment on just how to word my current brush with stupidity, I stalled a bit too long for Barrett's liking.

"Maxima!"

"I accidentally summoned Alistair to my basement," I blurted, my words semi-garbled in their rush to fall from my mouth.

"You did what, now?" Barrett asked, genuinely confused.

My words were even more rushed than they were before, the story tumbling from my lips like boulders during a rockslide. "I accidentally summoned a demon. Alistair in particular, and he's currently stuck in a bound circle in my basement. And also, I have no idea how I did it. One second, I was thinking of punching him in the face while I was drawing a salt circle, and the next, he was in the middle of a circle in my casting room."

I heard a whole lot of nothing on the other end of the phone. Barrett either muted me, or he hung up. Suddenly, sounds were back, and Barrett's low, menacing voice reached me. "I will be at your house in two minutes. When I get there, I better not find what I think I'm going to. I'm going to pretend you didn't just tell me all that bullshit, and you fix it. Do you hear me, Maxima?" he threatened, hanging up on me.

Oh, I heard him all right. I just didn't have the first clue of how to do that. Not without either leaving a dead body or a witness behind.

Instead of trying to figure out how to kill Alistair and dispose of his body in the two minutes I had left, I called my little sister. Since it was way past dawn, and I had seen neither hide nor hair of her since pancakes the morning prior, my big sister concern-o-meter was pinging.

When her voicemail picked up, I said, "Ria, darling, I have every confidence you are getting laid good and proper and not lying in a ditch somewhere. But to ease my sisterly worry, call me back, nerd."

Maria didn't officially live here—her words—but she'd been staying here enough nights over the last six months that she had a room dedicated to her and her alone. Plus, after our mother left her to fend for herself against a Corax demon, well, let's just say Maria wasn't feeling all too keen to keep the status quo with Teresa. After living nearly four centuries with someone, Maria was also not too enthusiastic about living alone. I'd been happy to let her figure it out, and it wasn't like I didn't have the space.

I was tempted to call Striker, but since he'd been spending more time at Aether and not less, I knew he wouldn't pick up. I somehow doubted he'd be knee-deep in frolicking witches, but Striker had been reluctant to disclose what he was really doing in the nightclub that hid the doorways to so many pockets of the Ethereal.

I was going to be on my own to face Barrett's wrath, and it was probably for the best. When my two minutes were up, I opened my front door to see Barrett's Mercedes pull up. Marcus was driving, so at least no one was likely injured or maimed on their way here. Barrett slammed out of the two-door coupe, stalked up my front walk, and squared off with me on my front porch.

"Look, I didn't mean to do what I did." I desperately hoped he understood. "I don't know how I did it. Please, just help me fix it."

Barrett's eyes narrowed into a condemning scowl. "Take me to him."

I nodded and opened the door wide for him and Marcus—who was laden down with a drink tray full of coffees and two bags of what was likely pastry heaven, if the smell was anything to go by—to pass through the additional warding of my front door. I didn't say a word as I led them down the steps to my casting room. Even from the outside of the heavily warded room, I could hear Alistair railing colorful obscenities and promising vengeance.

When I opened the door, I got to see Alistair in all his furious glory, throwing himself against the walls of the circle. No matter how hard he pushed, he didn't seem to be able to break through the magics holding him there. Moreover, every time he threw himself against the wall of magic, his clothes came away smoldering, and his phase took over more and more of his body. The blackened skin of his phased half—or more than half now—

crept across his face, the fiery runes glowing brighter. A pair of oddly angled horns jutted up from his head, peeking through the molten fire of his hair. It wasn't that they were jutting in weird directions, more that they were made of slate or some kind of stone instead of bone, chipped from time rather than sanded away.

"You actually did it. You really fucking did it," Barrett muttered to himself as the three of us watched Alistair toss his head back and let out an animalistic roar, his fangs sharp and gleaming against his charred skin.

And that was what his skin looked like: blackened like unspent charcoal. Like he was made from the sharp and pitted coals, and like he would burn just as bright.

Alistair's roar was loud enough and laced with enough power to cause the whole of my house to quake. I'd never been so happy I'd tuned my wards to muffle sound.

"Oh, knock it off," I yelled, causing Alistair to shut his trap for a bloody minute. "I was calling for help, no need to scream the house down."

Alistair bared his fangs at me like they would scare me. They would, they so totally would, but he didn't need to know that.

Barrett examined the circle for about two-point-five seconds before he reached for one of the coffees in Marcus' hands. "You have bourbon in here, right?"

I strode over to the apothecary cabinet and yanked open one of the lower drawers. Cracking open the bottle, I poured the bourbon into his cup until the liquid was nearly cresting the top. Barrett took a long pull before he dropped into the overstuffed chaise lounge in the corner.

"I have no bloody idea how you did that. There are no sigils drawn in the salt. There is no binding. There is nothing that tells me what kind of spell you used. There's nothing." He took another pull of his doctored coffee.

"You didn't use a spell at all, did you?" Marcus asked, and I shook my head.

"I swear, I just thought about punching him in his stupid face while I drew my salt circle. That's it. Then he just appeared."

Marcus frowned. "Why were you thinking of punching him?"

My smile was almost evil as I tattled on Alistair. "Because he had one of his paladins staked out in front of my house spying on me. Lucky for me, this douchebag didn't know I can see under glamours. By the way"—I turned to the douchebag in question—"Ren is plenty mad at you. He didn't like being used against his majesty."

Alistair flashed his fangs at me again. "What she is forgetting to mention, was that she summoned me from Hell. Not my house in New Orleans, not from this plane of existence. I was about to talk to someone important, and she ripped me from the bloody depths. I want out of this sodding prison, Maxima. Now."

I rolled my eyes. "What do you think I'm doing here?" I half yelled, throwing my hands up in frustration. "I called my mentor, didn't I? I didn't murder you and dump your body in the freaking ocean—which is still on the table, by the way—so how about you settle the fuck down? You pacing and throwing yourself against the damn circle every five seconds isn't helping."

A menacingly quiet growl passed his lips.

"Yes, because growling at me is going to make me move faster."

"Wait a minute." Barrett seethed. "He had someone from his household staff watching you?"

I nodded. "But don't take my word for it, ask Stalker over here."

"Don't try to turn this around on me. Spying isn't against the law. Summoning is," Alistair shot back.

"Spying with intent to harm a member of the royal family is against the law, Alistair, and you know it." Marcus seethed. "So is attempting to infiltrate a Council member's home. Both charges are treason, in case you weren't aware. You know, punishable by death."

Alistair's expression turned mulish, his charred jaw set in a firm line. "So much for the position being open, huh? None of this matters. She's an Arcadios witch. No matter what you say, no matter what you do, an Arcadios witch summoned a demon." His chuckle was almost pitying. "It is of no consequence what I did first. She's still going to burn."

Burn? What would burning do? And then I got it. He meant in Hell in a place I couldn't escape. He meant torture, endless, excruciating torture. Forever.

"What I want to know is, why everyone is raising such a stink about Arcadios witches? What in the blue fuck did these bitches do to get on everyone's shit list?"

"You should know, you are one," Alistair shot back.

Wow. He really knew nothing about me whatsoever.

"All this talk about brushing up on *my* history, and you know not *one* fucking thing about me. I learned nothing from my coven. I was never inducted, never taught. Not one single spell. I learned everything I know today from research and pure dumb luck. My mother knew I was too powerful. From birth, she kept me hidden away because of what I am. So, fuck you very much, Alistair, I know exactly fuck all about this coven you vilify so much."

"But—"

"I was cast out at fourteen, you idiot. Do you know why? Because I came back from the dead after being burned at the stake. I know nothing about the Arcadios witches. And for the last damn time, I am not an Arcadios witch!"

Pinching the bridge of my nose, I realized the only way I could get out of this—once I figured out how to get him safely out of the circle—was if he didn't remember it in the first place.

There was only one person I knew who could wipe someone's memory without blowback. It was time to call in my vampire assistant to pull my ass out of the fire.

CHAPTER THIRTEEN

This time, I did not make a phone call. I sent a text for my assistant-slash-grandma's assigned bodyguard to get her bloodsucking booty here pronto. Della was one of the few people who had keys to my place, the wards coded for her specifically. She couldn't walk someone in like Maria, or I could, but she could come as she pleased.

Last year, Della had saved my ass in a number of ways, first by streamlining my business when Striker had gone on his walkabout. The second, when she mesmerized my customers into getting the hell out of my shop when it was on fire. The added bonus of that, none of them had been the wiser that the fire happened in the first place. And third, when she'd gotten my shop back up and running, the building was rebuilt better than ever after the fire. Lately, the shop had been running smoothly without me, and I had to thank Della for that.

When I didn't get a text back, I called her, letting the phone ring until she finally picked up.

"You do know the shop doesn't open today, right?" she said thickly, her normally smooth French-Catalan accent rough with sleep.

"I kinda have a huge problem I need your help with."

Della groaned. "I'm still half-drunk. There is no way I'm driving. Can you make me a doorway?"

Della lived in my new-slash-old apartment above the shop, and luckily, making that door was one of the easier spells I knew. At least it was one of the few I couldn't fuck up.

"Sure, but don't freak out when you get here."

"*Quan sempre tinc?*" she asked in her native tongue. My Catalan was rusty, but I figured it was something like, "When have I ever?" or something close.

"Give me a minute, and I'll open a door in the living room. You don't have any midnight snacks there, right?"

By midnight snack, I meant humans. Della was a no-shit vampire, a species I thought was only relegated to fiction. I should have known better. All the other things were real—why wouldn't vampires be amongst us other freaks? But Della was one of the few vampires left on our plane. The way I heard it—and there wasn't too much written down about vampire lore in the first place —was that they left this plane and went to the Fae realm where they were more accepted. I didn't even know we had a Fae realm, and once that little tidbit fell out, I realized it was entirely possible to know too much, and I closed the door on investigating vamps.

Fairies had always freaked me way the hell out. Too many rules, and the accidentally owing them, and all the other shit I'd read in way too many Young Adult books. Nope. Hard pass.

"No, he went home after dinner." She giggled. "Get it? Because he was dinner."

I half-chuckled at her drunken joke. "I'm hanging up now. See you in a minute."

I ended the call and went back to the casting room, readying the ingredients for a doorway. Because I was at full strength—or more than full strength as I'd witnessed recently—I didn't need the blood of an animal or a wooden bowl of herbs. All I needed was a stick of chalk, a destination, and a whispered word of working.

But even that was too much.

Before I even said a word or thought of anything other than

Della, as soon as the chalk was drawn, the portal opened into Della's apartment. The darkened living room lay just past the wall, a woman in a ball gown lay sprawled on the couch, the tulle of her dress pillowed in a mass of fabric frothing over the side of the furniture. I wanted to walk through the doorway, and the silvery break in the wall where the chalk used to be seemed stable enough, but I didn't trust it.

"Did you… did you guys see that?" I whispered, not taking my eyes off the brand-new doorway in my casting room.

"What kind of manifestation shit is this? You didn't do a spell at all. You didn't even snap your fingers." Marcus marveled behind me.

"I've seen you manifest objects before, Max." Barrett chimed in. "This is nothing like that."

I just shook my head. I had no more of a clue of what was going on than they did.

"Della?" I called, and my assistant sat up like a Jack-in-the-box.

She yawned an "I'm up" before she rubbed her eyes, making unintentional mascara raccoon rings. Della half-walked, half-staggered through the portal, making a zombie shuffle beeline to the coffee perched on the apothecary cabinet that I assumed she found by smell alone. She sucked back a healthy amount of caffeine before she noticed the pissed-off demon in the circle.

She frowned, shook her head, and then downed more coffee, not saying a word until every drop of the brew was gone.

"I suppose the big problem is this." She gestured to Alistair. "Why do you have a demon in a circle? Isn't that frowned upon?"

Della herself frowned, and then swiped the last cup of coffee from the tray and plopped beside Barrett on the chaise. The carefully created up-do she'd had at the presentation was half-down in a mass of snarled curls. She also still had a bit of her midnight snack on the corner of her lips, the blood dried to a dark red that could have passed for smudged lipstick if I didn't know better.

I'd never seen the vampire less put together, but I supposed this was what I got for calling her at the ass end of dawn. The storybooks had it right; vampires were, in fact, nocturnal. Della just made do with daylight when she had to. Apparently, the myth that they burned in the sun was misinformation used to keep the zealots off their scent.

"Yes, this is the big problem, and I was hoping you could help me fix it. I was kinda hoping you could do that mesmerization mojo on him, so he forgets I accidentally summoned him."

Della snorted—which was unfortunate because she was drinking the last dregs of the final coffee. She coughed, sputtered, and let out the loudest cackle of all time. I swear, witches everywhere wished they had this kind of cackle.

"You know it doesn't work like that." She was still chuckling as she wiped her mouth.

I did not, in fact, know that. I knew exactly zero things about how that whole mind-melding forgetting mojo actually worked. "But all those people in the shop. You didn't use a spell or anything, you just looked at them funny, and they turned into lemmings."

Della gave me a wry smile. "Those were humans. Humans are easier to manipulate because they believe in magic. They believe in fairytales. Ethereals know better. Magic exists, but fairytales do not." She dropped that bit of wisdom on us and then gestured to Alistair. "Plus, he's a demon. His mind is likely too powerful for me to penetrate."

Alistair's menacing smile was almost smug. Add into that the fang he kept flashing, and he was becoming more and more irritating. At least he'd quit bellowing. For now.

Della was my last viable option for getting out of this the easy way. She was the only person I knew who could wipe someone's mind without side effects. But if Della couldn't help me—and as much as I liked my life as it was—I didn't want to mess with Alistair's mind. I'd seen it done too many times—Ethereals botching memory spells. It was too complicated and too delicate of work, and it almost always caused damage.

My remaining option seemed bleak. Alistair might not be the devil, but his shady ass was pretty close. And I was going to have to make a deal with him.

"Look, Knight, I have very few options here. The most drastic: I kill you and dump your body somewhere. You've been kind of a dick, but I doubt you deserve to die." I counted that option out on my finger. "The slightly less drastic: I perform a memory spell on you. Given that my magic seems to be going wonky, that would probably either turn you into a vegetable, or kill you, so I'm not a fan of that one. Then, shitty option number three." I continued counting. "I let you out and you tattle on me, which means I get deported to Hell and tortured for eternity. Also, not a fan of that one. So that leaves only one option."

Alistair's menacing smile turned practically malevolent. "You wish to make a deal with me."

"Bingo."

"You think I'm just going to let this go? You think I'm just going to stand here, and let you and your ilk carry on with your lives after you have dishonored me? You must be joking." He scoffed. "Do you know why Arcadios witches, in particular, are forbidden from summoning? Why demons will always look down on them? Why the Fates themselves were offended at you proudly displaying Arcadios blood? It seems your friends won't tell you, but make no mistake, Princess, I will."

"Don't," Marcus growled, his eyes flashing the iridescent blue of his wolf.

Alistair regarded the Alpha. "She deserves to know where she came from."

"Okay, Knight, spill it. Why is the coven who kicked me out for dying the worst ever?"

An expression passed over his face like something just dawned on him. "Your mother did you a favor. She excised you from a cesspool of corrupt witches that only thirsted for what they did not have. The Arcadios Coven was known for their necromancy, for their deals with demons in exchange for power. Centuries ago, it was a contract, a symbiotic relationship, a partnership. The demon lent power and life to the witch in exchange for service. But witches got greedy, and they started summoning and binding demons without consent. They drained them of all their power, turning them into no better than long-lived humans. Some were never heard from again."

So, the necromancer stories I'd heard—the reasons why it was so forbidden, the reasons it was illegal—was because the coven I'd come from abused their power.

"That says nothing of the children they sacrificed," Alistair added. "Did you know there actually is a special place in Hell for Arcadios witches? Your coven has its own wing."

"Does it matter to you at all that I didn't mean to summon you? Do you even care that I have no intention of binding you, draining you, or any other atrocity? Because I've had my will taken away." I suppressed a shudder. "I know how vile an act that is. I would never."

"But you did. And now you want to make a bargain. Have you ever dealt with a demon, Princess? The devil really is in the details."

"Oh, bloody hell, if you won't kill him, I will," Barrett muttered behind me.

But then it dawned on me, that was what he was bargaining for. His life.

"How about this? In exchange for not killing you and letting you out of this circle, you promise not to tell a single soul about my accidental summoning."

Alistair smiled, and then I added, "Also, you can't write, mime, sign, draw, or inform anyone in any way about the summoning. Ever."

His smile dimmed. "No deal."

I massaged my temples. "Ugh, why are you such a fucking prick?"

"It's a gift." He parroted my earlier words with a wry grin. "I require something for my mental anguish."

"What do you want, then? A pony?"

His expression sobered. "I want a favor. You owe me one for ripping me through the veil. That hurt, Maxima."

"Fine," I answered before I thought better of it, and if his expression was an indicator, I'd just royally screwed up.

CHAPTER FOURTEEN

"I want in on the investigation. I know more about this world than you do, and I could be of some help. That's not my favor. I want this from you as a courtesy since my name will get dragged through the mud right along with yours if you fail."

I pondered his request for a second before adding a stipulation of my own. "This favor can't get me into trouble, cause anyone's death, or harm anyone I care about. If any of those options are on the table, we can just squash all this, and I'll kill you right now."

Alistair sighed as if my distrust of him was taxing. "Of course."

"And no sexual favors," I added hastily.

He rolled his eyes and quipped, "I plan to earn those all on my own, thank you."

At his honest reply, my belly dipped. It was no secret Alistair was sexy as hell. The fact that he was half-phased and pissed off actually did little to deter my wayward libido. His scorched tuxedo jacket with the three spines punched through the shoulder, his half-open dress shirt that showed both his blackened phased side and his pale human form, the cut of his abdomen and chest, the runes carved into his flesh that glowed like embers. Yeah. He radiated power and abandon, and yet, somehow, he also exuded control.

If he'd quit being a complete dick, he could probably earn those sexual favors. Maybe. Granted, the odds of him not being a complete asshole for the length of time it would take to change my mind about him was pretty slim.

Still, the man was very nice to look at.

"Deal." I did my best not to let my voice wobble as I met his gaze.

"It's a deal then. Get me out of this infernal circle. Please." That "please" he tacked on at the end was more of an afterthought than anything else, but I let him have it.

All this might have been an accident, but I'd taken something big away from him. I'd hurt him. I could give Alistair the benefit of the doubt. At least on this one thing.

Still, I raised my eyebrow at him so he knew I wasn't having any of that demanding bullshit. I'd been pondering how to get Alistair out of the circle without hurting him, or me, or anyone else in the room. My only solid theory was to overload the circle.

To do that, I'd need to bleed.

Not exactly my favorite pastime, but if it got him out safely, well, I couldn't knock it. Heaving a sigh, I plucked my athame from the altar, debating on the best place to cut myself. I wasn't my mother, and I sure as hell didn't know the spell that could heal wounds in a matter of seconds.

Then I remembered the vampire in the room.

"Hey, Della?" I called over my shoulder. "If I cut myself, are you going to go bananas and bite me?"

I felt this was a legitimate question, but Della snorted in derision. "No offense, Max, but you're not my type. I prefer humans. Ethereals taste weird."

Super. With no other reason to stall, I put the athame blade side up in the palm of my hand, closed my fingers around it, and pulled. The white-hot agony of the knife slicing through my flesh didn't hit me all at once. No, the blade was so sharp, I didn't feel it until the rain of droplets hit the salt.

Gritting my teeth against the pain, I squeezed droplets of my blood on every few inches of the circle. Once the revolution was complete, the floor beneath us began to quake. I felt the spell overloading, and the burn of it racing over my skin like a flash fire. Then the spell snapped, cracked, and fizzled out, the green fire dancing high before snuffing out altogether.

The room was bathed in darkness, and only when Barrett snapped his fingers, did the remaining upright candles flare to life. I wanted to be happy I managed to fix what I had broken, but I didn't feel right. I staggered through the now-defunct circle to the door, and I was through and out of the room before I heard anyone calling my name.

I felt sick, and it wasn't the blood still falling from my fingers. My head ached, my body felt like it had been put through a meat grinder, and my stomach felt like a bag of roiling snakes. I staggered to the basement bathroom, barely managing to flip up the seat before I lost my pancakes in the toilet. I heaved until there was nothing left, only noticing my hair being held back after the worst of it had passed.

A cool washcloth was laid over the back of my neck, and I appreciated whoever was thoughtful enough to think of it. The same person who held my hair back flushed the toilet for me, and if I wasn't so exhausted, I'd hug them. After I brushed my teeth.

When I had enough strength, I opened my eyes, catching a glimpse of the blackness swirling away in the bowl. What the fuck?

I ripped the washcloth off my neck and wiped my mouth. It came away streaked with black.

"Backlash," a voice murmured behind me. *Alistair.*

"What?" I managed to look up to meet his eyes. It was a short trip since he was crouched behind me, but even that little bit was exhausting. He was back to his normal un-phased self, only his shirt was still half open, and his hair looked like it'd gone through a wind tunnel, the curls a riot of brownish-red corkscrews.

"You took the spell into yourself. You..." He trailed off, hesitating to say the words. "You stopped the spell from hurting me and hurt yourself instead. I never wanted that. I didn't ask for that." He seemed almost angry that I followed through with the break that freed him.

"Well, you said I hurt you in the summoning. Any chance we can call it even?" I joked, knowing his answer before he even opened his mouth.

"Of course not." He chuckled, shaking his head.

"I'm not dying, right? That would suck for you not to get your favor before I kicked the bucket."

Barrett elbowed Alistair out of the way, kicking him out of the bathroom altogether. "You're not dying, you just broke an enormous working in the dumbest—and likely only—way possible."

"Well, it's me, so you know, standard."

Barrett nodded with a raised eyebrow that meant he was judging me as he blew on his fingers. He rubbed the digits together as he blew on them, and I watched as his magic sparked. A blur of midnight motes swirled over his fingers, and then he touched my forehead with them. It felt as if I had been plunged in a cool swimming pool on a hot summer day.

The cold tendrils of Barrett's magic flowed through me, dousing the smoldering bits left over from my overloading the circle. My stomach unknotted, and I could take a deep breath again, my only discomfort the itch of my skin knitting back together on my palm.

I watched as the flesh closed, still mesmerized that such healing even existed.

"Thank you." I sighed, those two words inadequate to describe just how much I appreciated his help.

Barrett shrugged. "It was the best I could do. But your body still needs to finish healing on its own."

"I'm sorry I dragged you into this. I never meant for any of this to happen, Barrett, I hope you know that."

He stood, holding out a hand for me to take. "Yeah, I know that." He pulled me from the bathroom floor, watching me like a hawk while I washed my hands and rinsed my mouth. "Look, Marcus and I will pore over the grimoires. I need you to take a quick nap—just a couple of hours," he insisted when I began to protest. "You need your strength. We'll see what we can find out about the spikes."

Reluctantly, I agreed, letting Barrett lead me up to bed. But I didn't see Alistair, and Maria never came home.

After a three-hour nap and a cup of coffee, I checked on Barrett and Marcus. I felt marginally better than I did when I passed out, sprawled diagonally across my bed. Nevertheless, I managed to dress myself, brush my teeth, and put my hair in some semblance of order—even if my whole body ached while I did it.

The pair of them were poring over a crate full of ancient leather-bound grimoires, spread out over my entire living room. The couch, coffee table, and end tables were all filled with open books. Barrett's hair was a disheveled mess and Marcus looked ready to drop. Their expressions told the tale well enough. They had found exactly dick after their tireless searching.

"You guys need to get some rest." I startled Barrett enough for him to nearly fall off the couch.

Marcus didn't even glance up from his reading, his brow puckered in concentration. "We have forty-two hours, kid. Rest can come later."

"Said the man who made me take a nap." I noted the blatant hypocrisy in his statement.

"*I* didn't just have a spell blowback on me. *I* wasn't throwing up black goo. Therefore, *I* can do whatever the hell I want," Marcus shot back.

I had to give it to him, he wasn't wrong.

"Touché. You guys find anything?" I asked, diverting his attention.

Barrett growled before slamming a giant grimoire shut. "No. All the lore on the spikes is either too vague or too specific to the ones we already found. There isn't even a hint of where the other spikes might be, what was done with them after Perseus was killed, or what became of the Gorgons after they managed to kill a demigod. And I'd ask Atropos, but she won't answer my calls."

Well, that didn't surprise me at all.

"Is that something she would know? How much do the three of them actually see?"

Barrett shrugged. "I have no idea. The Fates are a bit tight-lipped about their abilities outside of the spinning, drawing, and cutting stuff. I don't think she'd even answer me if I managed to get her to deign to talk to me. She's probably still pissed at me for arguing for your release."

Surprise rocked through me.

"You argued for me?" My voice clogged with something I didn't want to name.

I didn't have too many people in my life who would argue with anyone for me, let alone the bloody Fates. Choking back tears, I carefully stepped over the ancient books to Barrett and attack-hugged him. He seemed surprised at my emotion, but I guessed he didn't understand. I'd been scarred by people abandoning me when times had gotten tough for the majority of my life. When I found a person willing to go to bat for me, I never let them go.

"Of course I did, hon," he whispered into my hair as he closed his arms around me to hug me back. "You can't get rid of me that easy, kid. I just started getting used to you."

Only a fourteen-hundred-year old witch could get away with calling me a kid.

I pulled back, wiping the tears off my face and sniffed. "Well, if she won't talk to you, I guess we need to pay her a visit. I need to inspect the crime scene, anyway. If we can't get clues from these books, maybe the killer left more than just a message behind."

But I didn't want to call Alistair. I didn't want to let him in on the investigation. And I couldn't figure out if it was because I didn't trust him, or if I just didn't want to let myself.

Because the idea of letting Alistair in scared the shit out of me.

CHAPTER FIFTEEN

One would think that a nightclub would be barren at nine o'clock in the morning on a Monday, right? Not Aether. The weathered outside of the derelict warehouse didn't show it, but the inside of the witch club was teeming with people—most of them in various stages of undress. I felt sorely underdressed—or overdressed, as the case may be—in my black jeans, black tank, and—you guessed it—a pair of sweet black booties. My only nod to color was my blue hair and the tangle of assorted amulets hanging from my neck.

I wondered if these people had lives, or if since they lived so long, partying was all that they did. Or maybe since Aether was the hub of the community, this was where they did business.

Without clothes.

Barrett and Marcus went their own way to see if they could get an audience with one—or all three—of the Fates. I wouldn't begin to know how Barrett could call the Fates. Did they have cell phones? And if they weren't answering his calls, would they be more inclined to speak to him in person? I hoped they had more luck than I did. Somehow, I figured I would prefer looking at a crime scene to talking to Atropos again.

Luckily for me, the club wasn't nearly as packed near the entrance, letting me have an unobstructed beeline for the hallway I was after. Aether itself was a maze of corridors. Some doors led to storage rooms, and others led to different cities, a few even led to different planes of existence. Honestly, the door juju really freaked me out.

I suppose it would freak me out more if I couldn't see the magics surrounding them.

I was ten steps into the hallway that would take me to the high courtroom, when a familiar voice sounded behind me.

"I knew you'd leave me behind," Alistair playfully scolded, causing me to freeze and whirl to face him.

He was as casually dressed as I was, only he pulled it off way better than I did. Screw a tuxedo, this man shouldn't be without jeans and a black T-shirt. If he weren't such a dick all the time, I could definitely see myself drooling. Pity.

"Tough to exclude you when you bail all on your own. I didn't see you staying to help Barrett and Marcus search through the grimoires."

His smile was snide as he pushed off the wall he was leaning on. "I had a contact to get back to after I was so rudely interrupted. Sorry I couldn't stay to spin my wheels getting exactly nowhere."

I wondered how he knew we didn't find anything, but I almost didn't want to ask. Too bad my mouth couldn't help itself.

"How do you know we didn't break the case?" I asked accusingly as I crossed my arms.

"You wouldn't be here looking like you were on a mission if you did," he answered simply, and I couldn't argue.

"Fine, you really want to help? I'm not going to stop you. I need to look over the scene. See if I can get any clues."

"That's pretty much where I thought you'd go. I can't open the high courtroom door, so ladies first," he said gesturing for us to continue down the dark corridor toward the room in question.

Wait a minute.

"You can't open the door? Then how in the fuck could you

have…" I trailed off. "Atropos is a bitch and a half. Trying to blame you for something you couldn't have done."

Alistair sighed and kept walking. "Don't take this the wrong way, because I'm just spit-balling here, but couldn't the killer just use Ruby's hand to open the door? You know, like in one of those spy movies where they steal the eye for the retinal scan?"

I contemplated this for about a second.

"I'm not sure if the magic is still tuned to her. I figure not since she was wanted for treason, right? But if it was still tuned to her, then she'd have had to have been alive when she opened the door, wouldn't she?"

He shook his head, not in denial, more like he wasn't sure what the right answer was. When we reached the ominously inscribed door, I paused before touching the doorknob.

"In the interest of scientific theory, I would like you to try and open the door. Not because I don't trust you—because let's be real here, I don't—but because if I see you can't open it, then I am more inclined to believe what you say."

Alistair's eyes popped wide. "You don't like to beat around the bush at all, do you?"

"Honestly, I don't have that kind of time. I don't trust you. You think I'm an evil soul-sucking witch. I mean, if we know where each other stands, then we are more likely to get our ducks in a row. I have forty hours and some change to solve this shit, and even if I didn't, minced words aren't my forte." I gestured for him to try and open the door. "Have at it, Knight."

Alistair sighed heavily before giving me a look that couldn't be any more pointed if it were a sword. Reluctantly, his fingers closed over the doorknob. The smell of ozone was our only warning before a loud *zzzttt* sound echoed through the hallway, and Alistair was thrown back. His body hit the other side of the corridor before he landed on his hands and knees, panting.

"Holy. Shit," I muttered, trying not to laugh as faint tendrils of smoke wafted from his hair. "Are you okay?"

His expression was positively scathing as he slowly looked up at me. "No. I am not okay."

A giggle slipped out before I could stop it, and I slapped a hand over my mouth to contain the rest of the laughter that was bubbling up my throat.

"Do you want to try it? Maybe it will shock you, too."

Still chuckling, I remembered the time I blew up this door in particular with my powers. Yeah, even if I couldn't open this door, I could *so* open this door.

"Are you forgetting I was in here last night? I know I can open it—one way or another. Trust me."

"What's that supposed to mean?"

I shrugged before holding out a hand for him to grab. "I may have blown this door to smithereens last year." At his bewildered expression, I elaborated, "I was under the mistaken impression Barrett sent a demon to burn down my tattoo shop with me, my customers, and my artists inside so he could steal the demon blade. I was a little miffed."

Alistair's bewildered expression didn't cease after my explanation. "What?"

"That's a Fae-built door." He said it like that was supposed to mean something to me.

"I know." I shrugged again. "But I put it back together, so it's good as new."

"No, you don't understand. They are supposed to be impervious to tampering and indestructible."

"I know," I repeated. "Barrett said the same thing last year. It blew up easy enough, so I don't know what to tell you. Impervious and indestructible really aren't in my vocabulary."

"Neither is impossible," he muttered. "Well, go on then. If you're going to get zapped, I want to be here to see it."

I worried for about a second whether or not the door would attack me like it did Alistair before I yanked up my metaphorical big girl panties and gripped the doorknob. I didn't feel anything but cool metal. The knob turned easily in my hand just like it had the night before. Pushing open the heavy wooden door, I stared into the darkness.

A part of me didn't want to illuminate the room. I didn't want to see the blood and gore, but I didn't come all this way for nothing.

"*Detrahet me in lucem.*" I snapped my fingers once again in the gloom. A white ball of light bloomed in my palm, illuminating the area closest to me. But it wasn't enough.

Instead of looking for the likely nonexistent light switch, I tossed the ball of light up in the air, repeated the spell, and snapped with both hands. The ball exploded, washing the entire room in light just like when I'd been here before. Maybe that *was* the light switch.

"Good god, woman, you're a menace." Alistair covered his eyes. "Warn a guy, will you?"

But I didn't give a shit that I'd likely seared Alistair's retinas. I was too busy freaking the fuck out that there was nothing here. Not a speck of blood. Not a single crack in the marble where Ruby's body was nailed to the floor. Not one single shred of anything.

"What did they do? Where is everything? Why?" I sputtered, rage washing over me.

How was I supposed to figure out who killed Ruby if I couldn't find them? And how in the blue fuck was I supposed to find them if there wasn't a single thing I could use as a tracker?

"They took everything," Alistair muttered, aghast. "It's like they don't want you to find out who did it."

He spoke the exact words that just flashed like a neon sign in my brain. Maybe not the Fates, but someone didn't want me to find out who killed Ruby, and basic logic told me it was probably her killer. Which meant, her killer likely had access to this room.

A shudder racked my body. My only charitable thought was the fact that at least the killer couldn't possibly be Alistair. I'd need to check a few facts, but I highly doubted the killer could have used Ruby to open the door. After what she'd done, there was no way Barrett or Caim or even Marcus would allow her access.

No. The man who murdered Ruby could come and go through

this room without injury. But rather than voice that uncharitable thought out loud, I kept it to myself. I'd ask Barrett later. If he had a leak—and this was a big fucking leak—then I wanted to help him stem it without prying eyes.

"He murdered a woman in this room. There has to be an imprint. I just have to find it."

"An imprint?" Alistair asked.

"Death leaves a mark on the earth the same way someone would notch a tree. Too many deaths and there is a spiritual groove scored in the earth. That's what makes ley lines. But every death—especially the brutal ones—leaves a stain."

"So, you would be able to see the murder then?"

I shook my head. "Maybe, maybe not. I've only done this once, and I was only able to see the point of death, and FYI, it wasn't pleasant."

I remembered the one and only time I searched for an imprint after a friend had passed under suspicious circumstances. I still remembered seeing Corrinne breathing her last breath as masculine hands choked the life out of her. If it weren't for the filigreed wedding band, I wouldn't have known who it was. Her husband said she'd drowned, and as the town magistrate, no one questioned him.

But I'd done much more than question him. And when the town magistrate had gone "missing," I'd been drowned in a lake for being a witch. Honestly, it was one of the less painful ways to go.

Alistair's hand on my shoulder made me jump, but when I refused to turn to look at him, he got in front of me and made me meet his eyes.

"What happened?" His voice was so soft, it made me want to answer him.

My smile was bitter. "A friend of mine died. I suspected the husband. I was right."

"No backlash, though, right?" He asked the question as if it mattered to him that I could end up hurting myself, and it finally made me realize I had absolutely no idea where I stood with him.

Did he give a shit? Did he think I was going to summon him in a circle again and drain the life out of him? Both? Neither?

Who the hell knew what was going on in that brain of his?

I shook my head. "No, but I was in a human house, not in a room made of magic. I make zero promises on what might happen."

I just hoped it ended a little better than the last time.

CHAPTER SIXTEEN

Eyeing the tracery magics in the room like they were coiled snakes, I bumped my slouchy satchel tote off my shoulder and started digging through it. I brought supplies with me like a good little witch. Maria would be so proud if she could see me right now. As many times as she'd scolded me for not being prepared, it made sense that the one time I was, she wasn't here to see it.

I made my way further into the never-ending room, stopping near the dais close to where I remembered Ruby laying. Kneeling, I started pulling out what I'd need: a candle, a small metal bowl, and a palm-sized vial of herbs and semi-dried flowers.

It was then that I noticed Alistair was still at the door and hadn't come any closer.

"What are you doing?" I asked. "Close the door and get over here. You saw the same thing I did last night, so I can use you."

Alistair's expression hadn't shifted one iota after he found out I'd blown up the door. Maybe I'd broken him?

"Yo, Knight, we're on kind of a time crunch here, so if you could get a move on that would be super helpful."

Alistair looked at me, looked at the door, and then back to me.

"I'm not touching that bloody door again, Maxima. Did you forget I was shocked not five minutes ago? No, thank you."

I got up, stomped to the door, slammed it shut, and then tagged his wrist, dragging him to my pile of supplies.

"Sit," I insisted, resuming my kneel as I continued digging through my bag until I found my vial of salt.

"Good dog," he muttered, but relaxed into a kneel similar to mine.

I really wanted to roll my eyes, but I didn't want to give him the satisfaction of annoying me, which was no doubt his goal. Focusing on the task at hand, I lit the candle with a snap of my fingers. Alistair jumped when the candle flared to life, and that time, I did roll my eyes.

"Calm down. Aren't you fireproof?" I already knew the answer—the only demon who wasn't fireproof was me.

"Yes, but with you, one never knows."

He had a point, so I kept silent as I dumped the herbs and dried flowers into the bowl. The scent of the lemongrass, sage, rose, and lavender wafted up as I sprinkled salt into the basin, and snapped my fingers again to set it on fire. At least this time Alistair didn't jump.

Beginning in an almost inaudible chant, I muttered the same words I had when I was twenty-four and lost the first person to ever show me a bit of kindness. "*Ostende mihi vitae labe cito sublatus est. Mortis signum ad revelare.*"

Show me the stain of life that was taken too soon. Reveal the mark of death.

I'd repeated myself twice before Alistair chimed in and broke my concentration.

"Why is it you witches always use Latin? You sound like you're trying to raise the dead."

"A, you are not helping. B, it doesn't have to be Latin, it's just what I'm most comfortable using because that was the language all the grimoires I started out reading were written in. It could be any language if it is used with intent. I've used French Creole, English, Catalan, Norwegian, Arabic, Tagalog, and Cantonese, but I understand Latin- or Germanic-based languages better because they are my first languages. Any other observations you want to make, because I have to concentrate."

His expression was almost sheepish, so I let it go.

"Give me your hands. It'll be easier for you to not interrupt me if you can feel the magic." I grabbed his hands, crossing them wrist over wrist.

He started again before relaxing, the warmth of him seeping into my chilled fingers. I held his giant hands loosely so my rings didn't bite into his flesh, but it didn't matter how lax my grip was, I could feel the jolt of power under his flesh.

Closing my eyes, I began my chanting again, letting the power of our joined energies flow back and forth between us like an infinity loop of light. With each revolution of the spell, the loop spun faster and faster until it spun into a bright ball of light in my mind. A chill fell over me, and I reluctantly opened my eyes again, knowing that the working was done.

I let Alistair's hands go and stood, staring at my new view. The room as it was five minutes ago was still there, but a diaphanous overlay of Ruby's last moments played out on the marble clear as crystal.

Ruby's breath was labored, her chest rising and falling in faint little pants, and she gritted her teeth against the agony of the spike in her chest. Her formerly silky blonde hair was matted to her head in spots. In others, the corn-silk strands were dyed red with her own blood. Mascara smudged under her eyes, she silently wept as her breaths came faster. I couldn't hear them, but I knew they probably sounded wet with the blood that stained her lips.

A silvery spike etched with runes protruded from her crossed feet, a twin to the one lodged just to the right of her heart. It was as if the spikes weren't meant to kill her, but meant to bring the ultimate pain until her body gave out on her. Blood pooled underneath her body, either from the mangled wings ripped from her back, or from the spike nailing her to the marble.

A hooded man knelt over her, one hand in the pool of blood as if he'd like to paint with it, and the other holding another spike. He leaned close to her face, and an amulet swung out of his cloak toward her. Weakly, she grabbed it, but something in her expression changed once her fingers closed over the metal. With her last vestiges of strength, she ripped the necklace from his neck, a snide expression on her face as she spit blood at the cloaked man. We couldn't see where it landed because of the darkness of the cloak, but for Ruby's sake, I hoped it hit the mark.

The hand that was once in the pool of blood cracked across her cheek, and Ruby's fingers went slack, the amulet slipping from her grasp. The circle of metal rolled to a stop a few feet away from her outstretched fingers, but the man paid it no mind. He gathered her wrists together over her head and rammed the spike through both of her palms. Then, he pulled a mallet from beneath the billows of fabric, hammering the spike through her flesh and into the marble.

I wanted to look at the amulet, needing to study it, but I couldn't deny the pull I felt to watch Ruby's last breaths. Somehow, I felt like I owed it to her, to witness this terrible evil done to this flawed angel. I may have hated Ruby, I may have wanted her to pay for what she'd done, but not this way.

No one deserved this.

The man stood and watched as Ruby gasped once, twice, and then went still, her face going slack. The rigidness of pain left her body, and I knew her life was really and truly snuffed out.

Only then did I look at the amulet. Only then did I kneel to inspect the round disk of bronze carved with a symbol I'd seen before. In fact, I'd seen it yesterday.

On Finn's neck.

"I have a lead," I whispered as I watched the cloaked man pick up the amulet, wipe the blood off of it, and slip it around his wrist.

"You damn well better have a lead after making me watch that. This guy makes the torturers in Hell look like my nana's knitting circle." Alistair's hushed voice almost made me smile.

Almost, because the vision of Ruby's death wasn't over, and wouldn't be until her spirit left her body.

So, I watched some more and waited, owing it to Ruby to see everything I could. The cloaked man stood by, too, only he wasn't waiting exactly. No, he was performing a ritual, bathing a small dagger in Ruby's blood, then plucking a feather from one of her ruined wings, and binding it along with the amulet to the bloody knife with twine. Then, just as suddenly as he rammed the spike in her hands, he plunged the dagger in Ruby's heart.

As soon as the blade made contact, Ruby's eyes opened wide, blazing with pure light. Then just as quickly, her light snuffed out, flowing from her body into the amulet. The amulet glowed for one brief second before it faded, and then the whole scene died.

"Holy shit," Alistair murmured.

Holy shit was right. I knew Ruby's death was gruesome, but had I known it was that bad, I didn't know if I would have had the courage to do the spell in the first place. A chill rolled through my whole body, and I shuddered at the wash of cold.

"You said you had a lead. What was it?" Alistair asked, but I didn't know if I could answer him.

Finn was in Marcus' pack. Didn't I need his approval? Would he give it on my word alone? And could I even question someone without his consent? Questions roiled in my brain, and I wished I had someone to talk this out with. Someone I trusted.

I wanted Striker. Or Maria. Barrett. Hell, I'd take Aidan at this point. For a split second, I thought it was funny that when I listed all the people I trusted, Ian didn't make the cut. A year ago, he would have been at the top of the list, but now I'd take the BFF who betrayed me, the sister who left me behind, or the former trainer who would rather I not subject his brother to my particular brand of trouble.

I'd take all of those over the man who left me in the dust. Funny how abandonment worked.

"Tell me, Maxima. What was the lead?" Alistair asked me, but it was less a question and more of a demand.

"I don't know if I can." I did my best not to look like a whiny teenager and bite my lower lip.

"What in the bloody hell does that mean? It was the amulet, wasn't it? You've seen it before, haven't you?"

Dammit, why did the man have to be so freaking perceptive?

"Maybe? It looks like an amulet I saw yesterday, but if I go question the guy who had it, it could cause some heavy tension, so I'm trying to be an adult and figure out what the fuck to do, okay?"

Alistair just blinked at me. "You're actively trying *not* to cause trouble? I thought trouble was your middle name."

More like it followed me like a lost puppy.

"Look, I need to make a phone call before we go question this guy," I said while I drenched the embers of the herbs with a dousing spell before packing them and the candle back into my bag. "Let's get out of here so I can get reception, and when I make my call, mind your business. I'm not looking to start a new war while we're trying to prevent the one already looming over us."

Alistair raised his hands in surrender, but I did notice he didn't answer me one way or the other.

Once we were out of the high courtroom and in a spot with a tiny bit of reception, I called Marcus. When he didn't answer, I called him again. And again. I called Barrett, too. As well as Caim, and Cinder. Gorgon didn't have a phone, but if he would have had one, I probably would have called him, too. No one was answering.

Growling, I dialed Marcus one more time, this time actually leaving a voicemail, which I considered akin to torture.

Before the voicemail picked up, I put a deafness spell on Alistair. Not my finest moment, but he didn't need to hear this.

"This is Marcus. Leave a message," the recording ordered in a tone that I'd never heard come out of Marcus' mouth. I did not have a good feeling about this at all.

"Marcus? Yeah, hi. It's Max. Look, I did a spell in the high courtroom that showed me Ruby's murder. I had to do the spell because someone had the entire room cleaned, and anyway, I saw an amulet the killer was wearing, and it looked like the one I ripped off of Finn yesterday. I'm going to the pack house to question him, so please don't kill me when you get there. I love you!" I hung up, managing to say all of that in one breath, the verbal diarrhea spewing freely.

Marcus was going to kill me.

I turned back to Alistair and remembered to lift the deafness from his ears. When the sound turned back on, he automatically seemed to know it was me, giving me a glare that could singe the surface of the sun.

"What?" I shrugged with a defensive stare. "Trust is earned."

Alistair crossed the few feet that separated us, getting right into my space. His blue eyes blazed golden as his demon peeked from his depths. "Yes, trust is earned, Princess. How exactly is a man supposed to earn your trust if you refuse to give him even an ounce of leeway to prove himself?"

I didn't have an answer for him. I wasn't sure if I ever would.

He remained in my space, still waiting for an answer to his question. Like a dog with a bone, he really didn't want to let this go. I couldn't answer him, and because I was a master at avoidance, I changed the subject.

"Look, we're about to do something highly stupid, and I need you to get on board, because this is going to suck in the extreme if you're not with me on this." Why I decided to lead with that, I had no idea, but I continued, not letting Alistair's searing expression hinder me. "Yesterday, I was attacked by a werewolf. Well, it was more like he charged me, and I didn't back down. Anyway, that werewolf had an amulet around his neck that looked very similar to the one we saw—"

"You're going to just blow right by what I said, aren't you? You're going to ignore the whole bit like I didn't even speak."

I heaved a sigh and forced myself to meet Alistair's gaze. The gold had receded, which made what I was about to say only slightly less painful. "I'm not a good bet, okay? I'm always going to be too something. Too loud, too rude, too whatever. You might like what you see now, but you'll change your mind. Everyone does. Every single person I've ever cared about has left me behind in one way or another. You will too. You'd be better off picking someone else to mess around with."

Every single word out of my mouth was the truth, and I could tell he knew it as well when he took a step back. Even though I was the one doing the pushing, it still stung.

"You would rather do the leaving, then?" he asked like he knew the burn of being left behind, like he knew the exquisite sting of always being the one no one wanted to keep.

I shrugged, swallowing past the lump in my throat, and if my eyes were a bit wet, well, that was just the light. “It hurts a whole lot less when I’m not the one being left.”

Gritting my teeth, I forced my tears back, stuffing that bit of pain that bubbled up to the surface back down to the depths of me. Why it made itself known was a mystery I didn’t have time to crack.

I wanted to get Ruby’s murder solved. I wanted to get out from under the Fates thumb. I wanted the threat of war in my rearview.

And I wanted the quiet burn in my chest whenever I thought of Alistair to go away. The only way to do that was to get him the hell out of my life.

“So, you want to go question a werewolf or what?”

CHAPTER SEVENTEEN

I eyed the guard to the dungeons—the same man who was barring my way, keeping me from questioning Finn. Honestly, I didn't blame him. I wasn't a shifter of any kind, so I shouldn't even be here. Plus, in no way did I have permission from his Alpha to enter these dungeons in the first place.

I knew it. He knew it. Hell, even Alistair knew it. The demon in question appeared as nonthreatening as a man that size could be, his hands stuffed in his pockets as he hovered to my right—behind me, but ready to fight if he needed to. Alistair didn't like being put in the back seat, but it had to be done.

But still, I needed to get past the guard, and I didn't want to resort to violence if I didn't have to. Especially since the guard in question had been a real stand-up guy when we sparred the day prior. His name was Hideyo, and if I remembered right, he was a Kitsuné. Hideyo didn't shift when we fought, but I'd heard the other shifters whisper about him. I'd never come across a Kitsuné in my travels, but I'd heard enough about them to know the phrase "sly like a fox" was their *modus operandi.*

"You know better than to ask me for passage, Max," Hideyo warned, the ancient spear in his hand at odds with his garb of black tactical pants, tight T-shirt, and gun belt. Likely, the spear was ceremonial, but I had no doubt he could use it if he needed to.

I sighed, not wanting to go through the entire spiel, but I needed to give the man something. "I'm trying really hard not to start shit here. You know about the angel that was murdered, right?" At his chin jut in the affirmative, I continued, "Well, I have to investigate her murder because the Fates decided to be dicks by putting me in charge and gave me a time limit. I have a feeling Finn knows something, although I seriously doubt he was involved since he's been locked up. I would really like to question him without violence or bloodshed, but honestly, I don't have the kind of time for diplomacy, so I'll shed it if I have to."

It was a threat wrapped in an explanation, but Hideyo caught it well enough. His face was the same picture of immovable stone he used right before he took someone down. I'd seen that expression first-hand before he landed me on my ass.

"Please keep in mind, I'm trying to be nice here. If I had the time to give the proper respect and go through the correct channels, I would. But I don't. So, pretty please with sugar on top, don't make me make you." I gently reminded him that I did, in fact, win our sparring session when I finally stopped trying to be nice.

"Fine, but if Marcus asks, you made me, deal?" Hideyo gave me a devious smile, tipping up his lips.

"Can do," I promised, and he stepped aside, giving us passage to the dank stairwell that led down to the cold sub-basement cells.

"And Max?" Hideyo called to my back after we'd taken several steps down. "Finn wasn't in these cells the whole time. We caught him trying to get a witch to reverse your curse."

My eye twitched at the word, and I wanted to argue that what I did to Finn wasn't a curse. It was punishment for being a sadistic prick, but I kept my mouth shut on that sticking point.

"Good to know. Thank you." I watched Hideyo's face for censure.

It was totally possible that not everyone agreed with what I did to Finn. Many shifters might think turning off their link to their animal was akin to death itself, only more drawn out. I'd considered that only after I judged Finn, but I couldn't lift the spell now, especially since he'd already tried to have someone remove it. Not unless I wanted to kill him.

The stone stairwell curved west the farther we descended, the walls practically weeping moisture the farther below ground we traveled. Even if I didn't already know we weren't in Colorado anymore, the wet sandstone walls would have been a big clue. Torches lit the arched ceilings, highlighting the fact that ninety-nine percent of the cells were empty.

That made total sense if you knew anything about shifters. They valued honesty and loyalty, even the ones who were considered shifty like the big cats and foxes. And to disobey an Alpha like Finn had done was usually met with a death sentence.

It was a hard way to live, but the togetherness in shifter clans made up for it. It was a promise to never be left behind, and Finn had taken his good fortune at finding a family and squandered it. Then, evidently, he'd taken it one step further by shirking his punishment. The fact that he wasn't already dead was likely a consideration Marcus had given to me, and I wondered why he didn't say anything about Finn last night.

But then I remembered the shitshow of epic proportions that was last night and gave him the benefit of the doubt.

The very last cell at the very end of a row of emptiness housed the pacing wolf. Or former wolf as the case may be. As soon as Finn saw me, he charged the bars—bars meant for wolves, shifters with immense strength and speed—and reached through them to grab at me. Human strength and speed or not, Finn was still fast and deadly enough to be a threat. His rough fingers grazed the front of my shirt before Alistair banded an arm around my middle and dragged me back out of Finn's reach.

"You stupid bitch." Finn seethed, his screams echoing off the stone walls. "I ought to rip you apart. I should rend you flesh from bone—"

Muttering under my breath, I twisted my hand like I was turning a key, cutting off his voice like turning off a faucet.

Locking Finn away from his animal was my only option aside from killing him outright, but maybe I was too generous with my judgment. But turning off his voice did nothing but make his anger burn brighter. His mouth moved with the words he wished to scream at me, I just had the added benefit of not hearing them.

"While I suppose that spell is handy, cutting off his voice will hinder the questioning a bit. You have an idea of how we can get his attention?" Alistair whispered his question in my ear.

That's when I realized his arm hadn't moved from my waist, and the heat of him was still at my back. Everything in me clenched for one hot second before I stiffened and stepped away from him. But that step took way more willpower than I thought it would.

"Thanks." I referred to his save, glad my voice didn't sound as breathy as it felt. "I can get him to talk to me, I was just trying for the least amount of bloodshed. Jokes on me, right?"

With a bit of concentration, I could get Finn's attention easily enough. I focused on his body, letting the weight of it coalesce in my mind. Then it was as easy as flicking my fingers to throw him into the dank stone wall. His whole body thudded against the rough surface, his head especially giving a solid thwack.

Attention achieved.

The bitch of it was holding him there, but I wouldn't let that stop me.

"Finn, I need to talk to you, so I'm going to need you to put away your idiot bullshit for a few minutes. Can you do that for me?" I asked sweetly, even though I could feel the sweat on my brow from holding a nearly three-hundred-pound giant against a wall with my mind.

Finn's eyes narrowed, and he gave me a little nod. I must have knocked some sense into him after all. Lucky me. But I wasn't a complete idiot, so I gave him his voice back, but kept him dangling from the wall with my mind. Finn, to his credit, kept his mouth shut.

Smart man.

"An angel was murdered last night, Finn." Fear crossed over his face, so I dissuaded the idea that I was here to blame him. "Now, I'm not stupid enough to think you killed her. For one, you're not smart enough to pull off something that clever, and two, the guy was closer to my size than yours. But the murderer had an amulet like yours, and I want to know everything there is to know about that necklace."

He gave me a hesitant little nod, and I gave him control over his body, letting him loose from my mental grip. Finn landed on the stone floor with a thump, but he kept his feet. The release of him caused my whole body to sag in relief. Doing shit the nice way was hard.

"You mean the necklace you ripped off my neck yesterday?" His voice was cold, bitterness leaking into every syllable, but I let it go.

"The very one." I nodded as I willed my body not to give out on me. Telekinetic spells weren't made for the weak.

"It's the Nordic rune for protection." He pulled the bronze disk from his pocket, the attached necklace's clasp still broken from when I'd yanked it. "My mother gave it to me when I left our pack at sixteen. Did you know what it was when you ripped it from my neck?"

"No. Honestly? It was waving in my face, and I was pissed off. It wouldn't have stopped me from doing what I did, Finn. Your punishment is not a curse. It's a chance for you to see what it's like to be weak, so you understand that it is your job to protect. Well, that, and to teach you that being a prick doesn't pay."

If I were being really honest, I just didn't want to kill him, and that's precisely what would have happened if I didn't punish Finn.

His attention was on the circle of metal in his palm. My focus was on Finn. So when Marcus' voice came from behind me, I nearly jumped out of my skin.

"What the fuck are you doing, Maxima?"

His voice had that low, growly quality that gave me a chill of fear. So far, I'd never really seen Marcus pissed. Miffed at a push, but never blisteringly angry and especially not at me. His eyes blazed the blue of his wolf, and all I wanted to do was cower behind Alistair.

I'd also forgotten just how big Marcus was. Barrett was six feet, but Marcus was a burly six foot four with shoulders wide enough to make you wonder if he could pass through a doorway without trouble.

"I'm questioning Finn," I answered meekly, and meek was never a word I associated with myself.

"In my home? Without my consent?" Marcus seemed calm, but I had no illusions he was anything other than murderous. I caught a glimpse of Barrett right behind him, and the "oh, shit" expression on his face did nothing to help my nerves.

"Yes? You didn't check your voicemail, did you? I tried calling you. And Barrett. And every other Council member. No one answered."

Marcus' scowl deepened.

"I swear, if I weren't under the gun, I would have waited. But I did leave a voicemail to tell you where I was going and why." I swore, lifting my right hand like I was going to swear over a bible or something. Not that anyone swearing over a book would keep them from lying—well, not without a *veritas* spell on said book.

"You left a voicemail." His accusing tone made my stomach bottom out, and I mentally crossed my fingers that the voicemail actually went through, and the cell phone gods weren't pissed at me, too.

Marcus narrowed his eyes as he took his phone from a pocket of his tactical pants, pressed a couple of buttons, put the phone to his ear, and listened. The scowl melted from his face, but the remaining expression was carefully blank. He was trying to keep me guessing, but I knew I had him. His eyebrows did that quiver thing that they did when he was trying to look stern, but really wanted to laugh.

Barrett, sensing the change in his husband, stepped around him to give me shit. "A four-hundred-year-old witch completely bypasses all her spells and mystical ways of contacting someone, and leaves a bloody voicemail. Humans have ruined you, Maxima."

I wanted to laugh at the joke, but all I could think was that they weren't the only ones. Ethereals had a hand in some of the worst of my ruin.

"You're probably right," I whispered, unable to laugh at the absurdity of it all, and Barrett's face fell a little. "Did you get an audience with the Fates?"

"Yes, but they either didn't have any information on the spikes or didn't want to share. I'm betting on the latter. Either way, we have nothing. You?"

"The whole courtroom was wiped. No evidence, not a speck of blood, nothing. I did a *revelare vestigium*, and it was brutal." I then launched into the tale of what we saw, stopping at the amulet. "I remembered Finn's, so we wanted to question him."

"We, huh?" Marcus huffed, staring at Alistair like he would rather crush him beneath his boot.

A sliver of hurt wound through me at that expression. Marcus had never looked at me like that, and I didn't know what Alistair had done to warrant it. Unable to stop myself, I stepped in between the two men—or further in between them.

"Yeah. He was there when I saw her. He helped me anchor the spell. We."

Marcus' eyebrows nearly reached his hairline, but he didn't comment any further on the "we" nonsense. "Very well, then. Finn, show us your amulet."

After hearing our every word, Finn was all too happy to help us. His only explanation was that he didn't want to get blamed for this shit. I had to give him that.

I studied the bronze disk Finn supplied—okay, he thrust it in my hand like it was on fire. The amulet was similar to the one I saw in the courtroom, but not the same. Finn's necklace was rough-hewn and ancient, the trident-like rune crudely carved into the metal. The amulet I saw in the courtroom was smoother, the three-pronged shape stamped instead of carved.

"This isn't like the one I saw, but it was similar. Like a trident, but without the recurve tines. Have any of you seen a necklace like that? On anyone?"

No one answered me until Finn piped up.

"Yeah. The witch I saw yesterday—the one who was supposed to undo your curse—"

"It's not a curse," Alistair and I said at the same time.

"Whatever," Finn shot back, exasperation written all over his face. "The witch. He had a necklace like that. I only noticed it because he tucked it away. He was going to help me, but then your Council found me and brought me back here. The guy split before he could even get started."

Barrett's face went white before color bloomed high on his cheeks. "What witch, Finn?"

Finn started to answer, then frowned, his mouth gaping like a fish as it opened and closed. Finn's face turned red, and I didn't understand until I caught the whiff of sea salt. I'd smelled that on the air last night but hadn't put it together.

Everything came crashing into place once Finn said the three words I dreaded most.

"I can't remember."

Memory spell.

Shit.

CHAPTER EIGHTEEN

Memory modification spells were the absolute worst. The last time I'd run across one, it had been done by a demon with limited to no finesse. More like a battering ram to the brain. The bartender's mind Micah had fricasseed ended up dead from me trying to pull the erased memories back. To this day, I still felt a heaving dose of guilt from my hand in Vaughn's death.

I could feel the horror cross my face at the thought of doing the same thing to Finn. I got it. Finn was a shit bag of the highest order. I still wasn't going to kill him unless I had to.

"Memory spell. The bad ones smell like rotten fish. This one is fresh—like salt water. I don't know what that means." My voice broke at my admission. I hated it when people messed with someone's mind. It was a violation.

"You can smell magic?" Alistair's tone was dubious.

I glanced over my shoulder at the idiot. "Of course I can. I see the threads of magic, too. Go ahead. Call me a freak. You wouldn't be the first."

I didn't have a lot of demon powers. I didn't phase into another shape like Alistair or Bernadette did. I didn't call to people like an incubus. What I didn't know about demons could fill a library, but I kind of hoped my weird extra-sensory shit was demon-based. The more disbelieving Alistair's face became, the less I reckoned that was likely. *Figures.*

I turned back to Barrett and Marcus who were looking at me like I'd lost my mind. "You guys knew this about me. Why is everyone staring at me like I'm a Martian or something?"

But the answer didn't come from my fellow Council members. It came from Alistair.

"Because that isn't a demon ability, nor is it a witch one." He said it like he knew what kind of power it was, and it wasn't good.

Honestly, I didn't want to know. If it was just another thing to knock me for a loop, I had exactly zero desire to pull that thread.

"Did you ever think that maybe since I'm the first of my kind, maybe I have powers no one else does?" I shot back, trying to cover, but the hurt scalded my heart.

Of course I wasn't like anyone else. I did so relish being one of a kind. I enjoyed not looking like my mother or my father. I loved not sharing many features with my sister. I adored growing up with no family, moving every so often, losing friends, losing myself.

Honestly, it was my fucking favorite.

Alistair blinked at me, his plump lips mashed together like he hadn't thought of my oddness in just that way. Aces.

"Now that my freakishness is all out in the open, can we focus on the matter at hand? Someone messed with Finn's memory. I… don't trust myself to recover the ones he lost. The last time I tried, the man died."

Finn squawked like I'd shot him, and I didn't blame him. After I was done recovering what I could, Vaughn's brain was oozing out of his ears. Literally. I shook my head at Finn. Dickhead or not, I wasn't that cruel.

"Granted, the job done to his mind was cruder, and there wasn't much left to him, but… I don't want to. Are there other, less deadly ways to recover stolen memories? Or can we just hand him over to the Fates and tell them what we have?"

Barrett and Marcus seemed to think it over, but their posture was not optimistic.

Alistair, however, voiced his concerns right into my ear. "You killed a man?" His question made my head whip up to look at him square in the face.

My eyebrows shot up as I went for broke. "I've killed several. On purpose. Most of them grace your Hell as permanent residents. His death, however, was accidental. I'd never taken an innocent life before, and while he was a pawn in something bigger, he didn't deserve to die. Truth be told, I don't think he would have survived even without my intervention, but I carry the guilt all the same."

I spoke low and measured so he knew I was serious. Ninety-nine percent of the people I'd killed deserved it. Vaughn didn't, and that was why I didn't want to do a memory spell. My magic was wonky as hell right now, and I didn't trust it.

"I want to go to the Fates with this information. Unless they intervene, I don't know how we can move forward. Our only lead can't remember anything, which leaves us exactly fuck all to go on. And a memory spell that expertly crafted?" I paused, still meeting his gaze. "I could end up killing him and still get nothing."

"You don't like killing." Alistair said it like a complete and absolute truth like he was looking into my soul to measure my worth.

"Not innocent people, no. Not even a little."

"But bad people are okay?" He tilted his head a little, like he was trying to figure me out.

"Asks the Knight of Hell." I tilted my head in the same direction, taunting him. *Gotta stick to your strengths.*

I turned back to Marcus and Barrett who were still discussing what to do. "I'm going to the Fates with this. I love you both, but I'm not asking."

"I want to agree with you, but I know them, Max," Barrett began gently. "They are going to tell you this is nothing to go on. They'll say you brought them nothing but circumstantial evidence and your word, which to them, is nothing. Going to those three is a waste of time. Time we don't have."

I wanted to rip my hair out, but it was slicked back into a ponytail tight enough to make my scalp hurt. This whole thing was bullshit. "What would you have me do, huh? Unless you've got a better plan, I'm taking Finn, and we're going to the Fates."

I locked eyes with Finn. "I'm trying to keep you alive, okay? If I don't do this, either Barrett is going to do the reversal spell—which might kill you—or someone is going to come looking for the loose end. Either way, none of those options spell good things for you. So I'm taking you to them, and hopefully three damn deities have more magic than I do. But I swear on everything I love, if you fight me, I will snap your neck without a second thought, you got me?"

Finn showed me his teeth, which didn't spark much confidence. Then Finn's gaze slid to the man hovering just at my back—the same way he'd been doing it all damn day.

"And when you go to Hell—and you will go to Hell if you leave this earth today—I'll be the one making sure you stay there. Choose wisely, wolf. There won't be any more chances." Alistair's voice was a soft bit of cool menace wrapped in a blistering promise. He meant every single word.

And although he was threatening someone, I still felt that warmth threading through me that he gave a shit enough to back me up—even if he couldn't make his mind up about me.

"Fine. What the fuck am I going to do against the two of you, huh? This one"—He pointed to me—"made me no better than a human."

"As opposed to killing you in front of your entire pack like the coward you are. You tried to kick me when I was down, and then shifted and charged me in wolf form, you prick. Get your facts straight."

Alistair let out a quiet menace of a growl. It wasn't his angry animalistic one. No, this was something different. This was a sound pulled from nightmares. This was the pit of Hell yawning wide and swallowing you whole.

"You are lucky I'm not your judge, wolf. But you'd better keep this in mind. When you go to Hell, there will be no place you can hide from me. Turn your life around before it's too late."

Marcus heaved a sigh before producing a key from his back pocket. "If he's going, I'm going to be there to make sure he doesn't lose his mind and try to escape. It's the least I can do for not watching him after he was sentenced."

"What else do I have to do today?" Barrett sighed. "Time to go get my ass handed to me again by a bunch of self-absorbed deities. Fun."

"Is it too much to ask that they come to us? We can't climb up Mount Olympus every time we need to check in," I griped, thinking of what kind of warding I'd need to put on Finn so he didn't do something stupid. Protection? Idiot-proofing?

The trip to Aether was uneventful. Mostly because it involved going upstairs and through one of the many doors that led to the underground witch club. The tricky part was not losing Finn once we got there. Even though Finn had human strength, speed, and abilities, I didn't put anything past him. I refused to get caught showing my ass because I was too lax on the wolf I'd spelled. Cursed.

Okay, it was probably a curse.

Bodies swarmed the dance floor as acrobats—or really skilled witches—swung and spun in the great swaths of fabric hanging from what seemed like nothing. They moved like they were underwater as lights flashed and danced over them. The sultry music had the patrons winding their bodies around one another.

The thing about Aether was, if you weren't a fan of nudity on an epic scale, this wasn't the place for you. It was almost as if the nakedness was to distract from all the doorways to other places. So far, it seemed like a solid protection. Who would notice the portals to other places with all the dicks hanging out?

Though, it also made me wonder if Dionysus was a witch, because this constant partying had to be supernatural.

We moved in a group through the throng, Barrett and Marcus in the front, Finn in the middle, and Alistair and I in the back, guarding our prisoner as we made our way to the right door. I felt uneasy, and I wanted it to be because I knew the Fates were going to be assholes. But something niggled at the back of my brain that Finn was a major loose end. And if the killer thought he was going to be able to lead back to him, he'd exterminate Finn without a second thought.

The crowd felt like it was closing in on us, like the swarm of bodies kept growing, multiplying until I almost couldn't breathe. A witch wearing nothing but a smile wrapped herself around Alistair, trying to get him to dance with her. Several people reached out and touched me, fingers tugged at my hair, pulled at my belt loops, stuck their fingers in my pockets. Hands reached for Finn, too, and that's when it became really fucking obvious something—or someone—might be behind this.

"Barrett!" I screamed when hands banded around me, yanking me off my feet and dragging me back into the swarm of bodies.

Then Marcus' training kicked in. I kicked up, throwing my legs up before swinging them back down, knocking my captor off balance before tossing him over the fulcrum of my hip.

But it wasn't just one. It was hundreds of people, some naked, some not. Some drunk or high or magicked out of their mind and all under a spell. Their faces blurred, swirled, as my breaths came in frightened pants. Their hands grabbed, held, and when my panic reached its crescendo, somehow my mind became sharp.

The ground quaked underneath our feet, the floor cracking and throwing people down as they tried to claw their way closer. Without a clear thought of why, I clapped my hands once, the concussion of that single motion knocking everyone within a twenty-foot radius on their asses. Acrobats slid from their ribbons, glass shattered, and still the earth quaked.

Barrett appeared in front of me, urging me to take deep breaths, to let the magic go. Pleading with me to stop because no one was attacking us anymore. But it was Alistair who managed to talk me down.

"Bloody hell, woman. You shake this building anymore, and the sodding roof will come down on us. You planning on killing us all?"

My panic throttled down, replaced with ultimate irritation. Granted, that made the earth stop quaking, but it wasn't like I was doing any of this on purpose.

"Don't tempt me, Knight," I growled through clenched teeth.

Barrett wrapped me in his arms, hugging me close for a beat longer than necessary. "You scared the shit out of us. But you saved us, too. So, thank you, Max, but can we never do that again?"

I let out a mirthless laugh as I pulled from Barrett's arms to look at the damage. Patrons lay on the floor in heaps. Unmoving.

"Did I kill them?" I murmured my question as tears flooded my eyes.

"No, Max. I put them under a sleeping spell. No telling how long it will last on some of them, so we need to go."

I nodded, surveying the sleeping bodies scattered like leaves on the dance floor. Someone had to know where we were going. Someone had to know we would bring Finn to the Fates. Someone had the time to spell all these people in a haven that was supposed to be safe.

"I hate to break it to you, Barrett, but you have one huge fucking leak."

CHAPTER NINETEEN

My gaze locked on Finn. He was cut up. So was Marcus, but Finn was hunched over, listing to the side like he'd been stabbed or was protecting an injured rib. Broken beer bottles and glass lay at his feet among the fallen bodies.

Human healing. Finn was going to die if I didn't do something.

"Finn?" I broke away from Barrett and Alistair.

He coughed once, red staining his lips as he staggered, and Marcus caught him. Scarlet blood leaked from the gaps in his fingers. Yep, he was definitely going to die if I didn't act.

Now.

"Yeah?" he muttered, his face going pale.

"If I give you back your wolf, will you get your shit together and stop attacking people you think are weaker?"

He appeared confused, so I continued, "Meaning women, you fuck stick. No kicking people when they're down, no beating up on the little guy, no being a boil on the butt of humanity. Can you do that?"

An expression of hope crossed his face for a split second before he masked it. He gave me a weak nod.

"And get some anger management for shit's sake. It's the twenty-first century. Being a toxic douchebag is out. Think you can do that for me?"

Finn chuckled, his bitter laugh almost thready. "Yeah. If I make it through the day, I'll get right on that."

"Good. Don't make me regret this."

My hand knifed to Finn's chest, the pinky and thumb spread wide as I chanted the words for unlocking Finn's wolf, calling the other half of Finn's soul back to him.

Locking it up was easy. Letting it out? Not so much. Sweat popped up on my brow, my limbs turning to rubber as I called the white wolf back to his home. Using much more magic than it took to turn them off, I gave Finn everything I'd taken away. I gave him his healing, his wolf, his life.

I just hoped I wouldn't regret it.

"Now try not to die, mm-kay?"

I ripped my gaze off of Finn's rapidly healing wounds when I caught someone's arm shifting a little out on the dance floor. "Barrett, lead the way. That spell is going to wear off, and soon."

The five of us shuffled off the dance floor, careful not to step on the unconscious but rousing bodies as we made our way to a corridor I'd never seen hidden behind a glamour. Everyone else saw a wall, but me? I saw the drafty hallway with no lighting and a cobblestone floor. Cobwebs fluttered in the corners of the entrance—either because no one noticed them, or because they added to the "get the fuck out of here" effect.

Barrett searched a bit on the wall, feeling for the break where the glamour met the real until I pointed out the opening.

"I always forget you can see through glamours. I swear it's like you have a Fae eye or something," he muttered, but I caught the words.

Fae eye?

"What the hell is a Fae eye?" I blurted, unable to hold in the question.

Barrett gaped at me like I was on drugs. "Some witch you are. Do you not read lore at all?"

I suppressed a shudder by the skin of my teeth. *Fairies.*

"Not about fucking fairies. They freak me out. All those rules, and they talk in riddles, and can't touch iron, and they trade for children's bones, and..." I did a full-body shudder. "Okay, so I watched *Pan's Labyrinth* one too many times and got freaked the fuck out. Sue me."

Barrett gave me a generous amount of side-eye. Whatever. That movie, along with every other one that had Fae shit in it was off the menu. Hard. Pass.

"Well, if you don't like trading for body parts, I'll keep my Fae-eye knowledge to myself," he quipped, leading the way through the pitch-dark corridor to the very last door.

I didn't even want to know.

He knocked three times and waited. Not a moment later, the arched door opened. It looked like the door to the witch's house in *Hansel and Gretel.*

Atropos stood in the doorway, not saying a word, barring our entry until I got fed up and walked up to her, not stopping until she obtained the good sense to move. The room was made of stacked stone, barren of everything that resembled comfort. No books, no chairs, not a single thing. Nothing but stone and more stone.

It was little better than a dungeon, and I'd seen enough of those to last a lifetime.

Atropos put her hands on her hips, irritated that I'd barged in. Whoops.

"What do you want? You can't be here to tell me *this* is the murderer."

So, I wasn't the only one she hated. Good to know.

"Atropos, meet Finn. Finn, this is Atropos, the cutter of the thread. She's super nice and loves all Ethereals."

She rolled her eyes at my blatant dig. "You're testing my patience, Maxima."

Testing her patience? Was she high? Sending me on a wild goose chase, and when I come to her all she can say is, I'm testing her patience?

"Awesome, you're irritating the fuck out of me, too. Glad we're even. Do you want to know why I dragged my entire friends list into your inner sanctum, or are you going to carry on being a complete jerk?"

She made the motion for me to carry on as she turned her back to us, seemingly leading the five of us down a spiral staircase. We followed, Finn in the middle of us all. I didn't begin speaking again until we reached the bottom.

This floor was much cozier than the last, the furnishings more cottage and less *Crime and Punishment*. Atropos took a seat on an overstuffed blood-red wingback chair, tossing her red braid over one shoulder so she could play with the strands.

"Finn here met with a witch yesterday after I cut him off from his wolf. He wanted this witch to reverse what I'd done. Finn remembers the witch having an amulet like the one I saw in a *revelare vestigium* I performed on Ruby's death site. Trouble is, this witch modified Finn's memory. I can't move forward with the investigation without knowing who the witch is, and I have a moral quandary with noodling with someone's noodle."

Lachesis crossed her feet on her midnight-blue ottoman which matched her wingback. "You say you cut him off from his wolf, but he has the animal roiling under his skin. You forgive him so soon?"

Lachesis could see Finn's wolf, then. Interesting.

"He was dying. He promised to behave, so I gave it back. If he doesn't hold up his end of the bargain, I'll kill him."

"For a little game of chicken? Surely, you're overreacting." Atropos sneered, downplaying what he did.

"No, I'm not overreacting," I said calmly, trying not to let this certified bitch get a rise out of me. "And I don't appreciate you saying so. Had I not done what I did, Marcus would have had to kill him. I know you thirst for death, but I don't. Now, are you going to help us figure this shit out, or what?"

Atropos' face was snide like she was going to throw in another dig. But I stopped her before she started.

"Look, the entirety of Aether just attacked us so we wouldn't get to you. They were spelled, heavily. So, whoever did it has more mojo than I've seen in a while. I have a feeling this witch doesn't want us coming to you with this, which makes me want to come to you. You can put us on the right path, so please, just do me a solid and quit your bullshit. I don't know what the fuck I did to you to piss you off, but honestly, I'm doing my best here."

"There is nothing we can do to recover the memory without killing him, but you knew that already. That is why you won't do it yourself," Lachesis said, not unkindly.

"Well, I thought you had more power than I did." I blew out a breath, throwing up my hands.

All three of them looked at me like I was a Martian, like I'd said something so absurd they couldn't believe my stupidity. Fair enough.

Clotho—who had been silent up to now, comfortable to let her sisters do the talking—asked a very important question. "What did the amulet look like? The one that was on the neck of the murderer."

I closed my eyes to make sure I described it right. "It was like a trident, but not. Three-pronged. The left and right angled inward, and the middle straight, but with no recurve on the tines and a single line under the trident. It had Latin stamped around the edges, too. *Cineres cineribus pulverem pulveri.*"

Ashes to ashes, dust to dust. I'd forgotten that detail until just now.

"I've never seen anything like it, I don't think. Have any of you?"

Silence reigned for a long moment.

Atropos sat up in her chair from her formerly relaxed position. "We cannot help you, and all you're doing is wasting our time. You performed a *revelare vestigium* which cannot be replicated. Who else saw this amulet besides the unreliable werewolf witness?"

"Me. I saw everything Max did," Alistair said from behind me. "She speaks the truth."

"And what is the word of a Quinn worth?" Clotho was not snide, not teasing. Like she really wanted to know how much stock he placed in his word.

"My family is not me." He stepped in front of me, and just for a moment, glancing over his shoulder like he was studying my face, reluctance on his. "And my word is worth quite a bit. It is worth blood and war, worth life and death."

Alistair sounded like he was making a promise to Clotho, but I didn't understand what kind of commitment he was swearing to.

"Be that as it may, we can't go on the testimony of a faulty mind, and we can't see the *revelare vestigium* for ourselves," Lachesis began.

Shit. Why did I do that damn spell?

Atropos picked up where she left off. "And our order stands. Bring the killer to us. You have thirty-six hours to complete your task. No exceptions."

Atropos and Lachesis stood, leaving the five of us with Clotho. She seemed reluctant to rise and follow her sisters, a frown marring her young face.

"This does not make sense. You don't make any sense." She seemed to mutter to herself before looking up at me specifically from her perch on her bubble-gum-pink chair. "You should know the symbol you described, but you do not. You should know your own power after these many centuries, but you do not. You should know these things, but you claim otherwise. I do not know if you are dishonest, or if you are just in the dark." She said these words in a whisper as if she didn't want her sisters to hear.

"I cannot help you find what you need, but you have someone close to you who can." She paused as if she was checking to see if her sisters were out of earshot before she began again. "Ask Teresa about the amulet you described. She will tell you everything you need to know." Clotho peered over her shoulder to the hallway her sisters had walked down. "I suggest you do not come back until you have found what was asked of you. Atropos and Lachesis do not do well with souls on their journey. We were never meant to interfere, and when we do, there is always a cost."

A cost? Atropos and Lachesis interfered in Ethereal business by putting me in charge of this, and now it was costing them. They put me in charge of this. Because they thought I could do it? Or as punishment for some slight I had no idea I was making? And every time someone came to them, it took a toll. I didn't know what I thought about that—or the fact that Teresa somehow knew about the amulet we had been searching for.

None of this set well with me.

"Thank you for the guidance, Clotho. I appreciate it."

The blonde Fate smiled at me—a sad, lonely little smile.

That wane upturn to her lips made me wonder if it had cost her, too.

CHAPTER TWENTY

Kicking up little puffs of dust with every step, I reluctantly inched toward my mother's farmhouse on the outskirts of Coeur 'd Alene. The last time I made this trek, I had a demon brand on my arm and a knife to procure. The demon was dead now, and so was the blade, and since that day, my relationship with my mother had taken a very different turn. Still, old habits died hard, and if I didn't have people with me, I likely wouldn't be here in the first place.

"If you move any bloody slower, you'd be going backwards. We're on the clock, you know."

Alistair's crisp British accent was like a knife in my brain, but I didn't say anything. I wouldn't give him the satisfaction of seeing me scared of my mommy.

But this wasn't a social visit, and I didn't actually have the time to be this reluctant, so I gave him a dirty look over my shoulder and picked up the pace. Marcus and Barrett were busy dropping Finn off in his new home of the dungeon—just until we could figure out what to do with him—so I picked up my vampire assistant, and the three of us—Della, Alistair, and I—made the journey the quick way.

Through another door. Sometime—when the Apocalypse wasn't upon us—I would have to talk to Barrett about those damn doors.

Unlike the last time, there was no bevy of guards between me and the porch. There was no one. The absolute lack of people protecting my mother did not sit well with me. It wasn't so long ago that there had been an attack on all the major coven leaders. Only two managed to survive, Teresa among them.

She was waiting for me on the porch—not in her bathrobe, at least—her foot tapping impatiently on the wood planks.

"You could have called, Maxima. I would have come to you."

This was a much better reception than the last time I was here, which immediately made me think she was up to something. Taking in her casual attire and almost happy expression, I figured I knew exactly why there were no guards here.

Automatically, my eyes narrowed. "My father is here, isn't he?"

Andras was my mom's first love, so the fact that they reconnected kind of made sense if you didn't look too hard at the last four hundred years of abandonment and general fuckery.

"He was, but I don't know why that would bother you." Her voice had that dreamy quality of a woman full up on orgasms, and I kinda wanted to deck her.

I had several reasons to be bothered, one of which was my parents getting back together. The last thing the universe needed was another one of me walking around. Plus, the last time they got all loved up, they completely forgot to look for my little sister, Maria. Stellar parenting right there. Honestly, I didn't have time to deal with my parents' relationship issues.

"It doesn't matter. Have bigger problems than what you two decide to do to one another." And there would be bloodshed and tears if history was anything to go by. "An angel is dead, Mother, I kinda need your help."

She invited us in, pouring me a cup of coffee, but mostly ignoring Della and flat-out refusing to look at Alistair.

I filled Teresa in on the gory details of Ruby's murder, along with the even further concerning task the Fates decided to fuck me over with. But the more I talked, the quieter my mother became until she stopped talking altogether.

This didn't feel right.

Especially since Andras knew all about the murder, and Mom was pretending like she was just now hearing of it. That, and when I took a sheet of paper and drew the amulet for her, she went gray.

"Mom. Clotho pretty much told me to ask you what this meant, so you're going to spill."

But still, she said nothing.

I got up from my stool and grabbed Teresa's shoulders, shaking the shit out of her, because honestly? I did not have the time or energy to get into a battle of wills with my mother.

But her head just rocked on her neck, and still, she didn't talk, didn't react. That's when I noticed the dark magic roiling in her hair. I would like to think I didn't notice because the magic was masked in the darkness of her hair, but it was more likely that I just didn't bother to look.

"What's wrong with her?" Della's voice was no more than a whisper, just in case my mother could hear us.

"Dark magic is swirling around her head, so I'm going with someone doesn't want her to talk."

I wanted to believe my father wasn't capable of something like this, but the black, smoky motes practically screamed Andras.

"I'm going to help you, Mom," I murmured. "Don't you worry."

Concentrating on the motes of power, I saw them like a snarl of knots in my mind. One by one, I worked to untangle them from her. Freeing her bit by bit, I only got angrier. Andras did a number on my mother, and I wanted to know why.

When the last knot was undone, Teresa sucked in a big breath like she had been held underwater, and then it was no longer me holding her up, but the other way around.

"What in the Fates? Max? What is everyone doing in my kitchen?"

Alistair gave the simplest of conclusions. "Your ex is a right bastard, that's what."

Teresa whipped her head in his direction, her eyes narrowing at the accusation until her brain caught up. Her face went slack for a split second before rage colored her very being. "I swear to the Fates, when I'm done with that man, he'll wish I could kill him."

I slumped into a chair at the breakfast nook table. "Good, you're on board. Now did Andras tell you what is going on? About Ruby?"

"The angel that was murdered? Yes, but he..." She trailed off. "I'm sorry, I can't remember much of what he said. Something about how the Fates were going to blame a demon..."

I nodded, wishing my coffee was in arm's reach. "You're looking at her. I have about thirty-five hours left to find the bastard, and I need your help. I'm assuming Andras spelled you so he could look for the culprit on his own?"

"That sounds like something he would do." Teresa rubbed a hand over her face like she couldn't believe her ex could be that stupid, even though we both knew that this was a case of history repeating itself.

"So, you're telling me your father would rather cut you out of finding the man who tried to frame you, rather than let either of you two help?" Della's husky accent curled her words in complete disbelief.

"It wouldn't be the first time," I answered her.

"I've been in your presence less than a day, and I already know better than that. He knows you even less than I do." Alistair's words weren't meant to be barbed, but they still stung.

"Mom, do you know anything about this symbol?" I showed her the drawing I'd sketched.

Her face went gray again, and I felt it on the air when she lied. "No. It doesn't look familiar."

I nodded and caught Della's gaze. We'd planned for this, my mother being tight-lipped. And while I had reservations about messing with her mind, I did not have any whatsoever about Della doing it.

Della stood up, holding her hand out for my mother to shake. "Teresa, we've never met, I'm Della."

As soon as Della's fingers closed around my mother's, she

yanked her closer, making sure she snagged her gaze. As soon as Teresa's eyes locked on Della's, Della started to speak in a haunting, almost hypnotic way.

"We are not going to hurt you, so you aren't going to be afraid. You will answer our questions honestly and without hesitation. You will not hide things from us. Do you understand?"

"Yes, I understand." Teresa's voice was monotone and dead. The sound made me shudder.

"Mom, do you know anything about this symbol?" I repeated, holding up the sketch.

Teresa nodded. "It is an Arcadios amulet—a necromancy symbol and motto. But it did more than that. It held the power of a harnessed demon. Only our elders had them."

No wonder she didn't want to say.

"Do you have one?"

Teresa shook her head. "I salted the bronze and burned it in a forging fire when I decided to turn the coven in the week before you were shunned. I watched it melt, felt the power return to the demon I was bound to."

I narrowed my eyes, studying my mother anew. My mother used to be a necromancer. She turned in her coven for a wrongdoing of some sort. My mother was bound to a demon, and I had a sneaking suspicion, my father was the one she was bound to. Maybe she still was.

"Does anyone else have one that you know of? Maybe one of the other elders?"

"All of the other elders were executed. You, Maria, and I are the only Arcadios members left."

That was news to me. What the fuck had they done to get a whole coven wiped out?

"Why was the coven..." I trailed off, trying to think of the appropriate word. "Disbanded? And why would you turn them in? Turn them in for what?"

"Necromancy wasn't always outlawed. It used to be frowned upon, but never against the law. Our coven was the reason it was. Our coven didn't just steal a demon's power. They made deals—

deals they never should have made. They promised bodies of our children to inhabit demons who didn't have a corporal form. In exchange, the demon would bring another to tether—to drain. The first time it was done, no one cared because the child had recently died. Then we learned the child was a sacrifice, and no one seemed to care but me. Drunk on power, they were offering up their children to slaughter. The night you were burned? They wanted you or Maria to be an offering, but I couldn't watch you both, and I couldn't free you both if you were chosen, so I only brought her."

There was more to the story, but I didn't have to wait for Teresa to continue.

"Everyone knew you were different. There was no way I could bring you. If the demon chose you, everyone would know what you were, because you wouldn't die. So, I brought Maria. Luckily, she wasn't chosen, so I didn't blow my cover, but another child was sacrificed. As I called the Keys, you dropped the ward. While you were burning, nearly every member of our coven, except for Maria and I, were carted off to the Council. The demon we were trying to put into the child's body was dragged back to Hell, and you were shunned so no one would know about what you were. I was afraid either your family would come looking for you, or the Keys would mistake you for a possessed child. As far as I know, no coven member survived."

"Well, someone passed one down or found one, because our killer had an amulet just like that." I pointed to the drawing. "They had to have missed someone. They missed me, it's entirely possible."

"What about the other children? Did they kill them, too?" Della's voice was horrified.

Teresa looked at her and nodded. "Yes. All of them. They burned our encampment to the ground. Nothing was left."

But that wasn't true. I had an athame from the refuse of that encampment. And who knew what Maria had taken with her as a child. Something could have survived. And as much as it worried me, someone could have survived as well.

I didn't trust that the Keys—not that I'd been in the presence of these Ethereals for more than the five minutes it took to cart me to a cell—killed every man, woman, and child.

Someone survived. Someone had an amulet, and he knew how to use it. And he didn't just kill Ruby. He drained her power and was using it.

I needed to call Maria again. If someone was targeting me and mine, it was entirely plausible they would target her, too.

Whipping out my phone, I had her contact up and was listening to her phone ring and ring. Why the fuck wasn't she answering?

"Della, have you heard from Maria? I haven't been able to get ahold of her and I want to make sure she's safe."

"No, I haven't talked to her."

For some reason, Della didn't look at me. She didn't even turn around. And while I felt the truth in her words, she was still hiding something from me.

My stomach dropped, dread seeping into every fiber of what made me who I was. Something was wrong. Someone was lying. And Della knew something.

Where the fuck was my sister?

CHAPTER TWENTY-ONE

I didn't notice the ground shaking until Alistair put a hand on my shoulder, and even then, the shudders that shook the house and everything in it didn't stop. I just knew about them now.

Magic bloomed hot over my fingers, twirling and writhing like snakes along my flesh and nearly as solid. The panes of glass in my mother's cabinets splintered and cracked, the sound of them shattering only adding to the disquiet that coalesced into a shroud of rage permeating every fiber of my body.

Something was wrong with my sister, and Della knew. She knew and didn't tell me.

"Della, where is my sister? And where is Striker? Moreover, what in my past behavior led you to believe lying to me was a good idea? Answer in any order you choose." My voice sounded calm, which wasn't a good sign. Calm with this much rage meant that killing people wasn't off the menu.

A part of me knew that I was probably overreacting. The other part of me gave the rational side the finger and went on displaying her fury.

"I didn't lie. I haven't spoken to her since the presentation." Della dodged my questions, still unable to meet my eyes.

The house shuddered again and plates fell from the cabinets, shattering on the stone floor. Wind whipped inside the kitchen, tossing all our hair into snarled knots, but I didn't care. I wanted answers.

"You still know where she is, though. And wherever that is, isn't safe. Where is my sister, Della?"

"I promised I wouldn't tell. I swore that I wouldn't distract you."

The ground shifted once again and then stilled.

"Promised who?" I asked, but I already knew.

Della bit her lips, shifting on her feet as she reached into the back pocket of her jeans. I'd never seen her so dressed down. It should have been a dead giveaway that she was in the middle of some shit.

"I promised Striker. I swore that I wouldn't let you divert yourself because you didn't have the time to look for Maria and the killer. But we didn't know. Not until we got this..." She trailed off, handing me a folded paper.

The rich lettering was on heavy cardstock, rough, like it purposely didn't have a finished edge. On the outside in a beautiful script, it simply said "For Maxima" in a scrawl I'd only seen once. Only the last time I saw it, the ink was blood.

I flipped open the card.

I gave you a gift.
Now, it's time to return the favor.

My mind blanked for a single hot second, and then the ground pitched, knocking everyone but me off their feet. The stone counter cracked, sliding off the cabinet below and shattering on the floor. And still, I didn't stop. Walls split, fissures erupted in the floor, Alistair and Della yelled for me. And still, I didn't stop.

I wanted to do what I had with Alistair. I wanted to summon Striker into a circle and then beat him to death with his own severed limbs. And because I knew he wouldn't be alone—let's face it, lately Striker was never without Aidan or Ian—I wanted them in their own circles just so I could smack them upside their heads.

"Maxima, none of this is helping your sister. You need to stop now." Teresa's arms encircled me from the side as she whispered soothing words in my ear. In all my life, I couldn't remember my mother hugging me. Not ever. Not even as a small child with a cut knee. But she did then, murmuring lies in my ear to calm me down.

That we would find her. That we would bring Maria home safe. That we could fix this.

But could we?

Could we fix anything? Or would we only make it worse?

The ground stilled again, and the house groaned once, and then settled. I met Della's fearful expression with one of my own. I had to give her credit. Even with me close to losing my control, she still kept her fangs put away.

"Take me to Striker," I ordered, and she complied.

The first thing I did once I saw Striker and Aidan poring over Arcadios lore books, was snap my fingers and watch gleefully as their heads knocked together like a *Three Stooges* skit. After that, I looked around the open-concept flat that took up the entire bottom floor of what used to be a warehouse. Striker's new abode.

Everything was high end. The mahogany table that could seat twenty. The Persian rug that had to be over twenty grand all on its own. The giant tricked-out kitchen with custom concrete counters. Modern yet traditional with the price tag to match. He always did have expensive taste.

Aidan gave me a dirty look as he rubbed his temple. But Striker was the one with some sense, because he took a few steps back and raised his hands in an attempt to placate me.

"Max—"

"Why would you cut me out of this?" I growled. "It's Maria, Striker. You know better."

"It wasn't like that. We had no idea—"

"What? That the cretin who killed Ruby was the same man who took my sister? Weird? It's like I could have given you that information if you'd have fucking asked me."

Betrayal like I'd never felt before stole through me. This wasn't the first time he'd done this— left me out of the loop. He'd done it with Melody, too, using me and my power to get revenge. He'd gone behind my back and done things because he thought he'd known better. It seemed they all did that.

Aidan stepped in between us and tried to come to Striker's defense. "It wasn't his idea to leave you out. We all saw what you were like when Andras took your mother. We thought you'd lose it and abandon your investigation."

"Oh, so it's your fault one of my best friends seems to have forgotten a century's worth of time with me to follow your lead. Good to know," I said sarcastically as I flicked my fingers at Aidan and watched him fly back, smack the closest wall, and crumple into a heap on the ground.

The said ground shook again, only this time fire sprung up with it, lighting all the candles that stood tall in candelabras and chandeliers. Thunder rumbled loud enough to be heard over the din of the earth shaking. The crack of lightning nearly split the whole world in two.

I drew the athame from the sheath concealed in my belt, pressing the rune just under the first curve in the hilt so the blade expanded into a short sword. The green of my magic raced down the metal to coat the edge in liquid green fire.

"As many times as you've betrayed me, I always took you back, always kept you with me, because I thought you did it out of love. But this... this is something else. This is you not trusting me to know something vital. This is you proving that you don't care about me."

I took a step toward Striker, lightning cracking outside as my heel hit the floor.

"No, Max. I know how much you love your sister. I know you would do anything for her. I didn't want you to put her first."

Selfish.

"You thought I would risk everything, drop everything, and what? Let the world burn?" I seethed through gritted teeth. "You don't know me at all. A century of you being my friend, and you know nothing."

A lightning strike hit once, twice, three times, the rumble of the thunder almost instant. The power went out in Striker's flat, as the candles' flames rose higher and higher. A line of fire raced for Striker before splitting to encircle him, caging him inside the flames.

"As many times as you have betrayed me, I should kill you," I whispered. "I ought to just snuff you out."

How many times had he done this to me? Ten? A hundred? Thought he knew better, and I was the one left on the outside?

"This isn't a betrayal. This is me protecting you, can't you see that? It's what I've done a hundred times, a thousand. It is what I've always done."

"Yes, it's what you've always done. And I'm not going to take it anymore. I'm not some idiot without a brain in her head, Striker. I'm a grown woman with centuries of life and death under my belt. It's not me who is in the wrong here. It's you."

The earth shuddered again, creating cracks and fissures in the floor. Some so deep, the heat of the earth seeped up ready to swallow us all. Then I felt a different heat at my back, and before I knew it, I had arms around me—one banding over my chest, the other around my waist. Not pulling, not containing, just holding.

"Love, I'm going to have to ask that you not kill the angel if at all possible. I'd hate to prevent a war by starting it, if you catch my meaning."

Alistair's words were soft, peaceful in the face of my destruction. I'd almost forgotten he was here.

"This isn't finding your sister, Max. Ramp down your magic, and then we can start looking. Together."

I didn't want to ramp down my magic. I didn't want my fire

snuffed out and shoved back in the box at the back of my brain. I didn't want to stop being angry. I wanted them to know that I wasn't going to take this shit anymore.

I wasn't going to be left out and left behind. I wasn't going to be the one no one wanted to confide in or trust with their secrets.

I wasn't.

"Let him go, love. He didn't mean to disrespect you. He didn't know it would hurt you so. He isn't your enemy, Max."

Alistair was right. Striker wasn't my enemy—it didn't mean he was my friend, either. But Striker never hurt me on purpose. He was just an idiot with a god complex.

So, I closed my eyes and mentally shoved all my unleashed power back into the little box that held it. I let the ground stop churning, let the storm clouds go so they could dissipate into vapor. And I let the fire die. In my mind, I sealed all the cracks and fissures, put them back the way they were before I lost my temper.

"That's good, love. Very good. Now, all you have to do is put that blade away, and you'll be all done."

I turned my head so I could look Alistair in the eye. "I don't want to."

"Yes, I understand that, but you're scaring the bollocks off everyone in the room, and I think you're going to have to, love. Common courtesy and all that rot."

Grumbling, I unseeingly found the rune and pressed it, letting the blade collapse in on itself, and then sheathed it.

Alistair gave me a soft smile like I'd pleased him in some way. "I'm sure I'll never forget this, but, remind me never to underestimate you."

I wanted to tell him that if the summoning incident didn't teach him that, then nothing would, but I managed to hold my tongue. Especially since Ian and Andras picked that exact moment to walk through a portal door in the west wall.

As soon as my mother saw Andras, she snapped her fingers and set his head on fire, which made him drop the bags of takeout he and Ian apparently left to procure. I held in a snort by the skin of my teeth, and my father gave my mother a scathing glare. The fire wouldn't hurt him, but it was hilarious to watch.

"What the hell was that for?" Andras grumbled as he batted out the flames.

I braced for my mother to lose her mind like I did, but she didn't. Instead, she ignored my father and held her hand out for the card that Della had given me.

"Give me that card, and let's find your sister before I figure out how to really hurt him."

I passed the card to her, but the message she saw wasn't the only one written there. It was just the only one she could see. As soon as my fingers touched the parchment the first time, another message began writing itself underneath the first. The magic in the swirling letters somehow telling me I would be the only one to know what it said.

But the message was clear enough.

Come to me. Come alone. Let's make a trade.

Me for Maria.

Hadn't that always been the way?

There wasn't a doubt in my mind that I'd come to him, but I didn't think he'd like what happened when I got there.

I was getting my sister back. The question was if I would get him to the Fates or kill him and fuck everyone else over.

Only one way to find out.

CHAPTER TWENTY-TWO

Watching the clock was my new pastime. While the rest of them argued about the right thing to do, I sat on a barstool and ate my way through a carton of orange chicken, watching said clock tick away. If I was going out—and I had a feeling I was—then I wanted the yummy goodness of fake Chinese food in my belly before I went. Then I was going to lie my ass off and go get my sister.

And hopefully, stop the lunatic who wanted to jump-start the apocalypse. And why was that always the goal? Evil super villains always wanted either the end of the world, or power and the end of the world. Honestly, what had power ever done for anyone except paint a massive target on their backs?

Aidan and Ian were whispering off in a corner, Della was refereeing my parents, Striker was pouting and trying to catch my eye—probably so he could apologize—and Alistair was perched next to me, trying to swipe the last cream cheese wonton.

Not on my watch, pal.

Like the lady I was, I slapped the fried goodness out of his hand and stuffed it whole into my mouth, much to Alistair's chagrin.

"You are all class, Maxima. Anyone ever tell you that?"

Was that a pout on his face? Surely not.

"Nope," I replied, but it sounded more like "noupf."

Alistair turned me on my barstool, fitting my legs between his. Surprised, I kept right on munching, but the man had my attention.

"The others might not get what you're about to do, but I know you're planning something. I trust you know what you're doing, but I want in—whatever it is." His voice was low and soft, almost a whisper.

I shook my head, but he put a hand over mine to further get my attention. I gave it.

"I saw your face, love. I've known you long enough to know when you're planning something."

I snorted—*totally ladylike, I swear*—and nearly busted out laughing. "You've known me for less than a day."

His lips twisted in an arrogant half-smile. "I pay attention."

I debated on what I should say—if anything at all. So far, Alistair was the only person in this room to not make me feel like shit. But I still didn't quite trust him. His earlier words filtered through my brain.

How exactly is a man supposed to earn your trust if you refuse to give him even an ounce of leeway to prove himself?

But this was a hell of a lot of leeway.

Sighing, I gave in. "He wants me. He'll trade for Maria."

"And you're thinking of going." Not a question. See? The guy really did know me.

I nodded before stuffing another piece of tart chicken in my mouth. "I don't know if he'll really give her up, but I don't gamble with Maria's life. I never have."

"You don't want them to know." Another not-question.

I thought of all the times I'd tried to make a plan, only to have it blow up in my face because of either Striker, my father, or my mother. Yeah... no. I shook my head. "The quickest way to see my plan go to shit is to tell one of these fools. I'd rather just do it myself and save the hassle." *Said every other Virgo ad nauseam until the end of fucking time.*

"Need any backup? I'm great at following directions." He gave me a wolfish grin that made one of his dimples pop.

Fates, was his smile made of napalm or something? I had the inexplicable urge to fan myself.

"I was told to come alone. I fully expect you to follow me though, so try not to get yourself killed. I'll feel really bad about it later." I was trusting him on this, because if he didn't follow, there was a distinct possibility I would get remarkably screwed.

"I can feel your concern, really," Alistair deadpanned, his sarcasm so thick you could cut it.

The truth of it was, I would feel horrible if he got hurt, the same as I would if any of them got hurt for me. Didn't Striker understand that? Did any of them?

But this wasn't about me. This was about Maria.

"You need a distraction? That why you've been staring at the clock like you're trying to set it on fire with your mind?"

Way. Too. Perceptive.

"Pretty much. I need a way to slip out of here with enough lag time so no one follows me for a bit. I have a feeling he'd know." By he, I meant the killer, but I had a feeling Alistair knew.

"I've got an idea on that, but you might not like it. Really, though, I have put in quite a lot of time considering the best way to get you out of here with no one following you, and this, by far, is the best way I can think of." He took the carton of chicken out of my hands, setting it on the counter.

His expression was earnest enough that I was willing to entertain hearing him out, but skepticism was my BFF and true love all wrapped up in one. Resting my chin on my hand, I leaned conspiratorially closer, waiting for this master plan he spoke of. "Go on."

Instead of answering me, Alistair moved closer—and I didn't think we could get much closer than we already were—his breath hitting my lips as he whispered a warning, "Don't freeze."

I didn't understand until his lips lowered, hitting mine in the most delicate of clashes.

"Kissing me is your master plan?" Our mouths were so close,

my lips brushed his as I spoke.

"Not exactly," he murmured before his fingers cupped my chin, and his mouth landed on mine.

No brushes. No teasing. Just his pillowy soft, yet oh-so-firm lips on mine. My hands somehow found themselves hooked on his nearly scalding biceps, heat radiating through every bit of him. I couldn't tell if that was my imagination or not, and once his tongue touched my bottom lip, I really didn't give a shit. Then I was up and off the barstool, with my legs wrapped around Alistair's waist, and at no point did our mouths not touch. We were moving, I was sure, but all I felt was his heat filtering through me and his hands on my ass as he carried me to wherever we were going.

Hopefully, it was somewhere with a bed.

In the back of my mind, I heard the soft snick of a latch closing, but again, I was busy making out with the hot-as-sin Knight of Hell. When was the last time I made out with anyone? It felt like it had been ages.

The heat of Alistair's hands—hell, his whole body—radiated through me on a visceral level, causing shudders of want to roll over me. My back met cool metal as Alistair pressed closer, the bulge in his jeans pressing on just the right spot. I moaned into his mouth as my arms wound around his neck. My fingers found their way to his hair, gripping the curls so I could get closer.

Alistair groaned, pressed himself against me once more, and then broke the kiss, the pair of us sucking in huge breaths of air as we stared hungrily at each other.

"I'm pretty sure no one is going to follow us after that. And while I would really love to see if you have tattoos in places I haven't seen, I'm going to be a gentleman and put you down."

The distraction. Right. I'd somehow forgotten that was his master plan. Disappointment crashed into me until I realized Alistair hadn't yet put me down and was still staring at my face.

"What?"

"This isn't me leaving you behind. This is me trying to do the right thing with only a slight benefit to myself."

His sly grin had me tightening my legs around his waist so the in-no-way-slight bulge in his jeans rubbed against me once again.

"I don't think slight is in your vocabulary." I unwrapped my legs from his hips, and he let me down. And by let me down, I mean he ever so slowly let my body slide down his, the heat of him wringing just one more shudder out of me. And even though he let me down, he didn't let me go.

His hands made themselves at home at the curve of my hip as he wound his fingers around my belt loops. "I'd say you have about a fifteen-minute head start. I wish it could be more, but with this lot, that is about as much privacy as they'll manage. How do we find you?"

I thought about it for a second before pulling one of the amulets off my neck and fastening it around Alistair's, it's twin still resting against my chest. I grasped the obsidian ovals, whispering the words I needed so he could find me wherever I was if I wore its twin.

"You'll find me just fine, I think."

I took a step back, but Alistair refused to let me go. "I want you to watch out for yourself while you're saving your sister. Take only the risks you need to take. As much as you say different, there are people out there who care about you, who want you, who need you. When you're thinking there is no one, you're wrong. I want you to remember that. Remember that I'm coming for you. Do you understand?"

I swallowed thickly as I nodded, trying to hold back the wetness that hit my eyes. "I'll remember."

Only then did Alistair let me go.

I pointed my feet east toward the beacon that had sounded in my brain once I decided to meet with the man who'd taken my sister. Who killed Ruby. Who in all likelihood, wanted to kill me.

I let myself glance back once and met Alistair's somber gaze with one of my own. I mouthed the words "I'll remember" at him, but that only earned me a slight tip to his lips.

Only then did I snap my fingers, taking me away from him and toward the darkness.

CHAPTER TWENTY-THREE

When my feet touched down on forest bracken, I knew without a doubt I'd already fucked up. I'd tried to adjust course, tried to arrive a few miles away so I could walk in undetected. No dice. Somehow, the spell he used on the parchment—which seemed coded to me specifically—hijacked my landing. Somehow, some way, he must have gotten ahold of my blood? That was the only way I knew how to tune a spell for just one person.

Trees surrounded me except for a small clearing, the moonlight barely filtering through them, but I didn't have to worry about the darkness. No, darkness wasn't an issue at all due to the lit torches dotting the landscape in regular intervals. It lit the center of the clearing perfectly.

The center of the clearing that had a stone altar. With my sister on it.

The altar was little more than a giant quartz boulder flattened either by man or by time—either way, it made a pretty clear picture of what was at stake. Maria was no longer in her pretty presentation day dress. Instead, she seemed to be dressed in some kind of old-timey nightgown with a high collar held together by threaded ties. I used to have one like it as a teen, the coarse linen always seeming to chafe my neck, and I was glad when modern sleepwear shifted from those puritan trappings.

I felt eyes on me even though it wasn't Maria. No, Maria was too busy looking at the back of her own eyelids, the motes of what appeared to be a sleep spell glittered and popped near her face. Sleeping would definitely be better than worrying about her potential for sacrifice. Which seemed high.

And even though I knew eyes were on me, I still had to try and get Maria the hell out of here. But every step seemed too loud, like the snapping twigs would summon someone here to stop me. I stepped more carefully, slowly making my way to Maria, but when I felt a shiver of magic race across my skin, I quit the careful bullshit and raced to her. Ten feet from the boulder that held my sister, I hit a wall of magic, tossing me off my feet.

My body airborne, it felt like lightning ricocheted across my skin. It burned and twisted, like when I'd gotten backlash with Alistair's summoning circle, only twice as bad. I hit the ground and skidded, the twigs and mulched undergrowth ripping at my skin, tearing at it like they had fingers with knives for nails.

"*Tsk, tsk, tsk*. I thought you'd know better, Maxima," a familiar voice called, but I couldn't place it. A young-ish man walked out from the cover of the trees. Or at least he looked young from twenty feet away and through the hazy lenses of the recently electrocuted.

"Knowing better isn't really my specialty." I said this from my hands and knees before I retched in the dirt—a testament to my statement if there ever was one. There went the orange chicken. One of these days I was going to be able to keep the food I ate in my stomach.

"That seems clear. You don't appear to pay attention, now do you? It took a hell of a lot of effort to get your attention, Maxima, and even then, it took you far too long to realize your sister had even been taken."

"I have stubborn friends and a very unhelpful batch of allies." I shrugged as best I could while still having a death grip on my stomach. "That doesn't always lend to timeliness. You wanted my attention. Now you have it."

The man came closer, and I studied him as best as I could while still hoping my stomach didn't decide to worm its way up my throat. He was slender, but not emaciated. Just small. No taller than I was, maybe five eight at a push. Dressed in a dove-gray three-piece suit, he seemed almost dapper, like he would be going to a business meeting after this.

Ritual sacrifice at seven, business meeting at eight.

He had medium-brown hair that hung to his shoulders and a heavy brow that made his face almost kind if it weren't for the crazy light in his eyes. Those were the eyes of a man that did not give a single fuck and wanted you to know it.

Yep. This was a horrible plan. Whose idea was it for me to go in alone? *Oh, yeah. Mine.*

"But do I? Do you know all the things I did to get you to notice? All the favors I racked up? You didn't notice when your old flame Enzo dropped off the map, now did you? He disrespected you so much when he left you, didn't he? But I didn't let that stand."

Enzo? It had been decades since I'd heard that name. Lorenzo Costa dated me for a very short summer in the 1920s. Everything had been fine until he'd found out I was a witch—or rather, when he'd found out I was a Rogue. I never saw him again after the day he learned who I was, but at the time, I didn't blame him. Our entire relationship had been one big lie. It was doomed to end as soon as it had begun, and I didn't blame him. Not one bit.

"You never heard from those incubi again, did you? Micah Goode had friends, you know. A family. They were teeming to take a crack at you, and they didn't care that you were royalty. But you never heard a peep. And Ruby. She betrayed you by working with your uncle. She tried to have you killed by siccing Micah on you. She wanted you out of the way. Did I let that stand? No. I didn't."

I didn't know what to say. I didn't want to say thank you for those things. I didn't want anyone dead for me. Not Enzo. Not Micah's cronies. Not Ruby. Judged, yes. Dead? No. And how long had he been doing this? Decades? A shudder of fear nearly wracked my whole body, but I managed to suppress it.

A change of subject was in order.

"You know so much about me, but I'm at a disadvantage. What's your name?"

His eyes brightened as if he delighted at being asked. "My name is Elias Flynn. You should know the Flynns, but you probably don't. We used to be a prestigious family until your mother had the lion's share of us executed."

I'd known he was probably an Arcadios witch… the thought trailed off into nothingness as something snapped in my brain. The smell of sea salt surrounded me in a miasma of memory. This was the man I'd danced with at the presentation. He was also in the hallway when the Keys carted Alistair and I off to the holding cells. He had a position of authority, too. Almost like he led them.

This man, Elias, was a Key. He had access to the High Courtroom. He had access to everything. I wondered how many of Caim's records he'd pilfered, how much he knew.

Barrett, I think I found your leak.

"Yes, I just learned of what happened. It must have been awful." My tone was pacifying, but it didn't work—my words only angering him.

"Awful?" He seethed. "Entire families were executed. Women, children. Men. Some of the women were pregnant, did you know that?" His smile was bitter as he began pacing in a short back and forth, even though he had a ton of room.

I had to keep him talking. If he kept talking, he wouldn't do whatever awful thing he had planned. It would give Alistair and the others time to find me—if they even could. Something wasn't right with my magic. Everything felt off—more than it had when I'd gotten slammed with backlash before.

"How did you escape?"

"I was an infant when the Keys raided our home. I wasn't more than a few days old. A Key wanted to kill me but couldn't. He took me under his wing instead, kept me as a son. Told me the story of my family when I was a teenager—with pride, like killing women and children was something to be revered. He didn't survive much longer after that. A dangerous job—being a Key."

Meaning he killed the man who refused to murder an infant. Elias was nearly as old as I was, and he'd been killing since he was a teenager. Nearly four centuries worth of bloodshed.

Empathy, Max, you know that emotion you rarely have? Time to blow the cobwebs off because this man is a bucketful of batshit.

"I can't imagine what you've suffered. I'm so sorry your family was taken from you. But why take my sister? Why summon me here? Why do all those things for me? Maria was a child when the Keys disbanded the coven, and me? I was burned at the stake. Neither of us had anything to do with your family being taken from you."

I'd thought the glint in his eye before was made of malice. Nope. That was a pleasant little preview. The new light in Elias' eyes was made from the very depths of Hell.

"You don't understand anything at all, do you? All you care about is you. All you care about is getting your sister back. Where is my 'thank you'? Where is my recognition? All these gifts you've been given, and you don't even have the good sense to express the slightest bit of gratitude."

Gratitude? He wanted gratitude for murdering people on my behalf. He wanted a "thank you" for killing an angel in probably the most brutal way possible. He wanted me to be thankful. He wanted me to lick his boots in gratitude.

No. *Hell*, no.

"Maybe because I didn't ask for those things. I didn't *want* Enzo to die. I didn't *want* Micah's friends to die. I didn't *want* Ruby to die. I would *never* ask for those things."

Elias' face fell, hurt staining the almost childlike quality to his pitiful brown eyes. Something was broken in him—even more than I'd previously thought. He assumed I would want these things. Why?

"Why would you think I wanted these actions, Elias?" My tone was soft, not pleading, but like a kind mother who wanted her child to answer a hard question. "Something made you think this. What was it?"

"I watched you, you know? The way you took revenge on the husband of your friend. You killed him. You've killed dozens of evil men and women in your life. You righted wrongs done to other people, but never yourself. You never got revenge on those who did you wrong. You deserved to have your revenge, too."

He began pacing again, but he never moved closer, never widened his track.

"I didn't get revenge on Enzo because there was nothing to get revenge for. He wasn't in the wrong, I was. I lied to him about who I was. When he left me, I knew I'd deserved it. I didn't get revenge on Micah's friends because they didn't kill Melody. And I didn't kill Ruby because she'd been a pawn in my uncle's games. It took me a long time to realize it, but Ruby didn't deserve to die. Get sent to prison for the rest of her life? Maybe. But not die, Elias."

His face twisted, rage painting his expression in slashes of red as he raised his arms up toward the full moon, dead center at the highest point in the sky. It was midnight-ish on the first day of the full moon. I had a feeling Elias was a moon witch. *Shit.*

"You don't like my gifts? You don't appreciate the sacrifices I've made for you? Fine. Then I guess I'll keep your sister. Since you don't like my presents."

The circle surrounding Maria flashed red, but it wasn't the only one.

No, what I hadn't realized, not until this very moment, was that there were three circles: one around Elias, one empty, and one around me.

And Maria was at the center of them all.

He never planned on letting her go. Because at the center of three circles always lays one thing.

The sacrifice.

CHAPTER TWENTY-FOUR

Have you ever done something so stupid the "after" you was stuck trying to figure out where the hell the "before" you went wrong? This was one of those times. The trouble was, I didn't know how I could have done things any differently.

I had to come alone—I didn't even know where to go until I decided to do this by myself. It wasn't so much as a location, more like a beacon in my mind. I still didn't know where I was, and I was pretty sure Elias weaved the spell to conceal his location just like he weaved a spell to hide his deeds from the Fates. And leaving Maria on her own just wasn't an option. I had a feeling this was all some massive catch-22. I was going to be screwed either way—at least this way I *might* have an option to save my sister.

But "might" was the operative word. Because I was stuck inside a three-ring circle made up of charged moonstones and salt, which meant it was a Venn diagram of awful. Not to mention, Elias was likely channeling the Arcadios amulet with Ruby's power and who knew who else. I had serious doubts Ruby was the only one he'd drained.

"You were never going to let her go, were you?" I asked, trying to break his concentration enough to stall him. I needed more time. I needed Alistair to come get me. I needed my mom.

"Well," he smiled, the quirky upturn of his lips almost boyish, "I may have fibbed a little. See, here's the thing about the spell I need to do, it requires a witch. A sacrifice, if you will. It's a trade, really. The demon I'm summoning, well, she's going to help me drain your power, and in exchange, this demon needs a body. She's incorporeal, a demonic whisper on the wind, and she wants to be solid again. And your sister, she will provide."

If I had anything left in my stomach, I would've lost it then. He wanted to kill Maria like the Arcadios witches did to those children. He wanted to stuff some demon in her body. All so he could drain me.

"But why do you need the demon? If it means my sister's life, you know I would gladly give my power to you. If you've been watching me all this time, if you know me as much as you say you do, you know this for certain."

I held back the wet that hit my eyes as I pleaded with him, the wet that wouldn't stay contained as he freely crossed from his circle toward my sister's.

"While you make a fine offer, I don't think it will work out too well for me." He lifted an iron spike from the quartz altar.

I knew those spikes very well. Those spikes—the same ones that the Gorgons used to avenge their sister Medusa, the same kind —if not the very same ones—that speared Ruby in her final moments.

"Why?" Hot tears scalded my cheeks as I watched him pick up a hammer.

Avarice crossed his expression before he squashed it. "Teresa Alcado murdered my whole family by turning us in to the Council. It has been my life's work to bring them asunder, the same as her. And after I kill one daughter and bring the other beneath my boot, I'll work on making sure she knows it was me who destroyed her. Soon, it will be her family who is gone."

He would punish us for something we had no part in, just to

satisfy his lust for revenge. Teresa's actions had screwed me over once again.

Figures.

I staggered to my feet, pain lancing every bone and every muscle. I couldn't get through the ward to Maria, but maybe I could get out of the circle that held me, and overload them all somehow. And maybe if I did that, the backlash would go to him since he was the caster and not me. I really hoped it wasn't me.

Sucking in a breath, I tried the only thing I could think of. I drew the athame that had been with me since the beginning, and I sliced the flesh of my hand. The same way I had to overload Alistair's circle, I tried dripping my blood on the moonstones and salt. But as much as I squeezed the droplets from my fingers, the blood refused to land on the barrier.

My blood couldn't get out. If my blood couldn't get out, then neither could I. I tried snapping, which only had me popping out and popping back in again.

Elias laughed at my efforts as he spun the spike in his hand. "I've been watching you for a long time, Maxima. I know all your tricks."

"If you know me so well, you should know I hate that fucking name. It's Max, shithead."

He chuckled once again at my complaint, kind of like how a father would look at a spirited child. "Oh, I know. I just really enjoy watching your eye twitch when I say it. Now, what do you think? Should I wake Maria up before I ram this spike into her flesh, or keep her asleep?"

I didn't want Maria awake for this. I didn't want to see her face when they pierced her skin. I didn't want those same screams to come out of her mouth that Ruby no doubt screamed.

"You don't have an ounce of mercy in you, do you?"

Elias' eyes danced as he shook his head, a smile stretching his lips wide.

The Keys had been searching for those spikes for centuries, but none were found. And yet, Ruby was murdered with them? I didn't think so. The Keys were dirty. Just like Elias.

"You're a Key, right? Are you their leader?"

Elias spun the spike in his hand again, pondering if he would answer me. "You mean, am I the Sentinel? I was wondering if you were ever going to ask me that."

"You seemed like a big shot when you hauled me to the holding cell. I bet you have a bunch of Keys as your acolytes, don't you?"

He frowned and stopped spinning the sharp spike. "I wiped your memory. You shouldn't remember me in the holding cell."

"I shouldn't remember you dancing with me at my presentation either, but here we are. Memory spells only work for so long on me, even in this circle. But I want an answer to my question. You have a bunch of them doing your bidding, don't you?"

Rage tinted his expression before he wiped it clean.

"Aww, come on, Elias. You've been planning this for the better part of four centuries. You had to have friends. Plus, the fact that the Keys swarmed us in that corridor when no one else knew we were there, well, it's telling, isn't it?"

Elias appeared almost pleased that I'd figured it out.

"You're right. I do have friends." Then he put two fingers in his mouth and whistled. As one, at least twenty men stepped to the tree line, each of them in the same dove-gray suit, and each holding an athame similar to mine. An Arcadios athame.

"Did you know that they only killed members of the Arcadios coven in *Virginia* in 1642? They did nothing to the members still in Spain. But that's the difference between the European Council and the American one. While the Flynn line ends with me, there were several lines that were much more fortunate. Each of them will relish this revenge the same as me. And when our vengeance on Teresa is done? Then we'll go after the Council."

Shit. Even if I could manage to get out of this circle, I couldn't take on twenty men. Not as drained as I was.

"Plus, I have one more friend. You should know her..." He trailed off as he tipped his chin to the western portion of the wood. That's when I watched Bernadette—her aging beauty mask in place—walk from the tree line, stopping just outside the circle.

At first, all I felt was relief. Backup had arrived. But the longer she stood there doing nothing as Elias readied himself for the ritual, I realized she had no intention of helping me. Her gaze was dispassionate as she looked me over, and the betrayal stung worse than if she'd cut me with the blade in her hand.

It wasn't like when we were in the courtroom. She didn't whisper in my head. She didn't change her expression. I'd killed Samael, and this was my punishment. I killed her son, and this was my comeuppance.

Thunder cracked overhead, and this time, I knew it wasn't me even though I wished it was.

I wasn't getting out of this circle. And the longer it took Alistair to reach me, the more I realized neither was Maria.

Not unless I quit this pity party and got my shit together. So what if Bernadette was a bad guy? So what if help wasn't coming? I'd done more with less and still kept right on kicking.

Kneeling, the cool, wet soil dampened the knees of my jeans as I tunneled my fingers into the dirt. I wasn't an earth witch or a moon witch, but both settled my soul. I didn't use anything but myself. And weak or no, I was still stronger than any other witch. I could get out of this. They hadn't made a ward yet that could keep me out, all I needed to do was pluck the strings. And if that didn't work, there were a hundred other things I could try.

Elias Flynn wasn't going to beat me. Not today, and not any other day, either.

I focused my sight on the circle containing me. Moonstones and salt at the base, but a web of tracery light formed a dome of magic around me, the red network of a complicated spell penned me in. It would take some work, but I could do it. If I could touch it. But maybe I wouldn't need to physically touch the ward to unravel it. I could maybe pluck the threads from here.

I concentrated on the first thread, using all my mental weight, I unraveled it bit by bit. Sweat snaked down my brow as I focused on that one thread.

Lightning flashed through the sky, a storm threatening to roll over the full moon. *If only*. Any help Mother Nature could send my way would be appreciated. A moon witch needed the moon to shine if he wanted to do a spell.

Once the first thread was undone, I focused on the second.

"Oh, Maxima," Elias called. "I wonder. Can you unravel my spell before your sister bleeds out?"

My concentration broken, I whipped my head up to watch Elias lift the sleep spell off of Maria. In the next second, the first spike was rammed into the delicate flesh of her right wrist, nailing it to the quartz altar at her side.

Her scream was louder than the thunder and tore at everything I was or ever would be.

In the next second, the other spike was in her left wrist, and even though both her hands were immobile, she writhed on the stone. Begging for help, begging for it all to stop.

"Ria!" I screamed, trying to let her know she wasn't alone. "I'm coming for you, baby sister. I'm coming."

Her screams spurred me on, as I tried to pluck the strings from this stupid ward. The second, third, and fourth unraveled, and I was working on the fifth when Elias produced a third spike. Maria kicked, and spat and fought, but he still caught her feet and hammered them into the stone, pinning her in earnest to the quartz altar.

Elias began to chant, the Latin words floating on the air as he yelled them at the sky. And then I knew without a doubt I wasn't going to break his ward.

I wasn't going to do anything but writhe on the ground as he began to syphon everything that I was from me.

CHAPTER TWENTY-FIVE

My screams rivaled Maria's as the power I was born with felt like it was being ripped from my very bones. I tried to focus on her. Tried to catch Maria's eyes. I wanted her to know she wasn't alone. It was stupid, really, but I'd died a hundred times.

She hadn't.

And unlike me, she wouldn't come back in a few hours or days. If Maria died, that was it. And if she died as a sacrifice, I didn't know if her soul would be gone as well or if it would be stuck, trapped in her body for a demon to feast on forever. Knowing what I knew about the other planes of existence, death didn't affect me like it did humans. I knew where souls went, I knew most of them—the ones who were sent on—would be reborn. On and on until the world ended, the same souls living hundreds of lives.

But loss touched me just like everyone else. And I didn't want to endure losing Maria. Not when I'd just gotten her back.

Bright red blood coated the pale stone, rivulets skating down the quartz to pool at the earth below, but the blood didn't stay there. No, it seemed like it was cycling back into the ground and up through the center of the stone, staining the opaque quartz red.

Movement caught my eye, and I tore my gaze from Maria to the empty circle. It was no longer empty at all. Black smoke swirled at the center, growing larger and larger, filling the dome like a macabre snow globe. Electricity crackled inside the dome, spikes of lightning from within struck the inside of the dome as if the summoned demon wanted out. I supposed it did. But if I had my history right, it was too soon to let the demon free. Maria was still alive, and Elias needed all her blood drained and her heart stopped if his spell was to work.

The agony of Elias' spell had almost abated, and I wondered if that meant I was going into shock. Honestly, shock would be welcome right about now. Then as one, the Keys began to chant, their words matching their leader, and I quickly realized the pain that I thought was agony was nothing in the face of this. This was being peeled alive, this was millions of fire ants devouring my flesh. This was worse than being burned at the stake, or drowned, or any other death I'd suffered.

I couldn't even scream, and I kind of wished that shock would come back because that was way better than this. I'd assumed being drained of power was kind of like being tired. Boy, was I wrong. Being drained was like someone decided they needed to shatter all my bones before fishing the shards from my body one by one.

And the fool I was, I looked at Bernadette, mentally willing her to help me. Wanting her to give a shit about either of us. But she did not do one single thing to help. In fact, she wasn't even looking at me anymore. She was staring off in the distance, as dispassionate as ever. If she would have stared at her nails and yawned, I wouldn't have been surprised.

I quit looking at her and focused on Maria. Her screams had stopped, and her blood coated the quartz altar like a curtain. She'd quit writhing, and I couldn't help but think that was a bad thing. I wanted her to fight. I wanted her to spit and scream. I didn't want her to give up.

If she was going to give up, then it had to be up to me. I sucked in a breath, and focused on the webbing above me, plucking the strands until I had no power left.

Out. I needed out.

A few threads came loose, but all too soon, I couldn't pull at them anymore. My entire body felt filled with lead, which would be awesome if that lead didn't feel like it was also on fire.

My power lay outside myself, and it called to me like a beacon—the same way Elias called to me when he spelled that parchment. Then it dawned on me. If I couldn't get out, maybe I could get someone in.

I focused on Elias as he chanted the stupid Latin words that stole my power. I focused on his hair, on his eyes, on his face. I focused on him like I'd focused on Alistair while I was drawing that salt circle in my basement. I imagined my fist burying itself in his face. I pictured his jaw breaking, blood pouring from his mouth, his teeth cracking with the force of the blow. I wanted him closer, in this circle with me. Wanted him away from Maria and close enough to reach.

Groaning, I struggled to my hands and knees as the flames of agony licked at my bones. I needed a circle. I needed to command him here. Digging the Arcadios athame in the dirt, I tore a trench in the forest floor, a three foot in diameter circle just big enough for one man. Then I ripped the filthy athame through the flesh of my hand one more time, letting the blood flow in the trench.

Green fire sprung up from the bloody furrow in the dirt as wind thrashed inside the dome of magic I was under. A tornado of soil and bracken whipped through my tiny little environment, rebounding off the magic before swirling some more. I staggered to standing, the world around me swimming. Storm clouds filled the dome as bolts of lightning struck the ground by my feet.

And just like I had with Alistair, I got my wish. Elias' scream as he appeared in my circle was as satisfactory as one would think a trapped enemy would be. This time, I had no intention of overloading the ward that held him in place. I had no intention of him leaving it at all. Shaking, I let my hand trace the boundary of the trap, allowing the power of it to warm my rapidly chilling body.

Only then did I reach inside the circle and latch onto Elias' wrist.

"You have something of mine," I growled through gritted teeth.

I could feel my power roiling under his skin, wanting out, and I obliged, drawing back what was mine. The electric heat of it filled me—nothing like when he was taking it. No, this felt like a warm blanket on a cold day, like hot cocoa, and fuzzy socks. It was the sun on my face and sand in my hair. I could breathe again, and I relished the relief for one moment before I split my focus to the bonds of the circle, snapping strings as if my mind was a sword.

But Elias wasn't going to let his master plan go to shit without a fight. He yanked, and all but tried to pry my fingers from his flesh. Screaming intelligible gibberish, he spat at the barrier between our faces, only to have it hit nothing. He flailed as he reached behind his back, producing a spike hidden in his belt. He slashed with the edged spike, the sharp blade of it ripping into my flesh.

Only then did I let him go. I had enough power back to fight. Leaving him in his prison inside my circle, I stepped through the sparking ward and into a melee.

The Keys were no longer chanting the words that would take my sister from me. No, they were a little too busy with my backup that had finally arrived. Teresa hurled balls of electric fire at a particularly large Key, lighting his dove-gray suit ablaze. Striker in all his phased glory, knocked into a Key with one of his wings, hurtling him toward Andras who suffocated him with his tar-black smoke. Della let out a screech of fury as she lunged for another Key, her fangs burying themselves in his throat as she ripped his flesh. Aidan smoked behind a Key, cutting through his neck with his blade before smoking out to find the next. A Key stumbled at my feet, scrambling away from a blackened and flaming Alistair. The burning runes etched into his flesh glowed in the night as he stalked toward his quarry, only pausing to flash me a smile before he continued on his quest for blood.

"Where's Bernadette?" I asked before he got too involved in the killing.

Alistair didn't answer me, he simply pointed to the circle that contained the smoke demon with his flaming sword—*not a euphemism at all, I swear.* I searched for Bernadette in the smoke —the woman that was probably the biggest threat of them all—but what I saw surprised me. She wasn't in her aging beauty costume. No, she was in her real form—the form of a young woman named Lilith. And Lilith was screaming at the top of her lungs, an unholy shriek that seemed to disrupt the smoke.

So, she was helping?

I'd need to talk to my grandmother about which side she was really on later. I had better things to do, like getting Maria out of here. From the outside, it was much easier to disrupt the circles—especially with an Arcadios blade in my hand. The dagger cut through Elias' circle like butter. I was about to cut through the demon's circle when a gray-suit-wearing Key tackled me.

We rolled in the dirt, me losing my athame when I fell. But that athame wasn't my only weapon. Gritting my teeth against the pain in my hand, I snapped both fingers and watched as his neck snapped, nearly twisting the head completely off his body. I noticed a circle of bronze at his ruined throat, the amulet of an Arcadios witch. Those amulets likely had more power than anyone knew what to do with, and I wondered how many souls were trapped in those little circles of metal.

Ripping it from him, I crushed the bronze in my fingers until it was dust. A wisp of glowing white trailed from the dust in my palm, crackling and fizzling into nothingness.

Elias screamed as the soul was ripped free, making me think all the amulets were tied to him somehow—like he was drawing power from more than just his. He was drawing from them all.

"Destroy the Arcadios amulets!" I made my way around Teresa burning a Key alive with her mind, and Andras ripping limbs off another. Gross. My parents were so fucking gross.

I needed to get Maria the hell out of here. I ripped through the demon's circle, caring a little that it might fuck with Bernadette's attack. But I should have known better than to worry, the smoke writhed at her feet as if in pain.

I shattered the rest of the circle that used to hold me. My last barrier gone, I sprinted for my sister. Maria's breath was shallow, the blood running from her wounds slowed to a trickle. Her eyes were open, though, and she stared off at the moon above us as she struggled to swallow.

Wetness hit my eyes, and for once, I didn't hold it back. I let the hot tears rush down my face as I wrapped my hands around the spike in her feet.

"I'm so sorry, baby girl," I whispered and then yanked, pulling the edged spike from her. I did it two more times to the ones at her wrists, and all the while she didn't so much as whimper.

Her breath stuttered, stalled, and then stopped.

Somehow, my hands found their way to her chest as I kept her heart beating with compressions.

"You don't get to leave me, little sister. Do you hear me?" I shouted, counting the compressions in my head. "I just got you back, and I'll be damned if you're leaving me again."

The green liquid fire of my magic glowed at my fingers as they interlaced at her sternum, pressing again and again in the rhythm of her heartbeat. I forced my magic into her, willed it to close her wounds and keep her heart beating, forced the power I didn't understand to keep my baby sister alive.

Then she took a breath on her own, and I couldn't stop myself from tugging her off that fucking quartz rock and hugging her. I also may have peppered kisses all over her face, which I hadn't done since she was a toddler, but if that was wrong, I really didn't give a fuck. My only wish was for her to open her eyes. I wanted to see those beautiful browns full of mischief. I wanted to see them sparkle, but mostly, I just wanted to see them open.

"*Aidan*," I shouted, searching around for the wraith I hadn't spoken to in half a year except to toss against a wall. I was going to have to apologize for that. Maybe. Later, though.

He smoked in right next to me, kneeling in the dirt. I wanted to look him in the eye, but I couldn't peel my gaze from Maria.

"Can you take her to Ian? I don't know how long my magic is going to work, and she needs blood and whatever other juju he can do to keep her alive. Can you do that for me?"

He pressed a hand to his chest. "I'd be honored," he whispered and gathered my sister in his arms, whisking her off to wherever his brother was.

With my main purpose gone, I felt almost lost until I caught sight of Elias trying to break out of his prison, slashing at the ward with the spike that could kill demigods. Funnily enough, it didn't make a dent in my magic. Interesting…

Elias screamed obscenities and promises of vengeance, and all I wanted to do was kill him. I wanted to snuff him out like he nearly did to Maria. The Fates hadn't specified if they wanted him dead or alive, now did they?

But I needed proof that it wasn't Alistair or I that killed Ruby. I needed him to confess all his misdeeds, unearth all of his dirt, and name every single one of his cohorts. Then, and only then, would I make sure he left this earth. Maybe I'd let Alistair escort him personally to the Arcadios wing.

But first, he needed to be neutralized.

Clenching my fists, I let my power go, enjoying his scream a little too much when lightning bolts speared him over and over. Elias crumpled in the dirt long enough for me to snatch the spike from his lax fingers with one hand and the Arcadios amulet with the other. I passed off the spike to Alistair and drew my athame. Only then did I slice through the circle, and this time, there was no blowback.

Sheathing the blade, I pressed my fingertips into his sternum, making sure my pinky and thumb were spread wide. Wind whipped at my hair and thunder cracked close to us, but I didn't worry. I'd done this twice already, hadn't I?

The ground quaked beneath my feet as I turned my hand to the right, and I gleefully watched as the red aura of Elias' magic that had been hidden when we met, sputtered and died.

CHAPTER TWENTY-SIX

Watching Elias' bloody face slide across the marble on the same floor where he murdered Ruby seemed just desserts to me. He would be lucky if I didn't spike his ass there, too, but he didn't move, the sleep spell I put on him keeping him down easily enough. The Fates stood at the wide steps of the dais, watching me with a peculiar expression on each of their faces. It was a little bit of proud threaded with a heavy dose of disbelief.

They didn't think I could do it. *Pfft. Rookies.*

I snapped my fingers, producing a chair for myself and gleefully dumped my tired bones onto the green velvet. Another snap provided the matching ottoman, and as soon as I placed my feet just so, I relaxed for maybe the first time since before I started getting ready to meet the three sisters in the first place.

"You want us to believe the Sentinel is the perpetrator in Ruby's death?" Atropos sneered.

Did that woman have any other expression?

"Well, since I ripped an amulet off his neck with the Arcadios emblem on it, and it likely contains Ruby's soul, and he tried to put an incorporeal demon inside my sister while draining my power for his own ends, well, *yeah.* I kinda do. But if you don't believe me, you can ask any one of the witnesses I have provided." I gestured to the mass of Ethereals behind me.

Teresa, Andras, Bernadette, Della, Striker, Aidan, and Alistair all stood in a line behind me. Bloody, dirty, and tired, the eight of us faced off against the three Fates and the rest of the Council. Barrett was fit to be tied, and Marcus was having a tough time calming him down. It seemed that Elias' specialty was cloaking and memory spells. I wasn't the only one who had been duped by the Arcadios moon witch, I was just the first one to break through his workings.

After I turned off Elias' power like a faucet, all of his spells had been broken. Every memory spell, every cloaking spell, everything. And without his amulet that housed I didn't know how many souls, he was no longer out of the Fates purview.

"And the eight of you decided it was within your right to exterminate the Keys in league with him?"

"Considering they were trying to kill us. Yep." I popped the "p" so they knew without a doubt I did not give a single fuck if they didn't like my methods. "You said, and I quote, 'We want you to resolve all of this. Immediately. You have forty-eight hours to bring the killer to us.' You said nothing about not killing anyone. You don't like my methods? Give me more than two days and fuck all to go on, and maybe you'd get a more conservative outcome. I did the best with what I had. And I'm not sorry. Every single one of those men had an Arcadios amulet with one or more souls inside. They were evil men. I did you a favor. You're welcome."

What I really wanted to know was—where the hell were they when all this bad shit was going down? Where were they when a phoenix leader was committing mass genocide? Where were they when Iva was stealing the souls of the aegis, or when Baron and Bella were trying to break their mother out of Hell? Where were they when Samael was trying to stage a coup, or Micah was trafficking humans? Where the fuck were they?

One angel was killed, and now they care? I wanted to call

bullshit, but I didn't. All I did was sit there and give them my best bitch face.

"You don't like the way we do things?" Lachesis asked, but it was more like a statement.

I could feel the sneer on my face when I answered: "*You think?*"

She continued on as if I didn't say anything, "You don't understand that we cannot interfere more than we already do. We provide visions to seers and oracles—we request tasks from some of our retinue. That is all we are allowed to intervene. The consequences are more than any of us could pay if we step out of line. So, when you think we sit on our hands and do nothing, I suppose you are right, but it is because we have been chained that way. Not because we desire to do nothing. It is just that nothing can be done."

I narrowed my eyes at the three sisters, studying them. Clotho seemed the nicest, Lachesis appeared the most apathetic, and Atropos was the angry one. But Clotho was only nice because everyone loved her. She made life, so everyone was on her side. Lachesis was the most ignored, so she ignored the world, and Atropos was pissed off because everyone feared her.

None of them chose their roles—of that I had no doubt—and yet they had the part they had to play.

I nodded to Lachesis and averted my gaze to Atropos. "I understand. We're all doing what we can, right? While you're evaluating what you can and can't do, a 'please' every once in a while wouldn't kill you. Not every job should be done out of sheer spite."

"I'll take it under advisement, and we'll discuss it at the next staff meeting." Atropos' smile was pure "fuck you." Meaning she would look into not being a royal bitch sometime between "never" and "go fuck yourself."

Fair enough.

"You do that, and while you're at it, maybe don't try and blame me or anyone else for shit you know we didn't do. Make no mistake, that isn't a request. You can make of that what you will, but I won't stand for that tactic again. Am I clear?"

Clotho put a hand on Atropos' shoulder, probably calming the Fate before she lost her mind at my challenge.

"You are honorable, that we understand. We also understand that it has been a lifelong mission of yours to protect the innocent." Clotho shifted her feet before stepping down from the dais so we were on equal ground. "You accepted the demon seat on the Council, but the three of us feel you might be suited for another position—one that appeals to your need to right wrongs. If Ruby taught us anything, it taught us that we have an internal problem. Samael, Ruby, Elias, the Keys... evil has somehow infiltrated our ranks. We need you to snuff it out."

Baffled didn't even come close to what I was feeling. "You want me to step down from the Council—a job I finally decided on a few days ago—to what? Fix your problem?"

"If you stay on the Council, it will be your problem, too. But if you take the mantel of Sentinel, you will be in a better position to make real change and stomp out the threat that poses to topple us from within."

I considered her proposal. Me, as some kind of supernatural narc? I couldn't see me doing anything like that. But if it meant being on the ground, if it meant helping people who needed it, then it couldn't be worse than the Council—even if I didn't exactly get a real shot of actually sitting in the seat.

"Would I have to wear the dumb gray suit?" I quirked a brow, and only Striker, Aidan, and Alistair snickered at my sort of joke.

"No. There isn't a uniform," Clotho answered.

"And who do I work for?"

Clotho smiled because she realized I was actually considering it. "You are your own boss. You take requests from the Council and we three, but you can choose what you investigate. We would formally request that you investigate any further Key involvement in the Arcadios mess, but that would be up to you to accept."

"I will take the job on a few conditions."

"What? You want a pony, too?" Atropos flicked her wrist, losing her grip on her attitude.

"While a pony would be nice," I tried to rein in my need to flip her the bird, "I'd want all of you to consider Alistair Quinn for my vacant demon seat. Out of the three remaining candidates, he wants the job, is well versed in demon politics, and isn't a complete dick. Whatever you think you know about him, I want you to accept him into your circle. Because I know honorable men, and he, without a doubt in my mind, is one. He will be a great addition to the Council."

I didn't look at Alistair while I sang his praises, but I felt his eyes on me all the same.

Atropos and Clotho appeared surprised at my request, but Lachesis only gave me a smile and a nod.

"Agreed. If he accepts, he can take your vacant seat. What else?"

I thought about what I would change if I could, and some like-mindedness in the ruling class couldn't hurt. "I want the Council to reach out to the other factions to fill the vacant seats. There is not a sitting phoenix or wraith on the Council, and I believe that this should change."

"I concur." Barrett interjected. "We've been asking for this for years. Now is the time to bring in new blood. Blood we can trust to do the right thing."

This time it was Atropos who agreed. "Fine. If they accept the mantle, then we will have them. Anything else?"

"That's all I have. As long as the job includes ripping every bit of knowledge from Elias before his sorry ass is deported to Hell, count me in."

Atropos' smile was practically gleeful. "Oh, don't worry about that. I think we'd all love to know his secrets, and luckily enough, you have a vampire as one of your paladins. Getting him to talk should be easy as pie."

Paladins? "What do you mean Della is a paladin? And what do you mean by 'one of'?"

Atropos frowned. "You're royalty, Maxima. You've had

protection since your Rogue status was lifted. I assumed you knew…"

I shook my head, willing her to keep talking, but it was Bernadette who stepped in between the Fates and me.

"I assigned you protection after Samael was…" She trailed off, her gaze shifting off of me and to someone at my back. "After Samael was judged, I made sure you had protection. I'd put Della in place before, but I added Striker and Aidan as extra protection after you rightfully took my son down. For the past six months, the three of them have been eliminating threats to your life. Della as your close guard, and the boys as your far."

I felt my eye twitching, and when the ground started its rumbling, I took a deep breath to make the earthquakes stop.

"You mean before you stopped talking to me altogether, you enlisted my friends to play bodyguard?"

"Not that I have to explain myself to you, but I needed that distance to infiltrate Elias' inner circle. I used Samael's death as a springboard. I couldn't be chummy with you and keep the façade, so I cut you off. Keep in mind, it was me who called in the backup. Keep in mind, it was me who destroyed one of my own tonight."

"No one is saying what you did wasn't awesome. All I'm saying is a heads up would have been nice. Maybe I wouldn't have been worried that you hated me, if you just would have said something. But that's not your style, is it?"

Glancing over my shoulder, I took a hard look at my bodyguards. "I expected more out of you three. We'll be discussing this at length later."

I stared past my grandmother back to the Fates, the act as much of a dismissal as I could muster. "Knowing now what I do about the Arcadios coven, I understand why you thought displaying that blood would be an affront. But I didn't display Arcadios blood. I displayed my witch side, my mother's blood. Alcado blood."

The three Fates frowned in confusion, but I continued, "I may not be a very good witch or a very good demon, but in presenting myself to you, I wanted to show both sides of me. Because I'm not one or the other. I am both. And maybe you don't like that, but that's who I am, and even though I'm just learning to accept it, I hope you can, too."

Atropos blinked in what I would call shock, but I couldn't be sure. Then she nodded, her head giving me an almost bow. When she rose, she speared my mother with a glare and then turned her gaze back to me.

"I think, Sentinel, what you are is still being discovered."

CHAPTER TWENTY-SEVEN

Soon after Atropos' cryptic pronouncement, we carted Elias off to one of the Key's holding cells. The shifter guard I knew there, Macallan, promised to keep him secure until I needed him for questioning—which would be after at least a full day of sleep and enough food to make my stomach burst. I gave him a way to contact me if any trouble arose, praying he wouldn't need it.

I didn't get a chance to see Alistair once I was done. The Council—which I was no longer a member of—was having a closed-door session. The fact that I was on the outside once again burned a bit, but I tried not to let my insecurities get the best of me.

Teresa, Andras, and Bernadette waited for me outside the holding area, the trio doing their best not to kill each other. I could tell that the tense détente wouldn't last.

"I'm sorry." The words from Andras caught me by surprise. "I should have gone to you when we got the letter from Elias. We should have included you instead of listening to others when they said you would lose focus. You have always put others ahead of yourself, and we—I—worried that you wouldn't do what I thought you should. I haven't been a father to you ever, but I want to try to not be such a raging asshole."

Okay, who was he, and what did he do with my dick of a dad?

Teresa stepped in front of him as she latched onto my hands. "And I'm sorry I didn't spill about the Arcadios stuff without vamp help. I thought it was behind me, and I wasn't ready to dredge it up. I'm glad you had Della yank it out of me."

My eyes narrowed at the admission. I turned to my grandmother. "Did you dose them with something?"

"This, my dear, is personal growth. They nearly lost you and Maria, and even though I owe you an apology as well, I'll wait a bit. Tea next week once you're rested?"

"You going to spill all the dirt and make sure I'm ready for this Sentinel bullshit?"

Bernadette rolled her eyes in the classy way only she could. "Of course."

"And the Quinn dirt?"

"Now you're just being a pain. Yes, I will spill all the tea while we drink some. Hopefully with some bourbon because I missed you to pieces. Okay?" She held her arms open for a hug.

I gave her a stink face but still hugged the shit out of her. "Quit keeping me in the dark, Grams. It sucks, okay?"

"I'll do better."

Once I breathed Aether-free air again, I pointed my feet toward home, only slightly irritated at the three bodyguards that tagged along. Since the sun was up, I opted for the passenger seat of Striker's obnoxiously overpriced car, nearly falling off my feet as I made my way to Maria.

Déjà vu hit me hard as I walked into the room, nearly the same scene as last year playing before my eyes. Maria in my guest bed—which was now her room—and Ian watching to see if she would wake up. Ian broke up with me in this room, and yet, the sting of it was gone. And Ian didn't look at me like I'd just betrayed him. Now he looked at me like I'd just brought him a gift.

"She wake up at all?"

Ian shook his head and stood, reluctantly releasing Maria's hand. He gestured for us to step out of the room like a good doctor would. But this didn't feel like he was a detached physician giving me news. This felt like he gave a shit, and not about me, but Maria. Good.

"Your spell to keep her heart beating lasted just long enough for me to get a transfusion into her. Physically, she will heal. I don't know what Elias did to her during the hours he had her. I don't know what she endured. She's likely going to need some assistance. I have a contact who helps Ethereals deal with these types of traumas. I can call her. When Maria wakes up."

After the ordeal with Micah, Ian tried to get me to talk to his contact, but I refused. I'd make sure Maria didn't follow my bad example.

"You care a lot about her, don't you?" I asked, not because I was jealous, but because I wanted to make sure what I was about to say came out right if something like this ever could.

"Of course I do."

"I know at one time you thought I was yours—that wraith bonding juju you guys have. But the girl in the club you kissed, she died. In your arms, if I remember right. We didn't work because I didn't trust that you could keep yourself safe. That you wouldn't leave me, that you wouldn't die. And looking back, we also didn't work because you thought the same damn thing about me. We didn't trust each other, and we never would. Not about those things."

Ian huffed and crossed his arms. The burn of him leaving didn't hurt anymore. He wasn't meant for me, maybe he never really was.

"I don't blame you for ending things. If I was honest with myself, I didn't give us even half a chance. But if you aren't pursuing Maria because of me, I will blame you. So, if you have feelings for her, I say go for it. But..." I trailed off, thinking of the exact way to phrase this so my meaning was clear. "If you break her heart? I'll kill you. Cool?"

Ian flashed me that blindingly white smile that I used to love so much. Now, I just liked that my friend was happy. "Cool. Can I go back to my patient now?"

"Yep. I'm going to go eat and then sleep for a week. But if my sister wakes up, I expect you to get me up."

"Will do."

I left the hall and headed for the kitchen, praying there were at least some leftovers in the fridge. Sitting at my kitchen table were the three people I did not want to see.

"I'm too damn tired for your apologies. The first one of you to give me food gets my eternal gratitude and a single freebie pass on being an asshole for not telling me they were assigned to be my bodyguard."

Della held up a greasy white paper bag with the *Mi Cosina* logo on it.

"Sweet mother in heaven, there had better be tamales in that bag," I whispered, the awe in my voice apparent.

Mi Cosina was a restaurant in Texas that had the best tamales on the planet. Someone had to have traveled to Texas to get them, and considering that it was too damn early in the morning, Della had to have compelled a cook to make them. This was a team effort.

"So, what did you bring to say sorry, you shit?" I asked Striker.

In answer, he produced a bottle of bourbon that had to have cost at least five hundred dollars in one hand, and the last Arcadios amulet in the other.

"I stole this," he said, handing over the amulet, "and I bought the bourbon. I kinda figured that you knew better than me what to do with the amulet, and I thought you might want to set her free. I didn't trust what the Fates would do with her, and..."

I felt the bronze in my hand, cold even though it had been in Striker's pocket for hours, and I could almost feel the souls roiling within it. A wave of sadness rolled over me, and I abandoned my guests, leaving them in the kitchen so I could do this part alone. I walked out to the courtyard under the wisteria trees and jasmine vines and spoke to whatever part of Ruby that was left.

"I don't know what made you do what you did. I don't know if you thought you were doing good or not. I guess it's not up to me to judge. Not anymore. I hope this brings you peace."

Closing my fingers over the circle of metal, I let my power rise in me as I crushed the amulet into dust. I could almost hear a sigh of relief when trails of luminescent smoke rose from my palm, fading off into nothing. And if I shed a tear at the gravity of it, well, that was just me being tired is all.

I dusted off my hands and headed back inside to eat.

I was going to murder whoever was ringing that doorbell. Groaning, I snatched off my covers, ripped the robe off my bathroom door, and stomped to the front door tying the robe closed over my rather inefficient jammies.

What the fuck were bodyguards there for if no one would answer the bloody door?

On my porch was a familiar face, and if I remembered right, I was pretty sure I told him he wasn't allowed back without an invitation. Alistair's paladin, shifted from foot to foot on my doorstep, nerves getting the better of him.

"Ren, I think I told you not to come back unless I asked."

He gave me a hesitant grin. "Yes, Majesty, but Mister Alistair asked me to deliver a present, and since I wanted to apologize for the part I played in your deception, I decided that—"

"You wanted to completely ignore what I told you to do, and do whatever the hell you were going to do anyway? Yeah, I caught that. I remember hearing something about a present? Gimme and then beat it. I need about three days more sleep." I held my hands out for the giant white dress box he had a death grip on.

"Yes, Majesty." He gave me a slight bow, handing over the box.

"Ren, we talked about this 'Majesty' shit. It's Max. Just Max."

"Right. Well, I'm off. I hope you enjoy your present." He turned off my porch as I slammed the door and locked it.

I attacked the cobalt-blue ribbon with a singular focus of a woman opening the first present that likely wasn't a blade of some kind in nearly ten years, with only a minor mental nudge that the ribbon matched my hair to the exact shade. Belly flutters hit me before I lifted the lid. Actual belly flutters.

The lid went bye-bye, and I gently pulled the cobalt paper back. Inside the box laid a set of supple fighting leathers with some kind of magic enhancement. I lifted the moto-style jacket out of the box, and a card fluttered to the floor. Hesitantly, I reached for it, appreciating Alistair's manly, nearly illegible scrawl.

But his words didn't quite make sense.

M—

LOOKING FORWARD TO WORKING WITH YOU. I KNOW WITHOUT A DOUBT YOUR ASS WILL LOOK FABULOUS IN THESE. CAN'T WAIT TO SEE IT.

—ALISTAIR

P.S. I HOPE TO CASH IN ON OUR DEAL SOON ENOUGH.

The deal? Didn't I already pay up when I gave him the demon seat?

But that wasn't what he asked for, was it? He asked for a favor. One of his choosing.

The devil really was in the details.

SISTER OF EMBERS & ECHOES

ROGUE ETHEREAL BOOK 4

CHAPTER ONE

My eyes narrowed over the rim of my teacup. My grandmother crossed her legs, matching my glare as she sipped her own tea. In all likelihood, she was holding in a laugh. Bernadette had seen oceans rise and fall, empires crumble to dust, entire civilizations wiped from the face of the earth. As one of the first demons in Hell, nothing short of a full-blown apocalypse was going to phase her.

Especially not my paltry little glare.

Fair enough.

Uncrossing my legs, I folded them underneath me, sucking down another sip of my tea as I settled deeper into the overstuffed armchair. I wasn't a big tea kind of person, but the herbal blend I'd concocted in a fit of nerves last week seemed to be growing on me. I'd been doing a lot of things like that—things that Maria would have done herself if she'd just freaking wake up.

"I'm not setting foot in Aether until Maria wakes up, and that's final."

Final.

Like that word ever stopped my grandmother. I was pretty sure if she had even a single shred less class, she'd have given the Fates the old double middle-finger salute while telling them to kiss her ass.

That last bit might just be wishful thinking on my part. At least it was amusing to think about.

"It's been a week, Maxima," Bernadette chided softly, her voice full of understanding, but her message clear. I couldn't wait much longer to interrogate Elias. The Fates were running out of patience, and I was running out of time.

"Have they gotten anything out of him at all?" I asked, unable to keep my gaze from shifting from Bernadette to Maria's closed bedroom door.

I didn't like being on this side of it. I didn't like that I wasn't watching her.

I didn't like that I couldn't figure out a way to help.

A week ago, Elias Flynn tried to use my sister as a sacrifice by offering her up to a demon as a host. Bernadette helped me stop him, but Maria still wasn't awake. The longer her sleep lasted, the more I realized we might not have been as successful as I once thought.

If we were successful at all.

"He isn't telling us anything we didn't know already. Della refuses to go without you, and very few witches are willing to do memory spells. Especially since he is no more magical than a human now."

I pursed my lips but refused to feel guilty. Elias used to be a very gifted moon witch. I say "*used to be*" because I turned off his magic like a kitchen faucet. I had a feeling I wasn't supposed to be able to do that. And since I was the only person I knew who was actually able to do that bit of magic, I wasn't a hundred percent on how it actually worked.

"I'm not sorry for nulling him. It was either that or kill him."

Elias wasn't the first person I'd nulled. I did the same to a shifter named Finn. Finn had deserved it, too, but no one deserved to have his powers stripped more than Elias.

"No one is saying you did the wrong thing, Maxima. But there are realities to this situation you need to be aware of. I'm not going to sugarcoat it just because you decided to take a holiday in the middle of a shit storm."

Bernadette uncrossed her legs, planted her feet, and stood. Her visage of an aging beauty slipped for a moment, showing her true face underneath. I always tended to forget that she put on the façade of an older woman rather than keep the unchanging one she was born with. And to see the face that she tried so desperately to keep hidden meant she was well and truly done with my bullshit.

I was acting like a child with no responsibilities instead of the four-hundred-year-old newly minted Leader of the Keys. Other than order takeout and watch my sister sleep, I had done little else besides tooling around my greenhouse and trying not to panic.

"She is in this mess because of me," I whispered, trying not to let all my sorrow fall from my mouth at once.

"No, Maria is in this mess because of a moon witch with an ax to grind. Maria is stuck in that bed because I didn't do my job of keeping you and yours safe. You want a pity party? Well, you're going to have to pass some around, kid. Put the blame on the prat who deserves it and find out what else he knows. That's the only way we're going to find out who else is with him. Letting him sit in that cell is just asking for the guilty parties to gut him in his sleep to keep him quiet."

Well, she wasn't wrong.

"Fine." I sighed, resignation pulling at every letter in that single syllable. "I'll go in. Tomorrow, though. Let me get an actual night of rest, and I'll go into Aether in the morning."

Bernadette huffed, but it was a good-natured one, so I shot her a smile.

"So now that that little drama is over, tell me about that big box of fighting leathers just sitting on your coffee table. I read the card. You made a deal with Alistair Quinn? Do I even want to know why?"

I thought back to the night I accidentally summoned a demon to my casting room. Directly from Hell. An act that should have taken an entire coven of witches with *not* a little bit of magic to accomplish. Bernadette would be the least likely to judge me for what happened with Alistair.

Probably.

"I may have accidentally summoned him into a circle. From Hell. In exchange for him not ratting me out, I owe him a favor. I kinda thought I repaid him by nominating him for the Council, but..."

The sigh coming from Bernadette's throat sounded like her soul was escaping. So maybe she would judge the shit out of me for making that deal. Super.

"You made a deal with a demon for a favor of his choosing, and because you gave him what he wanted without him having to ask for it, he essentially gets a freebie," she said, finishing my sentence.

"Pretty much."

"Didn't anyone ever tell you not to make deals with demons?" She said it like only an airheaded infant with no common sense could ever possibly *not* know this. To her credit, it should be a "no shit" kind of response, but being a Rogue for as long as I was, those little tidbits of wisdom were hard to come by.

"Since I didn't even know demons existed until a year ago, that would be a hard no."

Not that it took a genius to put it together, though.

Bernadette's visage flickered again, and the gravity of my particular predicament settled like a lead weight in my stomach.

"Making a deal with a demon is quite like making a deal with a Fae. They are concrete and binding, and there isn't a loophole big enough to wriggle through. And refusing to hold up your end of the bargain means nasty things. I hope whatever he asks of you, you can stomach."

Because I would be completing the bargain. Whether I liked it or not. *Got it.*

"Before I made it, I told him the favor couldn't include sex or murder, so at least there's that?" I said, wincing as I took another sip of my tea.

Bernadette's lips twisted like those caveats weren't enough

coverage for my ass that was currently swinging in the wind.

"At least that's something. Honestly, I doubt the Council would have charged you. Not for a Quinn."

I thought back at all the times I'd been charged for something I not only didn't do but was actually executed for. *Not that those executions took...* Yeah, I highly doubted the Council would have refrained from torching me on the spot. Even if some of them were my friends.

Trying to keep my skepticism off my face, I prodded my grandmother for info.

"Tell me more about the Quinns. What am I getting myself into?"

Settling back in her chair, Bernadette began sipping her tea. Not a good sign.

"I don't know much about Alistair other than when he helped take out the Keys, but if I had to guess, he's nothing like his family. Clotho sure hates him, but she hates all the Quinns. Not just Alistair. His father is a piece of work, and from what I've heard, his mother isn't much better. If you can avoid his family while you deal with Alistair, it would be for the best."

I tried to reconcile the man who'd stood up to me and stood by me in battle, with the man the Fates and my grandmother warned me off of. The man who'd given me the best kiss I'd ever received while also not treating me like spun glass. The man who'd made me take a deal to keep my ass out of hot water, but held my hair back when I'd gotten hit with a nasty case of backlash.

It made sense, and it didn't.

Everyone said Alistair wasn't like his family—not that I knew exactly what that meant—but I could see their trepidation, too. He seemed cold and aloof when I'd first met him, but he'd changed so much since then. I didn't know if I saw something he didn't show everyone else, or if I was making another mistake in a long line of epic blunders before him. But I couldn't help my disappointment —no matter how idiotic it might be.

"No Alistair. Got it." Was that my voice sounding that pitiful, or was I just tired? Yeah. Tired. I was totally tired.

Bernadette reached across my little side table to take my hand.

"I didn't say no Alistair. I said, avoid his family. But while I'm at it, I will say guard your heart, dear. There isn't a world or realm or dimension that will readily accept you two. Royal blood or not. So keep him around and fall in love if you must, but keep your wits. Yeah?"

That was about as much of a blessing as I was going to get. Bernadette's opinion on relationships was skewed by eons of neglect and pain. She was what I figured I would have been like had I not been forced into friendships and a makeshift ragtag bunch of family who refused to let me go.

But skewed by pain or not, her message was a hard kernel of truth I would just have to swallow.

"Yeah. Eyes open. I got it." I had a feeling keeping my eyes open wouldn't help me at all, but I was going to do it.

"Why don't you tell me about Maria?" Bernadette said, changing the subject. "Is she showing any other symptoms? Stirring, screaming, levitating?"

What was this, *The Exorcist*? Was that what real possession was like? Was Maria going to start crawling up the walls next?

At my stunned expression, Bernadette started laughing.

"Not. Funny." I seethed, setting my teacup down so hard I nearly cracked the damn thing.

"Come on. It was a little funny," she said into her cup, smiling like the demon queen she was.

"It would only be funny if it were someone else's sister. It is not funny when it's *my* sister. And no. As of today, there has been no puking up split pea soup or her head doing a full three-sixty. She's just… sleeping. Her heart's beating, her breathing is normal, her wounds are healing."

But I left off the last bit I didn't want to say.

She's fine. She just won't wake up.

But Bernadette knew exactly what I left out. She knew because, in the short span of time we'd known each other, she'd grasped just how precious having family was to me. After four centuries without one, I refused to go back to my island existence.

"If it will make you feel better, I'll check on her. But these things take time. She nearly died. Give her body time to rest. Give her mind time to heal. Dying might be old hat to you, but Maria's never done it before. She doesn't know how it changes you."

My eyes stung, my lips twisting in a grimace as I tried not to let myself cry. Maria's heart had stopped. What if we were too late? What if she never woke up? Those two thoughts had swirled in my brain all week, but I refused to say them aloud.

"She's going to be fine, Max," Bernadette murmured, squeezing my hand so I'd meet her gaze. "I promise."

All I could give her was a nod, so she released me to peek in on Maria. I let her do this alone since Maria's room was already overcrowded.

Teresa and Ian had camped out in Maria's room, bickering and sniping at each other every chance they got. I tried to steer clear, hence my constant greenhouse pursuits.

Bernadette seemed exasperated when she strode out of the room moments later, giving me the knowing side-long glance that said everything she probably couldn't say out loud because we had more than a few prying ears in this house.

"I'll come back later. Try to get them to eat and shower, will you?"

"I'll do what I can," I muttered, knowing full well I had no intention of telling my mother to do anything other than what she was already doing.

I liked my head right where it was, *thank you very much.*

But as I stared at my now-closed front door, Bernadette gone to do whatever it was Bernadette did, doubts flooded my brain all over again.

What if we were too late?

My gaze slid to Maria's closed door, Ian and Teresa's bickering only slightly muffled by the wood. I had a whole casting room downstairs with enough grimoires to sink a ship. Maybe they had something—hell, anything—that could shed some light on what was happening to Maria.

Or maybe I just needed to keep myself busy until I went into

Aether in the morning.

Yeah, I wasn't kidding myself, but a look couldn't hurt, right?

I soon found myself in the windowless casting room, the planked walls welcoming me. Snapping my fingers, I lit all the candles at once. As the flames flared, I pored over the spines to see if I had anything that might help. The grimoires were titled by family name. The books likely passed along the line from mother to daughter until the line either died out or was so diluted with human genes that their power was nil.

Sullivan, Goode, Morehouse, Alden, Bishop, Farrington, Wardwell, Parker, Miller.

I had more, but those were the most prominent witch lines. I didn't have any of the Flynn grimoires. Still, I started at some of the names I knew—the ones I was sure were members of the Arcadios coven at some point before it was disbanded. Snagging the Alden grimoire, I settled onto the chaise lounge and started reading.

When my neck started screaming in agony, and the candle's light was nearly spent, I gave up on the notion I'd find anything of value regarding my current situation. If I wanted to make a man disembowel himself or pluck out his own eyeballs, though, I had at least three different ways to do it.

And I thought I was vicious. Old-school witches made me look like a freaking saint.

If I couldn't figure out how demon possession really worked, I was going to have to finagle a workaround based on a locator spell I'd concocted. If I changed to word order, I could check on my sister, maybe?

If I could see into Maria's mind... If I could see she was in there and not the incorporeal parasite Elias summoned, then maybe I could coax her back to consciousness. Even to my tired brain that sounded like a bunch of hooey. Peeking into someone's subconscious seemed like an excellent way to find out shit I never wanted to know. Still, if it meant knowing my sister was okay, I figured I could risk it.

I selected a vial of Maria's blood from my apothecary cabinet, the contents clotted and dried, but still effective. When Maria started staying with me, I insisted on having several vials of her blood on hand. One sure-fire way to track a witch was by her blood, and since the last time I tried to track her ass down turned into a veritable shitshow, I wasn't taking any more chances.

Fuck scrying. I had a better way to find my little sister.

Drawing a circle of salt around myself, I settled in the center, relaxing my limbs as I began the chants with a slight modification to the spell. I knew where Maria's body was. I needed to find her mind.

"*Mens et animus, ut animam meam. Mentem mihi. Ostende mihi faciem eius meam.*" I spoke no louder than a whisper, closing my eyes so I could attempt to see inside my sister's mind.

Mind to mind, soul to soul. Show me her mind. Show me her soul.

I whispered the words until my voice became hoarse, and my ass went numb. All I saw was the blackness behind my own eyelids. I couldn't even get a glimpse of the faint glow of the candles. Opening my eyes, I checked to make sure they were all still lit. Fifteen candles stood with their flickering flames standing at attention. I closed my eyes again.

Blackness reigned. No light from the candles. Where Maria was —if she was anywhere but upstairs—was dark as pitch. Forcing more of myself into the spell, I tried to see something, anything, but I couldn't.

Something was hindering me. A barrier of some kind. I opened my eyes, and my gaze settled on the ring of white. The circle of salt... it was keeping me protected.

In a moment of complete idiocy, I kicked out my bare foot, scattering the grains and opening the circle. All at once, blackness clouded my vision, and the silence was no more.

Screaming. A woman was screaming like she was being tortured. Like everything she was and everything she would be was being ripped from her piece by piece.

What was more unsettling? That sound was *not* coming from me.

CHAPTER TWO

I let my magic fall as I dropped the link to Maria's mind. Shaking, I was barely able to stand, but I tore out of my casting room, anyway, nearly crawling up the stairs to the main level. I interrupted an epic sniping match between Ian and Teresa as I burst into Maria's room and fell to my knees at her bedside.

Grabbing her hand, I forced myself to utter the spell again. "*Mens et animus, ut animam meam. Mentem mihi. Ostende mihi faciem eius meam.*"

Magical wind whipped at my hair and face, the power of the spell raking over me as I tried to see inside Maria's mind again. Darkness shrouded me. Even with my eyes open, all I saw was the pitch black of Maria's mind. And the screaming was back—louder and shriller—as if Maria herself had sat up in the bed to shriek in my ear.

I dropped Maria's hand, crab walking backward as I scrambled away. My shoulder hit the doorframe as I scooted back into the hall, my back met drywall.

Then Teresa was in my line of sight, her fingertips wiping away wetness from my face, her voice calm and soothing. Teresa had never really been a mother to me—not like she'd been to Maria—so I nearly flinched at the kindness.

"Maxima, baby, I need you to come back to me. Look at me, child. Breathe with me," she coaxed, and I tried to do what she asked.

I held my breath at her count of four and then released it. In and out, over and over again.

"There we go. That's better. Can you tell me what just happened?" she cooed, and now that I wasn't about to hyperventilate and pass out, it took less than a second to notice the crowd of people in my hall.

Aiden and Striker were back from their perimeter run. Della looked like I'd just woken her from a hundred-year nap. Given that it was day and she was a vampire, the fact that she was even awake was no small feat. But it was Ian who snagged my focus. His eyes were wild like he was either going to rip the room apart or maybe the entire house. All of them waited on bated breath for me to tell them what I'd seen, but all I could do was shake my head.

I didn't mean no, it was more like I didn't know what to say.

"Darkness and screaming. That's all that's there." My lips trembled as I tried to get myself together enough to elaborate. "I did a spell to try to look into Maria's mind. To see if the exorcism worked."

Teresa's gaze sharpened, and I realized she'd thought to do the same thing I did but hadn't worked up enough courage to actually do it.

"All there is, is blackness and screaming. A blackness so dark there is nothing... Nothing but the wails of someone being tortured. I don't... I don't know what to do."

Teresa settled back onto her heels, her mask of calm slipping.

"I don't know if there is anything to do. Maybe she's healing. Maybe she's trapped. If we try to wake her, we could fracture her mind." Teresa's calm slipped even further, and a wash of grief clouded her face.

Elias did this to her. He took everything that was my sister and stuffed her into that pit of nothingness and screams. He stole from us—stole *her* from us. Flames of rage scorched through me, and my tears dried up.

"I can't wait until tomorrow. I'll purge every single thing Elias knows. I'll find out exactly what he did to Maria." I seethed, meeting my mother's gaze. "By any means necessary."

Spurred on by the single-minded focus of cracking Elias' mind open like a fucking walnut, I snagged Alistair's gifted leathers from the coffee table and got dressed.

I was in the middle of strapping my athames into the likely specialty-made sheathes that came with Alistair's leathers when Della burst through my door. Brandishing a phone like a weapon, she waved it at me, her face paler than her usual vampire pallor.

I knew, without a doubt in my mind, I wanted nothing to do with whoever was on the other end.

With a grimace, I snatched the phone from her when she impatiently waved it in my face.

"Hello?"

"Max, doll, I'm going to need you to come into Aether." Barrett's crisp English trill came through the other line. His voice was thready like he was trying very hard not to freak the fuck out.

Again, I was one hundred percent positive I did not want to hear whatever it was that had him in a tizzy.

Not. At. All.

"I'm already headed that way. What's up?" Because there had to be something. There was no way he'd insist on ruining my downtime unless it was of the utmost importance. Hell, he was the one who suggested I take time off in the first place.

"Elias is gone."

Uh, say what now?

I was pretty sure Barrett could feel my glare from across town. I said nothing, but I got a whole lot of explaining, anyway.

"He was heavily guarded in a null room. There should be no way he could get out, but it looks like a guard is dead, and he's..." Barrett trailed off.

My first thought was of the shifter named Macallan, who treated me decently when I'd been remanded to those same cells.

“Which guard?”

“What? That’s what you’re going to ask? Not how the fuck did this happen, not what we’re doing to stop it? No. You ask which guard.”

Barrett sounded hysterical, which was not his norm. Marcus must not have been close by. But still, a twelve-hundred-year-old witch should be able to keep his cool—or at least one would think.

“I know how it happened. You have a mole in the Council with access to the holding cells. I know what we’re going to do because it’ll be me that finds the fucker. And I want to know which guard died because I made a friend in that filthy holding cell, and I want to make sure it’s not him. Which. Guard?”

“Cyrano.” Barrett offered up the name like it hurt him to do it. He must have known the person. The name wasn’t familiar to me, but it didn’t matter. That guard was killed so someone could free Elias, and I was going to find them and string them up on a pike if I had to.

“I’m on my way. Keep the area clear for me, will you?”

“I’ll do what I can,” he muttered and then hung up.

Barrett seemed like he was leaving a lot out, but no one had time for me to drag it out of him. My questions would just have to wait.

When the four of us—myself, Della, Striker, and Aidan—arrived at Aether, it was evident something was amiss. The dilapidated warehouse looked the same from the outside—except for the gaping hole in the side of the building that appeared as though a giant had taken a can opener to it. Inside was dead silent. I'd never been to Aether without witnessing at least two orgies going on in the shadows—or in the wide-open dance floor to be honest—so the silence was more than a little jarring. Especially when all the patrons were where they usually were. The problem was, not a single one of them were alive.

Whoever had broken Elias out, did more than just kill a guard. He or she had slaughtered dozens if not hundreds of Aether patrons in the prison break. Men and women milled around the bodies, stepping through blood and viscera, tainting the crime scene like idiots.

White-hot rage shot through me. Elias had taken so much from me—so much from all these people—and there was nothing I could do to exact justice for all the lives he'd taken. But I *could* find him.

I shot a look at Striker and gave him a pleading expression. After a century, he knew exactly what I wanted. He did that weird boy whistle thing where they put two fingers in their mouths and magically make a sound that could shatter glass. Because this wasn't our first rodeo, I had the good sense to cover my ears first. Della and Aidan saw my motion and followed suit.

The rest of the room and their likely preternatural hearing weren't so lucky.

"Now that I have your attention, I want to know what you're doing here, why you all are contaminating my crime scene, and why there isn't a Council member in the middle of you idiots flicking you in the face for tramping through dead bodies? Do none of you have any respect?"

A tiny, pink-haired witch stomped over to me. Dressed in a belted floral dress and bare bloody feet, I tried to figure out why anyone would walk around a room like this without shoes on.

"We're looking for survivors, you heartless cow. Who in the Fates do you think you are?"

I blinked at the woman, properly chastised. I had to give her credit where it was due. I did sound heartless, and looking for survivors was a good reason to be stomping all over creation in an effort to save lives.

Too bad I had to inform her there weren't any lives to save. I took another sweep of the room to be sure.

"I don't mean to sound heartless, but there aren't any. Can't you feel that they're gone?"

I shot a look at Aidan and Della, my eyebrows raised for confirmation that what I sensed in the room was legit. There were no auras, no magic in the room outside of the people searching. There were just dead bodies and blood. Even the blood wasn't right. Like someone stole all the magic in the room and... ate it? That probably wasn't the right word, but my brain was stuck on it for some reason.

Aidan shook his head, confirming my suspicion that there was nothing. Della's nostrils fluttered for a few seconds as she scented the room, likely having trouble with all the blood stinking up the place.

"I'm not sure, but I don't think there is anyone alive in here that isn't standing. But there are so many scents I can't tell for sure, and the blood smells wrong," Della said, her Frenchy accent curling around the harsh words.

Turning back to the witch, I tried to soften my tone. I was never good at the hard-ass role, and I sure as shit wasn't going to start now just because I was some supposed leader.

"We'll help you look but clear your people out. If someone is alive, we'll find them."

The witch brushed a tear off her face, smearing blood on her cheek. She nodded at us and yelled at the room to clear out. Only then did I glance at Striker.

A year ago, we'd been under the impression Strike was an empath, a witch who couldn't cast but could feel the emotions of others. That impression quickly crumbled to dust when an Incubus came into our lives. Now we knew Striker was part angel, part something else, and everything he thought about himself was a big ball of bullshit. But that didn't stop those empath abilities, no matter how good he was at hiding them.

"You need to step out?" I asked under my breath, trying not to be an asshole. Not everyone needed their business broadcasted to a room full of Ethereals.

He was pale under his usual golden skin, his shoulder-length hair was pulled back in a queue. A wavy blond tendril that had fallen out of the elastic was shivering with whatever emotion he was picking up in the room. It was safe to say that Striker was in no way okay, and he most definitely needed to step out.

Was he gonna? Doubtful.

"No." The growled word sounded like it was dragged from him kicking and screaming.

Okey-dokey.

I sent a silent prayer to the Fates that Striker wouldn't lose his fucking mind in front of all these people. Not that I'd be embarrassed, but more so that *he* might. Striker was never fond of his empathetic abilities. Over the course of a century, I'd seen him shun them more than once. He purposely guarded himself against outside emotions on a daily basis.

I had to keep control of my own emotions. I didn't know what I'd do if I had to share an entire roomful of feelings at once.

But it turned out I had plenty of reasons to worry. I felt the frisson of Striker's change the second before it happened. I could almost feel Striker's scales erupt from his fingers, sense the exact rip of his skin when his lizardy-yet-feathery wings erupted from his back.

I should have been paying attention to my surroundings and not Striker. Maybe then I would have seen the Incubus step into the room.

Maybe then I would have been able to stop Striker before he did something stupid.

But then again, maybe not.

CHAPTER THREE

Striker's growl seemed to shake the room, and I couldn't figure out what had him so upset until I saw the dark-haired, red-eyed man emerge from the shadows. He looked nothing like the other Incubus I'd encountered. For one, he was skin and bone, like he hadn't had a meal in ages. The other, in no way did he seem like the kind of guy who would hurt a fly.

But Striker didn't seem to give a single shit about the man's appearance. He was an incubus—the same species of Ethereal who'd taken Melody from him.

Melody. Fates, that name still hurt to think of. It didn't make sense what we sacrificed for a girl we barely knew, but then again, it did. A pregnant woman had come into our shop with no way to help herself, no way out of the death sentence thrust upon her by loving the wrong man. Who *wouldn't* want to help someone like that? No one I wanted to know, that's who.

I never expected Striker to fall in love so fast and so hard. I didn't think Striker did, either.

We failed Melody. We failed her parents. We failed her son. We might have killed the man responsible, but I didn't think either of us had ever forgiven ourselves.

So, I *might* have hesitated a second too long, stunned by the sheer terror those red eyes caused.

"*You*." Striker snarled the single word echoing through the wide-open space like an accusation.

The man—no, he couldn't be classified as a man. The boy held up his hands like he was warding Striker off.

"I—I mean no harm, Mr. Voss. I swear."

At the use of his surname, Striker hesitated. The kid knew of him somehow. That little bit of hesitation allowed me to get in between them, snapping my fingers to transport myself within the room rather than walk over the corpses.

My gaze locked with Striker's, I stared at those glowing golden orbs. Phased, the pupil had elongated into a slit like a lizard. *Or a dragon's...* The thought pinged around my brain as I tried to make sure Striker wouldn't kill someone in the middle of all this death.

"He's a kid, Striker. Back off."

The muscle under Striker's left eye twitched, but he didn't move.

"Don't make me make you. Take a walk."

The sound coming from Striker's throat was like one of the dinosaurs from *Jurassic Park*.

Oh, fuck no.

"Don't you growl at me, Striker Voss, or I will turn you into a eunuch and sell your dick on eBay."

"Please don't make him go," the kid pleaded as he grabbed my arm. "I've come all this way to find him."

I did my best not to shake him off, but I didn't like to be touched on my best days and certainly not by an Incubus. Calmly—or as calmly as I was able—I removed the hand from my arm and took a step back. A sheepish look came over the kid's face, and his red gaze fell to the floor.

"I know your story. I know what the presence of my kind does. I'm not like them. Most of us aren't like them. Do you know what my parents do for a living? They're sex therapists." The kid blushed so hard his cheeks nearly matched his eyes. "They help couples fix their... *issues.* Most incubi never harm a single human. The men who hurt that woman? They are the scum of our kind, the scum of all Ethereals. *Please...*"

Incubi were said to feed off the sexual energy of others. If this kid was skin and bone, that meant he hadn't fed in some time—if at all, given his age, which I pegged at no more than sixteen. It would make sense to see an incubus in a club like this where sex was happening literally everywhere. But if he came today of all days, he might have seen something.

"What's your name, kid, and what in the Fates are you doing here of all places?"

"Keane, Highness. And I am here to ask for Striker's help."

The "highness" threw me a little, but the need for Striker's help threw me a whole lot more.

I turned back to Striker, my eyebrow raised, and he growled again before rolling his eyes. The action was more than a little unsettling. The scales receded from Striker's skin, and bit by bit, his wings folded back into his body. His shirt was toast, but he was calmer and less murdery.

Maybe.

"What could you ever ask of me that I would give you? Knowing what you know, how could you think I'd give you anything?"

"I don't know if now is the time," the kid—Keane—hedged, his gaze sweeping the death and destruction of the decimated Witch club. "You're needed here, and maybe... maybe what happened is for the best. I—I don't know what to do. I don't know what's best."

This kid had a point, but I still wanted to know what he needed so bad that he'd ask the man with the biggest grudge, and who was the least likely to help him. But the smell of blood was cloying in my nose and other scents as well.

"Will it keep?" I asked.

Keane's attention was yanked from the room around us and back to me. He seemed to debate the notion for about a millisecond, before nodding. "I—I think so?"

I decided clarification was my best course of action.

"Will someone die because you waited? Will someone be lost

forever? Will the world as you know it change for the worse because you didn't tell us right now?"

He lifted a skinny arm and waggled his hand at me.

"Okay, here's what we're gonna do. You're going to talk to this nice lady and tell her what is going on." I gestured to Della, who gave him a classy little wave. "No compulsion, no persuasion, no using your abilities. Just tell her straight up. If she thinks it is actionable, we'll see, okay? If not..." I trailed off as I gestured around the room. "It'll have to wait. Okay?"

Keane nodded vigorously, seeming glad he didn't have to talk to Striker anymore.

I pulled Della aside for a moment to make sure she knew to ask if he'd seen anything here while he was spilling his guts to her. I left it with a warning, but all I got was sass.

"He's an incubus. Be careful," I informed her, only to get rolled eyes in return.

"Only you two couldn't spot an incubus at fifty paces. Every other Ethereal knows what to look for. Plus, he can't get inside here." She tapped her temple as she swept Keane away from the wreckage of the room.

Fair enough.

One problem down. I gave Aidan the high sign, and not a moment later, he materialized himself right next to us.

"Go through the room. Consume any that you need to. Call in backup if you need it. Call Aurelia and get some phoenixes here. Knowing her, some are probably already headed this way, but this place is warded out the ass, so I don't want to assume. We're going to find Barrett and inspect Elias's cell. Call me if you run into any trouble. Cool?"

Aidan searched the room, not even a stitch of hunger on his face amid all this death.

"Anything else you want me to tackle?" he asked. "Maybe I should get on that whole world peace thing while I'm at it."

My eye started twitching, and it took all the meager decorum I possessed not to junk-punch him on the spot. I settled for stating the obvious.

"Barrett called me for help, but he's nowhere to be found even in the middle of this clusterfuck. This means something is holding him up, and that something is probably not good if a twelve-hundred-year-old witch can't handle it. Out of the two of us, I undoubtedly have the worst job, so when you decide to sack up, please let me know."

Aidan pursed his lips as he fished his phone from his leathers. "I'll call Aurelia."

"Aces," I muttered and pivoted toward the hallway that housed the high courtroom, dragging Striker behind me as I went.

The magic in the corridor felt off, like a spell was still in the middle of its cycle. I could feel the motes of it against my skin. All of a sudden, Striker let out a guttural moan. It was pained like something was being ripped from him.

A flash of red snagged my gaze, and I whipped my head toward him. His scales were back, his pupils slit like a cat's, and then his wings erupted from his back.

"Strike?" I hedged, backing away—not that I could go anywhere in this suddenly tiny space.

"Something... wrong... can't... control phase," he grunted as he crouched on the stone floor. His body whipped, his wings shivering as magic buffeted him.

Fangs I never knew he had, grew from his mouth as talons erupted from his fingers. Scales crept up his neck as his eyes glowed gold.

What. The. Fuck.

I debated a break spell for about a second before I cast it. Blowing on my fingers, I muttered the break spell as I spun the working breath on the pads of them, the spell strengthening with every widdershins—or counterclockwise—revolution.

Undoing, unraveling.

Subsisto, tardo, confuto, concesso, subflamino, insisto, conquiesco, finis...

But my spell didn't seem to have enough juice, and while it looked to be staving off any further phasing—turning Striker into... *I have no idea what*—it wasn't stopping him from advancing on me. Rising from his crouch, Striker took a single stuttered step and then another.

Through his fangs, he growled a single word: "Run." And so, I did, I ran directly for the high courtroom and threw the door open...

Only to see Barrett cowering against the dais with a phased and feral Marcus pinning him in.

Fuck.

The spell I'd felt against my skin, it must have affected the shifters. Made them feral. The club wasn't attacked by one lone witch... No, if I had to guess, that spell turned every shifter into a ravenous beast. And now Barrett and I were in a room with two of them... Ones we really didn't want to kill.

If I couldn't stop Striker—who was maybe half Marcus' age—there was absolutely no way I was going to be able to stop the Alpha without some serious repercussions.

You know, like death.

Watching as saliva dripped from Marcus' fangs, I begged the universe not to make me kill my friends—my family.

I tore my rapt attention off Marcus and met Barrett's gaze. He appeared unmauled, but he was holding his right arm funny as if the limb was dislocated.

"Ch-channel me. The spell is too strong," he stuttered—likely going into shock if his pale, sweaty skin was anything to go by.

I couldn't channel Barrett from this far away, though. Then he did something I didn't expect. He pulled an athame from his belt and sliced open the top of his forearm before tossing me the blade.

Somehow, I snatched the knife midair, wiping the blood on my palms as I gathered the ambient magic in the air. I opened my arms wide and then brought my hands together in a resounding crack, performing the only other spell that I knew worked on shifters.

"*Ipsum revelare*," I shouted into the cavernous room, praying to the Fates that this bit of magic turned my usually level-headed friends back to themselves.

Striker's guttural sounds of agony mirrored Marcus' howl of

rage. The pair lunged for me but fell several feet short when their phases hit them. Bones snapped in Striker's case, and Marcus' wolf body disappeared in a wave of mist, only to return in the shape of the man I knew.

Barrett slid down to his ass on the last step of the dais, his bout of shock getting the best of him. I left the knuckleheads to fend for themselves and moved to Barrett.

"What was the name of that healing spell you did on me again?" I asked, trying to make him chuckle. Barrett was an expert at several things, healing one of many. Living as long as he had, had given him all the time in the world to expand his repertoire. The one time he'd healed me was after I'd gone toe-to-toe with a prince of Hell and nearly lost, only healing my wounds after I'd broken into the high courtroom and almost killed him.

Luckily for me, Barrett was a forgiving man. He chuckled and then immediately groaned. Maybe laughing was better suited for later.

"*Sanitatem*," Barrett muttered, hissing when I put my hand over his cut to ebb the flow of blood leaking out of him.

I muttered the word and then snapped my fingers, only to have them do nothing. Frowning, I tried again. Maybe being what I was, I couldn't perform healing spells. Perhaps I'd taken all the magic in the room, and none was left.

"I don't know what's wrong," I mumbled, trying the spell again and watching it fail.

It was a tiny healing spell. I'd moved the ground beneath my feet, rendered ancient artifacts to ash and dust.

Why couldn't I heal a simple cut?

Why did it take so much effort to stop Striker and Marcus?

Why did I have to channel Barrett at all?

And what the hell was I going to do if the magic I needed was failing me?

CHAPTER FOUR

A hand on my shoulder startled the hell out of me. Marcus stood on the bottom step of the dais, bloody and rumpled, but seemingly fine. His gaze was laser-locked on his mate as he gently moved me out of the way.

I watched him closely to see if my spell—and his mind—held up. The fact that he was in his human shape spelled good things, but I had a sneaking suspicion the attack wasn't over yet. Or maybe because my magic wasn't working correctly, it was a macabre bit of wishful thinking on my part. I really didn't like that about myself.

Marcus helped Barrett to stand, and I hastened to collect Striker, the big lug still somewhat out of it as he tried to help me help him up. It was a mess, but somehow, together, we got him upright. Even if it wasn't on his own two feet.

"We need to get out of the pall of this spell. I can't cast in here, and I'm pretty sure my ribs are busted, love," Barrett murmured, unable to make his voice rise above much more than a whisper.

"Same," I told Marcus. "It took everything I had and some of Barrett's magic to get you guys to shift back."

"We're alive, and that's all I fucking care about," Marcus

muttered as he carefully guided Barrett to the door, holding his husband as if he might break in his arms. "Did you see the club?"

Solemnly, I nodded. "I had Aidan call in the phoenixes, and as soon as I inspect Elias' cell, I'll be tracking his ass down. By the way, what the fuck happened here? Was it...?" I trailed off, trying to figure out how to word what I wanted to say without casting blame. "Did all the shifters in the club get that same spell, or was it something else?"

Marcus' steps stuttered to a stop, and he leveled me with a look so searching I actually flinched at the weight of it.

"Both, Max. It was most definitely both."

Marcus led us to the door that led to the pack home. I still didn't quite know exactly where the house was located, but I figured it was rude to ask. If they wanted me to know, they would have told me by now. We paused there while Marcus put the pieces together for me.

"We noticed something amiss a few hours ago. Fights breaking out in the club, shifters and witches acting up. Usually it's all free love and excess, but it turned ugly fast. Witches tried to break up the drama only to find they couldn't cast. Then the shifters started phasing. I took one look at the room and locked Barrett and myself into the high courtroom. I thought the Fae-built door would protect us, but whatever the spell was had a way to combat Fae magic. I was sure I was going to kill my own husband until you walked in." Marcus let out a wet-sounding chuckle like he was holding back tears. "I couldn't control it. I tried so hard, but I couldn't... Thank you."

But I didn't want a thank you. I didn't want to even think of what might have happened. Marcus and Barrett had become so dear to me in such a short amount of time. I couldn't imagine my life without them, and that shot a bolt of fear through me that had more than a little staying power.

In my life, everyone left. But I didn't want to live that way anymore. I had people now. I just had to make sure they stayed alive.

"Why does the building look like a giant took a can opener to it?" Striker asked, echoing my earlier thoughts.

"Cinder," Barrett croaked. "She phased right along with everyone else. It affected anyone with another form. It turned them all."

A thought crossed my mind the same time it fell out of my mouth. "Where's the rest of the Council?"

It was bad enough we had a dragon to find. Trying to find a phased angel and demon would be so much worse. The image of Alistair's phased form flashed in my mind. I could just imagine the level of apocalypse drama that would be on the news if we had his blackened and burning form walking down Colfax. The collective internet would shit itself.

"Not here. Caim is in Brazil visiting some of his progeny, Alistair is in Hell making sure his replacement is trained, and Gorgon is doing whatever he does when he's not here. Since he's a warlock, I have absolutely no idea what that is. He tried to tell me once and I had a headache for like a week, so I don't ask him anymore. I kinda just assume he'll show up when he needs to. He's really good at that."

Knowing what I knew about Gorgon—and that wasn't much—that sounded about right.

"We should call the phoenixes off," I mused. "It's bad enough the building is ripped open. We don't need to burn the place down, too."

Then again, the spell didn't seem to be causing Aidan to phase, so maybe it didn't affect his kind. Maybe it wouldn't affect the phoenixes, either.

Striker and I left them to their healing and relayed the unintentional shifting problem to Aidan.

He simply shrugged. "I don't choose this form or the other," he explained, "I change to eat, but I live in this form. The phoenixes, though, will turn if they came here... which is exactly what Aurelia said when I called her. She said no phoenix will come for the dead until you remove the *grigri* pouches from the ledges of every door. She said they disrupted the magics of the doors and probably Elias' cell. She said for you to study the contents of them, but not to touch. She said the rowan tree shavings would hurt you, but she didn't want to tell me why. She wants you to call her so you can discuss it. She did leave us with a big clue. Aurelia told me that none of the ingredients affected the demon patrons."

That was a lot of info to digest, but I couldn't call her. Not in the middle of all this. Before I could open my mouth to ask if he'd started removing the *grigri* pouches, Aidan cut me off. "Yes, Della is collecting the bags now. I have no idea what to do with them once we have them all, but she's getting this place back to normal so the witches can cast, and the shifters won't go bananas."

"Do we need to look for all the shifters that went gonzo?" Striker asked, taking the words right out of my mouth.

"No," I answered. "If there were any Keys left in the building, they would have gone after them. This whole thing was one big diversion. We need to find Elias. Whoever he was working for is probably a demon, and if I can turn his Ethereal side off, maybe another demon can turn it back on again. Also... there may or may not be a dragon on the loose in downtown Denver. We might need to get on that."

Aidan stuffed his hands in his pockets and pursed his lips. "What do we do with the pouches?"

Most spells needed two elements to overload and break them.

"Fire and water. Set the bags on fire, drown the embers in water. Just do it away from anyone who is affected by the ingredients. The embers may be toxic. Before you do, let me inspect one. If there is something else that can hurt me in them, I want to know what it is."

Rowan. I couldn't remember a time I'd ever been in the presence of a rowan tree. I didn't use them in any of my spells. I was tempted to research them, but now was not the time. Now was not the time to do half the shit I wanted to do.

Shaking myself out of my swirling thoughts, I caught Striker and Aidan having a full conversation with their facial expressions alone. I had a feeling it was something about me, but once again, I didn't have the time to ask.

"I need to see Elias' cell. Has Della removed that pouch?" I asked, catching the boys off guard.

"It was one of the first ones she got rid of," Aidan answered.

"Fabulous."

Now I was going to do what I started the damn day trying to do, which was to go see Elias' cell. And while I was at it, try to figure out how in the blue fuck someone planted a veritable ass load of *grigri* bags in a place as highly populated as Aether without anyone noticing.

I did *not* like this job already, and it was my first freaking day. I wondered how much of a death sentence I would get if I told the Fates to shove this job where the sun didn't shine and go back to tattooing strangers for money. Like would they try to kill me on the spot, or would it be a wanted dead or alive sort of situation?

A question of the ages.

Elias' cell was nothing to write home about. Well, except for the dead witch with her head nearly torn off in the middle of it. The cell door was flung wide open, the nulling bars making my body ache even at twenty paces, which wasn't at all like what I felt the last time.

Last time, it had only hurt when I'd been *inside* the cell.

The locks didn't appear damaged, but I didn't relish doing a *revelare vestigium* to see who'd killed her so close to the nulling magic. If it would even work. If the witch was killed inside the cell—which the pools of blood said was likely the case—it was possible I wouldn't see anything at all.

The only clue I had was the faint smell of sulfur which *should* mean demon, but I couldn't be positive. None of this made any lick of sense.

"You got anything?" I asked Striker, at a complete loss as to what to do. The null bars were making my mind fuzzy and my whole body ache.

Striker leaned on the stone wall farthest from the spelled bars, his shirt still in tatters at his back, the lines of exhaustion clear on his face. I wasn't the only one affected by the magic-draining runes.

"If I had a guess, we're meant to chase our tails instead of doing the thing we need to do. Which, in case you forgot, is to find the bastard. I say we do that." He wasn't wrong. But Striker didn't stop there. "None of the spells affected demons. It smells like demon in here, which means we're probably looking for a demon working with Elias. We already know Elias had an accomplice. If it was a demon, I hate to say it, but Alistair might be the prime suspect. He's new to the Council, he now has access, and he's an unknown."

Everything in me charged to Alistair's defense. He was good, I knew it in my bones. Even if those bones at present felt like someone had taken a hammer to them.

"He helped us take out Elias in the first place. Something, I might add, he didn't need to do. He didn't need to help us at all. In all likelihood, there are other demons in the Keys. One of them could have done this. Elias could have made a deal with a demon in exchange for protection. Just because Alistair is an unknown, doesn't mean anything."

The pain in my gut wrenched again as I turned to leave, unable to stand being in this room another minute. Especially if all Striker was going to do was trash Alistair. The nulling magic had never felt this bad before, and I'd spent far longer in this room than I'd care to admit.

The tell-tale trickle of my nose beginning to bleed had me quickening my pace. Before I could hit the doors back to Aether's main room, Striker was holding me upright, and I was coughing up blood.

Rowan.

Rowan shavings disrupted the magic of the doors. Of the cell. It was how Elias had gotten out in the first place.

And Aurelia was right. It was most definitely hurting me.

CHAPTER FIVE

I was getting really tired of seeing my own blood. I'd gone centuries with little to no trouble. This one? Oh, noooooo. I was either dying, bleeding all over myself, or damn near getting eviscerated every six months.

It was bullshit.

Striker hit the door out of the holding area with enough force to crack the wood. He dragged me to the right, but I had enough strength left to pull on him a bit. Okay, so it was more like a baby yanking on his mother's shirt, but whatever.

"Not to the main area. I don't want them to see me like this. Take me to Barrett."

Or at least that's what I thought I said between hacking coughs that felt like I might actually be expelling pieces of my lungs. At one point, Striker had enough of my fumbling steps and just whipped me into his arms like I weighed no more than a child and took off for the pack home's door.

Not every touch could get through the wards—fucked up *grigri* pouches or not—and I had to actually open the door. I managed to inform Striker of that *before* he was electrocuted with me in his arms. I was super proud of that because consciousness and I weren't getting along. Be it blood loss or actual dying, I wasn't quite sure, but I endeavored to keep myself awake and breathing.

I should have called Aurelia. I should have made the time. She knew things—things I probably didn't want to know. She was a wealth of knowledge I tried to never use. Maybe because I didn't want to know the truth, maybe because I couldn't handle whatever it was that she had to say. I should have hugged my grandmother harder when she left, and I shouldn't have flinched when Teresa tried to comfort me.

A wrenching agony yanked at my chest, and tears welled in my eyes. I wanted Striker to look at me. I wanted him to tell me everything was going to be okay, but I knew it wasn't.

What if rowan was like morganite to a phoenix or bixbite to a wraith? What if this little tree was how I went?

I should have kissed Alistair one more time. I should have hugged Barrett and Marcus. *I should have...*

Maria.

Her name flashed in my mind, and I opened my eyes. *Darkness and screaming.* That was all she saw, all she heard, and those could even be her screams. Maria could be in agony right now. She could be torn apart and scared.

I coughed again, but this time I refused to let a little blood stop me. I gripped Striker's shoulders hard, and I forced the pain to keep me awake. The rumble coming from his chest was slightly comforting until his bellows for help finally reached my ears. If I had to guess, he'd been screaming since we opened the door. He sounded so far away, but I knew from experience that was the blood loss talking. None of your senses seemed to work right when you didn't have enough juice to run the engine, and either sight or hearing was usually the first to go.

Cold swept over me, and a body-wracking shiver nearly made me scream in agony. This was it. I could feel it. I'd died in so many ways, but it had never felt like this. It never felt so final, so permanent.

I managed to meet Striker's gaze, and I marveled at his gold irises with their funny little lizard pupil. I was glad if I had to go, it was with someone I loved close by. Too many times it was with people who hated me or in the middle of a battle. I just wished I had the strength to tell him that I'd miss him.

But then Striker was wrenched out of my line of sight and Barrett took his place. Barrett's blue eyes glowed with his magic as they filled with tears, the cool-toned motes of his magic swirling around him as he did his best to save me. Barrett was a good friend. I didn't like that I was causing him so much pain. I didn't like that I'd be leaving them all behind.

Would they look after Maria? Would they help her after I left? I liked to think they would. I wondered what they would get up to when I wasn't causing them so much trouble.

Barrett's nose began to bleed, the slow trickle of blood snaking down his chin until a single drop dripped onto my chest. The second Barrett's blood hit me, I sucked in my first real breath since I stepped near the holding cells. Oxygen scraped at my lungs, a sweet misery of healing that had me gulping at the air like a starving woman.

Barrett's warm, healing magic blanketed me, stealing my pain. In the back of my mind, I thought I could actually feel my organs repairing themselves, the tissues knitting back together. Then the coughing was back, and I had just enough strength to turn myself over as I retched up rowan dust.

Yep, Aurelia was right. Rowan shavings were definitely on the no-go list for me.

After I expelled the last of the poison and inhaled my first real breath, I took stock of the room. It wasn't just Striker and Barrett in here with me. Oh, no. It was Marcus, his lieutenants, and their wives. Not just them, but Aidan, Della, and my mother, too.

"How long was I coughing up blood?" I croaked, frowning at the gathered mass of people.

Damn near everyone was pale as a ghost, and that probably included me since most of my blood was on the outside of my body. Yep, I was really fucking tired of seeing that.

"About half an hour. I could have sworn I told you that I did *not* want to watch you die again, Maxima," a husky female voice replied to my left, and I slowly followed the sound with my gaze.

Aurelia, along with her twin sister Mena were sitting on the far end of the same couch I'd probably ruined with my blood. The sisters were the leaders of the phoenixes, and Mena was a healer of sorts… when she wasn't electrocuting people with her bare hands. Barrett had called in the big guns.

"I think I missed some things while I was dying. You weren't lying about the rowan shavings. That most definitely hurt."

Aurelia did not appreciate my joke, but I couldn't ask what I wanted to in a room full of people. What I really wanted to ask was why the hell were they all here in the first place, but I figured that question would be rude.

But Aurelia didn't disappoint, she answered my question without me asking. Which is what I got for having a powerful psychic for a best friend.

"We're here because you were actually dying, not doing whatever bullshit your body does when you're just going dormant. If it weren't for the complete lack of wings, I would've assumed you were a phoenix ages ago. But no, you have to be a 'witch' with no coven. But you were never really that at all, were you?"

I opened my mouth to answer her not-question when she cut me off, rising from the couch to stand in front of me to address the rest of the room. It wasn't much of a height difference since my BFF was only a few inches over five feet, but her presence was formidable enough.

"I don't know what kind of fuckery is going on here, but I'm not taking it for one more second. I didn't go through my last bit of apocalypse drama just to watch you guys fuck it up now. The governing body of all Ethereals on this continent has been hamstringed because they lack our resources. Phoenixes and wraiths will be joining the Council immediately. Is that understood?"

Barrett sighed in relief as Marcus hugged him close. I didn't understand what just happened. I thought the phoenixes and wraiths were already going to be members of the Council, but the way Barrett was acting, it was like he was relieved they were taking their seats.

Maybe I'd missed more than a few things while I'd been waiting for Maria to wake up.

Aurelia plopped back down on the couch—naturally she did it in the lone vacant space in the crook of my hips without even looking. She leaned down and whispered in my ear, low enough that even those in the room with super hearing wouldn't be able to hear her.

"You and I need to have a discussion, Maxima. Someone close to the Council knows what you are, and that is not a good thing for you at all."

She rose from my ear and pierced me with a look, which morphed into one of almost horror when she caught sight of my confusion.

"Everyone knows I'm a hybrid, Ari. Literally everyone. I did a huge debutant ball and everything. You were there."

Aurelia wiped every expression from her face in an instant and gave me a stony nod, repeating her earlier proclamation. "You and I need to have a discussion, Max. A big one," she whispered. "Stay away from rowan, sweetheart."

I snorted. "I'll scratch that at the tippy top of my to-do list."

"You do that," she muttered. "Come on, Mena, we have some news to break to our husbands and West. The lot of them will be spitting nails before the night is out."

Aurelia turned to face the room again and gave Barrett a tip of her head. I was proud that the man didn't flinch at her pale, pupilless gaze.

"Thanks for calling me. We'll be in touch."

With that, my BFF swept out of the room, leaving me with a mess of shifters and my freaked-out paladins.

Della swept through the throng and plopped on the couch in the spot Aurelia just vacated. "Come on, let's get you cleaned up. We have a witch to find, right?"

Relief raced through me. Della was nothing if not efficient, and she had just ended a mess of awkwardness with a single sentence.

. . .

After I was mostly cleaned of blood, I followed Della back to Barrett's drawing room, which was just a fancy name for a sitting room with booze in it. Barrett and Marcus were cuddled on the no-longer-ruined couch. Aidan and Striker were squabbling with each other in a corner, and only one of Marcus' lieutenants stayed. Hideyo, the kitsune guard, was leaning against a desk, fully decked out in fighting leathers like the rest of us.

My mother had also stayed, but she was pacing the room in front of the desk, eyeing the couch I'd soiled like it had somehow offended her.

When I strode into the room, all conversation ground to a halt. So the awkwardness was here to stay. Awesome.

The silence stretched to a breaking point before my mother decided she'd had enough and rushed me, tossing her arms around my shoulders and pulling me into a bone-crushing hug.

"Don't you ever do that to me again. Fates, Maxima. There is only so much I can take."

I couldn't recall a time where my mother had ever been worried about my well-being. Literally never.

"Okay, who are you, and what have you done with my mom? You might have met her. About yay high, stern expression, crazy powerful."

"Very funny, Max. You scared the shit out of all of us."

I tossed my hands up, frustrated at the blame aimed my way. It wasn't like I was trying to kill myself.

"It wasn't like I did it on purpose. I thought the room was clear. It wasn't like I inhaled rowan shavings of my own accord. Had I known that the air was permeated with the shit, I would have steered clear."

Striker appeared at my side, his silence only slightly creepy. "I think we're all just glad you made it, and everyone is on edge. We have a witch to find, right? Let's get on that."

I nodded, relieved someone was taking the heat off me. Striker led me to the desk where there was a scrying crystal and a world map, and I got to work narrowing down his location. Elias was still in Denver, not too far from Aether, still in the Ethereal district to be sure.

He was probably holed up in a safehouse warded out the ass. That was going to be fun to pick apart.

Once his location was found, I had the bright idea to make sure everyone was cloaked before we stomped around Denver in the middle of the day. Was it the middle of the day? Either way, hiding was a good idea—especially since no one but me could see through glamours.

Mostly, I wanted to do the spell so I could make sure my magic actually worked and I wasn't maimed for life from those fucking bags.

"I need four stones for glamours," I said to Barrett.

"Five," he replied, "Hideyo is going with you. After what just happened, you need all the help you can get, and kitsune are not affected by rowan or any other force-shift magic. Something about their trickster magic combating it on a cellular level."

Hideyo flashed me a grin that did nothing to settle the unease in my gut. His general demeanor was too close to Fae-like than I was comfortable with, but refusing the help seemed really fucking dumb at this point. I did, however, remember not to thank him. I wasn't sure if kitsune were actually Fae, but I wasn't going to chance it.

I gave him a nod and held out a hand to Barrett for the stones. Barrett slipped five onyx stones in my palm, and a quick flick of my fingers had them turned into necklaces in an instant. Each one I turned over and over in my hand while murmuring a hiding spell I'd used on several occasions. I didn't often hide myself, the obfuscation spells a bit tedious for my liking.

I passed the onyx necklaces out to the team and had Barrett test them to be sure. Each one passed muster, and I breathed a sigh of relief that my magic didn't shit the bed when I almost died. That would have been a mood killer.

Once we were ready, I pointed out the spot on the map where Elias' trail stopped. Refusing to go through Aether, I snatched

Striker's hand and snapped my fingers, transporting myself to a site a block away from Elias.

As soon as my feet touched the ground, I knew our plan was toast. Della, Aidan, and Hideyo arrived just behind me and I knew they had the exact same thought, especially when Aidan had a manly man hissy fit within earshot.

Flashing blue-and-red lights colored the gray warehouses even in daytime. And the warehouse I'd last placed Elias was surrounded by Denver police.

I did not have a good feeling about this.

Nary a one.

CHAPTER SIX

I wanted to be shocked, but really? It seemed about right that the building we needed to get into was surrounded by cops. I mean, why not? We already had an entire witch club full of dead bodies, an untold number of shifters on the loose, a dragon frolicking in downtown Denver somewhere, a poisoning, and some political unrest.

Why shouldn't we need to tiptoe around a bunch of human police officers?

I snorted a little and then started giggling like I'd lost my marbles somewhere between Barrett's house and here. Maybe I had.

My giggles turned into full-out belly laughter, but unfortunately for me, my belly laughs sounded like something one would use to frighten small children. I had a legitimate witch cackle, and it was pouring like a faucet from my mouth. I managed with some difficulty to rein in my giggles, wiping tears from my eyes as I assessed the bevy of cops.

"Are you okay?" Della asked me as she wrapped a cool arm around my shoulders.

"I'm peachy, darling. I promise. This is just a comedy of errors, and I'm wrapping my mind around it."

Aidan suddenly arrived right in front of me in a swath of black smoke.

"We have a problem," he announced, like we couldn't see the big, huge, honking problem barely a block away from us.

I gestured to the squad cars. "I can see that."

Aidan rolled his eyes before leveling me with one of his patented disgruntled looks. I used to remember a time when he was nothing but smiles. Those days were long gone.

He pinched his brow and sighed. "No. We have a bigger one. I popped in to see what was going on. Those cops are here for a reason. Apparently, there is a dead body in that warehouse."

Did Elias kill someone? Or more someones?

"Elias is dead," Aidan muttered, and my whole body went cold.

I needed Elias alive. I needed him to tell me what he had done to Maria. I needed to know who Elias was working with. Who he was working for. I had too many questions, and they wouldn't be answered by a dead man.

The ground rocked beneath my feet, and I could feel clouds gathering in the sky at my rage. As relieved as I was that it seemed my magic was back in full force, I was not even a little amused at the current situation. Three deep breaths later, I was able to stop the earth from shaking. The storm clouds, though, seemed to be here to stay. Lightning streaked the sky as I looked past Aidan's bright green gaze and stomped toward the warehouse.

I felt my companions follow, and I was grateful I didn't have to say anything, didn't have to apologize for the minor earthquake and storm clouds. I didn't have much control over either, even though they were both caused by my power leaking out of the stranglehold I kept it in. A part of me wondered if I should let the deluge come if the cops would get out of the way.

Probably not.

Picking my way through the throng of police, I managed not to bump anyone. My trek ground to a halt when I caught sight of a woman being hauled out of the warehouse doors in cuffs.

It took a few seconds to place her. Her usual white-blonde hair was streaked with blood. Her tailored blouse probably used to be cream, but, it, too, was soaked in blood and viscera. Mascara streaked down her face, mingling with the scarlet splatters.

Cinder.

Her expression dazed, she mumbled in a Slavic language of some kind—maybe Russian or Czech—as a gruff-looking cop guided her through the crowd by her upper arm toward a squad car.

I wanted to be happy we didn't need to find her, but I also kind of wanted to rip her head off for killing our only lead. If this was a result of the spell cast on the shifters, I couldn't stay mad at her, but… It was a test to my rationality to keep that little nugget of info at the forefront of my mind and not snap her neck.

But I had bigger problems than an arrested Council member. I felt a wall of Striker's rage hit me like a hammer, and I knew we didn't have the luxury of dawdling.

"Stay with her," I whispered to Aidan, doing this for more than a few reasons.

One, I planned on walking in that warehouse, and I didn't need Aidan eating Elias' soul before I was ready for it. Two, Aidan was cloaked and able to travel. Walls, car doors, and cell bars didn't mean shit to him, so he was one of the few of us who could keep an eye on Cinder besides me. And three, if I kept an eye on her, I couldn't guarantee I wouldn't lose my shit and give the cops a show.

I'd have enough of a problem with that without adding my rage to the mix. I snagged Striker's wrist and hauled him at a quick clip away from the huddle of cops and into the warehouse.

The inside of the warehouse was quieter than I thought it would be. I wasn't well versed in crime scene etiquette, so pretty much all I knew came from cop shows. I always thought there would be gabbing and a bunch of people milling about. Other than a few detectives close to the body, the place was empty.

One detective was kneeling near Elias' shredded corpse, examining the scene. It was tough for me to keep my eyes on Elias' dead body. Shredded was too kind a word for what was done to him. The only way I knew it was even Elias was because his face had been spared from Cinder's talons. But he had body parts flung in an intricate circle that looked like it had been done on purpose, if not brutal.

That was if she'd done the killing in the first place. I didn't trust anything when it came to this case. Nothing was as it seemed, and I wouldn't put anything past the former witch.

Even in death.

I couldn't tell exactly how tall the kneeling detective was, but he seemed huge, if a little on the thin side. A shock of white-blond hair fell over one eye, nearly obscuring the pale blue iris, and his skin was so fair, I'd have pegged him as an albino if his eyes weren't blue. Even from so far away, I could tell they were piercing.

The other detective broke off from the scene and headed for the exit.

"Hey, Durant," the exiting cop yelled when he reached the door.

"What?" the blond replied, his attention never leaving the parts of Elias that were scattered on the dirty concrete in an ornate, if macabre circle.

"You going to head back to the station and process the crazy, or do you want me to?"

I felt as well as heard Striker's menacing growl from behind me. *Fates help us.* The last thing I needed was a pissed off Striker losing his mind on a human cop.

"I want to process her," Durant replied. "Hang out for a bit but give me the space. I need to think."

The other cop shrugged at his partner and left. As a result, Striker's rage dialed down a few notches. I had a feeling I already knew what was going on with him and Cinder, but I wasn't positive. My inkling was that Cinder was related to Striker in some way. A grandmother, an aunt, a sister.

Something.

And Striker knew it. I didn't understand why he hadn't told me yet, but that wasn't unusual. I didn't know why Striker did half of the things he did. He hoarded secrets like it was his job. To this day, I still didn't know half as much about Striker as he did about me.

"See if you can influence this guy to leave," I murmured to Striker. "I need to do a *revelare vestigium*."

Meaning, I needed Striker to use his empath abilities—the ones he pretended he didn't have, ones he'd used on me—and make this dude move on out so I could see how Elias died.

"I can't," Striker muttered back. "He's too far away. And he smells wrong. Not like a human."

Durant stood, and I was proved right. He was well over six feet and had an air of self-importance I'd only seen on nobility. Already I was not a fan, and the man hadn't even spoken to me. Still, his gaze searched the room as if he could hear us, which did *not* sit well with me.

"That's because I'm not a human. What are you four doing in my crime scene?" Durant asked, shocking the shit out of me.

Did he just hear us? No. He said *four*. Della and Hideyo were silent as the grave, no way he heard them.

He could see us.

I'd thought I was the only one who could see through glamours. Maybe he was like me. Caim said I was one of a kind, the only witch and demon hybrid in existence, but he could have been wrong.

He'd been wrong before.

"You can see through our glamours. Interesting. I thought that ability was mine alone. What's an Ethereal doing on a human police force?" I asked, neglecting his question on purpose. I couldn't say why I didn't want to answer him. Maybe it was because he was an Ethereal, and that made it my crime scene, not his. Maybe because his eyes unnerved me.

Maybe I just liked being an asshole.

"I'm not an Ethereal. And you didn't answer my question. What are you doing here?"

That didn't make even a lick of sense. If he wasn't human and he wasn't Ethereal, what the fuck was he?

"I'm Sentinel. I've been tracking this man and the dragon you just arrested. She's a Council member under a spell from the attack on Aether where he escaped. That's what I'm doing here. Now, if you aren't a human, and you aren't an Ethereal, what the fuck are you?"

Durant stepped toward us, unwilling to shout across the distance. But he didn't make it within ten feet of me before Della and Hideyo were in his way.

"Paladins. How cute." He simpered before looking past them to me. "What else is there for me to be?"

I knew the answer, but I didn't want to say it. *Fae.* I suppressed a shudder and gave him a nod. If he was a Fae, then the verbal acrobatics were about to commence. Fae were rumored to only answer questions with questions. It was enough to give anyone a headache.

"You're a Fae, then? What's a Fae doing on a human police force? And better yet, if you know that this is an Ethereal matter, why are you here at all?"

Durant shrugged his shoulders and gave me a winsome smile. "Maybe I like being here, and maybe this case interests me. Or maybe I was assigned to this case, and I'm doing my job, the same as you. Though, I might be doing a better job at mine than you are at yours. I caught my killer, now, didn't I?"

My eyes narrowed at the slight, but I didn't immediately respond. Durant was speaking in maybes and mights. That was no better than answering me with a question.

"Could you have really caught your killer if she was under the influence of a spell? If there was a death at all. Elias Flynn was a murdering witch—or at least he used to be before I took his power away. Who says someone didn't use this circle as a way to put him into a new body? Possession was a specialty of his. I should know. He tried to have my sister possessed by an incorporeal demon just last week."

Durant's pale eyebrows climbed up his forehead.

"For someone claiming Sentinel, you sure seem to fail at having yourself in order."

Another dig. I didn't think I was going to let that one go.

"Well, since I wasn't Sentinel until a few hours ago, and I took that job from him," I said, pointing to Elias' scattered remains, "I'd say I'm not doing too horribly. Cleaning up messes and killing bad guys is a specialty of mine. Now, are you going to step aside so I can see who killed this steaming pile of rat shit, or am I going to have to get angry?"

I let just a little of my power go, loosening the reins on my rage the tiniest of bits. The earth quaked under our feet, wind whipped inside the warehouse, even with no open windows. Outside thunder cracked.

"I don't know, Princess. I think I might like to see you get a little angry."

CHAPTER SEVEN

He wanted to see angry? I could do that. After this utter and complete shitshow of a day, I had more than enough anger to spare.

"You asked for it," I muttered, using both hands to snap my fingers. At my snap, the ground opened up beneath Durant and swallowed him whole, closing over him as if he'd just disappeared into thin air.

"What did you do?" Della shouted, yanking at my arm. "Did you kill him?"

I sniffed as I inspected my manicure. My cuticles needed attention. "He has enough air to last him maybe thirty minutes. I should be done with the *revelare vestigium* by then."

If I let him out at all.

"Max. This man is a police officer. And if he's a Fae, there is no telling why he's here. He could be a royal for all we know. Having the ground swallow him whole is not the way to get on his good side."

I hated to admit it, but she was right. I had to remind myself that killing people who irritated me was bad form—especially with my new position. Kneeling at the mouth of his new home, I counted to ten and then snapped my fingers again. The earth opened over Durant but didn't spit him back out. I hadn't decided if I wanted him just walking around in my city.

Dirt-covered and pissed off, Durant eyed me from his hole. Oh, I'd made a friend already.

"You asked to see what pissed off looks like. I obliged. Now, are you going to continue irritating the fuck out of me, or will you agree to allow me into your crime scene to complete a *revelare vestigium? Please keep in mind,* my patience has already been stretched paper thin today."

I sarcastically batted my eyes at him, pasting a saccharine-sweet smile on my face. Striker always used to tell me that face was fucking frightening. It was like a murderous cheerleader on uppers. I mostly liked it because it showed all my teeth.

"Do your spell. Just let me out of this hole. Your lands have too much metal in them."

Oh, shit. I'd forgotten the Fae could be hurt by iron, and with the rebar running through the concrete, under the ground wasn't exactly his happy place. I kinda wanted to tell him I was sorry, but I knew better than to admit fault or say thank you to a Fae.

That was a good way to get in a heap of trouble.

I snapped my fingers again, and the earth spit him back out. Miraculously, Durant landed on his feet, making the inelegant task of emerging from a ten-foot hole in the ground look sophisticated.

After I looked him over to make sure I didn't cause actual physical damage, I rifled through the satchel Della prepared for me. I wasn't sure it had everything I needed for the spell considering we hadn't planned to find Elias dead, but I could probably make do with what was there. All I really needed was a candle, and a metal bowl. In a pinch, I could use some of the blood on the floor to fuel the working.

I brought my supplies to the edge of the blood circle, trying not to look too closely at the body parts scattered within it as I settled on the ground. The closer I stared at the boundary of the circle, the more I recognized runes written into the perimeter, each one painstakingly etched into the dirt with Elias' blood. And if I looked closely, they almost moved.

Fuck.

The runes were still active—the spell was still in progress.

I blew out my candle, careful not to let the smoke from it touch the boundary. If I performed any working so close to this circle, who knew what would happen. In an instant, I was on my feet and backing away.

A hand on my shoulder stopped my progress.

"What are you doing?" Striker demanded. I got it. He wanted to know what happened here. Wanted to exonerate his sister or cousin or aunt. But I couldn't help him. Not that way, anyway.

"The circle is still active," I muttered. "That's a working in progress. If I did a spell close to it, crossing it, it could disrupt that circle. It could kill us, blow the whole warehouse, or worse."

Striker gave me an incredulous look. "What's worse than killing us?"

"Blowing a hole in the dimension, opening the gates of Hell, imploding the world. I don't know what it does, but I sure as shit don't want to find out the hard way."

Durant chuckled, and my head whipped toward him of its own accord.

"You knew. What kind of prick just sits there and lets me almost kill us all?" I demanded. I really should have just left him in that hole.

"You seemed so determined to do your silly spell—who was I to tell you otherwise? There are very few things in existence that can actually kill me. No witch casting is going to do the job, *Princess*."

There was that word again. Princess. Was it just a condescending moniker like baby or sugar, or did he know who my father was? Regardless, the way Durant said it, it was most definitely an insult.

I was really starting to hate this Fae.

"It's one thing to gamble with your own life, it is quite another to endanger the people around you. How in the fuck did you ever graduate the police academy?"

"Who says I went?" Durant shrugged, shooting me an unrepentant grin.

I tried so hard not to roll my eyes, but I failed miserably and turned toward my team. Durant wasn't going to help us, so that meant I didn't need to acknowledge him anymore.

"A list of what we know. Elias is dead." I counted on one finger before continuing, "We can't see who killed him because of that fucked up working. We don't need to look for a whacked-out dragon anymore, but she's about to go to human jail. And we are no closer to finding out who broke Elias out of holding, murdered a club full of witches, and spirited a bunch of rowan-filled *grigri* bags all over the place to fuck up the Fae doors. Did I miss anything?"

I was out of fingers, and I was pretty sure I missed something.

"We still don't know what Elias did with Maria or who the traitors are in Aether. And possible shifters on the loose. Don't forget that one," Hideyo offered, the first time he'd spoken since coming into the building.

Aces.

"Any ideas how we can suss out a traitor other than rounding the whole lot of them up and questioning them one by one? Because that sounds exhausting." Yes, I was whining, but today had sucked in all the ways, and I just didn't have it in me to question literally everyone. Even with a vampire as a lie detector, that would take forever.

Maria didn't have forever.

"I could question Cinder," Della offered. "Marcus seemed cognizant of what happened while he was under the spell. She might know who cast it or have some details we missed."

I spared Durant a glance. "Are you really going to arrest Cinder? You and I both know she wasn't responsible for Elias' death."

Durant looked over his shoulder for a second as if he was

checking to see if I was actually talking to him. He feigned surprise, complete with a "Who me?" expression.

This guy was doing my head in. I'd never met anyone this annoying on purpose.

"Are you sure I can't kill him?" I asked Della. "At this point, no one would really blame me. And really, no body, no crime, right? No one is going to look under three feet of concrete and rebar."

Della's deadpan expression told me she was not amused. *Fine.* I wouldn't kill him.

Yet.

I wanted to be diplomatic, but I just didn't have it in me. Instead of answering him, I just glared.

"Of course I'm going to arrest her. She was caught near a dead body covered in what we assume was his blood, mumbling in Czech. There is way too much against your councilmember to not book her."

At Durant's flippant reply, Striker seemed to have had about enough. The transformation hit him faster than it ever had, full wingspan, dragon scales, talons and all. There went another shirt.

"You will release her," Striker ordered, his mouth full of fangs and rage.

I was tempted to intervene, but really, I didn't give a shit if Striker killed the guy. I had other pressing matters to attend to. I tugged on Hideyo's sleeve.

"Can you grab Aidan? See if he got anything from Cinder while we were dealing with this guy." Please note that I said "guy," but I meant "fuck stick." Look at me being all polite and shit.

Hideyo gave me a nod and took off.

Turning my attention back to the pissing match in front of me, I waited for Striker to make a move. I had no interest in cleaning up another one of Striker's messes. I'd done too much of that over the years. If I wasn't mistaken, he was supposed to be protecting me, not duking it out with a moronic Fae. Today was just not the day for that garbage.

"I will do no such thing. Thirty cops saw us arrest her. Thirty.

I'm not releasing her. Not until after she's booked, and an alibi can be produced."

Durant had a point. Thirty people were a lot to persuade. Even Della couldn't work over that many minds.

Begrudgingly, I spoke up in Durant's defense. "He's not wrong. Della can't mesmerize that many people."

Striker snarled and I scraped at the dregs of my patience.

"What did I say about snarling at me, Striker? I will sell the set on eBay," I threatened, but softened my tone to calm him down. "We'll talk to the Council. See what they can do."

Striker growled again, but I watched as his scales faded. He was listening at least.

Aidan and Hideyo picked that moment to grace us with their presence. Aidan took a big sniff, his nostrils flaring as he scented the wide-open space. I braced myself to talk down another man whose job was protecting me and not the other way around.

"There isn't a soul waiting here," he announced, and that gave me pause.

If there wasn't a soul waiting, then was Elias really dead? Or did whoever kill him—assuming it wasn't Cinder—take the soul with them? We'd considered that a demon was the architect of all of this. But could it be something else?

"Can demons abscond with souls? Or can you just not feel him past the circle?" I asked, pinching the bridge of my nose. My brain hurt and my patience was gone. I was tired of jumping through bullshit hoops today.

"There isn't a circle in this world or the next one that would stop me from feeling the ache of a soul," Aidan replied. "Someone took it. Or he might not have had one in the first place. I've seen that a time or two, but that's rare."

So, we had a soul-stealing person who may or may not be a demon. Great.

"Fabulous. Did you get anything out of Cinder? Has the spell worn off?"

Aidan paused, eyeing Durant like he didn't want to talk in front of him.

"He can see you and hear you. Durant here is a Fae and a cop. We're working it out. Just talk."

"I don't think she's under the same spell as the rest of the shifters. She kept saying something about her son. Protecting her son. I think she killed Elias, but I don't know if it was of her own accord, or if someone made her think she had to. Either way, Cinder isn't out of the woods yet, and I'm pretty sure she just committed murder."

My feet shifted, pointing me at Striker. I balled my hand into a fist so I wouldn't slap the shit out of him. The sharp sting of betrayal cut me deep, and it had lashed me far too many times from the same person.

Striker knew everything there was to know about me. He knew every sin, every boyfriend, and every death. I told him freely because he was one of my best friends.

Because he was family.

But I wasn't family to him, now was I?

"She's your *mother*?"

CHAPTER EIGHT

Getting one look at Striker's wide-eyed, guilty expression, I really wanted to punch him right in the face. My hands practically itched in anticipation, but I took one calming breath after the other. Rage and betrayal wouldn't help me right now.

Still, I couldn't help the hurt that seeped into my tone.

"No more secrets, huh?"

That was what we'd promised each other after he hid Maria's kidnapping from me. *He'd promised.* But he'd promised me the truth before and look at where we were now. But that was drama for another time. I couldn't let myself wallow. Especially since it seemed like Striker wasn't even going to try to defend himself.

Wiping at a tear that managed to escape my lashes, I turned back to the Fae, who didn't need to be party to our internal drama. We had enough on our plates to fix.

"Do what you have to do, Durant. We'll get someone to contact you after you process her, but I'd like to perform a *break* before you go. If she's still under the influence of a spell, there is no telling what she could do in a human jail. She ripped Aether apart like it was a tin can. I wouldn't want to be within a mile of her if she decides shifting is a good idea."

Durant contemplated my idea for a moment, his body shifting from one foot to the other as he did so as if his body was playing out his internal debate.

"I will allow you to perform a break on the dragon," he began.

I swore if there was a *but* after that statement, I was going to lose my mind.

"But, I was wondering if you happened to have a plan for what we are supposed to do with this?" Durant gestured to the macabre circle behind him.

No, I did not have a plan for that. That circle was witch business well above my paygrade. How Durant had gotten the forensic team to leave the circle as it was—the body where it was—was a mystery.

"I'll call Barrett and maybe Teresa. That mess," I said, pointing to the scattered remains, "is not in my wheelhouse."

Neglecting my cell phone, I fished a pad of paper and an ink pen out of my satchel, scribbling a note to Barrett about the shitshow we were now in. Once I was sure the message of "Get here right the fuck now" was successfully conveyed, I ripped the paper from the pad and placed the single sheet in my palm. Slapping my other hand on top of it, I twisted my hands and watched as the paper flashed out of the thin space between my palms and traveled to Barrett.

A week ago, Barrett scolded me that I relied too heavily on technology because I left a voicemail instead of doing a spell. Now, no matter where he was on the planet or what he was doing, that piece of paper would float in the air an inch in front of his face until he read it.

Let's see him bitch about not getting the message now.

Not five seconds later, my phone rang.

"Yes?" I answered, trying not to giggle. I really needed a giggle right about now, but I was pretty sure it would make Barrett rage out on me.

"Someone will be there shortly," Barrett said through what I suspected was gritted teeth. "Don't let anyone cross that circle, Max. And for the love of all that is holy, stop talking to that Fae."

"You know when you tell me not to do something, it just makes me want to do it more," I replied. I was just giving him shit, but Barrett being Barrett, didn't know that.

"His name is Rowan Marchand Durant, and he is the emissary to the Seelie Court. I specifically remember your Aurelia telling you to stay away from Rowan, darling. I think she means this one, too. Stop talking to him. Don't even look at him funny. We have enough problems without angering the Seelie Court."

I wondered if now would be the time to tell him that I may have buried him in a hole and threatened to kill him.

Nah. It could wait.

"The absolute last words I want you to say to that man is that someone will be there in less than five minutes to handle the circle. Then, I want you to get your bum back to Aether. The Fates want a word."

I wanted to stomp like a toddler and tell him no. I did not want to add a trip to the Fates on top of everything else. I might explode into a thousand pieces and actually murder one of them. Probably Atropos, if I had to guess.

But I didn't do that. Instead, I took a deep breath and muttered an insolent "*fine*" before I hung up.

I relayed the message and set off to fix Cinder before I did something stupid—like punch Striker in the dick and snap Durant's neck before he could tell on me.

I was nearly to the door before Durant finally spoke up.

"I'll be seeing you around, Princess."

I couldn't tell if that was a threat or a promise, but I kept on walking. Cinder needed me.

The scene outside the warehouse had cleared quite a bit, and only a few police officers were milling about. I did the expedient thing and snapped my fingers, arriving on the fake leather seats of Durant's squad car next to Cinder.

She couldn't see me, but her dragon senses made it so she knew I was there. To stave off an attack, I grabbed her cuffed wrist so she could see me. It took far longer than I'd have liked for my visage to register, and no amount of waiting for her to understand was going to help me.

Cinder's blunted human teeth grew into sharp points as her skin wavered between pale peaches and cream to a scaly ice blue.

I didn't have a lot of time.

The links between her cuffs snapped like dry twigs. Latching onto her other hand so I had both wrists in my grasp, I began the break, muttering the Latin as quickly as it would fall from my lips.

Subsisto, tardo, confuto, concesso, subflamino, insisto, conquiesco, finis...

The same snarl I'd heard earlier from Striker was all the more unsettling coming from his mother. I channeled more power into the break as I gripped her tighter. But even as I concentrated, I could actually feel her body growing, changing.

Subsisto, tardo, confuto, concesso, subflamino, insisto, conquiesco, finis...

I refused to let this woman—this dragon—expose herself to the public or get herself killed by the fear of angry men. I focused all my fear, all my betrayal, all my rage at the break. Thunder rolled outside the car, and I gritted my teeth against the sheer force of the spell.

It was big, and it was buried, woven through her body, through the cells of her consciousness like a parasite. I feared Cinder was much deeper into this mess than I initially thought, but I couldn't let her stay this way. I couldn't let her keep getting used by the machinations of a psychopath.

Subsisto, tardo, confuto, concesso, subflamino, insisto, conquiesco, finis...

The trickle of my nose bleeding was unsurprising. So was the guttural snarl coming from Cinder's throat. She wasn't fighting me exactly, but my break was hurting her.

Subsisto, tardo, confuto, concesso, subflamino, insisto, conquiesco, finis...

I felt the threads of the spell under her skin pop one by one, freeing her bit by bit as its hold loosened on her mind. Someone had been mining her for information, making her do their bidding for quite a while. Years, decades, centuries? I couldn't tell, but this working wasn't new. No, it seemed very, very old, and renewed over time.

Finally, the last string of the working popped, freeing her completely.

Cinder wilted, the fight bleeding out of her instantly as she melted onto the fake leather seat. So did I, but for a very different reason. She might be at ease, but I had a heavy dose of apprehension to deal with on top of enough exhaustion to make getting out of this car interesting.

I was contemplating just how to do that when Cinder grabbed my wrist.

"My son," she rasped, her voice thick from either emotion or from the spell, I couldn't tell which.

"Striker is safe, Cin. I can't promise he'll always be that way. He has a bad habit of getting himself into trouble, but I'll keep an eye on him even if he's determined not to let anyone in."

"You know?"

"His scales might have given it away. The bigger question is—which angel is his dad? But I'll leave it alone for now. I have bigger problems than who Striker's sperm donor is."

Cinder's eyes closed in relief. She didn't want to talk about her baby daddy, either.

"I need you to stay in this car and let Durant book you for murder. There were too many cops that saw you bloody and standing over a corpse, so..." I shrugged, letting her infer what she would about the situation. It wasn't good, I knew that much. "I'll leave it to you to make arrangements to get yourself out. Barrett is sending someone to deal with the circle Elias is in. Can you tell me anything? Do you know who did this to you?"

Her body went rigid as she pinched her eyes shut. What did she think I was going to do, force them open?

Cinder's blue eyes flashed open, and her expression turned pleading. "I don't know his name, but I do know one thing. He has spies in the Keys. Ones you didn't kill."

Tell me something I don't know.

She seemed to read that thought right off of my face.

"He is a demon. An old one. And he has ways to make you do things you never thought you'd do."

Again, it was something I figured, but her confirmation was like ice in my veins.

"I'll be careful," I assured her.

"Careful, my dear, may not be enough."

It took three tries to get out of the squad car without breaking a window—which I was in favor of but didn't do out of respect for Barrett. Who—if he didn't send someone—would be here shortly. Tired down to my bones, I met back up with my team and waited until someone showed up. Something about that funky witch circle—or demon circle, considering the information I'd just gotten—rubbed me the wrong way.

Of course, there was no right way to rub when we were dealing with a dismembered corpse, so there was that.

A few minutes later, Barrett himself arrived on the scene. Something about seeing his freshly healed self made me want to run across the distance between us and hug the man. I definitely needed a hug after the day I'd had. Plus, there was a chance I could con him into not making me see the Fates.

But I didn't have to run to him, he came straight to me, opened his arms wide, and let me hug the shit out of him. Barrett was like a big brother or stuffy uncle. And he gave the best hugs.

"How bad is it?" he asked, but it was more a demand for information than anything else.

"Pretty bad. I'm pretty sure we're dealing with an ancient demon with enough juice to mind-control an Alpha dragon. There were enough threads of compulsion to weave a fucking dress in Cinder's mind," I murmured into his suit jacket. "But I broke them. It is someone with access to her, someone ancient, and definitely a demon. Anyone you can think of?"

Barrett's posture was so rigid he could have been a statue, but still, he managed to answer me. "A few names come to mind."

My very first thought was Andras, but I dismissed it almost as soon as it came to me. He'd been on the run for the last four hundred years. He didn't have access to Cinder until very recently.

"Not Andras," Barrett clarified, pulling back from our hug to look me in the eye. "It isn't his style."

At my dubious expression, Barrett amended his previous statement. "Okay, it's totally his style, but he didn't do it."

That, I could agree with. I gave him a big squeeze and then let him go. "Let me know if you need help, and..." I trailed off, trying to think of another way to tell Barrett about my Fae booboo.

"And what?"

I winced at his knowing tone. "I totally fucked with that Fae before you told me not to."

Barrett rolled his eyes. "Of course you did. What did you do?"

"I told him to stop pissing me off. He said he'd like to see me angry, so I showed him what angry looked like." Yes, I was hedging, but Barrett was already turning purple.

"Is he still alive?" His voice was the cold menace of a predator about to strike. I'd never actually heard that tone come out of him before, and I was not happy to be hearing it now.

"Yes, and not a single scratch on him. All I did was open up a hole underneath him and bury him alive for a few minutes."

Barrett's eyes popped open wide enough I could see white all around the irises.

Not a good sign.

Well, I thought that, until Barrett started cackling like a loon. Still, I backed up a step or five.

"Are you mad?" Why again did I feel like a child? Oh, that's right. Because Barrett was twelve hundred years old.

He wiped tears from his face as his giggles petered out. "No, Max. I am not mad. You verbally went toe-to-toe with a Fae emissary and bested him. Better, you put him in his place because he essentially asked for it. I am fucking thrilled. Rowan Durant has been a thorn in my side for the better part of a century. This is fucking priceless."

"Okay, good. He said he'd have to book Cinder because of all the witnesses, so I'm leaving you to deal with that while I go talk to Larry, Moe, and Curly."

Personally, I liked my nicknames for the Fates, but Barrett gave me a half-censuring look before giving me another hug.

"Max? Go alone," Barrett advised. "Whatever they have to say, they want it kept to you alone."

Perfect. I so enjoyed going into the lion's den by myself.

CHAPTER NINE

Arriving back at Aether was a surreal experience. The outside of the building looked like it always did. The damage seemingly to have never existed in the first place. Everything was put back to rights, but I could feel the change in the air.

You could put the building back together, you could clean up the blood, but the lives taken today would always be lost to the people who loved them. The club was quiet when we entered, the silence deafening in a way that it hadn't been when there was at least a little hope when they were searching for survivors.

I hated so much that there weren't any.

Peeling off from the group, I went down the hidden hallway that only I seemed to be able to find without help. Striker had stayed with Cinder—hidden beneath his glamour—to make sure she stayed safe. I wanted to be mad at him, but at this point, I was just resigned. Aidan, Della, and Hideyo were off to get some food while I got to have a meeting with the Fates.

I would have much preferred a cheeseburger to talking to those three, but I knew better than to snub them. The last thing I needed was another mess to clean up. Walking down the cobwebby, unlit corridor, I steeled myself in preparation for verbal acrobatics. Honestly, I was just glad I wasn't talking to Durant anymore.

I'd take a bitchy Atropos any day of the week over that pompous prick.

This time the door opened before I could knock. Atropos waved me in like she'd been listening at the door for my footsteps. This was quite a bit different than the last time I was here. Sure, the entry chamber still looked like something out of a Grimm fairytale, but there was a fire in the grate, and I didn't have to force my way in.

I couldn't help but think it wasn't so much progress as they needed something.

"Took you long enough," Atropos grumbled.

Ah, there it was.

I really wanted to let it go, but something in me just couldn't let another magical being fuck with me today.

"Oh, I'm sorry. Were you undoing likely a century's worth of memory modification on an Alpha dragon? Or trading barbs with the emissary to the Seelie Court? Or trying to figure out who the fuck killed a shit-ton of witches in a single afternoon? All the while, trying to figure out what Elias did to Maria? And now all hope of saving her is in the toilet."

I crossed my arms and let my voice go hard.

"No. That was me working my ass off trying to figure out this web of bullshit you just let happen on your watch. What, exactly, would you say you do here? Sit on your ass, dreaming up ways to ruin my fucking day?"

Yes, the ground was quaking. Yes, the fire in the grate had spilled out into the room and up the wall. Yes, I may have overreacted to a simple snide comment.

I didn't take it back, though.

Three deep breaths. In at the count of four, out at the count of four.

The heat in the small chamber dissipated as the fire returned to its original size, and the ground quit dancing.

"Feel better?" Atropos asked, her tone utterly unbitchy for the first time probably ever as she gestured to the staircase that led to their main living space.

"Much," I replied honestly as I followed her down the stairs.

Three seats were gathered around a table this time, each chair a different yet ornate amalgamation of each sister's personality. Clotho, with her white hair and sunny disposition, sat in a baby-pink overstuffed chintz, the solid color making her hair almost glow. The center chair was empty, but I could tell it was Lachesis' without question. It was high-backed, covered in a lush forest-green velvet, and tufted with pretty brass buttons.

Atropos sat in the last chair, a seat fitting for the cutter of the thread. It was a cathedral-backed, ornately carved black monstrosity that didn't look even the least bit comfortable to sit on. However, the black made her fire-red hair pop, and really, that was probably the point.

Lachesis' absence was glaringly obvious. The only bigger tip-off that something was wrong was Atropos acting damn close to an approximation of nice.

I couldn't tell if I was about to be murdered or if they really needed something.

Clotho rose from her fluffy cloud chair as I entered the room. She greeted me like a guest, which was a far cry from the last time I was here.

"Would you like some tea or a bourbon?" she offered, and my suspicions rose.

I really wanted some bourbon in tea, but I also didn't want to be poisoned, so I declined.

"No, thank you."

As if reading my thoughts, Clotho snorted before pouring me a cup of tea and splashing a bit of bourbon in it. She passed me the teacup and gave me a censuring glare until I took it. I murmured a "thank you" and dutifully sipped the doctored concoction. The bourbon slipped down my throat like silk and warmed all the bits of me that were cold.

At my happy sigh, Clotho smiled, and that little upturn of her lips made me sad. It made me wonder if the woman who spun every thread of life got lonely. If helping create so many lives made her long for one of her own. If she desired a child or if seeing so many babies born satisfied her in a way a child of her own might never be able to.

A rueful smile crossed Clotho's face as she began to speak. "No one ever wonders those things about us. No one sees us as people. They see us as things they can't change, but my sisters and I aren't things."

I nodded before I realized that Clotho was referencing questions I had never spoken aloud. She'd either read my thoughts, or maybe her abilities made it so she knew quite a bit more than just her advertised talents.

"We've been around quite a while. Our talents grew over time. Just like yours."

I noticed she never answered the questions I mentally asked but decided not to mention it. She'd answer the questions she wanted to, and there was nothing I could do to change that. What I could do was move this bit along so I could get back to the tasks at hand.

"Barrett said you wanted to speak to me. What can I do for you?" I asked, my tone as polite as I could make it. I was proud I didn't sound the least bit exasperated, which I so was.

"You can do the job you agreed to do and find the traitor in our midst," Atropos griped.

And there she was. I knew she couldn't stay nice for long. I sipped my tea some more so I didn't have another super-adult hissy fit.

"What exactly do you think I've been doing today, Atropos? Twiddling my thumbs?" I shot back, unable to hold in my snark.

Atropos slammed her fists on the table, rattling the teapot and our cups.

"You have been a step behind at every single turn. You need to do more. Do better. If you keep following this path, you will lose everything. We will lose everything. Can't you see that?"

Did I know that I'd been a step behind all day? Yes, I sure did. And then something dawned on me that hadn't before now. A pit in my gut opened wide as Clotho gave me a slight nod in agreement.

Lachesis saw what would be: the span of lives from birth to death. And she wasn't here. So, the demon either had Lachesis' ear, and she was on his side, or he had a way to see what she saw.

"Am I going to fight her or fight for her?" There was only so much I could do if I had to actually fight a goddess. It wasn't like I had god power in my back pocket.

"Both, but not in the way you think. Come, child," Atropos muttered, holding out her hand as she rose from the table.

I took it, thinking it was funny that a woman who looked no older than a teenager was calling me child.

Atropos led me to a hallway with three doors on the right and three doors on the left. We stopped at the middle two doors, and Atropos opened the one on the left. The room was decorated as a bedroom in what I would call earthy chic. On the four-poster bed was a dark-haired woman, shrouded in a spell of gold gossamer. I used the word "on" very loosely since it appeared as if Lachesis was floating a solid foot above the covers, her dark mass of hair pooled on the fabric.

"My sister sleeps, and we cannot get her to wake," Atropos murmured, a sadness in her voice I had not heard before. It spoke of eons of time and heartache, of death, and pain. Atropos only cared for her sisters, and half of her heart was held in a spell.

"Is that why you're breaking the rules? Talking to me when you know you shouldn't?" I asked because it seemed she could not read my thoughts when her sister could.

"Yes." She said it simply as if the world owed her one. It probably did.

"Do you mind if I take a look at her?"

What I thought I was going to be able to do, I had no idea. I broke Cinder out of her confinement, but this was a literal goddess. What the fuck did I think I was going to be able to do for her? Did I think I was just going to roll up and fix this shit like I knew what I was doing?

Because I never did. I never knew what I was capable of. I

never knew what my power was going to do from one moment to the next. I pretty much guessed and hoped for the best.

Kinda like I was right now.

"Be my guest. Two ancient goddesses can't figure it out, but sure, you'll be able to fix my sister in a snap."

Somehow, Atropos' snark was a lot easier to bear than her niceties.

I stepped closer to Lachesis, the golden spell weaving into and through her, sparkling with magic I couldn't name. I didn't want to touch her, and rightly so. As soon as I did, the magic latched onto me in a spark of agony so acute I thought I might throw up.

But it took me less than a second to realize something neither of the Fates had.

Lachesis had done this to herself.

Gasping, I backed out of the room and headed back to the circular chamber, downing my now-cold bourbon-laced tea in one gulp.

"What do you mean, she did it to herself?" Clotho demanded, anger coloring her fair features pink. She'd read my thoughts again, and she was not happy at all.

"She took herself off the board. She might have sensed that someone had infiltrated her mind, so she did the only thing she could. I don't know how to wake her up, but I do know what I need to do next."

And I did. I knew exactly what I needed to do to get a one-up on the demon who had infiltrated even this inner sanctum.

Clotho seemed to steel herself and rose to her full height, meeting her sister's gaze with her own. Willowy and pale, I never thought of Clotho as a goddess I needed to fear. Maybe it was because I'd never threatened her sister—at least not in any real way. Her pale-blue eyes seemed to burn with wrath.

"I'll get my scissors ready," Atropos quipped, her smile practically diabolical.

She'd need them.

CHAPTER TEN

The ragtag bunch of Keys in front of me looked like a hodgepodge of every kind of Ethereal there was. There were a few witches, some shifters, a fair number of angels and demons, a warlock or two, and more dragons than I knew what to do with. Each of them gathered in a loose formation as I stood at the dais with the newly formed Council behind me.

Caim sat at his usual angel seat while Cinder's chair remained empty. The phoenix seat was occupied by Aurelia, even though she wasn't the leader of the phoenixes, and next to her, Barrett sat in his appointed chair. The demon seat remained empty with Alistair still in Hell. Gorgon and Marcus seemed antsy in their chairs, but that might be because they were sitting next to the biggest wraith I'd ever had the pleasure of calling a friend.

Kyle Brennan was neither a leader nor a follower. A hybrid like myself, he chose his own path. While I wasn't exactly confused as to why his King wasn't here—he did have a newborn at home—I did wonder why West had chosen him in the first place.

I was just excited to have a wraith as powerful as Kyle in the room.

I was going to need him.

Once the last of the Keys were in position, I sent out my consciousness to get a feel for the room. I'd felt the power that had chained Cinder's mind. I would definitely know if I felt it again.

Without a word, I marched through the throng, waiting to feel that putrid bit of magic that would tell me someone had been used without their knowledge. I didn't know what it was about myself that saw the good in people, that hoped for a logical explanation for the wrongs committed, but I couldn't change it.

No matter how hard I tried.

When I came up empty, I moved to phase two of my likely idiotic plan.

"You are gathered here today because we have a traitor in our midst." Starting with a bang, I raised both hands and flicked my fingers outward, locking the entire room down. The sound of a bolt turning was audible in the space, and more than a few people flinched.

They couldn't flee, but their reaction was telling.

"We aren't leaving this room until I find every single person in league with Elias Flynn. If anyone wants to come forward, now would be the time."

Silence reigned for several seconds, and I heaved a sigh.

"The hard way it is, then," I muttered, turning to Kyle.

Kyle's nostrils fluttered as he scented the room for yummy morsels to eat. Wraiths feasted on the souls of the damned. A person who was responsible for fifty-three witch deaths seemed pretty damned to me, so I waited for him to cough up the traitor.

Kyle stood from his chair and the room got a collective gander at the new wraith councilmember. Standing at a hefty six-foot-seven, Kyle Brennan was not exactly the tallest, but he was the biggest man in the room. Kyle paced in between Keys, sniffing out the juiciest, darkest soul.

I tried not to giggle when Kyle stopped at a particularly weaselly-looking dude and sniffed his neck. Maybe it was because I knew the big brute would never hurt me, but I had a tough time holding in my mirth when I saw all six and a half feet of hungry wraith sniffing the neck of a man half his size. And his height was only compounded by the swirling black mist that shrouded his body, coal-like eyes, and razor-sharp fangs.

Here was the thing about Kyle, he might have been half-wraith, but he was also half-witch. And witches were known for their love of fucking with the masses. *I should know.* So, when weasel-dude nearly bolted, the both of us were ready for him.

Despite the audible locking of the Fae-built door, the guy made a run for the ornately carved wood. He nearly reached it before I snapped my fingers again and the door disappeared altogether.

"So, this one?" I confirmed with Kyle before I started my interrogation. It was good to be sure before there was bloodshed. I didn't want to torture the wrong guy. What kind of message would that send?

"That one," he assured me as he nodded. "When you're done with him, pass him over. I need a snack."

Weasel-guy scrabbled at the now-empty wall where the door used to be before deciding to jump to his other form. I'd known he was a shifter, but the kind was a mystery. All I knew was he wasn't a wolf. Still, the odd-looking, medium-sized cat was hard to place at first until I pulled the name from the dregs of my *Animal Planet* days.

Lynx.

Maybe the size of a domesticated large-breed dog, the lynx prowled the room. Well, until I put a stop to that. My *ipsum revelare* was getting a workout today. The traitor seemed shocked when he fell to the floor in his human form, but anyone who'd seen my exchange with Finn was wholly unsurprised.

A few words in Latin and a snap of my fingers later, and the traitor was properly secured to the bone-white floor with invisible ropes.

"What's his name?" I asked the room. No one answered me until Marcus growled it from the dais.

"It's Embry Jacobs." The way Marcus said the name, it was as if the mere action of it was ripping him up inside. And that made sense. Marcus was the shifter Alpha, he took in all kinds, made them family. For someone to do what Embry did, it was likely breaking Marcus' heart.

Marcus rose from his seat, eyeing Embry as if he was less than dirt on his boot. "I know what you've done. I know that you have turned against your own in the service of someone meaning to do us harm."

"Shifters weren't to be harmed. He swore none of us would be hurt." Embry yelled in his own defense but damning himself in the process.

Marcus' face turned to stone, only the rage behind his eyes told the tale of a man betrayed.

"He lied. No shifters were injured, but plenty were hurt. Those were good men and women who now have the weight of death on their souls because of what you did." Marcus drew in a breath, steeling himself for what was to come next. "Embry Jacobs, I renounce you from this pack. Your name will never be spoken again by any member of the pack. Your family will forget you. Every image of you will be burned. Your children will renounce your name, striking you from every record. To the pack, you will no longer exist."

"No. I made sure none of the pack would be hurt. He swore," Embry shouted, his gaze swinging to the shifters in the front, his expression pleading for any of them to listen.

But none of them showed him even the least bit of pity. Every single one of them was betrayed today by one of their own.

"Mr. Jacobs," I said to the raving man who refused to stay still, even though he was stuck to the floor. "You have been a very naughty boy. I want to know who your boss is, and I want to know now. If I have to ask twice, I will turn you inside out piece by piece until you answer me."

Embry struggled against his invisible bonds, his weasel face screwed up in mulish defiance. What he didn't do was start talking. Too bad he didn't think of that earlier when he was trying to defend himself.

"So be it," I muttered, snapping my fingers. A fine mist of blood spattered the Keys closest to him as his left hand was turned inside out. Flayed skin and ruined bone were all that was left of the appendage.

I was a woman of my word, after all.

Embry screamed a high-pitched girly kind of scream until I silenced him with a snap of my fingers.

"Embry, Embry, Embry. Please don't make me make you. It is my least favorite thing."

I snapped my fingers again, giving Embry his voice back. "Who do you work for? Don't dawdle, my patience for fools has run rather thin today."

The whole of the Keys formation took a collective step back. Smart people. They knew what was coming as much as I did.

Embry once again refused to answer me, so I moved up his left arm, snapping my fingers once again. This time I was smart enough to silence him before the blood flew.

"Della," I addressed my wondrous vampire assistant, "please convince this man that pain is not my only alternative."

Della eyed Embry's ruined arm with revulsion. For a vampire, she didn't seem to have a taste for torture or the macabre at all. It made me wonder where all the sadistic bastards were that were portrayed in movies.

Della looked directly into Embry's wide, shock-filled eyes and asked him to stop squirming. Instantly, he quit his writhing and stood tall. I gave him his voice back and Della questioned him, the Keys and the Council witnessing every deed, every machination. How he'd worked with a demon to put the *grigri* bags at every door. How he'd nearly ripped his partner's head off with his claws, the rowan shavings in the pouches interrupting the nulling magic of the bars.

What he didn't do, even with Della's influence, was give up the name of his boss. We were going to have to get creative. If I couldn't find his boss, it was possible he didn't know his name. Just like Cinder, that information might never have been divulged. Our puppet master was covering his ass big time.

"Someone had to have made those *grigri* bags. Do you know

the name of the witch who made them?" I asked, trying to find a work-around for our puppet master problem.

That's when we hit pay dirt. We now had a name and a location. Now we just had to make sure there weren't any more traitors in our midst.

I pivoted on a foot, as I addressed the rest of the Keys. "In case you weren't aware, Elias Flynn was a murderous traitor, spelling Council members, possessing witches, and participating in all manner of naughty things. That's why he was sacked as Sentinel, and I took his place. My goal of this tableau is not to frighten you or intimidate you. It is simply to seek out traitors and eliminate them."

I paused then, watching their faces as I let the silence linger. No one shifted on their feet, no one looked away. I'd have to question them all. Every single one until I was sure. I'd have to search for the threads I'd felt in Cinder because there was no way it was just Embry.

"Too many are dead today because I wasn't quick enough to eradicate this threat. Too many shifters have those deaths on their conscience. Too many families are without someone they love. So, I will turn this man inside out piece by motherfucking piece until I know everything he knows. And I will search every little bit of your minds until I'm certain I can trust you. If you don't want to stay after that, well, I won't blame you. But if you do stay, just know that we've got work to do, and I expect you to do it. Anyone got any questions?"

No one did, but I sure as hell got some answers.

CHAPTER ELEVEN

I took stock of the party raging below me from the balcony of my hotel room. If ever there was a town I liked the least, it was New Orleans. Especially in the middle of summer. After the day I'd had, there was no way I wanted to be in witch-central with a hundred percent humidity.

As a Rogue, I'd avoided all manner of witch havens for the last four centuries. Being around other witches seemed like a really good way to get killed. Or tortured. Or worse.

It would be like waving a red flag in front of a bull.

No, thank you.

Even with my Rogue status lifted, the weird honor of being the last in the line of what was considered demon royalty, and the Sentinel moniker, I didn't feel right being here. This city was a hotbed of death and power, the politics of such I had no desire to navigate. There were too many covens, too many demon aristocrats, and too many other Ethereals all fighting for the same bit of land that was no more special than the next bit.

Plus, I'd left Maria, Ian, and my mother behind, and I didn't feel right about that, either.

"Are you coming, or are you going to be mosquito dinner?

We've got places to be." Aidan nagged from the ornate French doors, his shoulder resting on the doorjamb like he owned the place. I wasn't quite sure how he'd procured this hotel room at what was the definition of the last second, and I didn't want to know.

"I'm thinking it over." I snarked, staring at the street below. It wasn't a high tourist time, the summer being too warm for most people, but still, the parties raged, and the city seemed to pulse with activity.

Denver didn't feel like this. Denver didn't have this buzzing, this trill of magic on the air like a spell was being cast every minute of the day. Denver felt like peace. This place felt like I was a moment away from being burned at the stake.

"My contact is not going to wait forever, Max. Get the lead out."

He was right, but I couldn't quell the unease in my belly. Maybe it was because we were here, or perhaps it was because it was the first time I'd seen Aidan without his signature beanie.

I'd always assumed he was balding underneath, but that was not the case. The knit fabric was hiding something, however. A long, jagged scar ran from one side of his temple to the other, curving down the side of his ear and disappearing into his hair. The white of the scar tissue told of its age, and it was hard not to flinch at the sight of it. It wasn't a scar you'd get from an accident —not with wraith healing, anyway.

No, someone had done that to him on purpose.

"Did they ever pay for what they did?" I asked out of the blue, nodding toward his scar.

His expression tightened, but he answered me. "No."

"If you ever want me to make them, you let me know. Now, are you sure it's smart to go out like this? I've never wanted to be in fighting leathers more in my fucking life," I griped, gesturing at my outfit.

No offense to Aidan's judgment, but a pretty summer dress and heels seemed to be the last thing I should be wearing if I wanted to go after literally anyone. Never mind that it was a super pretty off-the-shoulder number with a flared floral skirt.

"Do you want to stick out like a sore thumb?"

To that, I gave him a scathing glance.

"I have blue hair, and I'm covered in tattoos," I retorted, my arms spread wide so he could take in all the ink. "Sticking out is my literal goal in life."

"That shit won't get you a second look in NOLA. There are all kinds of freaks here. You've got that handy dandy 'hide me' ring and no telling how many charms that do Fates know what. Just keep your athames strapped to you, and you'll be fine."

I wanted him to be right, but I never felt like my personal style was a hindrance until I took off my fighting leathers and put on this freaking dress. Fiddling with the giant cocktail ring Bernadette had given me, I watched as the aquamarine sparkled in the low light. The beauty of the stone totally distracted the eye from the etched runes that kept me hidden.

The only thing that kept me even a little calm was the pair of athames strapped to the outside of my thighs under my skirt.

"If we didn't have to mingle with the locals, I would have advised you differently, but word on the street is that this lady is no one to mess with. If we want to find out anything, we can't come off as a threat."

It sounded like an excellent way to get my ass kicked, but whatever. I let Aidan lead the way to a little hole-in-the-wall spot named Sonny's that should be quiet but was just as crowded as every other fucking bar in this town. Della and Hideyo shadowed us, hanging back on the street as they kept an eye out for trouble. There were people drinking everywhere, yelling to be heard over what I begrudgingly admitted was fabulous music. The smell of good food practically fell out of every restaurant, and the scents of a well lived-in city chased them through the salty air.

The battered bar miraculously had a single stool open, so I snagged it before another patron could. I managed to flag down the bartender and ordered three fingers of a really expensive bourbon. I felt the evil eye from Aidan, but I chose to ignore the wraith in favor of sipping the smoky goodness. Drinking on the job wasn't precisely prudent, but I was blending, right?

"Don't give me that look," I said, not even sparing him a glance. "We're in a bar in New Orleans. Not drinking would stick out far more than sipping yummy bourbon."

"I'm going to take a lap to look for my contact. You're in charge of pumping the bartender for info. I'll meet you in the alley in ten minutes. Do try not to get into any trouble between now and then."

I tried really hard not to roll my eyes, but I didn't quite manage it. I felt more than saw Aidan leave me as I brushed my long hair off my shoulder. Wishing I had opted for an updo instead of pretty waves, I fanned myself as I sipped a bit more bourbon.

Okay, I was playing up my cleavage and essentially waving a fucking sign for the bartender to come and talk to me. He was a little too human and a lot too hipster for my taste, but he seemed to like my boobs just fine, and that was all that really mattered. Breasts seemed to have a magic of their very own, befuddling men to spill their secrets.

Within a minute, the bartender was back. Like I said, boobs were magic.

"You need anything else, *chère*? A menu? More bourbon? A tour guide?" He flirted, and I let my gaze drift over him.

He probably thought it was in admiration, but, in reality, I was cataloging everything I could about him. First off, his nametag read "Byron," but it was probably something closer to Brian. He had dark-brown hair, but I could tell it was dyed and was likely a mousey brown or dark blond. He was also older than I'd pegged, closer to mid-thirties rather than the twenty-something I'd initially thought. He was a writer or artist of some kind, and he was left-handed. Ink stained his fingertips, especially on the middle and ring finger on his left hand, as well as the heel, which was characteristic of lefties.

Byron wasn't a hundred percent human, either. He had some witch ancestry based on the energies surrounding him, but he didn't practice. He likely couldn't, his magic was so small.

I gave him my best grin, the one that probably promised hot, sweaty sex—not that he'd be getting any—and plumped up my cleavage a little as I swirled my finger over the rim of my glass.

"I'll take a little more bourbon and some guidance if you're game."

Yes, I was looking at him under my lashes while I did it, and no, I was not proud of myself.

Byron refilled my glass and then leaned on the bar, his gaze never straying to my chest, which knocked up my estimation of him a few notches.

"What do you need to know, pretty lady?" He was laying it on thick, but I'd be giving him a huge tip, so I figured we were square or would be soon.

"Do you know where a girl can get an authentic voodoo experience? Not the touristy ghost tours and stuff, but the real deal. I don't come here often, but I love getting the skinny from the locals. Can you point me in the right direction?"

Byron did not like the way this conversation was headed at all.

"A pretty lady like you don't need to be messing with that kind, *chère*. Them's a bad crowd," he warned, a little bit of an accent filtering into his words. He seemed legitimately concerned, so I raised my glass to him.

"Just the bourbon then," I said to ease his mind. Something told me I wasn't going to get much more from him, so I fished a hundred out of my pocketbook and passed it to him.

"For the booze," I murmured, giving him a wink as I got up.

Heading toward the bathrooms at the back, I gulped the rest of my glass and took a right turn toward the alley exit. The alleyway was several decibels quieter than the bar, and I would have breathed a sigh of relief if I could see Aidan. But I was alone, and I had to figure that wasn't a good thing. I knew it had been at least ten minutes, if not more since he'd left me.

My hands itched to reach for my athames, but I held back, trying not to be a paranoid wreck. This little space was too quiet, and even though the entire city seemed to scratch against my skin, I felt the slight surge of magic when someone entered the alley. Surprisingly enough, I couldn't see them, but I knew they were there.

I pretended to scratch my thigh as I reached for a blade, trying to lift my skirt as surreptitiously as possible as to not give myself away. As my hand wrapped around the swirling hilt, I caught the barest glimpse of tracery magic out of the corner of my eye. There was more than one, and Aidan was nowhere to be found.

Awesome. What exactly was the point of having paladins if they were MIA when you were about to be attacked?

I could feel them moving around me, even if the magic that cloaked them was more powerful than my sight. Realizing propriety was out the window, I reached for my other athame, springing the button that turned my dagger-sized blades into full swords.

Yes, I was in a dress and heels and a strapless motherfucking bra. No, I was not going to be taken hostage or killed because I was afraid one of my girls might deviate from her assigned seat.

Priorities.

Over the faint strains of zydeco music, I heard the whispers of a spell in a language I hated on general principle because I'd died the last time I'd heard it used. I was not a fan of French Creole, which was another knock against New Orleans.

Kicking off my heels, I realized a bit too late that I was fighting against more than just invisible men. I decided I wouldn't wait for them to attack first. Striking as fast as my bare feet would carry me, I launched myself sideways at the closest figure I could see out of the corner of my eye. My blade plunged through his body like a knife through butter, the man appearing from thin air as he lost his concentration.

Mortal wounds would do that to a guy.

Hands grabbed at my shoulders from behind, but I ducked, bumping out my hip so I could use his momentum to toss him over me. Plunging my blade into what I assumed was his middle, I tried to control my breathing so I could hear the next one. There were more than two guys in this alley, and I didn't have the luxury of waiting for them to attack.

Storm clouds grew in the night sky overhead, lightning streaking the sky as I whispered the words that had served me well all damn day.

"*Ipsum revelare*," I murmured, letting the spell carry my intentions away on the wind.

Four cloaked figures appeared out of nowhere, their spell trumped by my own. And I should have felt accomplished by that—my spell overloading a coven's worth of witches, but I didn't. No, my eyes were drawn to the fifth figure.

A woman deigned to show herself, uncloaked and unperturbed, her dark skin like silk as she nearly blended into the night. Pale pupilless eyes stared at me from a face so beautiful it nearly hurt my heart. The skull of a small animal rested at the base of her throat.

She said nothing, but she smiled at me as if I was adorable. And I was so caught by that smile that I didn't notice the white powder in her hand until it was too late.

One tiny puff of breath from her lips and I was out.

CHAPTER TWELVE

No matter how kinky you are, no one ever wants to wake up tied to a chair. That fact was no more evident than it was right then, as I struggled to free myself from a hard-backed wooden chair. Ropes bit into my wrists and ankles, the workings bound into the twine burned me as they kept me still.

Rude.

The infernal chair was in the middle of a salt circle, and that circle was in the middle of what looked like a crypt of some kind. Arched stain-glass windows glittered in the candlelight, and those candles littered every flat surface. Window ledges, steps, the floor. Stuck in nooks and crannies, their wax littered the ground with the remnants of spells long spent. Vine circlets bound with twine hung from twisted nails, bones and the detritus of life caught in their webs.

The room carried the scent of the long dead and herbs only witches used.

Since we were in New Orleans, I figured we were in one of those spooky ass above-ground cemeteries that all the tourists walked through, like being surrounded by the dead was a good thing. Like they wouldn't drag you to join them if they could.

On the other side of this circle was a wealth of power, but on my side? All I felt was the burning of the ropes.

The fact that none of my spells to free myself were working might have also contributed to my stress.

A giggle like tinkling wind chimes yanked my gaze from my infernal bonds to the beauty sitting across the room. She was sitting on an apothecary stool in front of a cabinet with more drawers and cubbies than I could count at the moment. In her hands was a bronze bowl, and she ground a pestle into the contents before setting it aside. The woman's skin was so dark that it seemed to gleam in the low light, and I realized just a bit too late that this was the same woman who knocked me out in the first place. I could have sworn she wasn't there a moment ago, and it was completely possible she wasn't.

"What was in that powder you blew at me? My brain feels like it's on fire," I groaned, trying not to insult the woman who took me out with fucking dust.

She got up from her stool, moving like water on silk, and that was when I got the impression that this woman wasn't even in the realm of human. Not that I thought she was one before, but still. Witches walked like humans. This woman flowed like the ground moved with her and not the other way around.

She folded herself into a scarlet high-backed chintz chair that seemed to have come from nowhere. I could have sworn I remembered her eyes being pale and pupilless, but now they were a whiskey brown.

"A little bit of this and a little bit of that. I can't be spilling all my secrets before we're even introduced. I'm Deya Baptiste. A little bird told me you, Sentinel, were here in my city looking for me."

Her accent was hard to place. Maybe she'd lived so long, she didn't have one anymore. Then, her form flickered a bit. One second she was the woman sitting in the chair, and the next she was a winged monster with fangs for teeth and a permanent snarl. Then she was back again, fingering the tiny skull at her neck. Getting more than a cursory glance at it, it appeared to be a raven's.

And I focused on the skull at her neck rather than my current predicament.

Denial was my friend.

Had I known Deya was more than what she was billed as—a witch practicing voodoo in New Orleans—then I might have told Aidan to shove his wardrobe advice where the sun didn't shine. But as it stood, there was no fucking way this woman was a witch. No, she was something else. Something—or someone—I didn't want to cross. I swallowed the thick trepidation in my throat and answered her.

"That's correct. I came here for you," I replied, wondering if she was a demon of some kind or something else entirely.

Deya's smile stretched wide, as if my coming here was a delight, and she was finally having a good time. It was not a comforting smile.

"What does the Sentinel want with me?" she asked, her false coyness accompanied by an innocent expression. She was just fucking with me now.

My mind cleared a bit, and I did my best not to waste that tiny morsel of clarity. "That depends on what you did to my people. Because I'm not dumb enough to think they just disappeared into thin air."

Deya swept her braids off her shoulder, her expression turning simpering. "Big talk coming from a woman tied to a chair."

I knew better than that.

"I wouldn't be tied to this chair if you didn't see me as a threat. But I'm not a kill first and ask questions later kind of girl, so... Where are my people?"

"Sleeping just like you were. They'll wake up tomorrow in your hotel room with a headache. You woke up faster than I thought you would, or you'd be with them." So she wasn't a kill first kind of girl, either. I could respect that.

"And because I intrigue you, I get to ask questions, is that right?"

The simpering smile fell away and Deya gave me a thoughtful expression. "Do you talk to my sisters like this?"

Shrugging as much as my bonds would allow, I answered, "That would depend on who your sisters are, but probably."

Deya's face transformed into a beatific sort of glee. Oh, man. I did *not* like that smile. "You know them as the Fates. The Moirai. Clotho, Lachesis, and Atropos."

I doubted she was close to her sisters, or this conversation would be going a very different way. No, if I had to guess, Deya had no idea her sisters were the ones who sent me here.

"If I remember my Greek mythology right, the Fates have a lot of sisters. Nyx was a busy little bee on the making kids front. Which one are you?"

"Well, the historians didn't give us names since there used to be a thousand of us. We are known as the Keres—goddesses of violent deaths. But there aren't that many of us left these days."

Well, at least I was right about Deya not being a witch. But if she left my team alone, then she couldn't be what the storybooks said she was—a bloodthirsty thing with no remorse.

No, she was something more than that.

"You made *grigri* bags and gave them to a shifter. Bags that hindered Fae and witch magic and turned shifters into feral beings. I want to know who asked you to make them."

I had to at least try to get the information I'd come for. If she didn't answer me, then I would just have to think of something else.

"Contrary to popular belief, but I don't actually give a shit what humans do to each other."

Sure, and she was in one of the most dangerous cities in the United States for the food. I didn't believe that for a second.

"They weren't humans. They were witches. Shifters," I countered. Not if she did that to humans it would be okay, but she needed to get her story straight.

"Humans. Ethereals. You're all just monkeys with magic to me. What do I care if some idiot wants to destroy the world as you know it? Every few millennia there's something else that destroys you all. What difference does it make to me?"

"So a goddess of violent death doesn't care when people are

slaughtered? I don't believe you. And there's no way that demon made you forget who he was. So, who was he?"

Because I knew it was a demon. The same one who had enslaved Cinder's mind. The same one who kept himself hidden from Embry. The same one who pulled Elias' strings. He was a heavy hitter if there ever was one, and she knew him.

Footsteps sounded from behind me, and a welcomed voice had all my muscles turning to jelly.

"Yes, Deya, do tell." Alistair drawled in that crisp British accent of his. "What demon was making deals with you in my city?"

At that point, I didn't give a shit if I owed him a favor or what he'd ask to collect. He was here for me and that's all I cared about. This was the second time Alistair Quinn had come to my rescue. I couldn't say I liked the trend, but I sure as hell didn't mind him being here.

He was dressed in my favorite outfit for him—jeans and a T-shirt—the stitching on his leather jacket familiar, reminding me of the leathers he'd given me. He'd had those leathers made—probably by the same person who created the jacket he now wore. I wondered if it had the same protection spells woven into the leather. Protection spells that had likely kept me alive while I was being poisoned by rowan.

I owed him more than a favor. Not that I'd tell him that.

Candlelight flickered off an obsidian pendant hanging from his neck. Its twin hung from my own, the pair a homing beacon for the other. When I'd chosen my jewelry for tonight, I'd forgotten about its mate, and I hadn't expected Alistair to keep the charm once its purpose had been fulfilled. But there the pendant swung, and that's how Alistair found me.

He studied the circle of salt around me for a few moments, rage igniting behind his eyes as his gaze snagged on the ropes burning my skin.

"Your city?" Deya shot back. "Why would you think this city was ever yours? And what gives you the right to come into my domain?"

Her domain? Did she mean the cemetery? Because a crypt in

the middle of a cemetery totally seemed like a goddess of violent death's domain.

"You took someone that belongs to me. I want her back, Deya. Unharmed. On top of that, you actively participated in the deaths of fifty-three witches. I'm sure your sisters would love to know of your involvement. Shall I tell them?"

I was stuck on the "belongs to me" part of the conversation, so I was a little late on the uptake when Deya replied.

"Who's to say they don't already know?"

"Your sisters sent me here to find out who is behind this. Your sisters are in the middle of this. That demon has managed to tap into Lachesis' mind. That demon is actively attacking your sister as we speak. What do you have to say about that?"

Deya Baptiste was pissing me the fuck off. With my rage, I poked pin pricks through the threads of her spell. Elias Flynn couldn't hold me with the power of a hundred souls and neither would she.

The faint tremors could barely be felt at first, but they grew, sounding like a gong through the crypt. I didn't know if I was shaking just this chamber or the whole fucking city, and I didn't give that first shit.

A sliver of a crack popped free just under the circle, funneling the salt down and away, breaking Deya's circle. I pushed some more, feeling the burn of the ropes sizzle against my skin. Blood trickled from my nose as I flexed more of my power, but I wouldn't stop until I was free of those bonds. As soon as I felt the spell tear, I was up and out of my chair, wiping the blood from my face.

I was using too much magic, and in all the wrong ways, but I wasn't going to be her trophy. I wasn't going to sit idly by while she scampered off with the information we needed, either.

"I want that demon's name, and I want it now."

Thunder rumbled outside the crypt, and I could feel the electricity of the lightning racing across my flesh. The candle flames scorched higher as I took my first step outside Deya's ruined circle. And promptly wilted, Alistair catching me before I could pass out.

But while I was worried about getting out of that infernal circle, Deya had been cooking up a diversion of her very own.

Rushing to the apothecary cabinet, she snatched a bowl from the top. The bowl she was working on before I'd woken up. Whispering a spell I couldn't place, she tossed the contents at our feet. Perfumed mist rose from the ground, enveloping Alistair and I in a cloud of smoke.

And what she hit us with would change the course of everything.

CHAPTER THIRTEEN

There were a lot of things you could get away with in New Orleans. Things that could get you tossed out on the street or thrown out of clubs in most places. Stuff that could get you arrested elsewhere were simply a matter of course in the Big Easy.

Making out with a man in the back of a cab while you actively tried to remove his clothing was one of the things people just shrugged at here.

I couldn't tell you why I was making out with Alistair in the back of a taxi when we had more pressing matters to attend to—not that I could tell you what the more pressing matters even were. All I knew for certain was that I needed to put my mouth on his skin, and I didn't really care about anything else.

Okay, I cared about other things, but those things involved more of the skin-on-skin contact and not much else.

I couldn't say why we were in a cab—neither of us needed to use conventional transportation—or why exactly I could not stop tasting that spot just underneath his jaw, but my focus was acutely concentrated on causing him to make that sound in the back of his throat. It was like silk over gravel, and it rumbled through the close confines of the cab in the very best of ways.

I felt that sound everywhere.

"You're gonna hafta gimme an address, buddy. Either that or get outta my cab," the driver griped from the front seat, and I should have felt a teensy bit of something that I was all over Alistair, but I just couldn't bring myself to give a single shit.

"Prytania and Third," Alistair rumbled, and that rumble was almost as good as his groan.

A nip from my teeth had his grip tightening on my hips, the heat from his innate demon nature warming my skin. I wanted his heat everywhere. I wanted him everywhere.

Our lips tangled, fighting for dominance as our tongues danced together, tasting each other. I couldn't remember being kissed so thoroughly in the four centuries I'd been alive. Everything in my mind, my body, wanted Alistair, and I didn't care about propriety or social convention. I didn't give a ripe shit about anything except getting his shirt off.

"Max, love, you have to wait. Just a little longer."

I may have growled at that, but soon his mouth was back on mine. I may not have gotten his shirt or jacket off, but my hands did get to explore underneath both. The delicious heat of him seeped into my palms as I ran them everywhere I could reach.

"We're here," the cabbie practically shouted at us, and I felt more than heard Alistair settle up with him.

I wasn't paying too much attention, too busy wrapping myself around Alistair like a vine to really notice. I barely caught it when we somehow got out of the cab—with me still clinging to him like a barnacle.

But I sure as shit felt it once we crossed the ward onto Alistair's property.

Lust still clawed at my insides, but I could think. *I could remember.*

I managed to pry my lips from Alistair's. I didn't want to. I wanted to taste those lips until I couldn't breathe anymore, but I did it. I couldn't make my legs unwrap themselves from his hips, nor could I manage to pry my fingers from his shoulders. The lips would just have to do.

"Deya did this to us. She spelled us." I gasped out the words, holding myself back from kissing him again.

"*Amor diebus fatalibus*. She was saying that over and over again. I'm afraid my Latin is a little rusty. What did she do to us?" Alistair's lips brushed mine as he spoke, his steps picking up again as he carried us further into his property.

Amor diebus fatalibus meant *fated love*, but I wasn't familiar with the spell. Also, there was no fucking way I wanted to tell him what those words meant. It was embarrassing, and weird, and...

He opened the door and we were in his house, but he didn't stop at the foyer. No, he carried me up a winding staircase, the details of such I couldn't say because I could not make myself look away from him. I couldn't make myself stop brushing my lips on his or holding onto his neck for dear life.

"Tell me," he murmured. The soft rub of his lips on mine mingled with the heat of him nearly had my eyes rolling in the back of my head.

"I know what the words mean. I don't know what the spell does. Gimme your phone." If I didn't have the faculties to figure out the spell—even though I had a general gist of what it did—I would call someone who did.

Alistair gripped my hips tighter with one arm as he fished his phone out of his jacket pocket with the other. All the while, his gaze never wavered from my face, and his body never broke contact with mine. I wasn't alone at least.

It took me a few seconds to remember the number and a sight bit longer to dial it. I didn't want to look away from Alistair, but I had to. Three rings later, I got a sleepy, "What do you want?"

Barrett's accent was even crisp half-asleep.

"What does an *amor diebus fatalibus* spell do?" I asked as Alistair turned us and sat on his bed. Yes. The bed was a very good place to be.

"Wow, that's a throwback spell if I've ever heard one. No one uses it anymore. It's a fated mates spell. If you cast it on two people who aren't fated to be together, then they end up killing each other. Brutally. If they are—" He paused to yawn, but I had an idea of where this was going. "They can't pull themselves off of each other until the spell has run its course. Usually after orgasms. It's meant as a distraction, and it's very effective if cast by the right person. Why do you have Alistair's phone?"

I didn't want to say. Nor did I want to tell him I was in the fuck-like-bunnies column of that spell.

"Is there a way to null out the spell? Reverse it somehow?" I asked. Not because I wanted to. No, I wanted to rip Alistair's clothes off and taste every bit of his skin. I wanted to do every single naughty thing my mind could come up with and then check to see if he could come up with more. But even though I wanted those things, I couldn't be sure he did as well.

"Not that I know of. Max, why are you on Alistair's phone asking me about a fated love spell?" Barrett knew the answer, I didn't know why he kept asking stupid questions.

"Look, I'm not in danger, but I got hit with some pretty potent magic. If the guys call you, I'm at Alistair's and I'm safe."

Barrett was silent for a second.

"Oh. Wow. Okay." He paused before giving me a boyish giggle. "Have fun? Use condoms?"

"Goodbye, Barrett," I said before I hung up the phone.

Somehow, I would need to explain all of this to Alistair. But how? How do you tell someone that a deity cast a love spell on you, and the only way we weren't killing each other right now was because somehow, some way, we were fated to be together?

Was that even explainable? And could I explain it when all I wanted to do was rip his clothes off with my teeth? Especially when he cupped my jaw in his hands. Fates, I loved that. That gentle hold he had on my face, the way his thumbs fit just under my chin. The way his blue eyes flickered to gold and back again.

"I heard what he said, Max," Alistair rumbled, his breath washing across my lips in the most delicious of ways. "You can stop trying to figure out a way to tell me."

I couldn't help the roll of my hips that brought a delectable little hiss from his mouth as my center pressed at just the right spot over the fly of his jeans. The fact that I was wearing a skirt and his jeans were so easily adjusted made me marvel at the fact that we didn't end up fucking in the cab on the way here.

"At least we don't want to kill each other?" I said it like a question, but more I just wanted him to laugh. When it rumbled out of him, I felt that joy through my whole body.

"True, but... I don't want to make love to you under the guise of a spell," he admitted. Knowing how much I wanted him, he had to have been feeling the same. And still he wanted to wait—knowing it was almost like torture to do so.

And that knowledge made me want to sully the shit out of him.

Spell or not, I wanted him. Spell or not, I remembered our first kiss and how much effort it had taken to pry my hands off him then. Spell or not, he was the first man to touch me since Micah that didn't make me flinch or want to run away.

"Do you know how long it's been since I haven't flinched when a man touches me?" At the shake of Alistair's head, I answered my own question. "Almost a year. Not since Micah. I think I like your hands on me."

Micah Goode had damn near enslaved me. The things he planned for me haunted my dreams even to this day. I hadn't had a good night's sleep since the day he walked into my shop. Before him, I used to hug everyone. I used to be... someone else. Micah Goode changed me and not for the better.

I shook my head and peeled Alistair's leather jacket off his shoulders. The coat was hung up on his elbows because he still hadn't released my face from his gentle hold. Alistair's grip turned a bit firmer, wrenching my gaze back to his.

"Max, love. You don't have to do this."

I couldn't physically make myself not kiss him then, and when his hands dropped from my face to land on my hips, I took the opportunity to shove his jacket further down his arms. Step one was the jacket. Step two was get him naked.

I was super fond of step two.

"And no one's making me. You want me, though, right? You

felt this before. Not from Deya's spell. On your own without all the magic, you felt like this, didn't you?"

His grip tightened on my hips, pressing me to him like he'd prefer to merge our bodies together.

"You know I did. Still do," he growled, his fangs nipping gently at my bottom lip. Those fangs spoke of how close he was to losing control. And the way his accent curled around the words released something in me that I had been holding back until now.

Hope.

A week ago, I wanted him out of my life. A week ago, I told him I wasn't a good bet—that he should pick someone else. Now, after all he'd done to find me, after all he'd done to let me be me, I couldn't keep pushing him away. I couldn't let myself shove him aside like I'd done so many others.

"Good. Get naked, Knight," I ordered, using his former title. "I have plans for this bed."

His smile was a flash of fang before my back was pressed into the fluffy down duvet, his delicious weight on me from the waist down as he tossed off his jacket. Now onto step two. My fingers curled into the hem of his T-shirt, yanking it up his torso. With a little help, it was off, and all I saw was corded muscles under skin decorated with black runes. I'd seen those runes lit up with fire when he'd been trapped in my circle, but I'd never realized they were etched into his flesh.

The pendant I'd given him swung between us and I snagged it, yanking him back down to me. Alistair got my hint because his lips were on me then, his heat seeping into my skin. His tongue tangled with mine as I reached for his belt. Together, we worked the stubborn leather free, but rather than waiting for his pants to be unzipped, I slid my hand in his jeans, the heat of him filling my hand as I gave him one slow stroke.

His growl was more feral then, and he caught my questing hands, holding my wrists above my head in just one long-fingered hand.

"Don't jump ahead. I have plans for more than just this bed, Princess. I've had more than a week to dream up all the ways I want you. I'm not going to be satisfied with just this bed or just tonight. I have a years' worth of plans, love. Centuries, even. Maybe longer."

I felt those words everywhere, but especially in my sex. Those words alone made my center clench, aching and empty and wanting him.

Breathless already and we had barely done a thing, I replied, "So you're saying you'll be using me for the sex. I can appreciate this."

Alistair's grin was all fangs as he ran his heated hands from my wrists, down my arms, along my sides to my hips. There, I watched his muscles as he bunched my skirt in his hands until he reached the hem. Questing fingers found the lace edge of my underwear, divesting me of them slowly, carefully, dragging the lace inch by inch down my legs.

When they were free of my ankles, he kissed and nibbled his way back up my body, his fangs grazing my flesh as he went. Once he had me shaking and—*I'm not even a little ashamed to say*—begging, his fingers expertly found the tie to my dress. Within seconds I was nearly bare, save for a diabolically uncomfortable strapless bra and then that was gone, too.

Alistair's fingers traced my ink as his gaze lit me on fire. He was beautiful standing there shirtless, his open jeans and belt exposing his black boxer briefs, his runes stark against his skin. They seemed darker than any black-and-gray tattoo, the pigment part of him in a way my ink would never be.

I watched as he removed his jeans and underwear, making him just as naked as I was. Then he covered me with his body, the slide of his skin against mine causing me to lose what little bit of control I had.

I'd always needed a taker, needed someone who would let me give all the parts of myself without artifice or barriers.

And Alistair took.

He took everything I had to give him.

I just hoped I would always have something left to give.

CHAPTER FOURTEEN

I woke up to the feel of Alistair's lips on my shoulder. It wasn't the first time I'd woken up that way in the last few hours, but with the pale light seeping in from the windows, it might be my last for the day. His heat at my back was fabulous, and it took everything in me not to burrow myself against him and go back to sleep. Well, either that or turn around and have another round of mind-blowing sex.

Really, it was a toss-up.

But with the spell Deya cast on us lifted, I knew I had other problems on the horizon, and going back to bed or consuming more of Alistair's attention was not on the docket.

Not until later.

I knew at this point I probably didn't love Alistair. Fated love spell or not. But I knew enough about myself to know that I *could* love him. If he stuck around. If I let him stick around. And for right now that was enough. I wanted to see where this would go—which was more than I'd given to anyone else in a long time.

"I can feel your brain working from over here. Anything you want to share?"

His voice was rough, either from sleep or an emotion I couldn't name, and I had to smile at the sound. That sound was like coming home to a warm bed and roaring fire in winter. I couldn't explain it any better than that. It was more than comfort, more than safety. It was something else altogether, and I really, really liked it.

"No, I'm good," I murmured, unwilling to tell him just what I thought of waking up in bed with him.

"Interesting. Because I think you really like the fact that you woke up in bed with me, and you just don't want to say. If I had to guess, I think you like me and are wondering what the next step is. You're having the exact same thought I am—you just don't want to admit it."

Turning over to face him, I opened my mouth to deny it, until I took in the flicker of hope on his face.

I settled with humor because it was my default setting.

"I dislike it immensely when you're right. Can't you just let me bask in the afterglow and make me breakfast?"

"I will once you give me a kiss. Then, you need to answer your bloody phone."

"My phone?" Honestly, I'd thought I'd lost my purse—and my athames—to Deya, because after she hit me with that stupid powder, I was out of sorts until right about now. It was then that I noticed Alistair was fully clothed. Interesting.

"I just got back from getting your things. Your pocketbook and your athames were all you were missing, right?"

I checked the charms around my neck and my grandmother's ring. Nope, all there. Other than my clothes, I wasn't missing anything else. It vaguely occurred to me that Alistair found me even with my grandmother's *hide me* ring on. Somehow my magic superseded hers in the amulet I'd given him. Interesting.

"Right. How the hell did you get my stuff back? After what she hit us with, I kinda figured she wouldn't be too receptive to a kind exchange."

"She wasn't there. None of her stuff was. Not the apothecary cabinet, not the idols and candles, not the witchy woo-woo shite she had all over the walls. Nothing. All that was left was your things and the chair you were sitting in when I came to get you."

I didn't like that one bit.

"That is not comforting at all. I should check the stuff you brought for spells. After what she did to us, I don't trust anything about that woman."

"You know she isn't a woman, right?"

"I know exactly what she is. And I know she used the *amor diebus fatalibus* to distract us. My only hope was she knew it wouldn't lead to our deaths, but there's no telling. She is not a friendly, and I'm checking every speck of my stuff to make sure she didn't put a locator spell or some other nasty on them."

Alistair dropped a kiss on my lips that lingered long enough for me to want to strip him naked and forget about this whole Deya business, but he was smart enough to break it on his own. Then he was off the bed, which I only now realized was a giant sleigh style in the middle of an opulent room. He grasped my hand and pulled me to sitting, the devilish grin that crossed his face when the sheet fell to my waist was an expression I wanted to see on him often.

I had to shake myself. Priorities, Max. Sex later.

"Clothes?" I asked, pulling the sheet back up to cover myself.

"It doesn't matter if you cover yourself or not, Princess. I know what's underneath that sheet, and it'll be burned into my brain for the rest of forever."

I felt a blush rise from my center all the way up to my face. Why, exactly, I didn't know. Maybe because all the decadent things we did to each other flashed through my mind. Maybe it was the way his mouth curled up to one side as he said those words to me. Maybe it was both.

"Clothes," I demanded.

Alistair nodded to the pile of frilly fabric that was likely my dress. Only… it was a different print. No, this wasn't mine.

At my frown, Alistair explained, "Ren procured you new clothes. He also went with me to gather your things from Deya."

"Ren got me new clothes?" I demanded because those words were not a question.

"It was in between round four and five last night that I made sure you would have something clean to wear when we finally wound down, yes. Would you have rather me go? You remember round five, don't you?"

A full-body shiver snaked through me. Oh, I remembered all right. Flashes of Alistair's body practically steaming in the shower, of our bodies wrapped around each other under the spray. I nodded, my anger fizzling out as soon as it came.

"There's underwear in that pile, isn't there?" Was that my puritanical upbringing rearing its ugly head? Maybe.

Alistair's lips quivered as he held in a laugh. Yes, I was born in the 1600s. Yes, I had issues with men who I wasn't sleeping with seeing my underwear. Sue me. "Max, Ren is older than I am. I think he's seen ladies' undergarments before."

"Fine. But if he makes a comment about them, I'll set him on fire. Deal?"

Alistair's laugh was a thing of beauty. It smoothed his perpetual frowning brow, it stretched those beautifully full lips just so, and when he threw his head back and the laughter fell from his lips, it was just so fucking stunning to see.

"Deal. Now, as much as I would like to take you to bed and never leave, the both of us have to deal with a load of bullshit today. So get dressed and check your things. And answer your bloody phone. Your people are probably worried about you."

He dropped a kiss on my lips and left the room to let me dress. Amazingly enough, I wasn't shy about being naked in front of Alistair, but we both knew that we wouldn't be done with each other anytime soon.

I pulled on my new clothes—that I absolutely refused to believe Ren picked out for me—and brushed my teeth after finding a new toothbrush still in the packaging. There was more than just a toothbrush and toothpaste laid out for me. There was face wash, moisturizer, lip balm, and deodorant in a French boutique bag sitting on the counter of the en suite. I decided to think of these things as an awesome gesture rather than super weird. Denial was my friend.

At least the dress was similar in style to the one I'd worn last night, and the undies fit.

As put together as I could be, I felt ready to attack whatever nasty Deya attached to my stuff, but when I inspected the phone, purse, and athames, there wasn't one. I even slit the lining to the bag to make sure there wasn't a hidden *grigri* bag. I was positive that I would be able to see it if there was a spell—locator or otherwise—on them.

Interesting.

I strapped my athames to my thighs again and stuffed the pocketbook under my arm. I needed coffee, but answering my phone was priority. It had gone off roughly five times since I started my inspection. Answering it, I mentally prepared myself for an onslaught.

"Hello?"

"Thank the Fates. For the love of all that's holy, please don't do that to me again," Della whispered, relief coloring her every word.

"I didn't mean to do it to you in the first place. I got knocked for a loop. You?"

"*Sí.* We were set upon as soon as we parted. *Colpeu-nos per darrere.* They were silent as the grave."

While I was pissed that they hit my friends from behind, I was surprised Della couldn't hear her attackers coming. Silent as the grave. Acolytes of a goddess of violent death might just be silent as the grave.

"I'm glad you're okay. How is everyone else?"

"Aidan is furious. Hideyo is confused. I'm resigned to the fact that we are dealing with more than just wayward witches, yes?"

"Have you ever heard of a Keres?"

The line went silent for a few moments. Then Della was yelling. "You're telling me we went up against goddesses of violent deaths and lived? *Deu meu.* We need to get the hell out of this city, Maxima. Where are you?"

I was torn on answering that. While I knew that we needed to get the hell out of New Orleans, we still needed the info that Deya had. And without asking the Fates outright, I couldn't figure out another way to get it. I needed to talk to Deya. I needed to see if she meant for me and Alistair to kill each other, or if she meant something else.

And I needed that demon's freaking name.

"I'll consider leaving. I need to make a few phone calls and get some coffee. Maybe even get a beignet or two."

"You did not answer my question, Maxima. Where. Are. You?"

I debated on pissing her off more. The last thing I needed was the three of them showing up on Alistair's doorstep ready to kidnap me back to Denver. Not that Alistair would let them, but still.

"I'm safe. I'm with Alistair."

I didn't know if Della liked Alistair, but I sort of hoped she did. "The same one you summoned to a circle? Current head of the demon seat on the Council. Knight of Hell. That Alistair?"

"Do you know of another one?"

The sigh Della made was as if her soul was trying valiantly to escape from her body. "Do I need to be more worried about you than I currently am?"

I didn't know how to answer that. "No?"

"That tiny little inflection at the end is not comforting in the least. You have one hour, or I will enlist Aidan and Hideyo to help me rip this city apart looking for you. Do you understand, Maxima? I will give a kitsune and a pissed off wraith free rein on destruction. Don't test me."

She was worse than Teresa.

"Max..."

"Fine. I'm at Prytania and Third if you need to look for me. Just give me some time. Deal?"

I would have hoped Della would be reasonable, but instead she'd hung up. I'd give her five minutes tops before she got here. That had me shoving my phone in my purse and hustling downstairs.

When I hit the landing at the top, I heard the sound of raised voices coming from what I could only guess was the entryway. As the foyer came into view, I could see an enraged Alistair, a pissed off Ren, and a redheaded woman I'd never met.

"Get her out of here, Ren, or I swear I will see her out." Alistair fumed, his words passing through gritted teeth. I didn't think his flowery words meant anything less than pure, unadulterated violence.

The woman was refined, if a little stuffy. It couldn't be later than six in the morning, and here she was calling on a man who did not want to see her at all. But as soon as she saw me on the landing, she was skirting around Alistair and coming right for me.

If it wasn't for the saccharine-sweet smile on her face, I would have pegged her as a legit enemy. While I knew she was a demon from the energies radiating around her body, I had no idea what relationship she had with Alistair. This felt more like emotional manipulation than an all-out attack.

Still, I was ready for either.

"Maxima," the woman gushed, her crisp British accent so much like Alistair's. "I'm so happy to meet you. I can't believe Alistair hasn't introduced us. I mean, with the marriage and all, I thought you would take time out of your schedule to meet your future mother-in-law."

It was a blitz attack, reprimand, and back-handed compliment all rolled into one. But marriage? Say what now?

I managed to skirt around the woman—no, Alistair's mother, I was guessing—refusing to let her touch me as she moved in for a hug. It was a feat on the stairs, especially since I was still processing the little marriage tidbit, and I was in heels.

I refused to give this woman my back, so I took the steps one at a time backward until I was down them and closer to Alistair.

"What in the blue fuck is this woman talking about?" I whisper-yelled at Alistair, hoping with all the little bit of hope in my heart that she was just crazy and not his actual mother.

"The arranged marriage, dear," Alistair's mother answered. "I'm so happy you two are going through with it."

What. The. Fuck.

CHAPTER FIFTEEN

In what world would anyone want me for an arranged marriage? I was the bastard daughter of the demon Andras, yes, but I was a half-breed tattooed freak with wonky magic. Esteemed breeding and poise I was not.

"Surely you knew about the arrangement, dear. It was your grandfather that made it. And honestly, if you two weren't carrying on all over town, I wouldn't be here now."

Okay, not only did I not trust this bitch, she was a condescending piece of shit in a pretty package.

"Tough to know about an arranged marriage since I was made a Rogue at fourteen, lady."

Ren stepped in front of me, arms spread wide like he expected Alistair's mother to come down from those steps and attack. His behavior was not comforting at all.

"Isolde, please see reason. You are just making it worse. Coming here barely past dawn because you want to cause a scene is not the way to make your case." Ren's tone was soothing, but it made no difference to his target. She was still smiling, but the little stretch of her lips seemed brittle and ready to crack.

But Alistair had zero compunctions about riling up his mother.

In fact, he was dead set on smashing her reason for being here in a hundred bits. I could respect him for that.

"That agreement was made a millennia before I was even born, Mother, and I told you I wouldn't honor it centuries ago. As I recall, that was the reason I was banished to the boundary as a Knight instead of being brought into the family business. If you think that since I now have a higher station you can come in here and steamroll me, you have lost every last bit of your mind."

So he knew about this so-called arranged marriage and didn't tell me. I'd file that away for later. For now, I would focus on the fact that he'd already told her no—years ago if his argument was to be believed.

If it could be believed.

"I also recall that Andras murdered the last man to try and marry off his daughter without his consent. You remember him? Abaddon? Andras murdered his own father to void that damn deal, and I can guarantee if my father insists on trying to push it, this time Andras will have help."

I thought Andras murdered his father because he was killing innocents. Was that a lie or was this? The only way I'd know for sure was if Andras told me himself. Good luck on that happening.

"Don't force my hand, Mother."

Isolde feigned shock. She was a good actress, I could give her that, but I knew a bullshitter when I saw one. Plus, every time she faked an emotion, the energies around her head would turn dark. She was her very own lie detector.

"How could you threaten me? I'm your mother," she insisted, like being a parent actually meant something.

"Look, lady. I don't know what game you're trying to play, but I know your son. I know he is good and honorable and pretty much everything you are not. You are not welcome in his home, and you are not welcome in my presence. I suggest you leave and not come back until someone invites you."

Isolde took one step down the stairs and then another. Her movements were lithe and sinuous, like she was a predator stalking her prey.

Ren and Alistair were now somehow in front of me, either they were protecting Isolde from me or the other way around, I couldn't figure out which. Well, until Alistair grabbed me and yanked me behind him, herding me backward. They were definitely protecting me from her, and I couldn't figure out why.

"You think you have the right to toss me out of my son's home?" she murmured, her head cocked to the side like she thought I was precious. The gesture reminded me of Durant, and he'd had that same exact expression up until I buried him alive.

With my free hand—because my right hand was still in Alistair's grip and he wasn't letting go anytime soon—I fished an athame out of its sheathe and pressed the rune to expand the blade.

I wasn't going into this shit unarmed. No way, no how.

Isolde's advance stuttered to a stop as she eyed the blade in my hand.

"You need to leave, Mother. And don't come back. Whatever he put you up to, stop it before it gets you killed."

I wondered who *he* was. I also wondered what power his mother had that was so bad he'd put himself in front of me to stop. Even Ren—who might like me but didn't know me—was putting himself between us at my defense.

"She will be one of us. And he will have what he wants. Make no mistake." She said it like it was a threat, until I got a fleeting glance of an expression on her cold face.

No. Not a threat.

A warning.

Without so much as another word, she stalked out the front door. When the glass rattled with the slam, I pulled my wrist from Alistair's grip and backed up.

I wasn't mad at him, but I was wrapping my brain around everything that just happened. Alistair's mother came here at the ass end of dawn after she heard of us together. How she heard, I didn't know. Maybe from Deya herself. But either Alistair didn't speak to his mother or he didn't want her in his home, so she knew coming here would cause a scene.

She didn't have to announce the marriage. She didn't have to say anything at all. She didn't have to come here at all. If she knew about Deya's spell—which the longer I thought about it, made the most sense—then she knew we might one day come to that end. And someone wanted this? He. She said: *he will have what he wants*.

Who was this *he*, and who was he to her? Maybe *he* was Alistair's father?

In the middle of my musings, Alistair grabbed my hand—the one not holding a sword—and took it into his own. He almost cradled it, as if it were precious to him. Maybe it was.

"I didn't know she would do this. I thought I made it clear that I wouldn't go through with an arranged anything. I swear, Max."

"I know."

Alistair stood at his full height, straightening from a slight crouch that had him at eye level.

"What do you mean, 'I know?'"

I yawned before pressing the rune to shrink the blade of my athame. Within a moment, it was re-sheathed, and I was headed to what I hoped was a kitchen. "Exactly what I said. Is there coffee?"

"Yes, Majesty. There is a fresh pot in the kitchen," Ren answered, and I tried really hard not to roll my eyes at the majesty bullshit.

"Ren, we talked about this. Beignets?"

"Of course. I procured Café du Monde's first batch of the day," Ren replied, skirting around me to the oven where he pulled out a hot plate piled high with fried bliss. I was so tempted to let the majesty shit go if it got me Café du Monde beignets. I'd heard they were little bits of heaven. I couldn't wait to try one.

"Would you like to explain the 'I know' comment? I would love to know if my balls are about to be permanently removed from my body."

Alistair was being cute. After last night, there was no way I'd remove that important bit of anatomy, and he knew it. I didn't answer him until I had a steaming cup of coffee in front of me and a warm beignet on a plate. Sitting at the expansive island in the middle of the kitchen, I sipped my coffee before biting into the best thing I'd ever eaten. It was sweet but not too much, a little firmer than a donut, and so fucking good.

I may have made sex noises at a piece of fried dough, and I wasn't even a little sorry.

Alistair cleared his throat.

"Oh, sorry," I said around the beignet and sipped more coffee. "Right. I know because you told her as much and she acted like she'd heard it before. Rather recently if I was guessing, but that would just be intuition talking. She came here after hearing about us from someone, maybe even Deya herself. She probably doesn't actually want the marriage to go through, either."

Both Ren and Alistair looked confused. Men.

"She came here specifically to piss you off and do the opposite of what she asked. Duh. If she wanted us together, the best course of action was to leave us the fuck alone. By coming here, she is maneuvering us to the opposite. And the warning at the end there? Yeah. Who is she talking about? Who will have what he wants?"

Alistair sighed and poured himself a cup of coffee, sipped it, and leaned heavily on the island. "My father. Soren. He's the one who struck the deal with Abaddon."

Soren. I'd need to ask Bernadette and Andras about him. Granted, that was likely handing out a death sentence, but I wasn't too mad at that. Not if what I thought was true.

I was looking for an ancient demon with enough juice to mind-control an Alpha dragon. Who better than a wheeling and dealing criminal who was trying to force his son into an arranged marriage?

Okay, so the connection was thin at best.

"But why? What does he gain by us being..." I didn't want to say married. If I said married, then I would give a full-body shudder and maybe vomit a little.

"Married?" he answered, supplying the dreaded word.

I swallowed a sip of coffee and bit into another beignet as I nodded.

"He gets access to the royal family—what little there is left—

gaining the status he feels he is *rightfully* owed," Alistair said sarcastically.

"Perfect. That means we really need to snap up Deya and get her to talk. She knows who she sold those *grigri* bags to. While we're there, we can ask her why she sold us out to your mother."

Alistair's eyebrows crawled up his forehead. "Why would she sell us out to my mother? Are you saying that my mother set us up?"

"Maybe. Maybe not. But it feels awfully coincidental, doesn't it? We're hit with that spell and somehow your mother gets wind of it? I know we weren't discreet, but we're in New Orleans. A girl making out with a guy isn't news, and it sure as shit isn't gossip worthy. Especially at this hour. Either your parents have someone watching you, or she was told by the person who did the spell."

"And why that spell?" Alistair asked. "Of all the spells she could cast, why that one?"

"We're being maneuvered, and I don't like it one bit. We need to get Deya, and I think I might have a line on how to do that."

I fished my phone out of my pocketbook, and dialed Della. When she answered, I said, "I'll give you coffee and all the beignets you can eat if you come to Alistair's house and let us explain the situation. Do not try to make me leave this city without information, Della."

I could feel her eyes narrowing through her silence. "I assume you want me to tell the boys to hang back?"

"Nope. They can come, too. I just need you to listen."

Della growled before she gave me a terse "*fine*" and hung up the phone.

"You might want to brew more coffee," I told Ren. "We've got a goddess to find."

CHAPTER SIXTEEN

"You want to do *what*?" Della asked, but I knew she heard me just fine.

I wanted to find Deya. What was so hard to understand about that?

"Your grandmother is going to set me on fire, you know that, right? Vampires are flammable, Maxima. I will burn and die because you're actively trying to get yourself killed."

I'd never known Della to be dramatic, but here we were.

"Deya Baptiste might be a goddess, but she could have killed me a hundred times over and didn't. This makes me think she might not want me dead. Now, she has information I need. Fifty-three witches are dead because of the *grigri* bags she made. Not to mention we have a dragon in human lock up, and an ancient demon using the Council as his own puppet show. I do not have the luxury of sitting on my hands because my grandmother doesn't want dirt under my fingernails."

Protection was one thing, but I couldn't just sit there and watch people getting hurt. I'd never been able to and I sure as shit wasn't going to start now. Not with Maria trapped inside her own head. Not with so many murdered like they were nothing.

"You are going to be the death of me, I swear. And you two are no help," Della griped, chastising Aidan and Hideyo for just standing there.

"You realize she doesn't need your permission. She is Sentinel, and she has a job to do," Hideyo insisted, his tone harsher than I'd ever heard come out of his mouth. I wanted to defend Della, but the man wasn't wrong.

"And I don't see Bernadette burning you alive. She'd probably just stake you," I joked, trying to break the iron tension around her shoulders.

"Stakes," she scoffed. "How ridiculous. Anything will die if you bludgeon its heart."

That wasn't true. I wouldn't die that way, and I was pretty sure Alistair or Ren wouldn't, either. I didn't want to bring that up, though. I had a tough time figuring out why I needed a set of paladins if my bodyguards were more vulnerable than I was. Della could actually be killed. So could Aidan and probably Hideyo.

But dying wasn't the worst thing. My friend Mena had reminded me of that many times over. And now that we knew I was deathly allergic to rowan, well, maybe those bodyguards didn't seem so bad. And maybe now that Della had seen me nearly bite it—pun totally intended—she wasn't so keen on letting me out of her sight.

"I'm just going to see if I can even find the woman. If I can do that, then maybe we can talk to her. Nicely. She seems to like politeness."

"We're doomed," Aidan said under his breath, but I still heard him.

I had a giant city map spread across the island in Alistair's kitchen. An amethyst hung from a silver chain in my hand, and I was about to start scrying for a goddess. A tiny part of me thought this plan was not even a little smart, but I didn't have much else in the way of options.

What else was I going to do? Go back to Denver empty-handed? No, I didn't think so.

I drew a circle of black salt on the map. I had a feeling Deya was still in the city, but I didn't have the luxury of hunting all two hundred square miles for her. Letting the amethyst pendulum swing, I tried to locate the goddess. The black salt followed the pendulum as it swung until it fell in a general area of the Garden District, where we were.

I tried the spell again, but all I got was the vague as fuck coordinates and not much else.

Growling, I fished a phone out of my bag and dialed Barrett. If he gave me shit for calling, I was going to murder him.

"Done already?" he answered, and my gaze immediately met Alistair's as I blushed.

"I'm not talking about that with you. Maybe ever. I need you to give your phone to Atropos."

Barrett sputtered, "What?"

"Look, I need to find one of her sisters and she is the only person I can think of who can do that. Since I'm only getting vague as shit readings, I need her to narrow it down for me so I'm not searching every bit of the Garden District for a freaking goddess, mm-kay?"

"You left some things out last night, didn't you?"

I pursed my lips as I tried to think of a good way to tell him to hurry the fuck up. "I was busy. And spelled. Are you going to hand over your phone or what?"

"Why didn't you just call her yourself?"

I shrugged even though he couldn't see me, throwing my hand out in the process. "We aren't exactly best buds, Barrett. We didn't exchange numbers and I figured my pay-attention-to-this-note spell would be rude."

"Fine. Here she is."

Atropos' voice sounded down the line, bitchy as ever. "Maxima. Why are you calling me?"

"I need to find your sister. Do you know where she is?" Direct. To the point.

"I have a lot of siblings, Maxima. You're going to have to narrow it down." No shit, she had a lot of siblings. She had—or used to have—thousands of them.

"Deya Baptiste. Keres. Goddess of violent deaths. Currently residing in the murder capital of the United States. That sister."

Silence reigned for about half a minute, and I figured Atropos was either thinking through her mental Rolodex of siblings or stunned stupid.

"She's in Lafayette Number One. Where she always is because she was banished there ages ago."

I remembered getting knocked out by magic dust nowhere near Lafayette Number One. And the cemetery she had me in? That was in the French Quarter. Yeah... Atropos needed to check Deya's tether.

"Umm... she slipped her leash, then. Because if you think she can't leave, you are wrong. She knocked me on my ass in the middle of an alley, and I was nowhere near that cemetery."

"You don't say?" Atropos growled, and I was kinda glad I wasn't Deya at that moment.

"I do say. Where is she? Deya has information I need, like the name of the demon responsible for all this bullshit. She made those *grigri* bags, she damn near killed me. And someone paid her to do it."

More silence as Atropos digested the information. I was under the impression that anything having to do with death, Atropos would be in the know, but maybe that wasn't the case.

"She is currently in the cemetery, and I'll do you one better. I'll make sure she can't leave whatever tomb she's using as a home base. It'll be up to you to find her, though."

That was something at least.

"Thank you."

"A word to the wise: Deya is not allowed to take lives, so if you know what is good for you, don't take hers, either. Do you understand?" Atropos' cold voice sent shivers down my spine.

I got her warning loud and clear.

"I hadn't planned on trying to kill a goddess, but thanks for the warning."

"What you plan and what actually happens are hardly ever similar, Maxima."

She wasn't wrong.

"I'll do what I can," I conceded, knowing that was the best I could hope for.

"I suppose that will just have to do."

A faint bit of shuffling came over the line and Barrett's voice smacked me upside the head. "Goddess of violent deaths. Are you out of your bloody mind?"

I took a second to think about it.

"Maxima!"

"No?"

"Your grandmother is going to set me on fucking fire, you know that, right?" Barrett griped.

"Funny, Della said the same thing." Was that me snickering? Maybe. But the two of them were being the biggest pair of overdramatic ninnies ever.

"It's not funny."

"It's a little funny. Deya had roughly a thousand chances to kill me and she didn't. She had me in a warded circle tied to a chair. She could have killed me a hundred times over. You know what she did instead? Hit me and Alistair with a love spell. While I'm not going to just walk in there without backup, I'm not as concerned as you are."

I was a little concerned. Hell, I wasn't stupid. Deya not only made the *grigri* bags that damn near killed me, she also took me out with a puff of fucking dust, so there was that.

"Now I have a goddess to question, so do you have any other grievances you wish to air, or can I go?"

All I got back was a grumble.

"I love you, too. Say hi to Marcus for me."

Barrett gave me a reluctant goodbye and hung up. The man was twelve hundred years old and I was probably giving him his first gray hair.

"I've got a location. Who wants to do a little grave robbing?"

. . .

I was not a fan of cemeteries. It didn't matter how many times I'd been near one, I shuddered every single time. I didn't like cities like New Orleans or Savannah, not just because they were witch havens, but because they had too many dead just sitting there piling up on top of each other. The ley lines beneath New Orleans were hotter than a nuclear reactor.

Lafayette Number One was a tourist attraction, crowded with people looking to see the places where books were set, or movies were filmed.

Humans.

Della had to persuade the local police to insist that there was a gas leak and clear out the entire place. Not that there was even natural gas in this section of the city or that there would ever be gas lines underneath a cemetery. Whatever comforting lie the humans needed to hear to get the fuck out, I was totally fine with.

Now we just needed to find the goddess. Easy-peasy.

The biggest problem with this particular cemetery—or any others in this town—was nothing was organized. It was like a corn maze of death. Yes, there were rows, but they ended abruptly only to fork off into a dozen different directions.

And there was no hope of GPS helping me out. A human might think their signal was crapping out on them. I knew better. There was too much energy from the corpses of hundreds if not thousands of dead to interfere with anything with a battery.

Aces.

"You don't have to do this, you know. We could try to figure it out another way," Della offered as I looked up from my paper map and eyed the entrance to the cemetery like a coiled snake.

"Not fast enough. Look, don't discourage me right now. Just stick with Aidan and Ren, okay? Hideyo will be with Alistair and me. We'll come in at the Sixth Street entrance and meet in the middle. Not that this map is even a little bit to scale, but whatever."

Della grumbled something about being burned alive as she moved into position with Aidan and Ren, but I just didn't have the patience to convince her otherwise. The dead made me uncomfortable in my skin.

It wasn't bloodlust, but it was something like it. There was a power calling to me, begging me to hold it, play with it, and I just knew that if I let myself, it would turn bad. That didn't mean I didn't want to follow the feeling. Something told me that the incessant call for violence and blood was Deya—her power gearing up something awful.

It was the middle of the day in New Orleans, but as soon as we crossed the boundary into the cemetery, the day turned to night. It couldn't have been later than ten in the morning, but the moon was above us now. When I finally got smart enough to turn back, the entrance to the street was gone, a tomb stood in place of where it once was.

"That isn't creepy at all," Alistair muttered.

"Can you feel that?" I asked, wondering if the call for violence was just me.

"Feel what?" Hideyo piped up, gripping the hilt of his sheathed sword tight enough to make the leather creak.

I had a hard time putting the feeling into words. "It's like a call for violence, and it's coming from there," I said, pointing to what I hoped was the east, but with the artificial night and moon, I couldn't be a hundred percent certain.

Alistair's warm hand in the middle of my back eased some of my fear, but I still wasn't quite comfortable with the wrath calling for me. "Follow it, love. We'll watch your back."

Pulling an athame from its sheath, I pressed the hidden rune to expand the blade. I didn't feel comfortable walking through this place without it, but I left a hand free just in case I needed to cast. I was ten feet into the first row when I felt the violence rise in me. A hooded figure appeared at the corner of a large crypt and then disappeared. I didn't know if he was hidden or had traveled?

I should have been able to see through glamours, but the ones Deya made for her acolytes were expert-level sorcery. Narrowing my eyes, I squinted into the night, looking for a shimmer in the air that would give one of them away.

Unable to see anything, a fire in me peaked.

"Fuck this," I muttered. "Back up guys and stay behind me."

"What—" Hideyo began, but Alistair grabbed him by the leathers and moved the kitsune just in time for me to snap my fingers.

Gathering the ambient magic in the air, I snapped my right hand while whispering a little Latin.

"*Somnum*," I murmured, hearing the thuds of Deya's acolytes as they hit the pavement.

"That's one way to do it," Alistair muttered.

I shrugged. "Sorry, I should have given you both more warning, but their glamours were too strong. I guess that's what you get when you have a goddess running the show. I think the way is clear, but keep your eyes peeled."

I also hoped I hadn't put Della, Aidan, and Ren to sleep, but I doubted the spell was strong enough to cover the whole block.

Moving forward, I stepped over hooded figures, following the pull that yanked on my baser instincts.

I heard the clash of blades before I saw the form of a man attacking Hideyo. His swords were a blur of steel, as he fought the hooded man. And something about that yanked harder at the wrath in me. I wanted the attacker to die. I wanted to snap his neck, and when Hideyo cut him down, I was actually disappointed I didn't get a chance to hurt him. And a tiny part of me wanted to hurt Hideyo for taking away my quarry.

"Maxima, love," Alistair murmured, pulling my chin to face him. I met his beautiful blue gaze and flinched at the concern.

I was not okay. Not even a little. If this was how Deya's power worked, I wanted no part of it.

"We have to move faster. Her power is calling and it's messing with my mind."

"Ready to run, then?" Alistair asked, snagging my hand and pulling me along.

The crypts were a maze of monoliths, but soon, I overtook Alistair and ran full speed toward that awful bit of wrath that yanked at my insides. That was until it threatened to overwhelm me.

All I wanted was blood on my sword. I wanted broken necks

and bloody hands. I wanted shattered bones and ripped flesh. Was this what a Keres really was? Was this what she was capable of?

"Can you feel it?" I asked again, but Hideyo and Alistair shook their heads. "You have to stay back. I don't know what I'll do."

Hideyo shot that down as soon as it came out of my mouth. "No, Max, we'll follow but farther back. Maybe it'll give us time to run if you turn murdery."

It was the best I could ask for under the circumstances.

"Try to keep me from killing her?"

Alistair and Hideyo shared a dubious look. Yeah, I didn't see that going too well, either. Rather than debate it, I turned and kicked in the crypt door. A smiling Deya was on the other side, sitting on her scarlet high-backed chair. The same one she had at the other cemetery.

"You rang?" I said snidely. And I had planned to be respectful. Shit.

"I'd say you rang first. Binding me to this crypt? Rude."

Smiling, I shrugged.

"I didn't do that. Atropos says hi, though. What, no chair for me? That's okay," I said as I snapped my fingers, pulling an ottoman from nowhere and taking a load off. "Where were we? Oh, that's right. The demon's name. I would like it, please."

Deya's smile turned rueful. "Doing my sister's bidding. How do her boots taste, I wonder?"

"Says the woman confined to a crypt. By the way, is this wrath feeling you? If so, bravo. No wonder this city is practically killing each other. You're doing a fabulous job, sweetie."

Deya huffed, crossing her legs and throwing them over one of the armrests. "What will really bake your noodle is, am I here because it's the most violent city, or is it so violent because I'm here?" She shrugged. "A question for the ages."

If I had to guess, it was door number two. I had no illusions Deya was responsible for more than a little death. It was her calling after all.

"Your stalling tactics are epic, darling, but I still want that name."

"You don't want it. You *need* it. These are two very different things. You want tamales and bourbon and world peace, but you *need* violence. It's what makes you. Everywhere you go there are storms and blood, and honestly, I'm inclined to give you what you need. If you do me a favor, that is."

Another favor? Other than not killing her? Doubtful.

"I want Atropos to lift the leash. I want to go anywhere in the city. Not just this cemetery and not this crypt."

And how much of her influence would taint the rest of the world if she got what she wanted? Would more people feel this wrath, this call to kill?

"Not if humans feel like this when you're around."

She huffed again and rolled her eyes, the wrath fled me in an instant. "They don't. I don't do that anymore. That was just a little incentive for you to come here. I didn't infect your friends, now did I?"

"Anymore" was the sticking point, and she knew it. She was banished for a reason—not that I knew what it was, but still.

"I can ask, but you know your sister. She'll do what she wants to."

Deya twirled a braid around her finger, giving me a long-suffering sigh. "If that's the best you can do, I guess."

Stalling. Why was this woman always stalling? "The name, Deya."

"Fine, but you aren't going to like it."

I'd be the judge of that.

"Soren Quinn."

She was right. I didn't like it at all.

CHAPTER SEVENTEEN

Of course the man I was looking for was Alistair's dad. I mean, why not?

"I suppose he thought I would be a good ally. With a past like mine, anything involving the violent death of innocents would be a no-brainer. My sisters and I used to be a vindictive, bloodthirsty lot. We took lives that weren't ours to take. Soren asked me to make up the bags, and I did it. He said he could get me free from my banishment. And he did for about two days. Now I'm stuck again, and the only way out is to help you."

Help me? Deya Baptiste didn't want to help me. She only wanted to help herself.

But if she was coughing up information, I wasn't going to dissuade her.

"From what I can gather, Soren wants to dismantle the Council. I don't know why exactly, but I do know he wants to use his son to do it. Something about ruling Hell. That was all I could glean from him in the short time we were together."

Maybe she was a mind reader like Clotho, or perhaps she could see past what was to be.

"Why should I trust anything you say? You're the queen of

distraction, and I wouldn't put it past you to send me on a wild goose chase."

Her lips twisted, a rueful smile mixed with chagrin. "Because it benefits me to tell you the truth. If I lie, you won't talk to Atropos for me. And... I might be feeling a little bit of guilt. Had I known the magic would have affected the shifters like that I—"

I cut her off. "You would have done the same damn thing, don't lie to me."

"Make no mistake, I would have still made the bags. I just would have added protection for the shifters. Those people didn't deserve what was done to them."

"Are you sure it was Soren? If I go back to the Council with this information, it's going to cause more than a few waves. I want you to be sure."

How was I going to tell Alistair that it was his father that caused those deaths? How the fuck was I going to explain that?

"Yes, Deya. Do be sure," a crisp British voice called out. *Shit.*

The scrape of stone on stone should have heralded Alistair's entrance to the crypt, but there was nothing. He moved quieter than I had anticipated.

"You knew your father was bad news, Alistair. I assumed you suspected him already."

"You and I both know it is one thing to suspect someone, and quite another to learn he was directly responsible for fifty-three deaths right under my bloody nose," he gritted out.

The edges of Alistair's flesh took on the cast of blackened charcoal, proof positive that his rage was getting the best of him. Not that I could blame him. Had my father turned out to be a flaming asshole, I'd be in the same boat. Oh, wait. I was in the same boat.

"Let's just take this information back to the Council. If they didn't hold Andras' sins against me, I highly doubt they'd hold Soren's against you."

Alistair's laugh was mirthless.

"Have you any idea what it has been like to have that man as my father? He's practically the reason Ethereals as a whole think demons are worthless miscreants. And no matter what I've done, he still manages to find a means to worm his way into it and turn it to complete shite."

Deya's laugh was just as joyless as Alistair's.

"Do you want to tell him, or shall I?" she asked me, and I winced. If Alistair was about to phase with just his father being named, he'd probably lose his mind once he found out his father wanted to use his son as a stepping-stone to dismantle the Council.

"Tell me what?"

Deya, unable to hold in the tea any longer, spilled. "He wants to dismantle the Council and use you to do it. He also wants to unseat her family and rule Hell."

A wave of heat whooshed through the room as Alistair's phase went from minimal to full-blown in an instant. Horns pushed up from his shoulders, punching through his jacket as if it was a personal affront. His skin blackened like soot—glowing runes carved into his skin like liquid fire. His eyes burned like hot embers, the fire in them full of wrath.

Yep, Alistair had lost the last bit of his mind, and if I didn't act soon, he was going to try and murder a goddess. Without much thought on my part—because I was hella flammable and Alistair was practically made of fire—I thrust myself between his advancing form and Deya.

"You need to calm your shit, Knight. She's giving us the information we need, and Atropos wants her alive."

His eyes blazed brighter as he spoke through gritted teeth. "I don't give a fuck what Atropos wants. Move, Max."

"No. I didn't just get you for you to sign your own death warrant now. Sorry, you're just going to have to take your rage out on your dad. I'll help."

Alistair's growl was something out of nightmares, but I didn't show even a little bit of fear. "Do I need to put you in another circle? Because I'll do it and damn the consequences."

He stopped moving forward, but it didn't look like he was happy about it.

Then I couldn't see him at all because I had a wraith in front of me for about a second before Aidan's hands closed over my arms, and I was pulled from the crypt.

Via traveling.

I *hated* traveling.

When we landed outside of the crypt, I stumbled to the pavement and lost my beignets.

"Prick," I gasped before puking again in a potted plant in a stone urn. Traveling felt like I was being ripped into tiny little pieces and put back together wrong.

Aidan waved a phone in front of my face, his expression a mask of stony silence.

"Hello? Aidan? Did you hear me?" Teresa's voice sounded through the receiver.

"Mom?"

"Max, honey. You need to get back here right now. Maria is awake."

Maria is awake. I'd been dreaming of hearing that for the last twenty-four hours. Had it only been a day? I was already a mass of goo on the pavement, but those three words made me wilt even farther with relief.

"I'm coming, okay? You tell her I'm coming."

Teresa's relieved laugh trilled through the line, and for the first time in maybe ever, I wanted to hug my mother. "I will."

I hung up and handed the phone back to Aidan.

"A simple 'Maria's awake' would have done the job. I hate traveling."

Managing to peel myself off the ground, I watched with amazement as the night turned back into day. Deya had lifted whatever spell she had on the place, at least. Unless Alistair killed her…

I pushed my way through Della and the boys to make sure he hadn't done just that. What I found was a still-phased Alistair eyeing Deya like she was a snake and Deya paying him exactly zero attention.

"My sister is awake, let's go," I called to him and watched in amazement as his body reverted to his normal form. Heat still shimmered off of him, but I'd take it.

Alistair turned to me, confusion on his face. Okay, so maybe I might have forgotten to mention Maria's condition in the middle of all this. Whoops?

"She's been asleep this whole time? It's been a week."

"Yes. And now she's awake. Let's. Go." I turned to Deya. "I'll talk to Atropos. I can't promise anything, but I will do what I said I would."

Deya nodded. "I believe you. It's in your nature to be honest."

Whatever that meant.

A sort of sadness fell over her face for a split second. "Good luck with your sister, Max."

I wanted to say the sentiment was comforting, but it wasn't at all.

In the end, we used a doorway to get back home. There were too many of us who couldn't travel instantaneously, and no one but Della could handle Aidan's form of transportation. My casting room was lit up with candles. My grimoires were strewn all over the place like Ian and Teresa had been hard at work, trying to figure out Maria's condition. As soon as I stepped from my casting room, I knew something wasn't quite right.

The house was silent.

No ruckus in the kitchen for the woman who hadn't eaten in a week, no shower upstairs. No talking at all.

I pulled out my athame, extending the blade as I took the stairs two at a time. Now that we knew Soren was on the loose and likely had an unhealthy obsession with both his son and me, I was expecting the worst.

What I got was an empty kitchen and a silent living room.

That's not to say that the living room was empty. No, Ian sat on the couch, quietly sipping bourbon in the dark. I didn't know why it physically hurt everything in me to see that.

Maria was awake. So why did his face look like a car crash?

"Ian."

Was that my voice? Was that all the pain I'd been carrying around with me spilling from my lips with that one word?

Ian sipped his bourbon, set it on a side table, and then brought both his fists down on my coffee table, snapping it to bits.

It wasn't the shock of Ian tearing up my living room that shook me to my core. It was every possibility of why he could be losing his fucking mind. The athame slipped from my fingers, and I felt Alistair holding me up as my knees threatened to drop me. Aidan went to his brother, trying to get him to calm down, but it took Aidan, Ren, and Hideyo to make him stop ripping the place apart.

Blinking furiously, I forced tears back and stood on my own. Step by step, I walked to Maria's room, ready to find her dead. Ready to see the absolute worst.

It made me regret every second I spent away from her. It made me regret all the years I watched her from afar, unable to make contact because of who I was.

When I reached the threshold, I was more than a little surprised to see Teresa's dry eyes and Maria sitting up in bed.

Then everything became clear.

Since the ordeal with Micah, I'd been able to see more than glimpses of energies. As a child, I'd get flashes of it, but as I aged, I often knew what people were before they said. Since Micah, those flashes turned into something more.

Every species of Ethereal had a different energy.

The motes of magic around Maria weren't even in the realm of witch.

No.

The swirl of black and orange was more telling than the look on my mother's face.

Whatever Bernadette had done to save Maria hadn't worked.

All that we had done to stop Elias hadn't worked. Everything we'd sacrificed, every life we'd taken.

None of it did a damn bit of good.

Because there was a demon inside my sister's body, and I couldn't think of a damn thing to fix it.

CHAPTER EIGHTEEN

The demon inside my sister's body refused to look at me. I couldn't tell if that was because she was a demon in a circle—demons tended to hate that—or if she was confused about how she'd gotten here.

I doubted the second option. Elias made a deal with a demon—maybe more than one. She had to know where she was. She had to know what she'd stolen from us. She had to know what she'd done.

To me.

To my family.

To Ian.

To everyone who had ever loved her, ever known her.

A line of black salt surrounded the bed, sigils drawn with chalk marked the boundary, kind of like a double circle. Mom wasn't taking any chances then.

"Did you put up the circle before or after she woke up?"

The sheer fact that I could say those words proved I had control. Because I wanted to rip the room apart like Ian had. I wanted to rip that soul out of my sister and watch as it writhed in my hands. Luckily, I had better control than that.

Teresa looked away from Maria's face—the first time she'd done so since I walked in—and seemed to think about it for a second.

"When she started to rouse. After everything that happened and how long it took her to wake..." She trailed off, shaking her head. Teresa was going to break and soon.

She needed something to do.

"I want you to do me a favor, okay? Call Barrett and Bernadette. They might be able to help."

Did I actually believe that? Not in the least.

Was I going to tell my mother that? Absolutely not.

"You're right. They might have seen this before," she murmured, proof positive denial was a powerful thing.

Teresa stood and passed me at the doorway. I wanted to hug her, the grief in her so potent, I could see it weighing her down. But I knew better. If I hugged her, she'd break just like I would, and the rage was all I had to keep me going.

I skirted the circle, taking Teresa's seat. I couldn't look at the bed yet, couldn't meet eyes that were Maria's but not.

"When she was born, I was so excited," I began, my voice nearly a whisper. "I didn't get to play with other children much, and when Teresa told me that I was going to be a big sister, I couldn't wait. Teresa—my mother—didn't like me or didn't understand me or she was afraid of me. And sometimes looking at me, she'd get this expression on her face like it hurt her to look at me. So, when Maria was born, all I wanted was someone, anyone, to look at me like I was something." I swallowed hard, the lump in my throat growing by the second.

"From the day she was born, she was my best friend. She was mischief and wonder and giggles. She was the only person to love me. She was my only friend. My only family." I glanced up then, taking in all of Maria's features that weren't hers anymore. The press of her lips, the set of her shoulders, the wild, frightened eyes.

The tears I tried to hold in crested my lids, flowing down my cheeks.

"So when you sit there in her skin, wearing her face, I want you to understand what you took. You took the first person to love me. The first person to show me what family was. The first friend I ever had in the world, my purpose when I had nothing else to live for."

I couldn't go on, telling this demon what Maria meant to me. I'd only had her in my life for such a short time. Only a handful of years, really. And the rest had been me on the outside looking in on a sister who couldn't ever really know me because of what I was.

"So you'd better pray to whatever deity you find holy that I can get her back. Because I didn't abandon my sister when I had nothing and no one, and I sure as shit won't be doing it now."

The demon started laughing then. But it wasn't a happy laugh. No, it was a half-hysterical almost cry that chilled me to the bone.

Tears welled up in the demon's eyes—Maria's eyes—as her whole body shook, her hands practically vibrating. She curled her fingers under, balling them into fists, but she didn't stop that awful keening. When those horrid sounds stopped, she began to cry, but as she did it, she began to speak.

"I didn't ask for this. I don't want this. *I didn't ask for this,*" she screamed, her hands rough on her own face as if she'd like to scratch her skin off but didn't want to hurt the body.

"I hope that's true, because if I have my way, you'll go back to where you came from."

Then I got up and waited in the kitchen for Barrett and Bernadette, and I prayed to no one in particular that my sister could be saved.

I was putting my casting room to rights when Bernadette and Barrett arrived. My apothecary cabinet was a complete mess, and once the grimoires were in order, I needed to fix that. Then I needed to dry more herbs, and maybe I needed to charge more of my crystals or something. Maria was always on me about that. I never had enough charged crystals or dried herbs. I didn't have cleansed tarot decks or a proper altar, either.

And I was focusing on making sure everything was organized and put back together rather than what Bernadette and Barrett might tell me. Teresa was more versed in the possession angle than I was, and she wasn't too optimistic. What news could they give me that wasn't as clear and concise as Teresa's face when she told me she called them to help us?

Alistair and Della had tried to talk to me, but I couldn't seem to articulate what I was feeling, and if I caught even a glimpse of pity, I was going to lose it.

But it wasn't Barrett or Bernadette who came to get me.

"How you doing, kid?" Marcus called from the open door. Not a stitch of pity was on his face, but I knew it was a mask. What else could it be?

"Shitty. You?"

Barrett and Marcus had gotten to know Maria in the six precious months I had with her. I knew they were feeling this, too.

"I'm doing just a little bit better than you are. They're ready if you want to be there. No one will blame you if you don't. The way Barrett talks about it, this isn't going to be pretty."

I knew they were planning an exorcism. It was just about the only thing they could do. But from what I'd read in my strewn grimoires, it was nothing like the movies. It wasn't a bit of Latin, a priest, and some holy water.

If only it were that easy.

From the description in my books, an exorcism loosened the binding of a soul with a body, and more often than not, the host ended up dead. I knew what was at stake, but I didn't know if I could handle the consequences should it pan out that way.

My brain was pitifully trying to come up with alternatives to what was coming. Or maybe search for something the surviving exorcism witches had that the others didn't.

So far, there wasn't anything of note.

"I want to be there. I'm just—"

Marcus leaned on the doorframe and finished my sentence. "Trying to gather the courage?"

How did he always know?

"Maybe," I said from my disarrayed altar, watching as Alistair joined Marcus in the doorway.

Alistair gave me a sly smile and held out a cut crystal glass filled with amber liquid. "If I give you a glass of bourbon and a hug, you think you can pull your shit together?"

I waggled my hand at him.

"Good enough. Come on, love. We have a job that needs doing. Drink your courage, and let's go."

Reluctantly, I stood, dragging my feet as I reached for the bourbon. Alistair passed the glass over and wrapped an arm around me.

"We're not giving up on her, love. Don't you, either," he murmured against my hair before dropping a kiss to my temple.

I wanted to be optimistic, but I couldn't quiet the voice in the back of my head that said I should have stayed home.

I let Alistair pull me upstairs to Maria's room. The bed had been moved to the centermost point in the room, a circle of salt, herbs, and small bones surrounded the bed. A square of the same ingredients surrounded the circle, white pillar candles sitting at the four corners. The demon wearing Maria was at the center with Ian, a stethoscope around his neck. His face still looked like a car crash, but he had a little hope left in him, which was something I was lacking. Aidan, Della, and Hideyo were at the corners of the room, weapons drawn and ready.

Barrett and Bernadette were finishing up their preparations. When Bernadette saw me, she wrapped me up in a bone-crushing hug.

"I'm so sorry, Max. I thought I helped. I thought—"

"I know. We did what we could. That's all anyone can ask of us, right?" I didn't blame Bernadette or Teresa or Andras or anyone else.

I just wanted this mess to not be true. I just wanted it to be fixed.

"We're ready to start," Barrett murmured, elbowing his way into our little huddle so he could hug me. "We've been talking to the demon. She is more than willing to release the body.

Apparently, Elias summoned her without consent and never made a deal with her. All she wants is to go back home."

That was in line with what she said earlier that I may or may not have been too cognizant to hear.

"Ian is monitoring Maria's vitals. He'll be here to make sure her body can handle it. Too many exorcisms haven't had medical staff on hand. This will make sure we don't go too far," Barrett added, trying to ease my worry. "Alistair is here to make sure the vacating soul goes back where it belongs—the rest of your paladins are here as backup. You and Teresa will act as a familial bond, calling to Maria's soul to expel the demon's. Have you studied the exorcism spells?"

I nodded. "What point do you want me at?"

I had to ask because it wasn't like I was an air or water witch. I didn't draw on anything but myself. My position in the circle was up to the witch casting it.

"I think north will do given your penchant for earthquakes. Teresa will be south, Barrett east, and I'll take west. Ian will be in the center with Maria's body."

North signified earth. I could work with that. Not that this was like any witch circle I'd ever been a member of—not that I'd been part of many witch circles in my day. Not too many circles consisted of two-and-a-half witches and a demon and a half.

We took our positions, and Barrett began the incantation.

"*Projiciam vos a facie mea. Hoc corpore dimittere. Vade exiit daemonium relinquunt corpus. Vade exiit ad inferos.*"

The translation to English was rough, the form of Latin more obscure than I was used to, but the gist of it was, "Get your ass back to Hell and leave this body alone."

I could respect that level of directness in an exorcism.

Repeating Barrett's words, I added my magic to the working.

"*Projiciam vos a facie mea. Hoc corpore dimittere. Vade exiit daemonium relinquunt corpus. Vade exiit ad inferos.*"

The candles flared, their flames ratcheting higher as Bernadette joined in.

"*Projiciam vos a facie mea. Hoc corpore dimittere. Vade exiit daemonium relinquunt corpus. Vade exiit ad inferos.*"

When Teresa's voice joined the cadence, the flames reached waist-high.

"*Projiciam vos a facie mea. Hoc corpore dimittere. Vade exiit daemonium relinquunt corpus. Vade exiit ad inferos.*"

Salt and herbs and tiny bones swirled at the perimeter of the circle.

The demon flinched, and then her whole body flailed. It looked like someone was yanking her soul from her chest—which I guessed was exactly what we were doing. I felt a tiny bit of hope at that moment. Each revolution of the spell ramped up the flames, and it wasn't until she started screaming, that my hope died.

If the demon wasn't fighting this, why was it hurting her?

Maria's body shook violently, and then she retched, blood spilling from her mouth. Instantly, I quit my incantation, praying the others would follow suit.

"Stop, stop, *stop*," I screamed as the room quieted, and the flames died.

Aidan tossed Ian his medical bag, and he started working on Maria's body.

But I knew. I knew it before Bernadette said it. "This shouldn't happen. Hearts stopping, maybe, but... This is wrong. It's like Maria isn't there at all."

Because she wasn't.

And I knew exactly where her soul was.

In Hell. Where she'd been all along.

CHAPTER NINETEEN

"Darkness and screaming. I'd thought she was in a dream state not that—" I couldn't finish that sentence.

I hauled ass out of Maria's room back down the stairs to my casting room. All this time I'd been trying to find the demon responsible. Well, I'd summoned his son to a circle by accident. I wondered what I could do on fucking purpose.

I had a vial of salt in my hand, and I was two-point-five seconds away from drawing a circle on my casting room floor and summoning his ass when Marcus, Alistair, and Barrett caught up with me.

"Don't you fucking dare, Maxima," Barrett ordered as I flicked the cork stopper off the salt vial.

I felt my eye twitch, and outside there was a crack of thunder so fierce, it shook the house.

"He stole my sister's soul. He has her in Hell and has been doing Fates know what for a week, Barrett. He's responsible for the deaths of fifty-three witches, the brainwashing of a Council member, and Fates know what else. If I can get him contained, I'd be doing this realm and every other realm a favor."

"Only to be executed right alongside him." That was from Alistair, and he said it like the words burned as they came up.

"Why? Because I was born an Arcadios witch?" The betrayal in that statement stung. Why were they just standing there? Maria was in Hell right this second.

She was screaming.

Barrett sighed, pinching his brow in his fingers and shook his head. It was Marcus who answered for him.

"It was outlawed for a reason. It's one thing to do it by accident. It's a whole other animal to do it on purpose. And you want us to look the other way? Baby girl, we can't do that."

His soft, gentle steps across the room hit me like knives, and when he took the salt vial from my loose fingers, I wanted to scream.

"She's *screaming*, Marcus. My baby sister is screaming in Hell. If I can't summon him, I have to do something else."

Didn't he know? I'd never left my sister behind. Not when I was a child with nothing and no one. Not when Elias had her, and none of the times in between.

"No one is saying give up. Just don't sign a death warrant right this second. We—"

I cut Marcus off. "You're just telling me to leave the man who did this to her alone."

"What did you say to me when I was going to go after Deya, Max?" Alistair murmured, his arm wrapping around my chest from behind. "'I didn't just get you for you to sign your own death warrant now.' Don't do this, love. We'll figure out another way."

Wet hit my eyes as I let my head fall back to his shoulder. If I couldn't summon Soren, I would have to figure out another way.

All I knew was none of these men were going to like what I was going to come up with.

There was no other way around the wait for the demon to wake up. After Ian stabilized Maria's body, the whole of us waited for her parasite to recover enough for consciousness.

That was an uncharitable thought, and I wasn't proud of it. The demon didn't want to be here either, and she tried to give Maria's body back. As it stood, none of this was her fault. It didn't stop me from feeling that way, though, and it was becoming harder and harder to check myself.

Della made sure I ate, and Alistair made sure I at least attempted to sleep. Aidan and Hideyo patrolled the perimeter, and Barrett and Marcus pored over grimoires they'd retrieved from who knew where. My father had come sometime in the night to comfort Teresa, and Bernadette poured enough tea down my gullet to make me spring a leak.

The one person I thought would be here never showed up, but I never really expected him to. He had a family to look out for, and that didn't include me.

Not anymore.

A few people came that I didn't expect, however. Aurelia and Rhys showed up sometime in the middle of the night sans kiddos. A part of me wondered if this many people in my house was a punishment for wanting a full house. For lamenting at the emptiness and all the unused rooms. I didn't like being tip-toed around, and I couldn't make them stop.

All I wanted right then was for everyone to leave.

To stop hovering.

To let me plan.

But no one left me alone. Hell, if I had to guess, Aurelia was the one making sure I wasn't left alone for a single second. And as I stared into my friend's pale, pupilless eyes, I wondered how much of this she'd already seen. If she knew my sister was in Hell already. If she knew her body was dying in the next room.

I wanted to ask, but I knew better. There was a whole host of things Aurelia didn't say on any given day because she knew the outcome. A believer in free will, she didn't want to influence others.

I tried not to hold that against her. I really did.

"It's not going to turn out the way you want it to," Aurelia murmured.

I shook myself out of my plotting and refocused on her. She was sitting on the edge of my bed, holding my hand. Alistair was sitting next to me holding the other. I wondered when I'd gotten up here but decided quickly it didn't matter.

"What?"

"Your plan. The one you aren't telling anyone about? It won't turn out like you want it to. It's going to go bad."

I clenched my jaw to avoid violence. "What plan?"

"I may be a few centuries younger than you, but please don't pretend I'm stupid. You can't do what you want. It will have consequences you are not prepared to pay."

If she meant my life, I could deal with that. If it meant a lifetime—hell, a hundred lifetimes—in a null cell, I could deal with that, too.

I pulled my hand from hers and from Alistair's. I sat up in that bed and locked eyes with my best friend. "If it was your sister, what would you do? Would you listen to a warning and give up? Or would you go ahead, knowing that it might not work out?"

Aurelia's stoic expression melted into one of pain. Her eyes welled as her mouth twisted.

Yeah, that's what I thought.

"I'd do exactly what you're going to do. Even knowing what I know."

"Then there's nothing left to say," I muttered, my voice breaking as I looked away.

Aurelia snorted. "There's more to say, just not to you." She shifted her body, staring at Alistair like he was a bug on her boot. "You will listen to her plan. You will aide her in her endeavors. You will hate every single facet of this plan. But I expect you to bring her out of this alive or die trying."

Alistair recaptured my hand, studying it for a moment before he laced his fingers with mine.

"That was always the plan."

. . .

When the demon inside Maria's body woke up, she seemed devastated she was still here right along with the rest of us. The fact that she did wake up was a good sign—at least for the host body.

"It didn't work. Why didn't it work?" she asked Ian over and over again.

Each time she asked him why, it was like watching him get stabbed in the gut. Smartly, Aidan got him out of the room before he started ripping the place apart.

Bernadette took charge of the demon, and once she found out who Bernadette was, it was a free-for-all on information. Being the Queen of Hell had its perks, I guessed.

The demon—Selene—was a lower-level demon, an imp of some kind with little to no power. She was stolen from her home months ago and sold. Not that I knew what an imp even was or what they did, but trading souls for power kinda seemed like a bad thing.

Who knew there was a black market in Hell? Not this girl.

But Bernadette and Alistair knew, I could tell by their faces. The wince that came over their expressions as Selene talked about being taken and sold was all I needed to know.

"There is a demon who buys us, stealing whatever power we have. We call him *neque sanctiores animarum*. Destroyer of Souls. He uses us to power old magic. A spell with no name, no language, in a place at the edge of nothing and nowhere. It is blackness there—even for those of us who can see past the shadows." Her lip trembled as fresh tears snaked down her cheeks. She clutched the blankets tighter.

It made me wonder why she would want to go back there. Ever.

"Why would you want to go back?" Della asked, stealing the question from my brain like a mind reader.

"I don't want to go back there. I want to go home. I have a family. A life. It's nothing like this, but it's all I know."

That statement made me wonder what Hell was like for the demons. Was it just another job, another way of living? Or was it something else?

I had a feeling I was about to find out.

"Do you know the man's real name?" I probed. I had a good idea who'd taken her, but I wanted to be sure. No one was going to get on board with my plan if I didn't have evidence—confirmation from a goddess or not.

Selene nodded, but she eyed Alistair like she didn't want to say. "I saw his face when I was sold. It was the last time I saw anything until I was brought to the circle."

Alistair nodded, his jaw set. "If it's who I think it is, you can say, Selene. We'll get him. I swear it."

She twisted the covers in her hands, her jaw clenching as she seemed to gather the courage.

"Soren Quinn."

I nodded and left the room, heading back down to the casting room to get my supplies. I had his name and a location. I was a demon and a princess. I should be able to walk in there and get Maria's soul back. Shouldn't I?

And what other option did I have? Bernadette had spent all that time with Elias and didn't know who was behind all this. Too busy keeping her façade in place to dig deeper. Andras was persona non grata pretty much everywhere—including Hell.

The way Aurelia worded it, I wasn't going to be able to go with anyone but Alistair. So maybe Bernadette and Andras wouldn't want me to go. I filled vials with salt and iron shavings, others with holly water—not to be confused with holy water—and a few with the ashes of my burning tree. In a few other vials, I put my sister's hair in one—*don't ask how I got it*—and a few drops of her blood in another. I filled a velvet-lined pouch with my bounty and headed back upstairs.

Rifling through my weapons stash, I picked my favorite bladed implements and got dressed, tossing my hair into a tight braid.

When I made it back downstairs, my friends were waiting for me, but it was my mother who stopped me on the last step.

"You had better not be doing what I think you're doing, Maxima."

I snorted out a laugh before pushing past her. "What do you think I'm doing?"

"Going into Hell, child," Bernadette answered my question. "That realm is not for you."

"Either I'm a demon or I'm not. Either I'm Princess or I'm not. Either I'm Sentinel or I'm not," I fired back, tired of all of the double-talk and riddles. "Either you're going to tell me why or I'm going. You pick. Give me a good reason why I can't go."

"You don't know the way," she whispered, skirting around me to bar my way to the door.

"I have a guide."

Bernadette looked over my shoulder where I knew my parents were standing. "I haven't had the time to tell you all my secrets, Maxima. There are things you don't know and..."

"Are any of those things more important than getting Maria's soul back? Don't answer that, because I'll tell you now that they aren't."

"Very well," Bernadette murmured, resigning herself to my half-cocked plan. "Who is going to lead you?"

Alistair joined me in facing my grandmother down, lacing his fingers with mine. "I will, my Queen."

Bernadette nodded, moving out of our way.

That was way too easy.

"Oh, Knight?" Bernadette called to our backs before we could make a break for it.

There it was.

"If you get a chance? Murder that son of a bitch father of yours, will you? Consider it a freebie."

Oh, she didn't need to worry about that. If I had my way, there wouldn't be anything left of Soren Quinn.

Not even ashes.

CHAPTER TWENTY

It was one thing to say you were going to Hell, it was quite another to actually go there. There were several entrances to that particular realm, but only a few we could actually go through without dying first. Being demons, we didn't need the more drastic methods of entry, a door in Aether would do just fine.

Funnily enough, I'd once told Caim that I would never go looking for the door I was currently searching for. It figured it would be Maria to make a liar out of me. I supposed since I wasn't looking for the door exactly, it didn't fall into the realm of lying. I was being led—there was a difference.

"Are you absolutely certain you want to do this?" Alistair asked, the first time he'd voiced any concern whatsoever about this bullshit plan.

I had to give him credit where it was due, he listened to Aurelia's every word.

"No, this is a terrible plan that will probably end in my ruin, but I'm gonna do it to get my sister back. Sound good?"

Alistair stopped at a door I'd never noticed in a hallway I'd never traversed. There were a lot of corridors in Aether, more hidden than not. The door itself was unremarkable. No carvings etched into the frame, not an inch of prettiness or ornament. If that was the door to Hell, I worried some poor soul would end up where they didn't belong.

"No, it sounds awful, and I don't like it one bit. But we're going because I refuse to be the one who tells you that you can't fight for family. Maria is your sister. If it were you instead of her, I'd be doing the same, and no one could tell me different."

Was it wrong to swoon right now? Because I really wanted to rip his clothes off and lick him in naughty places.

His smile was positively sinful as he caught my lips with his. "Later, love. When this is all over, we'll spend a week in bed, and everyone else can sod off."

Best. Plan. Ever.

"You ready?" he asked, reaching for the door handle.

Ready to go to Hell? No. Not really, but just think of all the jokes I could tell.

I was about to tell him yes when Andras appeared in front of us, blocking the door. Of course, Andras would feel the need to stop us in the most dramatic fashion possible.

"Bloody hell, man." Alistair cursed with a start, shuffling me behind him. Why he would feel the need to protect me from Andras, I wasn't sure, but knowing Andras, it really wasn't too far of a stretch.

"I want to talk to my daughter, Quinn. I know you Quinns think you have a claim to her, but you don't." Was snarling really necessary right now? Andras thought so.

"You mean the arranged marriage business? Yeah, I know all about it. Alistair and I aren't getting married, Andras. You can unclench."

Alistair drew up to his full height, which was eye to eye with my father. "I am not like my family. Do not paint me with their brush. No one will tell Max what to do. Not me, and definitely not you."

Andras seemed to consider Alistair for a moment before giving him a manly sort of nod. Was that approval? From Andras? Color me shocked.

"I still need to talk to you," Andras said to me. "Alone."

"Are you going to try to stop me? Because that won't work out so well for you. If you think Mom setting your head on fire was bad, just you wait," I threatened, cracking my knuckles.

"I'm not going to stop you."

"Fine. Alistair, can you give us a minute?"

Alistair dropped a kiss to my temple and gave us some space.

"I won't be far," he said, making sure Andras knew that he was in earshot if things got dicey.

Andras rolled his eyes in a way that seemed almost petulant.

"You aren't inured to the flames, and that is my fault. When you were an infant, your mother locked away some of your abilities. Most broke free, but..." He paused, shame coloring his face. "She locked you away—inside your own body—because I wasn't there to teach you. That's my fault. You can't go into Hell still bound. Will you turn around and move your braid?"

I wanted to be surprised, but at this point, I just wasn't. I didn't know which stories were true. Did Andras murder his father because he was killing humans? Or was it because he promised his granddaughter away under his son's nose? Did my father care about me? Or did he abandon me to be burned at the stake?

Or did he do all of these things to protect me?

I didn't think I'd ever know for sure.

With no reason not to, I turned around, sliding my braid to the side to expose the back of my neck.

"This will hurt, my sweet girl, but it must be done."

I didn't get another warning before pain lashed through my skin like a firebomb. My scream echoed through the corridor as the ground quaked beneath our feet. The floor split, green light spilling out, until all at once, it stopped.

The pain, the earthquake, the whoosh of wind that somehow whipped through the building.

All of it.

I fell to my knees, gasping in relief.

I glanced behind me to see Andras held at the point of a scythe, with a phased Alistair looking ready to commit murder.

"It's done. It had to be done. Max, touch him while he's phased, and you'll see."

Using the wall for balance, I staggered to my feet. I wanted to believe my father. I didn't know why. He'd given me no reason to trust him. But then again, none of the people in my life had.

I reached for Alistair only to have him flinch away. "Don't, Max. You'll burn."

"Maybe, but if I do, you can hurt my dad. If not, then he did us a favor."

Alistair's lip curled. "If she gets so much as a blister, I will send you to the depths and set the hounds on you. Then, I'll throw you in the river and let the souls feast on the scraps. I swear it, Andras."

"You know, I'm really starting to like you. You might just be worthy of my Max yet."

"I'm honored." I wanted to laugh at Alistair's deadpan delivery, but I was too busy trying to make sure I didn't burn my whole hand off.

When my hand made contact with his phased skin, I felt the warmth of it first. The fire didn't burn, but I knew it was there. Then the texture filtered in past the heat. His skin was craggy and almost brittle like charred wood, but strong, too, like stone or some sort of mineral. It was like he was made of embers.

I ran my fingers over the smoldering sigils carved into the flesh of his cheek and then pulled it back to check for blistering. Nothing.

"I ought to punch you in the face for letting me get burned at the stake. That shit hurt."

Andras pinched the edge of Alistair's scythe, pushing it away from his neck, taking a healthy-sized sidestep away from the blade.

"Yeah, well, you would have met Soren much earlier if I hadn't. Be glad, child. At least now you have a fighting chance. I'd go with you, but if I go, I can't come back. It's the price I had to pay for killing Abaddon."

It was now or never. If I was going to find out why he did what he did, I had to ask now.

"Did you kill him because he was hurting people, or was it because of me?"

Andras' smile was sad. "Both, kid. A healthy dose of both."

I supposed that vague as fuck answer would have to do.

"Here," he said, holding out a hand. I opened mine underneath it, and he dropped a handful of gold coins into it. "For the ferry."

Without so much as a word, he snatched me into a hug, kissing my hair as he did so, and then he was gone.

I opened my hand to inspect the six heavy coins. Around the edge, there were sigils I didn't know. At the center was an upside-down triangle over an inverted star with another six-pronged sigil underneath.

"That's Lilith's seal," Alistair said. "It should buy you passage both ways."

I hadn't thought of passage at all. "Do you pay every time?"

Alistair shook his head, closing my fingers over the coins with his hand. "I don't require passage. I'm not allowed on the boat. Put those in your bag."

That didn't make sense to me, but I did as I was told. "Why am I going on the boat then?"

"Because you do. You don't belong in Hell, Max, and Hell will know it as soon as you step one foot into the place. You need those coins. It gives you a pass from Lilith herself. Don't lose them."

"I won't," I muttered, tightening the tie on the pouch. As an extra precaution, I whispered an anti-thieving spell on the bag and the leather tie that attached it to my belt.

Certain his warning was clear, Alistair put his hand on the doorknob and turned. The door opened to a cobblestone bridge over black water under a blood-red sky.

"Ready?" he asked.

"Lead the way."

As soon as I stepped over the threshold onto the bridge, I felt a frisson of fear race up my body. But the earth didn't quake, and fire didn't rain down from the sky. Trust me, I was seriously concerned about both happening. The door closed of its own accord and then faded from sight. Even I couldn't see where it had been.

That was not comforting.

"Where's the door? How do we get back?" Was that my lily-livered ass talking? Yes, yes, it was.

He had the nerve to chuckle at me. We were in Hell. There were zero chucklings to be had. "We have another exit planned."

"We have a plan?"

"Okay, I have a plan. You have gumption, and a 'don't give a fuck' attitude, how's that?"

I snorted. "You know, some people would say those were the same things."

Alistair grabbed my hand and started walking down the bridge. The structure was wide enough for a two-lane road. If it weren't for the complete lack of guard rails, it would almost feel safe. As it was, though, the sea underneath us seemed too close, the sky not far enough away, and the air too thick. Everything seemed too close, like in a single moment the sea could revolt and pull me under, the sky could rain down on us, the air could choke us if it wanted.

The sky itself roiled, scarlet clouds churning in the too-close shadows. The sea did the same, black waves crashed into the bridge, sending a spray up and over the stone.

I started walking faster, dragging Alistair behind me as I booked it toward land. Well, until I saw eye sockets in one of the giant cobblestones.

We were walking on skulls.

Ohshitohshitohshit.

It was then that I realized that the bridge wasn't made of stone at all, and my anxiety about being in Hell really hit me. I may or may not have speed-walked down that bridge just shy of an all-out run.

"Max." Alistair chuckled.

"You're chuckling right now? We're walking on the dregs of people, and you're fucking laughing? What the shit, Alistair?"

"We're walking on the dregs of child murderers. I plan to relish every step of my boots, grinding their bones to dust as they're tortured somewhere in this place. As should you."

I thought about that for two-point-five seconds, and then I smiled for a second. It fell just as quickly as it came.

Tortured.

Maria's screams echoed in my head.

She was waiting for me.

CHAPTER TWENTY-ONE

I couldn't afford the luxury of walking—not when Maria was out there somewhere, wishing she could die. I may have scoffed at Alistair a bit.

When he looked confused, I explained.

"My sister is waiting for me. Likely being tortured by your father. A sense of urgency would be appreciated."

Alistair blinked at me for a second before something like chagrin passed over his face. "Got it."

If I could have run in this getup, I would have, but as it stood, I didn't want to shatter the bottles in my pouch. "Tell me again why we can't just snap our fingers and get there?"

Alistair shuddered and shook his head. "Magic doesn't work here like it does anywhere else—especially on the Earth realm. Don't use it unless you have no other choice. And your magic? You nearly tear the world apart, and that was before your father took away whatever Teresa did to bind you."

Alistair's eyes widened as he shook his head again.

"I don't want you to snap your fingers and rip this whole place apart. No, thank you, love. I have transportation covered. It's not as fast as you'd like it, but it beats walking."

Alistair jutted his chin toward the end of the bridge, where a giant gate stood in the middle of a never-ending wall. On either side of the gate, the walls went on forever. The barrier itself was taller than I could quantify. It seemed to fade into the sky, so I hadn't noticed it as we crossed the bridge. The gate itself was made of a blackened metal threaded through with enough magic to make it light up like a flare, while the wall consisted of something different. Sooty bricks of stone—each had a sigil that I didn't know—the mortar between them shimmering faintly with magic.

"That's a big gate."

Weirdly, the gates seemed more warded than the wall itself. I wondered if Alistair could see the wall's magic dwindling. Or was it dwindling at all? Just because the magic wasn't as bright, didn't mean it wasn't as strong. Still, I didn't feel good about just letting the observation pass.

"There are hundreds of gates. This is only one of them. Luckily, I know a guy who can open it for us."

Alistair knocked three times on the enormous metal door and waited.

"You know the magic of the wall is fading, right?" I whispered the question, afraid of saying those words too loud.

Alistair's head whipped in my direction, surprise coloring his face before his expression turned knowing. "You can see it." Not a question, a statement.

I nodded, staring at my feet before glancing back to the bridge. The magic and mortar that held the bones together was fading, too. "The bridge, too, I think."

"It's been an ongoing problem. We think someone has been siphoning off the magic. We've been working on it for a while."

I gave him a mirthless laugh. "How much you want to bet your dad has a hand in this?"

There was a commotion at the door as Alistair answered me. "All my money and yours, too."

Aces.

Did I want to devote my brain power to the fact that the barrier to Hell was failing?

No, I did not.

Was I going to while I searched for my sister? Yeah, I was. "What does Bernadette say?"

"She thinks it has something to do with the barrier to Faerie. Someone might be trying to knock down the gate between them."

I had a shitload of questions.

Like, why the fuck was there a barrier between Faerie and Hell in the first fucking place? Who was responsible for that design flaw? And siphoning power? That sounded like a demon we both knew, and the more problems that came up, the more it looked like Soren was responsible for all of them.

I thought Samael was bad. Then again, he might have been in league with this asshole.

The biggest question of them all swirled like a maelstrom in my head.

What happened when the magic in the wall was gone? I had an idea, and it was not a comforting thought.

Gears turned within the gate; metal screeched as the sound of locks turning echoed through the air. The gate cracked open maybe a foot or two, and a familiar head poked out.

Felix looked a bit different since the last time I'd seen him on the dance floor of my presentation to the Fates. No longer did he have the debonair tuxedo and slicked-back hair. Now he sported fighting leathers and silver armor on the left side of his body. The silver had sigils carved in it that might designate his house or family line or maybe his commander.

"'Bout time you guys showed up. Come on, the horses are getting restless."

Horses?

Alistair led me through the gate. On the other side was a barren desert, backed by a craggy mountain range. No people, no buildings, no trees, no nothing.

Well, *no people* was a stretch. Standing next to Felix was the ever-irritated Donovan. His red hair actually resembled flames as it gave the finger to gravity and wafted above his head as if he were underwater.

Donovan held the reins to the pair of black stallions, their red eyes glowing in the perpetually dim light. The animals seemed friendly enough, and one pulled at Donovan so he could come sniff me. The horse snuffled at my ear before resting his head on my shoulder, almost like a hug. I'd never had a horse do that, so I sent a questioning glance to Donovan.

"He likes you," Donovan informed me, and was that a spark of niceness in his tone? "His name is Erebus. He will guide you to the ferry."

I reached up to the bridge of the horse's nose and ran my fingertips over the coarse black hair. "You're a handsome man, aren't you? I appreciate your help, Erebus."

Donovan looked on with approval. Huh. This was a very different reception than I'd gotten the last time we met.

"How are you these days, Donovan?"

He glanced past me, eyeing the wall like he could see the failing magics like I could.

"I've been better, but I suppose you have, too," he said and passed me the reins. "Go find your sister, Max, and good luck. And don't worry about Erebus, he'll find his way home once your task is done."

I muttered a choked "thank you" and mounted the horse. Alistair was already on his, and he waited for me to get situated before he started in on the directions.

"There will be souls that you will pass on this route. Do not converse with them. Don't even look at them. We will be going at a fast clip, so they likely won't be able to reach us. Don't stop until we get to the ferry. For any reason. This is not a safe place, Max."

I wanted to give him a "no shit" response since this was the entrance to Hell, but I didn't. He knew this realm, and I didn't. Listening and minimal lip was kind of necessary right now.

"Got it," I said softly, patting Erebus' neck.

"We're going to go fast, boy. I'll keep people off you, you worry about going as fast as you can, okay?"

Erebus tossed his head in what seemed like a nod, and we were off, the burst of speed wholly unexpected from any land animal. Honestly, it felt more like I was on a motorcycle with how fast we were going. I dared to glance behind me, and the pair of us were kicking up enough sand and dust that I couldn't even see the gate or wall anymore.

Soon we were passing people walking in the barren nothingness toward the mountain beyond. They looked nothing like the zombies I had dreamed up in my head when Alistair went on his rant about souls trying to get us. Still, I wasn't dumb enough to think the people futilely reaching for us were up for a chat.

We were in Hell. I was here for a reason, and I'd bet they were, too. Very different ones, mind you, but still.

Reasons.

The mountain stayed in the distance as if no number of miles traversed would bring it any closer. We went on like that for what seemed like hours, and I worried the steed beneath me would tire. But Erebus kept going, churning his legs faster and faster until the faint flicker of water came into view.

The closer we got to the shore, the more he slowed. Soon, we were at a canter, approaching a crowd waiting at the tiny dock with a carved wooden boat. The water was just as black as the churning sea that slammed into the bridge, only this ocean was calm as glass.

People milled at the dock, some sitting on the ground waiting, some yelling at an impossibly tall cloaked man holding a ferryman's pole.

"I've been here forever. I want to cross!" a burly man screamed at the cloaked figure.

I assumed the cloaked man was the ferryman, and if I were dead, pissing off the man who was taking me to my final resting place wouldn't be my first way to go. Then again, if my final resting place meant torture forever, I might be acting just like the burly guy, hoping my complaining added time to my stay on this side.

Alistair halted his horse and hopped off, and I followed suit. Granted, my dismount was ungainly and not even a little graceful.

Alistair took up Erebus' reins and led the horses to the shore closest to the ferryman. The horses drank from the river, and Alistair addressed the cloaked man.

"Charon, my friend," Alistair said, shoving the bellowing soul out of the way. The people behind the fallen soul murmured but didn't dare complain. "Please meet Max."

The arm of Charon's cloak reached for me, and a skeletal hand slipped out to grasp mine. There was little to no flesh left on the withered digits, but I nodded like I wasn't screaming inside my head.

"Nice to meet you, Charon."

Charon's head—or what I assumed was his head because I actually couldn't see into the cloak to make out a face—swung to Alistair.

"She is alive," he rasped, his voice like smoky gravel.

"That she is, but she has Lilith's permission to be here. She will ride the ferry with you, and I will meet you both on the other side."

"Very well. Max, do you have your payment for passage?"

I nodded and passed over two coins from my pouch, dropping them into his skeletal hand.

"Very good," he said, inspecting the coins I gave him. "Please board the ferry, and we will be off."

Alistair hugged me tight, whispering in my ear, "Remember what I said. Don't talk to anyone but Charon. Don't look at them, okay?"

"I hear you."

"Be safe, love. I'll see you on the other side."

The boat was small, closer in size to a skip than anything. There were four other passengers on my boat, two men and two women. Each of them appeared shell-shocked like they couldn't believe they were on the boat in the first place and didn't want to be there, second. I didn't blame them. I seriously doubted what was coming for them would be any better than a boat ride on calm seas. I followed Alistair's advice, not meeting the eyes of any of the passengers, and smartly, I sat in the back closest to Charon as we shoved off from the shore.

Everyone seemed to give the ferryman a wide berth, but not me. I was burning with questions. Was this the real River Styx? Had he always been the ferryman? Did he get time off?

Did I ask these questions? No.

Did I want to? So much. I had to fight to keep my lips zipped and not draw attention to myself.

Too bad, my silence wasn't helping me there at all. One by one, each of the passengers turned to stare at me. They whispered to each other in tones too low for me to hear, but soon their voices got louder and louder.

"She's different."

"Look at her eyes."

"Her skin is so bright."

The fourth man didn't say anything, but he kept moving closer, inching toward me like I wouldn't notice.

"Umm, Charon?"

The ferryman ignored me, continuing to push off the bottom of the river with his pole, hurtling us forward over the water.

When the man got within touching distance, I noticed the sky beginning to roil, the scarlet clouds twisting and turning, growing darker with a coming storm. The sea beneath us began to churn, tossing the boat this way and that. The man was knocked away when a particularly nasty wave smacked into the skip.

Lightning crackled in the sky, the rumble of the following thunder shaking me to my bones.

"This is you, isn't it, child?"

I winced. "Probably? It happens on Earth a lot when I'm riled."

Charon—or rather, his hood—nodded.

The shadow of a giant serpent slithered through the water, its body circling the boat, bumping it a bit with every pass.

The silent man and his compatriots began moving toward me again, inching closer despite the crashing waves.

Fear cracked through me. I sure as shit didn't want to make a swim for it with that thing in the water, and Charon didn't seem too concerned that his passengers were eyeing me like a snack.

Lightning cracked again, casting shadows on the souls' faces. The boat rocked from the serpent bumping the hull once again.

And I didn't know which was worse.

The water.

Or the boat.

CHAPTER TWENTY-TWO

Thunder boomed at the same time lightning streaked across the sky. Only this time, it struck the man closest to me, blowing him off his feet and tossing him into the water. Before he could sink below the surface, the serpent raised his head from the depths and swallowed him whole.

It wasn't a snake, more like a fin-headed dragon with blue-green scales and horns that curled into spirals. I wanted to think it was pretty, and if it weren't the most terrifying fucking thing I'd seen in my entire life, I would have. If this was what the Loch Ness Monster was crafted after, I could see why so many people stayed out of the water.

The serpent followed the boat, catching up and keeping pace. If I didn't know better, it looked like a puppy waiting for me to drop more food. Its snout came closer and closer to the boat, sniffing at the passengers at the front. But the other souls seemed to see the error of attacking me, preferring to stay seated.

The sea dragon almost appeared to pout when we made it to shore, but that didn't stop it from coming closer, barring my exit to the dock even as the other souls tore out of the boat. Fear laced through me for one hot second, and then Charon began to chuckle.

"He likes you, child. He thinks you're pretty."

I didn't know how comforting that was, but I think I'd take that over him eating me. The sea dragon snuffled at me before doing almost the same thing Erebus had done, resting his jaw on my back like he was embracing me. Only, this dragon was enormous, and it was more like a wet full-body hug.

"Zillah, quit accosting my woman," Alistair griped from the shore, the reins of our two horses in his hand.

The dragon—Zillah—chuffed at Alistair, ignoring him completely. I patted the dragon's body, which given that it was so damn big, was all I could reach.

"One of my friends is half-dragon, and he isn't nearly as majestic and fearsome as you are."

Zillah let out a dragony purr as he pulled back. I got an up-close-and-personal view of his face. Blue-green scales faded to purple closer to his fins, but each one was iridescent like a fish. His eyes were a fantastic midnight blue that faded to an icy color close to his slit pupil. Those eyes were intelligent in a way I hadn't seen on many other animals. Erebus had that same intelligence—like he knew exactly what I was saying, and if I tried hard enough, I could understand him, too.

"I appreciate the assist back there. Sorry, you didn't get more snacks."

Zillah bowed his head in such a way, it looked like he was shrugging. It was an odd gesture on a dragon, but it made me smile. Alistair held out a hand from the dock, and I stepped off the boat, the earth shuddering under my feet.

"Is that normal? Please tell me the ground does that for everyone."

"No, love, that's just you."

Aces. "The souls in the boat did not give me the option of not saying anything to them, by the way. They kept talking about my eyes and my skin. Do I look different here or something?"

Alistair was leading me to the horses like I couldn't walk on my own. Funny, he'd been doing a lot of that. Keeping a hand on me while I was on the ground.

"Something is going on, Knight, and you're going to tell me what it is before I get angry."

He sighed, glancing back at me for a second until we reached the horses. "Get on the horse, and I'll tell you."

"You're only saying that because you know I can't kill you while I'm on Erebus." Still, I got on the horse and absently started petting his neck to say my hellos.

"True," he said, mounting his own horse. "Your eyes glow, not with fire, but with magic. Your skin the same. And it did it before you crossed into Hell, so likely, Andras removed more than just a binder, he removed your glamour as well. The souls here can see you for what you are, a light, so they are drawn to you. It's why I've been a might bit more attentive than usual."

I huffed, wanting to be pissed at him, but just not able to scrounge up the energy for it.

"Fine. Just tell me next time, so I'm not blindsided by grabby hands, okay? So what's next on this plan of yours? Mine pretty much was get here. How to find Maria in this place is a little out of my wheelhouse. Unless I can use magic, but that might be a little dicey."

In a place where everything was amplified ten-fold with untested magic? Yeah, no thank you.

"We're headed to a market I know of. We've heard whispers that it has black market dealings. It might be where Selene was sold, and if so, they could know where Soren is. You up for that?"

The chance to fuck up a black-market dealer? Yes, please.

"Absolutely."

The journey to the black-market dealer was less than eventful. All I could see was desert, cracked, ruined earth, and the black mountain in the distance. There didn't seem to be a sun in Hell, just ambient light, so I couldn't tell how long we'd been here. The scarlet sky pushed in on us the deeper we traveled into the desert, and the mountain beyond never got any closer.

There also didn't seem to be a night, and I longed for a moon of

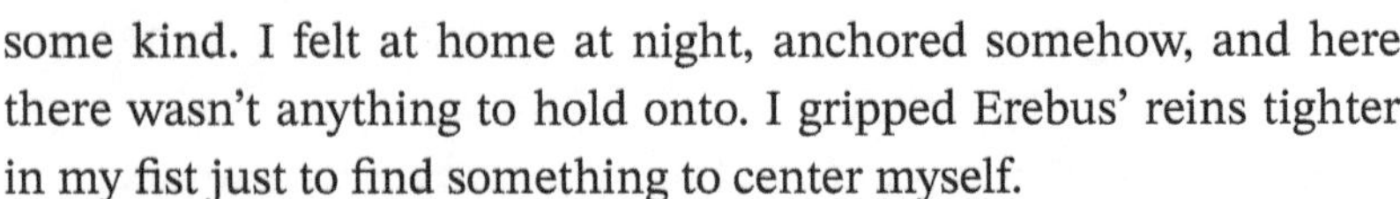

some kind. I felt at home at night, anchored somehow, and here there wasn't anything to hold onto. I gripped Erebus' reins tighter in my fist just to find something to center myself.

Occasionally, we would pass souls stumbling toward the mountain, and I had to think this was also somehow a punishment. I wondered if the mountain beyond was an illusion, and I figured it probably was. After a few more hours of nothing, Alistair slowed his horse to a trot before stopping altogether. There wasn't a marker or anything to suggest this spot was different than any other patch of cracked dirt.

But Alistair climbed off his horse, anyway. Despite my misgivings, I followed suit. My ass numb from the trip, I stumbled a bit. The earth beneath me pitched and shook as if it didn't like me being here. Erebus snorted and stamped the ground, stepping in such a way that his body corralled me closer to the other horse. The pair of them hid me for lack of a better explanation, and I couldn't figure out why.

"Stay where you are, Max," Alistair called, his tone wary if not a little frightened. I couldn't see him to check if he was okay, the horses blocking my view.

I wanted to do what Alistair said, but something in me wouldn't allow him to get hurt because of me. Not again. I used Erebus' saddle as a footstool and propped myself up over his back to get a better look. Three substantial black dogs guarded a door that seemed to have sprung up out of nowhere. The door wasn't attached to anything but air, and even still, it wasn't what I would call remarkable. It looked like one of those hollow-core doors one would see in a shitty apartment, and it was dirty, covered in soot and grime.

The dogs themselves were about the size of a shifter-wolf, their eyes red as fresh-spilled blood, and their teeth as sharp as knives. They growled in unison as if they shared a brain. Maybe they did.

I made kissy noises at the beasts, and instantly, they quit growling at Alistair. I didn't know if they were shifters or if they were really dogs. I didn't know if they were like Erebus and Zillah or if they were mindless. But I was in the presence of puppies, and I wasn't going to be scared no matter how sharp their teeth were.

I stepped down from the stirrup and managed to skirt Erebus despite his best efforts. Now level with Alistair, I knelt down on the ground, so I was face-to-face with the formerly snarling dogs.

"Hello, pretty puppies. I think we'd like to go through that door. Are you going to let us?"

Why I thought I could talk to Hell Hounds, I wasn't a hundred percent positive, but here I was.

The centermost dog sniffed at me before his tongue lolled out of his mouth. I let him sniff my hand, and he—or she, I couldn't be sure just yet—dipped his head under my hand for pets like any other dog would. The animals in this joint seemed to be super friendly. Soon, I had three noses in my face and was awash in doggy kisses. I gave as many pets as I could and a few scratches.

Did I turn into a fairytale princess when I wasn't looking?

"What in the bloody hell is with you and all the animals in this place?" Alistair broke in, wondering the same damn thing I was. "First it was Erebus, then Zillah, and now Hell Hounds? Really?"

Instead of answering him, I squealed when a particularly amorous hound licked me right in the ear.

"Okay, okay, okay, guys. Settle down." I got up off the ground, dusting off my leathers. "I'll give you more pats on the way out."

All three hounds sat down, but each one huffed as he did so.

Alistair snagged my hand, pulling me through the filthy door and into what looked like a tented bazaar. Stands filled with odds and ends littered the space. Each stand was unmanned, the trinkets dusty and unused. There was a still sort of silence to the place that didn't sit well with me. Not only had no one been here in a while, I had a feeling what we were seeing was a prop. No business was done in this place.

"Whatever you do, don't say anything, and please, for me, just look at the ground."

Alistair even pulled at the scarf I'd been using to keep dust from my mouth on the ride and pulled it over my hair like a hood.

"This isn't the place to be seen, love."

While I understood the wisdom in his words, I kind of wanted to punch him on general principle.

"Fine," I growled, petulant as fuck, but if it got my sister back, I'd do just about anything. Plus, eventually, I'd get to kick black marketeer ass.

He steeled himself and tightened his grip on my hand, picking his way through the rickety stands and narrow walkways. Eventually, we got to the front of the store—or maybe it was the back, considering how we entered.

Behind a particularly shabby counter, a behemoth of a man stood—if one could call this thing a man. With the face and head of a bull, the torso of a man, and a furred waist, I had no idea what this guy was. He didn't believe in shirts, either. He had hoops through his ears, nose, and nipples, and golden rings on every finger.

Alistair moved his hand like he wanted me to stand behind him, but the part of me that wanted to kick him for thinking I was the kind of woman who would allow that, only made me move slightly instead of completely behind him. Yes, that minotaur-looking motherfucker could see me, but he wasn't really looking at me.

No, his gaze was fixed on the Knight, and as he recognized him, he gave Alistair a toothy grin.

"Alistair Quinn, long time no see. Come to barter? Or maybe with the woman you're trying to hide, you've come here to sell."

Alistair shook his head, his voice just shy of a growl when he answered him. "Neither, Taurus. I've come for information."

Taurus gave him a smarmy smile. "Sorry, I'm not dealing in information today. Come back tomorrow, and we'll see."

Fucker.

"That doesn't work for me, Taurus. I want to know where my father is, and I want to know now."

Taurus chuckled darkly. "Too bad, I don't give a shit what you wa—"

Abruptly, Taurus stopped talking, taking in a huge sniff, scenting the air like he caught a whiff of something tasty.

Dread yawned wide in my belly, and I had to force myself not to take a step back. That plan went to shit almost as soon as I thought it, because Taurus was up and over the counter, knocking Alistair away with a flick of his hand. I flew with him, landing on a pile of junk.

The shattered edge of something sharp dug into the side of my cheek and the palm of my hand, spilling my blood on the ground. I struggled to stand, shock from the landing making me woozy. All too soon, my feet left the earth as a beefy hand yanked me up by my leathers. Giant hands turned me until I was face-to-face with Taurus.

Up close, he was scarier than he had been on the other side of the counter. His teeth were filed flat like a horse, but their edges seemed sharp, cutting. As he brought his face closer to me, I tried to struggle, but he was just too big. Taurus sniffed at me once, twice, before he snaked out a tongue and licked my cheek.

Oh, fucking gross.

"Who are you, and what are you doing in my market?"

Instead of answering him, I was distracted by Alistair coming at him with his scythe ready to strike. Taurus tucked me close and knocked Alistair away like he'd flicked a bug off his shoulder.

Alistair went flying again, and I had no choice but to answer him.

"I—I'm Max. Daughter of Andras and granddaughter of Lilith." I figured name dropping was okay, just this once if it meant this huge fucker would let me go.

Taurus chuckled mirthlessly, shaking his head. "You lie. I have tasted your blood, child, and you do not belong to either of them. No, you smell and taste of Fae."

I shook my head. "I'm not. My parents are Teresa Alcado and the demon Andras."

Taurus looked at me thoughtfully.

"That might be what they told you, child, but you aren't anything but Fae blood. I've tasted many of your kind, and you taste just like them." He said it like Fae blood was a favorite dish he missed because the restaurant had gone out of business.

Fae. There was no way. Taurus had to be lying, or mistaken, or… he was telling the truth, and everyone had lied to me.

My mother. My father. Bernadette. Caim. All of them. I didn't come up with the demon idea on my own. No, I'd been told I was a demon.

I wanted to believe the people closest to me wouldn't lie about something like that, but with their history of deceit, I just couldn't put it past them.

"I bet I'll fetch a pretty penny selling you," he purred in my ear, snuffling at my neck.

I shuddered, struggling to get out of his monster-sized hands. I couldn't reach my weapons, and Taurus was holding me so tight, I couldn't feel my fingers enough to snap them.

The growl coming from Alistair's throat practically vibrated in the space. "You will let her go, Taurus."

"Or what, Knight? Are you going to try to fight me? You won't win, and you know it."

"She is my wife," Alistair insisted, his voice a growl or warning.

Taurus huffed. "I smell no bond on her. She belongs to no one."

I met Alistair's gaze over Taurus' beefy shoulder.

"Remember that favor you owe me, love? I think I'm going to have to call it in."

CHAPTER TWENTY-THREE

He was bringing up that favor shit *now*?

"Are you fucking kidding me with that shit?"

Taurus, to his credit, bellowed out a laugh at my objection.

I didn't mean to protest quite so vehemently. Honestly, it just slipped out. But come the fuck on. *Wife*? I was no one's wife or wife material by any stretch of the imagination.

"Becoming my wife isn't the favor. Asking questions about this particular facet of our relationship is. *Trust* me, love. That's the favor. No questions, just do it."

Taurus took that opportunity to lick at the blood running down my cheek. It was either marry Alistair right this fucking second or deal with being sold. Or eaten.

Wild-eyed, I frantically nodded.

"Do you take me as yours?" Alistair asked.

"Yes," I croaked, and he sighed in relief before mouthing what I was supposed to say.

I sucked in a huge breath, steeling myself for something I couldn't name. Yes, I was being held against a wall by a minotaur. Yes, this was not how I'd planned this day to go, but still...

"Alistair, do you take me as your wife?"

"Yes, love." He seemed almost proud to say those words, and I supposed that went a little way toward making up for the ambush wife bullshit. Not a lot, but if it meant we got out of this, I was probably going to forgive him.

Someday.

"Fine. You've bound her. I hope you're happy." Taurus grumbled like Alistair had taken his favorite toy. Then, he dropped me like a sack of moldy potatoes.

I crumpled to the cracked earth, unable to stop myself from smacking face-first on the ground because my arms were numb from Taurus' hold. Alistair rushed to me, helping me up. Slicing his thumb with a fang, he ran the bloody digit over my wounds.

I couldn't figure out why he would do that when they would heal soon, anyway.

"We need to clean up your blood, love. The last thing we need is for another demon to smell it." He snatched a tablecloth from one of the stands and started rubbing at the blood on my face.

My breath whooshed out of me.

"Did you know?" I croaked, hurt lacing the question.

"No, Max. I would never keep that from you. Not ever." Alistair's phased golden gaze met mine, and I knew he was telling the truth.

"Aww, young love," Taurus trilled, sarcastically batting his bull eyelashes at us.

The fucker.

"Hey, Taurus," I called. "Want to see what a pissed off Fae can do?"

Without thought or a plan of any kind, I snapped the fingers of my left hand, binding his arms and legs with invisible restraints. The thunder that I'd wished for cracked outside the bazaar tent, the lightning flashing through the thick fabric.

"I'm not sure what my powers will do here, but I'm very interested in finding out. Aren't you? Now, I want some information. Since you aren't dealing in information today, I suppose I'll just have to figure out a way to entertain myself until you're inclined to give me what I want. Now, we're in Hell, so fire would be appropriate, but it feels too overdone. Hmmm."

I tapped my bloody fingers against my mouth, uncaring that Alistair had just scrubbed my face clean.

"Let me go, you fairy bitch. There's nothing you can do to me to make me talk. I've survived eons, and I'll continue on living after you're dust," Taurus spat, baring his teeth at me.

"You know, you're probably right," I murmured, my words like a threat.

I clapped my bloody hand to the side of his head, drilling into his mind to unearth everything I wanted to know.

Taurus was business savvy, plucking wayward souls like seashells. Every time he found a pretty one, he stole it. For the damned souls, that wasn't an issue. In fact, that was his actual job. No, the problem came when he found shiny souls that weren't damned at all. Demons, Fae traversing the realm, dragons, and the like. Shoving them in cages and selling them off to the highest bidder.

And typically, the highest bidder was Soren motherfucking Quinn.

Taurus delivered the souls personally to a place he called the Seam—the nothingness between Hell and Faerie.

I pulled out of Taurus' head and asked the question I knew he would answer. "Where is the Seam?"

Sure, Taurus' eyes, nose, and ears were bleeding, and Alistair was struggling to hold him up, but I was going to get answers.

One way or the other.

"P-past the mountain. Short—there's a shortcut in the back room. Too hard to take all those souls the long way," he answered, and I narrowed my eyes.

"Very good. Any traps I should be aware of?" Alistair asked. "Is he expecting a shipment?"

Taurus coughed, his blood spraying the air, but I managed to move out of the way before I got sullied.

"No and no. And it won't matter. What he's doing can't be stopped. Not by you, and surely not by this fairy bitch. What did he take from you, may I ask, to make you this stupid?"

I was sure my smile was feral, because even though his sight was slightly obscured with blood, he still flinched when I answered him.

"My sister."

As it turned out, there were several "shortcuts" in Taurus' back room. There were hundreds of doors back there. Some no bigger than crawlspaces, some so ornate, they had to go back to the human realm. And some, just like I thought, were black as night, and nearly impossible to see without eyes like mine.

Fae eyes.

Hadn't Barrett said something about my sight recently? How it was odd I could see magic? If I was a Fae—and I wasn't saying I was—it was possible that it made a whole hell of a lot of sense. I could see and smell magic when no one else could. I could draw power from myself rather than the earth or the moon. I could conjure from nothing...

I shook myself.

No.

I was the daughter of Teresa and Andras.

I was the granddaughter of Bernadette.

I was *not* a Fae, and the fact that I could see this door meant I was a special kind of demon.

Luckily, I'd decided keeping Taurus alive was a better plan than what I really wanted to do to him. That was to set the Hounds on him and see how long it took for them to get full. I was sure they would enjoy their feast, but that would have to wait until we returned with Maria.

Before we left, I made sure Taurus was secured, hogtying him with vines conjured from nothing. Vines that had poisoned barbs every few inches should he decide trying to escape was a good idea. Taurus wasn't too happy with me, but I had more than a few plans for him. The fact that he couldn't die, just made them all the more fun.

I studied the door that led to the Seam, unable to make myself just open it and file in. Yes, my sister was on the other side, but I knew better than anyone that just because I wanted to be able to get through this, I probably wouldn't.

"I need you to do something for me, okay?"

Something about my tone gave Alistair pause, and he snatched up my hand, yanking me around to face him.

"I don't know what you're about to say, but please, love, please don't. What did you say? 'I didn't just get you for you to sign your own death warrant now.'"

Regret washed over me. Regret that I wouldn't get a happy ending with Alistair. That I wouldn't get to tell my family I loved them one last time.

I pulled out a special jar I crafted from the ashes of my burning tree and my blood. It was fortified to hold precisely one soul. It was how I planned on returning her to our plane and past the walls. I knew all too well that there was no other way to bring her back.

Putting the jar in his hand, I closed his fingers around it.

"If for whatever reason I don't make it, this is how you take Maria back. And here are my coins for the ferry if you need them for her. I'm trusting you with this, Alistair. I'm trusting you just like you asked me to. If I don't make it, bring her back for me, okay?"

Alistair pressed his lips together like if he didn't, he'd scream at me. He looked like he wanted to smack the jar and coins out of our joined hands. Like he wanted to smash them to bits because if he had to use them, it meant...

"You're coming back with me," he insisted. "You are. There is no other option. Do you hear me, Maxima? I will pull you from the depths if I have to."

Then his lips were on mine, a fierce, hard kiss that made me feel like he was branding me with something I couldn't name.

"You're coming back with me," he whispered again against my lips. "No matter what. I didn't just find you after all these years to lose you now."

"Still. Hold onto them for me?" I murmured, my voice breaking as I looked into those golden eyes of his phased form. The charred, burning skin was starting to grow on me.

"I will, but only because you'll be getting them back. Understand?"

I only smiled.

I knew better than to make promises I couldn't keep.

In the end, it took both of us to open the door to the Seam. The doorknob felt like burning ice, and as I held it, it seemed to drain the very marrow from my bones. Stumbling back, I whirled, marching over to Taurus.

"Did you leave something out, you fuck? How am I supposed to open that door?"

Taurus' eyes held a malicious gleam, and I knew he wasn't going to answer me. Not without an incentive. My smile was feral as I clenched my fists in front of his face and watched his eyes bulge as the poison vines tightened around his body.

"F-fine! I'll tell you," he gasped.

I loosened his bonds only slightly as I waited for an answer to my question. He had five seconds to start talking, or I was going to make sure every thorn in those vines made their way into his flesh.

Five. Four. Three...

"It takes two. Usually, I use up one of the souls on the way, but if you want to live, it will take the both of you."

I didn't trust Taurus, but we were running out of time. We reached for the doorknob, and the metal siphoned magic from us faster than I thought possible. The two seconds it took to open the door felt like years.

Once the door cracked, we tossed it open together. The opening revealed a midnight path of cobblestones that were probably less stone and more bones and body parts. Beyond the path laid another door, only this one was ten-stories tall and at least fifty-feet wide. The arch of the entrance was an ornate stone carving of bodies in agony and devils torturing them with pitchforks.

It looked like the gate to Tartarus rather than the Seam.

And we were about to go through it.

CHAPTER TWENTY-FOUR

There was no way to stealthily open a fifty-foot-wide door. While I could most definitely snap my way into that room or castle or pit, it seemed like a horrible idea—even for me. The best I could do was see if my magic would let us pass through the damn thing without opening it.

I rifled through my pouch of goodies, hoping I was smart enough to bring chalk. When I finally located the bit of white underneath a shit-ton of vials, I breathed a small sigh of relief.

There was likely no way to go in there unnoticed, but I had to try something.

The chalk glided over the ornately carved door like butter, and as soon as I completed the drawing, the outer edges of it began to glow green. At first, I thought maybe the spell didn't work, but what I didn't realize right away was that the other side of the door was pure blackness. Uncertain, I held up a hand to see if it could pass through unimpeded. When my fingers drifted past the surface, I hazarded a guess that passing through this blackness was about all we were going to get.

Drawing back, I turned to Alistair, pricking my thumb with one of my athames and brushing the blood down the center of his forehead to the tip of his nose. *Ick*, but necessary as I copied a blessing my mother had given me what seemed like too long ago.

Alistair needed to be blessed before he followed me through that door. Staring into his eyes, I gave him what I could.

"I bless you with all that I am, and all that I will be. May you have safety on your travels. May your aim always be true. May you see what others cannot. May your victories far outweigh your losses. May your losses teach you, and may your love guide you."

I knew when my mother blessed me this way, she'd never expected to see me again. And now that those same words fell from my lips, I understood them for what they were. They were a wish for safety and security. A wish for someone you loved to keep breathing when you thought you might not.

There was more I wanted to say to him, more I wanted to experience with him, but we just didn't have the time.

Alistair pricked his thumb on his fangs and pressed it into the pad of mine to heal the cut, and all of a sudden, his eyes widened. His gaze passed over the door and the surrounding structure.

"Is this what you see all the time?" he whispered.

I nodded. "Don't get used to it, the sight will fade soon enough."

Together we approached the door once more, tentatively testing our hands with the barrier. When we felt no resistance, Alistair passed through first, and I followed. The ground beneath my feet seemed almost buoyant, like gravity was lax here. As my eyes adjusted to the darkness, I could faintly make out impossibly high arches and wall carvings, like we were stepping into a palace of some kind.

Maybe it had been once, but it felt almost abandoned now. And I said almost because I could feel the disturbance on the air of people—or souls, or demons, or things—moving around us. I couldn't see them yet, but they were out there. I wondered if it was good or very bad that I couldn't hear the screaming I'd heard both times I'd entered Maria's mind.

My gut went with bad.

I squeezed Alistair's hand, and we moved forward into the dark castle, stepping carefully as we traversed deeper into the blackness. I began to worry more when I realized a little too late that the fire under his skin couldn't pierce the darkness surrounding us. Even the runes carved into his flesh barely shone.

It was then that a man's hand closed around my throat, cutting off my air and ripping me away from Alistair.

"Max!" Alistair bellowed, his arms outstretched to find me in the dark, but I couldn't answer him.

Before I knew what was happening—okay, I knew I was caught, but still—or who had me, my body hit the wonky floor. I could barely see in this place, but I knew who had me, at least. A demon with shining eyes stood tall, looming over me like the god he thought he was.

Soren Quinn. It had to be. Phased he looked just like his son, charred skin, barely glowing runes and all. Only, his eyes were very different. Alistair's glowed with the fire of his demon. Soren's eyes were all black but still seemed to shine with magic.

My arms and legs brushed barely warm limbs of women huddled together in this dark place, and I wanted to search them for Maria. I did.

But I couldn't tear my gaze from Soren's. His smile seemed so smug, like he had a plan and I'd played right into it.

"Maxima Alcado. It's good to see you. I thought you'd never get here. Can I call you Max? Or should I call you by the name you were born with? Massima Bertrand Laffitte. The last living Elemental Fae in all nine realms. Do you know how long it took to track you down?"

I was still stuck on the bullshit name he called me. *Massima?* What kind of name was that? And *Elemental Fae?* Was there even such a thing?

Soren didn't like my silence and he reached down to close his hand around my throat again, picking me up off the ground like I weighed nothing. He shook me a little, bringing my face closer to his. He could see perfectly fine in the dim, and I realized all too quickly there was no way he was born with those eyes.

No, he'd stolen them. Probably from a Fae who could see in this place better than I ever could.

"*Detrahet me in lucem,*" I breathed with my last bit of air, snapping my fingers on both hands.

Light bloomed in my hands for barely a second before it fizzled away to nothing. He roared, the light searing his eyes for a few precious moments. The light was gone, but it was enough to get him to let me go, and that's all I'd really been after.

Scrambling backward, I quickly ran back into the cold bodies on the floor, the women shivering as they huddled together.

"Max?" a woman croaked, reaching for me with a weak hand. I grabbed at it as she searched in the dark for me. *Maria.*

I pulled her into a swift hug, and then I recognized the emaciated woman right next to her. *Lachesis.* Or rather, her soul.

Soren had stolen the soul of a goddess. A Fate.

I'd just made that realization before I was hauled up and away, flying through the air only to slam into a very solid wall, my skull knocking against the stone.

"You think one silly light spell is going to stop me? You stupid girl. Did you really think I didn't move all the chess pieces myself just to get you here?"

It made sense in a diabolical, evil mastermind kind of way. But I didn't know the details and I needed to stall him long enough for Alistair to find us.

"I kinda hoped you were just working on blind luck and a can-do attitude. Silly me."

Was it smart to antagonize the super demon? Probably not. Especially with blood running into my eyes.

"Your weakness is and always has been your family. Your parents, your sister, your friends. They weaken you. Make you stupid. I knew if I took your sister, you'd come right where I needed you. And I was right."

"What other chess pieces did you move? Besides Elias, Deya,

your wife, the attack on Aether, Cinder's brainwashing... Am I missing anything?"

I groaned as I tried to get my feet under me.

"Oh, wait, aren't you stealing the magic from the gate?" I added and watched with satisfaction as his eerie eyes went wide.

"So you aren't as stupid as I thought. I wonder if you've put together *why* I want you here."

"I gotta say, Soren, that I don't know. I know we're in the Seam, but other than that." I shrugged by way of answer.

I managed to stand, my balance completely fucked from the wonky floor and head injury.

"You're right we are in the Seam—the Seam between Hell and Faerie. Right now, it's a black void, a gate that lets no one through. But soon, it will be open, and you are the last Fae who can open it. Your parents thought they could hide what you are from me. Like I didn't strike that bargain with Abaddon because of what you are."

That didn't make any sense and I told him so. "You made that bargain before I was ever born."

"As if your Lilith is the only seer who can predict what's to come. I knew the daughter of Andras was going to be the key. I just didn't know you would be his adopted daughter. Then there was that mess with Abaddon, and I knew... I knew it was you. He killed his own father to keep you safe from me. As if killing him would stop the agreement. What really pissed me off was all the men I've sent to take you to me ended up dead right alongside him. That's when I knew I'd have to make you come to me."

And I had. I'd walked right into this fucked up castle and played right into his hands.

Faintly, I could see a figure standing at the archway between this room and the other. I wasn't sure if it was the entryway we'd come through, but it could be. The figure took small, measured steps toward the women huddling on the ground.

Alistair.

He needed to move faster. If Soren caught Alistair, he'd likely toss him into the void right along with me. And that was what Soren was saying, right? He wanted to open the gate, so sacrifice the last person to be able to do it. It was standard operating procedure for evil villains everywhere.

"Well, I guess you've won, then. Want to tell me why you want to open the door to a realm you've never even fucking seen, let alone could possibly be a big fish in? Tell me, how does that work? Is it a grass is greener situation, or are you just an idiot?"

Yes, I was taunting him, but I needed his eyes on me and not Alistair stealing back the souls that didn't belong here.

But Soren was too smart for that.

"Hello, *son*," he called before he flashed from in front of me and behind his son.

His fingers grabbed hold of Alistair's hair and Soren whipped him into the closest pillar, cracking the stone with a hiss. Soren wasn't done with him, though, because he picked Alistair up like a rag doll and slammed him into the ground over and over again.

White-hot anger surged through me, and without a thought, I snapped my fingers. I had no idea what my magic was supposed to do, but lightning arced through the room, a bolt shooting from my fingertips and knocking into Soren's chest. Soren flew off his feet, smacking into the wobbly ground.

I staggered toward the women and Alistair, falling to a crawl when my legs refused to hold me up.

"Maria," I croaked, "baby sister, we've got to get out of here. Can any of you walk? If so, you need to get up right now."

Using the last bit of strength I had, I performed a spell I'd been unable to do before.

"*Sanitatem*," I muttered, breathing health into my baby sister's soul. She had to make it. She had to.

"Get up, baby sister. Get the others. Get out of here."

With fumbling fingers, I clumsily yanked an athame from its sheath. Soren wasn't going to stay down. Not with all the power he'd adsorbed. He needed to die, and now.

"Max, what are you doing?" she asked.

I didn't rightly know. All I knew was Soren had to die. How I was going to accomplish that was a mystery.

"Killing the boogeyman, sweetheart. Like I've always done."

I had no illusions that cutting off the serpent's head was going to do any good. But I figured if that wouldn't kill him, it sure as hell would drain him of power. Maybe if I tapped his jugular like a keg, all that magic would come slipping out.

Only one way to find out.

CHAPTER TWENTY-FIVE

Standing was a bitch. A cold-hearted, miserable bitch. What little I could see of the room pitched, and I stumbled, nearly dropping my athame.

If I was going to do this, and by this, I meant cutting off Soren's head, then I needed to get my shit together. Steadying myself, I got within touching distance before he began to rouse. One would think a lightning bolt to the sternum would be enough to buy a gal some time, but nooooooo.

I was stuck with Soren the super demon and his plan for realm domination.

I didn't have the strength to lift the blade above my head, but I did have enough juice left in my limbs to stab the shit out of his belly. So that's what I did. Problem was, that little "poke" with my blade seemed to rouse him faster than anything I'd ever seen.

Okay, so I didn't "poke" him. I may have extended the blade on my athame and slashed his belly from hip to hip. One would assume that gutting a demon would offer her a little bit of dying.

Not so much.

Not a second later, Soren was on me, slashing at my fragile skin with abandon, his talons ripping into me like tissue paper.

Alistair charged him, knocking Soren off of me, but he fared no better than I did. Soren quickly got the upper hand, wrenching his son from him and tossing him away as if he weighed nothing. And then he was on me again.

"You will open this gate, Maxima, or I swear you will watch as I murder every single person you hold dear."

His talons squeezed my throat, as his stolen Fae eyes blazed with a magic I couldn't name. Unfortunately, I couldn't help but believe him.

"What will happen if I open it?"

"Does it matter?"

Did it? Yes. It did. If it meant Hell on Earth, if it meant millions of deaths, if it meant the end of us, then yes, it mattered.

"Yes." I seethed, putting as much venom as I could into that little, insignificant word.

"With your death, the wall between Hell and Faerie will fade away. Demons won't be beholden to our charges. We won't be forced to this life of servitude. Pigeonholed into a second-class citizenship because we punish the wicked. We will be free."

When he put it like that, I could see why he'd want to open the gate. Too bad I could smell the lie on him. It smelled sickly sweet on the stale air, and I knew he wanted more than freedom.

"Let Alistair, Maria, and Lachesis go. You let them go and I'll open the gate."

"Max," Alistair growled, "don't do this."

I could just make out Soren's smile, it was all fangs and falsehoods. He was getting what he wanted, why shouldn't he smile?

"If that is your bargain, I will accept. I will let them go."

That didn't mean he wouldn't find them again once this was all over.

"You let them go forever, Soren. You don't look for them, you don't have anyone look for them. You forget their names and faces. You forget they exist."

His smile was almost proud that I'd thought to cover my ass. "Of course, if that is what you wish, I will honor it."

"No, Max. He won't hold up his end," Maria insisted. "He'll kill us the first chance he gets."

I was counting on that.

What was the lore on fairy deals? If you made one, you'd better keep it, or your life would be forfeit. If I was a Fae, then he'd die the second he broke our deal.

"It's fine, Maria," I said trying to soothe her. "It'll be okay."

I might be dying in this deal, but I was taking him with me.

"Let me hug them one last time, and you'll have what you want."

Soren sneered at my request but set me down. "Foolish sentiment."

I staggered, barely holding myself up, but Maria caught me. Her soul was so strong. I'd gone into this knowing I wouldn't come back out of it. I just wanted one more hug. One more squeeze. One more chance to tell her all the things I couldn't before.

"You're going to make it, baby girl. You're going to go back and hug Mom and make babies and live an extraordinary life. That's all I ever wanted for you since the day you were born. So you do it, okay?"

"Not without you," she sobbed. "There hasn't been a time in my life that you haven't been there in the back of my mind. Driving me to question everything. Pushing me to make better choices. What kind of life am I going to have without you in it?"

"It doesn't matter, sweet girl. You'll have one, and that's what matters." I kissed her on the forehead, gave her one last hug, and stood on my own, swiping my tears away.

I moved to Lachesis, the soul of the Fate, haggard and far too thin. Soren had drained her, used her, and left her to rot.

"Tell your sisters I tried, okay? I didn't mean to fail them."

Lachesis' eyes gained a small spark of life. "I know, Maxima. It'll be all right."

I hoped she was right.

When I reached Alistair, he refused to look at me.

"You were supposed to come back with me, Max." He seethed, so mad that this was how it was going down, he could spit nails.

I'd tried to tell him, but he was so determined to be right, he didn't see that there was no way he'd get what he wanted.

"Come on, Knight, kiss me goodbye," I teased, even though my eyes were filling again, and my voice broke. "Please? I can do this if you're going to live. So kiss me goodbye and take care of my sister, okay?"

Alistair grabbed me, clutching me to his chest as if he never wanted to let me go. In turn, I cupped his face in my hands and kissed him with all the things I would never get a chance to say. When it ended, it felt too brief, not big enough for all the kisses we'd miss. But Soren wouldn't wait forever, and I had to make sure my people were taken care of.

Soren smiled when I started toward him. He reached for a piece of fabric I hadn't noticed with all the 'being tossed around' shenanigans. The fabric covered most of a wall, and when it was torn away, all I could see was a gilt-framed opening and the blackness beyond it. The nothingness appeared like pictures of black holes, the beauty of stars around a pit so deep nothing could escape it.

It probably wasn't the worst way to go. Out of all the times I'd died, it would probably even be peaceful. A sigh of resignation fell from my lips.

Four hundred years. Gone in a blink.

Without warning, Maria let out a screeching howl of rage, streaking across the room toward Soren with one of my athames in her hand. She'd extended the blade, turning it into a sword, and she wasn't stopping. She went right for him, ducking at the last second and shoving the blade through his middle to the hilt.

With a quick flick of her wrist, she brought the blade up, slicing toward his sternum.

Then everything seemed to slow down to fractions of a second that I only saw in flashes. Flashes of memories that would haunt me until the day I died.

Maria's vicious smile of triumph when she caught Soren by surprise.

Her dainty foot coming up to push him off the blade. Her pride at saving me for once.

Soren's shock as he fell backward toward the framed void.

His finger scrabbling at air until he caught Maria's wrist.

Maria losing her grip on the blade.

Maria falling with Soren into the nothingness.

We tried to reach her. Or at least I did.

But I wasn't fast enough.

CHAPTER TWENTY-SIX

I'd failed at a lot of things in my life. I failed at being a witch, at being a good daughter, at being anything but a blight on the universe. I couldn't recall a single thing I'd succeeded at in my long life that hadn't cost me more than I was willing to pay.

After Maria fell, I'd tried to get her, tried to reach for her. But I couldn't get close enough, fast enough. I'd been too late, and then Alistair hauled me away with his arm around my middle as I screamed for my sister.

Watching her fall.

I screamed for a long time, long after we made it out of the dark castle and back to the bazaar.

I tried bargaining. I tried threatening. But nothing I said made Alistair take me back to that castle. Alistair took every hit, every insult, every mean thing I could think of, and ignored it so he could haul me out of Hell kicking and screaming.

I petered out somewhere in the middle of the desert, but that didn't stop the tears. Alistair's way out of the realm was much faster than our way in, or maybe it seemed that way because I wasn't too lucid.

He held me close to his chest as we shared Erebus' saddle,

leaving the other horse for Lachesis. But these details filtered into my brain slowly, as if it took my brain far too long to process the fact that there was no going back.

I wasn't exactly sure how we got home, or how I made it from Hell to Aether to my bed.

Did it matter? Not really.

I didn't recall falling asleep on the trip, but I must have, right?

The tears stopped around day two, but that didn't stop me from staring off into space as I tried to wrap my brain around the fact that she wasn't here.

In fact, no one was here except Aidan, Della, and Alistair. Everyone kept a wide berth except Alistair. He made sure I ate, that I slept, that I sat up every once in a while. I couldn't say what my other friends did. I vaguely remembered them being here when we made it back, but when they realized we came back alone...

I wanted to care for their loss as well, but I just couldn't let my heart bend to another person's pain.

Not Teresa's, not Ian's. I couldn't care about them, or what was happening with Cinder, or where Striker was, or what would happen with Selene.

I wanted to be big enough to handle it—*them*—but I wasn't.

It wasn't until day three that Aidan made me go downstairs to eat. I sipped at soup and nibbled on crackers, but even I knew I was wasting away. I couldn't drum up enough emotion to care.

Numbness was my friend. If I stayed numb, then I could breathe a little. I couldn't even think her name anymore, that's how much it hurt. But I couldn't force myself to forget her, that was like drinking poison.

"Being your paladin is the worst job ever," Aidan griped, the first I'd heard anyone speak in days. Already I was missing the silence.

"Sorry you feel that way," I replied.

"If it isn't you trying to get yourself killed, it's you trying to save people who can't be saved. Or pissing off beings so out of your league, it's a miracle you're even still breathing. Corax, and Princes of Hell, and suped-up moon witches with axes to grind. Don't you care that your grandmother has a penchant for setting people on fire? And if you die, *I* would be next. Do you care? No, you don't."

"She's not really my grandmother, you know."

Aidan scoffed. "Just because you're adopted doesn't mean they aren't your family."

I huffed out a laugh. It was pitiful at best, but it was what I had.

"Bernadette lied to me, didn't she? She made you my paladin long before I killed Samael. You might not have hated me, but you wanted me out of your life. You tolerated me and then... you just pulled a one-eighty. What did she say to you to make you choose this job?"

Aidan stared at the carpet, his whiskey glass held loosely in his fingers as they dangled between his knees.

"She could see you needed help—"

"Don't lie to me. My father thought you were my mate because of the way you protected me, but I know better than anyone that you don't have those kinds of feelings for me. What did she say to you to change your mind?"

"She told me that if I didn't get my head out of my ass—or *arse* as she put it—that you'd get killed. That your blood would be on my hands because of my indifference. That I'd put my life on the line for my brother when he wasn't the one who needed saving. That I was meant for more than just saving Ian all the time. That you were more important than a promise I made a century ago."

"What promise did you make?"

"You know my scars?" he said gesturing to his forehead, to the puckered skin I knew was hidden under his beanie. "I got them for Ian. To get him free. His mother did that to me. It was my sacrifice to get him away from her. You know her. Her name is Deya Baptiste. I swore to her that I would protect her son. Swore that I would keep him from our father, and I have. But now I know that Ian never needed my help at all."

If Deya was the goddess she said she was, and Ian was her son, then no, he never needed his brother's help. Not even a little.

"But when I made my paladin oath, I didn't know what I know now. That you were as important as you are. But Bernadette is mighty convincing, and I made it because I needed more than just being a big brother. I needed more than just looking after him. I needed to be worth more than that."

"What will you do now?" I wondered aloud.

"My job, Max. The way you're glowing now, I need to hang around for a while."

That brought a smile to my face.

But it didn't last.

Anger came at day five.

They said there were five stages of grief: denial, anger, bargaining, depression, and acceptance. What they didn't say was that these stages could be felt simultaneously or out of order. Denial came first, but that only lasted for about a millisecond. Depression came next, and with it all the numbness that protected me. Bargaining was on a constant loop.

What if I'd have moved faster? What if she would have just let me save her? Was she really gone? And my personal favorite: *If I opened that gate, would she come out on the other side?*

Those thoughts were always there. Cutting at me every single second I was awake.

Anger came next, and the people in my life were feeling all the wrath I could muster and then some. Every stick of furniture in my living room was in shambles, the drywall scorched and cracked, the ceiling molding ripped from the plaster.

Nothing was safe.

Alistair tried to talk me down, but I couldn't quite look at him without losing it. I had a feeling he brought in Della because he knew I couldn't—or wouldn't—hurt her.

"You have to knock this shit off, Max," she said as she held a chair to fend me off like a lion tamer.

"Why? Why should I stop? I destroy everything I touch. I get people I love killed," I snarled, ripping a bookcase from the wall and watching as it smashed onto the hardwood floors. "Why shouldn't I rip everything I have apart?"

Della's tears didn't help my anger, it just made me madder, made me want to snap my fingers and destroy everything I could reach.

"I couldn't save Melody." *Smash.* "I couldn't save Maria." *Rip.* "All I do is kill and destroy, Della. Why shouldn't I rip this whole fucking place apart? Huh?"

Yes, I was screaming at the top of my lungs, hadn't showered in who knew when, and was in the middle of a living room's worth of rubble.

But what I said was still true.

I'd failed at everything. *Everything...*

I didn't realize I'd said those words aloud until Della contradicted me.

"You have not failed, Max. You went to Hell to save a soul that couldn't be saved. Maria died, sweetheart. She died and Soren stole her. She didn't belong in Hell, and she doesn't belong in that abyss, but you didn't do anything wrong."

That was all well and good, but I knew better.

"And Melody..." She trailed off, tearing a hand through her chestnut hair. "I wasn't here for that, but I know you did all you could. In fact, I have some news if you want to calm yourself down enough to hear it."

I eyed her warily, but I wasn't screaming or throwing things, so that was as calm as she was going to get.

"Remember that incubus that came to Aether? The one that wanted to talk to Striker?"

I carefully stepped out of a pile of rubble, wanting to be on solid ground for whatever she had to tell me.

"Yeah," I hedged.

"He has a problem. His parents adopted an infant. An incubus without a mother. A few days ago, the mother they thought was dead, came to their home looking for her son. A son she named Ronan."

I felt dizzy for a second, and I reached for the closest wall that was still sturdy enough to hold me up.

"She took him, the boy's mother, in the night while they were sleeping. Took him right out of his crib. But she left a note. Want to guess what it said?"

"Tell me," I ordered.

"It said that she'd taken him home with her. To Faerie."

Melody was alive.

I hadn't failed them all.

I hadn't failed her.

I was grasping all of this when Della asked her next question, one that hit me like a ton of bricks and buoyed me more than anything else ever could.

"So when are we leaving?"

PRIESTESS OF STORMS & STONE

ROGUE ETHEREAL BOOK 5

CHAPTER ONE

It was never a good sign to be drinking bourbon at ten in the morning, but after the week I'd had, I figured I was due. Self-medicating with alcohol wouldn't take the sting out of my grief, in fact, it was likely to make it worse. But I'd needed a teensy little breather from my housemates after the last truth bomb had been dropped, and wrapping my head around my new knowledge required booze.

I could feel Della's eyes on me, her acute vampire gaze boring a hole in the side of my face. She wanted an answer to her question, and she likely wasn't going to leave me alone until I gave her one.

When are we leaving?

That question echoed against the walls of my brain with enough force to give me a headache. Melody was alive. She was alive, and my sister was dead.

But that didn't make a lick of sense. Melody died right in front of me. I watched Aurelia send her soul on in a way only a phoenix could do. I watched her body burn in the flames of a funeral pyre. I needed answers before I could answer Della's question.

Because I wouldn't be leaving to hunt her down unless I was

sure this wasn't some kind of trick. I'd been tricked too many times in the last week, and I wasn't falling for another one.

"Melody is dead, Della," I whispered before taking another sip of bourbon, refusing to face my bodyguard. If I looked at her, I'd see either pity or censure, and I couldn't deal with either.

"Then why is her son gone?" Della pointed out a big hole in the "Melody's dead" argument.

Shit, fuck, and damn. I made a promise to Melody to keep her son safe. If it wasn't Melody who had her son—and I highly doubted it was—then I'd have to go get him.

In Faerie.

Aces.

But hadn't I earned a break? Hadn't I earned the right to let someone else take up the slack?

You made a promise. You swore. You can't turn away just because you're hurt.

Those words cut through my thoughts sharp enough to bring tears to my eyes. I did. I made a promise to make sure her son was safe. And I'd keep it. Maybe it would make my soul burn just a little less. Maybe if I did this one thing, losing Maria wouldn't hurt so bad.

Yeah, I doubted it.

I sniffed back the sting of tears, tossed back the rest of the bourbon, and managed to set the glass down without smashing it. I'd been on a smashing kick for the last little bit, and my living room had borne the brunt of it. At the time, I'd wanted to destroy everything Maria had ever touched. If I could just break it, burn it, wreck it, then it would have been like she wasn't stamped all over every molecule of my house.

Wasn't that stupid?

Like I wouldn't see her every time I closed my eyes.

"Okay, I'll give you that," I muttered, finally answering Della's question. "But I can't just bust down the door to Faerie and find her. If it is her. We need way more to go on than a note and a can-do attitude."

I peered down at myself. I had on black shorts and a black tank top. It was good enough for summer in Denver. All I needed was some flip-flops. Had I brushed my teeth today? Shrug. Was I wearing a bra? My tank had a shelf bra in it. It would just have to do. Plus, Barrett wouldn't give two shits about what I was wearing. I located my flip-flops in their spot by the door, shuffled my feet into them, and raised my hand to snap my fingers.

But Della pounced on my hand before I could complete the task.

"What?" My whole body was on red alert, my eyes searching my demolished living room and relatively untouched kitchen.

"You can't go out like that," Della whispered furiously, her face a picture of panic.

Frowning, I looked back down at myself. Yep, all my parts were covered.

"It's summer. Shorts and a tank aren't going to turn any heads no matter how much ink is on display."

A dawning realization lit up Della's face before she winced. "You haven't checked a mirror since you got back, have you?"

My eyes narrowed as a cold finger of dread raced down my spine. I tried to think of the last week since my return from Hell. I couldn't recall most of it, and the parts I could, I could say with the utmost authority that looking at myself in the mirror was not high on my list of things I wanted to do.

"I can't say that I have," I hedged, wanting her to tell me, so I didn't have to find out for myself. Who wanted to see puffy eyes and dark circles? And worse, who wanted to stare at the person who got her sister killed?

No, thank you. My psyche was fragile enough.

"You need to, Max."

I didn't want to, but I shuffled my feet to my bedroom. Sure, there were other mirrors I could use, but the one in the downstairs bathroom was right across the hall from Maria's bedroom, and I just couldn't. I couldn't see her touches everywhere, her favorite soaps, the spray of makeup brushes she kept on the shelf. I wondered if the brushes would still smell like her makeup, if the hydrangea blossoms she enchanted to never wilt or die would still be sitting in their vase on the counter. If her towel was still neatly folded on the rack.

I couldn't be in there yet. I wasn't sure I'd ever be able to.

I wasn't sure I'd be able to look up at the mirror either, and despite the murmured voices behind me, I hadn't yet gathered the courage. Warm arms surrounded my middle as a stubbly chin rested on my shoulder.

"You going to stand there all day, love?" Alistair's low voice rumbled in my ear. I couldn't explain the comfort I got from that voice. My body seemed to sigh in relief.

Yes, I could blame him. It was his father who stole my sister from me. Yes, it was Alistair who pulled me from Hell, keeping me from following my sister in death. I could blame him, but I didn't. The rational part of my brain refused to shovel the fault his way.

"I might. Is it bad?"

"There is nothing on this earth or the next one that could make you look bad. But you need to see, love. You need to know."

That sounded ominous. Internally, I counted to three and forced my gaze to move to the mirror. But the woman staring back at me wasn't me.

Her hair was blue, sure, but it was a color that you couldn't get out of a bottle if you'd tried. Her eyes were a shining golden hue, and her skin was practically luminescent. Her features were sharper, too, her cheekbones like a knife blade, her eyes just slightly tilted up, her lips a touch wider. And her ears... they were pulled into a rounded point.

This woman was a Fae. I was a Fae. Not a witch, not a demon. Not anything I'd thought I'd been.

"I look like a glowstick," I mumbled and watched as the light in those strange eyes flared.

And that was just a touch too much for me. Shoving out of Alistair's arms, I booked it out of my bathroom and down the stairs. I couldn't go outside like this—looking just like what I was.

A fucking Fae.

I needed Barrett. I needed Marcus. I needed to have a stern

talking-to with my mother about what in the unholy hell was going on. My chest burned with a scream that ached to be let loose.

Panic. This was a straight-up panic attack.

I needed Barrett. I needed him right now or I was going to lose it. And then I felt the pull—almost the same pull I felt when I'd accidentally summoned Alistair. It was similar to when I transported myself, but not. It wasn't like I was pushing myself through space, it was more like my mind was already where I wanted to be, and my body was just catching up.

Before I knew exactly what the hell was going on, I was standing in the middle of a Persian rug watching as Barrett screamed like a girl. Popcorn went flying, Barrett kersplanged off the couch, and if I wasn't so freaked, I probably would have laughed.

"What in the actual, all-encompassing fuck, Maxima?" Barrett griped from the floor. He was wedged between the couch and the coffee table, the remnants of popcorn in his hair.

I gestured at my face, my body, and my pointed ears. "You saw me when I got back, and you didn't tell me I was like this? I look like a glowstick."

Was that my voice sounding like a dying hyena? Maybe. But I appeared as if I took a bath in illuminator and followed it up with a glitter facial.

Okay, I was exaggerating, but still.

Barrett's delicate fingers plucked popcorn out of his hair as he leveled me with an expression so scathing my freak-out shriveled in on itself.

"You look like a Fae, Max. You look like an embodiment of magic so potent, it leaks out of your skin. You are beautiful, and just because you look different now doesn't mean you are different. You're the same as you've always been. A giant pain in my ass. So knock it the fuck off and get your shit together," he ordered and then paused. "Please."

That last bit was tacked on in a teensy effort not to hurt my feelings, and I couldn't help but laugh.

Then I asked the question that would burn me up inside if it was so. "Did you know?"

"That you were a Fae? Absolutely not. I definitely would have told you, though it does explain some things. A lot of things. It kind of makes me think we were bloody idiots for not putting it together sooner. It also makes me really want to tie your mother to a chair and peel her mind apart. The secrets that woman has." Barrett shook his head and I shuddered at the visual.

"Tell me how you really feel, Barrett."

"Oh, I will. Like right now, I'm feeling some kind of way about the bling on your finger. Is that a wedding ring?"

I chuckled for a second and then his words registered in my brain. My gaze traveled down to my hands to catch sight of a huge black diamond on my left ring finger. Shocked, I hid my hand behind my back like a child.

At my guilty-as-fuck action, Barrett's eyes widened as he sputtered, "Are you married?"

Was that a shriek? Yes, yes it was.

I rolled my lips between my teeth and didn't say a word, but I was pretty sure my wince gave me away. The diamond on my finger was most certainly a wedding ring because I'd married—or was bound to—Alistair on our little jaunt to Hell. Granted, it was so I wouldn't be sold into slavery or eaten by a Minotaur, but still.

Married was married.

There was a bevy of shit I hadn't told Barrett yet, but I'd been dealing with my own shit for the last little bit.

"How did I not know this? When? How? Moreover, who?"

At that second, the who decided to walk through the door, and I felt my eyes narrow. All Alistair gave me was an unrepentant grin.

"What the hell?" I asked as I waved my bling-laden hand at him.

"What the hell, what?" Alistair's grin widened on his face. That sneaky little shit. When had he snuck that ring on my finger?

I growled for a second and resisted the urge to stamp my foot. "When did you put this on my finger, Alistair?"

His grin faltered and he crossed the room in what seemed like an instant. "Do you not like it? You can take it off if you want."

His low whisper did something to my belly and I was struck with a pang of... of... it wasn't sadness, it wasn't regret, but it was something like loss at the thought of taking the ring off. I looked down at my hand, examining the ring more closely. The round black stone was three, maybe four carats, and it was haloed with tiny white diamonds and another halo of black ones.

It was perfect. If I'd ever thought of marriage—which I hadn't —it was the ring I'd have hoped someone would have picked for me.

"I don't wanna take it off. It's pretty," I muttered with a pouty frown. "I just didn't know it was there. When did you put it on me?"

"When you were freaking out about looking in the mirror. I figured if you didn't like what you saw, you'd like the ring. That plan backfired a bit, but I didn't want you to think I didn't honor what we did. And I couldn't find the right time to..." He trailed off.

He couldn't find the right time to give me the ring because I'd been too busy tearing my house apart.

I cupped his cheek. "What did I ever do to deserve a man like you?"

"Is that a good deserve or a bad deserve? One can never tell with you." His lips were once again pulled up into a devilish smile.

"Good, but don't make me change my mind."

A snap-snap-snapping broke Alistair and I out of our little love bubble, and we turned to face a stunned Barrett who was half-goggling at us and half-ready to have a full-on hissy fit.

"Married. Explain. Now."

I winced but held onto Alistair's hand as I began. "So, there was this Minotaur..."

CHAPTER TWO

"Let me see if I have this right. You came across a bazaar run by Taurus, who had been selling souls to Soren. He found out you were a Fae and threatened to either eat you or sell you into slavery, so you got married?" Barrett ended his summation on a question like he still didn't understand.

"Yes," I answered for the third time. It didn't seem that complicated, but Barrett was either actually confused or playing up his confusion for effect. My money was on door number two.

Barrett pinched the skin between his brows as he visibly tried to rein in his temper. "And this has nothing at all to do with the arranged marriage you two were supposed to have."

Ah. There it was. Barrett was looking out for me. I couldn't begrudge him that. But if Barrett understood how much Alistair hated his father, he wouldn't be pushing this.

Alistair stiffened at my side. "No. It doesn't. Taurus didn't believe she was my wife, and honestly, I don't know why he let us complete the bond. At the time, it seemed like the only way to keep Max safe."

Alistair stood and began to pace, something he did when he was supremely agitated. I shot Barrett a censuring glare. "Now that

I think back on it, I'm just glad he let Max go. Maybe it was a ruse orchestrated by my father. Maybe it was something else. I don't know and... I just wanted to keep her safe."

Alistair stopped his pacing, but I could see the steam rising off his shoulders. The fire he kept banked within him was about to burst from his skin if I didn't do something—say something. I'd been so preoccupied with my own hurt, my own sorrow, I hadn't thought what our trip to Hell might have done to him. What it cost him. What he might fear because of what it cost me.

Rising from the couch, I took the three steps to his side and pressed a kiss to his lips. "You did. You kept me safe. You kept me alive. You brought me home. No one could have done more. You did everything you said you would do and more."

When he refused to meet my eyes, I cupped his face in both my hands, sending a little jolt of magic into him. His eyes flashed open, the glowing fire in them overtaking the blue of his irises.

"I'm not sorry." I pinned his gaze with my own, and if my eyes were filling, then that's just what happened when you told your man you couldn't regret him.

Even if the victory was bittersweet.

"You lost too much," he replied. "I got my freedom from my father. We stopped him, and you lost Maria. It isn't fair. How can you not hate me?"

He was right—I did lose too much. But he was wrong, too.

"But you didn't make me lose her. You kept me from following her. And I can't be mad at you for that."

Even if it was his father that took her from us. Even if he couldn't stop what happened.

"Hate is the furthest thing from what I feel for you."

"Ugh. This is just too cute for words," Barrett huffed, crossing his arms and throwing himself onto the couch cushions. "What the hell am I going to do with you two? I can't even be mad at you for not telling me because you were dealing with... stuff." He let out a petulant growl.

"If it makes you feel any better, you knew before my parents." I tossed that little nugget out there like a lifeline.

Barrett thought about it for a second and then smiled. "Yes, that does make me feel better."

I breathed a sigh of relief and then brought everyone back on task. "So now that you've decided to forgive me, can we get back to the fact that I can't go outside like this? I mean, I super love that I don't have to dye my hair anymore, but I think the rest is gonna draw attention."

Barrett rolled his eyes, but it was Alistair who answered for him. "You can use a glamour, Max. Lots of Ethereals do. Do you think Gorgon goes outside looking like that?"

I thought of the stick-thin, seven-foot-tall warlock. Alistair had a point.

"Okay. I can do that." I nodded, trying my best not to freak out again.

Before I could even attempt a glamouring spell, Marcus shoved through the door with Aidan and Della in tow. Unlike his husband, who was still huffy on the couch, Marcus wrapped me up in his arms and squeezed me until I couldn't breathe.

"Missed you, kid," he muttered into my hair. "Glad you're back."

Gah! I freaking loved the big man. He and Barrett were like the parents I'd never really had. Sure, my parents were slowly making their way from being the absolute worst people ever—except for the whole "not telling me what I was thing" and generally lying their asses off with every breath they took. Barrett and Marcus were just better at being family than they were.

Marcus sniffed once, twice, and then pulled back, peering at me curiously. "You smell different."

"Yeah, I look different, too." I grinned. "Apparently, I'm a Fae. Surprise!"

Marcus nodded. "That... makes a lot of sense." He paused, the ramifications of my species hitting him all at once. "Your parents suck, kid."

I huffed in agreement. "Who you tellin'? On the upside, Andras did remove my glamour before I burned to death in Hell, so there's that."

"Oh, enough about the Fae bullshit," Della groused. "Tell them about the letter. About the baby. About Melody. You're Fae, you have pointy ears, *tot el que*. Let's get to the important shit."

Ah, the important shit. Della did have a point.

"Last week, when the attack on Aether happened, there was an incubus in the club. He was searching for Striker because his family adopted Ronan, Melody's son. Apparently, someone kidnapped the boy and left a note. The note said..." I trailed off, thinking. "Did you actually see the note?" I asked Della.

"No, but I can smell when someone is lying, and this kid was not. The note said that she'd taken the boy home with her to Faerie."

Barrett's eyes widened. "That's not good."

"I want to make sure it's Melody that has him. I have to make sure. I promised her I'd keep her son safe."

"That is literally the worst idea you have ever had, and that is saying something. Especially considering you were the one to go into an abandoned house by yourself with a Corax demon inside," Aidan growled before throwing his hands up. "You are bound and determined to make Bernadette light me on fire, aren't you?"

"Okay, for one, I didn't know there was a Corax demon in that house when I got there. And two, I saved your ass from a demon you couldn't see. You're welcome."

And while I did give a modicum of a shit about Aidan and his opinion, I really cared about Alistair's and Barrett's.

"I don't know, love. That seems more than a little risky, and we've had enough risky for a lifetime. Faerie isn't a place for demons." Alistair didn't broadcast that opinion. He instead murmured it in my ear.

"I made a promise," I whispered back. "What if the person who took him isn't Melody? And how could it be? I watched her die. I watched Aurelia send her soul on."

Alistair's brow pinched in a frown, and he gave me an infinitesimal nod. He didn't like it, but he wouldn't stop me. If I even went. I had too many questions to just jump in headfirst.

Barrett, on the other hand, was about to turn purple.

"No." He shook his head. "No, no, no, no, and no. We just got you back from Hell—where you definitely should not have been with your Faery ass. I agree with Aidan. This is your worst idea ever."

I threw up my hands. "It's not my idea. And I didn't say I was going to Faerie. I'm gathering information to make an informed decision like a rational adult. Stop treating me like I'm an idiot without a brain in my head. I'm sad, not a moron."

"People do dumb shit when they're grieving. Trust me," Aidan shot back, and it was then that I remembered he had a brother that was grieving Maria's death right alongside me. Aidan hadn't mentioned his brother since I'd been back, other than to drop the mother of all bombshells about Ian's parentage.

I wanted to ask him how Ian was doing, but I didn't know if now was the time to do it.

"I know. But I'm not them. I want to talk to Caim and Aurelia. See what they know. I don't see how Melody could be alive. Unless"—I snorted as the dumbest explanation ever popped in my brain—"Unless she somehow magically got turned into a succubus or something."

I watched as Alistair's eyes widened a bit.

"Wait, is that a thing?"

Alistair waggled his hand at me and winced. "Sort of? I'd need to know more about her situation to be sure. We need to talk to Caim. He's the keeper of the records. He'd know for sure."

At that moment, the door opened again, and Hideyo popped his head in. His features were drawn, and my concern for the man notched up about three degrees. I'd never seen Hideyo with anything other than an enigmatic smile on his face.

"Cinder's back. The Council is converging on the study, and they brought some guests."

That sounded ominous. Sure, I was glad Cinder was finally out of human jail, but if Hideyo's face was anything to go by, the guests were not—nor would they ever be—welcome.

Marcus and Barrett followed Hideyo out of the living room,

and the rest of us followed—me in the middle of Alistair and my paladins like they were protecting me from something.

"Would you guys quit it?" I hissed when Aidan tried to stop me from going around a corner first. "We are not in a war zone, and I am not a delicate flower. Stop. It."

Shrugging all three of them off, I hastened my steps to catch up to Barrett and shoved through the study door after him, leaving them to trail after me.

The whole gang was there. Caim and Aurelia were in a heated debate on one of the chaise lounges. Gorgon was in his usual leather wingback. Kyle was at the beverage cart, pouring himself a whiskey. And Striker and his mother were standing next to the couch, the pair closest to the door.

Upon seeing Striker's face, I had only one thought in my head, and I acted on it without a moment of reservation. Out of all the preternatural people in that room, only two knew what I was going to do before I did it. Aurelia, because she's a damn psychic, and Alistair.

Aurelia shoved off the chaise, standing faster than my eyes could track, and Alistair tried to grab for my hand. I ignored them both.

I stalked over to my former best friend, cocked my fist back, and punched Striker right in the face.

CHAPTER THREE

A long time ago, I trusted Striker. He was one of the only people I had, so of course I did. He was one of the few Ethereals I'd met who didn't try to kill me once he knew I was a Rogue. Striker didn't have a family either, and he'd been so closed off to anyone and everyone, that he needed someone, too. We trusted each other—or at least I'd trusted him.

But looking back, I realized Striker was never a good friend. He got me into trouble. He was selfish. He took too much and never gave enough back.

And he kept secrets.

For those reasons—and the fact he needed to not be here for the conversation I needed to have with Caim—I made the split-second decision to knock him out. When my fist made contact with the side of his jaw, I didn't expect to knock him out in the first go. Hell, I thought I'd have to pepper my punch with a sleep spell to do the trick.

Apparently, Striker had a glass jaw.

I appraised his unconscious form and stifled a giggle. Some paladin he turned out to be.

The room around me erupted. Okay, it didn't erupt exactly so much as Caim lost his mind.

"Have you lost what's left of your mind, Maxima? You just violated the Armistice in full view of every member of the Council."

I rolled my eyes. The fact that I currently looked like a disco ball with pointy ears should have shut him up, but alas.

"If I were a demon, sure. Since I'm not, you can take that Armistice you've conned me into protecting for the last damn year and shove it where the sun don't shine."

Shock colored his face for about a second before it hardened into a stern mask. Yeah, that wasn't going to work on me.

"As the keeper of the records, your feathery ass had to have known I wasn't Teresa and Andras' biological child. Armistice-shmaristice. You can eat a dick."

I ignored Caim's sputtering and turned to Cinder, who was looking down at her son like she couldn't understand a single thing about him—especially why he was passed out on the floor. I didn't blame her. I thought dragons were made of sterner stuff, too.

"Sorry for that," I muttered as I jutted my chin at her son, "but I was his family for the last century and he treated me like trash. He deserved that punch, and I'm not sorry. If you want to make a thing of it, we can, but I really hope you don't. I don't have any beef with you, and I want to keep it that way."

"You say he treated you like trash. How?"

I sucked in a huge breath and let her have it, counting his atrocities off on my fingers. "Well, for starters, he didn't help at all with Maria. He didn't come to see me when she died. He kept her kidnapping a secret which could have directly caused her death. He used and abused my power for his own gain. He constantly got me into trouble or nearly discovered by the wrong people when I was a Rogue. He almost got me killed on more instances than I can count, and he was a whiney bitch and deliberately antagonistic when he didn't need to be."

I paused before adding, "He also kept secrets. Ones he didn't need to keep. Not if I was family. Not if he trusted me. Not if he gave a shit."

I didn't throw in all the lying he'd done over the last century. I figured that was implied.

Cinder's eyes widened at the start of my tirade and only got bigger as I listed her son's misdeeds. She blinked, blinked again, and then looked at her son like she'd never seen him before in her life.

"You should have hit him harder," she muttered. "I did not get to raise him. I suppose that is my fault. But living with you for the last century should have molded him into a better man. I'm sorry it didn't."

While I loved that she was on my side, I still punched her son in the face hard enough to knock him out. I kinda figured she would have been a little mad. At my utterly confused expression, she snorted out an indelicate laugh.

"You don't know much about dragons, do you? We prize family over all things. You, my dear, were his family when he had none. He should have honored you, and he did not. Like I said, he is lucky all you did was punch him."

"That's all well and good, but the punching was a two birds, one stone kind of a thing. I would have knocked him out regardless, the connecting with his face bit just made me feel better. Della?" I called, turning to my very best vampire assistant. "You get to tell them this time because I'm still confused."

And wary. Everything about this situation spelled trap, and I was more than done with those for the rest of forever.

Della let out a sigh that sounded like someone was trying to snatch her soul before giving the room a rundown. She told them about the young incubus who'd come to Aether during the massacre. About his adopted brother who'd been snatched from his crib by a woman who was supposed to be dead.

"Now, what I want to know is how Melody can be alive after I watched her die. After Aurelia sent her soul on."

I wasn't looking at Aurelia as I said this. No, I was examining the angel who appeared guilty as sin itself. His face was pulled into an expression I'd seen on Striker's face a thousand times over the last century. Usually, when he'd done something wrong but was never going to admit it.

If I were ever on the hunt for Striker's father, I was pretty sure I'd found him.

"What did you do, Caim? What did you do when your son asked you for help? Does he even know you're his father, or did he get the bold-faced lying gene from you?"

Caim's eyes flared wide, colored with the magic of his other form. Like he was going to let his wings free in the middle of this room. Like he was about to attack.

I wish this motherfucker would.

Caim clocked the barely contained rage in my eyes and the curl to my lip that was almost a snarl but not quite. This asshole couldn't beat me when my power was half-chained with my mother's glamour. There was no way he'd get the upper hand now. Not when I knew what I was.

I practically watched those thoughts cross his expression as the light in his eyes ramped down.

"What. Did. You. Do." I seethed, but I wasn't the only one who had turned on Caim. No, it was Caim with his son passed out at his feet against the whole room.

"You had him pull her from Heaven, didn't you?" Alistair said from behind me when Caim still didn't speak. "How could you do that to her?"

"It's not that simple," Caim shot back. "She was fractured—her soul was broken. She was in the middle of a transition when she died. From human to succubus. The baby's blood in her veins was turning her. Half of her went to Heaven. The other half stayed here. I had Striker retrieve her, yes, but it was to put her back together. To put them back together. And why shouldn't I give my son some peace? Why not, when I could do that for him?"

Already on the defensive. That was a family trait if I ever saw one.

"But something went wrong, didn't it?" Aurelia murmured from her perch behind him, still seated on the chaise he'd vacated.

"You wanted to put the pieces back together, but you did it wrong. That's why it's taken almost eight months for her to want her son back. That's why you haven't told us what you did. You've been trying to clean up your mess."

Caim gritted his teeth and stared at his shoes.

"Because you weren't supposed to do any of it, were you?" I immediately jumped to the reason he'd kept it a secret. Because why else would he keep it from all of us unless he wasn't supposed to mend a fractured soul.

"No, he wasn't." Barrett seethed. "It's forbidden for a reason, Caim. How? How could you do this?"

Caim ripped his hands through his hair. "You didn't see him. You don't know. They'd already cemented the bond. He knew she was his mate from the moment he saw her. If I'd let him go on as he was, he would have gone mad. You don't know our stories, and why would you? No one gives a shit about angels. None of you know what happens to one of us when we lose our mates. Ever heard of the Fallen? That's what happens to us."

I actually hadn't heard of the Fallen, but I made the general assumption they were bad.

"But Striker is only half-angel. Who is to say he would have turned Fallen?" Barrett asked. "You stole a soul from Heaven, Caim. You ripped that woman from her peace, and what? Stuck her somewhere? And when you failed to join the two pieces of her soul, what was the result?"

I had an idea, but it was Alistair who answered.

"She would be crazed. Unable to function at the basest level. I bet she couldn't speak at first, right? Couldn't walk. But you taught her or had someone teach her. I bet you had a hell of a time when she finally started remembering. You fucking scum."

"Did he even ask her? In Heaven, I mean. Did he ask her what she wanted, or did he just take? Like he always takes." I shook my head. "Is she even lucid? Does she know who she is? And why would she take Ronan to Faerie?"

A white-blond haired man sauntered through the door like he owned the place. He was sipping on a Waterford crystal tumbler filled with what smelled like Scotch. In his other hand was a massive sandwich with an enormous bite taken out of it. He happily hummed as he swallowed his beverage before he plopped onto one of the open seats and propped his feet up on a coffee table like he lived here.

Our very own friendly neighborhood Fae detective wiggled his butt a little to make himself comfortable. Then he peered at us like he was settling in to watch the show.

Rowan Durant was an emissary to the Seelie Court—whatever the hell that meant—and he was a major thorn in Barrett's side. He was a prominent fixture on my shit list as well.

"Can we help you?" Marcus growled as he eyed the Fae like he was shit on his boot. For once, I did not mind this expression at all.

Rowan took another bite of his sandwich and shook his head. I had no idea what the hell he was doing here, but I didn't have a good feeling about it. I was proved right not even thirty seconds later when Rowan swallowed his bite.

"I just want to know what you're going to do about the half-crazed demon running around Faerie is all."

I could actually feel my eye twitching. Rowan Marchand Durant was a pain in my ass.

"We're having a little brainstorming session here, Ro. Why don't you come back in a bit once I've figured out the best way to retrieve our wayward demon? Best be on your way now." I lightly clapped my hands to get him the fuck out of this room before I ripped an angel apart with my bare hands.

"Oh, I don't think so," he said before taking another sip of his Scotch. "Demons shouldn't go to Faerie for a reason, and idiot Princesses should surely not follow them. Not if they like their heads attached to their shoulders."

I was so tempted to bury him in another hole and leave him there. Just like before, he wasn't going to help us. Just like before, Rowan was going to talk in circles and needle and poke until he had a bit of fun.

He didn't give a single shit about anyone, and I'd had about enough of men like that for a good long while.

Magic sparked over my fingers as thunder shook Barrett's home. Well, the magic sparked over more than just my fingers. It went all the way up my forearms and crackled and popped.

"If you live or die, it makes absolutely no difference to me. I am on the razor's edge of sanity, so I suggest you stop needling me. Because I'm one inane comment from eviscerating you in front of all these people, and I won't have even an ounce of guilt from it when I do. So, unless you can help, shut the fuck up. Mm-kay, pumpkin?"

I turned back to Caim. "You lied to me. You and your son. You let me believe I'd let her down. I never want to see you or him again. When he wakes, tell him I said so. I'll get Melody back. I'll keep her safe. Even from him if I have to. You make sure he knows that."

Before Caim could sputter a response, I snapped my fingers, sending him and Striker back to Aether and out of my sight.

CHAPTER FOUR

"Just out of curiosity, where, exactly, did you send them? No offense, darling, but if you dropped them into a volcano, we're going to need to go on a rescue mission." I wanted to laugh at Barrett's attempt at a joke, but I just couldn't manage it.

Someone I'd known for more than a century had betrayed me over and over again. I'd known I'd lost Striker. What I didn't realize was how much that loss would hurt until right at that moment.

The resolve I'd built up once I found out about Melody seemed to dim. I sagged a little before shuffling to a leather club chair and plopping onto it. Ever knowledgeable, Aurelia appeared at my side with a tumbler full of bourbon.

I took the glass and sipped it, letting the alcohol burn all the way down before I answered Barrett.

"I sent them to his office. Nothing crazy." Yeah, my voice sounded a little dead, but I just didn't have it in me to fake it right then.

Sensing my dour mood, Aurelia shoved my arm off the armrest only to pick up my still-sparking hand.

"Ooooh, shiny! Finding you in the dark will be super easy

now," Aurelia said, and if she wasn't one of my closest friends, I would have punted her little butt into next week.

"Be gentle with my feelings, dick. I'm still getting used to it."

"Oh, please. You look like mayhem and magic all rolled into one—which has been your aesthetic since the dawn of the wiggle dress. Own it," she ordered, leveling me with her pale-green pupilless gaze.

She did have a point.

Della let out a supremely unladylike snort. "Do you know how hard it was to not tell her she had pointy ears? I deserve a medal or a plaque or something."

I couldn't help it, I snorted too. Aurelia had the good sense to cover her mouth so she didn't bust out laughing. But I could totally feel the vibration of Alistair silently shaking with laughter even from a few feet away.

"You all suck," I muttered before taking another sip of my bourbon.

Aurelia slid her ass off the armrest and plopped onto my lap. Despite her tiny stature, she nearly squeezed the breath out of me when she attack-hugged me. "You love each and every one of us, admit it. Well, except for the Fae stooge, but he doesn't count."

She was right, but I didn't feel up to confirming her accusations.

"I have to go there to get her, don't I? Her son could be in danger. Now that we know it's Melody and what's been done to her, I can't just leave her there. Especially if demons are in danger just by being in Faerie."

Just thinking of Melody made my nose sting with tears. How could Striker steal her from Heaven? That hurt everything in me just considering it.

Aurelia rested her head on top of mine and wrapped me up in another hug. For two non-huggers, she sure as shit was turning me into a cuddler. A part of me didn't mind. The other part of my soul screamed for my sister in such a way I wanted to rip the room apart and watch it burn to ash. I didn't like that bit of myself—the destructive part that only wanted to destroy.

She squeezed me tighter, and it took everything in me not to start crying. I figured she felt it because Aurelia stood from her perch on my lap and went back to the chaise.

Rowan set his sandwich on the coffee table. No coaster, no plate. Just crumbs on the mahogany. "I could have sworn I just warned you that you'd be in danger by going to Faerie. Are you going to ignore me, or do you now have a death wish?"

I snapped my fingers and put the food on a plate—only slightly satisfied that Rowan flinched when my fingers made their tell-tale snap.

"First, eww. Use a plate, you heathen. Second, I heard you fine, I'm just choosing to ignore you because my life is not worth more than the people I swore to protect. If you had any shred of decency, you'd know that. Since you don't..." I trailed off.

"Fates forgive me, but I agree with Rowan," Barrett grumbled. "You shouldn't go, my darling girl. Someone needs to retrieve Melody and her son, yes. But it does not need to be you. Not so soon after losing Maria. Not after Hell."

Rowan coughed, pounding on his chest after his Scotch had gone down the wrong pipe. "You went to Hell." He choked. "Did you look like that when you went there because I can't see that going well for you."

"It went fine, Rowan. Thanks for your concern. You know, I only lost my sister is all."

He scoffed. "She wasn't your sister. You don't have any family."

Something snapped in me the moment he said Maria wasn't my sister. Without me telling them to, vines sprung from the upholstery of the couch and wrapped around Rowan's body. Each vine was barbed with two-inch thorns dripping with a viscous sap. When one of those drips touched Rowan's skin, he hissed in pain.

I hadn't even snapped my fingers. Huh.

"Was that me?" I asked Barrett because the only other person in this room who could conjure magic like that was him.

"Yes, darling." His eyes were wide as he stared at the poisonous thorns.

I studied the vines. They were so similar to the ones I'd conjured for Taurus. Neat.

"I'll ask you kindly to shut your fucking mouth about my sister. Just because I was adopted does not make her any less family. Her life meant something to me. Her loss hurt just as much as if she was my blood. Stop trying to get on my bad side, Rowan. You're there. Mission accomplished."

Rowan struggled against his bonds but only hissed when he scratched himself on another thorn.

"That's not what I meant," he backtracked. "You should know by now that you're one of us. A Fae. But your kind—the Elementals—have been hunted to the last. There are no more. You don't have any blood relatives because your kind has been hunted to extinction. You are the last. I'm warning you, Princess, not making light of your loss."

"Your delivery needs some work, Tinkerbell," Alistair growled, and it was then I noticed that he'd moved to stand behind me.

Rowan shot Alistair a baleful glare. "Tinkerbell is a fictional pixie. I am an air Fae, thank you very much. Any chance you'll be removing these bonds?"

I snorted. "Are you going to keep the asshole comments to a minimum?"

"I will now?" He said it like it was a question.

Whatever.

Snapping my fingers, the vines disappeared.

"I was trying to stress that just because you lost someone, that is no reason to risk yourself again. You should not have gone to Hell. You should also not go to Faerie. Don't get me wrong, someone should go retrieve that demon before all hell breaks loose. But it shouldn't be you."

Aidan asked a question that I hadn't thought of. "What's the deal with demons in Faerie? Vampires abandoned this plane centuries ago, and there haven't been any issues, so why are demons so taboo?"

Rowan sighed before he picked up his sandwich. "Demons can pass through veils that others cannot. Sure, vampires can pass to

Faerie with no issues, but they can't go to Heaven or Hell without getting stuck there because they're technically dead. Demons are living, breathing hosts that can pass to nearly all the realms without so much as a hiccup."

Aurelia snickered. "So, they could get a Faery parasite?"

"Faerie isn't just whimsy and pixie dust. There are beings imprisoned there. Old gods, monsters, anything too terrible to live in Hell or on Earth is locked up tight in Faerie." His face spoke of dark things that were too terrible to mention.

"If they're so 'locked up tight,' then what's the problem?" I asked, not understanding the issue. Maybe I was being purposefully dense, but if everything was sealed up nice and tight, and the only way to open the gates was killing, well, me, then all I had to do was not die, and we'd be good. Right?

Rowan sighed, shaking his head. "Nothing stays locked up forever. You think opening up the veil between Earth and Hell is bad? Let one of those old gods free, and we'll enter into a whole new era of shit."

I felt my eye twitch. Rowan seemed to know all about me—he knew what I was. He knew about our fight to keep the veils closed—the same fight that stole life from my body and damn near killed everyone I cared about.

I did not like him having that information. At. All. I did not trust this Fae one bit, and even if he was trying to help, he still gave me the creeps.

"Stalker. You keeping tabs on me, Ro? I don't think I like that. Not at all." Rowan went to sip his Scotch, and I snapped my fingers, making the glass and the sandwich disappear.

He rolled his eyes before leveling me with a simpering glare. "I'm the emissary to the Seelie Court. It's my job to know things."

Alistair's hot hands rested on my shoulders—either to steady himself or me. Or maybe if I was between him and the Fae, he wouldn't come across the scant space between them and set Rowan on fire. "You mean it's your job to spy on us and report back to your Queen. Are you supposed to sow dissension between Ethereals and the Fae, too, or is that just a failing of yours?"

"Oh, please. That little tidbit is no secret. She went up against an Eidola and lived. If you think no one knew about that, you're insane."

I shuddered, remembering the hoard of souls that busted through one of my wards like they were tissue paper.

But that was before I knew about demons.

Before I knew what I was.

"You've known who and what I was this whole time. It's why you call me Princess. You never meant demon princess. You meant Fae."

Not that it really mattered. Rowan didn't matter. My memories of that awful day didn't matter.

Only Melody mattered—her and her son.

Rowan shrugged. That wasn't an answer, but he'd probably met his quota of answers today.

"Of course, I knew. You think a witch can survive an Eidola and live? You were on our radar long before that, but we didn't know what you were until you started causing earthquakes and storms started popping up all over Denver. Way to have a low profile, Princess."

Just the name Eidola made me have to suppress a shudder.

The thought of thousands upon thousands of souls cobbled together to make the flesh-eating mist made me want to hurl. Technically, I didn't go up against the Eidola by myself. It just ate through the ward that I'd stupidly attached to my life force. Yeah, I was an idiot, and I for damn sure never did that again.

"One, I didn't go up against an Eidola by myself. Two, Kyle was the one who took care of that particular threat, not me. All I did was die."

Kyle snorted. "Granted, you died in the most dramatic fashion ever, while also saving my ass so I could do the spell in the first damn place. Don't sell yourself short, Sparky."

I took that opportunity to flip the wraith off from my safety across the room. That death hurt like a bitch. Luckily for me, all Kyle did was chuckle.

Rowan was just about to reply when Andras and my mother

walked into the study. It was still hard to call Andras my father—especially now that I knew for certain he couldn't be. I hadn't yet spoken to my mother to confirm my heritage, and I didn't know if I could bring myself to start that conversation.

Before anyone could even say a 'hi, how are ya,' Andras faded from his human form, turning into a man-shaped nightmare of black smoke and glowing eyes.

Then he launched himself right at Rowan.

It was then that I realized that the mass of smoke had teeth.

CHAPTER FIVE

Before I comprehended that my father was going full-bore demon on Rowan, Teresa latched onto my hands and yanked me from my chair. She used some sort of witchy transporting magic to get me from one side of the room to the other. The room exploded into chaos. Andras' form not only had teeth, but he also had talons, and he was slashing at the Fae like he'd very much like to rip him limb from limb.

The air Fae launched himself backward and began to fly, his body morphing into a kind of lizard? His body was as white as his hair, and he had wings of the palest blue. He appeared to be a sylph, but I couldn't be sure. All I knew was that even with fourteen-foot ceilings, he was not far enough from Andras. Andras' smoky mass was not bound by gravity, and those talons and teeth followed Rowan as he flitted around the room.

It was tough to watch—and even harder to stand idly by while it went down. Rowan was a pain in everyone's asses. If he was to be believed, his Court had systematically murdered every single member of my bloodline. It was difficult not to fault him for that—especially since he didn't seem to be too broken up about their passing.

But he didn't do the killing, and even if I wanted to punt him into outer space, that didn't mean I wanted him to die at my father's hands.

I was about a nanosecond away from stepping in when I heard a snap of fingers.

Everyone in the room froze. Andras' smoky mass, Rowan's lizardy body, every member of the Council.

Everyone but me.

My eyes locked onto the figure of a woman I'd only seen glimpses of. Bernadette was my grandmother. Straight back, British accent, carefully crafted silver bob, aging face and all. The woman before me didn't look more than twenty. Dark hair fell in waves down her back, and her tanned skin practically glowed with her barely restrained power.

This was not Bernadette. This was Lilith. One of the first demons and Queen of Hell.

As gently as I could, I pried my wrist from my mother's frozen hand and calmly shuffled over to my grandmother. A pang of loss hit me. She wasn't really my grandmother now, was she?

"I'm always going to be your grandmother, child. Quit thinking silly thoughts," Lilith said, reading my mind.

Good to know.

Her voice had dropped an octave or two, but it was still the crisp British I'd come to love. It made me wonder if the mouth to Hell really was in England.

"Why is Andras going after Rowan like a rabid animal?" I asked, curious about the complete lack of decorum. Andras was an asshole, sure, but unless he'd been attacked, I didn't think he just offed people willy-nilly.

"He's Seelie, child. He's a threat."

Well, I knew that much, but Rowan wasn't strong enough to take me on—especially in a room full of allies. I told her as much.

Lilith gave me a knowingly sad smile. "There is a lot that you still don't know, my darling girl. No matter how harmless a Fae appears, there are claws and teeth where you least expect it."

Well, wasn't that the fucking truth.

"Fine. I'll get him out of here, then. I'm not going to let Andras kill someone who hasn't done a thing to me—no matter how much of an asshole he might be."

I didn't even need to snap my fingers. All I did was think of where I wanted him to go. Granted, the place I was sending him wasn't far. I just hoped when he landed in Aether, he wasn't still frozen.

That would suck.

Lilith unfroze the room. Teresa latched onto my hand again, only this time she wasn't trying to yank me away from anyone. No, she was just holding my hand. I stared down at her fingers linked with mine, and couldn't remember a time when I'd seen that sight. It felt good and hurt all at the same time, and I struggled to swallow down my agony.

I almost couldn't make myself look her in the eye. I'd cost her Maria—her only daughter. Her only real one, anyway. She had to hate me just as much as I hated myself for failing her.

"Knock that shit off, Max," Lilith growled, the strange rasp to her voice highlighting the fact that she was in demon mode. "You aren't responsible. No one blames you."

I wasn't looking at Lilith, though. I was staring into my mother's eyes as Lilith scolded me, watching for any flicker of the blame I felt. If I saw it, I was going to wash my hands of it all. I would never see her again. I'd take the coward's way out and hide until the end of the earth or until I died. Whichever came first.

But it didn't come. The only thing in Teresa's gaze was empathy and pain. It mirrored my own agony, and I pulled her into a hug so tight it healed just a little bit of my soul.

"How can you forgive me?" I sobbed, breaking down. "I lost you your only daughter. She died saving my life. She saved all of us, and I couldn't save her."

Teresa pulled back from the hug and cupped my cheeks. "I have two daughters, Max. I've always had two daughters. Not birth, not blood, not death is going to change that. I'm not going to blame you for another man's choices, and I'm not going to stop calling you daughter. Unfortunately, you've been stuck with me for the last four hundred years, and you're just going to have to deal with me until we lose count."

Teresa had never really felt like a mother—well, only in the ways that made me loathe families in general. But for the first time, she felt like a real mom. Funny how finding out you're adopted will do that to you. Wait...

"Am I adopted, or did you get a little freaky-deeky with a pixie?" I blurted, not knowing which answer I preferred.

A laugh burst from Teresa's mouth, which was at total odds with the tears running down her face. Wow. We were a pair, weren't we?

"No, I did not get freaky-deeky with a pixie. But I can show you if you let me."

I considered that for a second before my gaze drifted to Alistair's.

"Come with me?" I asked, nervous about finding out where I'd come from. I wouldn't feel weak if I leaned on him, and I couldn't explain why. Trust—the thing he'd been asking for all along—was about to be shoveled his way.

"Of course, love." Alistair joined me in our tiny huddle.

My mother's eyes widened when she took in our joined hands —particularly the giant black diamond on my ring finger—and her head whipped up to stare at us. "You... How? When?"

I wanted to roll my eyes, but Teresa didn't seem displeased, so I refrained.

"Hell. Since no one told me I was Fae, I didn't know to be more careful. Taurus was going to sell me or eat me, so Alistair bonded us so he couldn't. And I kind of like the guy, so..." I trailed off, smiling at my mother in a way that told her I was really happy—even if that happiness was dimmed by Maria's death.

"Congratulations. I can't say it's a surprise, though."

Lilith broke in. "But that explanation will come once you see your mother's memories. Let's find a quiet place to do the spell, Andras," she called to her fuming son.

Andras wanted to go after Rowan, I could tell. I could also tell he was miffed at me for snatching his quarry away from him.

"We don't need to," I answered. "I trust everyone in this room."

Lilith smiled at me in a way that spoke of broken promises and too many betrayals to count. "That may be true, child, but some things are better seen alone."

I nodded, but it was Barrett who offered to clear out the room for us. He kissed me on the forehead, and Marcus squeezed me in a monster-sized hug before they left. Everyone else but Aurelia and my paladins left.

"I'm trusting you not to hurt her anymore," Aurelia said as she stared into my mother's eyes, the glow of them shining on my mother's face.

Teresa nodded, shame coloring her expression. "All I have ever wanted was to keep her safe."

"No more lies, Teresa. Tell her everything, or I will. Do you understand me? I will tell her all of it—the good and the bad. I'm giving you this opportunity to show her your side. Don't make me regret giving it to you."

With that, Aurelia strode out of the room with Della and Aidan following her.

"We'll just be outside this door, Max. You need us, yell," Aidan informed me, but I could tell he was giving a not-so-subtle warning to my parents. I knew, without a doubt in my mind that if I yelled, there would be some hell to pay.

Once the door closed, Lilith told Teresa and me to have a seat on the couch and get comfortable.

"You boys, stand behind your women and hold onto their shoulders. You'll ground them to the now while I perform the spell. Try not to let go," she instructed before addressing Teresa and me. "You two need to hold hands."

My mom clasped my hands, and Lilith moved closer. A dagger materialized in her hand, and in less than a nanosecond, an infinity loop was carved into the backs of our joined hands.

I hissed in pain. "A little warning next time, jeez."

Out of nowhere, Lilith conjured a piece of red ribbon. About two inches thick and made from some kind of silky material, the fabric floated in the air of its own accord before it wound itself around our joined wrists. The ribbon wrapped further down, soaking in the blood of the infinity mark before tying into a complicated bow.

She perched on the coffee table and began to chant.

"*Videre priores. Ad animi res et tempus.*"

I translated the Latin in my head, and the words didn't quite connect. It wasn't until the second or third pass did I get the spell. To see the past. To see the mind, circumstance, and time.

Lilith wasn't just going to show me what had happened. She was going to put me in my mother's shoes and make me walk the path as her. Oh, I wasn't going to like this at all.

I wanted to pull away, wanted to unbind our wrists, but I was stuck.

"*Videre priores. Ad animi res et tempus.*"

I felt like I was falling, even though I knew I was still on the couch. My open eyes were unseeing, blind to the here and now. I heard Teresa's sharp intake of breath and barely felt Alistair's hands on my shoulders as the ground swirled and tilted beneath my feet.

"*Videre priores. Ad animi res et tempus.*"

Everything fell away, and I landed in Teresa's memories—a place I never thought I'd be.

CHAPTER SIX

TERESA – SPAIN 1628

My feet barely made a sound on the moss-covered rocks as I navigated around laurel branches. This was the one place humans refused to go, and I was glad for it. The Inquisition had claimed some of my witch sisters. Forests like this one were a safe space for us to practice and live without fear of watchful eyes.

Humans were superstitious for good reason. The creatures they feared were real. Had we lived alongside the humans, I wondered if they would fear us as much as they did. I missed my mother's stories of when the earth was freer—less concerned with us Ethereals. Less worried about rooting out our magic or blaming fellow humans for powers they didn't even have.

The gentle shush of my shoes against the moss was quiet to my ears, but soon Andras would find me. We were playing a game, and soon he'd appear from behind a thick tree trunk, the tendrils of Hell smoke clinging to him.

I felt my lips curl at my little secret. No one in my coven knew about Andras—my demon Prince who was set to rule Hell one day.

No one had ever seen him. I'd kept him safe from witches who would try to use him and his power, and he kept me safe from humans.

It helped that we were madly in love with one another, but I couldn't wait for the day when he would take me away from this blasted country with its too-strict nature and watchful eyes. I wanted fewer rules, not more. I wanted freedom.

And I wanted Andras.

I heard a rustling close by, a gentle *shush-shush-shush*, followed by a whimper. The sound was unlike any animal I'd ever heard, and I stayed still trying to place it.

Feeling a trill of unease in my belly, I carefully rounded a tree. I wasn't the only one in this wood, for certain, but I didn't think there was anything in this thatch of trees that would hurt me.

Not that I couldn't hurt back, at any rate.

But when I reached the other side, there was no one there. The only thing I found was a pair of athames resting on a thick patch of moss. The metal wasn't shiny or dull but glowed with a power I couldn't name. The hilts were a delicate spiral, unlike any blade I'd seen before. The instant I saw them, I wanted to feel the metal in my hands. I wanted to cast with the power these athames would provide. I wanted to take them for my own.

I looked up, peering around me to see if there was anyone to claim them.

I knew better than what I was about to do. I'd heard stories of people who took things that did not belong to them in this wood.

But the metal called to me, sang my name and begged me to pick them up.

And so I did. I felt the weight of them in my hands, how balanced the weapons were, how light. Turning the athames this way and that, I saw a rune etched into the underside of the first turn. I pressed it, and the blade expanded into the length of a sword.

Shocked, I pressed the rune again, watching as it retracted into the length of a dagger.

Yes, I would keep these blades for my own.

"Do you like them?" a voice called from my left. Shocked, I dropped both blades, and they fell just so that the pointed end sliced into the dirt and stood straight up, sticking out of the ground.

"I'm sorry. They…" I couldn't finish that sentence. What could I say? The metal sang to me?

I studied the woman before me. She was covered almost head to foot in a green cloak, the same color as the moss that covered everything in this forest. Her eyes shown gold, the faint light catching them just so that the color gleamed. She was heavily leaning on a staff, and I predicted she was injured in some way.

So many who wandered into this forest were often refugees from the church, and I wondered if she was such a person.

"Do you want them?" she offered, a faint smile pulling at her mouth.

Of course I wanted them, but at what price? "Yes. How much?" I asked, as I offered her my hand filled with gold I'd conjured.

Money was easy to make. Jewels too. If the crown wasn't so hell-bent on destroying witches, they could have all the riches they needed.

"I don't want your money, child," she said, and at her use of the word "child," I studied her face harder. She didn't appear to be any older than my thirty years, but I knew I didn't look my age, either.

"Then, I can just have them?" I asked, not understanding.

"Of course."

My eyes widened, and I snatched the blades from the ground. "Th-thank you," I gushed, gratitude and pride swelling within me. I now owned something so beautiful I'd be the envy of my entire coven.

Relief colored the woman's expression, and she smiled beatifically at me. "I am so happy you said that."

Suddenly, the blades burned hot in my hands, but I could not drop them. My fingers refused to obey my mind, and they held fast to the twisted handles. I wanted to scream, wanted to cry out for Andras. I knew he was somewhere in this wood. He would save me. He would stop this agony.

But just as suddenly as the athames burned me, the heat and pain melted away.

The woman pulled the hood from her head, blue hair spilling around her shoulders as she did so. Her skin seemed to glow in the low light, and when she looked down, her hair parted just so, and I saw the point to her ears.

She was a Fae, and somehow, I knew I'd just accidentally made a Faery deal.

Fates, no.

"What did you do to me?" I whimpered, fear climbing up my throat.

She sighed before wilting to the ground. "I gave you a gift. You said, thank you. You must believe you owe me a debt. Now you must repay."

What?

Frantically, I shook my head. "But—"

"There is no going back." Her voice was a harsh command, cutting me off. "Only forward."

I pressed my lips together as tears gathered in my eyes. I should have known.

"You will repay your debt, you must do me a favor," she murmured, but her voice reached my ears, anyway.

Glistening tears fell from her eyes as she pulled back the sides of her cloak. Strapped to her breast was a sleeping baby in a sling. The fabric of it stained red from a wound in the woman's chest. It was packed with healing moss, but I could tell it wasn't working, and she was living on borrowed time.

"Take my daughter as your own. Keep her safe, keep her from harm. Don't let the Throne steal her away from you. Hide her from my kind. Conceal the features that peg her as one of us. The athames will show you the way. They are the last... She is the last of us."

My gaze snagged on the little bundle of life the Fae woman clung to. She snapped her fingers, and the baby was now in my arms, the bloody sling around my neck. I frowned at the rapidly cooling wetness against my skin, but more, I worried for the baby. Babies were fragile. She could catch a chill.

"You will need the blood to conceal her. Your demon will help you. Trust him. You will both keep my Massima safe. There are those that would kill her just because of what she is. Please remember, if she dies, you will soon follow her. The athames will see to that."

The woman wilted some more as blood dripped from her nose and ears. She was fading fast. Instead of raging against the bargain I made, I rushed to the woman's side, snatching moss from the closest rock and pressing it into her wound.

"*Sanitatem*," I murmured, drawing on this forest to try and mend her. When that didn't work, I tried to keep her awake. "What's your name? Can you tell me? Tell me about your daughter."

Her eyes fluttered, her skin dimmed, and she breathed her last.

Tears hit my eyes as I stared down at the Fae. She had just been a mother trying to keep her daughter safe. I had no children of my own, but I knew that bone-deep need to protect that every mother possessed. I knew because I now had it for this child—even though she wasn't mine.

I couldn't say if it was the deal I'd accidentally made or if it was Fate, but as I stared at the blue-haired infant in my arms, I knew I'd risk anything to keep her safe from harm.

Suddenly, the ground began to shake, lightning cracked across the sky, and the Fae's body began to dissolve from human form into blue light. The light grew brighter and brighter—so searing I had to protect the baby's face and my own eyes from it. Then the light exploded, blue streaks of smoke curled and roiled in the spot where the woman had taken her last breath. Slowly, it crept closer to me, surrounding us, letting me breathe it in.

Then the earth stilled, the sky cleared, and just as soon as it came, the storm was over.

But I knew the woman's name. Zeta. She was an Elemental Fae, one of the last of her kind. And in my arms was Massima, her only living child. The rest of her babies had been slaughtered. Her husband had been lost to the war that raged in Faerie. Her sister sat on the throne of the Seelie Court—a sister who shared her blood but not her power. A sister who stole the throne from beneath her under the guise of protecting the realm.

The Seelie Court would be coming for this child.

A twig snapped close by, and I extended both blades to fight, thankful that the child was still asleep in her sling—her mother passing just a bad dream. I whispered spells to keep others from hearing us, seeing us, and I hid.

Until I heard Andras calling for me. Only then did I creep from my hiding spot. Still, just in case I was mistaken, I held those blades, ready to strike if anyone so much as looked at us wrong.

"Teresa, my love, please," he yelled, his voice a desperate plea.

"Here," I called back, praying to the Fates that I wasn't wrong.

Andras' form slid like rippling water over the moss and stones, around laurel trees to find us in the hollowed-out trunk of a dying maple.

He sniffed, scenting the Fae blood on the sling and the tiny baby resting against my body.

"She's a Fae, Teresa. What are you doing with a Fae baby?"

"It was an accident," I began, telling him of the deal I'd inadvertently made with a dying Fae Queen.

Andras' face went white, and he gathered Massima and I in his arms and ushered us to the small cabin we'd made for ourselves in this neglected part of the forest. The trees were mostly overgrown, but we stayed hidden here. Away from his duties in Hell, apart from my coven, away from humans who would try to kill us.

When we were safely behind closed doors, I removed the sling, and together, we inspected the baby now in my care.

Our care?

"I have to summon my mother. She..." Andras trailed off as he stared at the babe. "There was a divination made ages ago, made long before I was born that my child would be promised to the Quinn clan. It was a way to appease a hated rival—to give him status where he had none. My mother told me we shouldn't worry, that my beloved would not be able to bear my young."

I nodded and sighed. Witches and demons could not reproduce. That had always been the way.

"But if this Fae babe is under your care—our care—then destiny has discovered a way around my mother's prediction. We need her help. If ever we are to keep this child safe, we will need all of her help."

Quickly, I agreed, and Andras sought out his mother. She came to us without delay, a beautiful raven-haired woman stepping from the forest mist as if from a dream.

She inspected the babe, cradled her in her arms, and sniffed her blue hair.

"I will help protect my grandchild at all costs, my son," Lilith said. "On one condition."

I'd already made one deal today, so I was not about to make another. Especially not with a demon—even if she was Andras' mother.

"Anything," Andras replied, and I felt my eye twitch.

"You shall call her Maxima."

In the end, we ended up saying her name was Maxima Christina Arcadios—Christina for my mother, and Arcadios for my coven. Lilith herself spoke to the angel who kept the records, and he swore he would keep her origins a secret—easy to do when we refused to tell him where the babe had come from or who her real parents were.

Only I—and maybe Lilith—knew her real name and lineage. Together, the three of us used the Fae blood to conceal her abilities, her appearance, and her location. But that didn't stop Andras from having to kill his father.

It didn't stop people from finding us. It never stopped. It didn't stop when I sailed across the Atlantic to the New World. It didn't stop when Maxima was nearly taken from me on that ship. When she died only to rise again—mortal and magical weapons never stealing her from us.

It didn't stop, and every time Andras traveled farther and farther, snuffing out the threats to our child until he stopped coming back. He stopped returning my missives.

He stopped talking to me. I became bitter, hurt, and mean.

I took another husband, had another daughter, but all too soon, that husband died from disease. And my bitterness grew. I was destroying the light inside this child. Day by day, year by year, I was snuffing her out.

And all the while, Andras never came back—not until we faced a threat inside my own coven. Only then did he return to help me hide the Fae child we'd been trusted with.

We had to get her away from us—from me. And once she was away from my coven, we took turns watching her from afar, watching her grow into a woman who would not stand idly by while others were suffering. A woman who would always help, always fight fiercely for those that needed it.

We let her flounder, we let her rise. We kept the biggest beasts at bay.

Until it was time for her to stand on her own.

CHAPTER SEVEN

I came back to myself as if I was sinking onto a mattress—which was by far better than how I left. Alistair's hands on my shoulders helped me find my body, and when I opened my eyes, I knew I'd cried through all of it.

For the life that was stolen from my birth mother. For the agony Teresa felt after losing Andras. For the missed opportunities and all the pain. And more, the love that Teresa felt for me, even when she was bitter, even when she didn't do it right, even when she had to shove me out.

All the wrong reasons and all the mistakes—I saw it all through her eyes. Felt her heartbreak, experienced the bitter agony of it all.

How she didn't hate me, I didn't know. I was the catalyst for all her pain, and on top of it all, I was responsible for Maria.

Slowly, I sat up, meeting her gaze with my own. "It's really tough to hate you now. I hope you're happy."

It was a terrible joke and not very funny, but I just couldn't express my… gratitude? My utter horror that I was the root cause of her pain?

"You should have told me sooner. I could have handled it," I murmured, trying to get ahold of the terrible ripping ache in my chest. We could have had years, decades even, as a family.

"It wasn't time yet. We had to wait until your glamour started dissolving on its own. We didn't know it at the time, but with the Fae blood, the spell we cast was too powerful for us to break. Not without hurting you," Lilith returned, the color of shame painting her words in a new light. "We couldn't show you—not until we had an inkling that the spell was breaking. Your powers finally started to show themselves, and only when we could wait no longer did Andras remove the glamour."

I pondered this for a moment. "It hurt like a bitch. I thought I was going to die."

Andras squeezed Teresa's shoulders before rounding the couch to rest on the arm of the sofa. "Imagine if I'd tried to do it four hundred years ago. You would have died."

"Did all that really happen?" Alistair murmured, still frozen in his spot. "Did you kill your father to save her?"

"Of course I did. She's my daughter. The only one I'm ever going to get. I'd die to keep her safe. I'd say I'd kill to keep her safe, but we all know I'd do that. Will you do the same, Quinn?"

Alistair's head whipped up, piercing my father with an expression so sharp it was as if he'd wielded a sword. "You know I will."

"Good. Then welcome to our fucked up little family," Andras said with a roguish smile. Leave it to Andras to welcome and threaten someone at the same time. Then he faced me, and his grin fell away. "If you still blame us, I get it, but we kept you alive as best we could. With a few hiccups here and there, to be sure, but we tried our best. You deserved better parents."

It was tough not to think of the mother and father that I'd missed out on. The ones that were stolen for someone else's gain.

"So when Rowan called me Princess, he meant of the Seelie Court. I was born a Princess, and the queen had my family and everyone like me killed. My brothers and sisters, my birth parents.

She stole everything, and now I'm going to have to hide from her ass when I go get Melody. This is a total shitshow, isn't it?"

Andras stood from the arm of the couch, his form flickering from black smoke back to human again, those flame-like eyes burning into me. "You aren't going, Max. You can't."

I stood facing him, my glow, my magic not sparking an inch because I wasn't mad—not after all he'd done, all he'd sacrificed. But he had to know. "I'm pretty sure we've discussed you telling me what I can and can't do. But you're forgetting something that even I hadn't realized until a few seconds ago."

"What's that?" he growled.

"I made a promise. I am bound to it, just the same as Mom was bound to her unintentional deal. I have to go. I have to help. There is no other way. I can't send someone else, and I can't sit here and let that baby be hurt." I sighed, my tone without malice or heat as I continued. "So, I'm going, and you can help by telling me everything you know, or you can get knocked the fuck out, and I'll go, anyway. You choose."

Andras narrowed his eyes at me, the demonic flames dimming. "I'm not going to be able to stop you, am I?"

Shaking my head, I grinned at him. "No, but you can help."

"Fine, I'll tell you what I know," Andras huffed and then glanced over my shoulder to Alistair. "Looks like we're going to have to sit this one out."

Alistair scoffed. "Speak for yourself, old man. I'm going to retrieve my kinswoman and support my wife. You can sit this one out if you want to, but I'm going. I drug her out of Hell. I'll drag her out of Faerie if I have to."

In all of this, I did not think about whether Alistair would go with me or not. But the danger of it hit me in the face like a two-by-four. Fear crawled up my throat as I reached for him. I didn't know if I could do this without him. I didn't like feeling weak, but there it was.

I couldn't do this without him, but I couldn't ask him to come.

Alistair must have seen the fear in my eyes because he leaned down to pierce me with his gaze. "I'm coming. Protect me with a spell if you need to, ward me until you are satisfied, but I am going with you, love. I won't be left behind."

Shaking, I latched onto his biceps, leaning into him until his warmth thawed me. I gave myself thirty seconds to calm down, and then I turned to my grandmother.

"There are anti-possession spells, right? A way to protect him?" My voice sounded steady, but I was fooling precisely no one.

"Yes. We'll need your blood for them, but I can show you how to perform the incantations. I would, but your magic far surpasses mine on that front."

I could feel the shock on my face. Lilith was one of the first demons in Hell. No way was she small potatoes.

"Believe it, dear. Why do you think we tried to keep you hidden?" Lilith chuckled. I found it strange that I thought of this woman as Lilith and the aging beauty mask as Bernadette.

"I'm both, but this form is Lilith, the Mother of Demons. Bernadette is a grandmother, an elder. Lilith is something to be feared. I'll need this form for now while you and your husband are gone." She was reading my mind again.

Not creepy at all, Gramma.

"Like you wouldn't use that ability if you had it. It's easier to suss out bullshit this way, dear," she said while giving me a conspiratorial wink. Then she faced Alistair. "And you are lucky you're pure of heart. Otherwise, no one would find you. Not even the Fates."

"Yes, Alistair is appropriately cowed into treating me with respect until the end of days. Good on you. The incantations? I've someplace to be."

Lilith went over the spells with me, of which there were three. One for protection, one for concealment, and one for anti-possession. Each one required blood, and each one took a whole hell of a lot out of me. Not nosebleed-worthy, but it wasn't a walk in the park, either.

Only after his protections were put in place did I notice that while he'd given me a ring, his finger was still bare. Call me silly, but that would just not do.

Pulling on a bit of strength, I conjured the best ring I could think of. A platinum band with an inlaid channel of pure obsidian. A ring that couldn't be made by anything other than magic.

Instead of asking—because why should I?—I snapped my fingers, and it was on his hand.

"There. Even-steven," I said and then stuck my tongue out at him.

Alistair growled at me, and I couldn't help but laugh. A real one this time. In answer, he cupped my face and brought our bodies close. "Stop doing things that make me want to kiss you in front of your parents, love."

I couldn't help it, I kissed the shit out of him in front of my mom, dad, and grandma. I wasn't wasting a moment with him, not on pleasantries or propriety. I was holding on to everyone and everything for as long as I had it.

Maria taught me that.

When we broke apart, I tugged on his hand. "Come on. Let's go watch Barrett's head explode when we tell him the news."

"I don't like this, Max."

I snorted. "So you've said."

Barrett huffed, stomped his foot, and then flopped onto the chaise like a pissy two-year-old.

All class, that one.

I was busy arming myself with every single bit of magic I had. Every potion, every magical weapon, every concealment spell I'd cooked up in the last four hundred years was either tucked away in a never-ending pouch or stuffed in my pockets. My athames were strapped to my legs in their handy-dandy weapon sheathes, and my leathers were slightly modified to blend in with the Fae realm.

Similarly, Della, Aidan, Alistair, and Hideyo were gearing up, preparing for whatever we'd need for however long it would take to find Melody and bring her back.

My plan included not being found by the royals, staying under the radar, and not making any enemies. I snorted to myself. Yeah, I didn't think this was going to go down like that at all. Hence, weapons.

I'd already snapped the rope dart to my belt and was in the process of stuffing a set of self-replenishing throwing knives in my boot when the door to my casting room opened. My mother popped her head in, and when her body followed, I knew what kind of discussion we were about to have.

She was decked out the same as me, only the leathers on her left side were covered by silver armor that protected her arm, half her breast, and her hip. Spelled leather shielded the other side, but her right arm was uncovered to her wrist, where her hand was encased in a bowman's glove. At her hip was a spartan-style sword, the hilt covered with a geometric guard and the tang starting skinny before curving wide again. And at her back was a quiver full of arrows, and a bowstring crossed her body.

If I didn't have my athames, I'd want a sword like that one. Also, I had no idea my mother knew how to use a bow.

I could tell just by looking at her face I wasn't going to talk her out of this.

"I made a vow to protect you, and I'm not letting you walk into the one place where they actually know how to kill you by yourself. Yes, I know you'll have backup, but—"

"Okay," I said, cutting her off. If I didn't say yes, she was just going to follow me. Better have her on our side now.

"Okay?" she repeated. "You haven't agreed with me since you were three."

That wasn't true. I'd agreed with her two weeks ago when she said Ian was a jerk.

"Then I'm turning over a new leaf. Maybe now that the truth is out, we can be... a family again?" I offered, tossing my mother an olive branch so fast she had no idea what to do with it.

"Yes, Max, I would love to mend our shattered relationship," Barrett answered for her using a mock-girl voice, rolling his eyes as he did it.

"Yes, Max, I would love to mend our shattered relationship," she croaked out Barrett's words before continuing in a clearer voice. "I'd like to be your mom again—if I ever really was."

I'd take it.

CHAPTER EIGHT

The door to Faerie was not ornate or obvious. In fact, I almost missed it entirely—especially since the door right next to it was about as ostentatious as a wooden door could be. The not-Fae door was carved to perfection, and several of the grooves were inlaid with gold. If I was going to pick an obviously Fae door, that would have been it.

Apparently, the ostentatious one went to a club in Vegas, and the broken-down almost-off-its-hinges one was the way to the Faerie realm.

"Is this some dumbass test to show me that nothing is as it seems?" I asked no one in particular as I studied the two portals. "Because I'll bet that lesson is going to get real old real quick."

Della jostled my shoulder, her tentative smile mired with a little bit of worry. "You'll see. Faerie is just like any other realm. People and things are trying to kill you, there are eyes everywhere, and don't ever give thanks or a promise. Really, it isn't so bad. Plus, the Fae taste positively scrumptious."

I thought back on all the times I bled around her, and she'd not so much as showed me a peek of fang.

"How come you never freaked out about my blood?"

Della scoffed. "I'm not a mindless heathen, Max. Plus, you used to smell different. Now you smell better, but I make it a point not to eat my friends. Kind of puts a damper on the relationship."

Well, when she put it that way, I kind of felt like an asshole. The sum total of what I knew about vampires was from TV and movies. And the occasional vampire romance novel. Okay, more than occasional. The prevailing theme in all of them was a vampire's nearly uncontrollable hunger.

"Good to know."

I reached for the door to Faerie, not eager to do the job I'd set out for, and nervous as hell that I would what? Die there? Lose the majority of my closest friends? Lose Alistair—who was my husband in a sort of loose sense, but also, he was someone I could really care about if I let myself.

I didn't quite love him yet, but almost.

What if I lost them all like I lost Maria?

That thought blazed through my head like a brushfire, and I snatched my hand back.

You promised Melody you would make sure her son was safe. You. Promised.

"Max?" Alistair's smooth rumble of worry hit my ears, and I reached for the door again, twisting the knob in my hand.

I stood there shaking, and slowly I managed to take the first step, then the second. One after the other until I was out of the way, and my companions could join me. Teresa was the last to go through, and she closed the door behind her. It blended in perfectly with a ramshackle little house that seemed to come out of *Hansel and Gretel*—complete with a thatched roof and scalloped shingles.

In a pique of worry, I slid past Teresa to open the door again. When we went to Hell, the portal faded away to nothing, and we were stuck. If shit went sideways, I wanted a way out.

I turned the knob in my hand and opened the door. The hallway in Aether greeted me, and I breathed a sigh of relief.

Okay, I can totally do this.

Turning back to the group, I shrugged. "I wanted to be sure we weren't stuck."

We crunched across the lawn, which quickly gave way to moss-covered trees and a brambling forest that seemed dark and full of things I wanted no interaction with—especially since I had no idea what was real in Fae lore and what was bullshit.

"Lead on, MacDuff," I said to Della, letting her take the lead on the rather thin footpath that led who knew where.

"Misquoting Macbeth? That's not ominous at all, Max. And that isn't the way," Della informed us before she latched onto my shoulders and turned me ninety degrees to the left. "That's the way."

The trees to the left were darker, thicker, and coated in a glittering mist. The mist itself was something out of an acid trip: it moved like fog, had the consistency of runny sap, and it clung and stuck to the trees yet passed over them all at the same time. And it glittered. Super.

"That fog is going to fuck with us, isn't it?" It wasn't really a question. I knew without a doubt in my mind that the glitter-slime-looking fog was gonna make this whole trip a thousand times more bullshit than it had to be.

"Oh, absolutely." Della emphatically nodded her head.

"This is going to ruin my whole day, isn't it?"

"Yup."

"Aces."

Groaning, I trudged behind Della toward the path, Alistair and Aidan behind me, and Hideyo and my mother behind them.

I knew Della had been here before—hell, she lived here since the beginning of the Spanish Inquisition, so that made her a couple of hundred years older than me. I wondered if Hideyo had ever been. He hadn't said as much, but since he was a Kitsune, I had to wonder if that particular species was more Fae than Ethereal.

"Don't let the fog get on your skin, guys. That is one acid trip that is guaranteed to be a bad time," I said, the knowledge filtering into my brain from nowhere.

Della stopped at the edge of the forest and turned back to me. "How do you know that?"

I wanted to be snide and say, "common sense," but all I could do was shrug.

Without me telling them to do so, my arms raised, and I began a complicated series of hand gestures before I snapped my fingers. The fog peeled itself back from the path as if I was Moses—okay, I was totally picturing myself as a young Charlton Heston and the fog was the Red Sea.

Surely that trill of fear was totally normal, right?

"What the fuck, Max? I remember coming through here the first time and damn near losing my ass in this forest." Della seemed both relieved and slightly miffed we wouldn't get to experience the full accoutrement of Fae horseshit.

"Your guess is as good as mine. I have absolutely no idea how I did that, and I probably couldn't repeat it if you held a gun to my head."

But I sure as shit wasn't going to look a gift horse in the taint. Skirting around Della, I took point and began our little march into the trees. The further in, the darker the forest became, photoluminescent mushrooms clustered at the bases of black trees, the leaves looking like spray-painted ferns with dayglow tips.

I wanted to inspect everything, but I also didn't know how long this barrier spell was going to last. I picked up my pace, walking at a steady clip along the path when I heard a rustling in the trees. A stupid person would go to check. A complete idiot would want to know what was beyond the tree line. I was neither of those things, so I walked faster.

"What is that?" Aidan whispered. Why he was whispering, I had no idea, but it seemed like a good idea.

Leave no trace. That was supposed to be the way, right? Just like in state parks and shit.

"It doesn't matter. Don't look at it, don't breathe at it. Leave everything in this forest alone, and maybe whatever it is that is most definitely following us, will not eat you."

Then I heard a chuckle coming from a dense thicket to my

right. It was dark, deep, and masculine. It was also way too close. It took everything I had in me not to start running. But I did ramp up my pace to the speed-walk range, kinda like the same one I had in Vegas when I wanted to get the fuck out of the crowd.

I shook my head and kept saying "nope" over and over again until the light at the end of the path grew brighter. The closer we got to it, the faster I walked until I was damn near jogging. There was a valley sprawled out below the end of the path and a mountain range beyond.

The giggles in the trees got closer. Fucking Faerie. Already I hated the damn place, and I'd only been here an hour.

I wanted out of this forest.

I wanted out of this stupid realm.

As soon as we cleared the trees, I did a full-body shudder and turned back to look at whatever the hell was following us. All I could make out were glowing eyes in the middle of dense branches. The trees were the ones chuckling at us. The trees were sentient.

I couldn't tell if that was comforting or not.

I noticed an all-white deer walking near the tree line. It stopped to nibble on the grass close to a broad trunk. Like a whip, a branch shot out and wrapped around the doe, dragging it into the thicket of trees.

Nope, not comforted by sentient trees at all.

Pursing my lips, I tried to ignore the decidedly unsettled exclamations from my traveling group and studied the wall of mountains in front of us. I had a sneaking suspicion I'd need to climb this bitch of a mountain to really get into Faerie, and I was not looking forward to it. I looked left and right, and unless there was some kind of hidden passage, the only way out was up.

"I do not recall anyone saying anything about climbing a fucking mountain, Della."

Della stopped her minor argument with Aidan—he was not a fan of not knowing there were carnivorous trees, either—to address me. "I decided parceling out information as we went was a better course of action."

If I had laser-beams for eyes, she would have been dead right there on that spot. I was done with people withholding shit. I was done with people keeping secrets.

I was not a child, and paladin or no, I was D-O-N-E with being treated that way.

"When has that ever worked for anyone in my life? Did it work for Striker, or Ian, or Caim? No, it didn't. In case you haven't realized, I've started excising people who keep important shit from me. Cutting them out like a cancer. So, I'll ask now, you got anything else you want to tell me before I climb this fucking mountain?"

Della had stiffened when I asked my first question, and she was what I'd call dead-still when I asked my last. She wasn't breathing, wasn't blinking.

"After living here so long, I forget that your realm is different. Here, there are more secrets than truths, and if the information will hurt the outcome, it is not given. That is how I've lived for six hundred years. Only when your grandmother called in her marker did I go back to your realm."

"Called in her marker?"

"Lilith made me. I am her progeny."

My grandmother could make vampires. That was news. Grandma had some 'splainin' to do.

"I used to be a nun until a rather vicious cardinal decided I was a witch infiltrating the church. He and his acolytes tortured me for a month, and every day I prayed to God to save me. No help came—just like no help came to the others during that time. On my last day, I stopped praying to God and prayed to Lilith instead. Swore I would serve her until the end of time if she would help me. She saved me. Pulled me from the depths of that Hell and turned me. Made me stronger. Faster. Lethal. She gave me fangs and talons, and she helped me end every single evil soul in that place."

Della paused, and the world around us was so quiet, I knew even the trees were listening.

"When we were done exacting my revenge, she sent me here—where my kind was allowed to rest, to thrive. And as long as my kind did not cause trouble, we were allowed to stay. My kind stays on the outskirts. We live in these mountains along with the Tandrirr. And all of us wait for Lilith to send for us."

Because Lilith didn't just make Della. Lilith was the mother of all vampires. I digested that leap of logic and nodded my head.

"So what you're saying is, you know a shortcut," I quipped, my anger melting away and my trust of Della growing by the second.

Della gave me a rueful smile. "Yes, Max, I know a shortcut."

CHAPTER NINE

I didn't know what I was expecting, but a tram was not it.

In my mind, Faerie was a place with no technology, no scientific advancement, no industrial progress. I was proved wrong in the first hour, which caused me to alter my whole concept of this realm.

Della led us to a path hidden by a waterfall. The waterfall itself seemed to be a river that passed over the edge of the mountain above but refused to pool at the bottom. Instead of the water collecting at the base of the mountain, it just fell through what I assumed was a never-ending hole in the earth. Maybe the water went to an underground aquifer that recycled through the realm.

Maybe it went nowhere.

I didn't ask, even though I wanted to. Della's pace was too swift to spare a minute on my ponderings. We followed Della through a winding footpath around the massive hole in the earth, ducking every so often so we didn't snag the trip wires and traps that kept this passage safe.

I didn't know how many people had access to the Faerie realm, but I had a feeling those safeguards were necessary. Maybe the carnivorous forest filled with psychedelic fog was, too.

Behind the cascading water was a Fae-style tram. Made from glittering metal and braided vines, the small car sat waiting for us to board. Inside the car was a tall woman with leather and armor on her shoulders. Her red hair was braided in rows on one side of her head, but the rest fell in a cascade down her back, some locks in braids, some in dreads, some wrapped in a thin wire. The red of her hair contrasted beautifully with her pale-bronze coloring which was a few shades lighter than my own. She wore two swords on her back, the weapons situated parallel with one hilt at the top and the other at the bottom.

Reading the motes of energy swarming around her head that she was at least part vampire, Della gave the woman a smile and approached her for a hug. They embraced for a long minute before Della made the introductions.

"Everyone, this is Idris. Idris, this is my charge, her paladins, and her family."

I noticed right away that Della did not introduce us by name, and I was all for that.

Idris looked us over like she was inspecting us for flaws. "Why have you brought them here? You know Father eschews outsiders and you've let a witch, a wraith, and a demon know where the safer passage is hidden," Idris scolded Della, and I noticed she did not say anything about Hideyo or me. I now knew Kitsune had to be Fae of some kind.

"We were the outsiders once, too," Della replied, squeezing Idris' hand. "They are here to reclaim a kinswoman. If you have her here, then we will retrieve her and be on our way. If you do not, my charge is bound by oath to aid her."

Idris shook her head. "Well, get on then. I'll have to take you to Father."

We piled into the tram, and other than being cleaner, and decidedly less clunky, it was like any other tram I'd been on.

"Idris, have you seen who we are looking for?" I asked, watching her face for any sign that she might not tell me the truth. "She would have come through here about a week, week and a half ago. Light-brown hair, pale skin, blue eyes. She would have been carrying an infant boy."

Idris shook her head. "I did not see such a woman, but I'm not always at the base of the mountain. Or she could have used one of the other paths. They are more treacherous, but a determined mind can traverse them. Father does not like me to be in danger, and the other paths have creatures that are most unpleasant."

Idris didn't speak to the group again until we reached the top, preferring to talk to Della in hushed whispers instead. The pair seemed close, and I had to wonder if they were related. That brought up a whole host of questions about vampire reproduction. Could vampires have babies?

Could vampires and Fae make babies? I tried not to think of vampire-Fae sexy times as I studied the Fae mountain city. There were whole tenements on individual peaks with bridges connecting them all. Closer to the base, the bridges were stone and wide as highways. Up higher, they were made of a kind of living metal and vines and no wider than a footpath. I figured these people had no issues at all with heights.

The tram let us off at one of the wider stone bridges, and we followed Idris into a glittering building that was part ivy-covered monolith and part glittering metal spires. The inside matched the outside, the dichotomy of metal and vines stamped all over the walls and giant ceilings that seemed to go on forever.

We walked for ages, finally reaching a council room where a bunch of people sat around a round table arguing. It was evenly split between men and women and Fae and vampires. One man was clearly the leader. His midnight skin gleamed against the overhead light, his pointed ears peeking out of a head full of silver dreadlocks. Idris went directly to the man even as the room continued their tumultuous yelling.

Some were shouting in Catalan, some in German, some in what had to be a Fae language because I couldn't place it and I'd been around for a while. I considered whether or not I wanted to know what they were saying. That was kind of a no-brainer, so I snapped my fingers as unobtrusively as I could, letting the translation spell I'd concocted in about half a second work.

"They encroach on more of our mountain every day. We cannot divide our resources any further. The dwarves will just have to move west. We must renegotiate," a pale vampire female said reasonably.

A giant of an elf stood up, slamming his hands on the table. "We promised them amnesty. We cannot go back on our word."

"It is not going back on our word. It is renegotiating a deal—which you know is perfectly acceptable." This came from an old tottering elf who couldn't be any taller than my shoulder.

"Friends," Idris' father called in English and the arguing stopped. "We have guests. Let us not frighten them with our shouting. Newcomers, wife, come closer."

Wife? I shot Della a look. She gave me the most enigmatic of smiles and sauntered toward her husband. At the last second, she took a running leap and wrapped her arms around him, kissing him for all she was worth.

"I missed you," he said when they broke apart.

Even though this was another secret, I held no animosity for it. Della had a family—she had a husband and a daughter and who knew how many children. The smile that had bloomed on my face fell in an instant.

Lilith had taken her away from her family because of me. I felt awful. I had no idea she would be leaving anyone behind in Faerie, but now that I was smacked in the face with it, I realized I'd never asked. I'd never asked what her life was like before she turned or what she left behind.

I was a first-rate asshole.

"Did you know that Della was married, had babies?" my mother asked, her question whispered in my ear.

I shook my head ruefully and vowed to myself that I wouldn't embarrass her in front of her people. Or at least I hoped I wouldn't.

"We are pleased to make your acquaintance. I am called Lothan, and welcome to Tandrirr. Please give us your names so we may be properly introduced."

Della smacked her husband in the stomach. "My charge is already wary of our realm. Don't start that Faery shit now."

I snickered, loving that Della went from proper to irritated wife in less than two seconds.

"I'm called Max," I replied, copying his phrasing, "but I feel you probably knew that considering your wife is my paladin."

Lothan's eyes widened and he sputtered, "Highness," before dropping to a knee. The rest of the vampires and Fae did the same. Well, all except the tottering elf who seemed a bit too old to start any bowing. I didn't blame him.

So much for flying under the radar.

"Please rise. I'm just Max. Not Highness. Not Princess. Just Max." I also may have flopped my hands around in a solid "no" gesture. Class, I was not.

Lothan and the rest of his retinue rose. "Lilith gave us our brethren, our families. Without the addition of the vampires, the Tandrirr would have died out. She helped us thrive. We will be forever grateful to her."

He thought I was a demon princess? I hadn't bothered with a glamour since the Fae could see through them, so I knew what I looked like.

At my skeptical expression, Lothan smiled. "We know your origins. Highness works in a variety of ways."

My earlier thought fell out of Alistair's mouth. "So much for flying under the radar, Della."

Della sighed. "You're safe here. It's once you pass the mountains that you're going to have to keep to yourself. The Court and the Tandrirr haven't seen eye to eye since before I came to this realm."

To ease Alistair's irritation, I slipped my hand into his and squeezed. "I trust her, Knight. It's okay."

Alistair pursed his lips together so he didn't say anything else, but his eyes told the tale all on their own. He was not happy. At. All.

"We are here searching for a kinswoman. She is called Melody.

She has brown hair and blue eyes, and she has an infant with her. Has anyone seen her?"

Lothan shook his head. "A kinswoman? You mean a demon."

"Yes, we believe she is part demon. I haven't spoken to her since she turned, and her soul is... She was brought back, and she is—for lack of a better word—fractured. I swore I would make sure her son was safe, so here I am."

"I'm sorry, but we do not allow demons to pass our borders. If she came this way, she would still be here. Demons are too vulnerable in the realm." Lothan's voice was smoother than silk and twice as nice.

He was being kind when he probably didn't have to be, and I was glad for Della to have a husband like that.

"I understand. Is there a chance you will let us pass to search for her? My husband is a demon, but I have placed every protection I can on him. He should be safe here—or as safe as I can make him."

Chatter in the room erupted. The giant table-slamming elf raged that demons had no place here. The sensible lady wanted to hear what protections we'd put in place. But I could tell no matter what I said, the real person I'd have to convince was Lothan, and he had already made up his mind.

"Your husband cannot follow you. It would be too dangerous for him. The old ones are restless, the chance of them breaking free grows every day. The risk is too great. The rest of your party can pass, but the demon cannot. He may stay here and wait for you."

Alistair gripped my hand tight, and the fear of being apart from him splashed me like a wave of dread. The rational part of me knew I sounded codependent as fuck. The irrational part of my brain told the rational one to go fuck itself.

Della must have felt my fear, because she did something she hardly ever did which was give me a hug.

"Don't worry, Highness. I know a guy," she whispered in my ear as she squeezed the shit out of me.

Della knew a guy. Yeah, I'll bet.

CHAPTER TEN

There were few things I hated more than being the center of attention. Okay, that wasn't exactly true. I didn't hate being the center of attention on Earth. In the Faerie realm with a whole bunch of mountain elves and vampires staring at me like I was some kind of messiah?

Yeah, no. That was a whole lot of something I wanted no part of.

"It is too late to descend the pass tonight. You will stay and feast with us," Lothan decreed. While I appreciated his distraction, the fact that I would have to be subjected to more stares sounded about as fun as having bamboo shoots shoved under my fingernails.

Still, I was smart enough to give him a conciliatory nod instead of the "Hell, no" I wanted to respond with.

"I'll show our guests where they'll be sleeping," Della announced and ushered us out of the room.

We walked for ages before we got to another part of the castle. That was the only thing I could think to call this place, and Della dropped Alistair and me off at a sumptuous room fit for legit royalty. The room itself appeared as if it were carved out of the heart of a tree. The walls seemed like almost living wood. There were no windows, but there was a chandelier with glowing orbs of magic that lit up the room as if we had our very own sun.

This said nothing of the bed. Constructed from vines and that same living metal that seemed to be everywhere, it resembled a canopy style with gossamer curtains and fluffy down bedding.

There was also a wardrobe, a dressing table, and two doors. I opened them both, inspecting the fully-stocked closet filled with anything a woman could need—be it leathers for war or an evening gown. The other door led to an interesting kind of lavatory. The walls were rocked in smooth stones veined with vines, and it had modern conveniences like a toilet and shower and sink. The only thing that was missing was the mirror, but I could live without it.

Alistair pulled at my hand, leading me out of the odd bathroom and closer to the giant canopy bed. It was the first time we'd been alone, really alone, since we spent that blissfully drugged evening in New Orleans. He sat on the edge of the mattress, pulled me between his legs, and wrapped his arms around me, resting his head against my chest. It couldn't be comfortable since I was still wearing leathers and bits and bobs, but it was the best fucking thing I'd felt in a while.

Without much consideration, I pulled the strap of my bag over my head and gently set it on the floor. It was full of potions and supplies, so I wasn't going to toss it. After that, I yanked at buckles and zippers until I was in the silver-threaded compression shirt and leggings that I wore to protect my skin. Once that was gone, I was in nothing.

I couldn't say why exactly I went from a hug to get naked. By the time I spared a glance at Alistair, he was riveted on my boobs and half-naked himself, his fiery runes calling me to touch and taste.

"I have no idea why you're getting naked, love, but I am all for it," he murmured, and I couldn't help but laugh—a real one this time.

I moved closer, putting a hand on his shoulder and pushing

him onto the mattress, following him down. "I'm getting naked because I want to kiss you. When I kiss you, I'm going to want to do all the things I've wanted to do to you since we were forced to deal with all my shit. When we do those things, that is going to lead to other things, and it's best we're naked for all of it. To save time. I'm being proactive, really."

A slow grin spread across Alistair's face, and I felt the heat of it in all my parts.

"I married a genius," he growled, cupping my face before planting a searing kiss on my lips.

Damn right, he did.

Hours later, I was in a scarlet gown that was half body armor and half fluffy confection. The bodice was constructed from golden scales that I sincerely hoped were metal that wrapped around my curves like someone had conjured it specifically for me. Which, in hindsight, could have been the case.

We were outside on a courtyard under a canopy of trees, the night sky sprinkled with a heavy hand of diamond-like stars. It was a different sky than I was used to, and while it didn't feel like home, it was more beauty than I'd seen in my many years.

People were clustered in groups, eating and drinking, talking animatedly about this and that. Many people stared at me as Della introduced us, but no one was rude. I'd felt silly in the gown Della had chosen for me, well, until I saw many of the women dressed like I was. Unearthly fire pits dotted around the courtyard, and Fae and vampire alike congregated around them. The air held a slight chill, and the brilliant purple flames warmed me as Alistair and I found a place to sit out of the way of so many guests.

The air held a sort of anticipation that made my stomach burn, and I didn't like it. It was like I could feel a hint of danger on the wind even though I knew that was stupid. I wasn't a Seer or a psychic. But I knew enough to trust my instincts.

Della handed Alistair and me a glass filled with a glowing sky-blue liquid. Neither of us took it from her. Before we started this journey, I told Alistair every single bit of Fae lore I'd read over the centuries. I had no idea what was bollocks and what was on the level, but I knew not to eat or drink anything here.

Exasperated, Della shoved the glass in my hand. "I'm not going to make you dance until your feet fall off, and you're hobbling on bloody stubs. I swear, Max."

It totally wasn't fair that she brought that up. I'd told her about that fear in confidence.

"You're the one who reminded me not to eat or drink anything here. Excuse me if I took you at your word."

"I meant when I wasn't there. Not when I'm the one handing you the food, dummy."

Okay, it was totally possible I may have read way too much Fae-themed horror books in my time. I took a tentative sip of the drink. It tasted fruity and delicious and mildly alcoholic.

"We distill that from the fog at the dryad forest. It's diluted about a thousand percent, so it won't make you see things that aren't there, but it will fuck you up. Use sparingly."

That one sip would definitely be my last.

"We'll begin the feast soon. Yes, it's okay to eat it," she said before I could even ask. "Just don't break bread before Lothan unless he asks you to. Which he might. He knew your family, your father. From before Verena took the throne."

She really meant before she stole it. Verena. I could only assume that was the name of the Seelie Queen, who'd had my whole line murdered. She sounded like such a sweet woman.

"So Lothan knew... Did you guys know I was alive?" Wariness filtered into my voice without my consent as I asked the question.

Della shook her head. "We all thought the Elementals were killed. It wasn't until you came back from Hell, did I start to put two and two together. Honestly, the fact that I didn't figure it out sooner just goes to show how good that glamour was. Lilith had to know I'd smell it on you as soon as we met."

Appeased, I relaxed some. After Striker, I wondered if I would always question my friends' motives, if I would always wonder if they were holding back secrets and lies. I was a Fae, so my die-hard penchant for telling it like it was wasn't exactly normal. But Della had lived with and married into a Fae clan. Honesty probably came easier to her than it did most people.

In the middle of my musings, a tall, dark-haired man approached us. He had strikingly cold blue eyes offset by bronze skin. His hair was long on top, shaved on the sides, and the tips of his locks were the same color as his eyes. I couldn't tell if that was the best dye job in the history of dye jobs or if his hair was naturally like that. Considering we were where we were, I figured it was natural. His lips were full, his nose slightly narrow, and cheekbones like mine—sharp and high.

He wasn't dressed like Alistair or the other men who were clad in half-armor, half dress shirt and slacks. Instead, he was in all-black leathers, his weapons at the ready at his hips.

Maybe I'd met my quota of new people, maybe it was the almost sneer to his mouth, but right away I could tell this guy needed to be knocked down a few or five pegs. Maybe even ten.

Della rose from the seat next to me. "Max, meet my son, Torren." She hugged her son, but he barely returned his mother's embrace. Okay, maybe he needed to be all the way at the bottom of the ladder with a couple of broken legs.

"Pleased to meet you." I managed to keep nearly all of my immediate hostility out of my voice. Go me.

Della had informed me of what the Tandrirr were. They were the guardians of the realm, keeping out those who would do it harm—especially if the carnivorous forest full of bloodthirsty dryads didn't do the job first. The Tandrirr took pride in their purpose, something they hadn't had in many years since the Seelie Court tried to steal their lands.

But Torren seemed less about the pride of it all. He wanted to hurt something. I knew that as sure as I knew my hair was blue. I couldn't say how I'd gleaned this information from him, but my mind was solidly made up that Della's son was a prick.

That ice-blue gaze moved from mine to Alistair's. "So, you're the demon who wants into Faerie. I had no idea demons were so stupid. Are all Ethereals like this?"

I prayed to the Fates that Della was not about to tell us that this POS in leather armor was our way out to Tandrirr. Like usual, the Fates were zero help.

"Torren will be sneaking us out at dawn."

I fucking knew it.

Della's son stiffened, his sneer growing. "I said no such thing. I said I would do it for a price. One of my choosing. It is risky going against Father—especially about this. And for Ethereals?" He scoffed. "I want a favor. If I need to, I wish to call upon you."

First off, his mother was an Ethereal. Second, another open-ended favor? I didn't think so. I got lucky that Alistair actually liked me when he called his marker in. Torren would ask me to go jump in a burning lake.

"Absolutely not." I tossed my thumb over my shoulder. "An open-ended favor is how I ended up married to this big lug." I turned to Alistair. "Not that I'm complaining, but you actually like me. This kid does not."

"That's my price. Take it or leave it. It's not my business to play lapdog to royals who can't find their own way."

That was another less-than-veiled dig at his mother. Oh. Hell. No.

"Oh, please," I blurted, knowing this kid better and better each second. I'd met plenty of this kind of asshole in my years. "You'd go against your father for a ham sandwich and a cold soda. Don't play me, junior. Do you know how many assholes like you I've met in four hundred years? A lot. They all have that same sneer, that same chip on their shoulder, and that same shitty attitude. You didn't even hug your mother back, and she's been gone for almost a year. And I'm supposed to trust you to do what you say? Not in this lifetime, pal."

Turning to Della, I said, "No offense, D, but your son sucks. I'd rather take our chances by ourselves than trust this turd."

What was it with shitty sons this week?

Della covered her mouth, but she couldn't quite contain her snickering. "Just like always, Max, you never disappoint."

I made a mock bow to Della but kept my eyes on Torren just in case he decided my honesty was a little too much for him. I felt his fingers twitch before I actually saw them move, and my athame was out and against his throat in less than a millisecond.

"Don't test me, son. I've put better and stronger men than you on their knees. I respect your mother, and that is the only reason I haven't gutted you in front of your entire family yet. You are very close to making an enemy."

It was then that I felt the ground quaking beneath my feet, and I tried very hard not to take the whole damn mountain down in my anger. The flashes of lightning and rolling thunder, though, could not be helped. The wind howled around us, and the flames in the fire pits flared high.

Yes, I was drawing a crowd.

Again.

The welcomed heat of my husband was at my back. I knew without looking that he'd phased into his demon form. Blackened skin, glowing runes, and all the fixings. If Torren wasn't scared of me, he sure as shit should be of Alistair.

One wrong move and Alistair would ruin this guy's whole fucking day.

"My apologies," Torren began, his Adam's apple bobbing as he carefully swallowed. His gaze did not stray from mine, and I could glean the faint hint of my eyes glowing in the reflection of his irises. "I was out of line."

"Accepted, and I'll make you a deal of my own. You will immediately start treating your mother like the fabulous woman she is and lead us out of the mountain unharmed, together, and on the safest route. In exchange, I will promise that if ever you are in mortal peril not at the edge of my blade, I will lend you my aid. Do we have a deal?"

Because unless Torren started getting real cool with a lot of people real quick, we were going to have a problem.

A big one.

CHAPTER ELEVEN

"Take the deal, son. You won't get a better one." Della spoke from my elbow.

The same elbow that was attached to the hand that had a knife to her son's throat. Just because he'd apologized didn't mean he wouldn't try some dumb shit.

Torren swallowed again. He didn't seem any closer to agreeing to my deal than he was before I'd put a knife to his throat.

"Torren, I don't know what you have against Ethereals, and I have no idea what has you so pissed at your mother. But considering you are half-Ethereal, you're doing yourself and your family a disservice by looking down on them."

His eye twitched. Ah, I'd hit a nerve. Torren was a not-so-closeted racist. He didn't like what he was, and because of that, he lumped his hate onto his mother.

What an idiot.

"I accept your terms," he muttered, insolence stamped on each word.

I rolled my eyes. "Yeah, I'm gonna need the words."

"It's a deal."

I sighed, stowing my athame without taking my eyes off

Torren. He was the type to do something stupid. "Was that so hard?"

His sneer was back in full force proving that, yes, it was hard. Without another word, Torren was striding away, and Lothan was taking his place.

Way to keep a low profile, Max.

I wanted to greet him, but I was too busy looking Della over to make sure she wasn't either mad at me or hurt by her kid. Why was it that family could hurt us more than anyone else?

"Please tell me you meant for me to teach him a lesson because if not..."

If not, she was probably ridiculously pissed at me right about then.

Della gave me that most tremulous of smiles, her eyes shining with unshed tears. "You did exactly as I expected. It was Torren who surprised me."

Her voice was clogged with emotion, and I was sorry I didn't kick Torren's bitch ass up and down this mountain for hurting his mother.

"What has our son done now?"

I wanted to brush it off, but it was Alistair who answered, his voice low enough that it couldn't be heard by prying ears. "He insulted your wife and our entire party. And Ethereals in general. Oh, and went for his weapon while speaking to my wife. If at all possible, could you have a word with your son? Before one of us do?"

Alistair nodded his head to Aidan and Hideyo, who moved out of the shadows at my left and right, and my mother—still in full body armor—marched up from behind him. I knew I was never in danger, but damn. I was *really* never in any danger.

Lothan's midnight skin turned gray for a second, the blood leaching from his face before his shoulders stiffened to stone. "He disrespected you in my house? He dishonored his mother?" Lothan whispered, menace coating each word. I wouldn't want to be Torren for all the money in the world right then.

I shrugged, used to people not liking me for whatever reason they had. "I handled it, but he does not like Ethereals. He said as much. If I were his parent, I'd want to know where he's learning this. From what I've seen, your species coexist beautifully. It's something we could strive to emulate on Earth."

Pride welled on his face before concern slashed through it. "We weren't always this evolved, and not all the species in this realm like Ethereals. Some think them as less than, but I thought..." Lothan paused, rubbing the back of his neck. "I don't know who has his ear, filling it with this nonsense. Everyone knows we are all the same. We all have the *hudau*—the magic—in us. It doesn't matter which realm we call home."

I couldn't do much more than nod. I didn't want Lothan to know why we were talking to his son, but the fact he was a racist ass needed to be dealt with.

"I know why you were talking to Torren. I know you want to sneak your husband past the mountains to look for your friend. And while I cannot publicly allow you passage, when I find the lot of you gone in the morning, we will not go looking for you. I wish I could do more for Dušan's daughter, but in this I cannot. If there is ever a time for you to retake your throne, please call on me. The Tandrirr will be here for you."

The wet hit my eyes before I could stop it. I'd learned my birth mother's name, but I hadn't known my father's. I'd seen a faint glimmer of him in my mother's memories, but nothing more.

Lothan took a step toward me, probably concerned that I'd went from normal to damn near crying in the space of a second.

Shaking my head, I tried to wave him off. "No one told me his name," I croaked, trying to smile even though the loss hit me like a hammer. Why did I feel the burn of it when I'd never even met the man?

"Dušan Lafitte was a great king and an even better friend. If you ever want to know more about him, ask. I will tell you everything. The good, the bad. His wins and his losses."

Lothan wouldn't sugarcoat it, either. He would tell me everything. I had to appreciate that about him.

"Come, my little Queen," Lothan said, breaking the tension.

"Bring your family and eat with us. I promise none of the food will make you dance."

You tell your friend one little Fae dream and she tells the world. Can't trust anyone anymore.

After a night of feasting and avoiding fog-booze, we were rested enough to begin our trek out of Tandrirr. Starting at dawn, Torren escorted us out of the castle, and in the early light, we got to experience the full wonder of the mountain elves home. The river that we thought went nowhere wove itself through the city. Tiny offshoots made even tinier waterfalls, the water pulsing through the city like blood in veins. There were clear pools filled with water lilies, and if I looked closer, I knew I would glimpse water nymphs swirling in their depths.

Everything smelled clean, the sky looked bluer, the trees greener.

But I knew that there was just as much blood spilled here as there was at home. There were just as many wrongs and just as many injustices. I wasn't fooled by the pretty façade.

Even if it was nice.

The waterfalls gave way to a rocky terrain, and it was slow going for a while as we free climbed over boulders bigger than city busses. One of the few things going for us was the fact that it was still cool. Wearing these leathers, this trek would be a balmy mess if the weather decided not to cooperate.

My mind kept snagging on the difficulties I'd been having with my magic. While some of my spells—not that I had to use spells anymore—were working just fine, all my attempts to locate Melody had me turning up bupkis. I almost wished it were like Maria, even if that thought hurt. I almost wished I could hear her screaming, crying, something.

But every time I tried, I couldn't find her.

I didn't know who to ask or what my questions might be. Who would be able to help me navigate the power running through my veins if I was the last one?

The last.

That thought hurt, too. I almost missed the identity of the first-born demon-witch—the hybrid no one thought could be made. Being the first was a much better feeling than being the last. The last meant that if I died, there would be nothing left of the family I'd never met.

Nothing left of the family who were slaughtered for a reason I didn't know and probably couldn't comprehend. I couldn't think of a good reason for genocide, and that was exactly what it was.

I wondered if I'd ever stop hurting. If the pain of all this death would ever wear away. I wondered if I could ever trust again. Then I mentally slapped myself as my gaze snagged on the black diamond on my finger.

Yes, I could trust a few.

I could trust Alistair. I'd given him the only thing he'd ever asked for and he refused to let me down.

"What's that smile for?" the man in question asked as we continued to traipse down the mountain. We were supposed to be headed to the dwarves to check if they had seen Melody.

"I was just mooning over my husband. Have you seen him? He's about this tall"—I gestured over my head—"has a snarky British accent and killer dimples."

Alistair smiled at me, showing off said dimples. "I may have met the fellow. He sounds positively dreamy."

The sound of someone gagging made me glance over my shoulder. Aidan was a little green. Someone hadn't steered clear of the fog-booze, and he was paying the price today.

"Fucking newlyweds," Aidan muttered, shaking his head before groaning at the motion.

I stuck my tongue out at him. "Party pooper. If anything, somebody should have pooped your party last night. How many drinks did you have?"

Aidan waved my question away like thinking of the drink made him want to die. "I only had one. No one told me what it was. I spent half the night trying not to float off my bed, and the other half trying to keep my insides from falling into that weird toilet thing they had in our bathrooms. Never trust Della when she says an alcohol isn't strong. She *lies*."

"Or you just can't hold your booze," Hideyo piped up from behind him.

The kitsune wasn't holding in his enigmatic smile as he razzed Aidan which I thought was a fabulous thing. Hideyo had been uneasy since the moment we stepped in Faerie, and I couldn't blame him. I didn't know his history—or even how old he was—but I knew without a doubt that this realm did not make him happy at all.

And why would it?

If he were Fae like me—and I strongly suspected he was—anything that sent him running to the Earth realm couldn't be good.

Suddenly, Hideyo stopped dead on the path, cocking his head to the side like he was listening for something. I trusted his and Aidan's ears a lot more than my own, so when he stopped, I grabbed Alistair's hand and froze, too.

Without a thought, something rose up in me and pulled Della and my mother to me—the magic in my veins activating on an instinct I didn't know I had. One second, they were thirty feet ahead of us, and the next, they were behind Aidan and Hideyo.

I realized my body's mistake as soon as I made it. Just a glimpse of Della's expression hammered that home. I'd pulled Teresa and Della to me, but Torren was still out there, and he was about to be found by whatever or whomever pinged Hideyo's ears.

Footsteps reached my ears before I could do anything about Torren. Out of all of us, he was the one least likely to be picked apart by another Fae, so I did the only thing my limited time allowed—I hid us. The glamour I tossed up was some of the most advanced magic I'd ever done, and it went up without much of a fight.

Keeping it up was the problem.

The longer I held the walls in place, the more drained I felt, the magic to keep us concealed syphoning everything I had. Moving mountains and causing storms was no big deal, but this?

This was… unnatural magic. It felt wrong, too big, and too much.

I knew Fae could see through glamours, but this one? I had a feeling even I would have had trouble seeing through this type of spell had I not been the one casting it.

I wasn't sure what anyone else was seeing, but me? I saw the exact second Torren was spotted by a group of six soldiers.

Each of them had white hair and pearlescent pale skin, their bare arms swirled with glowing blue magic. Their armor was the same living metal I'd seen all over Faerie, but it was limited to breastplates and shoulder pieces. They held spears, the tops a deadly sharp triangular head and the bottoms barbed like tiny maces.

Torren saw them, stuttered to a stop, before giving them a low bow, using that bit of movement to discretely check his six. He was searching the magic in the air for us, but his gaze slid off our hiding spot before he rose. If Torren couldn't see, it was completely possible these soldiers couldn't, either.

"Filthy half-breed." One of the soldiers sneered. "What are you doing off your mountain top? Here to muddy your blood even more by fucking a dwarf?"

The tips of Torren's ears turned red, and I figured his whole face matched them. He said nothing in response, but I knew without a doubt his face told them to go fuck themselves.

"Look how red his face is!" another taunted, his following laugh echoing off the rocks. "How can you tell a dwarf woman from a man? Or does it matter?"

Torren growled then, his anger getting the better of him.

And that's when the six Fae swarmed him, the magic in their glowing blue arms flowing like tentacles of power, slamming him onto the ground.

A whimper escaped Della's throat, and Teresa put her hand over Della's mouth before she could give away our position. As the soldiers thrashed Torren, Teresa and Della struggled, and I watched horrified as Della's fangs slid into my mother's flesh.

Where was a random bolt of lightning when you needed one?

CHAPTER TWELVE

Torren was in danger, I was scared, and I had no idea if I could hold this glamour much longer. So it wasn't much of a surprise when the walls of my spell crumbled to dust. What also wasn't a surprise? My nose pouring like a fountain as I fell to my ass in the dirt.

I was using my magic the wrong way. Not that I knew how to use it the right way, but whatever.

Della struggled against Teresa's hold for about a millisecond before she realized the glamour that kept us hidden from the six men kicking her son's ass was down. Then she waffled. She had a duty to protect me, but I wasn't going to stop her from defending her son. Especially since it was my fault he was out in the open.

"Go," I growled, pissed that whatever loyalty Della had to Lilith could possibly trump family. Della's gaze whipped to me, and with tears in her eyes, she gave me a single nod before she leapt at the closest man.

Every time I watched Della fight, I was reminded that she was not dainty or fragile. She tore into one man's throat, viciously ripping his flesh with her fangs. Then, I couldn't see much else because Aidan and Hideyo were in front of me, defending me from the soldiers that still hadn't realized we were behind them.

If I could've stood right then—or spoken complete sentences—I would have told them to help Della. As it was, I couldn't do either of those things. I'd thought I was done with this draining bullshit, but I was wrong.

"*Sanitatem*," my mother murmured, putting some oomph into the healing spell that I hadn't quite mastered as she snapped her fingers. The jolt of energy and healing had me shaking off the blood loss, but I could tell it took a bit out of her. Especially when I glimpsed the plant she'd drawn from crumble to ash in her hand.

Damn.

One of the soldiers tossed Della off his back, her body flying through the air back toward our still-stationary group. She landed in a crouch, hissing at the six of them like she could ward them off somehow, but it was already too late.

We'd been spotted.

The five of them were going to protect me. No matter what I said, no matter what I did, they were going to put their lives on the line for me.

I figured it was high time I should put my life on the line for them, too.

The sky darkened to pitch as storm clouds rolled in, the earth roiling with the magic that leaked out of me when I couldn't help it. Wind whipped around us all, creating spouts of earth as the dirt fell prey to the gale. Lightning streaked across the sky, and without my body telling them to, my hands reached for my athames, extended the blades, and met the bolts of fire. Energy coursed through the metal, and if I were a human, I'd have died from the voltage ten times over.

As it stood, my blades were a conduit, and I knew exactly where I wanted my power to go.

Two bolts of lightning flew from my blades into two men, the blue tentacles of their magic writhing under the strain of electric heat. I was too busy staring at the two dudes I was frying to pay much attention to the other four, which was a problem when an azure wave of magic knocked me off my feet.

The magic was so cold it felt like knives pelting my skin as it stole my breath, but I rolled, twisted, and landed in a crouch. Slashing through their thrall with my twin swords, the seemingly incorporeal tentacles bled easily enough. A hot hand yanked me to my feet, and I briefly took in the sight of Alistair's demon form before his scythe hacked through another rope of magic.

The two I got with the lightning were smoking mounds on the ground, but the other four were holding their own against my companions. Della was trading blows with the soldier she'd nearly beheaded with her fangs. Teresa's electric fireballs were keeping another busy, while Aidan smoked in behind to cut off his head. Alistair was going toe to toe with a monster-sized soldier, his blue ropes of magic nearly taking Alistair off his feet.

But the last one was tangling with a floating animal that looked like the biggest fucking fox I'd ever seen in my life. Then it dawned on me. Hideyo was a Kitsune. Duh.

Hideyo's seven tails moved independently of each other and were much longer than any tail of any animal ever. Four of the tails had wrapped themselves around a limb, holding his prey still as Hideyo's jaws clamped around the soldier's head and pulled.

Gross.

I looked away just in time to watch Della get thrown into Aidan. Luckily, the wraith had just taken the Fae's head, so he had enough time to catch her midair and set her on the ground. Unfortunately, her soldier was on the move, realizing a little too late that he was vastly outgunned.

He took off, moving so fast I almost couldn't track him. If we lost him and word got back to the Seelie Court, we'd be fucked. I tiredly summoned lightning once more, my pull on the element not as strong as I'd like.

"Stop, love. We'll track him and take him out," Alistair murmured in my ear, half-holding me up as I tried to wield the current.

But before I could do any more than sink into his waiting arms, the guard seemed to bounce off of air. He fell to the dirt, and then his back bowed as if an invisible giant pulled his chest with a string. He writhed, his pale skin turning red and then blue and then a sickly purple. He gasped, clawing at his neck and chest, but he couldn't pull in any air.

Not a minute later, we all stood shocked as the soldier stilled, the life in him snuffed out. When he couldn't be anything other than dead, I relaxed a touch, but couldn't rest easy until I knew what the hell made him die.

"Mom, did you do that?" I called to Teresa, watching as she wiped the blood off her face.

She shook her head, her eyes never leaving the soldier.

And for good reason. Not a second later, white smoke poured from the soldier's mouth. It kept coming and coming until it coalesced into the shape of a man, the form solidifying into a guy I'd hope to never see again.

Rowan. Fucking. Durant.

He didn't spare us a glance until he'd reached down with both hands, took hold of the soldier's head and yanked it clean off the body, the bones of the spine cracked and crunched until it was finally free. It was not a clean process, and it made me want to toss my cookies.

"What the fuck?" Aidan murmured, and I couldn't help but agree with him. This was definitely a WTF moment.

Rowan carried the head by the Fae's braid as he sauntered back to us, and I couldn't decide if I was afraid, pissed he was here at all, or grateful for his assistance.

He stepped over the mounds of soldier ash, giving them a respectful nod.

"What the fuck?" Aidan repeated, louder this time like he wanted an answer. Since I was on my ass in the dirt, I let him take the lead on this one.

"I'm sorry, did you want Seelie guards to make it back to the queen and tell her you're here? If so, I suppose I should have let him pass and saved myself the trouble."

This did not make even a tiny lick of sense. Rowan was a Seelie emissary. He belonged to the Seelie Court.

"Oh, dear. I suppose I'll just have to spell it out for you." He sighed, exasperated we didn't understand. "I'm a double agent, obviously."

Obviously. Like he wasn't a lying liar who lies. Yup, totally trusted him.

"That does not inspire confidence, Rowan. In fact, it makes it a little bit difficult to trust you—you know, with the whole lying thing," Aidan growled, moving more in front of me to keep the sylph away.

"Do you see this?" Rowan held up the guard's head. "This is a Seelie guard with direct access to the queen. I ripped his head off so he wouldn't tell his beloved majesty you are here. For which you are welcome. And why are you still on the ground?"

I rolled my eyes and pushed at the back of Aidan's legs so I could see the bastard. Aidan shuffled to the side, but he was tense and ready to fight if he had to.

"You try putting up a glamour not even a Fae can see through and see how well you do." I put a hand in the dirt to try to still my swaying brain, but it didn't work. My mother's healing spell was a Band-Aid, and it was failing.

Rowan crouched to see me better, his crystalline eyes flashing blue in the sun. "Why aren't you drawing on Faerie? Or are you such a complete moron that you think you can sustain using power like that?"

A fireball streaked across the air and exploded in Rowan's face. Surprised, he fell back on his ass in the dirt, coughing and hacking as he snuffed out the flames, his skin only a little pink from the heat.

"Stop speaking to her that way," my mother growled, stepping in front of Aidan, her sword in hand. Her right sparked with a fireball traced with electricity. "Or the next one won't be a warning shot. It'll stay glued to your sylph form, and I'll watch as you die screaming. Don't test me, Rowan Marchand Durant. I'll bind you in a heartbeat."

I had a feeling using his full name was significant, especially since Rowan stood, the magic rising in him. The men around me shifted their weight, preparing for a fight, but Teresa stood calm, ready to set a man on fire if she had to. Go, Mom.

"She had no idea she was Fae until a week ago. She knows nothing of the Elementals because there is no one to teach her. If you have any helpful remarks, I suggest you supply them. Now."

"Using concealment magic big enough to hide from Fae is more magic than her body can sustain. But just like when she was a conduit for the lightning, Elementals can draw from all elements to replenish their power and heal. So draw on the earth, draw on the air, something, so you don't look like a pitiful girl sitting in the dirt."

I thought about it for a minute and asked what he thought was probably a dumb question. "Will I hurt them—the elements? Will I take too much?"

Rowan's expression was like I'd hit him in the face with a two-by-four. "I just told you that you can draw on the whole of Faerie, and you're worried about taking too much. That you'll hurt the realm and, by extension, the beings in it?"

"Well, yeah. If an earth witch draws too much, plants around her die. If a fire witch does it, the air gets too cold to sustain life, the same with water and air. I never draw on anything, just myself, so I want to know what I'm doing before I take too much. The life around me matters, Rowan."

"I see," he muttered, his voice catching, and he cleared his throat. "No, you can't take too much. The elements are yours to wield. Close your eyes, put your fingers in the dirt, and pull. The earth wants to help you, sustain you. Breathe in the air, let it heal your lungs. Feel the fire crackling in the sky, let it warm you."

Worried about the truth in his words, I reluctantly did as he asked. Tunneling my fingers into the dirt, I felt the grit push under my nails as I closed my eyes. It was as if the earth was waiting for me. Power rushed into me, warming me up, healing me more than I'd ever been healed in my life. Aches and pains I didn't know I had eased, the rupture of blood vessels in my nose sealed shut, the lancing pain in my lungs that I'd ignored lessened until it went away altogether. Then I breathed in, letting the air heal me even more.

My heart raced as I drew on the lightning still cracking against the clouds. My body felt alive for the first time since... since... I couldn't remember.

Was this the way I was supposed to feel? Was I supposed to feel this good?

I forced myself to ramp down the connection, knowing that if I cut it off, it could hurt me. Slowly, I disconnected, opening my eyes.

Night had fallen sometime since I closed my eyes, and I searched for Alistair, for my mother. I was in a forest, alone. They wouldn't leave me alone. Something was wrong.

"Rest easy, child. No one has left you," a man's voice rumbled, and I searched the trees for it. A giant of a man sat on a rock to my right, his purply black locks waving above his head like he was stuck underwater. His hand held a ball of flame, and if I focused, I could see the shape of a woman dancing in the center of his palm. She twirled and bowed and blew him a kiss as he stared at her with a mournful pull to his mouth.

I should know this man. I should, but I didn't.

"You were a baby when last I saw you. You look so much like your mother," he murmured before closing his fist on the fire. "I knew if you drew on the elements, I would be able to find you—even if I'm stuck here."

I wanted to ask who he was, but I didn't know if talking to him would be bad or not. The rules in Faerie were different and complicated and...

"I won't harm you, Massima. You are of my blood. You are the last."

"You can hear my thoughts like Lilith can. I have to say, I don't like that power."

His face split into a grin. "Only here, my child, and only because we are in a small pocket of the spirit realm. You accessed this element to help heal you—even if you didn't mean to. My name is Dušan, and I am your father."

Tears hit my eyes, and I tried to swallow them down. "They said you died."

Dušan nodded. "I did. But I carved out this little place for myself before I left so I would have somewhere to go to. Your mother decided to stay with you, so I wait here for her to come back to me. Her spirit will find me eventually. I just have to be patient."

"Is patience a family trait? Because if so, it skipped a generation."

He grinned bigger this time. "It is not, but we do what we must. I brought you here so I could deliver a message. And to see your face, if I'm to be perfectly honest. Your brother and sisters are out of my reach, and I miss my children."

My eyelids gave up the ghost, and my tears fell. The loss in his voice spoke to me, spoke to my grief and pain.

"I lost someone recently, too. I've lost plenty, but..." I trailed off, shaking my head. "My sister. She is lost to me."

"Maria, yes?"

I nodded, my chest feeling like it was going to cave in on itself. Her name burned. "She was pulled into the Seam. I can't get her back."

Dušan stood from the boulder and sat in front of me in the dirt. His face was kind, with eyes like mine and my same too-wide mouth. "No, you cannot. But she doesn't feel pain where she is. She doesn't feel sorrow or fear. She is... gone. There is no coming back. She is at rest."

I couldn't explain why, but that made it almost hurt worse. I would never see her again. Never see her smile, never hear her voice. Why hadn't I taken more pictures? Why hadn't I recorded her voice so I'd always have it?

Because I thought I had more time. I thought I had forever.

Warm arms surrounded me, and Dušan pulled my head to rest on his chest. He smelled like hickory smoke and leather and magic, and I felt the hug deep down in my soul where it was ragged and torn. It took me a second to realize I was crying, the keening wail of a pain so deep it had to come out. These were tears that could never be silenced.

And Dušan didn't try.

He hugged me tight until they petered out on their own.

He kissed my forehead and let me go, relief on his face so acute I had no idea he'd been in pain. But then again, why wouldn't he be? He was stuck here alone, waiting for his family to come back to him.

"Thank you for giving me that, Massima. I haven't felt like a father in a very long time."

My heart broke for him, but I gave him a smile, anyway. It was the best I could do. Then my brain caught on the "thanks."

"I am in your debt, my child. Your tears were a gift that I have every intention of repaying. I'll start by giving you the message I sought you out to provide," he murmured, the warning in his voice clear. "She knows you're here. Verena is coming for you."

CHAPTER THIRTEEN

"You are not safe where you are. You need to get back to your family, your protection."

But why? Why is she coming for me? What is so special about me?

Okay, I knew I was supposed to be able to open a door, but I thought that door was in Hell.

"There are many doors, Massima, but that is not why she wants you. She'll say that you could free the old ones, and that is true, but she wants you dead because you're supposed to be on that throne. Not her."

Freaking politics. They were the same on every realm—complete bullshit.

"Can't I just tell her I don't want it? Because no offense to you and your realm, but I don't. I have a home and a life and a job. I have a family I built bit by bit. I don't..." I trailed off, not able to tell him why exactly I didn't want to be here.

Dušan sighed and rubbed his brow with the palm of his hand. "She will not believe you."

"I thought the Fae can't lie."

"We can't. That doesn't mean we don't talk around the lie to weave it into a truth. She murdered her sister in cold blood. She slaughtered every single Elemental and all the Fae that stood up to her. She's still letting her men do whatever they want to half-breeds and any that she deems unworthy. Verena is poisoning Faerie, and she will use any means she has to stay right where she is."

I sighed, the peace I felt a moment ago long gone. "You want me to kill her. To take her place or—"

Dušan shook his head. "No. I want you to stay alive. If not you, someone else will save this realm. It is not up to you, and I would not ask it of you. You deserve better than to inherit this war."

The waterworks came again, but I did my best to hold them back. I'd been a tool my whole life—something to wield, something to gain. This was a man who had every reason to want me to kill his rival, and all he wanted was to keep me safe. He reminded me of someone.

"Your Alistair? Yes, we are much alike in that way. All he wants is you safe and happy. As far as husbands go, you chose well. Get back to him. Find your charge and get out of Faerie. This is not your war. I won't ask you to fight it."

Dušan gave me a soft smile, snapped his fingers, and…

My eyes flashed open, and I was now staring into blue irises I knew so well. Alistair was cupping my cheeks, worry etched into every line of his face.

"Fates, love, don't do that," he hissed, pulling me into his arms. "You weren't breathing. Fates, you weren't breathing."

Aidan chuckled. "Ah, so this was your first time seeing that. Just wait till she actually dies on you. It's super fun and not at all frightening."

"That happened one time," I grumbled, sinking into Alistair's arms.

"Twice. You forgot about Micah," Aidan reminded me, and I shuddered, remembering both times the bastard almost killed me.

"Oh, right. Is Torren okay?" I asked, changing the subject.

Alistair snorted. "No, love. Teresa is trying to help, but it doesn't seem to be working."

Worried, Dušan's warning that we couldn't stay here replayed in my head. I needed Torren up and moving. I needed him to lead us where we were supposed to go.

"Let me try," I whispered into Alistair's ear and he reluctantly let me go. I could tell he wanted to say no, but wouldn't on general principle. Smart man.

I stood, noticing the lack of creaking to my joints, the sheer absence of pain in every part of my body. I wondered how bad off I'd been, drawing off of nothing or myself for four centuries. By the way I could take a deep breath for the first time in a while, I figured pretty bad.

Alistair stopped me, his hand at my elbow as he drew me back to him. "You look different. You… you glow. More than before. Did Faerie heal you that much?"

I widened my eyes at him, lowering my voice not much more than a whisper. "You have no idea. Let me see what I can do to help, and then we have to move. Verena knows I'm here."

Alistair's gaze cut to Rowan and then back to me, the unspoken question lingering between us. *Did he tell her?*

I shrugged at him and made my way over to Della and Teresa who were putting everything they had into Torren. I stilled their hands, moving them away and replaced them with my own. Pressing one to the skin above his heart and the other on his head, I willed some of my strength into him.

Information streamed into my brain, hitting me like a brick. Torren getting beat up as a child by Seelie for having fangs he couldn't retract. Getting made fun of because he didn't have his father's powers to move earth. Being slower than other elves, being taunted, being hurt, someone attacking, tearing, shredding his throat. Fear, so much fear. Someone—he couldn't see who—hurting him in ways no one should ever be hurt. *No one will believe you. No one will believe you. No one will believe you.*

His father's disappointment. His mother's abandonment. His sister's fear of his anger.

Painpainpain.

I willed myself to back out of his mind, and pulled on the earth beneath my feet to seal the wounds in his body. Some of them were fresh from the Seelie. And some were old—ones that had never healed right after…

Giving it less than a second's thought, I drew on the spirit element, willing just a little into him to try to mend his soul. I was working off of instinct and hope.

Hope that this little bit would help.

Torren's eyes opened slowly, a languid set to his shoulders, his jaw relaxed. He was beautiful—the ravages of his past momentarily absent from his face. Then he caught sight of my expression, and, somehow, he knew what I'd seen.

I saw the instant his face shuttered, and I willed just a little more spirit into him.

So no one would hear, I brought my face to his ear. "I'll find him. I promise you. I have his voice, his thread. He won't hurt anyone ever again."

I wanted to tell Della, but I knew I couldn't. That wasn't mine to share—that pain, that brutality, that stealing didn't happen to me. And it was a secret I would keep until I couldn't keep it anymore. Preferably after whoever hurt Torren was a smoking pile of ash.

I shifted back, pulling Torren up with me. "I keep my promises."

His crystalline eyes shone with an emotion I couldn't name. "I believe you."

No wonder. No wonder he wanted nothing to do with vampires. If one did that to me, I'd probably be just like him—livid at a whole species for the actions of one.

"Good. Take us to the dwarven caves. We can't stay here."

I'd wanted to elaborate, but I didn't. I couldn't say why I didn't want to tell them about Dušan in that tiny pocket he'd carved out for himself.

Maybe it was because I wasn't sure it was real. Maybe it was because I wanted that little piece of him for myself. Maybe it was because I didn't want someone to tell me he was wrong or lying or…

I had to get over it. I trusted these people—or at least I trusted most of them. I wondered why I still didn't trust Rowan. He had given me the information I needed to heal myself. But after Striker, my trust button was broken big time.

Following closely behind Torren, we kept our eyes peeled for more Seelie guards. Rowan overtook our little group, beckoning for us to follow him. This didn't feel like a trap, and yet it did at the same time. Once we entered the mouth of the cave, I felt a ripple of magic against my skin.

Immediately, I went on high alert, which ended about three seconds later when I caught sight of the walls of the cave. Crystals of every color jutted from the walls as they pulsed with magic as they lit our way. A soft voice in my head told me not to touch them —not because they would hurt me, but because they did not belong to me.

Bad things would happen to those that took without asking.

"Don't touch the crystals," Rowan and I said at the same time, and he whipped his gaze back to me.

All I could do was shrug. It was like the forest and the lightning. I had no idea how I knew what I knew, just that whatever—or whomever—was guiding me, they had my best interests at heart. A part of me wondered if it was Dušan whispering in my ear, our spirits connected over space and time. Or maybe it was the knowledge Zeta had given my mother in her passing, filtering down to me.

It was completely possible that it was both, and my spirit was bolstered a bit by that thought.

The caves seemed never ending, the tunnels snaking around stalactites which appeared to be made of the clearest crystal and stalagmites of a living, breathing metal. They were almost molten, but no heat came from them.

Alistair and I moved closer to Rowan. I wanted to be there if he struck out on us. I was stronger now—thanks to him—but my trust had limits.

Rowan seemed to sense when I was behind him because he began talking like we were continuing a conversation. "The Seelie have been searching these caves for years trying to find us, but they never do." His chuckle was dark as he hopped over a set of Fae bones propped against the cave wall—the breastplate marking him as a Seelie guard.

I wanted to inspect them to see what killed the man, but Rowan wasn't slowing down.

"Seelie magic doesn't work in these walls. The crystals keep the taint out. The Resistance might have cells all over, but here is where we do most of our work. Helping those that need it, trying to repair the damage wrought by the queen and healing the wounded." Rowan's steps faltered for a second as we came to a fork in the trail. He seemed to be searching for something before he chose the third tunnel from the left.

"I thought the Seelie were supposed to be the good guys. That's what all the stories say," I wondered aloud, my questions multiplying in my head too fast to keep them in.

"History is written by the victors, Max. That's as true in Faerie as it is on Earth."

Rowan shuffled to a stop again, turned ninety degrees to his right and knocked on the cave wall three times, paused, two times, paused, and then five more times. The cave wall rippled, the rocks moving like blocks as they peeled themselves back to make a person-sized hole in what used to be a solid wall.

Was everything in Faerie creepy as fuck or was that just me?

Without another word, Rowan marched through the newly made doorway, and against my better judgment, I followed. This new cavern was dark, and even though I'd had no trouble seeing in the tunnels, it was black as pitch now.

Unable to make myself wait for Rowan to turn on a freaking light, I snapped my fingers. The goal was to put light in my hand. Instead, I managed to light every torch, ignite every candle, and flare every single non-lit crystal in the immediate vicinity.

Which would have been super awesome had we not been completely fucking surrounded.

CHAPTER FOURTEEN

The brightly lit cave was filled with every manner of Fae, but dwarves took up a large portion of the populace.

I was no stranger to Fae lore. I'd had a fascination with their stories since I'd heard my very first one. Ethereals—even the ones I hadn't heard of—were easy to figure out. But Fae? There was always some convoluted reason for skinning someone or stealing a child or gnawing on bones. And there were so many kinds and so many variations. And I wouldn't even start on fantasy books.

But none of them had pegged dwarves correctly.

Yes, they were short—the tallest one was no more than chest-high. Yes, they were stout—their thick legs and strong arms seemed fit for hauling rocks or mining gems. But they didn't have bushy beards or jolly faces. No, these dwarves were battle-ready in head-to-toe armor. But they didn't carry axes or swords. Each one had a war hammer in their hands, the dual-sided mallet fit for crushing rocks or skulls depending on their mood.

And the mood in here was three steps past hostile.

We were not welcome. *Message received.*

My first instinct was to draw on the earth to see if I could steal their weapons away from them. But I knew if I did that, they would never trust me.

No, I couldn't win them over by force.

The best course of action I had was to see if I could talk them down. It wasn't my strongest skill, but it was what I had.

Elbowing past Rowan and ignoring Aidan, my mother's, and Alistair's whispered threats, I walked closer to the horde, raised my hands, and sat in the middle of the floor.

"I'm called Max. We mean you and yours no harm." Glancing around the room, I spotted a bevy of split lips and black eyes, a few broken arms, and other injuries. "What happened here? Are your people okay?"

The dwarf closest to me seemed confused, not expecting the question at all. His eye was swollen shut, his nose a bloody mangled mess. His left arm didn't look right, either—like it wasn't quite attached properly. He shifted his weight before dropping the hammer to his side, his one good arm barely holding onto the heavy weapon. Through what was close to a thick Scottish brogue, he asked, "You worry after my people?"

I covered my mouth with a hand, worried I'd made a mistake. Nowhere in Fae lore did it say compassion was a bad thing. "Is that not done here? I meant no offense."

A few more warriors lowered their weapons, eyeing me with a suspicious air.

"I'm called Aramal, and no offense taken. A lass blew through here a night or so ago carrying a wee baby with her. She wanted past, but she was of demon blood, and Faerie is a dangerous place for people of that sort. When we wouldn't let her through, she put a spell on us. Made us want to fight our own."

None of this was good news. Like none of it. Why in the blue fuck was Melody in Faerie in the first place? She said she was going home, but Faerie wasn't her home at all. Her home was a massacre sight in Bumfuck, Indiana.

"We're looking for that woman. She's called Melody, and she —" How could I possibly explain a broken soul to these people—that she was broken and put back together in such a fashion there was no way she was even lucid. "She is fractured. Her soul, I mean. I'm not sure she's cognizant of what she's doing."

Aramal scoffed, his dubious expression telling me he in no way believed me.

"She was stolen from Heaven and put back together wrong. I don't even know if she's in her real body or…" I shook my head, trying to find the words so he would know just how broken she was.

"Someone nicked her from Heaven? Who would do such a thing?"

"A complete fucking moron, that's who," Alistair growled, his feet shuffled behind me. "Look, I know my kinswoman hurt you, but she isn't in her right mind. We're looking for her, we're trying to get her home. Do you mind lowering your weapons? We're not here to make trouble."

Aramal raised his fist, and as one, the dwarves and assorted Fae lowered their weapons.

I thought of the only thing I could do to endear me to these people, and asked, "Are there any severely wounded? I can help if you let me."

Aramal didn't seem convinced, so I held out a hand to him. Reluctantly, he wrapped his rough fingers around mine. Gently, I pulled on the earth element, feeding it into his body. Almost instantly, his swollen-shut eye began to deflate, his nose cracked before righting itself, and his shoulder seemed to go back into its socket. He stood taller, taking a deep breath—the first one I imagine he'd taken in a while. Years flew off his face, the deep grooves of pain melting away.

"Elemental," he whispered, his eyes shining. "I haven't felt the earth like that in some time. Please help my people, and we'll return the favor in kind."

His emotions pulled at me. Why could he not feel the earth when he was at the center of it? "Of course. Lead me to the worst ones, and I'll do my best."

The lot of us moved through the throng of people to an alcove where the really injured were. I had no idea, but that swarm of warriors were protecting their wounded. And there were a lot of wounded here. Some with missing limbs, some with split skulls. I had no idea if these Fae were like me, if they could regenerate over time. Based on the stench of fear clouding the air, I had to bet on no.

"Alistair? You're with me. Aidan? Della? Help me triage these people," I ordered like the general I was so not. "Everyone else, help them make sure they have clean water to drink and a way to prepare the dead."

I held Alistair's hand as Aramal led me to the worst off. The woman was barely breathing, her skin sallow as she clutched a dirt-covered rag to her abdomen. She was septic, and I knew that from years of watching humans kill each other. Alistair was there to protect me, but also, he was there just so I could hold his hand as I surrounded myself with this much pain. I could feel it seeping into my toes, it was so big.

"I'm new at this, so I'm going to do what I can. You understand, right?"

Aramal's newly fixed face gave me a sad sort of smile. "We can only do what we can do, my Queen. If you can help my people, we will follow you until the end."

This was the second person to call me Queen in the last twenty-four hours. I didn't know if I liked that or not, but I had bigger fish to fry, and this woman wasn't going to last much longer.

Putting a hand to the cave wall, I drew on the earth, feeding it into the woman by my fingertip at her forehead. In a flash, she opened her eyes, pink coming back into her cheeks, her wound drying up.

Like a whip, the element flitted through me, and I knew the answer for so many wounded.

"Everyone, touch the ground, a wall, something with your bare skin. Your foot, your hand. Something."

The ones who could move, did. The ones who couldn't, we moved them before I sat in the middle of them all. I buried my hands in the earth, the rocks jagged and sharp, and the sand between them so smooth it was like butter. Air pulsed through the room, fire bloomed from the crystals, water dripped from the stalagmites. I pulled all the elements into myself, letting my body taste them before I pushed them all back out to the wounded.

At first, they didn't want to go, like rusty gears, they forgot how to turn. But I pushed and shoved and manhandled the elements to do what I wanted. I gave them back to Faerie.

Something told me these people hadn't had a real breath of air, or fire in their blood, or earth under their nails, or water in their veins in some time. They were empty, and they needed to be filled.

"Max?" Alistair called from what seemed like far away. "You're hurting yourself, love. You have to stop."

That's when I felt the blood dripping down my chin. I was doing it the wrong way. I was supposed to draw in as I gave it back. It was supposed to be a circle. A give and a take.

I could almost feel Rowan rolling his eyes at me.

"I'll fix it. Just let me fix it." My voice was barely there, and I had no idea if he even heard me, but I switched course, taking the individual elements into myself so I could heal these people.

The power almost burned as it flowed through me. The molten heat of Faerie's core, the frisson of energy raked across my mind as I gave it back to the people who were in such dire straits, they couldn't possibly do this for themselves.

When I couldn't hold it anymore, I mentally snipped the threads tying me to each of the wounded, gently titrating them off the power one by one until it was just me. The ruptured blood vessels in my nose and ears sealed shut, the damage I'd accidentally done to my organs healed, and I breathed in a steady breath.

Opening my eyes, I met Alistair's gaze. Concern and something like pride was stamped all over his face.

"I was doing it wrong at first. I fixed it. I didn't mean to scare you," I whispered so no one could hear, trying to ease his worry.

I didn't want him to tell me to stop. I didn't want him to tell me I couldn't help when I could. Not that I'd listen, but it would hurt if he were like the rest of them.

Alistair didn't say a word. Instead, he cupped my cheeks in his hands and kissed the shit out of me. I could feel the fire in him calling to me. I'd never felt the element that lived in him like that before, and something in me wanted to bask in it, wanted to roll in it, wanted to drink it down, and let it fill me forever. I wanted him, all of him, in all the ways.

This is what love feels like. You love him.

That thought streaked across my brain, not snide or unkind. It was a gentle missive to the wholly uneducated, a soft reminder that this was what I'd been missing.

I deepened the kiss, wanting him to feel everything I was, hoping that I wasn't alone. I didn't think I was. I was sure I was arriving at this party late as usual. When the kiss ended, he drew back from me, pinning me with his gaze, the fire of his demon in it.

"I'm so bloody proud of you, love. I can't—" Alistair cut himself off, disbelief and awe coloring everything about him. "I'm a lucky man having you as my wife."

The pride that he felt was like a warm blanket, and I felt cozy and safe and so full, I couldn't possibly wait for a better time when we weren't surrounded by people.

"I love you."

Those three words slipped past my lips for the first time ever. I'd never told a man that I'd loved them—not the way I meant it right then—and for a split second, I felt more vulnerable than I ever had in my whole life.

But he didn't let me down. No, Alistair was the kind of man who would never let me down.

"I love you, Max. To the ends of the earth and far beyond. Vaster than Heaven or Hell or any of the worlds in between."

That was it. That was the exact feeling, and I could tell he meant it because his boyish grin most likely matched my blisteringly bright smile. I could see a lifetime—hell, a hundred lifetimes—in that grin. Mischief and mayhem and laughs and worry. I could see all of it like I was taking a tiny peek into our future.

Alistair raked a thumb across my cheek, catching a tear that fell from my eye. I didn't know why I was crying. I was the happiest I'd ever been in my life. In the middle of Faerie searching for a half-crazed succubus while on the run from a mad queen.

Only I could tell the man I was bound to that I loved him for the first time in the middle of all this mess.

"I know you guys are having a moment, but I don't think the dwarves are going to wait much longer to talk to you, Max," Della said, popping our little love bubble.

The sounds around us rushed into my ears for the first time since I opened my eyes. Excited whispers of joy buzzed around the cave, and as much as I didn't want to, I let Alistair pull me to my feet.

Aramal took that opportunity to approach. "I haven't felt the earth like that in centuries, child. Not since—" He cut himself off as something dawned on him. "You aren't just a queen, are you? You're Dušan's daughter."

I knew Dušan was a king—the last true King of Faerie—but the way Aramal was putting it, was he more than that? I didn't understand, and for a second, I was afraid.

Alistair sensed this because I was behind him and surrounded by Della, Aidan, Hideyo, and my mother in a blink.

"I mean no disrespect, your Maj—"

Alistair cut him off. "She doesn't like that. She's Max. Just Max."

"Right. I meant no disrespect. Dušan was rumored to be a god in hiding. One of the first old gods. He made this world from nothing, molded it, shaped it, gave it life. From it, all Fae emerged."

That sounded like a cool story, but Dušan was dead... and living a half-life in a pocket world he'd made for himself.

Aramal saw my utter disbelief and dialed up his legend to the nth degree.

"Have you ever heard of the god, Chaos?"

I was the daughter of Chaos? Yeah, that sounded about right.

CHAPTER FIFTEEN

"Are you trying to tell me that I'm a demi-god?"

Aramal blinked at me. "Well, yes. Do you not know who your father is, lass?"

According to Greek mythology, the god Chaos was the void that the primordial gods sprang from. Chaos was supposed to be the beginning of everything. If what Aramal was saying was true, then Dušan was way more than the stories suggested.

"If he was a god—not just a god, one of the first gods—then why is he dead? How could Verena kill an immortal?"

Dušan said so himself. He was dead. But why hadn't he told me what he was?

Aramal sighed, the pain in it hitting me square in the chest. "It was a rowan arrow that hit him in the heart. There is only one rowan tree in Faerie. It was his only weakness, and he was said to have kept it just in case he needed to die. But that was before he met Zeta and his children came. Before your brother and sisters, Dušan was a different man. A god hiding within his own creation. He was sad and tired and alone. His type does not do too well by themselves."

Aramal spoke as if he knew my father. As if he'd sat down and chatted with the man. Or god. Or whatever.

"Why was he in hiding? Why make Faerie at all? And how in the fresh hell can he possibly think he's hiding if he's making whole realms? Who could he be hiding from?"

"Well, that depends on who you believe. Some say he was hiding from his brothers and sisters. Some say he just wanted peace, that the wars took too much out of him. Some say he wasn't hiding at all, that he just desired to make his own way without man muddying it up. There are a lot of stories, Maj—Max."

I couldn't quite wrap my head around what Aramal was saying, but he couldn't help a realm full of mumbo jumbo.

"I don't think I'm a demi-god—even if Dušan is my father. But I kept my word, your people are better, right?"

Aramal scoffed at me. "Not a demi-god my wrinkled arse. Take a look around, Max. See what your "non-god" abilities did for my people."

Looking around the cave, I spotted people who were on death's door five minutes ago smiling and laughing, hugging their fellow dwarves.

"All I did was tap into the elements and give them back. Rowan?" I called, spying the sylph talking with a fawn woman, her antlers and cloven feet a dead giveaway.

He sauntered over, unaware of what we were talking about.

"Tell him what you told me, that Elementals can draw from the elements. You told me what to do to heal myself."

Rowan looked like he'd been caught in a snare. He'd known this whole time—before even I did—that I was Fae. He knew I was an Elemental. Did he know I was a demi-god, too?

"Elementals can draw on the five elements, yes. But they cannot conjure objects from thin air, they cannot give the elements back to heal others, and they cannot heal an entire cave full of injured at once. You wield the elements, yes. But you can do things I've only seen a god do."

Aramal nodded, crossing his arms over his barrel chest like what Rowan said made it a done deal. "The last time we felt the earth move within us, the air touch us, the water fill us, the fire warm us, was before your father passed. No other Elemental could do that, lass. Not even your mother."

I started laughing, that not-right laugh of a woman at her limit. It was part-hysterical giggle and part-exasperated irritation. "Yeah, I'm done talking about this. Aramal, I'm glad your people are better. If you need help, give me a shout. Someone needs to lead me out of this cave before I lose it."

Alistair wrapped his arm around me, and I leaned into him. Only then did I think to glance at my mother.

She felt my gaze and threw her hands up in surrender. "Don't look at me. I didn't know any of this shit. Zeta's memories, or instructions, or whatever that was did not include your father's information. I didn't even know his name until Lothan told you."

"Not everyone believes that Dušan was a god. I know Lothan would have said something if his best friend was a..." Della trailed off, seeming to consider what her husband would and would not have told her. She blinked hard, shook her head, and then winced. "Okay, it is completely possible he would have kept it from me if Dušan said to. Fuck." She groaned, rubbing her face with her hands.

Yup, I needed to get out of this cave. To keep myself calm, I buried my nose in the crook of Alistair's jaw and inhaled. He drew me tighter to him as I counted to ten. When ten didn't work, I counted to fifty, the silence stretching as I refused to explode in a room full of people I just helped.

"Lass," Aramal began, his voice pitched low as to not irritate me. "You shouldn't head out into the forests without warriors with you. That is where the girl was headed. I'll send some of my best to help protect you. We owe you more than that, but I have a feeling that will be all you'll accept."

I didn't want to accept even that. We were fine. I was fine. But those Seelie guards nearly kicked our asses. If Verena knew I was here, I was a sitting duck. And when Verena came for me, she wouldn't just hurt me. She'd destroy all of us.

Begrudging, thy name is Max.

"I accept your generosity. It would be helpful to have more warriors."

Look at me being all adult and shit.

I did growl a little under my breath but gladly followed Aramal as he took point to lead us out of the maze of tunnels, his ten best warriors following us. I was half-tempted to see if Rowan was right, and I could conjure shit and make myself a bottle of bourbon.

I didn't even need a glass. The bottle would do just fine.

But I had a freaked-out slightly homicidal fledgling succubus to find, and I needed my wits about me. Denial was going to have to be my friend for a little while longer.

When the mouth of the cave yawned wide, I was aggrieved to find that it was now night. Della said that we shouldn't travel after dark. Then again, if Melody was out there causing mayhem, we might just have to contend with the darkness.

The tunnel we exited didn't seem to be the same one we entered. The other was surrounded by craggy rock and black sand. This entrance was spongy grass, with a copse of trees not too far away. I could even hear the tinkling of a stream nearby. It seemed almost peaceful if it weren't for the creatures I knew were within the wood.

Aramal was conferring with the fawn woman Rowan had been talking to in the cave. She stood tall, at least three feet taller than Aramal, dressed in a leather skirt that covered until the first bend in her knees. Her top was an amalgamation of living metal armor, dangling feathers that glowed even in the low light, and several clusters of animal bones.

Or at least I hoped they were animal bones.

Her antlers flowed up and back, almost like a ram's, and she had an additional knife-edged bone that protruded from either side of her neck. But none of that compared to her face, which was beautiful and frightening all at the same time. Her cheekbones were high, sweeping back like knife blades from her cupid's bow of a mouth. Her eyes were thin and wide, her irises and sclera blending together to make it look like the cosmos were in them.

And her skin—the part that wasn't furred—was an unusual shade of gray, threaded through with veins of glowing green magic.

She was quite possibly the most stunning creature I'd ever encountered in my life.

Aramal and the woman moved closer, and she made her introduction, not bothering with typical Fae customs as she thrust out her heavily ringed hand.

"My name is Maireen. I am the leader of the fawn people. I came to Aramal because your Melody has come through my lands. Her destruction has been great. I won't mince words. Can you help us?"

I wondered why she didn't say as much in the cave. I would have gladly said yes then.

"I will do what I can," I replied before pausing, asking the question that was at the forefront of my mind. "Can you guarantee our safe passage? I was told the night was not friendly to us."

"A demi-god is worried about a few Faeries? You have nothing to fear from the night or the inhabitants of my forest."

Shrugging, I gave her a wan smile. "I don't know if I believe the demi-god theory. And I'd rather not fight or hurt people when I don't have to."

Maireen turned to Aramal. "You're right. She is very different from Verena." To me, she said, "Your aunt is my enemy. Is that a problem for you?"

I stood there speechless for a moment, struck dumb from Maireen's direct questions. I'd never met a more direct Fae.

"She murdered my whole family. I grew up not knowing what I was, not knowing how to live in my own skin. Alone. Without anyone to hold my hand or love me or look out for me when I needed it. I do not care that Verena is your enemy as long as I'm not."

Maireen gave me an enigmatic smile that could mean she was plotting my murder or lending support—I had no idea which.

"That is good. And no, I do not consider you an enemy. We'll see if you are an ally if you can help my people."

So somewhere in between, then.

"Fair enough."

Maireen led us deep into the forest where the air warmed just slightly. Usually, with deeper tree cover, the air cooled down, but not here. The farther into the woods we walked, the hotter it got.

I soon found out why.

Parts of the forest were burning, a magic sort of fire that did not spread. Instead, the tree sat smoldering, the flames killing it bit by bit. Maybe there was a spell holding it in place, perhaps the fire could not be put out. Maybe the tree couldn't die.

"Did Melody do this?" I asked as I squeezed Alistair's hand. He hadn't left my side once since we'd said our I love yous, and I didn't mind one bit.

Sadness rolled over Maireen's face as tears collected in her eyes. "No," she croaked before shaking her head. "This is Verena's doing. Because we would not pledge loyalty to her. It was a sacred tree, thought to be one of the first that Dušan made when he created Faerie. It was our holy place."

"That bitch. I mean, who burns down a church? Honestly." I knew humans did the same, sure. I'd seen the aftermath of smoldering churches of all religions. It seemed like the biggest dick move, and it never worked out how the perpetrators wanted it to. It just made for a fiercer enemy with rage in their veins.

I let go of Alistair's hand and walked closer to the flames. It was hot, but it didn't burn, and I closed my eyes to try and sense the fire. The flames were sentient, they did not want to burn the tree, but they were under a spell. A crude and hastily crafted one. Plucking the threads of it, I unlocked the flames from their unwanted mission, drawing them into myself so they wouldn't go rogue and spread throughout the forest.

But the flames were too much for me to hold—the power too great for my body to sustain. The magic fire wanted out, it wanted to live free, not trapped in my body, so I gave it what it wanted. I filtered the energy back into the ground—into the center of Faerie, where it could be of use but also where it could flit around in the core of this world free as any fire could be.

It was crude, sure, but it was better than the whole damn forest burning down. Plus, with as formidable as that fire was, it would burn more than just the wood. Verena wasn't being smart. Conjuring flames like that was an excellent way to rule over ashes.

When I opened my eyes, all I saw was the charred tree. It was still standing, but the damage was considerable. I wondered if I could heal the tree itself. If Dušan was Chaos, if he was a god, then this tree was a piece of him. Could I even make a dent?

"Only one way to find out," I muttered to myself as I put my hands on the sizzling bark.

The embers glowed with heat, but I didn't feel it. No, I felt the tree's agony, the seared fronds, the blackened branches. I could feel myself screaming—the tree's pain lashing through me. It wasn't like with the others. I could sense their pain, sure, but not like this.

This felt like I was burning at the stake all over again.

Alistair's arms circled me from behind, but I couldn't appreciate his support. All I could do was feel, all I could do was flail in the mindless agony of it all.

"Max, love, you have to let go."

Didn't he know that I couldn't if I wanted to? Didn't he understand that this tree was alive?

"Then heal it, love. Give it earth, give it water. Give it the elements and then let it go."

His voice called to the sensible part in my brain that had decided to fuck off and hide while the pain lashed at me. Following his words, I did what he said. I pulled from the earth, the air, the water in the lake nearby. I gave it to the tree, gave her all the tools she needed to heal herself because I couldn't do it all.

The water hit first, the relief of the cool wetness dousing the smoldering bark made me almost lose our connection. The earth hit next, the green shoots of new growth overtook the charred bits, absorbing them into itself as the tree shot up, towering over all the other trees in the forest. Buds of fresh flowers sprouted, their petals opening to the moon. Air hit last, as it ruffled the leaves, and carried its pollen on the gale.

There would be more trees like this one popping up all over

Faerie soon. A whole family so she wouldn't be alone anymore. I smiled at that, severed the link, and opened my eyes.

Alistair was holding me up with one arm as he guarded me, his scythe in his hand as he kept people back.

"What did I miss?" I whispered, my eyes scanning the crowd.

"You were healing that tree for twenty minutes, love, and at first, it looked like you were killing it."

I peeled my gaze from the rather weapony people in front of us to look at the tree. It was bigger around than it had been when I started. Ten men couldn't reach their arms around it. It had started the size of an ancient oak, and now it was more like a redwood.

Whoops?

The bark had healed, the branches flowering in the night.

"But it's fine now, so?"

"You stole water from the lake. They are not pleased."

I rolled my eyes so hard I almost gave myself a headache. I stood up, the pain a distant memory as my anger made a sashaying appearance.

"Are ya'll fucking with me right now? Didn't you hear me screaming? That tree was in pain, and you would rather be pissed I took water to douse the flames than be happy that tree—which is your holy place—isn't dying? This has to be the dumbest shit ever."

Growling, I stomped over to the nearby lake. There had to be a water nymph or whatever I could talk to to get this shit sorted.

"Knock, knock," I called.

And that's when a familiar water dragon popped his head out of the water.

"Zillah, you beautiful beast, how are ya?" I wasn't quite sure how the giant water dragon got from Hell to here, but I decided not to question it. He was his own man—or dragon—and he could do as he pleased.

Zillah gave me a gentle purr and rested his head on the shore so I could pet him. I'd missed the scaly monster, and I was glad I could see him again.

"You pissed I took some water? I'll make a storm and give it back if you need me to. But that tree was dying. You understand, right?"

He gave me an "obviously" expression, which I took to mean he didn't mind I took some water.

"See, Zillah doesn't care," I offered to the still-antsy crowd of warriors—a crowd that seemed to have multiplied since my encounter with the tree.

"Zillah is not in charge of the water Fae. I am," a voice called from my left.

But when I turned, it wasn't a person, it was a seaweed-maned horse.

A pissed off kelpie. Fabulous.

CHAPTER SIXTEEN

It was said that kelpies tricked passersby to jump on their backs before luring them into the water to drown. I had zero intention of jumping on the back of the water horse, and I couldn't imagine a world where anyone would do it, either. This kelpie looked mean. Horses always appeared regal to me, but this one was one irritating comment away from stomping me into next week, and I knew that just from the expression on her face.

"What do I call you?" I asked because I liked to be introduced to people I was arguing with, and I had a feeling I was going to be arguing with this filly for a minute.

"You want my name?" She sounded offended. Oh, joy. It was going to be like that.

"I don't give a shit what your name is. I want to know what to call you. If you don't pick a name, I'm going to start calling you Karen and be done with it." She sounded like a Karen.

She whinnied, and I really hoped she understood the insult. Still, no name was supplied.

"Okay, fine. Look, Karen, I took water to revive a sacred tree. If you would like it replaced, give me a minute and I'll make a storm. You'll get your water back and you can fuck back off into the lake.

Honestly, I thought the Fae were a little more understanding than that."

Alistair gripped my hand, trying to get my attention. "A diplomatic approach might be better suited, love."

I agreed, but I was pissed. "A diplomatic approach might have been not to pull weapons on my husband when I was doing them a favor. A diplomatic approach might be to introduce yourself. Did I get either of those things? No. All I wanted to do was keep that tree from hurting, and what do I get for it? Threats and weapons and bitchy attitudes. No. Hell, no."

"You take most of what is likely the only clean water we have, and you have the nerve to be offended?"

My head whipped back to Karen the Kelpie. "What do you mean? How is what I took your only clean water?"

She stomped her hooves as she whinnied. "Verena is poisoning our water—our lifeblood—because we will not join her. Now that you have taken our good water, we will die. Just as your aunt planned."

Oh. Shit. I could totally understand the brandished weapons now. Whoops?

"Fates, that woman sucks." I growled for a second, wracking my brain for a solution. I didn't have one, but I could at least see if I could fix this problem, too. "Okay, let me see what I can do."

I made for the lake, but Karen stomped in front of me.

"Look, lady, I fixed the tree." I waved at the massive fucking thing at our backs. "Let me see what bullshit my aunt of doom has pulled, and maybe I'll be able to fix that, too."

Karen's eyes narrowed at me, but she backed off when she saw my steely-eyed glare. I was one thousand percent done with her attitude. Understood it, sure. Willing to deal with it? Absolutely not.

I snapped my fingers, swapping my leathers for a dress so my bare feet could go in the lake without the undignified rigamarole of getting my boots off. Wading into the water, I felt the poison immediately. It wasn't close, but the black fingers of it reached far. Fae were sick, some were dying. I knew the bad stuff had to get out of the water, but what I was going to do with it once it was out, I wasn't sure.

Could I burn it up? Encapsulate it in the earth? And what was it?

I concentrated harder, trying to get a fix on it. Iron. Verena poisoned the water with iron. What a dick. Lucky for me, I wasn't hurt by iron. At least I didn't think I was. Pulling on the element, I drew out the iron-tainted water, leaching it from the lake so it did not poison anyone else and let it evaporate. What iron there was left, I let the air take it to me.

The object poisoning the water was an iron dagger not much bigger than one of my athames. Of course it was. Because why wouldn't she poison the water with the very thing that could kill her. I drew it to me, fusing the particles of it in the air with the stupidly ornate dagger.

Iron hurt the Fae, but I could change it. All I needed was a little alchemy. I snapped my fingers, molding the metal into what would least hurt the Fae, and when I was done, the dagger was a crystalline weapon so clear it looked like glass.

"There. No more poison. Your waters are clean again."

Zillah purred from his perch on the shore, and I was half-tempted to give his head scratches. Instead, I snapped my fingers again, putting my leathers back in place complete with a new belt loop which now held the crystal dagger.

Karen the Kelpie was less gracious. "Your repayment of debt is adequate. We hold no issue toward you."

"That warms the cockles of my heart, Karen, let me tell ya. Next time you have a problem, ask instead of brandishing weapons. I'm a mostly reasonable kind of gal."

I gave her my back, now facing the Fae that used to be pointing weapons at us.

"When you kill your aunt and become Queen, we will work well together," the kelpie said, her words like a slap.

My feet stuttered to a stop, I turned, and marched back to her. "I don't play well with people who threaten my family. Keep that in mind."

With that, I about-faced, marching toward Maireen and Aramal, pissed that they, too, drew down on us when I was doing her a favor. My face must have said as much because both of them bowed to me.

"Quit it," I said, exasperated. "Had I known there was an issue with the water, I would have fixed it. Maybe, just tell me next time. Cool? And quit bowing. It's weird."

"Apologies. We thought... Verena..."

I filled in the blanks myself. "You thought that even though she is an evil bitch from Hell, and she killed my entire family, I was siding with her anyway? Ya'll didn't think that through, did you?"

"I suppose we didn't," Maireen replied, her hooves shuffling with unease. "But not everything is as it seems here—even for us. We didn't know if we could trust it. You, your coming here, seemed too good to be true. Too much to hope for."

That, I understood perfectly—the not wanting to hope because it hurt too much when nothing panned out. "Don't worry about it. I get it, just... trust me when I say I have no desire to hurt good people. What Verena has done makes me sick. Living under a thumb like that, I can see how you wouldn't, but I'm not her."

A part of me wanted to march into the spirit realm and give Dušan a piece of my mind. How could I let these people suffer and do nothing? How could I leave the fight for someone else? The other part of me realized all too quickly that if I unseated Verena, I would have to take her place. I would stay here in Faerie, and that thought hurt my heart, too.

Faerie wasn't my home and I had no desire to be a queen. Not here, not on Earth, not in Hell, nowhere.

"Please, just take me to your people. I want to see if I can help." I may have said those words, but the fight had left me for a moment. I was weighed down by everything that was happening here. Their pain wrenched at my heart, and I didn't know if I could leave this place with so many suffering.

Warm fingers threaded through mine as we followed Maireen further into the forest. I hadn't noticed the chill in the air with the fire gone, and Alistair's grip on my hand was a comfort in all the ways. For a moment I was buoyed, breathing air again after a harsh minute of drowning.

I wanted to look at him, but I couldn't. He would see the fight within me, and I didn't know what I thought about it enough to have that discussion.

"I know what you're thinking," he whispered in my ear when I didn't meet his eyes.

My stomach dropped—I wasn't ready.

"You're trying to figure out how we can keep Zillah as a pet. Well, I hate to be the bearer of bad news, but you live in Denver, love. There is no way we can keep a water dragon in your backyard, no matter what you say."

I couldn't help it, I snorted out a laugh. Zillah would be the very best of boys.

I tapped my finger on my chin, pretending to ponder the ridiculous situation. "I see your point. We'd need to move to a lake or something."

He bumped me with his shoulder, and I peered up into his face. "I know you're thinking it, love. Helping these people. Staying. I know it's ripping at you, the sense that if you can do something, you should."

Wetness hit my eyes and I groaned. What was with the waterworks all the time? Hadn't I cried enough?

"I'm with you, Max. Whatever you decide, and if you want to, say, run some ideas past me, that couldn't hurt, either. You don't have to do this on your own."

"Okay," I whispered, and that was the only thing I could say around the lump in my throat. I wanted to kiss him, but we had things to do. Instead, I squeezed his hand and bumped his shoulder with mine and felt safe in our little bubble for a moment.

That moment was obliterated the second we rounded the next copse of trees. The magic high on the air, I couldn't quite make sense of what I was seeing. The whole of the area was under some sort of stasis spell—for which I was supremely grateful, but the rest...

Fawns were floating in the air—some eviscerated, some intact.

Wood sprites were frozen solid or in burning embers. There were pixies that had been turned into objects and some that had morphed into floating, pixie-shaped drops of water. Some Fae had their insides turned out; some were contorted into shapes no body should ever make. There were more things that were screwed, but my brain refused to process them all.

And that stasis spell wasn't going to hold them forever.

It was a complete and utter shitshow. A clusterfuck of epic proportions. I didn't think even me, my mom, and all the magic-users in the realm could fix this shit.

I stared at Della, wide-eyed, and afraid. "We need backup. Contact the elves. We need everyone they can send to help. This... this is..." I couldn't even finish.

"We do not need elven help," Maireen hissed, her stomping hooves too close to my feet for comfort.

Rounding on her, I threw my hand out, wildly gesturing at the complete dumpster fire of the situation we had on our hands. "Yes, lady, you do. I cannot possibly fix all this myself. Not after healing everyone and their brother, fixing the sacred tree, and unfucking the lake. If people are willing and able to help you, no offense, but you need to get your head out of your ass and fucking take it."

"They will shit on us every chance they get. They will lord it over us. My people are proud—they will not want elven help."

"Then they are idiots and so are you. You'd rather let your people suffer than accept help? You'd rather them die? How about this, when the elves come—and they will because I asked—they will treat you with respect, or answer to me?"

Maireen backed up a step in surprise. "You would do that? You would defend our honor?"

"I'll make a speech and everything. Cool?"

She smiled at me, that same enigmatic one that could mean death or friendship. "You are kind, Max. I did not think a goddess like you could be this kind."

I stuck my fingers in my ears and did a childish "lalalala."

"I'm not listening to god, goddess, or demi-god talk right now. Let's just get this fixed."

Maireen scoffed but cast her gaze on her injured people. “Denial is not your friend, little goddess. Everything you shove away will come back to you before you’re ready. Best to meet it head on.”

We both knew she was right—which is why I did the only thing I could think of.

I blew a raspberry at her and walked off to find Della.

Adulting could wait until tomorrow.

CHAPTER SEVENTEEN

The elves came faster than I thought possible, arriving from a portal someone or other conjured. I wasn't positive what kind of abilities the elves had, but I knew they were potent magic-users and we needed all the help we could get. And yes, I had to make a speech like a teacher over kindergarteners about showing respect and treating everyone with kindness.

It was super well received by everyone. It totally wasn't at all going to backfire on me.

Honestly, I probably would have been better served to knock out the first asshole that started some shit and moved on with my day, but I was trying on my diplomatic hat. It was bullshit.

Once the elves realized that I wasn't joking about the non-assholery, we moved on to undoing each curse, counter curse, hex, jinx, transmogrification, and plain old fuckery done to the forest-dwellers. By the time I was ready to pass out, we weren't anywhere close to halfway through them all. It would take days to fix the havoc Melody wrought, and we didn't have that kind of time.

I was staring at a map of Faerie, my eyes burning from

exhaustion, as my vision swam. Maireen pointed to the glowing spots. "This is her destruction. This is what she has done."

The glowing dots of affected creatures looked like a forest fire the way it spread, heading straight for the Seelie Court. This was the definition of not good. Della had said that Melody was going home. That was what she'd written in her note—that she was going home to Faerie. Why would Melody think that Faerie was her home?

And how did she get through the LSD-trip-from-Hell forest? I knew the answer was staring me in the face, but I just couldn't think.

"You need to rest, Max," Teresa said, pulling on my hand and away from the makeshift war room that was little more than a tent with a table in it. "You aren't doing yourself any favors. Running yourself ragged is not helping anyone. Alistair set up a tent for you two. Go to sleep."

I was just tired enough to do what she said and not argue. Without a fight, I let her lead me to our tent and shove me inside. I caught sight of Alistair passed out on a two-person cot, his body curled around my space, and I crawled into the bed with my boots still on, passing out as soon as my head hit the pillow.

I woke up with a start in a wash of blackness. It was still night, but something had pulled me from a deep sleep. Alistair was still out, his face peaceful, his brow smooth and unfurrowed. I refused to wake him and made my way out of the tent. Torches burned around the affected Fae, offering only a meager bit of light. A force I couldn't name was calling to me, the need to go to it almost visceral.

"Where do you think you're going?" Aidan whispered, scaring the shit out of me. He was perched on a cut stump outside my tent, his weapons drawn like he was guarding me while I slept—which when my lagging brain finally caught up, I realized that was exactly what he was doing.

"Christ on a cracker," I hissed. "You scared the shit out of me."

"And you avoided my question. Where are you going?"

I let my mind wander, listening for the call that woke me from exhausted sleep and pointed. "That way. I need to go that way. I don't know why. I just need to go."

Aidan made a low whistle and Hideyo jumped down from a nearby branch, also scaring the ever-loving shit out of me. "You need to go somewhere—you aren't doing it alone. Let's go."

I contemplated this for about a millisecond and decided just to roll with it. Following the thread of calling, we left the clearing to a denser part of the forest. At the base of a gnarly oak, Torren sat curled in a ball, rocking back and forth. He held onto his knees with one arm, shaking as he rocked. He was quietly having a meltdown, that only possible because he held a hand over his mouth to quiet his sobs.

I knelt at his feet, afraid that if I touched him, it would only hurt him worse. "Torren? Sweetheart?"

But he didn't answer, his gaze unseeing as he rocked himself. Gently, I put a hand on his shoulder, and even though he flinched, he didn't stop rocking.

"One of you get Della or Lothan. Now," I ordered, and I heard the faint wisp of wind as Aidan did as I asked.

I'd put spirit into Torren. Maybe that tied me to him in some way. Maybe if I funneled more in, he could show me what happened. I glanced up, catching Hideyo's concerned gaze. "I'm going to look to see what happened since he isn't talking. Watch my back?"

"Always, my Queen," he replied, his voice no more than a faint whisper. He said it with such sincerity, such conviction, I couldn't say anything back.

Harnessing my courage, I felt myself sink into the ground, letting the earth energize me, the air wake me up, the water revive me, the fire warm my tired bones. Then I tapped into spirit, the element ephemeral and hard to hold as I gave Torren a little, trickling it into him as I tried to read him.

It was that same voice I'd heard in his memories. *No one will believe you.*

And then I knew. The man who had brutalized him was here.

He was here and Torren had seen him, or had been hurt by him again, or... he was hurting someone else.

That was it.

The man who'd hurt him was hurting someone else, and Torren was trying to get back to us—trying to tell someone, but either he couldn't, or he'd been stopped. Plucking at the magic that held him down, kept him quiet, I freed him from the prison of his own mind.

Blurry images hit me, but I couldn't place the faint outline of the man—Torren's mind protecting itself from remembering. Gently, I pulled back. "It's okay. I'll find him."

Torren didn't respond, but that was fine. Lothan had arrived. Brought by Aidan to this little thatch of trees, he knelt to take care of his son.

"There is someone in this forest hurting a fawn. I think it's an elf, but it might not be. Torren was trying to tell me, but he can't right now, so I'm going to search for them."

Lothan stiffened, every line of his posture gearing toward a fight. "This is madness. No elf would hurt a fawn. We are civilized. You think one of my people are..." Lothan began but trailed off when he saw my face.

"Do you want to see what this man is capable of?" I asked but didn't wait for Lothan to answer as I touched his forehead, giving him what I'd seen. Letting him see what had been done to his son, his blood.

Lothan fell back, turned, and retched. When he could breathe again, tears were in his eyes. "No—no one should ever go through that. My boy," he whimpered as he reached for his child, pulling his adult son in his arms.

"I swore I'd find who did this. Take care of your son. I'll be back soon."

I felt the pull again, the thread I'd cast out to find the man who broke Torren, who stole his innocence and his mind. Following the thread, Aidan, Hideyo, and I picked our way through the forest, turning back in almost a full circle, coming around the other side of the camp.

How far had Torren run as he'd lost his mind? How far had the man sent him, letting Torren's brain deteriorate into mush?

The thread pulled at me harder, and I began to run, the faint strains of a woman in distress hitting my ears. Before I knew it, lightning was streaking across the sky, dipping down into the trees like a playful puppy, begging to be used. When I saw them, when I saw the poor fawn woman scrabbling at the tree as a giant of an elf hurt her, I let the fire in my veins loose.

Light grew in my hands until electricity yanked free from its tethers and poured into the elf.

I'd seen him before. He was on the Council, demanding they give the dwarves more access, more space—a kind gesture that was now tainted by what he'd done. He was a rapist, an abuser, a monster. A man of power who abused those who he was supposed to protect.

The fawn fell to the forest floor, the poor woman crying as she told us thank you over and over again. I wanted to vomit. I sure as shit did not want to be thanked for this.

The earth roiled beneath my feet as a storm of rage lashed us with biting rain and booming thunder. I knew I'd woken the entire encampment, but I didn't care. They needed to see this. They needed to witness what happened next.

Soon enough the elf stirred, crawling to standing as he tried to defend himself.

He shouted arguments I'd heard before from men—from men I'd killed. From husbands with murdered wives, and boyfriends with abused girlfriends. From big shots who thought no one would care that they'd hurt children, and from magistrates with no one to keep them in check.

His defense was no different from theirs and would be met with the same fate.

"I don't care what your reasons are. There is no excuse you could give me that I would accept. I told that woman's leader they would have respect, or the violators would answer to me. This is what that looks like."

The elf growled and shot forward, but he didn't make it very far. I snapped my fingers, enjoying his split-second scream before I turned his body inside out. A fine mist of blood sprayed outward, coating the forest floor, and I watched as the earth soaked most of it up, taking the sacrifice as an offering. Lightning snaked through the treetops and fire bloomed over the elf's carcass, taking its due before the air swept through, consuming some of the ashes before dropping the rest into the lake.

My elements were just as bloodthirsty as I was, and they were appeased by the offering.

But I was not okay. Rage still coursed through me. Unsatisfied at the elf's quick death, I wanted more blood for the innocence stolen. I wanted justice for those wronged.

But I had no one to hurt, no blood to take.

So instead I screamed. I screamed for every woman I'd failed, every death I couldn't stop, every brutality I couldn't prevent as the world roiled around me.

I didn't want to hurt anyone else, but I was ravenous for blood, hungry for violence, starving for a fight. I fell to my knees on the wet earth, unable to hold myself up anymore, and when I opened my eyes, I was back in a familiar forest.

Dušan crouched in front of me, his face a mask of pain. All I wanted to do was cry.

"How do I make it stop?" I croaked, the hunger for violence still coursing through my veins.

"You breathe in the air, you feel the rain on your skin, you dig your fingers in the earth, feel the fire in the wind, you let spirit flow through you, and you wait. There is no answer for brutality like that, and that scar must be healed, too."

An easy answer, but sometimes, that was the way of it. I took one shuddering breath after the other, letting the spirit of this place heal my soul just a little.

"You're a god, aren't you?" I asked when I could think again. "Chaos? Why didn't you tell me?"

"Some things are better learned in small doses. I wanted you safe more than anything else, and so I told you what you needed to know."

I snorted. "That's a shitty parental habit you need to break. I've had enough of that garbage to last ten lifetimes."

Dušan smiled the indulgent smile of a father negotiating with a feisty toddler. "I'll remember that."

"I'm glad to know, though. I'm glad to know you a little. Glad to have a piece of you here. I'm sorry it's a prison for you."

I tried to focus on the particulars of this place, this little pocket he'd carved out for himself, but I couldn't exactly make out the details. We were in a forest at night. Fireflies popped up every now and again, but the edges were blurry, like a crude drawing.

"It is and it isn't. I get to see you, don't I? That alone makes it worth it."

So I didn't dissolve into a puddle of tears, I settled on sass. "You are determined to have another cry-fest on your shoulder, aren't you?"

"It's my mission in life," he replied dryly, and I couldn't help giggling. "I'll look forward to our next visit, Massima. Stay safe."

When I opened my eyes, I was staring into my mother's brown ones. She was crying, and I didn't know why.

"What's wrong?" I croaked; my voice rusty from disuse.

"Oh, thank the Fates," she breathed, cupping my face in her hands. "Don't do that, baby. You scared the life out of me."

"Don't do what? What did I do?"

Teresa pulled me into her arms, the leather of her armor softer than I thought it was going to be. "You stopped breathing for an hour. Where did you go?"

"Promise you won't think I'm crazy?"

"Of course you aren't crazy. Tell me."

I worried my lip, debating on what I could say that wouldn't flag me as certifiable. But then I remembered that this was Faerie and crazy shit was its modus operandi. "I was in the spirit realm. I was talking to Dušan. He's a god, Mom. This is real. All of this is real."

"Of course it's real, baby. This is the land of possible."

"Max!" Alistair called from behind us. He sounded frantic like he was two seconds away from lighting people on fire.

I stood from my perch in the muck and Teresa tugged at my hand.

"I'm sorry in advance for what he's about to tell you. He was losing it, so I knocked him out for a little bit. But it was so he didn't go full monkey shit on the elves that were pissed you killed one of their own. Lothan told them what happened, and they backed off, but—"

My mother was cut off when Alistair crashed into me, clutching me close to his chest like he was never going to let me go.

"I'm sorry I wasn't there, love. I'm sorry—"

I kissed him to make him shut up. I was the one who left him to sleep like an idiot. I wondered how much spirit I would have needed to take if Alistair had been with me. Would I have unleashed that much rage?

I figured probably not.

He would have calmed me. He would have helped.

We sank deeper into the kiss, uncaring of those around us. This was the peace I needed.

A faint rustling hit my ears, and I broke the kiss, whipping my head toward the sound. It pulled on me like Torren did when he was stuck in the forest. It was a call for help—a familiar one. One I did not want to answer. Not ever again.

But I had to follow the thread, and I did.

Only to find my former best friend shivering at the base of a tree. He was wet, ragged, and beaten. His bloody cheek looked red and puffy with infection, and he was holding himself all wrong.

"Heya, Maxie. Long time no see," Striker croaked before passing out on the forest floor.

Aces.

CHAPTER EIGHTEEN

"Wake up, you idiot," I muttered, snapping my fingers at my freshly healed former best friend.

Striker's eyes flashed open as he sprang up from his cot, only to meet resistance at the end of a chain. Yep, I'd chained him to a stake in the ground—one my mother assured me he couldn't break—and I wasn't sorry.

I didn't trust him—not even a little.

Striker stared at the chain, at his manacled wrist, at the stake in the ground, and then at me. "First a punch to the face, and now this? I'm starting to think you don't like me, Max."

He said this like he hadn't earned that punch or his current confinement. Like he hadn't done anything wrong. Like he hadn't stolen a soul from Heaven.

"I don't. You've seen me cut a lot of people off, Striker. People who have abused me, taken things without asking, lied to me, treated me like dirt. It might have taken me a century to get smart, to remove the blind spot you made, but I see you for what you are. And no, I don't like you."

My words seemed to have hit him like a slap, because he reared back, yanking at the manacle around his wrist.

"I was protecting you." He put his feet on the floor like he was going to stand up and face me. He didn't make it very far until he was staring at the pointy end of Alistair's scythe.

"You were doing fuck all. Have a seat, Striker, my wife has more to say."

Striker sneered at him. "You won't use that blade, demon. The Armistice prevents it."

I laughed for a good long minute at that one. "Pumpkin pie, you are in Faerie. There is no Armistice on any realm that will save your ass if you start acting cute, so sit the fuck down. No one gives a shit about your excuses. No one is ready to listen to you wheel and deal like you have a good reason for stealing a soul and lying about it. And don't think you can use your abilities to try and convince us to listen. I turned that off as soon as you passed out."

Yes, I fiddled with his powers some to prevent his mojo from affecting us. Again, not sorry. I didn't know if his abilities affected me differently with the glamour gone, and honestly, I wasn't going to chance it.

"You turned off my abilities? Like I'm some pup that needs to be put down?"

Was he high?

"You. Stole. A. Soul. From. Heaven," I growled, punctuating each word with a clap right in his face. "A soul that I have been cleaning up after for two fucking days now, and I'm tired. Do you know what she's done? Do you know how many people I couldn't save all because she wanted to walk through Faerie like she was tiptoeing through the fucking tulips? People are dead, Striker. Dead."

I wasn't even going to get into all the other shit he did. The list was too long.

"It wasn't supposed to be this way." His body melted back into the cot like I'd deflated him.

"Like that makes it any better. Just like always, you turned off the empathetic part of you. You turned off the part that actually has a conscience. You did what you wanted and fuck everyone else. Did you even ask her if she wanted to come back? Or did you just take?"

Shame made his face haggard—a feat I didn't think possible on a mug like his. He had always been beautiful, but now he just appeared lost. Lost and ashamed.

"I didn't ask her," he admitted, his voice so low I almost didn't hear it. "I saw her, and I was so happy that I just took. She was at peace. I knew that, but I wanted her with me."

I knew it. I knew that was what he'd done. I was just so disappointed that I didn't want to even look at him. Still, I needed to know why he was here and who beat him senseless.

Unable to look at his face anymore, I peered up at the canvas tent wall as I asked the questions I needed. "What happened to you in the forest?"

A little moan of pain had me turning back at him, even though I didn't want to. Tears filled Striker's eyes and he shook his head. Not like he was telling me no, but more like he couldn't process what happened.

"I've been following you since you got here. I figured you would find Melody before I could, since no matter what I did, I couldn't use our link to find her. I heard a woman in the forest. She wasn't screaming, but she was making this horrible noise. But sound here doesn't make any sense. The sound of her was everywhere and nowhere, I couldn't follow it, so I dropped my emotional warding." Striker covered his eyes, shook his head and sniffed like he'd shove tears down by force of will alone.

"She was... she was being hurt. An elf had tied her wrists together around a tree and he was..." Striker shook his head, unable to go on.

He didn't have to. I knew what he saw. I'd seen the same thing before I turned him inside out.

"I attacked him, or at least I tried to. With my wards down I couldn't do much damage—I was too affected by her pain. He stomped my ass into the dirt and went back for her. Then you came."

But that had always been his problem. He shut off his emotions and turned himself into a flaming asshole only to be hindered when he turned them back on again. We'd been going through this cycle for a century. I knew the only reason he turned his emotions on again was because he wanted to find Melody. I held no illusions about that. But it was a tiny point in his favor that he actually did something for someone else.

Even if it would never heal our friendship, I was glad he wasn't a total monster.

"Do you have any idea why Melody would come to Faerie in the first place? That's the one thing I can't figure out. She called it home in her letter. Why would she think Faerie was home?"

"When I brought her back to Earth after trying to repair her soul, she kept saying that—that she wanted to go home to Faerie. But as far as I knew, she was human. If she was part-Fae, that could explain why..." Striker trailed off, but I knew what he was thinking.

If Melody was Fae, it would explain why the spell he used to fuse the two parts of her soul didn't work.

It would explain why she was still broken.

"Was she adopted? A changeling? What?"

My mother was the one to pipe up with an answer. "She could have been part-Fae from a distant line. There are plenty of humans with a fair amount of Fae blood. Fae come to the Earth realm all the time. Where do you think the lore comes from?"

"So, what? Her brain gets scrambled in the re-fusing process," Alistair offered, "And then it somehow gets stuck on the Fae setting like a homing beacon? I don't buy it."

I didn't buy it, either. "There had to be outside influences. Who did you leave her with to try and rehabilitate her?"

"I didn't. Caim had people lined up—they took her to a convent-type place. It wasn't until she broke out that we realized there was a problem."

Aidan popped his head in the tent. "Hey, the Fae are going nuts. You'd better get out here."

We filed out of the tent to see Fae scrambling. The fawns were trying to gather up their wounded and get them out of here. The elves were on high alert, and the dwarves were readying their weapons.

I turned back to Aidan and Hideyo. "Keep an eye on him. If he fucks up, knock him out. I'll be right back."

Alistair and my mother followed me as I sought out Della and Lothan. Or Maireen or Aramal. Really, I'd take anyone at this point. I found Della and Lothan in the "war" tent—the one we'd used to look at the map of doom.

"What's going on?" I asked, likely breaking up a heated discussion.

"Seelie are coming. We need to move or get ready to fight," Della answered, her accent thicker with either fear or rage. It all seemed the same on Della.

"How do you know?"

Della stiffly pointed at the map. Blue dots clustered in groups in an arrow-point formation heading right for us. Shit on a stick. Melody's destruction glowed gold. The two were headed right for each other.

"How can I help?" I asked the question because I had minimal battle experience, and even less with military tactics. But I could be a weapon. I was real good at that.

"I don't know, Max. How can you help?" Della's tone was biting, and I knew why. I didn't tell her about the atrocities done to Torren.

"It wasn't my secret to tell," I murmured, my voice pitched low so she would know I didn't want a fight. "If it had happened to you, would you have wanted me to tell? He was scared and ashamed. It wasn't my place."

"But you told Lothan. You showed him."

"That was more so he wouldn't stand in my way while I killed his council member. That man was hurting someone, and I didn't have a chance to explain."

I met Della's gaze, hoping she saw how much it hurt not to tell her. Hoping she knew I couldn't betray a trust like that. Not ever.

She raised her chin, her mouth tightening as she pressed her lips together. When she spoke again, it sounded so raw, I felt her despair in my bones.

"I'm angry, but I know you can't change it. I know you did what you thought was best. But I'm just so mad. Mad that I can't kill him. That I can't... He hurt my baby."

I wrapped my arms around her shoulders, knowing it may be a long time before Della could process this. "If I'd had more time, I would have urged him to tell you. But we didn't have time then, and we don't have time now. How can I help?"

She shook her head. "I don't know. Lothan and the other elves are making portals so we can house everyone on Tandrirr. Some fawns won't go. I don't know what we could possibly say to convince them after what Irion did. A part of me wants to throw his whole family off a cliff, but I know they couldn't possibly have known—or if they did, they were just as cowed and abused as my son."

No one will ever believe you.

I shuddered. "One problem at a time. I'll see if I can talk to the fawns. They might listen to me."

I turned to go, but Della stopped me with a hand on my arm. "Thank you, Max. Thank you for healing my son, for finding his attacker, for meting out justice even if I couldn't. I won't forget it."

"You would have done the same."

"Damn right I would have."

I kissed her temple, squeezed the shit out of her, and sped off, searching for Maireen with Alistair and my mother in tow. I found Maireen close to the lake, trying to coax an injured pixie to come with her. Pixies were bigger than I'd have thought, close to a foot tall with ephemeral wings, so faint they were practically invisible. They were human-ish shaped, with longer legs and arms, their faces spritely and beautiful except for the razor-sharp teeth.

This pixie had a broken wing and a bum leg, making traveling almost impossible, but she didn't want to go with Maireen.

"Goliah, you have to come with me. The others left for Tandrirr. If you don't come, the Seelies will kill you. Stop being so stubborn," Maireen argued with the pixie, but based on the mulish expression on the pixie's face, she wasn't budging.

"For the love... Goliah, is it?" I asked, startling them both. The pixie nodded. "Do you have a death wish? Do you wish other people dead?"

The pixie shook her head. Maireen could hear the pixies in her mind, but not many others could. Pixie's didn't have vocal cords for some reason, so communication was mostly sign and head nods.

"Then get your stubborn ass up and get to safety before you cost someone their life. Do you hear me?"

Goliah nodded, but she didn't seem happy about it. She held out her tiny hand to Maireen, who gently scooped the tiny lady up, placing her in a pocket.

"How many more will not come?"

"Not many. Even the fawn you rescued is coming with her family, granted she's staying away from the elves themselves, but Torren is looking after her. He hasn't spoken yet, but he's helping where he can."

I breathed a sigh of relief. "Good. I need to get my people out of here. We need to find Melody and get out of this realm. Maybe Verena will settle once I'm gone."

But I knew she wouldn't. I knew she would just keep picking off her opponents until the whole of Faerie was fully under her thumb.

Maireen's face told me she was thinking the same thing I was—that Verena would never stop, that it didn't matter if I was here or not.

Fuck.

What do I do?

"You save as many as you can, love."

I glanced up at Alistair, unaware that I had asked my question out loud. "How do I do that and keep my promise? She's heading right for an army." By she I meant Melody. "How am I supposed to keep her and her son safe in the middle of a war? And she's killing people, Alistair. What..." I trailed off, unable to finish the sentence.

What am I supposed to do with a woman who doesn't appear to want to be saved?

Alistair reached for my hands and enveloped them in his—sharing a little bit of peace and warmth with me. "You fall back and regroup. Reassess when we aren't looking down the barrel of a loaded gun. Yes?"

"Okay. Go help Maireen round up as many Fae as you can. We'll get Striker and meet you in the war tent?"

Instead of answering, he pulled me into his arms and gave me a quick, blistering kiss.

We broke apart, heading in opposite directions.

"You know, when I heard the prophecy about you two, I was against it, but now it all makes sense," my mother muttered—more to herself than to me.

"What prophecy? The one where we would be married?"

"The very one. Had I known then that he would be your match, I might not have been so against it."

I chuckled, remembering how I'd been under her roof. "Or maybe we wouldn't be together at all because we had our parents' blessing. Fate's a funny thing, Mom. Let's just be happy it turned out like it did."

We approached Striker's tent, and I slowed to a stop. Where were Aidan and Hideyo?

I held my hand out to stop Teresa from going any farther. Our eyes met and she nodded. Without a word, we separated, circling the tent on opposite sides. On my side, I found a decidedly gnawed upon Aidan, his arms bloody from sharp teeth, his sword drawn and coated in red. He was unconscious but breathing.

"Max," my mother called from the other side of the tent, and I rounded to find a bloody Hideyo half-in and half-out of his kitsune form.

My heart stuttered in my chest until I noticed he was breathing. But if Hideyo was stuck this way, he was not doing good at all. I knelt on the ground, willing the earth to rise up and greet him, begging it to heal my friends. Hideyo's other half melted away, and his breathing became less shallow.

I wanted to feel relief, but I knew I couldn't. We were in danger here.

"Who did this?" Fear leaked into my mother's words as she scanned the forest for an attacker.

I shook my head. Could it have been Melody? Why would she come back here? She was supposed to be heading to the Seelie Court...

Without thought, I stood and slashed the tent canvas rather than rounding it. The inside was empty save for a lonely cot and Striker's broken manacle.

Suddenly, blistering pain bloomed across the back of my head. I staggered, and then the ground rushed up to meet me.

Before darkness took me, I saw a familiar pair of black boots stop in front of me. I knew them and the man they belonged to.

Striker.

CHAPTER NINETEEN

Being chained to a tree was about as fun as one would think. As in, it was not at all fun, not even a little bit. Being chained to a tree with a spiky wooden collar around my neck was even less fun. Especially when I could sense that the wood was carved from a rowan tree.

The same rowan tree that had killed my birth parents.

Each carved spike pressed against my throat, their sharp tips digging into my flesh. If I moved the wrong way, I was going to get a rowan spike jabbed in my throat.

Awesome.

My brain caught up to the last thing I remembered. Aidan and Hideyo were hurt. Aidan looked like he'd been attacked by a wild dog? Or could it have been a kitsune? And Hideyo had looked like he had been slashed by a blade and got stuck trying to turn back to his other form.

Wasn't that how all the others had been hurt? They'd attacked each other. Was that Melody using her succubus influence, or was it Striker?

It didn't sound like my former best friend, but then again, I couldn't trust what I knew about Striker to be true. The man I knew could have never done that to his friends. The man I knew would have never bashed me on the head. Or chained me to a tree. Or made sure I was restrained by the one thing that could really, really kill me.

I wanted to believe that the man I knew was still in there, but as I stared at Striker scratching sigils into the dirt, I was certain that the man I knew was long gone.

As it stood, Striker's blond hair was loose around his face, the strands in disarray as he used a steel blade to carve into the dirt. From this vantage point I couldn't see the design, but I could sense it. It wasn't a language I knew—or a language I thought Striker knew, either.

He was muttering to himself, but not in a sane way that said a person was in charge of their mental faculties. No, it was as if he was arguing with himself as he carved into the dirt and then smoothed out the furrows before starting all over again.

Staring past my former best friend, I took in our surroundings—well, as much as I could without turning my head. We were in a deep fissure in the earth, the sides coming up and over us with only a thick sliver of sky overhead. Even though it was night above, there was light down here. An eerie blue light was coming from a closed pair of doors in a cracked-and-craggy archway set in the smallest part of the crevasse—the light leaking around the seam of them like it was begging to get out.

That wasn't to say that the doors were small. No, those doors made the ones at the Seam look doll sized. Each one was easily a hundred feet tall and thirty feet wide, the design etched into them a seal that seemed in danger of cracking.

"What are you doing, Striker?" I called to the mumbling man who was on his fifth pass of carving and erasing sigils in the dirt. Well, it could have been more than his fifth since I'd been knocked out for a bit.

He twitched like he heard me, but he didn't answer. Instead, he drew the sigils again, expanding them this time until they made a whole circle of carvings in the earth.

"Why are you doing this? Why did you hit me?" When he still

ignored me, my anger grew enough that the ground shook beneath us—well, not beneath me, but the earth roiled under him, disturbing his drawings.

"Answer me!" I yelled and then hissed as a rowan spike dug into my flesh. It didn't draw blood, but it was a very near thing. Screaming was out.

Striker looked up then, his face a mask of haggard lines, and sunken cheeks. He'd aged fifty years since I saw him last. Like something was stealing the life out of him. His eyes—normally a beautiful hazel—were now milked over.

Could he see me? Could he even hear me?

"What happened to you?" I breathed, not expecting an answer to this question, either.

He shook his head, turned back to the still-trembling earth and began carving again. The dirt where he dug his knife stayed still, but everywhere else moved with my anger, with my fear. Lightning lashed the sky above us, one bolt hitting a tree on a nearby outcropping. The tree burst into flames, and I wondered if I could coax a bit of lightning to do the same to this tree.

The fire wouldn't hurt me, and if it burned this wood up, all the better.

I closed my eyes, trying to convince the fire to come closer, but it did not heed my call. By the time I reopened them, I was sweating, and the lightning drew no nearer than a few feet away. It stabbed down in the middle of Striker's sigils, but refused to come to me.

Was there something about this particular tree?

Then I understood. This was the tree—my father's insurance policy against eternity. Striker had chained me to a rowan tree, before clamping spikes to my neck.

What a dick.

If fire was too scared to come over here, would earth help me? I did my best to read the earth, letting myself sink into it. The element accepted me, embraced me, but could not work against the tree. It wasn't magic or a spell I could break that prevented the element from coming closer. It was more than that.

It wasn't magic or a spell or a curse. This tree was a void of nothingness housed inside the gnarled branches. It was an instrument like the Seam—a place where nothing could exist, so it took all life indiscriminately.

The elements couldn't free me.

Undeterred and in total denial, I decided to keep reading the earth, keep working the problem. I focused on Striker's sigils. On the surface, they just looked like furrows in the dirt. But below, where no one but me could see, blue tendrils of magic snaked toward the giant door.

Was he trying to open it? Well, duh, of course he was trying to open it. But why? What purpose could Striker have for opening the door where monsters were kept? Why would he care what was behind that door?

Or was someone making him?

I looked closer at the magic as it trailed sickly blue fingers toward the door. That magic wasn't coming from the sigils like I once thought. No, that power, that magic was coming directly from Striker. Each furrow in the dirt poured more magic in the earth, and each furrow sucked the wealth of power from Striker. It was draining him dry.

No, someone was definitely making him do this. There was no good reason for him to open this door—not when no one knew the horrors behind it.

Was this it? Was this how I went?

Rowan had said that I was the only person able to open the door, and just like with Soren, I had been led to the one place I did not want to be.

No.

I wasn't going to survive four hundred years of bullshit just to let myself get knocked down by a stupid fucking tree.

I could stop this. I could. Maybe.

I was too busy contemplating the likely instrument of my death to notice when Striker stopped drawing his sigils. Not until he was right in front of me. Brandishing an athame—one of mine, the prick—he snatched up one of my chained wrists and slashed down. His aim hit true, and my forearm split down the middle. Blood poured from my arm, the pain waiting a few moments to make itself known. But when it hit, I suppressed a scream that tore up my throat and would have shook the whole realm if I let it out.

But I couldn't scream, even though that was all I wanted to do. The last thing I needed was a neck full of rowan.

I should have hit Striker with lightning when I had the chance. I should have killed him. That would have been better than letting him hurt me, than letting him start the working to open that door. It would have been better than letting him be used this way.

The *plink-plink-plink* of liquid hitting metal had me groggily peering down. Striker had put a bowl under my arm and was collecting my blood. That was not good. I had a feeling I knew where that blood was going to go.

"Striker, don't do this," I begged, my voice barely above a whisper. I hated it. I didn't need to beg—I wouldn't. "You don't know what's behind that door. Fight this. I know this isn't you. I know you wouldn't do this."

Striker shook his head like he was trying to clear it. It wasn't working—whatever had ahold of him was stronger than he was. He slapped his own head, his face, but it wasn't working.

Maybe I should try and hit him with lightning again. That thought streaked across my brain an instant before a fiery bolt slammed into him. Being a dragon—at least in part—should protect him from the heat of it. Maybe. Okay, I didn't think that action through even a little bit, but it was what I had, and if it could get him to stop trying to open the monster door, then I was all for it.

Two other bolts of lightning slammed into Striker, his arms reaching for the sky as the electricity surged through him. He was screaming at the top of his lungs, the agony of it lashing through the air so hard I could feel it, too. And then the bolts titrated off, the electricity spent, and he crumpled to the ground.

I hoped I did the right thing. I hoped I didn't just kill him, even though I knew opening that door was going to kill me.

Wasn't that stupid? It felt stupid. I was such an idiot for

trusting him so long. For letting him get away with dumb shit, for letting him lie. And now that he was a puppet for someone else—even though he'd been shit to me—I still hated that he might be...

I shook my head. He wasn't dead. Couldn't be.

Still, I watched to see if he was breathing, to see if his chest moved even a millimeter. It didn't.

Tears hit my eyes even though I didn't want them to. I didn't want to cry at all. I wanted out of these chains. I wanted one of my very best friends to actually be a best friend and not die on me in the middle of the ass end of nowhere Faerie while I was chained to a death tree bleeding the fuck out.

Tears were not helpful.

Trembling, the cold of blood loss hitting me hard, I begged the earth to do me a solid. I coaxed it to feed into him a little bit. Not enough to heal him all the way—just enough that he wouldn't die and maybe break whatever bullshit spell was poisoning his mind.

Earth did not want to help Striker. It wanted to heal me, it wanted to reach me, but the tree's roots stopped it from coming to my rescue.

Stupid. Bullshit. Tree.

I begged the element to help—if it would do as I asked, maybe Striker wouldn't be such a dumbshit and take these fucking chains off me. Yeah, that would be good. Reluctantly, the element heeded my call, threading just a little bit of power into the idiot. I watched as Striker took his first breath, his second, and then earth backed off.

It refused to help anymore, but that was okay. Striker was alive at least—even if I couldn't tell if that was a good or bad thing.

As intently as I was watching Striker, I still heard the footsteps that crunched through the crevasse heralding another's approach. They were light, careful steps, and the earth told me it was a woman. I couldn't turn my head too much—the collar of death spikes keeping me immobile—but I hoped it wasn't the woman I'd search the whole damn realm to find.

I hoped it wasn't her that put Striker up to this. I prayed it wasn't all a big trick.

But when the tiny woman came into my line of sight, all my hopes were dashed.

She stood at the base of the tree, her gaze shifting between me chained to a tree and Striker's still-but-breathing body.

"Melody?"

She sighed before giving me her full attention. "I knew he was going to fail me." She shook her head. "But you know how it goes. If you want something done right"—She snatched up the athame Striker had used to cut me open—"you have to do it yourself."

CHAPTER TWENTY

Betrayal at this point should be second nature to me. Really, it wasn't such a stretch to figure out why unseated Kings and Queens were paranoid as fuck. I mean, when you had so many people in your life not telling you shit, hiding ulterior motives, and straight-out stabbing you in the back—or in the arm as the current case may be—paranoia was just smart.

The Melody before me only slightly looked like the one I remembered. Granted, the last time I saw her she was bleeding out on a battered pool table while Ian attempted to put Humpty Dumpty back together again, so I supposed I couldn't gauge her on that. Gone was her giant baby belly and swollen pregnancy cheeks. Gone was her sweet smile, and the playful glint in her eyes. And gone was any semblance of the sweet girl that sat in my tattoo parlor so long ago, her eyes begging for help.

No, this woman and the one I remembered were vastly different.

But if she took her son to Faerie, where was he? Because he sure as hell wasn't in her arms right then. It wasn't like Faerie had a list of babysitters on call.

So where was Ronan?

"Where is Ronan, Melody?" I asked, my voice pitched low because I was talking to a woman that in all likelihood was severely unbalanced.

She hummed in answer as she fiddled with my athame, pressing the sharp point of it into the tip of her finger—not like she was trying to draw blood, but more like she just wanted to see how sharp it was. When she drew her finger back with the flesh only slightly marred, she smiled.

Yes, the edges were sharp as fuck, and no, I did not have to sharpen them. The metal hadn't rusted or tarnished since I'd owned them, and I supposed the same could be said for the matching blade my mother had carried with her all these years.

I tried again to get her attention. "Micah's dead. I killed him. His puppet master is dead, too, and the one above him."

Granted I didn't kill Elias, Ruby, or Soren, but I'd taken out Samael and Micah at least.

Melody nodded and hummed again as she found the rune to extend the blade—only it was as if she already knew where it was. A sinking feeling hit my belly, and I couldn't decide if it was blood loss or the realization that this woman was nothing like the one I remembered.

The Melody I knew wanted her son, loved him even though she hadn't met him. The one I knew begged me to care for him as she took her last breath.

This wasn't Melody. Couldn't be.

"Where is Ronan, Melody?" I asked, insistent, the flash of lightning punctuating the question like a threat.

"Around." She shrugged, like leaving an infant to crawl around Faerie was top-notch parenting. That was if he was even still alive.

Not-Melody abandoned her inspection of my athame and moved to Striker, kneeling at his side. "Striker, my sweet, you must get up. Our job is not finished."

I felt the power in her voice. A power I definitely felt before in Micah. Shit. Maybe it was Melody after all, because that persuasion wasn't something just any kind of demon could do. No, that kind of powerful mind-control was something only the incubi and succubi were able to wield.

Striker's body jerked, stilled, and then jerked again. He groaned long and low, kind of like he was recovering from a lightning strike or three.

Okay, so I was only a little sorry about that—especially now that I knew he was alive.

He rolled away from her, putting his hands in the dirt as he struggled to stand. His hair was still smoking from the electricity I'd pumped into him, the color now less blond and whiter.

Whoops?

He kept his face turned away from her, groaning in pain as he staggered on his feet.

"You must finish what you started, my sweet," Not-Melody called in a saccharine-sweet way, shoving more power into her words.

Strike stumbled closer, his feet nearly tripping over each other as he made his way to me. He was between her and me, and only then did he raise his head. His face was still aged and sunken, but his eyes were a different story. His hazel gaze was clear as crystal as he bore it into me.

And then he winked.

I tried not to let the relief show on my face, tried to coax the earth and fire into him, to bolster him a bit more because I knew my best friend wasn't under Not-Melody's spell. Not even a little.

With each step, I watched as his face filled out, the wrinkles erasing from his skin, his cheeks pinkening.

He was healing right in front of my eyes and I was glad for it.

Because I was about to pick a fight.

"So how long have you been inhabiting Melody's body—if that is what you're doing? Because I know you aren't her. Drop the act."

Not-Melody's gaze flicked to me, an expression close to grudging pride on her face. She didn't think I would figure it out so quick?

"What tipped you off?" she asked, confirming my suspicions.

I wanted to list them all on my fingers, but my wrists were

chained, so I had to make do. "Melody loved her son. She wouldn't leave him unless she had to. She loved Striker. She wouldn't use him. Ever. And Melody hated Micah Goode, and she'd be jumping for fucking joy that I murdered that rat bastard."

"Too bad you're not the one I needed to convince. Your friend here believed it all too quickly. It was rather sad, actually, how easy he was to fool. Is that what blind love and devotion does to people? Makes them gullible?"

Yep, definitely not Melody.

"Sometimes. Sometimes the havoc that love does to us can make a sane man crazy. Then again, he isn't the one impersonating someone else to try and open a door that should stay shut. So, who's really the idiot here?"

Not-Melody smiled wide, her lips not quite right for her face. "You think I don't know what is behind that door? Oh, you child. Of course I know what is beyond that seal, dear. And it's the reason no one will mind when I kill you. No matter how much support you've gained, no matter how much people love you now, no one will once that door is opened wide."

"Why would you give a ripe shit about the support I ha..." I trailed off, knowing exactly who she was.

I was an idiot. "Verena, I presume?"

Not-Melody smiled wide again, her whole face melting and rearranging as her body grew. Melody's light-brown hair fell from her skull and blonde hair replaced it, growing in quick-time. Her skin darkened a touch—after it rearranged, that was—her nose a touch wider, her eyebrows dark slashes over piercing, unearthly blue eyes. One side of her cheek and mouth puckered around an old scar that cut a jagged path over her cheekbone, down through both lips, and curved back along her jaw. Still, she was pretty, the scar only adding to her appeal.

Verena was at least six inches taller than Melody had been, so I was glad to see her illusion came with new clothes, too. Granted, those clothes consisted of a floaty medieval-style dress and golden circlet of a crown. Verena wasn't built for a fight, nor was she dressed for one, and I hoped that would work in my favor.

"Shapeshifter?" I offered, worry filling me. Shapeshifters could turn into anything they wanted—they weren't limited to just one animal as long as whatever they turned into was of similar mass. But if she was one, then Melody could be long dead—if she was ever brought back to begin with.

Striker looked like his world was ending all over again, but he didn't stray his gaze to Verena at all. He didn't even twitch. Instead, he knelt at my feet and retrieved the bowl of blood.

She smiled and shook her head. "Changeling, actually. It means something a little different than the way humans use it. Yes, I was born in your realm, but I had a touch too much Fae in my blood. My human parents put me in a Faery circle and left me—not knowing if I'd die from exposure or if I would get taken. I was eight. Changelings can do just that—change—so I can be anyone. My parents didn't like when I impersonated my sister. They dropped me in that Faery circle and never looked back."

Like that could excuse four hundred years of bullshit. I wanted to feel bad for her—I did—but I just couldn't muster up the empathy for someone who had killed as many people as she had.

"And I was burned at the stake and shunned at fourteen. You don't see me murdering people en masse." I wanted to roll my eyes, but I was too tired. "Is Melody even in Faerie, or did you kill her on Earth and take her place there?" I asked this not just for my benefit, but Striker's as well. He needed to know.

Verena seemed so pleased that I'd taken such a leap in logic. "Oh, you must think me so devious. No, I can't leave Faerie anymore. That doesn't mean I didn't call her home—rather insistently, I might add—but I suppose that is beside the point. You want to know if she's alive?"

"Yeah, that'd be great. I would love to know if the person I've been searching for all over this fucking realm is actually breathing. Her son, too."

"Last I saw they were, but then again the dungeons in the Court aren't exactly the best at keeping people alive."

I could actually feel my eye twitching. I needed out of these chains so I could slap the shit out of this woman.

"Were you not loved enough as a child? I mean, come on, being adopted is not that bad." I paused, thinking about my own experiences. "Okay, so sometimes being adopted is a complete shitshow, but honestly? Did you have to kill everyone and be a total she-beast? Were you just jealous? What? Is there an evil plot you can explain to me because I am not getting it at all?"

Verena sighed. "I would, but what's the point? You'll be dead soon just like your parents and anyone else who opposes me. I'll finally have the throne—not the watered-down version I have now because you're still breathing. Eventually, I'll get some other poor soul to open the Hell gate. I may have fibbed a little bit to Soren about that, by the way. I don't need an Elemental to open it. I didn't even need you. I just wanted to see how far he'd go to get you there. Bravo on killing him. I really appreciate you taking out the trash for me."

I was still processing the implications of what she'd just said, when Verena snatched the bowl of blood from Striker's loose fingers and flung it toward the furrows in the dirt.

The thick, red liquid flew out of the bowl, dousing the sigils. As soon as the blood hit, the earth trembled, and I knew it wasn't from me.

CHAPTER TWENTY-ONE

As the red droplets hit the dirt, Striker lunged for Verena, his phase catching him on the fly. The pair of them tumbled to the earth, but Verena managed to scramble away mostly unscathed. Striker's change was hitting him hard.

The few times I'd seen Striker phase, his form had stayed mostly human-shaped, and it most certainly did not cause pain. In fact, the limited times I'd seen him in his other form, he hadn't even known it had come over him.

This time, not so much.

He screamed in agony as his body grew and grew, his form morphing into a giant winged beast that put Zillah to shame. His scales were still mostly scarlet, and he'd kept the scaly yet feathery wings—they were just a hundred times their previous size.

Striker opened his mouth and roared at Verena; the deafening sound punctuated by blistering flames that swept the ground as she did her best to dive out of the way.

Striker was a fire dragon. Good to know.

The last time I'd seen Striker phase, he hadn't nearly been this size. Did I do this to him? Did I accelerate his abilities somehow with my weird demi-god mojo? It kinda looked like it.

But I couldn't count Verena out. She hadn't spent four hundred years in Faerie sitting on her ass. I had no doubt that she'd changed into a bevy of creatures in her time as Faerie's supervillain, and she was morphing into one before my eyes.

Gone was her circlet crown and pretty dress. No, now she had a bone-like face and delicate wings—topped off with talons that could rend flesh and glowing yellow eyes that nightmares were made of. Tiny bones hung from leather strings at her waist like a macabre wind chime.

Bone Fae.

If I had a list of Fae that freaked me out the most, Bone Fae would be at the tippy top.

She dove at Striker's legs, digging her blackened talons into his scaly flesh. He roared again, spitting fire as he kicked, but Verena stayed glued to his leg like a barnacle, climbing up his flank.

A part of me wished he would blow some of that fire onto me. I wouldn't burn—at least I didn't think I would—and I'd love to see this tree be reduced to ash.

Plus, someone had to deal with the cracked seal on the door that I had a feeling was going to open any second now, and I was pretty sure the only person that could deal with that bullshit was me. I wanted to be free from this stupid death tree. It was too close to my burning, too close to the first time I was helpless.

I didn't do helpless. It was bullshit.

I got my wish about thirty seconds later as Striker reached down with his giant clawed hands and ripped Verena off his leg, tossing her away from him like he was flicking a bug. She flew, her Bone Fae body twisting in the air, but she failed to land on her feet. No, she smacked into the wall of the crevasse, crumpling to the ground.

Solid distance. If I had a scoring card, I'd give him a ten.

"Yo, Lizard Boy," I called, trying not to yell so I wouldn't jab myself in the throat and kiss this fight goodbye. "Any chance you wanna let me outta here?"

Striker curled his neck down so he could look at me, his belly resting on the ground. Jesus fuck, he was huge.

"I'm thinking you need to breathe fire on me. I can't call the elements closer, but I can still wield them. So gimme. Cough it up."

Striker's lizard face frowned at me, and it was majorly disconcerting that even in this form, he still looked like himself.

"Just do it before I hit you with lightning again." Not that it would hurt too much in this form, but whatever.

Dragon-Striker rumbled out a little growl.

"Sack up and do it, dick," I taunted, praying he would get his head out of his ass quick enough that I had enough time to get the hell away from this tree.

Striker's growl grew louder, shaking the ground with its power. Any minute now.

His jaws opened wide, and I heard a tiny little click before he bathed me in flames. I'd never been so happy in all my life that I was fireproof. The heat of them was blistering, sure, but I barely felt it. What I did feel was the way the collar jangled around my shoulders as the wooden spikes burned away. The chains at my wrists and waist melted, and then I was free.

Without me telling the element to, it filled me, strengthened me, replenished the blood I'd lost, and the blow to my head.

The only thing Striker's flames didn't do was burn the stupid tree. Coated in a fire that could liquefy metal, the tree stood tall without so much as a wilted petal or singed bark. I wondered if I could dig it up and drop it in the Seam. Punt it into outer space. Something.

Stepping away from the roots, I could feel all the elements fill me again, the power in my veins humming as I breathed them in.

I looked up at Striker, giving him a nod of thanks before I searched the spot where I saw Verena fall.

She hadn't moved, and I was tempted to ask Striker to eat her or blow her up before she sat up like the killer in a horror movie. Just as I was about to ask exactly that, the ground shuddered beneath our feet, the source of the quake cracking the seal that held the giant door closed to who knew what.

I'd heard whispers about what was behind that door—or behind one of the many portals in Faerie—to the hidden part of this realm. Some said Unseelie. Some called it the dark place. All I knew was, I was perfectly happy with my ignorance. I had absolutely no desire to know what was behind it.

Too bad I was a pro at not getting what I wanted.

The seal on the doors was a giant ram's head, the horns curling up and back to flow into the ornate design engraved into the stone. Down the center of the ram's face, the crack grew wider, the stone hissing as air passed through.

I didn't know what I should do. If I hit it with lightning, it might crack the stone further. If I hit it with pure fire, I feared the same. Earth, maybe? Would that help?

In the middle of my ponderings, I saw movement out of the corner of my eye. Verena was up and moving fast, her dark gossamer wings only adding to her speed as she ran full tilt right at me. Before I had a chance to react, she caught me in a flying tackle, her talons ripping into my shoulders as the pair of us landed in the dirt.

But Verena hadn't been training for the past year with a guardian, and even though she tore at my skin with her stupid Bone Fae talons, I still had the upper hand. I landed on my back and immediately rolled, taking her with me, and we switched positions—her on the bottom and me on top. The earth rose up in greeting, climbing over her face, filling her mouth and nose with soil. She coughed, breathing in dirt as I scrambled off her to my athames. One was at the base of the tree, and the other was in the middle of the weird sigils frozen into the earth.

I extended the blades, rounding just in time to greet Verena as she wrenched herself free. She opened her skull-like mouth, screeching at me like something out of a nightmare and lunged. Only it wasn't a lunge so much as her taking flight. Her delicate wings were unexpectedly powerful, and she shot at me like a bullet.

I slashed with my swords, marking her chest with a bloody "X" as my aim hit true, but still, she came at me, reaching for me as I rounded out of her way. My shoulders were tingling where the flesh was already knitting back together, my body pulling at the elements without me telling it to.

In the middle of all this, I could feel Striker's stomps and hear his roars, but this was the first time I'd had a chance to glance at him. He was roaring at the gate, breathing fire on the black smoke that was leaking from the cracked opening. On the upside, the fire was burning up the smoke—odd, I know—and driving it back.

The downside?

The gate was cracking more, the fissure in the ram's head so deep, light was pouring out of it.

The ground bucked, tossing even Striker off his feet. And I tried my best to figure out how to stop the door from opening all the way.

I asked the wind for a gale to blow away the furrows, but no matter how hard the wind pushed, not a single grain of dirt moved.

I called rain from the heavens, and fire from the clouds, and begged the earth to move, but nothing touched the sigils—nothing moved them. And I could feel them reaching for the door. I could feel the magic in them breaking the seal on the doors, chipping away at it bit by bit.

While I was busy trying to break the opening spell, Verena had her own problems. Somehow healed from the "X" I'd placed on her chest—she batted the black smoke that coalesced around her like a shroud. Verena ripped and scratched at her own head—her talons falling through the smoke. Try as she might, she could not fight the smoke, and she ended up rending her own flesh.

Black tendrils filled her nose and mouth, and she choked, stumbled, and fell. It reminded me of when Rowan had killed the Seelie guard, and I worried if we had a dark sylph on our hands. The vapor rose from her, and she gasped a breath.

So it didn't want to kill her? I couldn't say if that was comforting or not.

The ribbon of shadow crept back down to the earth before punching into it, the blackness disappearing altogether.

Nope, not comforting at all.

The earth bucked again, and neither of us knew if it was coming from the door or the black smoke that decided to make the earth its home. Striker screeched at the moving door—the seal now ripped wide.

Rather than try to figure it out for myself, I bolted for Verena and wrenched her from the ground.

"What did you do?" I screamed in her face, shaking her a bit to get her attention.

Even half-dead, Verena was a diabolical bitch because she just laughed—her bone jaw open wide in a macabre smile.

"Only I can close it. Only I can stop the monsterssss," she hissed, which shouldn't have been possible since she didn't have a tongue or lips.

I flung her away from me, watching with no small amount of satisfaction as she flew, bounced, and hit the ground with a decidedly pleasant thud. When she landed, blackened hands shot up from the earth and grabbed at her, their talons ripping at her flesh.

And, I hated to say, I felt good about that for about point-five seconds.

That was until very similar hands reached up from the ground and latched onto me as well. I yelped as I ran to Striker, but they gripped my ankles, using me to rise from the earth like eyeless zombies. Their enlarged heads and skeletal bodies crawled from the dirt like the worst sort of nightmare.

We were well and truly fucked.

CHAPTER TWENTY-TWO

If I ever made it out of this, I was never watching another zombie movie for as long as I lived. I had no idea what kind of Fae these bastards were, and I didn't want to know. All I wanted at that point was a shotgun and a gas mask, so I didn't have to be subjected to the stench.

Like anyone who had seen even ten minutes of any zombie movie, television show, or hell, even glimpsed the first pages of a comic, I knew to cut off their heads. The problem was, my athames were working full-time, swinging like helicopter blades, and I wasn't making a dent in the horde of whatever the fuck that was coming out of the ground.

"Striker! Anytime now you can flame their asses," I yelled, hacking through a zombie's neck like butter. And the next, and the next. My cuts and scrapes were healing on the fly, but this shit was no picnic.

The glorious feeling of Striker's flames washed over me, and I had enough time to do the sensible thing and call down enough lightning to power a small country. And because my lightning was enough to kill damn near everything, I didn't want to hit Striker with it. Instead, I did the friendly thing and picked off the zombies attacking him—or trying to—one by one, until they were all basking in the same flames as their brothers.

Zombie ash filled the crevasse for a moment before I whisked it away on a gale, shoving it back through the cracked door. A tiny bit of relief filled me until the world pitched again. This time the gate didn't just open a crack. Oh, no. The doors flew open wide, shoved open by a blackened figure bigger than any human.

Easily eight feet tall, the thing was made of shadows and smoke. If I didn't know any better—and I did—I would've believed it was a demon. His face coalesced into the shape of a ram, with horns curling back from his head, twisting with smoke. This thing looked so close to Andras' phased form it freaked me out a little. Especially since the very first thing it did was go after Verena. The giant reached down for her as she tried and failed to scramble away.

It roared at her in a language I couldn't name, and even with my translator spell, I couldn't understand what he was screaming at her. Verena's form shifted while she was in his hold, turning back into the scarred, blonde queen. She squirmed, fighting him until he flung her away from his body.

Verena landed on her feet and screamed at him some more. "I will have what I am owed. You nor she will take it from me."

She changed shape as she ran at him, growing twice her height as she morphed into a tree-person. A dryad, maybe? They clashed, Verena's limbs smashing into him. Or almost. The monster dematerialized right as she swung, moving out of the way before reforming behind her, his talons digging into her bark and wrenching her to the ground.

I kinda wanted to watch them duke it out, but more things were coming out of the wide-open gate. Shadows fell upon us as hands grew from the ground. Again. The zombies were back, and they'd brought friends.

Fates, would these things just fucking die already?

But the zombies and shadows weren't alone. Grotesque and monstrous things crawled from the open portal, things I couldn't name or describe. Things that there were no words for. A horde of them poured into the crevasse, overtaking us with mindless determination and razor-sharp claws.

Striker and I poured flames into the land—and that worked on most of the surreal beings that hacked and slashed and snapped at us. But some were made of flames, made of smoke, made of air, and that element did nothing to hold them back.

A particularly nasty thing made of noxious purple smoke and gnarled teeth took a hunk out of my arm—the venom in the bite enough to nearly bring me to my knees. A burning yet freezing agony tore through my veins—so bad I didn't think I'd keep my feet. My body slowed, failing me in battle as I tried to hack and stab my way through the horde.

A shadow fell over me—Verena's smoke monster, and I thought that was it. I wasn't going to make it out of this chasm. But instead of hitting me when I was down, the smoke monster stabbed at it with its claws before ripping it away from me—his talons able to cut through it when my sword could not. This lone monster appeared to be on our side as it helped us push back the horde.

My arm hung useless for a few harrowing minutes as I stabbed and hacked with one lone sword until the elements filled me again. But as much as I was drawing on the elements themselves, I wasn't healing fast enough, wasn't moving fast enough. I was flagging and I couldn't see a light at the end of the tunnel.

The earth began to pitch again, a gentler vibration than the ones before it. It felt like hoofbeats pounding on the ground, and soon I saw the giant head of a kitsune barreling toward us, his seven tails fanning out behind him like a banner of an army.

And Hideyo wasn't alone.

Beside him—hacking through monsters like it was his happy place—ran Alistair, his scythe rending through the crowd like butter. Behind him was Aidan and my mother, bowling through nefarious beings with the single-minded focus of warriors. Rowan and Aramal and Maireen and all their retinue followed with Della and Lothan not far behind. Lothan and his elves blasted the horde with magic as Aramal and the dwarves swung their battle hammers and the fawns shot their arrows.

The cavalry had arrived.

Alistair wrenched his scythe through three bodies before he got to me, yanking a sightless zombie-thing off my leg before wrapping me up in a swift hug.

"I leave you alone for five bloody minutes and you've gone and caused the apocalypse," Alistair quipped before smashing a quick kiss to my lips. "I swear from now on, I'm not leaving you alone. Ever. You get up to too much trouble on your own."

I'd never been so happy to see him in my life. I would be kissing the shit out of him if we weren't in the middle of the biggest shitshow I'd ever seen.

"You cannot possibly blame this on me. Also, the dragon is Striker. Don't ask, just don't kill him."

Alistair pondered that for about a second before he gave me some sage advice. "You might want to make an announcement, love," he insisted as he ripped through another body, "otherwise they might assume he's just another monster."

He had a valid point.

"*Audite me*," I whispered, pressing my fingers into my throat. *Hear me.* "Don't hurt the dragon. He's a friendly. Drive the horde back to the gate. We can't let them gain any more ground." I released my throat and glanced over to Alistair. "Did that work?"

"You mean did I hear that in my bloody head?" he asked, ripping his flaming sword from the scabbard at his back and beheading a crawling thing that looked almost inside out. "Yeah, love. It bloody worked."

"Good," I muttered before pressing into my throat again—the action like a walkie-talkie. "Anybody got any ideas on how the fuck to close that gate? The sigils are immovable. Cutting these guys down is great and all, but if we don't get that gate shut, we're screwed."

My mother's voice sounded off in my brain and I understood Alistair's shuddering reaction. "If you can't rebuild the gate you've got," she began, grunted, and then continued, "Why don't you just make a new gate?"

I wanted to slap myself upside the head. *Duh, Max.* To my credit, I was fighting monsters and kinda failing, so I gave myself a teensy break.

"Anyone want to watch my ass while I do that?"

Yes, Alistair was doing a fine job, but we were going to be overrun in about a minute if things stayed as they were.

"Everyone, back up." Striker's voice sounded in my brain, the volume ten times what my mother had, the sound rattling inside my skull like a gong. "Fire in the hole."

Everyone but Alistair and the monsters scattered. Striker let out another ear-splitting roar as the flames bathed us in heat. Alistair and I fell into step, the pair of us back to back as we hacked through the ones that the flames didn't touch. The ones that we missed and weren't reduced to ash were attacked by a white sort of miasma—the familiar shape of a sylph running through the remaining creatures, stealing their lives in a manner I couldn't name.

"Your ass is covered, love. Figure out a way to make a new gate," Alistair prompted, his flaming sword whirling around his body like a dervish.

The only thing in this whole crevasse that hadn't been touched by flames or wind or earth was the death tree—the rowan my father had made as an insurance policy against forever. If I couldn't kill it, and I couldn't remove it, could I convince it to work with me?

I made a beeline for the tree—or at least I tried to. The way was blocked by clashing bodies and carnage, only the spot right outside of the root line was clear.

"Ah, fuck it," I muttered before latching onto Alistair's hand and snapping my fingers. I hadn't traveled here like I'd had on Earth—too scared to use that particular power because I had no idea where I'd end up. When we landed at the tree's roots, I breathed a sigh of relief.

"Did you—did you just travel us without knowing if it would

work?" he asked, a might bit cranky for a man who had been in his happy place a second ago.

"Maybe? We're under a time crunch. There were people in the way."

Alistair leveled me with a stern expression.

"Okay, fine. I'm sorry. That was rude."

He muttered something under his breath, shaking his head as he readied himself for attackers. But it was as if no one wanted to be anywhere near the giant tree. Even Alistair's flaming sword sputtered and died as he stepped closer to the bark.

No one came near the tree because they couldn't—even the elements refused to come to me here.

Alistair snagged my fingers, pressing them to his mouth. "You're safe, love. Do what you need to do."

Shaking, I pressed my hands to the one thing that could kill me. The tree was warm to the touch, the fire we'd poured into the crevasse heating it but not burning it at all. The rough bark pressed into my skin and I sank down to the gnarled roots that peeked up from the dirt, resting my forehead against the trunk. I felt myself slipping away, separating from my body as my consciousness fell into the tree.

I'd thought the tree would be blackness and death like so much of Faerie was—like the creatures that had once been held back by the ruined gates—but I was wrong. It was bright here, so bright I could barely open my eyes, even though I knew I didn't really have "eyes" here.

"Hello? I hate to bother you, but I need help." I couldn't see anything, all there was to the place was brightness and white.

"First, you want to burn me down or rip me up or punt me into —what was it called? Oh, yes. Outer space. And now you want my help?"

The woman's voice shocked me. I thought I would get a feeling or something, not a full-on conversation. She had an accent I couldn't place, but that wasn't important.

"You're right. I was rude. I had no idea you were a sentient being, and even if you were, I would still hold a grudge. Your bark nearly killed me. It did kill my parents and siblings. To me you were a symbol of my family's death."

"Ah," she said as a shadow moved through the whiteness.

A woman's form took shape, her coloring not much different than the world around her. She seemed to pull the brightness into herself and she became clear. White hair topped albino-white skin and glowing ice-blue eyes. Her lips were radiant blue as was the crescent moon in the center of her forehead. A pair of horns peeked out of her hair, the bones curving forward toward her brow like a kind of crown.

A formidable woman with a face like stone, she contemplated me, sizing me up before she spoke again. "Am I not still a symbol of your family's death?"

I thought about it for a minute, weighing my words carefully. "You are, but you cannot help how you were used. Unless you gave your branches freely, someone took them to use as weapons. Someone used you as an instrument of death. On Earth, rowan trees are symbols of life and perseverance. They grow on mountain tops in barely any soil. On the sides of cliffs where nothing else can flourish. I have a tough time believing you ever intended death—even if that was what my father made you for."

She smiled then, as she gave me a bowing nod. "You are intuitive, but I would expect nothing less from the daughter of Chaos. I am Aiyana the Eternal. I cannot be burned or chopped or dug up. I cannot be moved, and I can never die. But my branches do fall occasionally, and people use them in horrible ways. Ways I cannot predict nor understand."

She was confirming my suspicions in a roundabout way, and I understood that she had not conversed with anyone in some time. I needed to ask direct questions in the hopes that I might get direct answers.

"You cannot be moved, but can you move yourself? Can you reach out your roots?"

"Perhaps. If I have a good enough reason."

"The gate to the dark place is open—broken in a way I cannot repair. I can't fix the old gate, but I thought if your roots dispel magic, then you could grow a new door, one that could not be opened by magic. One that—"

"Yes, I know what you want me to do. But why? What do your people say? What's in it for me?"

Oh, shit. Aiyana wasn't a Fae, but she also wasn't a goddess—or maybe she was. I still did not want to make a deal with anyone ever again.

"You would have a purpose other than just sitting still in a crevasse. You would be holding back things that kill."

"Anything can kill, child."

Boy, was I getting really tired of people calling me child. Granted, Aiyana was older than time itself, so to her I was probably a fucking embryo.

"Okay, so I don't understand the things beyond that door. I don't know why they are there, and I don't know if they can be reasoned with, so they don't mow down an entire realm full of creatures. I don't know what I don't know. I need time to get smart, and to do that, I need you to close that damn door. Better?"

Aiyana's smile grew as she twirled a ring on her first finger. It was a plain band of wood no thicker than my fingernail.

"You remind me of your father. He is just as direct and impetuous as you are. I will do what you ask and make a gate no magic can open, and when you are settled, you will come to me. I will educate you on what you do not know. That is my bargain."

I'd get a closed gate and answers. I couldn't agree fast enough.

"Sold. I will agree to those terms with the caveat that this moves fast. My people are being hurt out there. I can feel it."

And I could.

Aidan and my mother were bleeding. One of Hideyo's tails was damn near ripped off and might not grow back. Della was being held up by Lothan because her belly was pouring blood, and the list went on. Dwarves were dying, fawns were being cut down.

"Agreed," she murmured, her body right in front of me. I hadn't even seen her move.

Aiyana pressed two fingers to my forehead, and I fell backward, my body following suit when I returned to it.

I gasped in a lungful of air, the world swimming around me like I was caught in a dervish. Alistair grabbed me by the shoulders and stood me up, and I struggled to hold my own weight.

"You all right, love? Can you stand?"

I gripped his shoulders for all I was worth. "Get me away from the tree," I croaked, and as soon as he put me on the soil outside of the drop line, I could breathe again, the elements filling me until I could stand on my own.

"She said she would help us. We need to get all the monsters on the other side of the gate."

"She? You mean the tree is a she?"

"Yep. Aiyana." I pressed into my throat again, calling to my people. "Get all the monsters back on the other side of the gate."

"What do you think we've been doing out here? We can barely hold them back," Aidan growled, his voice sounding in my mind like a slap.

The elements weren't enough to drive them back, but I wasn't just an Elemental, was I?

No. I was a fucking demi-god. My father was Chaos.

It was time to cause some.

Drawing on all the elements, I filled myself full until I could draw no more. Then I pushed, not using the elements themselves, but me and my magic. The power that resided in me since birth. The power that no one could name or quantify, the abilities that marked me as an outcast, and got me burned.

I pushed them all, the things in the ground, the smoke in the sky. Anything and everything that belonged on that side of the door, I shoved it back. Zombie Fae were plucked from the ground like daisies, blackened smoke-like things flew back to where they came from. Every monster and ghoul, every unnamed grotesque thing, all of it.

A few things scrambled at my people as they passed, trying to hold on to something as they were forced back into their prison, but nothing was stopping them. They all went, every single one.

And I watched as roots grew up out of the ground like climbing vines, the thick bark widening, stretching, weaving into itself until nothing could make it out of the new gate. The vines solidified, turning into a new carved door, blue like the darkness of space and with a larger seal.

This time, the lock that held the two doors closed was a carved rendering of Aiyana's face, her horns like a crown and all.

I turned back, searching for Alistair, only to find him crumpled just outside the drip line of Aiyana's tree. Forgetting everything else, I ran to him, pushing my hands to his chest ready to fill him with every element I had at my disposal.

But as soon as I touched him, he grabbed my hands—gasping awake.

"Are you okay? What happened?"

Alistair's brow furrowed in confusion as he stared at me and then at his surroundings. Shaking his head, he blinked and rubbed his temple. "I'm all right, love. I'm okay. Just a bump on the head."

Unable to hold in my relief, I tackle-hugged him, clutching him to me like he was life itself. We were okay. It was going to be okay.

For the first time since we'd set foot in Faerie, I finally felt just a little bit of relief.

"My Queen, what would you have us do with the usurper?"

I pulled back from Alistair to give Hideyo the stink-eye. "Usurper? That's just—" I couldn't even think of the right phrase. "Weird. And quit with the queen shit. You know how I feel about that. I'm Max. Just Max."

"You should start getting cool with it real quick, Majesty. You have an entire realm full of people who will refuse to call you by your name. Think of this as a crash course."

"Whatever," I grumbled. "Bring Verena to me."

Usurper. I rolled my eyes.

Hideyo shot me a wide grin that was all teeth, and he was off to collect the former queen.

My eyes drifted over the battle-weary Fae, and without me telling them to, the elements reached for them, restoring my people. We had casualties, and those would have to be honored.

I stood, searching the crowd for my mother, for Della, for Striker, and Aidan. Striker was harder to find since he'd gone back to his human form. I spotted the lot of them grouped around a woman until Hideyo joined them. He reached into the middle of the group and plucked the former queen from the earth, dragging her struggling body to me.

I saw the instant she was about to let a change come over her and pounced.

Pressing three center fingers against her chest, I turned them like a key, shutting off her power like a faucet. "I don't think so. You're changeling days are over."

She was about to scream at me, her mouth opening as she sucked in a breath, but I snapped my fingers, shutting off her voice. Her body bucked with rage, and I decided to do Hideyo a solid.

"*Somnum*," I murmured, putting her to sleep, her body sagging in Hideyo's hold. "That'll make the trip easier."

"What trip?" my mother asked, pushing her shoulder under my arm to give me a hug. I squeezed her, so happy she was okay—so happy that they were all okay.

Alistair answered for me, knowing exactly where I needed to go.

"We're going to the Seelie Court."

CHAPTER TWENTY-THREE

I couldn't imagine what the Seelie guards were thinking when they saw roughly four hundred of their enemies show up in the middle of the Court like they had a right to be there. I would assume some shitting of pants was involved, but I couldn't be certain.

When Striker hit me over the head and took me to the Unseelie gate, it had taken a minute to rally the troops. Striker didn't just hit me when he broke out of the encampment, and Teresa had been knocked unconscious. Once she managed to get the word out that I'd been taken, the Seelie soldiers were nearly upon them. The Tandrirr, dwarves, fawns, and water Fae banded together and drove them back.

Only then were they able to come to my aid with Alistair using his obsidian charm once again to save my ass. I didn't want to think of what would have happened if they hadn't shown up. Striker and I wouldn't have survived it.

Striker seemed to be more himself than he'd been in nearly a year. I didn't understand it until I touched his forehead, diving deep into his brain to make sure I could trust him. After the events of the last year, I wasn't taking any chances. I could feel traces of old magic in him—the same spells I'd found in Cinder after she'd been controlled by Soren. The lightning I'd poured into him seemed to have knocked something loose, but there was still lingering magic there.

"This is going to hurt," I told him before I burned out the last vestiges of the spell that held his mind captive. I may have made his nose bleed a little, but it was better than him not being in control of his own brain.

I saw flashes in his mind of when he'd been taken, and I had a feeling it was in the hours he'd been missing while we were on the hunt for Melody before she'd died. That's when he'd really gone off the deep end, but it could have been before that. Striker had been acting off for some time now.

That was the only reason he was by my side as we walked through the Seelie Court like we had a right to be there. The walled city took up nearly half the realm, the walls moving by magic as more land was conquered. That wall would be the first thing to go once I had things settled.

A castle sat at the center of the Seelie Court—the giant stone structure spanning much more land than a single building should. The turrets touched the clouds, the tops hidden from the naked eye. Each stone was such a brilliant white that I wanted to muddy them up a little, and the whole of the structure gave me the creeps with how pretty and perfect and just wrong it was.

I led the charge through the streets, climbing the last set of steps to the closed castle doors. In front of them was a set of four guards and a stuffy-looking fellow with twigs for horns, line-drawn face paint, and pointed ears. He wore clothes that were out of a regency romance novel, and he appeared no happier wearing them than I was seeing him in them.

"Who—"

"I'm going to stop you right there, Jeeves. I am Massima Bertrand Laffitte, Dušan's only living daughter. I have come to take my place as Queen of Faerie. Oh, and to throw your shit rag of a queen in the deepest, darkest hole I can find."

The guards got the message. Jeeves did not.

"Y-you can't—" he began again, yanking at his cravat like it was choking him.

"I am the daughter of Chaos. Are you going to come over here in your pretty pantaloons and stop me?" I crossed my arms over my chest and sized him up. Jeeves didn't seem like he wanted to challenge me, more like he was scared of what would happen if he did.

"I turned off her magic. She can't hurt you or anyone else."

Relief made his shoulders slump like I'd deflated him. He straightened again. "Are you sure?"

"Hideyo, show him his former queen," I called, wanting this poor Fae to see his boogeyman incapacitated.

Hideyo grabbed Verena by the hair, showing him her face. Jeeves wilted again, one of the guards having to catch him before he fell.

"She can't speak, she can't wake, and she cannot turn. She has no power."

Jeeves spoke again, only this time, his words were clogged with tears. "She has our families' as prisoners. If we make a false step, she..."

"Then, lead me to the dungeons. I figure I have some prisoners to free."

Jeeves—whose real name was Warrick—led us down too many flights of stairs until we reached the dank and freezing dungeons. It took forever, but he told me what each prisoner was remanded for. Almost none of the prisoners stayed in their cells. There were a few exceptions, men who were in there for murder or torture, but I planned on revisiting their cases to make sure they were there for the right reasons.

In one of the very last cells sat the woman I'd been searching the whole damn realm for. Melody sat on a lone stool, holding tight to her son, who was sleeping against her chest. I worried she might not remember me—or Striker, for that matter. Worried that her soul was as broken as they said it was.

"Melody?" I called, hoping she knew me.

"Max?"

I couldn't help it, I teared up a bit. I never really thought I'd see her like this—alive and holding onto her son. "Yeah, sweetie. It's me. Are you… you?"

I wasn't sure how much Verena had influenced her, how much she made her do. I shouldn't have worried over Melody's sanity.

"You mean, am I planning on pitting people against each other for my own gain? No, Max, I hadn't planned on it."

A relieved sort of laugh bubbled up my throat, and I gave Warrick the nod to open the door. Striker was right behind me, so Melody passed me her sleeping son, stepped around me, and then socked Striker right in the face.

Aidan and I exchanged a glance before busting up into giggles. Yes, the big man giggled. I didn't care what he said.

"You had no right," she hissed before shaking out her hand.

Striker nodded, his face the picture of bliss even with a bloody lip. "You're absolutely correct. No one has the right to take you where you don't want to go. I have no defense, but I will do anything in my power to make it right."

"He does too have a defense. He's just too worried you won't believe him to use it. Verena mind-controlled him just like she did you. Granted, he might have done it, anyway, but…" I piped up for Striker, hoping he at least got a little bit of happiness.

"Really?" she asked him, mostly ignoring me.

When he gave her a gentle nod, she lunged at him, kissing the shit out of him in the middle of a damn dungeon. Now I knew how other people felt when Alistair and I kissed in inappropriate places. I snorted to myself and hugged Ronan closer.

"Hideyo, drop off our package, please?" I asked him as I handed off Ronan to his mother.

He dropped her in the middle of the dungeon floor, her skull hitting with a solidly satisfying thud. Warrick locked the door, and I took the key from him. Verena wasn't going anywhere, and I was going to be sure of it.

Calling on all my magic, all the elements, everything I had, I weaved a spell so tight around Verena's cell, no one but me could open it. There was no escaping, no conning her way out, and no one would kill her before I could question her.

I refused to let history repeat itself.

Pretty much the entire Court was relieved that Verena was the dungeon's newest resident. But speeches had to be made, and I wasn't going to live in a place where people were going to poison my food or stab me in my sleep. I kept it simple, letting them know she wasn't coming back except for judgment, and if they were her supporters, they had five minutes to get the fuck out.

"If you feel I am not the rightful Queen of Faerie, then I suggest you get out of this castle and out of the Seelie Court post haste. Because if you decide to rise up against me or mine, it will be the last thing you ever do." I said it with a smile, but I got the feeling they knew I wasn't playing around.

"Warrick here will instruct you on your new tasks. None of which include working yourself to the bone, starving, or worrying about the safety of your family. If you have family recently freed from the dungeons, please go to your homes and welcome them. Take all the time you need to come back—but only if you want to. Everyone is dismissed for the day. Please go home and relax. Tomorrow is a new day."

My stomach dropped at the end of my speech, and I knew why. Queen. I was acting like a queen. I'd never wanted that kind of responsibility. I'd always wanted something small. My tattoo shop, my greenhouse. My little family that I made for myself.

But a kingdom? No way.

I wanted to hold Alistair's hand, but he was all the way on the other side of the throne dais, too far away for me to snag his hand.

"Warrick, if you could find rooms for us and directions to the kitchen, that will be all for the day. If you want to come back tomorrow, I would love to have you, but it is up to you."

Warrick looked like I just gave him the biggest Christmas present and topped it with birthday sprinkles.

"Of course, Maj—err—Max. I will be back in the morning." I nodded and dismissed him, almost everyone following the Fae down the hall for some grub and a decent night's rest.

I plopped onto the throne—a place Warrick insisted on taking us to make the speech to the household staff. It was cold and lonely, and I wished Alistair would come talk to me.

He'd been weird since the crevasse, and I hoped all of this wasn't too much. I'd meant to talk to him about accepting this role —about all of it—before, but nothing had turned out how I wanted it to. It all seemed to be happening so fast.

"Are you mad? That I took the throne? I know we were just supposed to get Melody back, but I couldn't just leave them here like this."

"I know that. I don't think you did the wrong thing. I think I'm just tired."

I stood, making my way to Alistair and snagging his hand like I'd wanted to. I was ready for a good night's rest in something other than a cot. Hopefully, in a room with a decent shower and maybe a tub.

A tub would be glorious.

"Come on, Knight." I pulled him to me. "Let's find us some food and a bed."

I pressed my lips to his for one brief moment.

In an instant, my whole body ran cold. On instinct, I reached for my athame. In the next second, I'd shoved him into the closest wall, and my blade kissed his throat.

My whole body shook as fear and rage and horror filled me.

"You are not Alistair," I said through clenched teeth, tears pooling in my eyes. "Who the fuck are you, and what have you done with my husband?"

QUEEN OF FATE & FIRE

ROGUE ETHEREAL BOOK 6

CHAPTER ONE

They say the first year of marriage was the hardest. If the blade to my new husband's throat was any indication, they—whoever *they* were—would be right.

But this wasn't my husband—not really.

Sure, this was Alistair's body, and sure, he was probably hidden somewhere, crouched low in the recesses of his own mind, but the man looking through Alistair's eyes, and wearing Alistair's skin was not my husband. He was some kind of dark Fae, and he'd taken over.

"What have you done with him? Where is he?" I'd meant it to come out as commanding, but I didn't quite hit the mark. I was a frantic mess at best, and the monster wearing my husband's skin knew it.

This was what I got for coming to Faerie. Literally every single person with any lick of sense said demons could get possessed here. They said it was too risky. They said Alistair was in danger by following me to this place.

Did I listen?

Of course not. I smiled, nodded, and did whatever the fuck I wanted to anyway, and look where we were. Look at what happened to the man I loved.

I should have known something was off the moment I saw Alistair fall in the gorge. We'd been trying to keep the Unseelie Fae back. We were trying to stop Verena and whatever cracked plot she was trying to carry out. I'd thought we'd succeeded. Peering into the strikingly blue eyes of Alistair's hijacked face, I'd say we missed one.

I saw the lie cross his face before he opened his mouth. *No. Not today, buddy.*

"Think very carefully about what you say next." I could practically feel my molars cracking from how hard I was clenching my jaw, and if my blade happened to nick his neck, well, it was just a sign that I meant business.

And yeah, this was far too close to home for me. Not just that it was Alistair—not that it was the man I loved being used in such a fashion. No, this was Maria all over again. This was everything I'd buried bubbling up to the surface.

And if Alistair's face wavered a little due to some unshed tears, well, I'd say I'd earned them.

Not-Alistair took that moment to pounce, bringing the sword from his scabbard up and knocking my blade away from his neck.

I scrambled back a step, before our swords clashed—or rather my athame went from dagger-sized to short-sword sized after I pressed the rune on the handle, and I attacked. My fencing skills were weak at best, but no-rules swordplay? Aidan had once said I was a natural.

Still, this guy was parrying every single strike like he was humoring me rather than fighting for his life.

"I am not your enemy," Not-Alistair's mouth said, but his voice was no longer my husband's. It had a burr of something else I couldn't place. A smokiness that had never been there before—not even when he'd been phased.

"Really? You got a funny way of showing it." My frustration bubbled up inside my chest as I slashed and parried. I couldn't say why I didn't want to use the power that roiled beneath my skin, but I didn't.

I could kill him. I could hurt him. But I didn't want to because of the face he wore. It was a weakness I knew I had, but I didn't have the luxury of time to analyze it.

"I didn't want to take over this body," he grunted, staving off the edge of my blade with a bit less finesse than before. "It was the only way I could talk to you. I tried in the valley. But you couldn't understand me. I helped you, remember? I am on your side."

I had a tough time remembering the battle. Everything from the last twenty-four hours was a blur of one shitshow after another.

"I tossed Verena into a cliff face like she was—what do humans call it? A frisbee?" he offered, not unkindly.

That rang a bell. A huge monster of a Fae had taken Verena out for us, and then helped us fight the rest of the zombie-looking Fae back to the door. "Smoke guy?"

All the while, our blades were spinning as we slashed and parried and stabbed at one another—or rather I did the stabbing and slashing, and Not-Alistair, AKA, Smoke Guy parried and danced around me. Granted, I was wearing him down, but he still hadn't had so much as another nick from my steel. Or whatever the hell these blades were made of.

"Niall, little goddess. My name is Niall."

I found I liked the use of the goddess title no better than "highness" or "majesty" and growled at him. "I don't care who you are. Give me back my husband. *Now*."

If he even could. I couldn't get Maria back. Who was to say I could get Alistair? Who was to say that this would be how everyone left me? My nose began to sting, and his face wobbled and distorted.

"I will. I have no intention of staying in this body. I will return him to you alive, intact, and unharmed. I promise. I just need your help."

For some reason, even though his words made sense and his tone was kind, I brought my sword down harder, my slashes sped up, my jabs grew sharper. He was lying. Alistair had been taken away from me just like she had.

"I don't believe you." With that, I shoved at him with my mind, causing his body to fly back into the wall as my blade kissed his throat.

I didn't even hear the footsteps behind me before my mother started speaking. "You know, I'm all for setting my husband's head on fire, but I've never actually tried cutting it off. You think that would work, or is that just a good way to become a widow?"

I couldn't help it, I snorted, a sharp bark of laughter bubbling up my throat. Still, I didn't move my gaze even a millimeter from Alistair's stolen ones.

"This isn't Alistair." Yes, I knew I probably looked like I'd cracked. Here I was holding a sword to my husband's throat insisting that he wasn't my husband.

Like a crazy person.

Which totally explained why Teresa was shifting her weight from foot to foot as she tried to decide what to do next. "It's his body, but it's not him. Remember how everyone said demons could be infected by Fae? Meet Niall, Mom."

The heat of fire blooming in my mother's hand swept over me, and I relaxed just a smidgen. She didn't think I was crazy.

"Like I told your daughter, I need your help. This was the only way I could speak to you. Please. I don't want to quarrel with you or yours, and I will give this body back unharmed. Just listen to me. Please. The fate of Faerie depends on it."

It didn't matter how much I wanted to believe him, I didn't know if I could. I didn't know if I could trust Niall.

"Go on," my mother prompted. "If you say the fate of Faerie depends on you delivering a message, give it to us and then return Alistair."

Niall's lips—so different than any expression Alistair had ever shown me—twisted in indignation. "You won't listen. You won't do what I need you to. My only leverage is this body. Faerie and all Fae will die if you don't. I can't risk it." He shook his head like he was coming to a decision. "I will not leave this body until the task is done."

"Sure. I'll just drop everything and let an Unseelie Fae lead me on an epic quest. Who the fuck do you think you are? Give him back to me, or so help me, I'll kill him to save him from you."

Niall shook his head, his pitying expression pissing me the fuck off. "No, you won't. You love this man too much. It is a harsh thing I do, Little Goddess, but it is what I must. I pray you might forgive me one day, doing this horrible thing to you. But maybe not. Stealing him away—even for such a short time—is cruel, I know. I do not wish to do it. But there are many things I have done in service to your family that I had never wished for. Still, these things must be done."

None of this smelled like a lie. It didn't mean any of it made sense or was the truth, either. The Fae were a tricky lot, and they could lie without trying. Still.

I couldn't help asking a question that had been on my mind throughout all of this. "Is he okay? Is he hurt?"

"No, child. He is safe. Right brassed off at me for stealing his body, but he is safe inside his mind."

I couldn't say why that gave me a bit of relief, but it did. "So he can see me? Hear me?"

Niall nodded before pinching my blade between his thumb and pointer finger and gently pushing it back. He did this with enough power that I knew there was no way I could have bested him in a sword fight—or any other fight for that matter.

"I am not here to hurt you. I am not here to injure you or yours in any way. Please listen. Please. We don't have much time."

"Tell me what he's saying to you," I ordered. "Tell me what he's saying, and I'll listen. I'll believe you that he's okay in there. I'll let you speak."

Niall considered me for a second before his eyes went unfocused. He looked like he was listening to a far-off voice. "To the ends of the earth and far beyond. Vaster than Heaven or Hell or any of the worlds in between."

I couldn't help it, I started crying in earnest, relief making me wilt to the stone floor. Those were the words Alistair had said when he told me he loved me. He was in there. He was.

When I'd gotten myself marginally under control, I touched the rune on my athame, collapsing the blade into a dagger and sheathed it.

"I'll listen. I can't promise to do what you need, but I will listen."

Niall considered me, a faint trace of approval in his half-smile. "I appreciate a goddess who doesn't make promises she doesn't think she can keep. You remind me of your father."

"Lying pisses me off. What can I say?" I shrugged before indelicately wiping my eyes and nose. "You knew Dušan?"

"No, child. I *know* Dušan. And we need him back before this world and everyone made from it collapses into nothing."

I couldn't help the half-crazed bark of laughter that bubbled up from my throat. I sounded like I needed a straitjacket STAT. "Well, that's tough shit, Niall. Dušan is dead. Has been for about four hundred years."

I kept giggling as I turned to my mother. "I guess we're fucked then, huh?"

I personally felt I had every right to crack. I mean, hadn't I stopped one Apocalypse after the other? Hadn't I lost enough? Sure. Let's add in an entire realm of people and my life while we were at it. Absolutely. That would be the cherry on top.

So, there I was—giggling like a loon as I sat splayed on the floor of a Faerie castle that I was now the apparent Queen of, and my husband was possessed by a dark Fae.

Someone just shoot me now.

Niall crouched at my feet, concern etched in Alistair's face. "I don't know where you heard Dušan was dead, but I can assure you, he is not. For one, we're all alive. If he were dead, this realm would have collapsed in on itself. Secondly, I have no idea where you got the idea that gods were so easily killed, but one little changeling who is more human than anything else does not have the power to murder a god—especially not the father of all gods."

I supposed Niall could be right. Dušan was in a little pocket of existence he'd made for himself, so I assumed it was possible that he could be alive. How I thought I could possibly convince a god older than time that he was wrong was anyone's guess.

"Again, child, we don't have time. If we do not get Dušan back before the Blood Moon rises, this realm will be lost."

I snorted, rolling my eyes. *Blood Moon.* How fucking cliché. "Fine. How much time do we have until this *Blood Moon*?"

"Three days."

Yeah, I started giggling again, but could anyone blame me? I had three days to get my birth father back from the brink of existence.

Piece of cake.

CHAPTER TWO

After I stopped giggling—which probably took far too long considering my current time constraint—I did what any rational person would do when given a task far too big to tackle. I conjured myself some top-shelf bourbon and drank that shit right out of the bottle.

Okay, so a more rational person would probably brainstorm ways to complete said impossible task, but I was tapped out on brainstorming sessions for the time being. Once I was sure I wasn't dreaming, nor could I find a logical reason not to believe the ancient dark Fae trapped in my husband's body, I handed the bottle off to my mother, conjured myself a paper and a pen, and got to writing.

My succinct letter to Barrett was written and off to annoy him in two minutes flat. His response was terse, but I could feel his relief at hearing from me through the note he sent back.

Meet us at the door. We have much to discuss.

I really hoped he was referring to the portal door that brought us here, because after I latched onto my mother's hand and grabbed Niall's sleeve, that's where I took us. Yeah, there probably should have been a discussion about where we were going or who we were meeting, but I just didn't have the energy.

I left my mother to her cursing and Niall to his spluttering, walking straight toward the portal door. Yes, for a split second, I thought about walking through it and going to my house and taking a nap. I thought about just giving up on it all. But then Barrett walked through the door with Marcus behind him, and I just fucking lost it. I sprinted to them, letting the pair of them fall all over me in a group huddle. I then vaguely noticed Andras, Bernadette, and Atropos had followed them through.

Out of all of them, I expected my grandmother and father the least. I'd specifically requested Atropos' presence, and the fact that she actually came made me think hope wasn't actually lost. Maybe. Honestly, it was a crapshoot and we were all probably going to die. Who knew at this point?

After a few moments that seemed way too short, Barrett pulled back to look at me. "Darling girl, you look like you've been put through the wringer." He clucked his tongue as he tucked me under his arm, pulling me toward another door to the cottage. "How about some heavily laced tea and a chat?"

It wasn't like I was going to tell him no. I had reached the very end of my rope, and if Barrett was going to make me tea and give me a hug, I was all for it.

The cottage itself appeared ramshackle on the outside and a cozy little space on the inside. The furnishings were straight out of the 1950s but they seemed to be in good repair and clean. I wasn't going to turn my nose up at any of it. To the left of the room was a couch and several armchairs with cute little throw pillows dotting the corners. To the right was a bare-bones kitchen with an avocado-colored refrigerator, butcherblock counters, and a mammoth farm sink. In the window above the sink were several thatches of herbs tied together with twine which hung from a wooden shelf, their corresponding pots above each.

Someone appeared to live here. Took care of the place, too. Everything was clean and in good repair, and it had the distinct air of home. Not my home, but somewhere I could rest. Because we were in Faerie, I immediately assumed it was a trap, but Barrett was the one to suggest the place, so I let that go.

Before I could say "boo," Barrett had me curled up on the couch with a blanket tucked around my leathers, a cup of tea in my hands that was mostly booze, sandwiching me in between him and Marcus like they were holding me together by sheer force of will. That assessment probably wasn't too far from the truth.

I let Teresa do the explaining because I was tapped the fuck out. Over the last two weeks I had traversed Hell, lost my sister, gotten married, trekked through Faerie, found out I was a demigod, sealed up the Unseelie Court, and gotten my husband body snatched.

I was d-o-n-e—done.

"It seems that the warnings about demons in Faerie weren't bullshit," my mother began, and I snorted into my cup. She wasn't lying. "Alistair seems to be possessed by an entity known as Niall." She paused to let everyone process, and the Fae in question waved at the room like it was NBD.

I took that opportunity to snap my fingers and refilled my cup. It was straight booze this time, but could anyone really blame me? I was lucky I was self-healing, or my liver might have a few things to say. See? Silver linings were all around.

"Niall insists that he only possessed Alistair because he cannot communicate with us. Given his dire warning, I suggest we hear him out." At that, Teresa took a seat so Niall could have the floor. Andras, however, was not too keen on that.

"Do you know what she's gone through? Do you have even the faintest fucking clue?" Andras said, and I could only guess he was referring to me. I could've been wrong on that front, though. I wasn't the only one who watched Maria's mouth talk with another person's voice. I wasn't the only one to watch that get stolen from her along with everything else.

"I can't say I do. The only thing I know is if we don't retrieve Dušan before the Blood Moon rises, this plane and everyone sprung from it will cease to exist. If you're too busy worried about *feelings*, then I can't help you." Niall wasn't wrong, but it was likely the wrong thing to say to my father.

"My wife watched her daughter get possessed and we couldn't get her back. Max watched her sister die. And here you are, thinking we'll just hop-to with no assurances, no promise that the Alistair you stole will come back to her. Fuck you. Fuck you for thinking that my daughter can pursue another cause when she's been broken. Fuck you for thinking my wife can watch another one of her daughters' fight and die for a realm that has no love for them. Fuck you, buddy. Fuck you and the horse you rode in on."

If my hands weren't full of booze, I would have clapped. As it stood, I still had tears in my eyes, and I wanted to hug the shit out of him. Andras had never really felt like a dad, but dammit if he was vying for father of the year. Okay, maybe he wasn't the best dad on the planet, but he was trying.

Niall's eyes widened, affront written all over his face, but Andras didn't appear to give that first shit. "You are asking too much of her to watch you parade around in her husband's body. You ask too much of her... wait... who in the bloody hell is Dušan?"

I snorted in my cup again before speaking for the first time since I arrived. "He's my father. You know him as the god, Chaos. You know, the father of all the gods, where the Titans came from, Zeus' granddaddy. That guy. Supposedly he was dead, but according to Niall he isn't." I shrugged, taking another drink of my booze. It was yummy.

Everyone seemed surprised except for Atropos. She scowled at me. I was just drunk enough to give her a finger wave. "What's up, 'cuz? Wait, that's not right. Nyx is your mom, so that would make you my niece? This is one fucked-up family tree, am I right?"

Atropos sputtered before she broke out into a laugh. "You don't know the half of it."

"A daughter of Chaos. Really, it's not even a little surprising," Barrett volleyed, and I gave him a patented raised eyebrow. "Okay, so it's a little surprising, but just like the Fae business, it makes a whole hell of a lot of sense. You have way too much power for a simple Fae, Elemental or not."

"You're just mad you didn't know from the get-go," Marcus muttered, and squeezed me into his side.

"Fabulous. Her parentage is out in the open. How about we talk about the end of this realm and every single Fae that walks among the other eight." Niall was very interested in making sure we stayed on task—which considering the time frame, was a good call.

"She isn't going anywhere with you," Bernadette hissed, tossing a black lock off her shoulder as she stood. She was tiny compared to Niall, but the power held under her skin made her seem eight feet tall. "You say that she must retrieve Dušan, but he has other daughters. He has other sons. You want her to go, but you offer nothing in return. You want her to help you, but you offer no proof, nothing. We are to just trust you? After what you have taken and how you've injured her? I think not."

Ruh-roh. Gramma was pissed. It was about to get heated in this little cabin. Which was sad because it was so nice and cozy.

"He speaks the truth." Atropos sighed. "The Fae Blood Moon only happens once every five hundred years. If Dušan is not here for it, there could be dire consequences."

"Way to be vague, Atropos," Marcus growled. "What kind of Fate are you? Yeah, let's just let a whole fucking realm tank and not say anything."

Then it was Atropos standing in anger, her red hair flying about her head in a halo of rage. I wondered if we should all start standing when we had a grand statement to make. "I do what I can. You know the laws I am bound to. You know, Marcus. So, don't sit there and tell me I'm doing a shitty job. I'm doing what I freaking can, okay? I'm here, aren't I?"

"Oh, for fuck's sake. Settle down. I'll just talk to him, okay? I've done it a couple of times already. I'll talk to the guy and see if we can get him out of whatever pocket dimension he made for himself, and we're good, right? Easy-peasy, lemon squeezy and shit." Yep, I was slurring the shit out of my words, but I had a feeling my message was clear enough. "Then you can give me back my husband, the world won't end, and things can calm the fuck down."

I took a little sip of what was left in my cup, and gently set it down on the coffee table. Okay, so I had to close one eye and aim extra careful, but I at least attempted to set it down gently.

Then I snuggled into the blanket and closed my eyes, calling on the element that was as elusive and ephemeral as smoke. Spirit wasn't like the other elements. Those I could feel all the time here. They were like breathing or my heart beating—they seemed to flow into me without thought. Spirit only wanted to touch me when I was at my lowest, when I didn't have enough strength to go on.

Kinda like right now. I felt the pull at my chest, the heat of all the elements filling me, healing me... stealing my damn buzz, but whatever. Then it felt like I was falling for a second, a sensation I hadn't yet felt while contacting Dušan.

I opened my eyes, but he wasn't there. The forest that was blurry at the edges, the night sky that was too close and too far away at the same time, the wooden stump he sat on—those were all there.

But he wasn't.

Frantic, I called out, "Dušan! Come out. I need you!"

My eyes swept the tree line for the giant of a man with purple hair and lightning in his eyes.

But no one came.

Pulling out of the little pocket world took far too much effort, and by the time I made it back to my body, I could tell something was wrong.

Teresa and Andras were holding onto me, forcing my arms to my sides as I thrashed. Also, I was on the floor—that was another clue that something was amiss.

"He isn't there," I croaked. "I called and called, but he isn't there anymore."

"We know, baby," Teresa murmured, pulling me to her as she wrapped me in her arms.

"What are we going to do?" I asked, but no one answered me.

CHAPTER THREE

"You can't do that anymore. You can't try to visit him again, Max." Bernadette's warning was clear, the command laced in every single syllable. "We almost lost you."

Lost me?

"What the hell are you talking about?"

Bernadette's—or rather Lilith's face—twisted, fear lining her expression. "If your parents hadn't have held you down, if I wasn't using all my power… Wherever Dušan was, it was pulling on you. I don't know the particulars—not really. Just… don't do that anymore. Maybe if he isn't there, the pocket world requires a new host?"

Well, that wasn't frightening at all.

"Not a host," Niall huffed. "Dušan is a creator of worlds. If he only managed to make a pocket world, then he has been recharging his power for centuries. It is possible that if he heard my call, then he has left that scant space he made for himself—it may be collapsing. You have to go back. If we know where that world is, we might be able to use it to find Dušan."

He wants me to go back to the place I almost got stuck in?

Eff that trash.

"Hell, no. Moreover, fuck you very much. I would very much like to not be stuck in some random pocket world with exactly zero exit strategy, thank you." I thought about what he said for about a millisecond before I added, "What do you mean "heard your call?" Does Dušan's pocket world have a landline, and I missed it?"

Niall leveled me with a glare so scathing, it was a wonder it fit on Alistair's face. "Do you honestly believe I have been waiting for four hundred years in the Unseelie realm without trying every single thing I could think of to bring him back? Do you think I have been twiddling my thumbs on vacation while I rot over there?" He brought up a good point, but he wasn't done. "I was Dušan's paladin. I was supposed to suss out things like this. I was supposed to protect him. If you think I'm going to let a piece of changeling trash bring down my charge, you are sorely mistaken."

Niall advanced on my parents as we knelt on the floor, a stance so threatening, it had the hairs on the back of my neck standing on end. I could feel the crackle of unspent magic in the air—the energy rising fast enough it felt like ants on my skin—but it wasn't me. No, that honor was reserved for Lilith. And make no mistake, this was *Lilith*.

Bernadette was a gorgeous grandmother. Lilith was the Queen of Hell. Ancient, ruthless, powerful.

And she was *pissed.*

"You would do well not to threaten her, Niall," she whispered. "Not by word or deed. Do we understand each other?"

Niall sneered—an expression quite at home on Alistair's face, but never with this much vigor. "I will do whatever I need to do to bring my King home. I will threaten, I will bargain, and I will kill. Do not mistake me, demon, I will complete my task or die in the trying."

And that was the point when I'd had just about enough. The tiny cottage was so pretty, it was too bad I was about to shake it into rubble. The ground danced a jig beneath us as I heard the crackle of lightning fizz and pop. And not outside, either. No, somehow, it raced over the walls before circling Niall's feet like a puppy.

"Do not mistake us, Niall. If you want us on your side, you're gonna have to be a bit less of a dick. We have the same goal. Getting ourselves killed in the process is no way to go about it. And offering me up as a test subject to a likely collapsing world is not going to win you any favors in this group. No matter whose face you're wearing."

I managed to pull myself up off the floor and walked out of the cozy little cabin.

Holding back tears, I took huge gulps of air as I tried to calm myself down. All that was Faerie smacked me in the face as I talked myself down from a rage. I was tired of feeling weak. I was tired of feeling like I had no control.

I was tired of the world throwing me under the bus time and time again.

It wasn't fair that so much had been taken from me—from us. It wasn't right that I couldn't—even for a full day—be happy with the progress we'd made.

I had a horrible thought right then. That I should just lay my sword down. That I should just plop down on my ass and let the world burn. Let Faerie and everyone in it burn to ash.

Maria was gone.

Alistair was overtaken.

I was tired. So tired.

"Don't do that," Lilith said from behind me, startling me so bad I jumped. I had been pretty far down on the shame spiral, so I wasn't too hard to sneak up on. Her black hair hung down her back as fire danced in her eyes.

"Don't do what?"

"Give up," she answered. "Don't you dare. You didn't come this far—you didn't sacrifice this much to lay down and die now. I will get your husband back to you. We *will* win this fight. You *will* be happy again. I swear on everything in me, I *will* make this right for you. This doesn't get to happen to you. Not on my watch."

I wanted to believe her. I wanted to stand up and dust myself off and convince myself that I could press on.

I wasn't doing a very good job of it, if I was being honest.

"I want to believe you, but..." I couldn't even finish that sentence. How could I explain it so she would understand?

"But this was just one hit too many." Not a question, a statement of fact.

I nodded solemnly, turning away from her to stare at the enchanting forest filled with trees that could swallow me whole if I stepped wrong. The fog glistened against the leaves, little dots of light—which looked like fireflies but was probably a pixie of some kind—blinked in the darkened recesses of the foliage. It was beautiful and still. Creepy as all get out, sure, but beautiful.

This is what I'd be destroying if I sat down. This and every Fae I'd ever met. Every person of Fae blood that lived on Earth. This whole realm. It would all be gone.

I didn't know if I could be that callous, that oblivious to my own culpability and power to let everything burn while I watched. I didn't know if I could sit down and let it all go.

That's it. Get your shit together in that little brown paper sack you call a soul and fight, dammit.

Theeere she was. That was my conscience rallying for one more bout.

"That's better," Lilith said from behind me. "I was worried there for a minute."

I glanced over my shoulder at her, my expression probably more scathing than I intended, but whatever. "So glad you approve. Do you think we can come up with a different plan that doesn't involve me getting trapped in a collapsing pocket dimension to find Dušan?"

"Probably."

"Good."

It was then that I heard a smattering of running feet. Without a thought in my brain, I drew both athames, extending the blades to turn them into swords as I turned to the sound. Not a second later, Della, Aidan, Hideyo, and Striker bolted from the trees. Della had a dripping cut on her cheek and Striker looked like he'd been accosted, one of his sleeves was torn open and hanging from his shoulder.

Relief crossed each of their expressions when they saw me.

"What the fuck, Max?" Aidan barked after he caught his breath, resting his hands on his knees as he sucked in air.

"What the fuck what? You're gonna have to be more specific."

Did I need to be that contrary?

No.

Did that stop me?

Also no.

"Why are you here? What is going on? Why does that forest of freaking teeth hate us? What. The. Fuck." All good points, I'd give him that.

"I needed to go to a meeting—that's why I'm here. The world is ending, is what is going on. And I have no idea why the forest hates you. Your guess is as good as mine." He opened his mouth to reply, but I held up a hand to stop him. "No, I don't want to go into it right now. Yes, you will get an explanation—just not from me. No, I'm not going to do something stupid—unless you think not stopping the world from ending is a good idea, then yes, I will totally be doing something stupid. And no, in case you were wondering, I am not okay. Did I cover everything?"

Aidan slowly closed his mouth, leveling me with an expression so concerned it was a wonder I didn't burst right into tears. Emotions were bullshit. "Yeah, Max. You covered everything. I'll talk to Lilith, yeah?"

"Yeah," I whispered, blinking furiously as I broke eye contact.

I let my gaze drift back to the forest. It was a wonder that just a few days ago I'd been more freaked about those trees than anything else. But it was Della who asked the question that brought me to my knees.

"Where is Alistair? We need him."

And then I was in the dirt, my knees and fingers digging into the earth as I just lost it. I could hear them asking what was wrong. I could feel their confusion and fear as the world churned beneath me and lightning cracked, and the wind whipped.

But I had nowhere to go.

No pocket place where my father calmed me down.

No husband to go to.

No Maria.

"Fine," Niall bellowed, yelling over the din. "If I give him back to you, will you cease this bloody temper tantrum?" It was said so scathing, I wanted to light him on fire. Granted, the world did settle down, so I couldn't exactly fault the guy…

Since he'd hijacked my husband, I so totally could.

Niall crouched in the dirt in front of me wearing Alistair's face like he had the right. It pissed me the fuck off.

"You take and take, and you still want more. You steal from me and have the nerve to say my grief is a temper tantrum? Give him back." I was shaking, my words barely passing my gritted teeth.

Niall sucked in a sharp breath through Alistair's nose. "I cannot communicate with you without a host. It is how I am bound." He swallowed thickly, remorse flitting over his face for a second before it was gone. "But if someone volunteers, I can use them instead. Had I known how important he was to you, I would have picked another host. I'm sorry, Massima."

I was full-on shivering then as hope bloomed in my chest. And then it was gone. Someone would have to take Alistair's place. I couldn't ask anyone for that.

"I'll do it," Andras offered, his booted feet stopping just in my line of sight. I stared up at him, watching as his golden eyes flashed.

"I can't ask that of you," I whispered, my face threatening to crumple.

"You didn't. I offered. I'm not going to let you down, Max. Not ever again."

I wanted to hug him, but I didn't get the chance. Niall opened his mouth and black smoke poured from it, exiting Alistair's body in a matter of seconds, his large frame falling in a heap on the dirt.

It coalesced into creeping fingers, snaking into Andras' mouth and nose, filling him before I could blink.

An inky-black color filled the whites of his eyes for a second before he blinked, shuddered, and fell to his knees. Andras shook his head once, twice, and then stood.

When Alistair had been possessed, he'd been out for a minute. Andras' body seemed to be taking it in stride. I met his gaze, a not-so-small tendril of fear snaking up my spine.

"I'm still me, you know," he said, probably trying to allay my fear but I wasn't so easily swayed. "I'm older and stronger than your Knight, kiddo. Niall is speaking to me and not through me. I know what we need to do."

A gust of a sigh passed my lips as I wilted in relief. I hadn't realized how tight I'd been wound until right then. Then my gaze fell to Alistair.

Now I was stuck waiting for someone I loved to wake the fuck up.

Again.

Aces.

CHAPTER FOUR

Time stretched like taffy as I watched Alistair's eyelids for movement. What was probably no longer than a few minutes felt like days. Years. Eons.

At the first flutter of movement, I held my breath, sending out a silent prayer to whatever deity that would hear me that he'd just wake up unharmed. And then I was staring into his baby blues, confusion clear in them for about a millisecond before they dialed themselves to pissed the fuck off.

Did I care about his rage? Hell. No. I cared that he was cognizant enough to be pissed. I pounced, my hands clutching his face as I looked him over. "Are you… you?"

His anger flowed away in an instant. "Yes, love. I'm me."

And since he was the smartest man alive, he brought his mouth to mine. I'd known after a single touch of his lips that he wasn't him. This kiss confirmed every hope I'd just prayed for. Inexplicably, I started crying. Even as happy as I was, the whole of the day had finally taken its toll on me. But all Alistair did was hold me to him, wrapping me in his arms and squeezing me tight.

When my tears ramped down, and after I'd likely scared the

shit out of our entire party, I kissed him again. A sweet little kiss because I could. Because he wouldn't stop me.

Because it proved he was him.

I broke the kiss, met his gaze, and quipped, "The first year is always the hardest, right?"

Alistair snorted before squeezing the breath out of me as he crushed me to his chest. "I have to say, being married to you hasn't been dull at least." He pulled back to whisper in my ear, "I need to talk to you. Alone."

I gave him a slight nod and we stood. It was then that I realized everyone had gone back inside the cabin, leaving us to our reunion. I had half a mind to steal Alistair away so I could have him in a safe place without all the threats that loomed over us here. "We are alone."

"No, love, we are not. Eyes watch us here. What I have to say requires no audience."

That can't be good. "Okay. Do you remember everything?"

"I do. And I know quite a bit more. Let's talk to the group. If Andras is anything like me, he'll know quite a bit as well."

I nodded and he took my hand, leading me back to the cabin. My reluctance to go was gone now that he was with me. I wasn't okay—I might never be—but I could do this. I could press on.

The cabin was crowded with the addition of my paladins, every seat was full and even some choice floor real estate. They spoke in hushed whispers that I knew were about me. I had no illusions their choice of discussion topic, and I was fine with it.

Did they decide to lose it in the middle of a crisis? No. That was me.

I wanted to say sorry, but how does one apologize for flying off the deep end? "Sorry I'm a basket case" wasn't a greeting card I could just pick up at the grocery store.

"So, what did I miss?" I chirped, a fake sort of happy infused into my words. It rang false to me and everyone else in the room, but they had the good sense to ignore it.

"Niall suspects that Verena knows quite a bit about Dušan's whereabouts and what can be done to retrieve him," Andras began.

"We will need to interrogate her. We have to know what she did to him before we can plan to retrieve him."

That meant I'd have to wake up Sleeping Beauty. This was not going to be fun.

The dungeons of the Seelie Court were unchanged since I'd walked out of them less than twelve hours ago. Funny. It had felt like years since I'd been down here. Since I'd freed the prisoners so wrongly detained.

Since I realized that Alistair wasn't Alistair. I squeezed his hand again, reassuring myself that he was really him and he was with me. Call me codependent if you want to, but I'd lost a shit-ton in not a large amount of time and I could not bear losing him.

Not after everything else.

Was I a nut-job right now? Absolutely. But hey, at least I was self-aware, right?

Verena lay sleeping on the stone floor of the cell Melody had once occupied. She was the only occupant of these cells, and other than Alistair and Aidan, I was alone to speak to her.

Verena didn't make sense to me. Not one bit. She had a family that abandoned her, but was accepted into a new family, in a new world. She'd gone from nothing to the ruling class in a place filled with magic, and still, that wasn't enough.

She wanted her booted foot on the throat of this world. And for what? Because her mommy didn't love her?

If that was a valid excuse, then I would have been razing cities and collapsing Hell by now.

I had to gather the courage to wake her and wondered if I could peek inside her mind without actually talking to her first. My honor wouldn't let me do that—stupid honor—and I contemplated the bars once more.

"What are you doing?" Alistair whispered in my ear, and even though I was troubled by the working I'd put on the cell, I smiled.

"Gathering courage, figuring out how to unravel my own

magic, and questioning my life choices," I whispered back without taking my gaze from the Fae metal that housed Verena.

Alistair snorted, squeezed my hand, and said, "I have a feeling if you wanted in that cell you could just walk in there. No unraveling necessary. You are the daughter of Chaos, Max. Do you know who else is the daughter of Chaos? Nyx. Do you think those bars could keep her out?"

No. No, I did not.

Puffing out my cheeks to let out a huge breath, let go of Alistair's hand, and closed one eye, I winced and stepped forward. There was a fifty-fifty shot of this going horribly wrong. A rush of cold washed through me as I took another step, but then it was gone, and I was inside the cell.

One obstacle down.

I stared at Verena some more. With her Changeling magic gone, she had aged some. Not in a bad way, just in a way that spoke to how vain she was. There were faint lines fanning out from her eyes, a deep groove between her brows, and a pair of parentheses bracketing her mouth. Her scar was redder, too, like it was fresh instead of ancient. I vaguely wondered how she'd gotten it and why she chose to keep it.

I sat down on the stone bench, resting my elbows on my knees. Snapping my fingers, her eyes flashed open, the sleep spell I'd cast breaking, even though this room wasn't supposed to allow magic. Either I'd worked the spell wrong, or...

Or it was exactly as Alistair said. This cell would keep most out, but not someone like me.

Once Verena's gaze landed on me, she scrabbled backward—not because she feared me, but because she wanted time and space to make her next move. There was no fear on her face. None in her posture. She didn't care if I was able to take away her power with a snap of my fingers.

And why would she?

She killed the father of gods. Why would she believe anything else?

"I want to know what you did to Dušan." It didn't really matter if my statement was whispered or not, the power that leaked from my words made them a command.

A smile bloomed on her face as her eyes got that hazy quality of a fond memory. "You know what I did to your father, Massima. I killed him."

Dick.

"No, you didn't. I've spoken to Dušan. I know he managed to hold on. I want to know what you did to him specifically and in great detail."

She shrugged as if being in the cell with me was no skin off her nose, and I had the fleeting desire to turn her limbs inside out one by one until she told me. I'd done it to others. I couldn't say exactly why I did not relish doing that to her.

Was it because she was a girl? Was it because I had an inkling that torture wouldn't work? I couldn't tell, and I didn't like it.

"No, I don't think I'll tell you," she replied blithely. "I think I'll let you stew in your own ignorance."

This was a stalling tactic if I'd ever seen one. A stalling tactic that would earn her no favors from me. Rather than going the torture route—even though I really, really wanted to go the torture route—I snapped my fingers, yanking her to me. Fingers closing on her throat, my ass on the bench, her on her ass on the floor, I peered into her eyes. I'd peeked inside a Minotaur's mind without half the knowledge I had now. And he'd been a magical being.

Verena was no more magical than a human—not right then, anyway—and she knew it. The fear she'd eschewed before flooded her face.

"I've had a very bad day, preceded by a very bad few weeks, and a shit life. I'm pissed, tired, and hungry, and you are working my last fucking nerve. Answer the question, Verena. I'm not going to ask again." My whisper was as cold as ice, and if she had any sense in her brain, she would comprehend just how fucked she was.

Her face screwed into an expression that was three steps past mulish.

"So that was a no, then? Fine," I growled, clamping my hands to her head and drilling down into her brain. With no wards and no magic to stop me, I was bombarded by what she'd done.

The lives she'd taken.

The pain she'd caused.

And the pleasure and sick need she had to create more destruction. I didn't know what it was that caused this need, couldn't fathom the impetus that tipped her, but I didn't need to know that.

All I needed to know was what she'd done to Dušan.

She'd stolen power after power, changing into one creature after another, taking their power for her own. She started quietly at first until it started to snowball. Then she made her move. First by killing my brother and sisters, then by stabbing my father with the rowan branch before banishing him to the Unseelie Court.

But she didn't see him die. She'd only assumed he was dead because he hadn't come back. After that, she hunted my mother to the edges of Faerie, stabbing her too with the same branch that she believed killed a god.

She hadn't expected my mother to fight back. She hadn't prepared for the athame that ripped into her face. My mother had gotten away with me, but Verena had to recover, and since Zeta never returned, she assumed her dead as well.

She was right about my mother.

But I was becoming more and more certain, my father was alive.

I pulled back out of her head, only slightly aggrieved to find that Verena had not fared too well from my extraction. Blood dripped from her nose and eyes and ears, blood vessels had broken in her face, and with no magic to heal the likely ruptured organs and damaged tissue, she would die right here on the floor of this dungeon.

I was sort of fine with that. Then again, I wasn't fine. She hadn't suffered. She'd gotten off easy.

"Don't heal her, Max." Aidan's voice was a command from the other side of the bars. He knew me well enough to know that I would contemplate this course of action. I didn't know if I liked that or not.

"And why not? She needs to pay."

"She deserves to be in Hell, love," Alistair answered for him. "I'll get word to the Knights. Make sure they know where to put her. I have a few friends who are very good at their jobs and enjoy their work. She will pay for what she's done. This I promise you."

I let his words appease me, and the bloodlust that I'd felt ramping up in my gut faded.

So we watched Verena take her last few labored breaths, the air squelching a bit as it passed once, twice, a third time between her lips before her body wilted and died.

And while I did this, I made a plan.

CHAPTER FIVE

After the day all of us had had, it was tough to slip my leash and enact my roughly formed plan. And while I appreciated everyone's need to check in on me to see how I was doing, their attention grated. I'd had to resort to saying I needed to go to the bathroom. Only Atropos leveled me with a look before taking her leave of the realm, insisting she needed to get back to her sisters.

This was likely the only reason no one figured out my bathroom gambit was a ruse.

Well, not exactly. I *did* need to go to the bathroom. It was just that after I'd taken care of business, washed my hands, and gave myself a stern pep talk, I did not go back to my friends and family. I snuck out of the castle and made my way back to that craggy crevasse where the rowan tree stood.

Well, I didn't sneak. I snapped my fingers and appeared where I wanted to be. I'd contemplated snapping my way to Dušan, but I had a feeling that it would not only *not* work, it would also maybe sorta kinda kill me.

The rowan tree appeared no different than when we'd left it

those scant hours ago. Still tall, still whimsically mysterious. But the rowan tree wasn't exactly a tree at all. It was a sentient being named Aiyana the Eternal. And just as the name suggested, she was as cryptic and enigmatic and fucking ominous in a way that had the teeny tiny hairs on my arms standing on end.

And I would need to converse with this beautifully frightening being if I wanted my plan to work, because like an idiot, I'd made her create a gate to the Unseelie Court that no magic could break through. Not that I wanted to test that theory at all. My magic did not work near her, so I had a pretty good inkling that my abilities, as vast as they were, would do exactly bupkis to the scant door to the realm of monsters.

Rather than draw it out, I approached the trunk of Aiyana's tree, letting the power that made her suck me in. Instead of the blinding whiteness I'd experienced before, it was now a star-filled night. Galaxies peppered the sky with brilliant stars and swirling nebulas. I was so busy standing in awe of the beauty that it took a minute to realize Aiyana was standing beside me, her pale skin and blue horns glowing in the night.

"I see you appreciate the beauty of the night, Massima. I, too, enjoy the burn of the stars." It was as if she thought of the stars as her own personal crackling fireplace. I tipped up my lips at that oddity.

"I didn't expect you so soon after our last visit. Or maybe I did. With the Blood Moon so close, it would make sense why you would come to me. I take it you've come to make a bargain?"

That was the thing about conversing with a being that could read your mind. Subterfuge was futile. "I hadn't planned on coming this soon. I'd planned on eating, going to bed, and resting for a week. Then, only after I'd gathered the courage, would I come here. Today has not gone to plan in a bevy of ways."

Aiyana's smile was small but there. She thought I was cute, I'd bet. Like a Chihuahua or a Poodle.

I kinda wished she would have spilled the beans about the Blood Moon before we'd left the crevasse in the first place, but I wasn't going to scold her about it. I had a feeling there was a lot of shit she knew and hadn't shared.

"If you are willing to share, I would like to know about the Blood Moon. What it is, why Dušan needs to be here, what the consequences are for skipping this year, etc."

"I see."

"In our deal, you spoke of teaching me about this realm, I figure since my tiny bit of knowledge says that this realm will cease to be in three days if I don't get my father back, this could be our first lesson." I paused before tacking on, "If you're amenable, that is."

Politeness was key here, but I may have been laying it on a little thick. Oh, well.

"What if I said I wish to skip over discussing the Blood Moon in favor of explaining how pixies were created, or whether worms were actually good for the fish to eat?"

I sucked in a breath, prayed for calm, and answered, "I would try to steer you back to the current matter at hand so I didn't die. Probably. Unless time dilates in here, then I'd pull up a seat and listen."

Maybe. But with my impatient ass, I'd probably fuck that up a little bit.

"You are one of the most self-aware deities I've ever encountered," she remarked, a ghost of a smile playing at the corners of her lips. "You do your best to be honest, not just with me, but yourself as well. You do not shy away from introspection, nor do you relish death and destruction. I wonder what you will become in a millennium or three. Will you be jaded? Or will you stay as you are, doing better, trying to be better?"

I kind of hoped I would be the second option. I didn't ever want to be the jaded demigod with a thirst for blood. But did anyone really want to be the first option?

I doubted it.

But it didn't matter if I could technically live another year or a thousand more years if I couldn't get this Blood Moon bullshit sorted out. Me—right along with the rest of Faerie—wouldn't be breathing.

"Ah, yes, the Blood Moon. I suppose I shall tell you what you wish to know. Yes, the Blood Moon is real, it is a sacrifice to the universe. A payment Dušan must make every five hundred years to keep this realm whole."

"How does he pay it? What is the price? Who does he pay it to?" I thought those were good questions. Maybe I didn't have to break into the Unseelie Court and search for him. Maybe I could pay the price myself.

"The payment is never the same, and it cannot be a descendant of Chaos. It must be Chaos himself. He tried with one of your sisters, and even though she produced what was asked, the sacrifice was not accepted. Had Dušan not been there to right it, I fear we all might have been lost. As for who he pays it to, that I cannot say."

Not like she didn't know, but more like she couldn't tell me. Something dawned on me—it really should have before now, but I was working on little sleep and a boatload of trauma, so I excused myself.

"You'll be lost, too, won't you? If I do not succeed."

Aiyana's smile stretched wide. "Perhaps. But perhaps not. I am here and not here. And I am not Fae, so I am not sure if I will go if Faerie collapses. I try to stay optimistic about these things."

I kinda wished she had the same level of motivation as the rest of us, but I could accept her honesty.

"So, to recap, the Blood Moon is real, it's dire if Dušan isn't here to pay the price, and I can't pitch-hit for him. Anything else I should know?"

"You have three days. If Dušan is not at the rowan tree by the time the moon hits its apex, the bargain will be void." All good things to know.

"Do you know where he is?"

She shook her head, her eyes sad. "I do not. Not exactly. I know he is beyond the wall. But the Unseelie Court is vast and treacherous. And dark. The light that shines here does not shine there. I cannot see."

"Well, at least there is a general direction. Will you let me pass? I won't insult you by trying magic on your roots. I know it won't work."

Aiyana contemplated this for a full minute. Well, I could only guess she was contemplating it because she was silent, her eyes downcast.

"No. Not without a sacrifice of your own. I think I would like the life of a fawn—no, wait—a water dragon. Your friend Zillah will do. Yes. Bring me Zillah's head, and I will let you through."

I reared back, disgusted. "Absolutely not. I'm all for killing out of necessity, but you don't need a sacrifice. You want one. What the fuck is wrong with you?"

Aiyana smiled, lips pulled into a no-shit grin. "Do you know how many times I have asked that of deities and they just nodded without question? Do you know how many people in your shoes would not hesitate to kill a friend?"

I crossed my arms. "That better be pride in your voice, woman."

"I am no woman, and yes, it is pride. The fate of our world—your life—is at stake and you refuse to murder. Yes, I think I can make something of you yet, Massima."

"I hope that's your vague consent for passage. I've got a deity to find and not a lot of time to do it."

Aiyana nodded. "Three days. Don't let time slip away from you."

I wanted to say thank you, but I thought better of it. Fae or not, Aiyana was not a being I wanted to owe. "I appreciate your help."

Aiyana smiled wider and muttered, "Smart girl."

I didn't know if I felt all too smart, but I at least had a vector and a general plan. Go to Unseelie Court. Find Dušan. Haul ass back to the gate. Pray we make it in time for the Blood Moon.

As far as plans went, it was absolute shit, but it was what I had. I came back to myself at the foot of Aiyana's tree, the dirt sifting through my fingers as I wobbled to standing. Instantly, the hairs on the back of my neck prickled, and I knew I wasn't alone in this crevasse.

Shit.

Slowly, I glanced over my shoulder to see not just my husband but my parents, my grandmother, my paladins, Barrett and Marcus, and Striker all staring at me like I had just shit on their birthday cake. My mother, in particular, looked like she was ready to open-hand slap me.

Didn't they get that I was leaving them behind for a fucking reason?

Alistair approached cautiously because he was a smart man and he knew me. How long had we been together? A week? A month? How did he already know the right things to do?

How did he know that I was a stupid, fragile creature with too much power at my disposal and the emotional control of a toddler?

I picked the best person in the universe to marry, and it was by total accident.

"We won't be left behind, love. You are heading into enemy territory. You need more than just your power as backup."

"Three of you are demons. One of you is already possessed. What happens if I fail? What happens if I can't protect you? What happens if we don't all make it out? I can't handle one more person leaving me, but especially not you. You're asking me to take my whole world with me—put you all in danger right alongside me. I don't... I can't..." I shook my head. I was positive I'd rather die than do that.

"I have a working to circumvent the possession thing, darling," Lilith called. "We fudged it a smidge during Alistair's warding. I've fixed the error and tested with Niall. It works."

Teresa, who appeared calmer now that she'd gotten my explanation, stepped up beside my husband and said, "Everyone has protection charms and warding. We are armed, ready, and have a good idea where Dušan might be. With Niall's help, we might be able to find him sooner than we thought. But we need numbers, Max. Don't leave us behind out of a need to protect us. We are all signing up for this. It is our choice."

I wanted to rage at her that I couldn't keep her safe—that I couldn't keep anyone safe, but that wasn't what she'd said. She knew the danger. She wanted me to allow them to accept it and fight anyway.

"Okay," I whispered, conceding even though it burned my soul up to do it. "Let's go."

CHAPTER SIX

Aiyana saw much more than I'd given her credit for, because no sooner had the giant-assed group of us walk up to the tangle of roots that made the gateway to the Unseelie Court, did she part them so we could walk through. The hole was small, no bigger than a tractor tire, and all of us had to tuck ourselves into a ball to climb through.

Once on the other side—and only after the last of us crossed—did the roots seal shut again. The slight problem I found was I had no idea how to get back to the Seelie side once this was all over. The wall of roots that was visible from that side was gone, replaced by a stone cliff face complete with moss-covered boulders and ferns jutting out of the cracks.

Nope, not frightening at all.

The landscape was a dark forest, fog mingling at the bases of trees—and not the sparkly glitter fog either. No, this was a dark mist that seemed oily and caustic. The trees were gnarled and twisted like out of a fairytale nightmare, battered leaves and bracken littering the forest floor.

If I were being honest with myself, this was exactly what I'd figure the Unseelie Court would look like. Dark, ominous, threatening.

Super.

"We must go this way." Andras pointed to what I assumed was south if my internal compass was on point. Not that I trusted it completely in a place like this. I was tempted to leave breadcrumbs *Hansel & Gretel* style, but I was fresh out. Andras had a far-off expression on his face like he was listening to Niall speak inside his head. "Niall says that he has searched the Unseelie Court for four centuries, looking for Dušan. The pocket world he created for himself made it hard to pinpoint his location, but he can find him better now."

I didn't know how much faith I had in Niall, but if he had a lock on Dušan, we needed him. That was the only reason I followed after Andras as he listened to the Fae parasite inside his head. We, as a group, marched into the trees, and I was certain everyone—like me—was keeping an eye out for danger. Honestly, I was just waiting for one of those zombie-like creatures to pop out of the ground and fucking eat us.

But the farther we moved into the trees the denser they got. It was as if they were moving in closer to us, uprooting themselves to hem us in. I didn't like this. It felt like a trap. Like one of those military operations that funneled people into a centralized location before opening fire.

We were the fish and the trees were the barrel.

Unless I was being paranoid. That was an option, too.

I tugged on Alistair's hand as I whispered, "Is it just me, or are those trees getting closer to us?"

I was having a tough time not staring at the craggy bark, so when he squeezed my hand back, I peered over my shoulder at him.

"No, love. It's not just you. We are being herded."

I was super tempted to flex back, but I knew if I exploded this forest—which was probably filled with sentient trees—I would be taking lives and earning a whole host of attention we likely did not want.

Still, the trees moved so close it was getting harder to move forward. I was about to say fuck it and do something stupid when a thick tree no-shit pulled up its roots from the ground and stalked over to us. What was this, *The Lord of the Rings*? Hell, for all I knew it was a historical account.

The tree rumbled out a command, but because none of us spoke tree, we had no idea what he was saying. Well, that was until Andras started translating. Likely it was Niall in his head translating, but that was just too confusing a concept to think about.

"He says that he is the Guardian of the Gate. Don't ask me what they call the gate because I cannot possibly pronounce it. Anyway, he says we do not belong here and may not pass. We are to go back where we came from and never darken this forest again. Essentially."

I wondered how much I should tell the tree about our business. It wouldn't do if everyone and their brother knew about what we were doing here. Then again, what kind of hope did we have if he didn't peacefully let us go?

"Does he have a name? Because calling him Treebeard would probably be considered rude."

"Not that he's said, but I think he can understand you. It's you who cannot understand him."

Fabulous.

"I'm Max," I called to the giant tree. Seriously, he was a moss-covered, gnarled mammoth tree with twisted bare branches and at least a hundred feet tall. "I am a daughter of Chaos and we need to find him. This is the only reason we are here. If you let us pass without incident, we will be peaceful. If not, I cannot say what will happen. If we do not get Chaos back, this world will end. All of Faerie will die. I want to be peaceful, but I'll cause a ruckus if I have to."

The tree spoke in his grunted language, the garbled consonants low and vicious.

Andras didn't translate immediately, so I stared at the side of his face until he started talking. I could tell he did not want to tell me whatever the tree said. I was also pretty sure I did not want to know whatever it was that Andras didn't want to tell me.

I had a feeling, though, that whatever Treebeard said was sort of imperative to the current situation, and if Andras didn't spill the beans, I was going to get pissed.

"While he understands your plight—and our mission—no Seelie Queen has stepped foot in the realm for four hundred years. Verena imprisoned them here, and..." Andras trailed off. I was pretty sure I was going to start yelling if he didn't get the fucking lead out and cough up the rest.

"What's the rest, Andras? Kinda on a time crunch here," I snapped, but I didn't let my magic loose, so at least there was that.

Andras mumbled the rest, his words coming out in a rush, but I still got the gist. And I better not have heard what I thought I did. "Say again?"

"He requires a person to stay behind as collateral so you will do as you say."

I was about to start yelling at a sentient tree that he could take his request, fold it up into little corners, and shove it up whatever gnarled bark hole he called an ass when Striker spoke up from behind me. "I'll stay."

Mouth hanging open, I whipped my head to stare at him. He was already shifting through our little crowd. He stopped when he reached me, pausing to speak low into my ear. "You need someone to make sure the way back is clear, Max. It wouldn't hurt to have a fire-breathing dragon as your clutch player if this decided to go sideways," he offered, and if our history was any indication, things always had a way of going sideways on us. Then he continued, and his next bit broke my heart a little—not because it wasn't true, but because it was. "Plus, it's not like anyone trusts me. For good reason, I know, but still. I have to earn that back. I can do this."

I really hated it when he spoke logic and I was being the emotional one. Really. It was so rude of him. Heaving a sigh, I let him pass, leveling the tree with my very best of glares.

"He had better be in the exact condition I left him in when I get back. No spells for sleeping, no immobilization, no nada. Do not torture, maim, injure, or kill him. There better not be so much as a splinter in his finger, or you will answer to me. Do you understand?"

The tree, with his craggy face appeared kinda surprised a woman less than a tenth his size was threatening him. Still, he nodded, muttering some grunts and warbles to Andras.

"He agrees about everything but the splinters," Andras interpreted, and I couldn't help it, but I snorted.

"Fine, if he gets a splinter in his finger—as long as it's not poisoned and will kill him or make him sick or whatever—then I won't raze this entire forest. Happy?"

A few more grunts which Andras translated, "Yes, he agrees."

Fabulous.

One tree negotiation down, one member of the team sidelined, and one monster of a trek to go.

Once the tree guardian—or whatever the hell he was—let us pass, it was easier going. The trees backed off from us, and soon we were out of the forest altogether and following a rocky outcropping that had to be a cliff. A wide gorge sat to the east, the craggy rocks sharp and foreboding. It was way too wide to cross in some places—even with magical assistance—so we continued south for a bit. I was tempted to just travel, but I had a feeling expending magic here was a good way to pop up on someone's radar, and the walk had been smooth so far.

I didn't want to spoil it before we'd found our bearings.

That was until we came upon a slender vine bridge at one of the thinner spots in the gorge. It seemed rickety, sure, but if it would hold, then we could get this show on the road, and maybe get Dušan back before the world imploded.

That was before I noticed the figure standing in the middle of it, blocking our way.

"I swear to the Fates, if that's a troll, I'm out of here," Aidan griped, and I had a tough time holding in my snicker.

"Nah, too skinny to be a troll," Hideyo remarked. "Probably a river Fae."

I hadn't noticed it before now—because I wasn't stupid enough to get close to the edge—but the gorge housed a pretty substantial river. Holding onto the vine railing for balance, I peered over the side. Swirling azure water raced swiftly through the crack in the earth, the white froth of rapids pummeling the sides of the nearly kissing mountains.

The water roared at us, and I wondered why I hadn't noticed before now. Still, I did not want to bargain with a river Fae, and I did not want to potentially lose another member of my team to whatever bullshit sacrifice or riddle or whatever such bullshit was in store for us.

Still, I was the de facto leader, so I yanked up my big girl panties and tried not to vomit as I made my way to the Fae barring our way.

I was shaky, sweating, and close to freaking the fuck out by the time I made it to the middle of the bridge. Okay, so sue me. I did not like rickety bullshit vine bridges that could snap at any second and leave me plummeting to my eventual drowning.

The river Fae—or that's what I was assuming they were—was silent. It was tough to put a finger on their gender, so I mentally settled on they. With green skin and bulging black eyes, they should have been ugly but weren't, and while their features were dialed to fish, it was in conjunction with pouty lips and cheekbones sharp enough to cut glass. With their iridescent scaled neck and flowing purple hair, they were weirdly beautiful.

Still. I did not want to be on this bridge, and I did not have time to dawdle.

"What do you want?" I asked impatiently, while the fish-person blinked at me, bored.

Bored. Like being on this stupid vine bridge hanging over certain death was a super-fun way to spend a lazy Sunday. Fucker.

The fish person regarded me a few moments longer before I got really pissed off.

Don't use magic. Don't use magic. Don't use magic.

A sly smile crossed their fish lips before they spoke. "I want what all dark Fae want. Death and blood. Give me the life of who you hold most dear, and I will consider letting you pass."

"Yeah, those terms don't really work for me, so I'm gonna have to decline. Have fun on your bridge, though," I said snidely, snapping my fingers and transporting myself to the other side of the gorge.

And then I got cocky—which thinking back on it was probably why what happened, happened. I gave the fish person a shitty little finger wave and blew them a kiss, flaunting the fact that I did not need their fucking bridge.

About three seconds after I did that, the ground eroded away from beneath my feet, and I was falling into the churning waters below.

CHAPTER SEVEN

The fall seemed to take for-fucking-ever. The river hadn't appeared to be that far down, but in the fall itself, getting to the water seemed to take a bloody age. I actually had the time to kick myself for being an asshole, forgive myself because they asked for blood and death, and then fret about what the fuck I would do when I actually got to the water.

Maybe I was processing shit at lightning speed. Maybe time dilated. Whatever. The closer I got to the surface, the more I could see the creatures thrashing beneath the water's depths.

I had a whole host of not-okay thoughts about that. I wanted to call on the water element, wanted it to help me, but as my feet broke the surface of the shockingly cold water, I couldn't think of anything else besides the needle-like sensation of near-freezing water slamming my senses like a wrecking ball.

In a moment of panic, I kicked, trying to get to the surface, but no matter how hard I kicked, I couldn't reach the air. Not quick enough to save my lungs from burning like molten lava in my chest, I realized that I'd gotten turned around in the fall. I tried turning myself around, but shadows surrounded me, the churning rapids kicking me about as I struggled to just go up.

I couldn't find the surface, I couldn't...

A flash of blue scales had me trying to back up. Well, that was until I saw a familiar face. Some might fear a giant blue sea serpent reaching out to grab you, but Zillah was a friend—a friend who had saved my ass in Hell, no less. His giant, yet gentle talon wrapped around me and we went up.

I coughed and sputtered as I broke the surface, vomiting up water when Zillah gave me a gentle squeeze. Only when I could breathe again, did I assess our surroundings. We were on a craggy shore. Or, I should say I was on the craggy shore while Zillah filled up the whole of the cove, his long dragon body curling in on itself like a pile of snakes. The river rushed past us, the gorge so far in the distance it wasn't even funny.

"River Fae are dicks, am I right?" I croaked, pushing myself up from the rocks, my leathers and weapons squelching as I did so. I was of the opinion my "no magic" edict was complete bullshit. Zillah gave me a low snuffled sound that I took as agreement. "Want to give me a ride? I need to make sure that bridge prick isn't trying to bargain with my friends."

Zillah gave me another snuffled grunt and bowed his head. When I hesitated, he reached out with a clawed foot and plopped me on his crown. I used his spiraled horns as handlebars—even though they were the size of freaking tree trunks, so I really only held onto one—and we were off.

Zillah had absolutely no trouble snaking up the thrashing river, the rapids churned against him. His huge body took the force in stride. Luckily, he kept his head above the surface—otherwise he probably would have lost me he was going so fast. The spray of the water hit me in the face, but I didn't care. This felt like flying, like soaring, and in a way, I was.

When the bridge came into sight, I realized a couple of things. One, my group of friends could not be left unsupervised, like ever. And two? I was really fucking happy they were on my side.

Aidan and Alistair were sawing at the fast-growing vines on the east side of the gorge, trying to unseat the water Fae. Andras, Della, and Bernadette had already traveled to the other side and were sawing from their end. Teresa and Barrett were concocting some sort of spell on the cliffs from twigs and fucking berries, and Hideyo and Marcus were in their other forms ready to throw down.

All through this, the river Fae seemed unmoved, and while I figured they saw something like this quite often, I had to admit, I was more than a little touched that my friends were ready to burn a motherfucker down if need be.

The Fae yawned—no shit, *yawned*—at them until they caught sight of me rolling up on a fucking water dragon. Now, I knew the gorge was deep, but I had no idea how big Zillah was until he rose up as high as he could go, and the both of us were looking down on the river Fae.

"That. Was. Rude," I said finally after waiting for the apology I was owed. Seriously. That water was fucking cold.

Giant fish eyes wide, the Fae knelt on the vines—do not ask me how, that lone action defied everything I knew about physics as a whole—and stuttered out a hesitant, "Ma-majesty?"

I really hated that title, but if it got this prick to move, I was all for it. Then I had a thought. "How do you know who I am?"

Fish-person frowned in confusion. "The water serpent, Majesty. Zillah only serves the children of Chaos. He is bound to protect them."

Huh. Well, you learn something new every day. "Are you going to let my friends pass and quit being a monstrous dick? Seriously. *The life of who you hold most dear?* Was that even necessary?"

Trembling, they answered, "I was charged with keeping people out of the Court. Very few wish to sacrifice their loved ones, Majesty. I was just doing my job."

I thought about that for a second and realized I couldn't fault them for it—especially since I'd been a bit of a dick about it.

"Those rules do not apply to me and my team, let them pass, but keep your post. We'll be coming back through soon enough. If we have a tail, you can drown as many of them as you want. Cool?"

Fish-person nodded and snapped their fingers, transforming

the rickety vine bridge into an arched stone one that was about as wide as a single-lane track. I pulled a Striker move, letting out a whistle for my friends to get the lead out.

Things were tense as my team from the east crossed over to the west side of the gorge, passing Fish as they went, but Fish never moved, only kept their head low.

When Alistair and Aidan passed, though, I got an expression of relief from my husband and a censuring "What the fuck?" from Aidan.

That was fair. I probably should not have antagonized an unknown Fae in the Unseelie Court. That was my bad.

"Do you have a name?" I asked the Fish-person and they hesitated. I amended my statement. "Rather, what can I call you?"

"Pip, your majesty. I appreciate your leniency." They paused, their big eyes filling with relieved tears. "The Seelie Queen was a monster in a pretty dress."

I almost wanted to cry at that admission. Jesus, fuck, Verena had deserved to die.

"She's dead, you know. She isn't coming back."

Just like the people in the castle had, Pip wilted in relief. This bit of Faerie had been locked away for centuries, and even this one river Fae was relieved she was dead. What the fuck had she done to these people?

"I will keep my post, Majesty. I will do as you say. I give you my word. Thank you for not..." Pip trailed off, unable to finish the sentence.

"For not being a raging bitch on wheels? Yeah, glad I could be of service. Stay safe, Pip."

With that, Zillah and I moved to the other side of the gorge, and I disembarked his head. He rested his chin on the ground, his eyes pleading as he moved no closer. That made me have a thought. Striker could change between his human and dragon form. I had yet to see Zillah in anything other than this. Even when it seemed he had something to tell me.

Even when he had time to change.

And he had no issue going from one realm to the other. Hell,

Faerie. He could have probably shown up on the Earth realm if he wanted to.

"Are you stuck like that?" I asked, unable to just walk away from the serpent who saved my life. I couldn't say why exactly. It was like I needed to make sure he was okay.

Zillah let out an answering chuff, giving me a slight nod.

"Do you have a human form?" I whispered, hurt in a way I couldn't explain at this big beast being caged in his own skin.

Zillah nodded with more vigor, his motion dislodging rocks and earth from the side of the cliff.

"Do you need help changing back?"

Zillah's face was a picture of pleading: his giant scaly face, and huge blue eyes. Shit. I totally had to help.

I thought about it for probably less time than I should—the spell was probably older than I was. But I had to help. Zillah had saved my life twice—well, probably a third time if that Kelpie was planning on killing me.

"Max, what are you doing?" Lilith called from a few feet away. She sounded wary and censuring.

"Trying to figure out how to turn Zillah back to human again," I answered simply—like what I was doing was a totally normal thing to be doing in the middle of the Unseelie Court with people probably clocking our every move.

Still.

Faintly, I caught sight of the tracery magics weaved into his flesh. I was right. The spell was older than I was. Hell, it was older than Andras, probably. And done by a demon?

"It is not smart to meddle in these things, Max. He is likely that way for a reason." Andras' tone was more wary than his mother's had been.

Bullshit. I smelled bullshit. A heaping pile of it.

"This dragon has saved my life twice now. I know he's a friend. Would you stand idly by when one of your friends was hurting?" At his abashed expression, I pressed on. "I thought not."

I turned back to Zillah, studying the magic once more so I could unravel it. Yeah, I probably had god-power and could undo it with a snap of my fingers, but this spell was delicate and intricate, buried in his flesh for centuries, eons maybe.

"Maxima, do not mess with that dragon."

Funny. When she told me not to, that was exactly what I wanted to do. Far more than ever before. I looked her in the eyes, leveling her with a glare as I wondered why she didn't want me to free a sentient creature of a prison.

Then I raised my hands, snapping my fingers in open defiance of her warning.

At that, her face went white like I'd drained all the blood from her body and then some.

It was entirely possible I had just fucked up.

Again.

Go me.

CHAPTER EIGHT

Okay, so pissing off my grandmother seemed to be a pastime of mine. And maybe I'd never gotten those dick toddler moves out of my system when I was a kid. But I couldn't pay too much attention to the fit she was about to throw. No, I was watching an impossibly large water dragon that had been stuck in his animal form for who knew how long, condense his body into a human-sized pocket of a person.

Zillah's transformation was hurting him if his blood-curdling-roars-turned-screams were anything to go by. His body bent, contracted in on itself, slithering further onto land before the trunk of his body shrunk to the appropriate size. He writhed on the ground as his body changed shape, and when it was done, he appeared no bigger than I was and no older than a teenager.

I knew for certain Zillah was older than I was by likely eons.

Gasping for breath, he stared up at the sky with his odd blue eyes. Still with their slit pupil and strange too-bright-blue hue, he blinked there for a few minutes, unmoving. A shock of dark hair topped his head, and coupled with his pale skin, his eyes seemed to glow. He was dressed in fighting leathers that looked ancient, and how they'd held up this long was anyone's guess.

"I can't believe you did that, Maxima. I can't believe you just…" Lilith trailed off, shaking her head. "You just stared me right in the eyes and snapped your fingers. What the fuck?"

I sighed, the disappointment clear in my tone as I replied, "Do you know that with how many times you have lied to me in the last year, I can tell when you're doing it now? That I know when you're hiding shit and being an untruthful snot? I don't like that I know what your tell is, Lilith. So if Zillah is some crazed beast, now is the time to state your case."

Lilith huffed before crossing her arms. Defensive much? "He is not a crazed beast. He just should not have been turned back. His job is not done, and that is not the bargain we agreed upon you slithering little snot," she said, turning from me to address Zillah directly. "You knew you agreed to watch over him until the war, Zillah. I can't believe you conned your way out of it with a pair of doe eyes and a whine. Honestly. Is nothing sacred?"

Zillah took that moment to quit blinking at the sky and speared Lilith with a glare so cold it was a wonder she didn't freeze on the spot. He didn't appear much older than sixteen. He cleared his throat—after years of disuse, it made sense—and growled a single word in a thick accent I couldn't place. "Conned?"

"Yes," Lilith insisted. "Conned."

Zillah took a few seconds to get his bearings and stood for the first time on two feet in who knew how long. He was unsteady as he came back to himself, but he quickly rose to his full height. He was my height, but then again, Zillah didn't seem full-grown, either. "You are the cheat. You neglected to mention that the war would never come as long as Lucifer stayed in his cell. That I would be stuck in my dragon form until the end of days, patrolling the rivers until the worlds ended. You tricked me, and you know it, Lilith. I will not watch over your father's cell another minute. I don't care if he is a child of Chaos."

That was a lot of info to digest. To combat the utter shock, I conjured myself a chair—the same green velvet one I'd conjured myself plenty of times when I was stuck some place I did not want to be—and a tub of popcorn. This firework show wasn't over, and I was going to listen to every fucking word as it played out.

My husband, however, was not as inclined to watch the show.

"Lucifer's daughter? Child of Chaos? What in the bloody hell is he talking about, Lilith?" Alistair growled.

"That's what I'd like to know as well," my mother hissed. "Tell us, Lilith, what is this poor soul talking about?"

There was a lot of rage directed at my grandmother. Well, except for my paladins who were digging their hands in the tub of popcorn as all of us stuffed our faces with buttery goodness. This was better than reality TV. Andras seemed torn, like he wanted to defend his mother, but there wasn't anything to say.

This was a big fucking secret.

"My father is Lucifer, yes. My mother is Nyx. Yes, I'm the bastard child of two gods. Yes, Lucifer is remanded to the pit, which is located underneath the river Styx, which Zillah patrolled daily as was his bargain."

Well, that was a story not in any religious text I'd ever heard of. Wait a minute.

"Isn't Nyx a daughter of Chaos? And Lucifer is a son of Chaos, and they did the nasty? *Ewwww.*"

Lilith rolled her eyes. "They were not conceived and born. They were made into existence with a snap of Dušan's fingers. It isn't like you. You were born, and had they been the same as you, then you'd be right. *That* would have been gross."

Okay, I could see that. Plus, it wasn't like there weren't more instances of straight-up weirdness as far as gods were concerned.

"So, you're like... my niece? That's super weird. I don't like it. I'm gonna ignore that piece of our relationship, cool?"

"Please do. The last thing I need is you lumping me in with Atropos in the family territory."

I snorted. "You're sisters with Atropos. How does that feel?"

Lilith sighed and searched the heavens for what looked like patience. "It feels like Lucifer is my father, and since he raped Nyx, and that's one of hundreds of reasons why he's in that bloody cell, I have to say, I could do without it." Lilith shifted her gaze from me to Zillah, whispering words that hurt my heart. "I did a lot of not-so-nice things to get him locked away, Zillah. I know you remember what it was like under his rule. I know you remember those days, even though they are far behind us. I don't want to go back there. Ever."

Something dawned on me as the popcorn in my mouth turned to sawdust. "The angels helped, didn't they? That's why the Armistice is in place—why you refused to break it. Even for me."

"It was a dark time for all the realms. Dušan could not bear to kill his son, but he was out of control, so we made a bargain with the angels that there would be no more bloodshed in exchange for..." Lilith paused, seeming to steel herself against what she was about to say. "In exchange for one thousand angel souls, we promised that Lucifer would be locked away. Guarded forever by a being that could not die. And no more angels would ever die at our hands."

Wow. Just... wow.

"I reinfused the magic over time, making it stronger as the years pass. I do this so my mother doesn't have to—not that I know where she is these days. Nyx has a bad habit of not staying in touch."

The demons and angels sacrificed a thousand souls to keep Lucifer in his cage. Holy. Fucking. Shit.

"I think my brain just exploded," Aidan muttered, and I agreed wholeheartedly.

"Way to bury the lead, Lilith. I take it these sacrifices were done the hard way?" The pain in her eyes when she finally met my gaze felt like a brand. Yeah, the sacrifices were done the bloody way and she didn't like it one bit. Even eons later, she still regretted them.

I wanted to be charitable about it, but *fuuuuck*. I also wanted Zillah not to be imprisoned, but holy fucking shit, he needed to get back to his post.

That thought was dashed almost as it filtered through my brain.

"I can't go back," Zillah whispered, wilting almost on the spot. "I'm supposed to stay with Massima. I'm supposed to be here."

Alistair plopped his ass on my ottoman and pinched the bridge of his nose. *Yeah, my brain hurt, too.*

"Why must you stay with her, Zillah?" my mother asked, her eyes scanning our surroundings for threats instead of looking him in the eye.

Zillah ran a hand through his short hair before patting it down in a gesture that was probably a nervous tick before he no longer had hands. "I don't know why I must. I know you put me in that river because my mind is safe from Lucifer. I know any other dragon would have succumbed to his whispers ages ago. I know that is the only reason why I got the job. *I know.* But something told me to stay with Massima. Something calls to me when she is in trouble more than any other child of Chaos. I am supposed to be here. And that is where I'm going to stay. Bargain or no bargain. Cage or no cage."

With that, I stood, snapping my fingers again to get rid of the chair and popcorn. There was no way I could eat another bite after what he'd revealed.

"Welcome to the team, Zillah." I offered him my hand. Instead of taking it, he took a knee instead. "No, no. No bowing. It's weird. And call me Max."

We left the cliff, moving west toward whatever the hell directions Andras was getting from Niall. I hadn't heard too much on Niall's opinion about Zillah and the current predicament we were in. Lucifer's cage—while reinforced with magic—had been left unguarded. Given what we knew about Soren and his draining of the boundaries to Hell, I wasn't super confident we didn't need to investigate that shit pronto. Too bad we were stuck following a Fae parasite into enemy territory.

The barren cliff gave way to more gnarled forest which then gave way to a craggy valley filled with razor-sharp rocks and slippery slate. Honestly? If I didn't know better, I would have confused the joint with Wales. It reminded me of this little town with too many damn consonants in the name that I couldn't pronounce if I wanted to. It was all sharp mountain inclines and slippery wet slate. One wrong step and you could fall off the fucking mountain. This was exactly like that.

That little town was beautiful but deadly. Just like this.

We'd been walking for a little while, the silence only broken by displaced rocks or the odd snuffling from Zillah that seemed so out of place when he wasn't a giant water dragon.

Alistair hooked his hand at my elbow and drew me back. Worry was stamped all over his features, the pair of lines between his eyebrows carved deep.

"I still need to talk to you. And, love, I think it might be urgent. Can you"—He mimed snapping my fingers—"and make them not be able to hear us?"

I nodded and snapped away—not taking their hearing away completely, like I'd once done to him, but making them not hear us as a whole.

"That should do it. Go on." To say that I was nervous was an understatement.

And I was proved right not a second later when Alistair confirmed the pit of dread I'd been feeling since I turned Zillah back to human.

"I don't think Lucifer is in his cage anymore."

CHAPTER NINE

I wanted to have a stiff upper lip about the current situation, but I was skating the razor's edge of sanity. First Micah, then Samael, Elias, Soren, and Verena... Was this the natural progression? Why not just get to the big boss and call it good?

Lucifer was probably out of his cage. *Yeah. Because that's exactly what we needed. Were locusts and murder hornets coming too?*

I was really glad no one else but Alistair could hear my crazed, semi-hysterical laugh. Still, the expression on Alistair's face when my cackle reached its crescendo probably threw in the final nail in my sanity's coffin.

I had officially cracked.

After wiping up my tears of mirth, I focused on his face, willing a teensy bit of sanity into myself. If this was actually a thing, trying to fix it should probably be penciled in at the top of my to-do list.

"Why do you think he's out?" I managed to ask, trying not to bust out in a fit of giggles as I pondered the idea of ding-dong-ditching a Fate's doorstep. Seriously. They'd shit all over my life, it was their turn.

Alistair shook his head as he frowned at me, his brow screwed up like he was searching his mind. "Niall was in my head. When you possess someone—or someone possesses you—sometimes you can access their mind before they throw up their wards." Alistair winced because whatever he was trying to access in his memories wasn't an easy thing to get to. "Before he shut me out—I caught a glimpse of something. I didn't know what it was at the time. It was a metal box, broken open. The box was old, under water, with the door thrown wide. I didn't put it together until after Lilith said where Lucifer was. I think Niall has known where Lucifer is for some time. I think this might be a ruse to... To I don't know what. But I don't trust him, and I don't think you should, either."

In a way, it made sense. Too many bad guys led to another bad guy. Too many were interconnected in a web of conspiracy and lies. Too many threads tied to the other.

"I think Lucifer slipped his leash when Dušan became stuck in his pocket spirit world, and I think he's been biding his time or... maybe gathering power. I think he's here, and I think Niall might be leading us into a trap."

"But the Blood Moon. Aiyana said it was true. Did he just use it to his advantage?" I asked because it was important to note that we still needed to get Dušan back—probably more now than before if Lucifer was on the loose.

Barrett took that moment to break into our little huddle. I knew he would probably be the first person to notice when he couldn't hear a particularly juicy conversation and come investigate. The snoop.

"I know you did something to my ears, Maxima. Fix it," he ordered, and I rolled my eyes as I snapped my fingers.

"You're too nosy for your own good," I griped once he could hear me. I pressed a kiss to his cheek as I skirted around him. "Alistair is going to fill you in. I have a pot to stir."

I threaded my way through our group, not walking too quick or too slow, not tipping my hand as I got closer to Andras. There was no way I was going anywhere without some cold, hard answers, and I'd pry them out of the Fae's mind myself if I had to.

That said, Teresa was going to be a problem. Rather than go

into everything, I whispered, "*Somnum*," rendering her unconscious before I enacted the next part to my hastily constructed plan.

Andras whirled, his gold eyes flashing before he started to dissolve into smoke. *Not today, buddy.*

Before he could completely devolve into his other form, I pounced, clapping my hands together, sending my power out to stop his change. The shockwave of the spell brought him to his knees, and before he could move against me, barbed vines sprung from the earth, wrapping around his limbs all the way up his body.

Now, all I had to do was get Niall out of my father's brain.

Should be a piece of cake.

I glanced over my shoulder to find that not only had I knocked my father on his ass with that little clap, I also brought just about everyone else to their knees as well. The only person left standing was Lilith, and she was none too happy about my current renegade antics.

"What in the bloody hell was that, Maxima?" Her voice was so loud nearby birds took flight and a bit of the ground around her feet shook. I guessed I wasn't the only person to inherit that bit of magic from Dušan.

"Andras has a parasite in his head, on that we agree, yes?" I asked her calmly, using the same tone I'd affect if I were calming down a feral dog.

"*Yes*," she hissed back, no calm in the least.

"Now, I assume since Niall is Dušan's supposed paladin, he would know about Lucifer and his cage. Yes?"

Lilith pressed her lips together so hard they were white around the edges but gave me a short, terse nod.

"Well, Alistair informed me he saw an open cage in Niall's mind when he was possessed. An open cage at the bottom of a body of water. Meaning Lucifer is out. Meaning Niall knows this. Meaning this whole fucking thing is likely a trap or a ruse or some other such bullshit." I took a deep breath before my voice turned cold. "Meaning I'm getting his parasitic ass out of my father's brain, and I'm not going to be nice about it. Any questions?"

Lilith's eyes flashed coal black for a single second. From pupil to sclera, everything was black as the very pit of Hell before she took a single, measured breath to quell her shaking. Lilith feared her father. I had never seen her scared. Not once.

That was not comforting in the least.

"Knowledge is power, right? We can't know what he knows if he's inside Andras." She nodded, a single, sharp bow of her head, and I got to work.

With Alistair, I was hesitant to do this—forcibly evicting Niall —but with Andras I had no such compunction. Now that I knew his lineage, my worry about his survivability was practically nil. So I flexed my power as I slapped a hand to Andras' head, drilling down deep into his mind where I knew Niall resided.

Don't get me wrong, I tried not to see the bevy of images flooding my brain. The death, the sacrifices, the—*gag* —relationship with my mother.

Only when I felt the Fae writhing in his mind, did I start my spell. "*Exiens e tenebris in lucem prodeunt.*" *Come forth out of the darkness and into the light.*

I repeated these words over and over, forcing my will into Andras' brain until it reached Niall, until I felt my spell wrap around him. Until I snared him in my thrall and yanked, pulling him free of Andras' brain.

Niall began to materialize. Black smoke fell from Andras' lips and nose just like it had when Alistair was freed. Only then did I pull out of Andras' mind, only then did I snap my fingers, binding Niall to his corporeal form with a single thought.

I was glad I did because he tried to dematerialize, likely trying to inhabit someone else.

Not on my watch, buddy.

With a wretched scream, I leapt at Niall and tackled him to the ground. But Niall had been fighting a lot longer than I had, and he rolled with me. I was up and over his body and flying through the air in less than a second. I may have tasted dirt there for a little bit, but I found my feet, ready to face him.

Only I wasn't the only one on my feet. No, Lilith and Andras flanked his left side, Aidan and Hideyo his right. Alistair and Barrett were bearing down on his front while a phased Marcus, a still half-asleep Teresa, and still-human Zillah were covering his back. Weapons drawn, teeth bared, talons at the ready, no one was letting Niall get anywhere.

Not today.

I loved my little family.

I approached the group, squeezing in between Alistair and Barrett to face Niall. His odd smoky face was scared. Hell, I would be too if I were facing down this lot.

“You don’t get to do this to us. You don’t get to lead us into peril. You don’t get to hold everything back while we risk our lives,” I whispered, knowing he could hear every single word I was saying. “You do not get to lie by omission. Not about this.”

Niall began speaking in that guttural language that tree-Fae had used. Either because he had to, or because he wanted to possess someone else, and that had been his reasoning before, right?

At the time, he had already possessed Alistair and there was nothing I could do about it. Now, I wasn’t in that boat.

As fast as a snake, I whipped my hand out, pressing two fingers into the smoky mass that masqueraded as a throat. It wasn’t solid, but it didn’t feel like nothing, either. It was like liquid smoke, and it felt wrong. Not evil, not sordid, but... Wrong. Like he wasn’t supposed to be in that form. Like he wasn’t supposed to be this way at all. Without much in the way of a spell so much as a thought process and a force of will, I pumped magic into him.

His form flickered a bit, a flash of something pale before it was back to the roiling mass of smoke.

“Try to speak,” I ordered, not bothering with niceties.

“I don’t know what you think is going to—” Niall muttered. In English. “I can talk! Fates save me, I can talk.” He reached to grab me, and a flaming sword was at his throat before I could even blink.

“You would do best to keep your hands to yourself, Niall. No one in this group is going to let you run amuck. Least of all me.”

Niall's hands went up in surrender. "Of course, of course. I was just excited. I haven't spoken to a person that wasn't trying to kill me or lead me to my own peril in four centuries. You don't understand what it's like here." He tilted his head back and sighed in relief. "It's like heaven."

"Let's not get off topic, shall we? Lucifer. You knew he was out of his cage. Cough up the details before I drill it out of that smokestack you call a skull."

Niall brought his head back to rights, tilting it down to stare at me, his odd orange eyes piercing me where I stood. "You wouldn't have come. You wouldn't. Dušan is in danger. I can't fight this fight on my own."

"That isn't giving us details, Niall," I said through gritted teeth. "That is giving me excuses. I don't *want* excuses. I want to know what you know so I can be prepared. Also, I'd like to know whose side you are really fucking on. That would be real good information to have. Just saying."

Niall seemed to wilt in on himself before he folded his limbs and sat on the craggy ground. "I'll tell you, Princess. But you aren't going to like it."

I had no doubt in my mind that statement was true.

I just had no idea how much until it was too late.

CHAPTER TEN

By the time Niall was done with his story, I had not only conjured a bottle of bourbon for myself, but I'd started passing it around. Honestly? There wasn't enough booze in the world to deal with a problem of this magnitude, nor was there a solid solution past "don't die."

"He has been free for four hundred years? Are you fucking kidding me with this bullshit?" Lilith growled for maybe the fifth time before she snatched the decanter out of my hands and started pounding it straight out of the bottle.

Classy, Grandma.

"Well, technically, more than that?" Niall corrected, and personally, I thought it was the way wrong time to do so.

Especially when Lilith's whole body started vibrating with rage. "Then what have I been reinforcing for the last few centuries? A bloody illusion?" she screeched before smashing the decanter on the rocks at her feet.

This was the third bottle she'd thrown, and I was getting tired of conjuring more alcohol. "Would you desist from throwing away good booze? Honestly. And why are you throwing a temper tantrum? This is not a 'temper tantrum' moment. This is a 'devise a plan before the embodiment of evil decides to kill us' moment. Sooooo," I scolded before snapping my fingers in quick succession, "Get the lead out and plan, woman."

"Fuck Soren Quinn. I swear I wish I could rip open the seam, yank his bastard ass out, and kill him all over again. And fuck Abaddon, too. Making that deal. That miserable shit only wanted more power. *More, more, more*. And Samael and Verena. Hell, all the way down to Ruby. If I could resurrect each and every one of them, I would, just so I could kill them myself."

Lilith was a hairsbreadth from losing her mind.

"Well, that's all well and good, dear," Barrett muttered, his tone just a touch snide. "But if you could stop your ranting for a moment, the adults in the room might be able to think of an actual plan. Also, when it is your life's mission to keep an ancient fucking Titan locked away forever, maybe it would be a fabulous idea to, oh, I don't know, *bloody well tell someone*." Barrett started that tirade so calm, but he ended it shouting at the top of his lungs.

Marcus wrapped an arm around Barrett's middle and hauled him back because he was less than a foot from Lilith's face, and that was a deadly place to be. "You losing it is not helping, babe. And quit yelling at Lilith. We all have a blind spot when it comes to family."

Barrett harrumphed in protest.

"We could bring up your parental drama and dissect it for faults if you like."

Barrett narrowed his eyes at his husband, crossing his arms in affront.

"Yes, we all have family drama. None of that explains how we'll keep Grandpa Luci from killing us all. Anyone have a plan for that?" Andras chimed in from his perch on a rather craggy piece of stone. He was pinching his brow like that action alone could stave off the mother of all headaches. Apparently ripping a Fae out of someone's brain hurt.

Who knew?

Okay, I felt a little bad about it, but it was unavoidable.

Probably.

Niall raised his hand like a kindergartener. This was particularly humorous since he was sitting crisscross applesauce in the dirt, his huge mass as foreboding as ever. "I do? Well, it's the same plan I had before. Get Dušan home safe, make the sacrifice, and let him deal with it?"

Lilith rolled her eyes. "Yes, because that worked out so well before. Dušan refused to kill him. Why do you think he got locked away in the first bloody place?"

Lucifer had many names just like Lilith and Dušan. Lucifer was the god, Cronus, and despite tales to the contrary, he had not, in fact, been killed by Zeus and thrown into Tartarus AKA the Seam.

Locked away, yes. Dead? Not so much. Homer was a lying piece of shit. Good of him to leave out half the damn story let alone the freaking truth.

"Yes, but that was before Lucifer had Verena kill his wife and children," Niall whispered. "Before Dušan was locked away in a pocket world he couldn't get out of for four hundred years. Before Lucifer systematically infiltrated every single part of the world Dušan created, poisoning it. He can't let that stand. *He won't.*"

Niall seemed to have so much hope. So much faith that Dušan would do the right thing. And I wanted to believe him.

I did.

But Lilith brought us all back down to earth.

Lilith snorted. "You think you know my grandfather, but you don't. Lucifer raped Nyx and Dušan did nothing. He flooded the earth, and nothing. He brought wars and destruction to the realms, and nothing. He orchestrated mass genocide, oppression, and misery to all nine realms, *and nothing*. Dušan will do nothing now. He will be silent just like he was when my mother cried at his feet and begged for help."

I wanted to throw up. I wanted to rage. I wanted to...

"He did not do nothing, Lilith, and you know it," Niall countered, and stood for the first time since he began his tale. "Just because he refused to kill his son does not mean he did nothing. Dušan leant his power to the cage. He resurrected the dead—he fixed his son's destruction. And he told you how to lock him away. He told you who could guard the cage. He gave you everything because he couldn't kill Lucifer. Do not lie and say he did nothing. It might have been eons ago, but I was there."

Lilith speared Niall with an expression so scathing it should have set Niall on fire. "Now who is the liar? Hades was the only other person in that room with me, and he's been dead for four hundred years. Abaddon saw to that."

Niall snorted, but took a step back, sitting on a craggy rock next to Andras. The disparity between their two bodies was hilarious. "Not dead, sister. Just stuck in this stupid form, looking for our grandfather and trying not to get myself killed in this absolute travesty of a realm."

At that point I had a thought which my husband voiced aloud. "Is anyone in this bloody realm not a god or goddess? Fates, love, your family tree is fucking bananas. Soon, someone will roll up and say, 'I'm the long-lost son of Apollo' or something, and then we'll all be in trouble."

I wanted to laugh. Really, I did, but I couldn't help but think he was right. Lilith was the daughter of Cronus, Niall was Hades, I was the daughter of Chaos…

"Okay, if anyone else has god lineage, now would be the time to speak up. Seriously, I don't think we can take another one," I called. Yes, I was shouting, but fucking fuck balls, honestly?

Andras raised his hand, "Mine is obvious, but I thought I'd put my hat in the ring so no one is surprised later."

"Not me. My dad is a plain old bastard wraith. Not sure about the mom bit, but I doubt she was a goddess. Then again…" Aidan trailed off. His brother, Ian, was the spawn of their mutual father raping a death goddess, so it wasn't totally out of the realm of possibility for Aidan's mother to be something other than a wraith.

Della was a human before she started out. Alistair was pretty sure he was not of celestial lineage. Barrett and Marcus shook their heads. The only person in question, really, was Zillah and Hideyo. Zillah could not be swayed or influenced by Lucifer. That kinda seemed like a god-like power.

Plus, Zillah's expression was hella guilty. "I don't want to say. You'll look at me weird."

I threw out a guess because, *water dragon*. Duh. "Poseidon? And a dragon?" I may have made a few hand gestures that implied sex, and Zillah blushed all the way up to his hairline.

"I don't know for sure of my mother's name, but she is an ancient. If she's still alive, that is. I've been doing this job a long time. She could be dead by now for all I know."

"But your dad?"

Zillah groaned before parking his ass on a boulder. He seemed ill at ease being out of the water, but I figured that was just because we were in enemy territory. Maybe. "You guessed correct. I don't know him very well, though."

That was messed up, but it made a whole hell of a lot of sense. It seemed a lot of gods didn't feel the need to actually raise their children.

Collectively, the rest of us turned to stare at Hideyo. His eyes widened and he shook his head. "Neither of my parents were a god of any sort. Trust me. If they were, they'd probably still be alive." He said it flippantly, but no amount of sarcasm or sass could hide the pain that leaked into every syllable of that statement.

"Damn," I whispered. "I'm sorry."

He shrugged before looking away. "Yeah, well, this place has always been bloody. Even before Verena."

Damn.

Hideyo had never come out and said he was Fae. Sure, I figured we all knew by now after the not-so-subtle hints that had been dropped, but he'd never said it.

"All of this is well and good, but are we just going to gloss over that you are directly related to Hades?" Alistair griped, staring Lilith down. "Or that your father is running around the Unseelie Court untethered and has been for how long? Or that we need to somehow find Dušan, get him back to the gate, *and* convince him to kill his son in, oh, I don't know..." He trailed off while glancing at his wrist that in no way had a watch on it. "...three bloody days. Less than, if I remember right."

And then, without the least bit of prompting, Alistair stood from his perch on the ottoman I'd conjured and phased. He went from a regal pale-skinned, almost-redhead to a charcoal-skinned devil in an instant. The burning runes carved in his skin glowed like embers, their light brighter with his anger.

"We are losing time. We are losing the element of surprise—if we ever had it—and I will not let you lot put my wife in danger any longer. Get off your asses and let's go. For all we know, Lucifer knows exactly where we are."

None of this was incorrect. Not a single word of it. I almost felt bad for stopping. Almost. Instead of yelling, though, I stood, sidling closer to his rage, and wrapped my arms around his middle. His skin might be made of burning embers, but he was warm, and his heat was welcome. I rested my head on his chest and listened for a heartbeat. It thumped under my ear in a steady clip before it started to slow bit by bit.

There didn't need to be any scolding or yelling. He was right, and now he needed his cool back. The only way we were going to get that was if he got a hug and a deep breath. I was giving the hug. I was still waiting on the deep breath. I gave him until the count of ten before I said something.

"Take a breath, Knight," I whispered, peering up at him. The distance was short, but I still perched my chin on his chest to look him in the eye. "Just one, and then we'll get a move on. You're right, and I'm glad you've taken us to task. One deep breath and we'll go."

Alistair narrowed his eyes before he let his arms surround me, eventually sucking in a huge gulp of air. When he let it out, I saw it all behind his phased eyes. The fear of losing me. The absolute terror at the thought of us not making it.

The loss he was preparing himself for.

I wanted to allay his fears, but they echoed my own. We'd lost a lot. Too much. And this didn't feel like a battle we were going to win.

But damn if we weren't going to try.

CHAPTER ELEVEN

Alistair never got calm enough to phase back to his human form. I didn't blame him. There was little in the way of happy thoughts in a place like this one. Even as calm as I could make myself, thunder still rolled in the distance. I knew without a doubt in my mind that that thunder was mine, and as much as I wanted to project a façade of calm, I was failing pretty miserably at it.

It was possible that it was because Niall—AKA, Hades—was leading us to a mouth of a cave. Maybe it wasn't that it was a cave. Maybe it was that this particular cave resembled a skull. In fact, I wasn't too sure that the rock formation that yawned wide *wasn't* a skull. Out of all the skulls I'd come across—*don't* ask—I could tell it was humanoid with only a slight prominence to the brow. Add in the razor-sharp teeth, and the creep-factor was turned up to eleven. I supposed it was totally possible that someone could have carved that shape out of the rock, but...

I had the sinking suspicion Niall was leading us into the literal mouth of a long-dead beast.

Yeah, calm had waved bye-bye to me somewhere before I fell off the damn cliff and hadn't come back yet.

"There is absolutely no way I am going in that cave," Barrett hissed, and I couldn't help but nod.

In fact, I had to look away from the damn thing because it creeped me out so bad. My gaze fell on the ribbon of a stream we'd been following for the last little bit. And by little bit, I meant hours. The stream we'd been following fell from the mouth of the skull like some kind of macabre tongue snaking through the realm.

Unsettled didn't even cover it. The Unseelie Court was vast, and this trek didn't seem to have an end. The cave was supposed to be a shortcut, but I couldn't see myself taking this path no matter how much time it might save.

"Seconded," Marcus agreed with his husband.

"Thirded," Della chimed in. "Lothan told me about these things. The bones of the old gods—the ones that died to make the new crop. About how the new gods brought down mountains on them, crushing them in the rock. There is no way I'm traipsing around the belly of an old god, Hades. I don't care how much time it will cut off."

Niall huffed, his big body almost wilting at our refusal to go into the cave. Granted, it would cut more than a day off our trek, and the Unseelie castle was still almost half a day away with the shortcut. We did need to save time, but no one—and I mean no one—trusted Niall.

I hated to think it was because he looked like an evil smoke monster, but it wasn't exactly a stretch of the imagination, either. It was also possible it was because he kept a veritable shit-ton of information from us and hid what he was. That wasn't even getting into the whole "possession of two of our people" thing. Yeah… that could be it.

"I can't make you go into the cave. I can't make you do what you said you would. All I can do is…" He trailed off, likely at a loss. "I can't think of what else I'm supposed to do. I spent my whole life serving my grandfather. I sacrificed everything so this realm was better. So that this realm was what my brothers could not make on Earth. That there was very little war, that there was peace. But I failed Dušan, and I'm stuck like this."

Because Niall was a giant smoke monster, it was tough to discern his features unless he made them prominent. But right then, I could almost catch a glimpse of who he used to be, and all of that culminated into a deity that was so sad, so alone, he would risk anything to change it.

I wanted to say something, but Niall continued, "My father is the worst being imaginable. Some of the stories are even true about him. Not all of his children survived. Many of us did not. He did not care. In fact, I think he reveled in it. He won't—he can't—stay in power here. He can't open the gates to Tartarus. And that is exactly what will happen when Faerie collapses, you know? The gate? The one that separates Hell from Faerie? That will crumble to dust. All the Fae doors, all the pockets of worlds, all of the seams holding the realms together. All of it will be gone, leaving the doors wide open for him to walk right on through. Lucifer will rule it all. We don't have the luxury of stopping. We don't have the luxury of time. So, stay out here and walk around the bloody mountain if you want to. Take your time and perish right along with this world. I'm going to get my grandfather. Do what you want."

I felt like I'd been slapped right in the face. Here I was thinking it would just be Faerie that went. And that was bad enough. But Lucifer with a freebie pass to the rest of the realms? Hell's gates open wide with no one strong enough to stop him?

Yep, that was the kick in the ass I needed.

"Welp, can't argue with that," I quipped and moved to follow Niall. Or Hades. Or whatever the fuck we were calling him now. This two-name shit was confusing. I was halted not a second later by Alistair's hand on my elbow. His brow was creased in worry, or maybe it was anger. Maybe it was both. His charred appearance did not lend itself to too many expressions.

"How do we know he's telling the truth, love?" Alistair asked under his breath, and I could feel the trepidation in him calling to me.

Fates, I wanted to comfort him, but I couldn't. I couldn't do anything else but tell him the truth. I sighed, the doubt in me almost too much to bear. "We don't. But I'd rather follow him and kill him later if he's lying than ignore him and let the universe implode. It's a failing of mine, sure, but I figure we can work on it at a later date... yanno, when the world isn't ending. Sound good?"

Alistair growled low and long, his eyes blazing for one tense moment. "Fine. But I expect his death to be bloody and brutal if this is a trap."

It figured that my Knight wasn't going to lose his demon ways anytime soon. I kinda loved that about him. I, too, thirsted for vengeance. What a pair we made.

"So noted." I planted a kiss on his phased lips. The texture of his skin reminded me of brittle stone, but I didn't care. Alistair needed to know that I was in this shit with him. Together, the pair of us followed Niall closer to the mouth of the cave. *Mouth.* Pun totally intended.

Lilith copied Alistair and growled under her breath, stomping behind us. With much grumbling, the rest of our party followed. They weren't happy about it, but they did it. Hell, I wasn't happy about it, either—especially the closer we got to the fanged teeth that made the entrance. Barrett was the most vocal about it, and it was a comfort to me that his bitching would persevere.

The only person who seemed less and less trusting was Zillah. I couldn't blame him for it, either. He'd been caged for eons and probably wasn't looking to get dead before he'd had a chance to actually live.

I felt a shiver on the wind before I ever heard the rumble. It was like the wind was trying to get my attention this whole damn time, but I was just too stupid to realize it. In fact, I'd thought it was the thunder that had been roiling in the distance since I got to this side of Faerie. But when the earth began to shake, and the stream that carved its way through the land began to rise, I knew that this was totally not me.

Water poured from the mouth of the cave in a rush before drawing down to a trickle, and still, the level of the stream rose. I —along with the majority of our group—whipped my head back in the direction we'd come from, searching for whatever it was that was causing the disturbance.

It took far too long for my brain to cobble together what I was seeing. The water was rising all right. In a wave that crested at least fifty feet high, the water changed shape, morphing into a kind of serpent. The dripping jaws opened wide with surprisingly sharp-looking teeth for a thing made entirely out of water. The thing let out an unearthly screech as it barreled closer, translucent as rippling glass except for a pair of glowing red eyes. My brain snagged on the fact that that noise shouldn't be possible, nor should it be able to come out of a being with no freaking vocal cords.

I knew firsthand what damage water could do. I'd been drowned in a lake a few centuries ago, and it was one of my least favorite ways to go—especially since I'd just barely survived a watery grave. And while I should totally be thinking of how to kill this thing, I was still stuck on the memory of my breath burning in my lungs.

How in the high holy hell were we supposed to fight this thing? It looked like fucking water. Were we supposed to talk to it? Be diplomatic?

Alistair took the choice right out of my hands because he yanked on my arm, and yelled, "Run!"

Yep. Alistair had a way better plan than I did.

Pulling me into the mouth of the cave, his hesitation over this particular path was long gone. The tunnel was black as pitch, the light of the Unseelie Court failing to reach us in this pit. It wasn't until I'd tripped over what I *hoped* were rocks did I toss up a ball of light.

"*Detrahet me in lucem*," I yelled, volleying the light in my hand in the air where it stayed, illuminating our way. Without much time to assess our surroundings, I still caught sight of the spine and rib bones of a giant long-dead creature as we slogged through a rapidly rising stream.

Yup, we were running for our lives from one monster into the belly of another. 'Cause there was no way *that* could go wrong.

Alistair and I were at the back of our little group, so we were within spitting distance of the creature—water monster? Thing?—that was hell-bent on devouring us whole. Though, I didn't see how exactly it was going to do it with water for teeth and no stomach.

I was just absolutely sure it was going to do its damnedest to try. Water rose higher up my legs as we ran, adding to my panic as I tried to keep my feet as the water did its best to trip us. The monster was right behind us, and I didn't think I had time to wield any sort of magic before it would be on me. And I didn't want to find out what would happen when it finally sank its water teeth into us.

And I was so worried about the damn water monster and its glowing red eyes at my back, I wasn't paying any attention to what was in front of us until Alistair and I slammed into the back of Della and Hideyo.

It was as if we froze for a second, balancing precariously on the precipice of what I hoped was a cliff but was more than likely *not.* Then we were falling—or rather *sliding*—hurtling toward the belly of whatever long-dead beast we were stuck inside.

Personally, I would have rather dealt with the damn water monster.

CHAPTER TWELVE

One would think sliding down the spine of a giant skeleton would be sort of fun, right? I mean, slides were always fun. Unless you didn't mean to slide down that particular slope and were now hurtling toward imminent doom. The ball of light had not followed me down the proverbial rabbit hole, and my panicked brain couldn't decide if not knowing what was coming was a good thing or not.

When the ground finally rose up to meet us, I settled on bad. I landed on who I hoped was Alistair, sprawling awkwardly on a body as I heard a pained "*oof*" when I hit the ground. It took a couple of seconds to get my bearings, the darkness and fall doing nothing for my equilibrium.

"What in the blue bloody Fates is this place, Niall?" Barrett demanded, a light blooming in his palm. It illuminated an expression of absolute loathing. "'I know a shortcut,' he says. 'This will be faster,' he says. Did you actually intend us to fall into this bloody pit, you absolute wanker?"

Barrett was not handling this shit any better than I was. I couldn't say why that was a comfort, but it was.

"Fall? No. But this is the way. There isn't usually water in the cave—or at least there wasn't the last time I was here. And there *were* stairs to get down here, but we missed them when that *thing* chased us."

"Speaking of," Andras piped up from his perch on a slimy rock, a place he appeared to have fallen after his initial slide. He paused before yanking on his left wrist. There was a squelching pop and he winced for a moment before breathing a sigh of relief. "What was that thing?"

A screeching roar sounded above us, punctuating Andras' question. And as far as we'd slid, that sound was a little too close for comfort.

Niall sighed, shaking his head. "I don't know. Don't you think if there was a river monster hanging around the shortcut, I would have told you?"

I snorted at the straight absurdity of that statement, but it was my husband who answered him, his voice a quiet ball of rage. "No. Honestly, I think you would have kept us in the dark as long as you possibly could have to ensure the outcome you wanted. Which is what you've done this whole bloody time." Alistair was already phased, but in the low light, his runes glowed with the fire in his blood. "Is there anything else we should be on the lookout for, Niall? Cave dwellers? Stomach monsters?"

Niall growled long and low at him in response but managed to speak a single coherent sentence that was all threat, even though it was not likely intended as one. "I am not your enemy."

"Well, mate, if this is how you treat your friends, I'd hate to see how you treat people you actually dislike."

Antagonistic as fuck, but the statement was still true.

"All right, boys, none of this is getting us closer to our goal. I'd like to get a move on before that damn thing figures out how to get down here." Leave it to my mom to get everyone back on task.

Teresa muttered a few words in Latin and clapped her hands together. Light bloomed bright between her palms, and when she threw her hands wide, dancing bits of light floated from her fingers to cling to the cave ceiling. It was a gifted bit of magic, a simple spell I'd seen her do a thousand times in my youth, made fantastical because of the showmanship. The bits of light cast an eerie green glow in the cave, making what was already a creepy place that much more sinister.

The water monster picked that particular time to roar again. I didn't know if it was just the cave or if my ears were playing tricks on me, but that thing sounded a whole hell of a lot closer than it did a minute ago.

"We need to move. *Now*," I ordered, but I didn't really need to. Anyone who was still putting themselves to rights was up and getting their shit sorted.

Our clip was in no way slow as we followed Niall further into the cave. In fact, I was practically jogging over craggy stones and slimy things to keep up with the group. My mother's spell hovered over our heads, keeping pace with us as we traversed the winding tunnel. And that's the best I could call it. There was nothing special about this particular bit of earth. No pretty crystals, no runes, or carvings. Nothing but bits of rock and slick stones.

Granted, we were in the belly of a long-dead being that in all likelihood could be a god. Why would there be pretty crystals or cave drawings in here? If people were smart, they'd stay as far away from this place as they could get. We—like the idiots we were—thundered through the tunnel, following Niall as he led us deeper and deeper into the earth. The air got cooler and wetter, the moisture in the air clinging to my face and hands, hell, even my hair. And the deeper we got, the less I felt like this was the way to go.

I didn't want to be the whiner of the group, but I was super tempted to ask if we were there yet. I didn't, though, but maybe I should have. Maybe if I would have asked something—*anything*—we might have stopped.

We might have heard the quiet shuffle of footsteps creeping closer in those tiny bits of silence afforded to us between the water monster's roars.

And maybe, just maybe, we wouldn't have been slowly surrounded by what had to be dark elves.

I used the term dark elves very loosely. They did not have dark skin or hair. In fact, they fell into more of the albino spectrum with white skin and hair, their red eyes glowing in the dark. They had the same bone structure as the other elves we'd met, and that was the only reason I would even classify these dark creatures as elves in the first place. Alistair was light years past tense, and I knew he could feel the frisson on the air that told of the elves that crept up from behind us.

I wanted to be diplomatic. We were in their home, stomping around after all. It wasn't cool to just bust down the door to a joint that wasn't yours and start blasting magic. Crown or not, that was just not done. Okay, so it was totally done, it just wasn't going to be done by me.

Alistair tried to stop me by yanking on my hand, but I yanked him right back, pulling him behind me as I weaved through our people to talk to what had to be their leader.

The only reason I thought this dude was the leader was because he had a crown of—*gag*—teeth circling his head like some kind of macabre headband. Add that to the bones hanging from leather thongs at his belt, the still-bloody skin stitched together to make his clothing, and… was that fresh scalps on his belt?

"We mean you no harm or disrespect. We wish to leave this place without violence." I was pretty sure more flowery words were needed, but it was the best I could do under the circumstances. I mean, the guy had fucking scalps hanging from his belt and teeth for a crown. You couldn't be one of the good guys with that much murder on your belt.

"That'sss funny. You breathing is disssressspect," the elf hissed like a snake, his head moving in those sinuous yet jerky movements of a serpent about to strike. "The firssst one to bring me her head will have all the favor you desssire."

Okay, so the diplomatic approach was out. At that moment I should have felt fear. We didn't know how many of them there were. We didn't know where they were coming from or how to get out. One could assume the way out was past Mr. Snaky McTeethcrown, but that wasn't a given.

What *was* a given was the fight we were about to have on our hands.

I think I was looking for that little bit of permission because I didn't hesitate to clap my hands together, unleashing my power in a wave. A fan of lightning sprang from my fingertips, hitting several of the elves in the chest—all except the leader who'd anticipated my actions. He blocked the bolt with a wide sword, the edges and tip jagged as if he'd pulled it from the earth just that way. The metal glowed blue for a short moment, and then he flung the lightning back at me.

I dodged the bolt, yanking Alistair down with me as it arced over our heads. The electricity slammed into an elf that had overtaken Barrett, and the ancient witch shoved the elf off as he writhed. There was a bellowing roar from behind, and as one, the elves converged on us. In close quarters, magic sailed around us—balls of lightning-laced fire from my mother, red arcs of magic from Barrett, my own magics, but it was Lilith's that was the real showstopper. Icy-white bolts of power found their way to the eyes of our opponents, their consistency as solid as knives as they buried themselves into dark elf brains.

An elf sailed past Alistair's defenses—which were formidable since he was slashing at anything he could reach with his flaming scythe while keeping me behind him—burying his fetid teeth into my shoulder. An enraged growl was ripped from my throat as I latched onto the elf's head and twisted, snapping his neck before throwing him off of me.

But more and more elves came. We were in a sea of bodies, all fighting in close quarters while trying not to harm our own side. Well, our little pocket of twelve were doing their best. The elves had no compunction about harming their own. A fact proven when their leader rained down bolts of electricity on us. I was hit by one before I managed to throw up a makeshift sort of shield, but it barely held up against the onslaught.

"Max!" Lilith screamed, and I turned toward her voice to watch her hack at an elf with a sword she'd conjured. She cut down elf after elf as I struggled to hold up against the dark elf leader's bombardment. "When he slows, take my hand. We must—"

Lilith's words were cut off as another wave of elves pressed into us, and she didn't explain after that. She dove for my hand, latching onto it as a jolt of power flowed from her into me. It gave me the strength to shove at the leader's onslaught, his power snapping like a dry twig at the flex.

"Everyone!" she called, but it was inside our minds and not out loud. "Take cover." The command rang inside my head before another surge of power hit me. This time, it flowed out of me in a mindless wave. I was merely a conduit for Lilith, hers mingling with mine before it poured out of me.

The earth pitched beneath me, but I was no longer on the ground. My feet hovered over the roiling cave floor as a scream was ripped from my lips. Golden light nearly blinded me as it whipped from my chest, from my skin, from my hands and feet and mouth. As soon as the light touched a dark elf, it seared through their flesh leaving nothing but ashes.

This lasted for far too many too-long moments, and when it died, the walls of the cave shuddered, and then the walls caved in on us.

CHAPTER THIRTEEN

Coming to under a mound of crushing razor-sharp rocks was decidedly my least favorite way to return to consciousness. It was dark, a pitch blackness only reserved for the very pits of Hell. The Seam was brighter than here, and that was saying something. I tried to draw on the earth—hell, I was surrounded by it, might as well use it to my advantage—but the element did not answer me.

I struggled, the first faint strains of claustrophobia setting in as I fought to move. A particularly jagged bit of rock gouged into my side, and every time I jerked, it dug further into my flesh. Panic came fast, and it wasn't until I heard someone else whimper, did I scrape my shit together in the tattered brown paper sack that was my brain.

The earth was not responding because this was not earth exactly. It was the decaying body of a god or goddess. Meaning that it was possible that the element would be dormant here just like it was near Aiyana and her stupid tree.

The elements are not your only powers, Max. My brain supplied that thought, and if I could have slapped my forehead, I would have.

I breathed a few words in Latin, and the rocks closest to me wiggled. I heard a few rocks topple somewhere above me, but that was about it. After what Lilith did to me—*through me*—I was about as strong as a day-old kitten. My breaths came in shuddered pants, and I did everything I could to not start screaming like a lunatic. This was what I'd always feared—being trapped in the dark, unable to move or escape. This was like every single time I'd died. Stuck in a never-ending thrall of blackness.

Help me. Help me. Fates, please I can't get out. Someone, please, help me.

I didn't know if I just thought those words or screamed them, but my throat was raw and aching, so I probably knew the answer to that. It wasn't until I felt the wash of cool air, did I snap out of what was likely the mother of all panic attacks. It wasn't just cool; it was an icy blast of almost slithering air. If I could have seen anything at all, I had a feeling it would have looked like smoke.

The frigid air hardened, solidifying into the shape of a man? Niall. Pressure and weight lifted off of me as he took shape, creating space between my prison and my body.

"Shh, child. I'll get you out. Don't fret, dear. You'll see your family again. You'll see them all again. Shh."

It wasn't until I heard Niall's smooth voice, did I realize I had been screaming. Still. After this I was going to need a mental health day... or year. Or decade.

Niall's arm looped around my middle and tugged, pulling me out from under the rocks and debris. Well, not pulled out completely, but a large majority of the heaviest boulders had been moved. I shoved off the last few rocks, positively blissful when I reached unencumbered air.

A familiar warm hand found mine, and Alistair pulled me from the pile. I clung to him and him to me. I wanted to take the time to look him over—check him for injuries—but I didn't. He, on the contrary, ran his hands all over me to assess if I was okay. I knew without his assessment, I had a couple of broken ribs, some bumps and bruises, and probably a concussion. I was a hell of a lot better off than I should be after something like that.

I hurt all over, and yet, I didn't hurt at all because I was with Alistair and he was okay.

"Fates, love. *Fates.* I thought I'd lost you." He pressed a kiss to my forehead but refused to unwrap his arms from my torso. He didn't press on my injured ribs at all, but his arms were an iron cage. I didn't mind. I was shaking like a leaf, leaning on him for support. Only when my eyes focused, did I notice I could see again. It was lighter out from under the rocks, an eerie green glow hovering at the new roof of the cave.

My mother's magic. She was alive. Thank the Fates.

"Who are we missing?" I asked because I didn't see anyone else.

Alistair swiped at his nose—which was bloody and swollen. He had a cut over his right eye and a blooming bruise on his cheek. He'd have a shiner if he didn't heal soon. That said, he seemed better off than I was. "Aidan, Marcus, Hideyo, and Zillah. Niall is looking for them since he can dematerialize with Teresa's help, but Barrett and Teresa can't locate them all. They need your help, love."

Each of those names was like a blow. I took a shuddering breath and touched one of the boulders. The earth was still not talking to me, but I did have other abilities.

"*Invenietis illos,*" I muttered, snapping my fingers. All at once, four balls of light bloomed in the cave above mounds of packed rubble, and we took off. I wanted to ask about the dark elves. Wanted to know what happened after I...

What had Lilith done to me? Through me? She'd said she didn't have time to explain, but whatever she'd done had sapped my abilities to a level that had left me damn near helpless.

"Here!" I yelled to no one in particular.

Alistair and I reached the first light and began yanking rocks—Alistair with much more strength and gusto than me. Then it wasn't just the two of us. Barrett gently moved me out of the way as he scrabbled at the stones to locate his husband. Or at least that was what I'd have been doing if my husband was still under a pile of rocks. With all of our help and Niall's assistance, we unearthed

Hideyo. He was conscious and mobile, but he was holding himself funny. Likely he had a dislocated shoulder or maybe a broken collar bone. I couldn't tell in the low light.

His injury didn't slow him down at all, and we came to the next mound. After some tricky maneuvering, we found Zillah. He was unconscious, but breathing, his forehead bleeding like a stuck hog. Once he was mostly unearthed, Barrett sprinted to the next light, yanking boulder after boulder off the mound. Half of us went to help as the rest worked on getting Zillah out of his stone prison.

I could practically feel Barrett vibrating with fear.

"Bloody Fates-forsaken elves. Fucking shortcuts, why did he do that? Why did he push me? I swear to everything I find holy if you're dead, I'll pull you from the depths myself. You aren't leaving me. You bloody well aren't." Barrett muttered his litany of curses as he searched for his husband, and I didn't blame him one bit.

Then the pile of rocks began to vibrate before the mound moved on its own. Niall materialized next to us as we backed off. Just in time, too, because in the next second, there was a giant gray wolf emerging from the mound, and he wasn't gentle about it, either.

Barrett latched onto my hand and yanked—which hurt like a bitch, by the way—pulling me away from the Alpha wolf.

"Marcus?" I asked, before quickly realizing that the wolf in question might have been Marcus' animal, but that animal was in charge now. He growled at me, snapping his jaws near where I once stood. Alistair shifted me behind his back and began herding me toward the rest of our party.

"Get back," Barrett murmured, his low tone likely used to not startle the giant apex predator. "You're safe, my love. No one is going to hurt you. Please give him back to me."

Barrett stepped fully in front of me and Alistair, making sure the wolf saw him and not us.

"Give him back to me," he pleaded with the animal. Marcus' wolf stared at Barrett for a few tense seconds before he nodded. A thick mist of white magic swirled for a moment, and Marcus appeared a second later, gasping on his hands and knees on the rocky cave floor.

Barrett tackled him—possible injuries be damned—and we left them to their moment to search for the last of our party that was unaccounted for. A pit of dread opened wide within me. Aidan could travel, which meant if he hadn't already saved himself, he was either too weak to do it or he wasn't conscious.

I didn't like either of those options.

Aidan had saved my ass on more than a few occasions, pulling me out of more scrapes than I could count. I couldn't lose him. Not here. Not now.

Soon we got help, and it wasn't just Alistair and I yanking rocks away. It was all of us—at least those of us who were conscious, anyway. We found Aidan at the bottom of too many boulders, his arm covering his head. But that arm was obviously broken, the radial bone protruded from the skin as the rest of the arm hung limp. He was breathing, sure, but he had more than just a broken arm. At least one of his legs was broken—if not both of them—and he had more than a few gashes that poured too much blood.

"We have to get him out of here. I can't draw on the elements in this stupid cave," I muttered under my breath, but Alistair heard me.

"Let me try," my mother offered, laying a hand on Aidan. She dug her fingers in the dirt, whispering a healing spell. It did little to slow the blood seeping from his wounds. She shook her head and tried again, stopping when her nose started to bleed. She growled under her breath before she stood, swaying hard once she reached her feet.

"That's the best I can do. You're right. We need to get out of here. Who knows if there are more dark elves lurking around this Fates forsaken cave? I doubt you vaporized them all."

Vaporized? I wanted to ask to be sure, but I could figure it out for myself. Who knew what spell or power Lilith had used me as a conduit for? Speaking of Lilith, where the fuck was she?

"She's tending to Andras and Della," Alistair whispered, and I whipped my head to him. How in the hell did he know that was on my mind?

"Did you just read my mind? Because that is not cool, man. Not at all."

"I read your face, love. Lilith is bound to care for them. They both are her progeny—in one way or another. Trust me, I want a word with that woman, too. She should not have used you like that. You were never made for death magic. I cannot believe she did that to you." Alistair pulled me behind him as we picked toward what I hoped was an exit. If I never saw another cave again it would be too soon.

I was still processing his words when light filtered into the half-collapsed tunnel. It was slow going with two unconscious members of the team, and by the time we made it to the mouth of the tunnel I was steaming mad. I barely took in the gray sky or slate-blue water lapping at the rocky shore.

Death. Magic. Death magic. *Death magic?*

I had the strangest urge to slap the shit out of my grandmother when I saw her kneeling over Andras' wounded side. I had half a mind to tackle her into the rocks and pummel her with my fists until she cried uncle.

Instead, I settled on the tried and true: "What the fuck, Lilith?"

Hasty and rude, sure, but I hadn't used her as a conduit for death magics, which was likely fucking up all my other magic. No, I didn't. She did. And I wanted to be all understanding because yeah, we were in dire straits in that damn cave, but honestly? What. The. Fuck.

"Oh, I'm sorry, should I have run down my plan with you and hammer out the details while those bloody elves were gnawing on our flesh? Or maybe you should just say thank you and shut up about it. I saved our lives." Lilith took that time to tie a field dressing on Andras' abdomen before moving to another wound. She wasn't healing him. Maybe she couldn't.

"Or maybe you could use your own fucking body for death magic and leave mine out of it? How'd that be? I can't draw on the earth, Lilith. None of the elements are responding to me. What the fuck did you do?"

"I did what I thought was best, and—" I never got to find out what excuse she was going to give me.

The world seemed to pitch under our feet. I didn't want to, but I looked back at the mouth of the cave.

Death magics or not, we still had an enemy, and it was coming for us.

CHAPTER FOURTEEN

It seemed like a lifetime ago that Striker and I watched sickly pale hands sprout from the ground like daisies. Unfortunately, it took an inordinate amount of time to remember that top-notch event was only yesterday. Or at least I figured it was yesterday. We'd been on this trek long enough for one day to pass into the next no matter what the sun and moon said.

And just like yesterday, these eyeless monsters with their rancid and rotting flesh were too quick. Erupting from the ground, it took me less than a second to fall back, trying desperately to call on the elements that had served me so well the day before.

But unlike my last battle, when I called on the elements to heal me—to fill me even a little—they refused to answer.

Staggering toward Zillah, I heard Hideyo and Della shout for us to fall back. Teresa and Barrett tossed up feeble barrier spells that wouldn't hold the monsters for very long. I didn't have much power, but if I could get him up, it was one less person to carry. One less person to protect. Zillah wasn't on his feet, but he was sitting up, his eyes wide and fixated on the horde spilling out of the ground.

"Fates-forsaken death magic. Bloody fucking Faerie. Of course, this would be the backlash," Lilith muttered to herself as she finished tying the splint on Andras' leg.

I wanted to ask, but we had more pressing problems at the moment. Kinda like getting the fuck out of here.

"We have to get to the water. Those shades won't follow us in the water." Lilith said that like she not only knew what those zombie-like creatures were but knew what to do about them.

And then it dawned on me—death magic. Verena was using death magic when she opened the gate. Those things were borne of death magics.

Zillah was having trouble focusing on my face, so I grabbed his cheeks and made him look at me. "We need to get into the water. Can you shift? Can you carry us?"

He blinked at me; his face so young for a being so old. He inhaled a sharp breath, his eyes gaining just a little bit of focus. "Yes. I can—I can shift."

He shook his head once as if to clear it before he stood. "You have to cover me while I change. I do—I don't know how long it will take. I'm not at my best."

I nodded, not promising him anything. I wanted to, but I couldn't. Anything I promised him right this second would be a lie. Because one thing was clear: I was under no illusions that we would make it out of here. That we would make it off this beach.

Fear leaked out of my pores as I readied myself. Barrett and Teresa's spells wouldn't hold. Nothing short of Aiyana's magicless tree would keep them at bay. Especially if they were called by death magic. I had a feeling the foul sorcery my grandmother had used me for was still coursing through my veins, still roiling beneath my skin. I wanted to think on it a little, but I had trouble focusing on myself, and a bit too busy refusing to let my skin crawl at Zillah's agonized cries. Like Striker the day before, Zillah's change was not sunshine and lollipops. It was a brutal agony of the highest order.

It had to be.

Anything that caused him to make that sound had to be the

worst pain in the universe. Instead of letting that sound shake me to my core, I helped the others clear the beach for the giant sea dragon. Andras was a heavy bastard, but he tried to help as he limped along with his splint made out of gnarled driftwood.

"Let me get him, love. Help the others with the shield," Alistair offered, and I passed off my father before adding my magic to the fight.

My mother and Barrett were doing a complex *obice* spell, the barrier like a mesh of magic keeping the beasts at bay. I added my little bit of magic to theirs, solidifying it to something that might give us enough of a head start into the water.

I didn't trust what Lilith said was true—that they wouldn't follow us. I hoped so, but I didn't believe it. These things seemed to be drawn to death magic, and they wouldn't stop. What I wouldn't give for some of Striker's fire right about now.

Too much magic poured out of me as I lent it to the wall, my legs barely holding me up as I kept the eyeless monsters back. But I didn't fall. My mother and Barrett stood by me, holding me up as we all kept our family safe.

"Zillah is in the water, dear. We need to go," my mother whispered in my ear. But was it a whisper? I had a feeling she was probably yelling it at me.

And then I was up and over a shoulder, a shoulder I knew well enough, as my husband hauled me to our makeshift ride across the water. The spell fizzled out almost immediately, the zombie-like things leaping toward us like they'd just heard the starter pistol.

"Take her," Alistair yelled, and I was given to someone as the light around me promptly went out.

"I can't heal her. The death magic in her blood is too potent. I don't know what to do."

My mother was trying to whisper, *I think*, but she was doing a shit job of it. Granted, we were riding on the back of a water dragon, so it wasn't like there was a lot of real estate to have a private conversation. Well, there was, just not too much above water.

I peeled an eye open, my head rocking a solid eight-point-oh on the Richter scale. Dear sweet mother of all that was holy, why did I feel like I'd been run over by a truck? Oh, right, because my grandmother poured death magic into me like a nut job.

"I can hear you," I groaned, realizing belatedly that I was in Alistair's arms as he kept us firmly fastened to Zillah. I studied what he was holding onto and realized someone somehow must have conjured a harness of some kind so we didn't get pitched overboard. "I don't think that magic agrees with me. Let's never use it again, mm-kay?"

"No bloody shit, love. You stopped breathing there for a minute. I am decidedly not a fan." Alistair's face was haggard with worry, the dirt and blood and fear carving deep grooves into his skin. His nose wasn't swollen anymore, so at least he was healing.

I… wasn't. That couldn't be good.

My mind was as fuzzy as cotton candy—only way less nice—and I hurt all over. Yep. Not good at all.

"Is that why my chest feels like someone sat on it?" I asked because it did. It felt way worse than that, actually. My actual heart hurt, like every beat was a struggle, like someone had a fist around it and was squeezing with all their might.

"Your chest feels like that because I am a first-rate asshole and didn't realize what my magic would do to you." My gaze zeroed in on Lilith, who appeared like she was on death's door. I had a feeling I looked about the same. "I thought that if I pushed my magic through you, with as much power as you had, it would strengthen both sides of the coin. I didn't know that it would attack you, too."

Wait. This was Lilith's power? And my body was rejecting it.

"Take it back. If giving it to me caused this, then take it back." It seemed only logical to me. Uncertainty rose in my gut as I watched Lilith's expression morph from sorrow to abject fear.

"I tried," she whispered. "It won't come back to me even though I called for it."

"So, we're just giving up then?" I scolded her, which in hindsight might not have been the best thing, but whatever. If I was about to kick the bucket, then I was going to be as salty as I wanted to be. "You tried once, and even though this poison in my veins is burning me from the inside out, you're ready to throw in the fucking towel? How about, fuck that?"

I wanted to quit, too, but did she see me doing that? No. I hurt all over. *Alllll over.* Everything from my scalp to my toes felt like it had been put through a fucking meat grinder, and *she* was the one who wanted to quit.

In a spurt of energy I so didn't feel, I sat up. Reaching across Zillah's giant body, I latched onto Lilith's forearm, meeting her shocked expression with my steely gaze. "Try again, or so help me I will haunt your ass until the end of time."

Now that I knew it was there, I could almost feel the poison in my veins. The death magics roiled under my skin like snakes, killing my body faster than it could heal itself. I might not have the elements to heal me, but I wasn't powerless. Pushing, shoving at the blackness that yawned wide within me, I gave Lilith back what was hers.

It was like the steel bands around my heart were snapping one by one. Each bit of power I gave back to her released a tiny bit of the biting pressure in my chest. I sucked in a full breath—my first one since the cave-in—letting the blessed oxygen into my lungs. Air filled me, healing the ravages of Lilith's power. A lightning bolt streaked across the sky, and I could almost feel the deadly yet playful electricity welcome me back. A clap of thunder was all the warning we got before the rain came. Normally, I'd hate being wet, but the droplets hitting my skin were like kisses from the elements.

It was as if they were sentient. As if they missed me. As if they were worried.

I closed my eyes, tilting my head up as each drop healed me bit by bit. I had spent the last four hundred years without these elements—the last four hundred years without them to sustain me—and I couldn't last one day without them now. Hell, less than that. I'd nearly been keeling over after an hour.

Finally opening my eyes, I settled back in the cradle of Alistair's arms. I didn't look at him, but I still pushed healing magic into him. I knew he needed it even if he didn't say. Again, I never took my gaze off of Lilith. She no longer looked like she felt like day-old garbage.

"No more death magic in the Unseelie Court. Noted."

It was a shit apology under the circumstances, but I was trying very hard not to be a shit about it. "Who hasn't healed yet? I can help."

The worst off was Aidan, his body refusing to heal his shattered arm or broken leg. I did the best I could while we were on Zillah, pulling from the air to push life into him. Still, he screamed like I'd branded him when his radial bone went back where it was supposed to go. I had a feeling me drawing on more than one element would have helped more, but it was the best I could do. Nevertheless, he did not wake, and that worried me more than what would happen when we got back on dry land.

Andras and Hideyo had mostly healed on their own, and Zillah had improved quite a bit when he shifted. But we were all a little bit broken, a cobbled-together band of misfit toys going off into the unknown. Not knowing where we were going did not fill me with joy, but if it meant that we weren't being gnawed on by eyeless zombie things, then I was all for it.

"You said those things were shades?" I asked Lilith, my question startling her out of silence.

Out of the two of us, I recovered a sight bit better than she did. Her skin wasn't sallow, but even though she appeared much better, she was still less than tip-top shape. She shook her head, seemingly to clear it, and answered, "Yes. Shades are the result of death magic. Blood magic can also call them. They look different in every realm. It is not something I do lightly—taking life like that. I suppose if I didn't have a consequence, I could have turned into something like my sisters. But Nyx—knowing who my father was—made sure that I would not be able to use that bit of magic without a steep price to pay."

"But we fought those monsters in the crevasse. They were

summoned to the gate when Verena opened it. I don't think Nyx put that limitation on just you," I informed Lilith. "No matter what I did, they would not go away. They just kept coming. Are you sure that the water will keep them back?"

Lilith digested my words for a moment, a green cast to her face as she did so. But her next words chilled me to the absolute bone.

"No, I'm not."

CHAPTER FIFTEEN

The sea churned around Zillah's big body. The dragon knifed through the seemingly endless body of water as if he knew where he was going. I supposed he was getting decent directions from our fearless leader. Niall said he could feel Dušan, and I hoped that was true. I hoped he could lead us to my birth father. I hoped this wasn't just a long line of missteps that took us nowhere.

I couldn't say why I wanted to trust Niall. Nothing he had done so far should allow me to trust him, but something about Niall called to me. He was family in a roundabout way. Not that family hadn't done me wrong. They so had. In fact, ninety percent of the shenanigans that had resulted in my utter ruin resulted from familial intervention.

It was official. I was a crazy person. Only a crazy person would be riding on the back of a water dragon as they ran away from shade-zombies on her way to rescue her literal god of a father from the ruler of the Unseelie Court, AKA, the head honcho of evil: Lucifer.

This was the actual definition of bat-shit insane. I chuckled to myself as I shook my head, embracing my insanity. Niall needed my help, and somehow that edged out my trepidation. I didn't know how it did, but it was a little too late to back out now. Especially since I couldn't actually see an end to this body of water.

Niall's smoky form rested at the scant amount of real estate between Zillah's horns. As fast as we were moving, I had no doubt that he had given Zillah a heading. Or maybe—unlike me—they could sense Dušan in this crazy backward place.

I wanted to climb Zillah's back and have a little logistical meeting with the pair of them, but I also wanted to take a tiny bit of a rest that wasn't mandated by involuntary unconsciousness. Plus, a little brainstorming session over what we would do if we actually met up with the literal devil should probably be penciled in at the top of the docket at some point.

I bet each member of my family was kicking themselves for deciding to ambush me at the gate. None of them should have followed me here. And no amount of positivity was going to make me think we were going to get out of this with just the damage we'd already sustained. Aidan was still out, and the longer time passed without him waking, the more worried I got.

I'd decided to try to heal Aidan a little bit more—if I even could —and was untethered for maybe a millisecond when Zillah's big body thrashed. The unholy roar coming from his mouth chilled me to the bone. And that bone-chilling was happening even though I was hurtling toward the churning water. In the next instant, someone snagged my hand, keeping me from falling into what I now knew was monster-infested water.

The monsters themselves were something out of a Lovecraft novel, miniature Leviathan things with needles for teeth like a piranha. And there were thousands of them thrashing in the water as they attacked Zillah.

I was too busy staring at the growing pool of red staining the water to really worry too much about the hand that held me. I knew it was Alistair. I also knew that if he dropped me, I was going to be a monster's dinner.

Zillah let out another unholy roar, one that should have scared these parasites off if they knew what was good for them, but they paid him no mind. Alistair yanked me up onto Zillah's back, fastening something to my waist before he said a single thing to me. Rage painted his face in his fiery runes, his charcoal skin overtaking his human form.

"Help Zillah, love," he yelled before tossing a rope over the side of Zillah's colossal body and jumping after it.

"Alistair!" I screamed, trying to reach him but failing once I'd reached the end of my tether. I could see him, though, and he was hacking near the water with his flaming scythe, trying to knock the monsters away from Zillah's side.

Help Zillah, love.

Okay. I could do that. Crouching on his big back, I shoved my power into the big lug, letting the air and water heal as much as the monsters took. But they were attacking too fast, too much. Zillah's speed and my power couldn't keep up with the damage.

I changed tactics, calling on the water to help. But the water didn't answer me this time, too busy taking the blood offered for itself. A flash fire of rage made my skin prickle, and that was my only warning before lightning rained down on the water, stabbing like knives.

With surgical precision, brilliant blue bolts of lightning speared the Leviathans burning them to ash. The problem was there was not enough lightning in the entire realm to take care of the horde attacking Zillah. We had to get out of the water. There was nothing else I could do. Not unless... Unless I pushed Zillah where I wanted him to be.

As insane as it was, I didn't see a whole lot of other options. Pulling on Zillah, on the elements, on everything in this realm, I pushed, forcing Zillah out of the water, out of the horde, out of it all. All I thought of was land—we needed land.

The push felt like I was ripping myself in two. A sensation that was not wholly unexpected since I was shoving a giant serpent and all the little fleas attached to it through space and time. When we landed with a giant splash in a rocky shallow—so not quite land, but close—I may or may not have vomited on his scales.

Zillah did not notice. He was too busy thrashing, trying to get the last of the Leviathans off of him. Alistair, Andras, and Hideyo jumped in to help, stabbing at the remaining monsters with their blades. Zillah shuddered, thrashed once again, and then began to shrink. His body shifted back to his human form, likely without his consent as unconsciousness pulled at him.

Niall and Lilith were carrying Aidan to shore while Teresa and Barrett were volleying fireballs and inky-purple smoke bombs at the few surviving monsters. The rest of us were doing our level best not to drown in the crashing waves and swift undertow. I knifed through the water, latching onto Zillah's ravaged human form as I hauled us both toward the shore.

Zillah—I could tell without even being out of the water yet—was in bad shape. Inky-red blood stained the water around us, wafting through the waves like red ink. If we didn't get this bleeding stopped, I didn't know if the kid would survive. And I knew Zillah was older than me by several thousand years, but he looked so young. Stuck in his dragon form so long, he'd likely been arrested at the age he'd made the bargain. Zillah had a teenage-boy build, fine-boned with a hint of the man he'd become—the man he'd become if he made it through this mess.

The rocky beach was mostly black sand interspersed with razor-sharp green glass and gnarled driftwood. I tried to find a clear spot, kicking away a few larger pieces of wood only to realize that they were not wood at all but bones.

I refused to ponder that too hard, focusing on Zillah and what I could do for him. Huge chunks of flesh were ripped from his body, parts of his leg cut all the way down to the bone. He was missing fingers on his left hand. I tried very hard not to look too closely at his injuries as tunnel vision hit me hard.

Unlike when he was being attacked, this time when I called on the water for assistance, it answered, funneling power into Zillah's battered body. But the water only answered for so long, the mercurial element leaving me to patch up the rest of Zillah's injuries on my own.

"Where in the bloody hell are we?" Barrett demanded, shoving sodden hair off his face as he knelt next to me as we tried to patch Zillah up.

"I have absolutely no idea. All I thought was we needed land. I can't say I deliberated too much on it." I was the queen of not looking before I leapt, but in this one instance, I didn't think I did too bad.

"I'm not complaining," Andras muttered, kneeling next to me and wrapping an arm around my shoulders. "You did good, kid. We need to stop his bleeding and then move. We can't stay on this beach."

I agreed with him even though I didn't say it out loud. There was a hum on the air, a pulse of power raking across my exposed skin. We were too exposed here. Instead of the water—who was being an epic shithead right now—I coaxed the earth into Zillah. Letting the element fill him, I watched as the largest of the injuries repaired themselves. But there was only so much the element could do here in this muted place, so when the bleeding stopped, I did, too, hoping that what I'd done was enough.

It didn't feel like it.

"We need to move," Niall echoed, pulling the injured dragon from the shore.

Andras helped Hideyo with Aidan, and we followed Niall to an outcropping of barren trees. I took in my surroundings for the first time since I'd dropped us in the shallows. The sun was dimmed by a green cast, the sky a gangrenous roiling of clouds. Further up the shore were ruined stone buildings, their roofs caved in some places. A crumbling bridge led to a dark castle, foreboding spires reaching up to the sky like a clawed hand.

If I could pick a place that embodied a "*fuck that*" vibe, this would legit be it. It wasn't cold enough to snow, but little tufts of white fell from the sky—which considering where we were—did not fill me with joy.

Niall led us within the tree line, and I appreciated the little bit of cover. "We have to leave them here," he murmured, setting Zillah down on a bed of slimy leaves and black moss. "The maze is too treacherous. They could die."

"Maze?" Alistair asked, echoing my thoughts.

Niall seemed to nod but did not take his eyes off the wounded dragon. "You took us to the right place, Max. This is the Unseelie Court. But it isn't like we can just break into the castle to find Dušan—if that is even where he is. This whole bloody kingdom is full of booby traps. We have to make it to the castle first."

I was still stuck on *"if that is even where he is"* part of the convo to get too mired in the booby trap portion of that statement. Teresa, though, was on the ball.

"Booby traps? Maze? What is this, *Indiana Jones*? What in the blue fuck did you get us into, Niall?"

"What I want to know," I broke in, interrupting what was probably going to be a spectacular motherly tirade, "is what do you mean by *'if that is even where he is?'*"

Niall growled at us, and if the man had hair, I was sure he was three seconds away from ripping it out. "I don't know. All I had was a heading, but now that we're here, I feel Dušan everywhere. Don't you? Like a buzz on my flesh. He is here, I feel it. But I don't know where."

That was understandable. I felt that buzz, too, and I told him so. "But a maze?" I asked, wanting to clarify that little nugget of info.

"Lucifer is a grade-A prick and loves to fuck with anyone attempting to access the Court. You had to have seen the bones on the shore. Had I known the maze started in the water, I would have suggested another route. But it's like I can't think in this body anymore. I know I've been here. I know I've seen everything there is to see. I've been trapped on this side of the wall for centuries. I knew this day would come. But everything is so bloody fuzzy." Niall shook his head. "I don't know how much help I will be to you anymore. I don't know if I can find him."

A whimper fell from his mouth, the sound practically gutting me.

I had to do something. Again, without much in the way of forethought, I put my hand on Niall's shoulder. The giant smoke monster was nearly solid to the touch, and he shuddered at the contact. Like I'd done to so many others, I pushed, searching for the thread of whatever it was that held him down, kept him locked up.

The blackened thread of magic was old. Old and fetid. Slowly poisoning him as it tied itself around and around his mind. It reminded me so much of the threads on Cinder, on Striker. It had a similar signature. But Soren was dead, and so was Verena. What had Niall said? Abaddon had done this to him?

And this was a magic that could not be broken by death or time. This was a magic that could only be broken by someone like me. Like so many other spells, I plucked at the oily threads, snapping them one by one.

Even before my glamour was lifted, no one could keep me out. And Abaddon wouldn't be able to, either.

CHAPTER SIXTEEN

Niall did not look like himself. Or maybe now that he was no longer an eight-foot-tall smoke monster, he looked like himself for the first time in four centuries. He was still impossibly tall, but that was about where the similarities ended. Golden hair cascaded down his back in a sheet. And by golden, I did not mean blond. I meant gold. Little flecks of metallic radiance glinted in the low light. His skin was paler than the palest human, without so much as a hint of pink or yellow undertone.

His eyes matched his hair, and although they were eerie in the extreme, the shade also fit him. His nose was like a knife blade, his cheeks sharp like mine, his jaw matching them both. A pair of jagged horns peeked out of his hair, too large to be called dainty and too small to be foreboding. A thin line of black indented his face from one temple, over his nose to the other temple, a trail of three dots underscoring the curve of his cheeks. His lips were full but held no color, the flesh just as pale as the rest of him. He had dark slashes for eyebrows, the hair in no way matching the rest of him, but somehow it pulled his features together.

He wasn't pretty, nor would I call him handsome, but he was

unearthly attractive in a way I couldn't name. The smoke monster was Niall. *This* was Hades.

He stared at his hands for long moments—moments we probably did not have—in awe of his body now returned to him. "You actually did it. I didn't think you would be able to break that spell, but you actually bloody did it."

"Brother," Lilith breathed, pushing between Barrett and Marcus to get to the tall man. She wrapped her arms around his waist and hugged him. "I didn't believe you when you said... Fates, how can you forgive me? I didn't look for you. I thought you were dead. I thought..." Lilith began to sob, and it was the first time I'd ever seen her show that kind of emotion. Bernadette had always been that stiff-upper-lip kind of British woman, even though she was neither British nor the aging grandmother she portrayed herself as.

Andras just blinked at his uncle, his expression blank. Just like the rest of us, Andras hadn't believed Niall when he told us who he was, hadn't believed him when he said he could feel Dušan calling him.

None of us had believed him at all.

I wanted to apologize to him, but time was of the essence, and it was running out. Plus, in that dark part of myself I so desperately did not like to acknowledge, I was jealous. Lilith had thought her brother was dead. And now, by some weird turn of events, she had him back. I wasn't ever getting Maria back. There was no spell to do, no voyage to traverse. Maria was gone, and as happy as I was that Lilith got her second chance, I was bitter as fuck about not ever getting mine.

Which is probably why I was bitchy as all get out when I said, "I love a family reunion as much as the next gal, but I was under the impression we needed to *not* be caught here. We need to hide Aidan and Zillah and pray no one finds them. The elements are wonky as fuck here and have no desire to help me out. I can't heal them any more than I already have."

Alistair squeezed my hand, and instantly, I felt terrible. Lilith's face fell, and that gutted me more than I'd care to admit. I was an asshole of the highest order.

"I'm sorry," I murmured. "That was a bitchy thing to say, and I'm a dick for ruining your moment. I'm a jealous shitbag."

Lilith didn't give me any shit. Like the grandmother I'd come to rely on this last year, she broke away from her brother and enveloped me in a hug. "You're healing, dear. You can be a jealous shitbag every now again if you need to."

"I'm glad you got your brother back."

"I'm sorry you lost Maria. I'd get her back for you if I could."

"I know. You're awesome like that."

"Okay," Barrett broke in, "this is touching and all that rot, but we are in enemy territory. Maze? Booby traps?" He snapped his fingers like we were supposed to hop to, and I, for one, adored his peeved nature.

"It will be an unfortunate follow-the-leader sort of thing," Hades answered. "There are too many traps to count, and the route is long. The only good thing is I don't believe they are altered too often, so my last foray into this batch of idiocy should provide us with enough information to stay alive. Not getting caught is the name of the game here, boys and girls. And there are plenty of ways to do that."

Hades' speech was less than comforting, but honesty was appreciated, especially here.

"I don't know where Dušan is. He could be in the maze. He could be in the castle. He could be roasting on a spit in Lucifer's kitchen for all I know. So keep your eyes peeled."

I looked down at our wounded. I didn't want to leave them behind, but I didn't see another option. Zillah wasn't going to come to anytime soon, but Aidan seemed to be rousing. As much as we needed to move, I couldn't—we couldn't—without making sure they were protected.

Aidan's bottle-green eyes flashed open, fear filling them as he struggled to sit up. Hideyo and I put a quelling hand on his shoulders. "Easy there, friend. Easy," Hideyo murmured.

"Where are the elves? What happened?" Aidan croaked, and

for the first time since we found him unconscious, did I breathe a little sigh of relief.

"Vaporized. You missed the zombie-shades and the piranha sea monsters while you were out."

Aidan's eyes flew wide. "Zombie-shades and piranha sea monsters? What the fuck kind of place is this?"

Alistair huffed from behind me, and I glanced up to see him scanning the tree line for threats. "An offshoot of Hell would be my guess. Bloody Lucifer. How in the Fates-forsaken fuck did he build this much power and hold it under wraps for this long? Do the Fates not care one whit about the rest of us?"

I followed his gaze to the Unseelie Court and its destroyed landscape. He had a point. Lucifer had either built this from scratch—which I thought was unlikely—or he'd taken over someone else's kingdom. The air had the feeling of the downtrodden and long dead. The only thing I could equate it to was the same feeling one got when traversing near the decommissioned concentration camps in Europe. It felt like torture and death and persecution.

If I squinted, I could envision what this place once was—before it became the devil's playground.

But I also knew that the Fates had their hands tied. But who or what, I wasn't sure. Nor was I sure what bargain they made that kept them shackled to silence.

"You and Zillah are hurt," I began, unable to explain the how's or why's. "There is a maze we have to go through, but you aren't well enough to—"

"No," Aidan growled. "Not without me, you're not."

His vehemence made me want to cry. Aidan took his job as a paladin more seriously than I realized.

"It's bad enough you went to Hell without me. I'm not letting you do this, too. Your grandmother would skin me alive if you got hurt."

Lilith huffed. "While under normal circumstances, you'd be right, I can't under good conscience let you go in there. Max will want to save you instead of the other way 'round, and then she'll end up getting hurt because of it. No, my dear boy, staying here and keeping watch over Zillah is a much better plan." Lilith crouched next to Aidan. "You have done everything I have ever asked of you and more. It is not a shame to do what you must to survive, dear."

Aidan did not appear appeased in the least, but he sat up and put on a brave face.

"We're going to hide you, okay? But you are in charge of Zillah." I knew that if I didn't give Aidan a job to do, he would end up following us, anyway. It was in his nature to protect—to care for someone other than himself. Maybe if he stood watch over Zillah, I wouldn't have to worry about him hobbling through booby traps on his own.

"You're just making me watch him because you don't want me to follow you," he grumbled, guessing our motivations easily enough. "I used to do the same shit to Ian when I wanted him out of the way."

"Oh, get over it. You're hurt, and Zillah is unconscious," Della griped, totally done with Aidan's bullshit. "We can't carry him and worry about you, too. Watch over the man who carried your ass on his back to safety and quit bitching about it." The vampire was showing quite a bit of fang, and I didn't blame her one bit. This shit was stressful.

Properly chastised by Della's epic "Mom voice," Aidan snapped his mouth shut, giving her a nod. "Fine, but everyone better come out of there or else."

I wanted to smile at his empty threat, but I couldn't. There was too much at risk, too much to lose if we failed.

"We'll do our best," I muttered, unable to lie even in this. "Now sit still. I need to ward you two against harm. If you ever feel up to it, try and travel out of here. Take Zillah home with you. Don't leave him to this place. He deserves a life." *And so do you,* I thought, trying not to make this sound like a goodbye. Aidan had sacrificed his whole life for someone else. Protecting his brother, in service to a king, trying to keep me from dying for the thousandth time. If he made it out of here and I didn't, he needed to live.

"Don't push it, Max," was all he said back, and I had a feeling that was the best I was going to get.

Without anything better to say, I began my wards, offering protection and concealment, and health. When I was done, Teresa added to them. When she finished hers, Barrett added to them both.

Unable to voice just how much I did not like leaving him to the dangers in this rotten place, I got up, walking away from one of the few people in this universe who hadn't yet let me down.

"Stay safe, mate," Alistair murmured before joining me, and the pair of us stared at the crumbling city at the base of the castle. That would be our maze, our obstacle. For a split second, I wanted to cry. Here I was about to head into the unknown, and as mad and scared as I was, I was glad Alistair was here with me.

How fucking selfish did that make me?

"Stop it," Alistair scolded, and I really had to wonder if he could read my mind.

"You really are going to have to tell me if you have somehow turned telepathic. It's rude not to, you know."

Instead of answering me, he pressed a kiss to my mouth. And not a quick one, either. It was slow and full of promise. It felt like a promise for a future, and I so wanted that with him. "Not telepathic, love," he finally answered when we came up for air. "But you had that guilty look on your face like you wanted something you knew you shouldn't have. We can't know what is waiting for us, love, but I'd rather be at your side fighting with you than knowing you were off on your own any day of the week. Don't regret me being here, because I wouldn't have it any other way."

I wanted to joke, but I just didn't have it in me. Instead, I told him I loved him, because who knew how many more times in this life I would get to. "I love you to the ends of the earth and far beyond. Vaster than Heaven or Hell or any of the worlds in between."

And I'll do that in this life or the next.

I thought it but didn't say it. Still, I figured he heard me.

CHAPTER SEVENTEEN

Hades informed us that there were several paths into the maze as well as several exits. I found that fact comforting, even though it offered a high probability that we would get lost. Mazes meant we could get out. Labyrinths were a whole other story. The absolute last thing we needed was a labyrinth with only one entrance that led us to the middle of who knew what.

Hades led us to a nearly blocked off entrance close to the copse of trees where we left Aidan and Zillah. It was hard to gauge how far we would need to travel, and no one wanted to think about what we would need to do while we were in that maze. It was possible Dušan was stuck in there somewhere, but I didn't think we would be that lucky. What were the odds an immortal being with eons of life would get tripped up by a damn maze?

Us? I could totally see that happening.

This path was bisected by a fallen stone monolith, the crumbling rock blocking half of the entrance. As soon as we crossed what I considered the threshold of the maze, the biting power that had raked my skin since we'd gotten here sizzled against my flesh. I hissed at the pain, but shook my head when

Alistair gave me a questioning look. If what Hades said was true, then this was Dušan's signature. Or at least I hoped this was him. If it wasn't, then we had a whole host of other problems.

The maze walls were higher than fifty feet, and as craggy and pitted as they were, they seemed too steep to climb. It wasn't like we could just scale to the top and walk this bitch. No, this would have to be done the old-fashioned way.

I just hoped Hades remembered the damned path.

The maze floor was littered with bones and other unsavory things. Like ruined armor and broken weapons. Whatever obstacle or trap that had been here before did not seem to be here now. Not that I was complaining, but it did fill me with a sense of dread as we waited for the other shoe to drop. It was too quiet here—the only sound was our shuffling feet as we carefully stepped where Hades told us to. In Faerie proper, there was always a bird cawing or a babbling brook or *something*. Here in this little pit of doom? Nada.

The earth vibrated under our feet, nothing like what I did when I was mad, more like the concussion that radiated outward when an elephant stomped. A looming shadow fell over us, and I stared *up, up, up* to find the biggest creature I'd ever seen resting his shoulder against one of the maze walls. Easily twenty feet tall, the giant wore a sleeveless tunic and breeches, and other than the bands around his wrists and ankles, he wore nothing else.

No shoes, no belt, no weapons. Which I supposed was good since if this guy had a weapon it would have to be enormous, and we would be ten times more screwed than we currently were. Shaggy haired with an unkempt beard, the man's face boasted only one eye at the center of his forehead, with two divots in his face where his other eyes should be but weren't. A single eye that locked gazes with me and refused to blink. Well, I was so small in comparison that he could be looking at any one of us, but I had a feeling he was looking at just me.

I should have felt a healthy amount of fear—I mean, this was a fucking cyclops—but something inside me whispered that this giant was not a threat exactly. Greek mythology told of three different types of cyclops. The imprisoned children of Gaia, the Homeric ones that were raving monsters, and the wall builders. Since Homer had been full of shit in regard to Cronus, AKA Lucifer, I had little in the way of faith that any of his other bullshit tales were true.

And that was probably why I stayed where I was when my other compatriots decided to try and rush the giant. Andras attacked first, his smoky demon body all talons and teeth as he raced toward the cyclops. He didn't make it very far, though. With a bored flick of his hand, the cyclops flung Andras back to us, his smoky body phasing back to his human one when he landed in a heap.

Then the rest attacked at once—well, Hades, Lilith, and I didn't. Hades and Lilith just stood there, not lifting a finger or saying a damn word. Hades, the sod, had a little smile playing at the corners of his mouth.

I rolled my eyes and snapped my fingers, transporting myself in front of my family. The group as a whole took a few seconds to skid to a stop.

"What the fuck, Max?" Barrett scolded, the purple-red magic on his palms fizzling out. The rest of them seemed to share his sentiment, but I answered Barrett all the same.

"What the fuck, what? Has this man attacked you in any way? Has he done anything but defend himself? Do you see Hades or Lilith attacking? No. I don't know what kind of bullshit game this is, but attacking is not the answer, so..." I turned my back to my family and craned my neck so I could stare at the giant. "What do you want?"

"You're no fun, you know that?" the cyclops muttered before plopping down in the middle of the path. And when this dude plopped, the whole of the earth shook. It was similar to when I made the earth pitch, and I barely kept my balance.

"So I've been told. You got a name, dude?" I sighed, pinching the skin between my brows. This was going to be a riddle or a bargain, I could just feel it.

"Argus," he answered, seemingly pleased I asked. Argus was

one of the three cyclops that made Zeus' thunderbolts. Or at least that was the way Hesiod told it. Who knew how much of that was bullshit?

"Okay, Argus, I would like to go past you so I can get my father back. Are you going to let us pass?" Yes, my tone was exasperated as fuck, but come on. Unless I bargained my ass off, we weren't getting past this guy. Like ever.

Argus put on a show of tapping his bottom lip as he pretended to ponder something. It was ripely overdone and dramatic. Who knew cyclopes were such bad actors? Not me, that's for sure. Granted, I didn't think about cyclopes in general, so I couldn't judge.

"Maybe," Argus said in a sing-song voice, which was disconcerting as hell because no man who was that big and that menacing should ever sing-song anything. Ever. "But maybe not. You did take all the fun out of smiting you all. No one ever comes to visit me anymore. How am I supposed to enjoy myself if I don't get to squash people?"

I wanted to roll my eyes, but I managed not to. Argus was acting like he was a third grader reading from a shitty script. "Have you tried knitting? I've heard that's a cool hobby. Plus, if I don't find Dušan, then it won't really matter, now will it? This little slice of Faerie will all go poof, and you probably with it."

Argus' face lit up at my joke, but his frown was real when I mentioned I was Dušan's daughter. "A daughter of Chaos? You shouldn't be here."

I shrugged. "No shit. I should be on a beach sipping booze from an umbrella drink and enjoying my honeymoon. Instead, I have to stop a civil war, an apocalypse, and rescue my father all at the same time. I'm tired. I'm cranky. I want this over with so I can go sleep for a decade or three, but I can't until you. Move. Out. Of. My. Way. So, what's it gonna be? You want something, so spit it out."

Argus regarded me for a long moment. "I lost my brothers because I would not give myself over to Cronus. Because I would not bargain with him. He killed them in front of me as punishment for the cell we made. To further twist the knife, before he killed them, he made me create these manacles. He said he would spare my brothers if I made them, wore them, and remanded myself to this maze." He gestured to the bands around his wrists and ankles. "They keep me here. Unable to leave. Unable to die. Unable to hide. And then he killed them anyway. You lost your sister. You understand my rage."

How he knew I lost Maria was anyone's guess, but it didn't matter.

"Here is my bargain, daughter of Chaos. Remove my bonds, and I will step out of your way. Don't, and we'll both sit here until this world is no more."

A freebie pass through the maze in exchange for removing a man from bondage? No contest. I would gladly remove those manacles if it meant he would be free.

Just like me, he'd earned it.

But I wasn't a sucker either, so I made sure to clarify. Alistair had taught me that the devil really was in the details after all. "And by step out of my way, you mean what? I think I'm going to need some details, bud."

Argus' smile was damn near boyish. He was absolutely delighted that I called him on this little bit of almost deception.

"How about this," I offered, "I remove your bonds as best as I am able, and you step aside and let us through the maze. You may not harm anyone in my party, nor may you inform anyone that we're here." I paused to turn to Alistair, "Did I forget anything?"

"You might want to add a caveat that he cannot impede us when we exit the maze, nor lie in wait for us to murder us after we exit. Just to cover all the bases."

I turned back to Argus. "What he said. Deal?"

"A goddess married to a demon? I wonder what your father thinks about that," Argus remarked as if he had all the time in the world. Wasn't this the same guy who wanted to burn this bitch to the ground two seconds ago?

"He likes my husband just fine, thank you. And what does that have to do with anything? Quit stalling. Do we have a deal or not?"

Argus stared at me for a long second, his lone eye piercing me where I stood. What? I had a limited amount of time and he was wasting it. "You are very rude, daughter of Chaos."

"And you're wasting my fucking time. I have until the Blood Moon to get Dušan back or else Faerie goes bye-bye. What about that time constraint is lost on you? Do we have a deal?" I repeated, you know, just in case he fucking forgot what we were doing here. Did he not want his bonds off or what?

I was super tempted to just snap my way around him, but I was hesitant to do that after the whole bridge incident. Who knew what was behind his giant body or what kind of traps were just chilling back there? I knew I was going to find out soon enough, but still, I didn't want to trip one if I didn't have to.

"You've played enough, Argus," Hades called as he sidled up next to me. "Stop torturing her and complete the bargain. Time is of the essence."

Even with the backup, I wanted to smash something. It shouldn't take Hades' intervention to get Argus to make the deal he'd specifically requested—even if it did have a few caveats.

"But it means I can't play with them when they're through. How am I supposed to have any fun if I can't try and ambush them later?"

I blinked, blinked again, and then completely lost the very last shred of my mind. Snapping my fingers, I shoved Argus up to his feet and pressed him against the giant wall. I wasn't a hundred percent sure what I'd put into that spell, but I was for damn certain he wasn't going to be able to move anytime soon. A few weeks ago, I'd had trouble lifting a single wolf, now I was just pissed enough to move a whole fucking giant. Granted, that was before my glamour was gone, but still. I was kind of proud of myself.

"You could have had your bonds off if you were actually willing to deal. Now you get nothing," I scolded Argus, readily admitting to myself that I had just likely made an enemy.

Did I care at that point? Absolutely not.

Would I care later? Probably.

"When you decide to get your head out of your ass, come find me and I'll help you. Until then, Argus, I want you to think long and hard about how much your *fun* is worth." I turned to the slack-jawed group of people behind me. "Let's go."

Out of all of them, the only ones who were not even a little surprised at my antics were Alistair, Barrett, and my mother. In fact, Teresa and Barrett were trying their level best not to start laughing.

Hades was miraculously paler than he had been moments earlier—a feat I didn't think was possible—his mouth open wide in shock. "How? Bu—*how*?"

Barrett snickered before slapping him on the shoulder. "First time? No worries, mate, you'll get used to it. How about you lead on then?"

Barrett guided Hades past Argus, and the rest followed them. I stayed back to impart one last thing to the cyclops. "I am not an enemy. When you come for me—and I know you will—remember that."

With that said, I brushed past him, releasing him from his confines as I went.

But he didn't come after us, and he didn't say another word. I couldn't tell if that was a good thing or not.

With my luck? I was likely in for a world of hurt.

CHAPTER EIGHTEEN

Hades was still stunned at my exchange with Argus by the time we'd rounded the second and third turns in the maze, which I supposed I didn't blame him for. Still, he needed to get his head in the game before we accidentally stepped on Faerie's version of a land mine and blew ourselves to kingdom come. We arrived at a weird three-pronged fork in the path. One way seemed to go below ground, the other went up, and the third stayed the course. All three seemed to be sucky options, but Hades was giving us nothing.

He just stood there and blinked, his shock getting the better of him.

"Okay, Obi Wan, wanna tell us which way we're supposed to go?" I quipped. I'd practically skipped when I came back to the group, but the longer we walked the less joy I felt. It was probably a bad thing that I felt a sense of satisfaction at pinning Argus to the wall. I mean, he was stuck here against his will and had watched his brothers die. Then again, if I had watched Lucifer kill my sister, it was unlikely that I would be dragging my feet on the deal that would free me to take him out, so there was that.

"Obi Wan?" he finally answered.

I shook my head. "*Star Wars* reference. Unless you're up on your pop culture, you won't get it."

"Pop culture?"

"Popular culture. What the kids are saying these days? Never mind. What I mean is, do you want to get over your shock and get to the leading portion of our endeavor? Is that clear enough?"

Hades' stunned expression didn't waver. "But you just picked him up and shoved him against the wall."

Ah. So he was still stuck on that.

"She also lifted a giant water dragon out of Siren-infested water and saved us all. How are you confused about the cyclops and not that?" Teresa quipped, and I had to hold back a snort. Leave it to my mother to get to the meat of the issue.

Hades' face paled. "You're right. How did you do that?"

I shrugged and shook my head. "I don't know, man, I just work here. Time crunch? Dušan? Can we go?"

It was a little disconcerting that my display of power was shocking. I mean, I thought he needed my help. Wasn't that what he said? That he needed me to find Dušan. He needed me to do this job. If he needed me so bad, wasn't it a good thing that I was coming through for him in a clutch?

"But you are a demigod. Not a goddess. How are you able to do all this? I was there the day you were born. I knew your mother. I —" He shook his head. "Those are not demigod powers, Massima."

A shrug was as best as I could come up with. "When we find Dušan, you can ask him. He would know better than I would. For now, I'm just trying not to be an asshole about the powers I do have, and that's about all I can do. Now, that path?" I pointed to the one that went up. The castle itself was on a higher elevation than where we were currently standing, so it sort of made sense, but I couldn't be sure in a place like this.

Hades shook his head, gesturing to the path that went below ground, the path lit by unearthly blue torches that seemed to be fueled by magic alone. "That is the way, but follow my feet. One wrong step will bring you a world of pain." He shuddered at the thought, and I figured it was best not to ask him why. The tunnel itself gave me the creeps. I didn't want to know what else would make a god shudder.

In a straight line, we followed Hades, stepping where he did as we made our way further underground. The walls were a wet, slimy mess, the still-rotting corpses of other wanderers lumped in the corners. I tried not to heave, but the smell was horrendous, the air thick with decomposition. I was definitely getting *Temple of Doom* vibes from this place and that was not comforting at all.

Especially since my connection to the elements seemed... just *gone*.

Hades made one sure stride after the other, only stepping on the wide tiles that had an hourglass etched into them. A part of the floor possessed a deep crack, the fissure several feet wide. Hades attempted to jump it—which he succeeded—but he fudged the landing a bit. Hades stumbled onto another tile, and even though he tried to pull his foot back, the tile depressed with an ominous-sounding hiss.

I—along with the rest of the group—stood stock-still, waiting to see what kind of horror the maze would subject us to. I had a feeling it had something to do with water—at least based on the water-logged and rotting corpses, but what did I know? But no water came.

Instead, a smoky fog crept up from the fissure, coalescing into the shape of a woman. The woman stared at her transparent hands for a moment before turning to us. When she locked eyes on me, she partially solidified, and I nearly hit my knees.

"Maria?" I croaked, wanting to reach for her, but something held me back. Not something, someone. Alistair's arm was banded around my middle, holding me to him so I couldn't move. It reminded me so much of our trip to Hell. How he wouldn't let me fall into that great abyss.

I wanted to be comforted—that he wouldn't let me fall—but all I wanted was to reach for her. Why wasn't he letting me go?

Maria's face was a grayed-out ghost of what she once was, her expression sad and accusing all at the same time.

"You didn't follow me, sister. Why didn't you follow me?" she asked, her words hitting me like a slap. It was a question I'd been asking myself since she fell into that abyss. To have her voice it now when we were in this place, hit me harder than anything else she could have asked.

"I tried." My voice sounded like broken glass. "But I couldn't reach you before you fell. I tried," I pleaded, begging her to understand. "But you're here now. Come back to me, and we'll find Dušan. He said you were gone, but maybe he can get you your body back. He can help."

She smiled a sad little smile, a bitter pull of her lips that told me just how disappointed she was in me. "You were supposed to follow me. You were supposed to die, not me. I was meant to live, not you. Isn't that what you promised me? That I would live?"

I wanted to vomit. Of all the things Maria could say to me, I never thought she would want me to die. I tried to pull out of Alistair's arms, but his hold was iron-clad. Maybe if I could hug her, touch her, then she would realize that we could fix this. We could get her a body—if not the one she had, then maybe Dušan could make her another one. I could fix this...

"Please, just let me try to help. I can help."

Maria's face twisted, her lips snide, her eyes cruel. "You do nothing but cause pain and destruction. That is all you will ever be good for. Lachesis told me so. Sitting next to me in that frigid darkness she warned me of what you would bring." Maria tossed her head back, a mirthless laugh spilling from her lips. "All you bring is death."

Those last words were a hiss as her face decomposed right before my eyes. Her cheeks hollowed out, her skin shriveled to rot, her eyes yellowed before morphing into glowing embers, their light unearthly and cold. Maria took a shuffling step toward me, reaching for me, as if she wanted to drag me back down into that fissure with her and keep me there.

A sharp crack of a slap whipped across my cheek and I blinked. I shook my head, searching the room for Maria's corpse. Instead I found freezing waist-high water and my mother shaking the shit out of me.

"Wake the fuck up, Maxima." She yelled right in my face.

I blinked hard, shaking my head, slowly coming to the realization that Maria wasn't there. She wasn't... Loss hit me like a slap as my mother raised her hand again to knock some sense into me. Before her palm could connect with my already-sore cheek, I caught her wrist.

"I'm awake," I croaked, trying my best not to cry even though I knew it was likely inevitable.

Maria wasn't there. She was never there.

Alistair's hold on me turned from restraining to a kind of hug.

"Good. Now, remove the spell you cast to keep you entrenched in the corridor so we can pull you out." Teresa said it like she was talking to a half-crazed toddler on a sugar high.

Confused, I peered at my wrists. Glowing blue ropes were wrapped around them, their ends attached to the wet walls by nothing but magic as I hung between them. Sure. Yep, I could totally see myself doing some dumb shit like this. I pulled on the bonds, but they would not come undone. I mentally plucked at the spell, trying to rip the threads of it until I was free, but the water was rising and my mother and Alistair were still in here, and I had no idea how we were going to get out.

We didn't have enough time. There was never enough time.

Fear and shame hit me like a one-two punch, and I pulled again at my bonds. I yanked and wrenched, but they were immovable. Whatever magic I'd cast without realizing it was potent as hell because I couldn't break the spell.

"You guys have to go. Follow the others. Get out," I ordered. "I can't—I can't break the spell I cast."

Neither Teresa nor Alistair moved an inch, but it was Alistair who spoke. "Go, Teresa. I'll stay with her. Make sure the others get out."

He said it so calmly, so serenely. Like resigning himself to my fate was no big deal. Teresa blinked, her eyes turning lazy for a second before she nodded and half-slogged, half-swam away. Even in the low light, I could still see the threads of the working he'd cast with his voice. He'd spelled her so she would get out. I didn't know he could even do that.

And he'd done that for me.

I was still stuck on the wonder of it when he removed his banded arm around my middle and sloshed in front of me so he could look me in the eye. "Now, my love, I want you to call on whatever elements you have in your arsenal. I want you to do whatever it is you have to do. But you and I are getting out of this bloody tunnel. There will be no dying. There will be no conceding. You are doing this, Max."

He wasn't going to leave. He needed to leave. I couldn't protect him. I couldn't protect anyone. Everyone got hurt because of me.

"No, love. I'm not leaving you. And no one gets hurt because of you. You can't control Fate and you can't take responsibility for everyone."

Until he said those words, I'd had no idea I voiced my concerns aloud. Unless he was reading my mind. That was always an option.

"Now think. What can you use to break a spell?"

Shivering at the aching cold seeping into my leathers, I tried to think. My athames could cut through spells. Maybe. Unless it had to be me that used them, and then we were likely fucked. "My athames?"

Alistair nodded, grabbing one blade from its sheath. In one swift motion, he sliced through the blue magical rope that held my right wrist and then moved to the left. Once I was free, the pair of us began the slog down the corridor, the water chest-high on us. But swimming in leathers and weapons was about as ineffective as carrying a bowling ball in a swimming pool.

Wanting to slap myself, I snapped my fingers, pressing the water away from us, shoving it against the walls. Alistair and I fell to the tunnel floor, but he grabbed me up, setting me on my feet.

The power I needed to shove at the water was substantial, the use of it draining the shit out of me because there was just so much of it. No element could help me here, and it was too much water, too much power, too... I nearly fell, and rather than ask if I was okay, Alistair yanked me off my feet and tossed me over his shoulder, breaking into a run.

He was right to run, right to haul as much ass as he wanted.

Because I wasn't going to be able to hold this water for much longer.

CHAPTER NINETEEN

My poor, feeble spell began to break down almost immediately, the walls of water falling like dominoes as Alistair sprinted as if our lives depended on it. They kind of did, so I didn't fault the man. Instead I tried my level best not to pass out or let my magic fail. The trickle of my nose pouring blood was not at all comforting, though.

Again, we were running out of time.

Despite the water, the blue-flame torches flickered their eerie light, highlighting just how vast the tunnel was. And just how fucked we'd be if we didn't get out of here.

A commotion behind—or rather in front of Alistair—had a rush of relief hitting me even as I struggled to keep the water away from us.

"Run, man!" Barrett yelled, his voice frantic as it rang out over all the other voices.

Alistair picked up the pace, and then he pushed off the sodden ground and we flew the last hundred feet or so, his feet leaving the ground as he shoved off the tunnel floor with an enormous boost of power. Brightness bloomed across my vision right before we hit the ground. Somehow, Alistair not only knew how to fucking fly, but he'd also managed to turn us midair so he took the brunt of the fall and not me.

Still, his landing was not the best, the pair of us groaning at the impact before several hands yanked us away from the torrent of water rushing at us. I barely found my feet before I was unceremoniously plopped on the ground. My mother's hands patted me all over, searching for injuries, pressing healing talismans into my flesh wherever she could reach.

Damn, I must look really bad.

"Can't believe he did that to me. Damn demons and their bullshit mind control. I ought to skin him alive for that." My mother's tirade only got louder when I coughed and bloody black goo poured out of my mouth. "Taking me away from my daughter. If I knew it would hurt him, I'd set his demon ass on fire."

I wanted to tell her it looked way worse than it was, but not only could I not articulate that particular statement, she wouldn't believe me even if I did. It was true, though. As soon as we were free of the tunnel, the elements made themselves known. Bit by bit, they filled me once again, their presence so welcome I would have sighed in relief if I weren't so busy yakking up bloody remnants of a spell gone bad. Alistair probably knew it would hurt me to sever the spell in that way, but he'd done it to save my life.

"Fucking backlash. Fucking demons. Just fuck this whole realm. Honestly. It's bad enough this maze is out of a bad imitation *Indiana Jones* movie, then I have to hear you scream Maria's name, too? I can only assume you saw her," Teresa hissed, not really asking me as she searched her bag for healing draughts and whatever else she thought she needed. "Stupid illusion magic."

I gasped an, "I'm fine," but she didn't even heed my words.

She kept searching for something in her bag. Letting out a blissful, "Ah, ha!" when she found what she was looking for.

"Don't make me shove my blood into you, Max," Della chimed in just as my mother unstopped a vial of glowing purple liquid of some kind.

All at once, she shoved it in my open mouth and then did a thing that I'd seen Aurelia do with her son when he refused to take a nasty bit of medicine. As she shoved the vial in my mouth, she then tipped my head back and plugged my nose. The noxious liquid fell down my throat, and I had no choice but to swallow. I gagged, but there was nowhere to go and nothing to do. I couldn't spit it out, and I also couldn't shove my mother off of me.

As soon as the liquid was gone, she let me go so I could shudder at that particular injustice in peace.

"I was healing," I croaked, barely able to stifle a gag. "That was unnecessary."

Teresa rolled her eyes before leveling me with a "Mom look" so fierce it could have incinerated me on the spot. "You were not healing fast enough, and backlash can be fatal. Don't fuss at me, missy. It's bad enough I had to leave you in that damn tunnel. Don't push your luck."

"I'm not sorry, you know," Alistair groaned, flat on his back as he tried to catch his breath. "I couldn't have carried you both."

Teresa let out a growl which was only tempered by Andras wrapping her up in a hug. Andras whispered something in her ear and she sort of melted into him, letting out a shuddering breath as she buried her head into his chest. I'd scared her.

I looked around at the faces of my makeshift family. Each one was a mask of fear and uncertainty. I met Barrett's gaze, his blue eyes shining with unshed tears as he rested his head on Marcus' shoulder. I'd scared them all.

"I'm sorry. I don't know what happened. One second Hades was jumping over the fissure and the next... it was Maria telling me I'd failed her and saying her death was my fault."

Hades let out a growl so fierce it was a wonder that my insides didn't shrivel on the spot. "It's one thing to do that to someone like me. It's quite another to make you think... I'll kill him. I'll fucking kill him."

I could only assume he meant Lucifer. I'd inferred this maze was concocted by Lucifer as a security measure for his castle. Or just a way to torture people. Really, it was dealer's choice at this point.

"What do you mean someone like you? You're no different than me."

Hades shook his head and stood, pacing a few steps away before he spoke. "I've been alive a very long time. When you've lived as long as I have, you do things you aren't proud of. Things you regret. The last time I sprung that trap, I saw something like what you did, a death I regretted but could not stop. I couldn't tell you how long I was in that tunnel, drowning over and over again, watching as the specter of my guilt bombarded me with shame."

Hades swallowed hard, like he was shoving his emotions down deep where they would never see the light of day.

"But that death was my fault. That blood will forever be on my hands. What happened to your sister was a cruel twist of Fate, and no matter how much guilt you feel, you are not responsible for her death."

I didn't like the way this conversation was going. I didn't want to hear one more person say I wasn't the reason Maria wasn't here anymore. Which was probably why I lashed out the way I did.

"And how in the fuck would you know? Were you in the Seam, watching us? Were you there when she fell?" I hissed, unable to stop myself from standing to confront him, getting right in his face like he wasn't an ancient deity. "Were you there when I didn't catch her? When I didn't protect her? When I waited too long to look for her? When I let myself get caught up in all the Ethereal drama and forgot that my first responsibility since the day she was born was to keep her safe? She's dead because Soren wanted to hurt me. She's dead because he saw her as nothing more than bait—as a way to trap me. So yes, I'm responsible for her death. Her blood is on my hands and will be until the day I die—whenever that will be. There is nothing you can say that will make me think any different."

For some reason, I hoped that my tirade would have pissed him off. I wanted to fight something. I wanted to hit something—anything—as hard as I could. But Hades wasn't mad at me. Instead, his expression was awash in something like pity and it made me want to scream. It was tough, pulling myself out of the need to destroy, but I managed to refrain from hitting him and walked away.

I knew I shouldn't stray too far—the traps were likely everywhere—but I couldn't stay in that huddle being bombarded with everyone's grief and pity. The sky rumbled above us, the impending storm roiling with unspent raindrops. Soon, the clouds would burst, and lightning would slash the air overhead. I wondered if the rain would wash away this heaviness in my chest. If it would heal me like I wished it could.

Probably not.

I felt him coming long before I heard the steps, the finger-light touch of Alistair's power that I'd become accustomed to after such a short period of time. I was proved right a second later when his arms closed around me and he rested his chin on my shoulder. Having him at my back was a balm in a way I couldn't explain. Every time I was overwhelmed, every time I thought I couldn't press on one more step, Alistair was there to egg me on, push me just a little farther, make me push myself.

"Being possessed was no picnic, love," he began, his voice a gentle whisper in my ear. "But Hades saw everything I did in my memories. He saw us lose Maria. He saw what it did to you through my eyes. He knows all of it, love. Probably more than you want him to."

Great. Now I felt like more of an asshole than I already was.

"He—along with the rest of us—are allowed to be incensed at the atrocities done to you, love. We are allowed to mourn for the losses you've sustained. We are allowed to grieve with you. It is not pity or fear or shame. It is empathy, love. You don't have to go on like you were before—with only a few to care for you. You have a family now. You have people that love you. It's time to let go of the belief that you have to suffer this burden alone. Because you aren't anymore."

I wanted to be funny or deflect or something. I was ill-prepared for conversations such as these. Especially with someone I couldn't tell to fuck off. Turning in his arms, I gave him the unvarnished truth, staring into the beautiful blue eyes of his unphased form as I did so. "It's going to take some work to believe it," I admitted. "And then it will probably take a century's worth of reminders, so I don't forget. But I'm going to try. Okay?"

"That's all anyone can ask of you."

"Good. Now on to more important topics that have absolutely nothing to do with feelings or emotions or whatever," I quipped, waving my hand like I was wiping the slate clean. "You can fly?" Yes, it came out like an accusation, which was exactly as I'd intended.

Alistair blushed, his dimples popping as he gave me a shy smile. "I'm not very good at it yet. It'll probably take another fifty years or so to master the art of it. But we were in dire straits, and well, I figured it was better to try than not."

"So, you can *fly*." Again, the accusation was clear.

"I bet you could, too, if you tried hard enough. I'm sure the air element would likely help in that endeavor. I also assume with time you could breathe under water or move mountains. You can already do so much with so little time under your belt. Think of the possibilities."

For the first time, I stopped thinking of the time crunch we were under. About the maze or what would happen when we got Dušan back. Instead, I thought of our possibilities and what kind of future I wanted and who I wanted in it.

"That, love, is what I've been waiting for you to realize since you talked to me about fighting werewolves when we first met," he murmured against my lips, his breath mingling with my own as a sort of tentative peace washed over me. "The possibilities for you and I are endless. Just as we are endless."

It was a hope I didn't have before then.

A hope that would be dashed long before it could ever come true.

CHAPTER TWENTY

Before we really had a chance to rest, we were off again following Hades down a path that we hoped would lead us to Dušan. I felt no closer to the power that radiated across my skin, and even though the hope Alistair coaxed me to feel buoyed my spirit, I was sinking fast.

The sky swirled above us, the green-cast clouds churning with an impending storm that was not mine. I tried to think on the bright side. At least we weren't stuck in that stupid tunnel filled with rotten corpses or trying to bargain with a giant cyclops. Walking wasn't too bad—especially if I tuned out the ache in my feet and the nagging headache that had been building behind my eyes. The best I could do was draw on the elements to heal those aches and pains and press on, but the toll on my body and mind was wearing me down.

We slogged farther into the maze, following Hades as he picked his way through obstacles, stepping carefully in several places. Other than his misstep in the tunnel, we had yet to see another sprung trap.

We became complacent.

The time passing and aches in our bones and too many steps on too little sleep, made us forget that we were in enemy territory, playing a game built by the worst of the worst.

The path seemed clear, the sky above was ominous, sure, but it had been that way since we stepped foot into this section of the realm. There were no arches, no tunnels. Just a clear walkway unimpeded by anything. Which was why I was so stunned when Alistair shoved me from behind, knocking me to the ground. A slab of stone fell from nowhere, cleaving one part of our group from the other.

On my side was Lilith, Hades, and myself. On the other was Alistair, my mother and father, Barrett and Marcus, and Della and Hideyo. Somehow, I didn't think that was an accident.

"Alistair!" I yelled, hoping he could hear me through the slab. I only got that one yell out, though, because soon, my grandmother's hand was over my mouth, and she was dragging me away from the barrier. Darkness swept over my vision as she enveloped us both in a cloak of black smoke.

In the next instant, stone doors appeared in the walls where the rock had been solid moments before. Out of them poured dark elf soldiers, their weapons at the ready. Lilith's hold did not waver a single inch, and she dragged me with her as she attempted to put distance between us and the elves. I had no desire to be a conduit for her power ever again, so I didn't quibble, moving with her without so much as a peep.

I studied the elves. Their pale skin glistened in the low light. They looked so much like the ones in the cave, only less dirty, less unkempt, less feral. These elves had plaited hair, the braids smooth and unsullied by the filthy cave and decorated with silver wire and beads. While their features were just as sharp as their brethren, they moved with more purpose, as if they were on a mission from Lucifer himself.

"If you think we won't find you," an elf hissed, "you don't know your brother very well." His lips pulled back from his teeth as he spoke, showing shark-like incisors that made me glad I'd never gotten up close and personal with the cave dwellers. His warning was clearly meant for me, since Lucifer was my brother in the very loosest of senses. Somehow, they knew I was here. My only hope was that they didn't catch us before we found Dušan.

Yeah, I figured that was too much to ask the universe. I mean, why the fuck wouldn't it throw me a damn bone every once in a while, right?

"You can't hide from me, daughter of Chaos. We will find you," the dark elf called, and Lilith stopped moving, taking that moment to speak inside my head.

I can't stop them from finding us, Max. The best Hades and I can do is distract them while you run, but even that might not be enough. Dark elves are Lucifer's creation—they are imbued with his magic.

I wanted to tell her no, but I couldn't do it silently. I settled on shaking my head, willing her to understand that we should just stay put.

"Tick, tock, daughter of Chaos. If you don't show yourself, I will be forced to do something rather unpleasant. Maybe I'll find your fake mother and gut her in front of you. Would you like that? Or maybe your joke of a mentor. Barrett would make lovely noises when I strip his flesh from his bones."

That fucker was trying to get me to show myself, but I knew enough to know that if they planned on torturing the people I loved, they would do it whether I showed myself or not. I just had to pray my family didn't get caught.

"Very well, then." He sighed, seemingly resigned to doing things the hard way.

The magic in the air sizzled against my flesh as the elf pulled it into himself. His hands and eyes glowed an icy blue as he sucked the power from the air. Lilith's shroud flickered and then died, the darkness falling away from us.

Immediately, Lilith shoved me behind her, shielding me with her body as death magic erupted from her hands. The swirl of black magic hit the closest elf, withering his body to a husk where he stood. In less than a second, he was ash, crumbling to the ground. Lilith then let the magic spread outward, the noxious black tether jumping from elf to elf. It looked so different from the awful magic that erupted from me in the cave, but I could feel what it was—could see it.

Lilith knew the consequences of using this magic, but she was doing it anyway.

Hades jumped into the fray to help his sister, cutting down the elves closest to her that she hadn't yet touched with her magic. I would have, too, but Lilith suddenly had a hold on my wrist, her grip like iron as she pulled my power into herself. She fueled herself with it, draining me rather than pushing her power through me.

It ached. It burned. It felt like she would use me up, and I'd be no more than the husks of elves she'd already killed. I tried to yank my wrist away, but my weakness leveled me, knocking me to my knees as she took and took.

But just like her shroud of shadow, the head elf stole that power from Lilith, too, absorbing the dark magic into himself. He advanced, grabbing her by the throat. And as much as I wanted to, I couldn't stop him. All I could do was hit the dirt and pray that the elements didn't abandon me when I needed them the most.

There was only so much a girl could do against an army of dark elves—especially when said girl was unconscious. Cracking an eyelid, I groaned as a bolt of pain lanced my brain. Consciousness did not like me and was making that fact known. When I could blink both eyes open without wanting to either throw up or die, I studied the ceiling of what had to be a castle. Chandeliers filled with brilliant blue lights dotted the room. It wasn't until I could really focus that I realized the lights weren't flames at all.

They were caged sprites, their innate light flickering as they withered in their bonds. Just that alone made me want to throw up again, but I settled on letting my rage fuel me instead.

I could feel someone staring at me, the slimy caress of their attention sliding over my skin. Again, vomiting seemed like a good option, but I held my face expressionless. Something about the power signature in the room was both familiar and not, all at the same time. It wasn't the same as the bite of magic in the maze. No, that had to be Dušan. But this—unless I was way off base—was more than likely Lucifer, or Cronus, or whatever the hell he wanted to call himself these days.

As discreetly as I could, I pulled air into my lungs—a feat much different than merely breathing—drawing as much power as I could from the element. It came to me willingly, as did earth, trickling into me as I pressed my hand to the stone floor and shoved myself up to sitting.

Stalling, I cracked my neck, rolled my shoulders, and stretched my arms over my head, letting the elements heal me as much as they were able. Lilith had pulled too much from me, and I knew without a shadow of a doubt in my mind, I was at a severe disadvantage.

The room was cast in the eerie blue glow of dying sprites, and I studied it rather than let my gaze stray to the man whose eyes I could feel boring a hole in my cheek. High domed ceilings reminded me of the grand ballroom where I'd had my presentation to the Fates. Other than the fact that they were painted, that was where the similarities ended. The scenes depicted on them were ones of torture and pain, eviscerations and beheadings.

The walls wept with moisture, the stone crumbling in some places from neglect, and the floor was filthy, strewn with leaves and detritus of inattention.

"Quit stalling, sister. Not looking at me won't delay the inevitable," a smooth British accent called, the power in it beckoning me to turn my head.

It seemed like ages ago when Micah Goode had transfixed me with his voice, and I wondered what would have happened if my glamour was gone like it was now. Because even with my power drained near to empty, I still gave Lucifer a mental *fuck you* and ignored him.

Rather than do what he said, I pondered if that was the reason so many did as he asked, why so many fell to his power. Was it his voice that lured them to do dark things, that convinced them to stray to the darkness in their own souls?

Or did people already have that darkness in them, and he just coaxed it to come out?

I supposed it was a question for the ages.

"Ah, so you are immune. No matter. My children are not. Would you like to see them attack each other? Or maybe you'd like to witness them gutting themselves?" He was so calm as he said this, like watching his children die was of no consequence.

As if he welcomed the idea.

Sighing, I tried to affect a bored expression. I met Lucifer's gaze, raising my eyebrows at him in the universal symbol of "what do you want?".

I didn't trust my voice at the moment because he was absolutely frightening in a way I could not name. It wasn't that Lucifer was ugly—he wasn't. In fact, he looked like a model. Chiseled features, blond hair, piercing blue eyes—nothing about him said grotesque. On Earth, he would be lauded for his beauty.

And it wasn't that he was huge—he was—but his size wasn't terribly foreboding. Close to six and a half feet, he wasn't even as large as Hades.

It had to be the air of utter confidence mixed with the crazed light in his eyes all combined with the blissful smile of a man at peace with the world—and his world was murder, torture, and death. It was the same quality I expected serial killers had when they'd found the perfect prey.

And his sights were set on me.

"That's better. I do so enjoy looking people in the eye when I torture them. It adds to the experience."

I snorted out a laugh that was so unladylike, and so totally me, it only made me laugh harder. What was he, a comic book villain? When my fit of giggles subsided, I couldn't help the zinger that fell from my lips. "What's next? Are you going to conjure a mustache just so you can twirl it? Honestly. Get better material."

Yes, I totally just laughed in Lucifer's face. The man who had kidnapped me, cut me off from my family, and was likely planning on killing me just as soon as he could.

Yep, no way that was going to backfire on me.

CHAPTER TWENTY-ONE

I didn't know exactly what I was expecting, but the gentle smile that bloomed across Lucifer's lips was not it. While I knew that smile was in no way a good thing, it was appreciated over an immediate smiting.

He sat forward on a black throne, the high-backed monstrosity playing at foreboding without hitting the mark. "Oh, I think my material is quite fresh. I mean, I've directly caused you to die one hundred and fifty times—give or take—without you even the wiser. I'm positive I'm doing just fine."

I blinked, stunned for a solid minute, but he kept talking, filling the gaps in my silence with his Machiavellian schemes. "First, I just wanted you out of the way. As Dušan's last-born child, you held claim to the Fae throne, and with it, the last true parcel of his power. I knew he wasn't true dead, but where he was, I couldn't follow. With you gone, I could claim your power as my own and snuff out Dušan once and for all." Lucifer tsked and shook his head, propping a booted foot on his knee, the picture of relaxation. "But you proved hard to kill. Like a weed, you just kept coming back. So, I decided to have a little fun. If I couldn't make you stay dead, I could make you miserable instead."

He sighed; his face wistful as another deranged smile bloomed on his face. "Humans are so easy to manipulate. I mean, burning you at the stake took practically nothing. And the stoning?" He chuckled at that one, shaking his head. "That was so simple, it was damn near criminal. And that hack of a doctor that dissected you while you were alive? Man, you took a long time to die. And on and on until Micah and Ruby and Samael and Elias and Soren. You know, all told, Verena was the hardest to convince to go along with my plan. She wanted more than the throne. She wanted the whole bloody realm. Silly girl. I do appreciate you killing her, by the way. Saved me from doing it."

All the times I'd died, it was Lucifer who was responsible. It was Lucifer as the puppet master the whole fucking time. I snorted before letting out the loudest fucking witch cackle I'd ever laughed. I was pretty sure his goal was for me to be pissed off and attack him or something, but all I could do was wipe my eyes as I just kept on laughing. I'd died *a lot.* And to find out none of it was my fault was a relief in a way.

"How annoying was it that I just kept coming back? I mean, at some point it kinda has to sting, right? I've been killed in *a lot* of ways, and no matter how many times you tried and no matter how many ways, I just kept giving you the middle finger and coming back to life. It is a relief, though. So, thanks for explaining it. I kinda just thought I was a little bit of an idiot. I kept getting myself into scrape after scrape, and lo and behold, it was you the whole time."

I dissolved into another fit of giggles, only this time, Lucifer was no longer a happy camper. No gentle little smile pulled at his lips, his genial nature long gone. "I tell you that I've killed you a hundred and fifty times, and you laugh? What's wrong with you?"

"What's wrong with me? More like, what's wrong with you? You're the chicken-shit bastard who can't gather the sack to kill me himself, and you wonder why I laugh in your face? You failed a hundred and fifty times to kill me. You failed in killing Dušan. You got locked up in a prison by your own children, and even when you escaped, I'll bet you couldn't worm your way out of this realm. Of course I'm laughing at you, Luci. You're utterly hilarious."

A booming guffaw practically shook the earth, the sound coming from behind me. I glanced over my shoulder to see Lilith and Hades tethered to the stone floor by glowing blue manacles. Hades was doubled over laughing, and I was sure he'd wipe the tears of mirth off his face if he could reach it. Lilith was trying to hold in her snickers but eventually gave up the ghost and began laughing with us.

I mean, what else was there to do? Lucifer had us, we were damn near out of time to get Dušan back to the tree, and all my family could be dead for all I knew. Why not laugh in the face of death himself? Why not knock him down a peg or two?

Because that was exactly what a man like that feared the most, wasn't it? People laughing at his worst?

"What else do you have for me, Luci? Are you going to kill me again? Ooh, or better yet, you'll torture me and make me watch as you rip out my liver. Or maybe you'll tie me to some train tracks or some other bullshit evil super-villain cliché. Again, my dear brother, you need better material."

Lucifer's rage ramped up so high I could feel it whipping against my skin. It swirled in the air around us without him so much as moving an inch. Out of the three of us, I was the only one untethered, but that was likely because I was the lowest threat. Lilith had syphoned off most of my power when she'd called her death magic forth. As much as the elements were feeding me, I wasn't at full strength yet.

"I have much more up my sleeve, sister, just you wait." With that he rose from his throne, his booted feet nearly shaking the ground as he descended a crumbling dais and made his way to his children. He stopped in between Lilith and Hades, his head waffling back and forth as he seemed to ponder something.

Lilith didn't wait for him to make a decision. She struck out with her booted foot, catching Lucifer right in the stomach before she yanked a no-longer-glowing manacle out of the stone floor.

With the chain still attached to her wrist, she swung the links at her father's head, smiling with satisfaction when the chain wrapped around his throat. She yanked the other manacle out of the ground, lashing it at one of his wrists before she lifted herself up, planting her feet against Lucifer's chest.

Hades snapped his manacles, and instead of helping his sister, he ran at me, yanking me off the ground and taking off in a dead run. I tried to fight him—we couldn't leave Lilith alone with Lucifer—but Hades slapped me and roughly tossed me over his shoulder, never slowing his stride. Hades pumped his legs faster, but before we could even fully make it out of the room, we seemed to hit a brick wall, the force of the impact depositing the pair of us on the ground.

Lilith let out a frustrated screech, and instead of staying where I was, I ran back to her. Hades and Lilith had worked this out—trying to use her as a distraction to get me out—but it had failed, and I wasn't going to let her get killed if I could stop it.

I might not be at full strength, but I could help, dammit. The sizzle of electricity bloomed in the air as a bolt of lightning streaked across the room, hitting Lucifer right in the chest. He flew backward, sliding out of Lilith's hold as he hit the floor. I didn't make the same mistake as I'd made with Soren. Oh, hell no. I called down bolt after bolt, striking him over and over.

Lilith tried to get me to stop, tried to yank me away, but I wouldn't let her. Only when Lucifer began rousing, starting to stand up even though I kept hitting him, did I take in when Lilith had probably been screaming at me the whole damn time.

He is absorbing the power from the lightning. Stop hitting him!

My miscalculation was about to cost us, because no sooner did I stop hitting him, did he strike, volleying the electricity back at me. It would have been awesome if I could have absorbed it like he had, only I wasn't that lucky. The bolt slammed into me, making Lilith lose her grip on me as I flew back. I smashed onto the floor as the lightning arced over my body, sapping my meager strength and polluting me with Lucifer's special brand of poison. Whatever he'd done to it after he'd drawn the electricity into him, he'd changed it somehow, making it so instead of helping me, it hurt.

I couldn't help it, I let out a scream of agony as bolt after bolt sizzled against my flesh. When the torture abruptly stopped, it took a second for me to get up. More like several seconds.

I managed to pull myself up to my hands and knees, my arms and legs shaking with strain. I nearly heaved when I struggled to standing, but I did it.

Lilith and Hades were trading blows with Lucifer, the siblings attacking in tandem. Lilith's death magic swirled around Lucifer as Hades' slashed at the ancient god with a glittering sickle. Black blood ran from Lucifer's cheek, as he fell to a knee.

And then it was like everything just stopped. The whole of the world stopped turning, the air stopped moving. Everything but Lucifer's hand as it whipped out, burying itself into Lilith's chest. Lilith froze, Hades skidded to a halt, but Lucifer kept right on moving, jerking his hand back, Lilith's heart now in his fist.

I couldn't say for sure if it was me that screamed or if it was Hades. Maybe it was the both of us. All I could see was Lilith's face. Her confusion. Her shock.

The color draining from her face as her body finally caught up to the fact that it no longer had an organ to keep the blood pumping. And then all at once the muscles in her face went slack as she fell, crumpling to the stone floor, her heart still in Lucifer's fist.

The ground quaked under our feet, the earth answering my scream of rage and pain as it split the floor in two. Hades pulled Lilith in his arms, dragging her from Lucifer, protecting her body with his own, even though she was gone.

She was dead. Lilith was dead. It's my fault. I taunted him, I filled him with power, I did this.

Hot tears hit my cheeks as I screamed, letting the earth pitch and quake. I hoped it would take this whole realm down. I hoped it would split this whole place in two, crumble it to ash and dust.

My rage only intensified when Lucifer started laughing. "You think a little earthquake is going to stop me? I've been alive since the dawn of time, and I'll be here after you taste clay, little girl."

That might be so, but dammit, if I was going down, he was coming down with me.

I didn't care if I had to bring this whole fucking realm down when I did it, either.

CHAPTER TWENTY-TWO

ALISTAIR

There were many things I would do for my wife. I would go to war for her. I would battle with her at my side. I would swallow my worry and fear and keep my promise to never stand in her way. But I swore to myself if she didn't make it out of this bloody maze, if she was lost to me, I would scour the dregs of this realm and every other until I found her again.

I didn't care what favor I'd have to call in, what deal I'd have to make. I was getting her back. *I was.*

Why did you push her? You should have grabbed her, pulled her back. Why did you do that?

My self-flagellation had been running on a solid loop for the last little bit, ever since that stone slab cut me off from my Max. *My Max.* She was mine, and Lucifer himself wasn't taking her from me. Not if I had anything to say about it.

Max and I had never discussed what happened to a demon when they mated. The bone-deep need to protect, to possess, to make a home in their soul and never let go. So few demons mated, the process arcane and little used anymore. There was no such thing as divorce. No such thing as irreconcilable differences—not that didn't result in death, anyway.

I supposed it didn't matter since Max was likely a goddess and not the demon princess we'd thought she was. The signs had been there, sure. Her perceptions of magic, how it smelled, how she saw the threads of it. The way she could bend the elements to her will, even under a glamour so powerful it locked most of her abilities away.

As soon as Andras removed it, I'd figured she was a Fae—I mean the ears were a dead giveaway—but her power signature was so much more than what she appeared. I wasn't the only one. The whole of Hell knew it, too. The ground rose up to meet her, the animals treated her as if she was their queen. The souls wished to touch her, share her light.

And then by an odd twist of Fate, she became my wife. I didn't know how I'd gotten so lucky—to have her love me, accept me. Even with the blight of my family, of my father.

Somehow, she didn't even blame me for Maria. Even though it was my father who dragged her down with him. Even though his blood still flowed through my veins.

A shove abruptly knocked me into the maze wall as a minotaur nearly gored me to death, the pungent scent hitting me harder than the wall. Della wiped blood from her nose before reaching out to help me up.

"Get your head in the game, Knight," she hissed and readied her sword, preparing to get the damn thing once and for all.

So far, we'd come across a hydra, a minotaur, three flooded passages, a fissure in the ground that probably went all the way to the heart of the realm, and a fucking Arachne. All of us were either hurt, tired, or just plain pissed off. Mostly all three.

The minotaur scraped back a booted foot, readying himself to charge when I heard the telltale snap of a witch casting a spell. Barrett's hands were coated in the reddish purple of his magic before the spell flowed to fruition. Not a second later, the minotaur's head exploded like a watermelon at a Gallagher show, blood and gore hitting the maze walls and floor in a gut-churning splat.

"You could have done that the whole bloody time, you

bastard," Andras griped, wiping mushy organ remnants off his face and flicking them off his fingers in disgust. "Way to go exploding his head right when I'm next to him."

I kind of wanted to laugh. I knew without a shadow of a doubt in my mind Max would have been laughing if she'd seen it. But that fleeting thought brought back the fact that she was out there somewhere, maybe hurt, maybe dying, and I could not get to her. I thought about all the times Max had been in trouble. All the times when I felt it down deep in my bones that she needed my help.

Absentmindedly, I rubbed my thumb over the obsidian pendant she'd given me right after our first kiss. It was how I found her that night in the clearing. It was how I found her in New Orleans. It was how I knew where she was after Striker had taken her. I wanted it to work right now. I wanted it to tell me where she was so I could go get her. Why wasn't it bloody working?

"Alistair?" Marcus called, and I shook myself out of my musings to glance at him. Like me—like all of us—he was several steps past worry. Max had a family now, and all of us cared for her. All of us were frightened that we wouldn't see her again.

"Yes?" I replied, my throat clogged with all the fear and rage and worry I'd tried so hard to shove down deep.

"She gave you that pendant, yeah? Maybe—"

"Do you think I haven't already tried?" I hissed. "All I can feel is that burning power against my skin. All I can see in my head is this bloody maze. I don't know if it's Dušan or her or if she's... if she's..." I couldn't finish that sentence. Not out loud. Not where the universe in all its cruel twists of Fate could hear me. If I said it aloud, the Fates might make it so. They might take her from me.

Teresa approached, threading an arm around my waist and giving me a squeeze. It was a wholly mom gesture, one I'd never felt from my own mother. Isolde Quinn had never been the mothering kind. Neither had Teresa if history told the tale, but she was trying.

"We will find her. I know in my soul we will. We will find her healthy and whole and she will outlive us all. Now, instead of thinking the worst, tell me what you see when you hold the obsidian. If it doesn't lead to her, it could lead to Dušan. Maybe if we find him, we can find her."

Teresa was talking sense, but I had no illusions that this would work. We'd likely find more of the same—more monsters, more obstacles, more risk to our lives because Lucifer was a petty cunt with nothing but time on his hands. She could see the apprehension on my face, because I got a scolding only a mother could provide.

"Stop stalling and do it, Alistair. Whomever we find is a step in the right direction—is a step toward my daughter."

I gave her a sharp nod, shoving my trepidation down deep where it couldn't spill out of my mouth. Closing my fist around the obsidian amulet, I shut my eyes and waited for that pulling sensation I'd felt each time I needed to find Max. My feet moved me, knowing the direction even when I didn't. In my mind's eye, all I saw was the craggy stone maze walls and the detritus of bones of the other travelers scattered about. Without my telling them to, my feet picked up the pace, hopping from one side of the corridor to the other, dodging obstacles as I ran.

The zing of power raking across my skin got sharper, the feeling so much like Max but wholly different. I knew this wasn't her deep down in my bones, and I hoped her magic wasn't leading us into a trap. I opened my eyes as I rounded the final corner, braced for whatever we would find.

Max's athame practically vibrated in my hand, the power in it calling to someone or something else. I hadn't had the chance to give it back to her after the tunnel, and even though it hurt to hold onto it, I knew I couldn't let it go. And as soon as we turned the corner, I saw exactly what had been calling to me, calling to the blade.

A giant of a man stood stretched between the maze walls, his arms pulled wide by glowing blue ropes. I'd seen those ropes before. They were the same damn magic that held Max in the tunnel and damn near let her drown. The man—whom I could only assume was Dušan—was easily seven and a half feet tall. His short dark-purple hair waved in a nimbus cloud above his head as if he were underwater. Glowing gold eyes reminded me of his daughter's, his wide mouth too much like hers as well.

Before him was a grayed-out woman holding a baby, the faint blue cast to her hair a less vibrant version of the swaddled daughter in her arms. The woman was being stabbed in the chest over and over by an unseen hand, the shock and betrayal on her face warring only with the pain. She screamed, pleading for the unseen person to stop, to not take her away from her daughter, but the scene continued to play out, never changing as it stopped, reset, and played again.

All the while, Dušan begged his wife to run, to not trust her sister, to take their daughter away from Faerie. He screamed as he struggled against the bonds, but they did not waver, and he could not get out.

I met Teresa's gaze and gave her a sharp nod. Teresa had done what I could not in the tunnel: slapping Max to snap her out of the illusion. Teresa appeared wholly unprepared to slap the shit out of the father of the gods, though. She visibly swallowed before she sprang into action, sprinting through the illusion and leaping up to knock the ever-loving shit out of Dušan. Teresa didn't give him a piddly little slap. Oh, no. She cocked her fist back and slammed her knuckles into his jaw, whipping his head back hard enough to give the man whiplash. Deity or no, that punch looked painful.

Dušan sputtered, shaking his head and blinking furiously.

He locked eyes with Teresa, her tiny body dwarfed by his. His expression wasn't angry, though. No, Dušan seemed relieved, his shoulder sagging as much as the magical ropes would allow.

"Thank you, kind witch," he rumbled, his voice exactly what I would have thought the father of gods voice would sound like. "You are my Massima's mother, yes?"

Teresa took a step back, her chin jutting high before she nodded.

Dušan's gaze swept over us all. "You all are her family." He nodded as if he was coming to grips with something before he yanked on his bonds. The blue ropes stretched but did not break. "My son's power is formidable," he murmured to himself before gritting his teeth and yanking again. The ropes refused to let him go.

"Max was under a similar spell. I can get you out," I offered, pausing before tacking on a condition. "But only if you are here to help. Only if you're going to stop Lucifer from killing Max, unless you are going to act against him. Lucifer does not deserve your mercy, and if you're just going to let him get away with all that he has done, then I won't help you."

Dušan appraised me for a few long moments, his unsettling gold gaze leveling me where I stood. "Lucifer will die today, my son. He will pay for his crimes. I swear on the soul of my beloved, on the souls of my lost children, on the very fabric of this realm, and all the others I helped create. He. Will. Pay."

I must have hesitated a touch too long because Barrett snatched Max's athame out of my grip, striding over to the giant god with a purpose. "Well, that's good enough for me, Dušan. How about we get those bonds off you? Be warned, your daughter experienced an unhealthy dose of backlash from this, so... gird your loins."

Barrett cleaved through the blue magic, and the earth was still for one blissful moment before it pitched, knocking us all to our feet. A shockwave of power blasted from the cut bond, knocking Barrett away as spent power exploded through the corridor. Dušan bent, snatching up the athame, the blade dwarfed in his big hand. Without warning, he slashed through the other bond, a twin blast ricocheting off the walls as it settled over us all. Dušan fell to his knees, sucking in huge breaths.

And then we heard it.

Somewhere—even though she had to be miles away—all of us heard Max screaming.

CHAPTER TWENTY-THREE

Tiny dribbles of blood fell from Lucifer's fingers, the minuscule drops inaudible as they hit the stone. But I felt each one. Each drip scored wounds into my soul in a way I knew I'd never heal.

The ground pitched violently under my feet, the whole of the realm reaching up to those drops of blood. Wind whipped through the chamber, carrying debris on the gale as it thrashed around us. Lightning stabbed the ground around me, the fire and electricity reaching for me. Clouds roiled against the domed ceiling, the water in them begging to be set free.

Maybe the elements thought I needed their comfort. Perhaps they waited for me to send them to do my bidding. Or maybe they were just as mad as I was and wanted their revenge.

Lucifer didn't spare me a glance even though I was the biggest threat in the room. Instead, he dropped Lilith's heart, his careless fingers flinging her blood on the stone floor as he studied his son. Hades was still clinging to Lilith, her slack limbs akimbo as he dragged her lifeless body back with him, refusing to leave her to their father.

Lucifer advanced on his son, but not for long. The floor opened up between them, cracking the earth so deep it reached the heart of the realm. Flames rose from the earth, forming a wall separating father and son, answering my call. The fire changed shape, the flames morphing into the head of a dragon snapping at a startled Lucifer. He fell to his ass on the stone as the fire coiled around Hades, protecting him as I should have protected his sister.

Lucifer whipped his head to me, focusing on me like he should have before. He might want to spite his children, but I was the threat in the room. I was his undoing. I was his punishment.

"So you want my attention, sister? Well, now you have it. So eager to die?"

Now was not the time for pithy dialogue and witty banter. There was nothing to say, no reasoning that would change his mind. No stalling. It was him and me, and we were at the end of a very long road.

"You know whatever you do to me, I will just steal your power for my own. I'll twist it against you." His voice was a sing-song taunt, reminding me how I'd gotten Lilith killed in the first fucking place. He didn't need to recap my failure. I'd remember until I stopped breathing.

No, I had no plans to hit Lucifer directly. My intentions were to hit around him, encasing him in a living prison until one of us died, or I figured out a way to seal him away forever.

Because he wasn't doing this to anyone else. He wasn't taking any more lives. He wasn't going to poison another soul. Not if I could help it.

Lightning streaked across the room, the bolt hitting the stone just at his feet instead of striking him directly. Each bolt was one spoke in a wheel-like cage, drilling into the ground, burrowing deeper into the earth. The burgeoning clouds began to burst, their water falling in a torrent before each drop moved to reinforce the cage. Fire was next, the flame dragon swirling around Lucifer's makeshift cell in a maelstrom of heat.

Lucifer began to scream obscenities at me, but I couldn't hear them over the howling wind that added itself to the barrier, carrying bits of earth with it. Each layer whirled in a widdershins circle, each one undoing, unmaking. Each layer a *break* all on their own, denying him power. He wanted to try to use my elements against me? He wanted to sully them, spoil them? I didn't think so.

I pushed the elements as hard as I could, giving everything to the cage, taking nothing for myself. I couldn't let him out—not after what he'd done, not after what he intended to do. But I'd already been drained by Lilith, already had spent too much of myself.

The telltale trickle of my nose bleeding gave me my first niggle of doubt. I didn't have enough power to hold him. I'd gotten cocky, already planning Lucifer's checkmate before reality set in. Lucifer was older than time, older than this realm or any of the others, and I thought a *break* was going to hold him?

Lucifer's lips curled in a triumphant smile as he studied my face, his grin stretching wide when he caught sight of the blood on my skin. He knew—just like I did—that I wouldn't be able to keep him caged.

That I would fail.

Slowly, he found his feet, fighting my *break* far easier than I would have thought he could. Lucifer began pushing against the walls of his makeshift cell, not even flinching as the power of the spell abraded his skin. It brought me to my knees when—even though he shouldn't be able to—he began drawing the elements into him.

I wanted to rip them away, steal them back from him, but I couldn't. Even in that cage, Lucifer cut through my elements like a hot knife through butter, liberating himself and stealing from me all in one fell swoop. The shockwave of the cage crumbling swept through the chamber, lifting me off my knees and slamming me against a far wall. I landed flat on my back, air refusing to go back into my lungs.

Lucifer took his time coming for me, letting me claw at my own throat as I struggled to breathe. Oh, but when he did? He gave me back my elements ten-fold, each one poisoned.

Each one wrong, tainted.

The fire raked across my skin—not the loving caress that

healed, but a blistering flame that would have wrenched a scream from me had I been able to make one. My skin burned away, my hair. The spells in my leathers no match for Lucifer's brand of poison. Bits of earth pelted my ruined flesh, the wind carrying them like tiny knives that embedded into my skin. And then the water came. It was like acid, burning away any flesh that the fire had left behind.

I could feel the elements try to reach me, try to heal me, but they were no match for Lucifer. The man in question practically giggled as he watched me choke and writhe, my body refusing to let him win, even if my brain had finally caught on that I wasn't ever going to. My legs pushed my body back, my hands scrabbled, looking for purchase on the stone floor so I could get away.

But I knew.

I would die just like Lilith had, like Hades would as soon as Lucifer remembered he had a son.

Lucifer knelt at my side, his still-bloodstained hand reaching for my heart. All I saw was a streak of gold and black as someone tackled Lucifer, knocking him away from me.

"You will not harm her," Hades screamed at his father, his form fading back and forth between the gold visage of Hades and his former smoke-monster shape. He stood tall, blocking Lucifer from killing me. "You might be able to steal from her, but you and I both know you can't steal from me, old man."

Lucifer tossed his head back and laughed, and Hades didn't waste that opportunity. He morphed into smoke and flew at his father's chest, knocking Lucifer farther back. When he recovered, Luci's smile was long gone.

"If I have to go through you to get to her, I will. Just like your sister, you chose the wrong side. You would think after centuries as you are, you would have learned that there is nowhere you can go, nothing you can do to deliver yourself from me. I will *always* win. I am inescapable."

The earth suddenly pitched, nearly knocking both Hades and Lucifer to the ground.

"As am I," a voice boomed. A voice I knew. A voice that was as welcome as the scant air in my lungs.

With my last bit of strength, I managed to turn my head to the voice, the weight of pain nearly crushing me, but I did it. A giant of a man stood there along with some very welcome faces. Dušan. My family.

I would have breathed a sigh of relief if I could have. Alistair broke ranks, coming to me and ignoring everyone else.

"Fates, Maxima. *Fates.*" His voice was clogged with tears, and I couldn't figure out why. I was so happy to see him, so happy. "Someone help me," he screamed. His hands fluttered over my body, as if he couldn't figure out where to touch me that wouldn't hurt.

Barrett and my mother's heads entered my field of vision, their forms swimming since I was crying tears of relief. Lucifer wasn't going to win. They had found Dušan and he would fix this. He would stop his son. I likely wasn't going to be around to see it, but I could feel the weight of expectation lift from my shoulders.

Struggling to swallow, I wanted to tell them how much I'd miss them. How much I loved them.

"Don't you leave me, Max. You hold on. We can fix this," Alistair ordered, his voice a fierce whisper as he laid on his belly right next to me, his face now on my level. He wouldn't touch me, but I could feel him anyway, and his presence was a relief even if the agony of my wounds were stealing the life from me.

He would live. They would all live.

And then with a single booming snap, the pain went away. My body started healing itself, Lucifer's poison leaving me instantly. It should have hurt—the re-growing of my flesh and hair, the healing of my muscles and organs—but it didn't. I sucked in one glorious breath after the other, my tears of relief falling in earnest. My body lifted on its own, Dušan's power giving me back everything Lucifer had taken.

I watched as my skin knitted back together, my tattoos blooming once the flesh was healed. I was naked for a single moment before a scarlet dress covered my body.

Alistair scrambled to standing, reaching for me. His fingers closed over mine and he pulled me to him, wrapping me up in his arms as his lips fell on mine. Our kiss broke almost instantly as the room's vibe hit us.

"You dare try to take another child from me?" Dušan growled, his power whipping through the chamber. "Of all the atrocities you've done, and you try this, too?"

Lucifer took a step back, his gaze searching the room for exits.

My gaze fell on Andras. He, too, had broken ranks and was cradling his mother's lifeless body in his arms. Lilith's dark hair fell in a waterfall over his arm as he buried his face in her neck. As happy as I was that I was alive, that we could win, that I wasn't alone anymore, my heart broke all over again.

"What was it you said to your son?" Dušan boomed, "'There is nowhere you can go, nothing you can do to deliver yourself from me.' I know it was you, my son. I know you did all of this. I know what your plans are. And no, you will not succeed."

Hades and Dušan moved in tandem, launching their huge bodies at Lucifer. Hades' smoke form wrapped around Lucifer's like a vine, binding the man so he couldn't move.

"Massima?" Dušan called. "I require your assistance."

Confused as to what I could do that they could not, I slowly picked my way to them, careful of the bits of sharp stone until I was smart enough to conjure myself a pair of combat boots. Say what you want about fashion, but a Grecian-style dress and combat boots totally went together.

Apprehension twisted in my gut, but I stood tall as I approached, my Knight just behind me. The heat of him seeped into my skin, warm and comforting and steady.

"You, alone, can stop him in a way I cannot. You, alone, can end his reign of terror." At my baffled expression, he continued, "Unlike any other god, you can alter Fate, bending it to your will. You have done it many times already. To Finn and Elias and Verena. You can change the threads of Fate, turning the long-lived mortal again."

Realization dawned. "Did you do this on purpose?"

Dušan shook his head. "I am master of many things, but I cannot alter Fate. Only you can. I ask that you use that power now."

With pleasure, I thought, not knowing if Dušan could hear me but hoping he could. Just like with Finn that first time, I pressed my three center fingers into Lucifer's sternum, my thumb and pinky spread wide.

"This is for my sister. My mother. For Lilith. This is for every life you've taken, everyone you imprisoned. I hope you fucking choke on it."

And just as I did with the wayward werewolf, I turned my hand to the right like a key in a lock, cutting Lucifer off from every ability, every power. The putrid motes swirling around his head like a macabre crown, the ones that told of his god-like power, fizzled and died.

We enjoyed the bliss of our win for one fleeting second.

And then the world began to fall apart.

CHAPTER TWENTY-FOUR

Lucifer's laugh could be heard over everything. Over the walls of the dark castle crumbling, over the ceiling cracking and falling in. Over the whole of the Unseelie realm falling apart.

Even mortal, Lucifer was a crafty fucker, and he'd already thought of the one thing that could checkmate us all. He'd created the Unseelie realm, and with his magic turned off, this whole fucking place would crumble to nothing.

That laugh grated, and I had the good sense to take his voice away with a snap of my fingers.

There. That was better.

"Time to get the fuck out of here," Alistair muttered, grabbing my hand and yanking us body and soul out of the castle.

I'd known he could transport himself, but like Aidan, I'd assumed his traveling would make me vomit. It was nothing like that—or maybe after Dušan healed me, I was different now. It wasn't like when I transported myself. It wasn't a blink-and-you-miss-it kind of thing. Instead, an ephemeral black smoke propelled us through space and time, unmaking and remaking us in an instant.

Alistair landed at the entrance to the maze where we'd left Aidan and Zillah. Their protections gone, as Aidan faced off against Argus. Argus' bonds had to have fallen off when I'd cut off Lucifer's magic, and he hadn't hesitated a minute in finding mischief. Aidan's sword was drawn as he protected the seemingly young Zillah against the cyclops.

"You dirty fucking rat," I yelled, getting both their attentions. Argus spared me a glance, but it was the relief on Aidan's face that made me mad as hell.

Others in our party landed seconds after we did, but it wasn't until Dušan stood tall next to me, a struggling Lucifer in his grip, did Argus stop advancing on Aidan. Oh, so now that Daddy was here, he was acting right.

Well, fuck that.

But before I could hand Argus his ass, the world pitched and swayed, the cacophony of the castle and maze crumbling in earnest stole my attention.

"Leave, son of Gaia," Dušan rumbled, his voice louder than the realm falling apart. "Do not make me tell your mother what you have done to those under her protection. This realm is not for you. I suggest you find other accommodations before your choice is taken from you."

Argus' face paled, and without so much as a word, he gave Dušan a truncated bow before loping off into the trees.

Without mercy, I stalked over to Aidan and thumped him right on the head. "You were supposed to get out of here, stupid. Facing off against a fucking cyclops. Gah! It's amazing you made it this long."

Aidan rubbed his temple, staring down at me like a big brother would when taken to task by his little sister. "You weren't back yet."

Frustrated, I let out a growl but still touched his forehead with a single finger, fully healing his idiotic ass. Then, I did the same to Zillah, only he still refused to wake up. "Pick him up and find a buddy. It's time to blow this popsicle stand."

"Daughter?" Dušan called, snagging my attention. "I will carry us to the bridge. Do not try to travel across it by magic. The river keeper is not one you should cross."

I rolled my eyes. *Now he tells me.* "Pip is a friend and should be expecting us."

Dušan's smile was knowing, and I had a feeling he was reading my mind right now as I thought about what happened the last freaking time I tried to cross that damn bridge. I only got to enjoy that smile for a moment before all of us were pushed through space and time, landing at the edge of the bridge.

Pip appeared surprised to see us, especially the magically neutered Lucifer. Their fishy eyes went wide as they studied the lot of us. The bridge was not the one I wanted to cross, the vines rickety and rotted. Nope. Even though I knew I wasn't going to die, I needed a solid surface to walk on.

"No time to waste, Pip. The bridge, please."

Pip blinked in shock, but snapped their fingers, the vined bridge morphing to stone. The majority of us crossed, but Pip stood tall in front of Andras, his arms curled around Lilith's body as he tried to bring her with him.

"The dead cannot cross here," Pip commanded, their staff hitting the ground at Andras' feet.

Andras' whole body shook as he yelled at the river keeper. "This whole bloody place is falling apart, you damned fish. I am not leaving her here."

Fates, his pain was my own. I wanted to sob, but it was Pip's next words that shook me.

Pip's eyes turned sad but repeated themselves, sadness laced in their tone. "The dead cannot cross the river, son of Lilith. Kiss her goodbye and leave this place. She would want that for you. It is what I would want for my child."

Andras looked like his soul was being ripped in two, but he placed a kiss on his mother's forehead, laying her at Pip's feet.

"I will watch out for her, son of Lilith. She will be safe with me." Pip reached to hold Lilith's limp hand, sitting in the center of the bridge, ready to settle in for the end.

"Pip? You need to cross. This realm isn't going to make it." That should be obvious. The ground was trying its level best to fling us into space.

Pip looked over their shoulder, their large, sad gaze meeting mine. “The dead cannot cross here, daughter of Chaos. Those without a soul cannot traverse Styx. It is forbidden.”

Two things became clear. One, the river Styx flowed through Faerie, specifically the Unseelie realm. And two, Pip was dead and soulless. And trapped in a crumbling realm. Tears hit my eyes for them.

“It’s time for you to leave this place, daughter of Chaos. Do not fear. I will be at rest soon enough.”

And then we were swept away, Dušan carrying us through the forest of sentient trees to the gate. Naturally, the gate was blocked by a host of pissed-off trees and a phased dragon ready to breathe fire.

It was Striker who saw us first, a relieved expression on his dragon face.

A sharp whistle assaulted our ears a split second later, and Marcus—who looked like he was fed the fuck up—marched toward the horde. His words were garbled as he let loose his tirade, likely because he had too many teeth in his mouth, the phase changing his features even though it shouldn’t.

“Listen up,” he commanded. “Unless you want to die, I suggest you knock it off and let us pass. This realm is collapsing, and you are very dangerously treading on your word.”

The trees parted, and rather than have their deaths on my soul, I figured amnesty was a better course of action. “It isn’t safe here. If you are deemed worthy by Dušan, you may enter the Seelie realm and set down roots. If you would rather stay, I won’t stop you. Make your decision quickly, though. This place won’t last much longer.”

I glanced over to Dušan, a proud smile on his face at my pronouncement. He nodded slightly, and I had a feeling most, if not all of the trees would be making a new home in Faerie proper.

The giant sentient trees moved to let us pass, and we

approached the gate. Striker, proving he was a man of his word, stayed put, guarding the portal like he swore he would.

"Yo, man. You aren't gonna fit. Time to phase back," I called to him.

I watched in amazement as his form shrank, his limbs and body forming his human shape once again. Unable to help it, I gave my friend a hug, grateful he was still here.

As our party approached the cliff face where the portal had once been, my apprehension about how we would get back to the Seelie Court ramped up. Aiyana had said she could not see this side of the gate. If she couldn't see this side, how was she to know we were here? And if she couldn't see, would the gate even open for us?

Dušan swept past us holding a still-struggling Lucifer in one hand and laying his other against the rock. I felt a pulse of power in the air, and I hoped Aiyana could hear his beacon. All at once, the stone cracked, the cliff face splitting. I had a sudden worry that Lucifer's removed powers were affecting this, too, when light poured out of the crack. The gate was opening, and it was larger than the one we'd had before. Stretched a few hundred feet tall and just as wide, it seemed tailored specifically for the beings walking through it.

Huh. I guessed that whole "no magic" credo for the gate only applied to beings that weren't Dušan. I was sort of fine with that.

He turned to the trees, speaking in that guttural language I did not understand. I sort of hoped he was telling them all to come with us, but I had no way of knowing for sure. Well, until Hades leaned over to whisper in my ear.

"He's letting them come to the Seelie realm. Well, his actual words were, 'There is no way I'm telling a creation of Gaia that they must die so we can live. If she disagrees, she can kill you herself, but it won't be me doing it.' Which is smart. Gaia really hates it when her creations are destroyed."

Good to know. I didn't understand exactly, but we were so close to the end, I did not give that first fuck. We traversed the gate, me holding Alistair's and my mother's hand, and we stepped into the

Seelie realm for the first time in what seemed like eons. We couldn't have been gone more than a day, but it felt like we'd been gone years.

The crevasse was dark, the sun gone and a full red moon above us.

The Blood Moon.

CHAPTER TWENTY-FIVE

Dušan wasted no time with ceremony or pleasantries. There was no discussion or lighting of candles or whatever. No. The Blood Moon was overhead, and we had officially run out of time. With Lucifer in tow, he strode to the ancient tree that had almost brought his demise. Dušan laid a giant hand on the bark in an almost gentle caress, coaxing Aiyana to answer him.

But confusion hit me hard when he began to speak.

"Gaia, mother of worlds, I seek your audience."

Gaia? But I thought… She introduced herself as Aiyana. Then I snorted. It totally made sense once I remembered that half of the people I'd met had two names. Hell, even I had two names. Dušan was Chaos, Bernadette was Lilith, Niall was Hades, Lucifer was Cronus, and I was Massima. The pain that still throbbed in my heart lanced sharper when I thought of Lilith.

We would never be able to bury her. Never be able to put her to rest.

My thoughts were stolen when a fissure of light cracked in the tree's trunk. The light grew wider, as a delicate bare foot stepped out of the bark followed by the rest of the goddess I'd once thought of as Aiyana. Clad in a midnight-blue floaty dress, she emerged from the tree in a way only a goddess could.

Okay, only in a way that a goddess who was not me could.

Her silvery-white hair flowed down her shoulders, the strands decorated with cuffs and braids and intricate loops. Her horns glowed blue in the low light along with the crescent moon on her forehead, her shining arctic eyes searching the crowd. Only after she met the eyes of each of us did she finally land on Dušan and the struggling Lucifer.

Even at the end, Lucifer was hell-bent on not being in Dušan's arms.

"The Blood Moon is nigh, Chaos. What have you brought me to pay your debt?" she announced, and it took a second for me to understand.

The bargain was with her. *She couldn't say,* my fabulous ass. She didn't *want* to say when I'd asked her who the bargain was with. But what they had bargained for didn't make sense for what —*and why*—they would have made one in the first place.

Dušan rose to his full height, staring Gaia down with an expression so formidable I wanted to take a step back. "This bargain was struck because you refused to end our son's life. In exchange for his imprisonment, you bade me to give you a sacrifice every five hundred years. Cronus is no longer imprisoned, so I will sacrifice no longer."

Gaia appraised her son, her face not the kind mask she'd worn before, but the bitter judgment of a disappointed mother. I knew that face all too well from my youth.

"You had to have known our son had broken free long before my family was killed, my former wife. For that you will owe me until the end of days. Your omission cost the lives of thousands. Your deception nearly unmade everything we created. Nearly took everything from us."

Oh, Dad was *pissed*. I was, too. Gaia's omission killed my birth mother, my sister, Lilith, and how many others? How many times had someone lost their lives because of Lucifer?

"Our union ended before time began. All I have of it are my children," she murmured, and I about lost my fucking mind.

Somehow, Alistair knew I was about to lose it because he wrapped his arms around me from behind, his gentle, calming touch ramping down my rage to a burning simmer of hatred.

All she had was her children? And what about all the other children Lucifer had taken? What about the ones he locked away or forced into servitude or straight-up murdered or...

"And how many of our children and grandchildren has Cronus injured? How many has he tortured or raped or played with like toys for his own amusement? Your refusal to see what he is, isn't going to change him. Caging him did not change him. He must be no more, Gaia."

Gaia shook her head in denial, her gaze landing on her son once more. She finally seemed to realize that he wasn't like he'd used to be as he struggled with human strength against his father.

"What have you done to him?" she asked, affronted.

She had the actual nerve to be *affronted*? I had to focus on Alistair's arms around me so I didn't pop off on the mother of creation, but the threat of me doing that was so real, it actually hurt my insides not to.

"Not me, former wife. My daughter did what you could not. She took away Cronus' power, took away his immortality. He will live and die as a man—as he should have eons ago when we discovered his vile nature."

Gaia's gaze moved from Dušan to me, and I couldn't help myself, I gave her a finger wave and a shitty grin. If I couldn't tell her to fuck off, that was the next best thing. Still, I hoped she could read my thoughts. I hoped she could see what her son had cost me—cost us all. If she believed I hadn't done the right thing after all that?

Well, then she was complicit—which made her worse than her son in my book.

Just in case she could read me, I made sure to remember each and every atrocity I'd witnessed that had a direct tie to Lucifer. Each murder, each torture, each chess move that brought about so much pain and suffering. I willed it to her mind, hoping she would see, hoping she was the mother I thought she was. Despair hit her expression—a loss so great it showed on her ancient face.

"I see," she whispered, her tone defeated before she turned her full attention to her son. "I will accept Cronus as the last sacrifice. The Blood Moon bargain is complete."

Gaia reached out, caressing her son's face for one long moment, her eyes studying him as if she would never see him again. Tears gathered in her eyes for a moment before they spilled down her face. In that next instant, a black web of magic bloomed on Lucifer's cheek where she had touched him. His mouth opened in a scream of agony, and as bad as the thought might make me, I was glad I'd turned off his voice.

Lucifer's skin began to die, the flesh necrotizing in quick time, spreading out down his neck and across his face. He fell to his knees, the blackness snaking down his arms and torso. He brought his hands up just as his fingertips began to crumble to ash, his body quickly following suit.

It happened so quickly, my brain couldn't process it. So soon was he snuffed out that my mind and body were still waiting for a villain in the wings to come out and kill us all.

Gaia wailed for the loss of her son, but as soon as Dušan wrapped her up in a hug, she quieted. He whispered in her ear words none of us could hear, and I hoped she was comforted. I didn't envy her in this, and even though I knew she did what was right, I still felt an echo of her pain.

Gaia swallowed hard and pushed Dušan away before striding over to our huddled group. She stopped right in front of me, her pale-blue eyes assessing me for a long moment. "My complacency and omissions have injured you and yours. For that, I will give you a gift of my choosing. It is too difficult a task to ask you to choose your own gift, and I would not ask it of you. Instead, my gift will be given freely. In addition to that gift, and although you may not want it, my previous offer stands. I will tell you all the things you do not know. I will impart my wisdom to you in the hopes that you will be better than me. I refuse to be your enemy, daughter of Chaos, and I hope, one day, you can forgive me."

I accept. And... I'm sorry for your loss.

"And that's why you're already a better goddess than I ever was," she answered my unspoken thought. With that cryptic statement, she raised her hand and snapped her fingers.

Nothing happened at first, but then a light bloomed in the formerly dark gate which had shrunk to the size of a door in our inattention. Despite Gaia's insistence that she was giving me a gift, I had a tough time believing that anything good could come out of the realm Lucifer had made. I actually flinched when the doors cracked open. Even Alistair's arms tightened around me—either in answer to my flinch or for protection.

A man with a head of white hair strode through the gate first, his face more haggard than what I'd seen in the previous times we'd interacted. Rowan Durant looked like he'd been put through the wringer, and as fun as that was to see, it wasn't what I'd call a gift.

That was until I saw who he was holding hands with.

Two women walked with him, both dark haired, both beloved, and both lost to me. In his right hand, he clutched Lilith's hand, and in his other...

I fell to my knees in the dirt, unable to handle the unexpected joy that punched me in the gut.

Maria.

And then I was up, sprinting across the crevasse to meet her. I probably wasn't the only one, but I was getting to her first. The stupid dress hindered my steps, but I yanked it up and kept on running. It was completely possible I may have accidentally tackled my sister to the dirt, but the way a laugh peeled up her throat, I didn't think she minded.

"I can't believe it. I can't believe it. Fates, Ria." I squeezed the shit out of her, clutching her to me like she could be taken away at any moment.

"I'm okay, Max. I'm okay. Everything's okay," Maria cooed, rubbing my back like she was comforting a child.

It was then that I realized I was sobbing, but I couldn't give a single shit. My sister. I had her back. Dušan said she was gone, so I never thought it would be possible to have this. To see her again. To have her in my arms.

Maria giggled, and I pulled back to stare at her face. "Are you really you? Do you remember what happened? Tell me something only Maria would know."

Please don't let this be a trick. I don't think I'll be able to handle it if this isn't real.

She smiled at me then, the gentle curl to her lips as mischievous as my Maria always was. "Yes, I remember what happened. I stuck that bastard like the pig he was, and then fell for a really long time. I remember everything, Max. Everything. Like when we were kids, you would occasionally slip an inordinate amount of dandelion in our mother's tea to turn her stomach."

I snorted out a laugh and then winced, hoping Teresa didn't hear that. "Okay, I believe you."

"No need to thank us, Max," a voice called—one I had not expected to hear in this place.

I glanced up from my and Maria's roll in the dirt to see Ian in full-battle regalia smiling at the pair of us. He looked different here in Faerie, his once-dark-brown eyes blazed bright, their amber cast telling of his death-goddess heritage. He stood next to Rowan, who I had a feeling was not who he appeared to be, either.

"Everyone in this damn place has two names," I griped. "So I figure you're what? Hermes, Thanatos, one of their kids? What?" A staff appeared out of nowhere in Rowan's hand, the two serpents and spread wings a dead giveaway. "Hermes it is then," I muttered.

It really did make a ton of sense—especially the trickster nature and air abilities. Plus, he always seemed to be at the right place at the right time.

Rowan's hangdog expression lifted, and he gave me an elaborate bow. "At your service, Max. I must say, you did a sight bit better than I thought you would."

I only nodded. Rowan was the king of backhanded compliments, and I refused to rise to the bait.

Not today.

Not when I'd gotten such a gift.

"Don't antagonize her, Hermes, she's had a trying day," Lilith scolded, and I couldn't help it, I laughed.

I got up, dusted myself off and pulled Maria with me, dragging her to Lilith as I gave her a one-armed hug. I had a feeling I wasn't going to let Maria go anytime soon. Lilith's arms closed around me, the zing of her power racing across my skin, letting me know she wasn't just a figment of my imagination.

I wanted to ask how they were back. I wanted to know everything.

But they were back, and safe, and alive.

And it could wait.

CHAPTER TWENTY-SIX

"Maxima Christina Alcado, if you don't get out here right this second, you are going to miss it!" my mother called, fit to be tied. I had to say something about my mother, it didn't matter if I was a goddess or not, she was still my mom and wasn't going to let me get away with squat.

Especially when we had a schedule to keep.

I didn't have a good reason for stalling, but here I was, trying to calm down and failing miserably. Nerves rose in my gut, the same ones that had been plaguing me all damn day. And the previous night. And the week.

Warm arms closed around me from behind, one banding around my shoulders and the other my belly. Without even opening my eyes I tilted my head back, resting it on Alistair's shoulder.

"You're doing the right thing, love. You were so confident a week ago, don't let your need to fix everything ruin it for you."

Alistair was right, of course, but all I could do was smile as I remembered the expression on my birth father's face when I told him and Lilith in no uncertain terms that I was retired, and they could take the crown they wanted to saddle me with and shove it where the sun didn't shine.

After the reunions in the crevasse, Gaia bestowed amnesty to the trees, letting them live with her in the deep fissure in the earth. Since it meant that they didn't have to die, and they were mostly peaceful, they had no problems with the arrangement. After that mess was done, Gaia returned to her tree, leaving Lucifer's ashes to blow in the wind. I had a feeling she would be grieving his loss a lot longer than she would ever let on.

Dušan took that opportunity to whisk us back to the Seelie Court castle where there was food and wine and more conversation than I really wanted, but I didn't quibble. The only one of us who got out of the revelry entirely was Zillah who was still unconscious. I'd started to worry about him, but Dušan informed me that he hadn't slept a single minute since Lucifer was remanded to his cage, and he was taking a well-deserved nap.

During our feast, I'd caught Lilith and Dušan talking about what I would do with the crown, and what changes I would make to the Seelie Court, and I fucking lost it on the both of them.

Lilith, I understood. She had no idea how much I did not like being an authority figure, nor did she have a single inkling of the conversation I'd already had with Dušan in his little pocket world. About how I didn't want to stay here in Faerie—no matter how beautiful it was. About how I had a family and life back home, and I wanted to live it.

Even with as much that had transpired since that talk, I wasn't going back on it.

"You should know better," I scolded my birth father, the creator of worlds and gods, one of the most supreme beings in the whole universe.

Yeah, I said what I said.

"You know good and damn well I'm not a Queen, and I never will be. *You know.* As of this very moment, I am retired," I announced, standing with my hands planted on the table, staring down my birth father and adoptive grandmother. I also may have knocked over my chair in my haste to stand up, but that was neither here nor there. "I will not be Queen. I will not be Sentinel. I will not be anything. As soon as I can, I'm going home. Do you two hear me? *Home.*"

Dušan's lips stretched into the most mischievous of smiles, the little sneak. "I know, daughter. We just wanted to see how soon you would announce this. We figured a little push wouldn't hurt. It's time for you to start living for you, my beloved daughter."

When would those two ever learn to quit with the maneuverings and just ask me about shit? I considered how old they were. Likely never, would be my guess.

Many drinks and much food were consumed, and when we reached the ends of our energy, we all paired off and went to sleep. I did notice—even though I'd kept her to myself for the majority of the night—Maria peeling off from the group to go with Ian at the end of the night. He'd been occupied by his overprotective brother for most of the evening, so I didn't feel too bad about stealing her away.

I was just glad they were together finally.

Over the coming days, I learned how Ian and Rowan broke into Hell, rescuing Lilith and Maria from the Seam. Well, it was more like Ian—with his new knowledge of who his mother was—went on a hair-brained adventure which most certainly could have gotten him killed, met up with Hermes in Hell, caused mayhem and mischief, but also managed to get the job done. Hermes had been sent by Gaia to retrieve my sister, her gift set in stone before I ever took a step into the Unseelie Court.

That particular story scared about a century off my life, and ended with me socking Ian and Rowan in their respective arms before hugging them until they couldn't breathe. Yeah, I was grateful, but dammit those two were idiots.

But the rescue itself was more than two-fold. Lilith had known when she went up against Lucifer that she would die. Blessed at a very young age with the ability of foresight, she knew just how she would lose her life, her die cast long before I was ever born. She also knew when she did die, she wouldn't go to Heaven or Hell, but the Seam—or rather Tartarus—where all gods go in death.

Lilith also knew that if she managed to find Maria, she would pull her from that place if she ever discovered a way out.

The other major thing that came about was Dušan's decision to retake his throne. I was happy to abdicate my position, but rules dictated that there be an event so the Fae could accept their new ruler.

The Fae were sticklers for rules, after all.

So here I was, in a very pretty dress, getting ready for my father to retake the Seelie throne. I couldn't say for certain why I was nervous. Maybe it was because I was still waiting for the other shoe to drop. I'd had a lot of joy in such a short amount of time, my natural inclination was not to trust it.

Hadn't that been the way my whole life? My mother and Della and Lilith were working with me on this—Lilith especially since she reminded me that every time the shoe dropped it was because Lucifer himself had done the dropping. Now that he was no more, there would be very little in the way of major catastrophes in my life for a while.

We hoped.

"Come on, love," Alistair whispered in my ear, "The sooner this is done, the sooner we get to go home and lock ourselves in the house for a good long while. I figure doing my part to help save the realms from Lucifer should buy me at least a month of vacation."

I spun in his arms, rising up on my toes to meet his lips with mine. "Maybe two."

By the time we heard a throat clearing in the doorway, my lipstick was a mess and so was Alistair's face. Whoops. Around my husband, I should definitely always have on smudge-proof lipstick. I snapped my fingers to right us before letting my gaze fall to the door. Della and Aidan were in their Faerie finest, likely coming to collect us because my mother had zero intention of walking in on Alistair and I. Again.

"Honestly, you guys," Della huffed good-naturedly, "It's like you're newlyweds or something."

"Yeah. And when you're on your honeymoon, you can jump each other's bones as much as you want, but until then, we've got a job to do," Aidan griped, pulling at the collar of his shirt, grumpy as ever. I was going to need to find him a girl.

Later, though.

Della and Aidan, along with Hideyo had decided to stay on as my paladins—refusing to renege on the promise they made to Lilith. Della, however, would stay in Faerie, watching over me when I came to visit, while Hideyo and Aidan stayed on the Earth realm. I was going to miss Della being around all the time, but with the newly installed Fae door in her Tandrirr home, we could see each other anytime we wanted without the freaky trip through the trippy fog-filled forest.

It wouldn't be the same, but I was so happy for her. She'd missed her family while staying with me. I was glad she could go back to them.

"We're coming." Alistair sighed, his hand tightening over mine as we swept from the room, ready to begin our lives together.

The Faerie event brought us all manner of creatures in my father's retinue. The elves from Tandrirr, the dwarves and fawns. Even the pixies and water Fae made an appearance, and the party moved outdoors to one of the many pools of water so they could be comfortable. A few of the sentient trees—which one of the fawn called Gnarus—managed to come to the party, too. I was glad they were being included.

A vast majority of the Fae were happy with how the monarchy had shaken out, and Dušan's re-coronation went off without a hitch. Many of the Fae were glad someone like me—an outsider—was giving up the crown. I could tell they were wary, especially after Verena, but most remembered life under Dušan's rule and the prosperity that was found during that time. I was delighted that they would have that back. Well, that, and the fact that it wouldn't be me dealing with the headache it would be to fix all the shit Verena trashed under her rule.

I was slow dancing with Alistair, so freaking happy I could burst when Andras tapped on Alistair's shoulder.

"Mind if I cut in?" he asked, and I pressed a kiss to Alistair's lips before going to my father.

It was weird that I thought of both Andras and Dušan as my fathers. Neither had been with me for the majority of my life. But knowing what each had sacrificed, what the pair of them had gone through to keep me safe, I figured they both deserved the title of Dad. Plus, I supposed it was like any other adopted kid or stepparent situation. I had two Dads, a mother that had sacrificed everything to keep me safe, and a grandmother that was as badass as they came.

It was more than some people got, and I'd take it as the gift it was.

"Are you happy, Max?" he asked, a faint thread of worry in his expression.

My smile had to be radiant as I answered him, "Yes. More than happy. More than anything."

He nodded before taking me through a turn. "Do you think your mother would want to stay with me? Even with my new position, I mean?"

The vulnerability on Andras' face made me pause. Lilith and Hades had decided to co-rule Hell, which had been their purpose and position before everything went pear-shaped. Now that Lilith no longer had a husband to oppose it, and Andras was no longer in exile, she restored him as a Prince of Hell.

And Andras wanted to know if my mother would stay with him? After four hundred years without him, I had a feeling my mother would be with him in a heartbeat.

"Have you asked her?"

Andras shook his head, a blush rising on his cheeks. "What if she says no?"

"She's not going to say no, Dad. Mom loves you. She's always loved you. Even when you were being a secret-keeping, manipulative dick. Just ask her. Ya'll will work it out. I'm sure of it."

Andras smirked at my dick comment, his dubious smile stretching to a grin when he caught sight of my mother dancing with Striker. The pair whirled toward us, and we switched partners in a move that was so smooth it had to have been a spell. I let my mother have it and settled in with Striker.

I hadn't spoken to the man much since we'd returned, me too busy with coronation shenanigans and him too busy with his reunion with Melody. He was learning what it meant to be a father to a succubus infant and a real partner to someone. All of which was probably blissful for a man like Striker as much as it was trying. I had a feeling Ronan would be a big brother sooner rather than later, and that made me so fucking happy I could burst.

"You going home still, right?" he asked as he led me through a turn, his tone apprehensive.

If he meant Denver, then the answer was yes. Alistair had no qualms about making Denver our home base—especially after he found out how much NOLA grated on me. "That's the plan. After some time off, I'll head back to the shop, too. I really miss the old place."

My fingers actually ached to hold a tattoo machine again.

"Do you think..." He trailed off, took a breath, and tried again. "Do you think I could come back? Melody would like to go home to Denver, and I really would, too. Now that she's no longer getting mind-bended by Verena, she has no desire to stay. We don't know which line her family is from, and there isn't really a need to find out. I think we'd all like to get back to..." He paused again, leaving his thought dangling in the breeze.

"Normal?" I offered.

"Yeah."

I thought about it for maybe a millisecond. "I think I'd like that."

Instead of staying another night in Faerie, after the party—that had to have lasted at least two days, I didn't give a shit what the sun and moon said—we traveled to Tandrirr to test out the newly built Fae door. The door—my first—led to a room in my basement adjacent to the casting room. I'd put more than a few protections on the thing, as did Dušan and Hermes. I had a tough time trusting

Hermes—especially since he was considered a trickster by many—but since I'd found out who he really was, he'd become way less of a dick.

Especially after I gave him a hug and said thank you. I had a feeling not many gave him credit for helping us. I'd never be able to repay my gratitude for bringing Maria back to me.

Never.

I'd never been so glad to see my basement in my life. Exhausted, Alistair and I trekked up the stairs, heading to bed. Tomorrow—or whenever Maria and Ian came up for air—we'd meet for brunch or dinner.

We had time. Lots of it.

That's all I'd ever really wanted—time with the people I loved. And now we had an infinite amount of days ahead of us.

Together.

This concludes the Rogue Ethereal Series.
Thank you so much for reading. It has been an absolute pleasure sharing Max with you.

However, if you would love to see a special glimpse of Max & Alistair, turn the page for an epic Rogue Ethereal Bonus Scene. I hope you enjoy it!

If you love Max, you'll adore Darby...
Stay tuned for the Grave Talker series, starting with ***Dead to Me****. I hope you're buckled in to see Darby contend with the dead, the Arcane Bureau of Investigation, and a slippery agent ready and willing to get her into trouble.*

Want the skinny on future releases without having to follow me absolutely everywhere on social media?
Text "LEGION" to (844) 311-5791

BONUS SCENE

Dear Reader,

I hope you enjoyed the Rogue Ethereal Series. Max has a very special place in my heart, and I am absolutely ecstatic for you to read more about her.

I have an extra special bonus scene for you as a thank you for reading. All you have to do is click the link below, sign up for my newsletter, and you'll get an email giving you access!

SIGN UP HERE:
https://geni.us/qff-bonus

DEAD TO ME

Grave Talker Book One

Meet Darby. Coffee addict. Homicide detective. Oh, and she can see ghosts, too.

There are only three rules in Darby Adler's life.
One: Don't talk to the dead in front of the living.
Two: Stay off the Arcane Bureau of Investigation's radar.
Three: Don't forget rules one and two.

With a murderer desperate for Darby's attention and an ABI agent in town, things are about to get mighty interesting in Haunted Peak, TN.

Grab Dead to Me today!

Want more in the Arcane Souls World? Check out...

NIGHT WATCH

Soul Reader Book One

Waking up at the foot of your own grave is no picnic... especially when you can't remember how you got there.

There are only two things Sloane knows for certain: how to kill bad guys, and that something awful turned her into a monster. With a price on her head and nowhere to run, choosing between a job and a bed or certain death sort of seems like a no-brainer.

If only there wasn't that silly rule about not killing people...

Grab Night Watch today!

SPELLS AND SLIP-UPS

The Wrong Witch Book One

I suck at witchcraft.

Coming from a long line of famous witches, I should be at the top of the heap. Problem is, if there is a spell cast anywhere in my vicinity, I will somehow mess it up. As a probationary agent with the Arcane Bureau of Investigation, I have two choices: I can limp along and *maybe* pass myself off as a competent agent, or I can fail. *Miserably.*

Worse news? If I can't get my act together, I may not only be out of a job, I could also lose my life.

Whose idea was this again?

Preorder now!

Coming June 7, 2022

THE PHOENIX RISING SERIES

an adult paranormal romance series by Annie Anderson

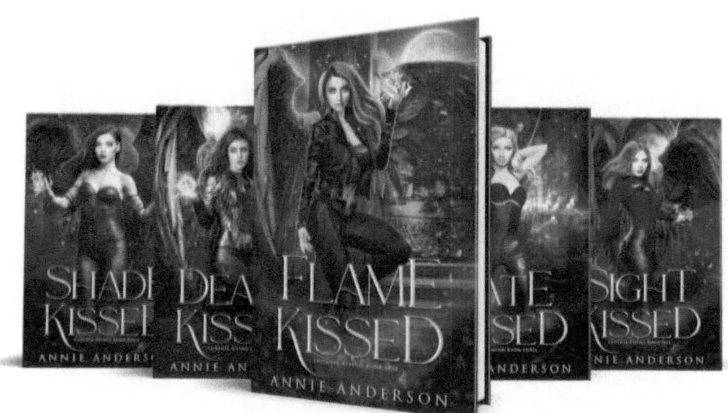

Heaven, Hell, and everything in between. Fall into the realm of Phoenixes and Wraiths who guard the gates of the beyond. That is, if they can survive that long...

Living forever isn't all it's cracked up to be.

Check out the Phoenix Rising Series today!

To stay up to date on all things Annie Anderson, get exclusive access to ARCs and giveaways, and be a member of a fun, positive, drama-free space, join The Legion!

facebook.com/groups/ThePhoenixLegion

ABOUT THE AUTHOR

Annie Anderson is the author of the international bestselling Rogue Ethereal series. A United States Air Force veteran, Annie pens fast-paced Urban Fantasy novels filled with strong, snarky heroines and a boatload of magic. When she takes a break from writing, she can be found binge-watching The Magicians, flirting with her husband, wrangling children, or bribing her cantankerous dogs to go on a walk.

To find out more about Annie and her books, visit
www.annieande.com

facebook.com/AuthorAnnieAnderson
twitter.com/AnnieAnde
instagram.com/AnnieAnde
amazon.com/author/annieande
bookbub.com/authors/annie-anderson
goodreads.com/AnnieAnde
pinterest.com/annieande
tiktok.com/@authorannieanderson
patreon.com/annieanderson

www.ingramcontent.com/pod-product-compliance
Lightning Source LLC
Chambersburg PA
CBHW020534310726
48979CB00014B/2324/J

* 9 7 8 1 9 6 0 3 1 5 0 4 5 *